Sails & Sorcery

Tales of Nautical Fantasy

Edited By
W. H. HORNER

Illustrated By
JULIE DILLON

Fantasist
Enterprises

Wilmington, Delaware

Fantasist Enterprises
PO Box 9381
Wilmington, DE 19809
www.FEBooks.net

Designed by W. H. Horner
Cover designed by Julie Dillon and W. H. Horner

Sails & Sorcery: Tales of Nautical Fantasy
Copyright © 2007 by Fantasist Enterprises
ISBN 13: 978-0-9713608-9-1
ISBN 10: 0-9713608-9-8

First printing: August 2007

10 9 8 7 6 5 4 3 2

This book is available for wholesale through the publisher and through Ingram Book Group. It can be ordered for retail at most booksellers, both online and off, and is available from the publisher's website.

Fantasist Enterprises grants a discount on the purchase of three or more copies of single titles.

For further details, please send an e-mail to bulkorders@fantasistent.com, or write to the publisher at the address above, care of "Bulk Orders."

TO GRANDMOM AND POP,
IT'S NOT THE TROPICAL
ISLAND YOU WANT,
BUT HOPEFULLY, IT WILL
TAKE YOU SOMEPLACE CLOSE.
~WHH

Contents

Contents

We Sail with the Tide
Lawrence C. Connolly

Listen! Hear the breakers? Listen carefully. The sound is there, throbbing at the edge of your awareness, the steady rush and crash of your own private waves. The tidal forces are within us, rising and falling with the beating of our hearts, sustaining us with the salty remnants of the sea that enveloped our primordial ancestors.

The sea flows inside us. It sustains us, influences us, and makes us who we are. Not surprisingly, its mysteries permeate our art.

Consider the oldest work of written literature, a 5,000-year-old proto-novel in which the Sumerian hero Gilgamesh discovers that the ocean holds the power of death and life: death comes in the form of waters that kill any man who touches their surface, but life lies deeper, in the form of a plant that grows on the floor of the sea. To win the promise of eternal life, Gilgamesh ties weights to his body, leaps in, and plunges to the bottom where he finds an ancient watercress named Never-Grow-Old. He plucks it from the rock, carries it to the surface, and takes it to the shore where he loses it before accessing its powers. Thus the Sumerian King learns what many sea-faring adventurers would learn after him. In the end, it is the quest and not the treasure that makes us who we are.

The joy of such ancient stories lies in discovering the ways in which they resonate with our lives. Indeed, you will find the streams of Gilgamesh running through the stories in this collection, for each in its own way deals with the mortal dangers and ephemeral promises of the sea. Beyond that, however, you are likely to find that such stories, rooted as they are in primordial archetypes, inform your life by illuminating day-to-day experiences.

I recall a night when I felt such a touch of the primordial, when deep waters served as a conduit between classic literature and real-life experience. It is the story of a Gilgamesh-like discovery at the bottom of a flooded abyss that came shortly after I completed my scuba certification.

It was late summer when I traveled with a group of more seasoned divers to a flooded quarry in south-central Pennsylvania. We arrived at the rock-rimmed hollow after sunset, unpacked our gear, and walked to the water's edge. I wanted to catch a glimpse of the bottom before agreeing to the dive, but the water taunted me. Looking down at the still surface, I saw only a wide swatch of reflected sky. To see what lay beneath, I had to commit to the quest.

I suited up and went in. The bottom fell away sharply. One step and I was under, drawn down by the lead belt I had fastened to my waist.

My first impression was one of disgust. The quarry was an aquatic trash dump, littered with debris: washers, refrigerators, tires, engine blocks—the detritus of a throwaway world. But as we swam on toward the center, away from the overhanging cliffs and into the lake's deeper regions, we encountered a surprising number of living wonders: disk-shaped fish and rock-clinging plants that swayed in our passing. But the most intriguing thing of all lay at the quarry's bottom, thirty feet beneath the skin of reflected sky in a rock-lined grotto that ran along the lake's limestone bed. Here I found myself swimming above a garden of discarded books, a sunken library strewn across the flooded limestone, pages swaying like leaves of albino watercress.

I picked up one of the books. It seemed beautifully preserved. I closed the cover and swam to the surface to examine it on the shore. And there, within minutes, the pages deliquesced in my hands, crumbling to sludge and leaving me with only the memory of the quest.

Like Gilgamesh, I had dived deep to discover a treasure that slipped away when I carried it back to the land. There is an ancient lesson here, a bit of wisdom that transcends verbal summary. The details, I believe, speak for themselves.

The crumbled book had been an edition of Dante's *Il Inferno*.

———⚓———

When asked to name the masters of nautical adventure, readers will readily identify Homer (*The Odyssey*) or perhaps Virgil (*The Aeneid*), two works that certainly convey the sense of wonder and mystery of the sea. Few, however, will think of Dante Alighieri, the fourteenth-century Tuscan best known for the work that is often referred to as *Dante's Inferno*, Book One of *The Divine Comedy*.

In Canto XXVI of that work, Dante relates a harrowing adventure of Odysseus (whom he calls by the Latin name Ulysses). The story is worth considering here, not only because it features imagery that you will encounter elsewhere in this anthology (see, for example, the mysterious black tower that rises from the horizon in Chun Lee's "Stillworld: Sailing to Noon") but because it speaks to our primordial unconscious, informing us with images that transcend words.

In Dante's high-sea adventure, which does not appear in any of Homer's texts, Ulysses incites his men to sail beyond the Strait of Gibraltar and into the ocean that lies beyond the known world. As the shores of Spain and Morocco sink below the horizon, the Greeks steer their ship into uncharted waters that flow beneath nameless constellations, coursing southward until they behold a monstrous tower rising from the Earth's southern pole.

Ulysses soon realizes that the tower stands on the center of an island heretofore unglimpsed by living man, and, with the shore of that island in sight, he urges his men to sail faster toward the undiscovered country. But just as the ship comes in reach of the shore, a terrible squall blows in, drowning all on board and plunging Ulysses into a circle of Hell reserved for those who encourage the attainment of goals beyond the ken of mortal men.

Does Ulysses deserve such a fate? Certainly Dante (a Roman Catholic from Florence) had historical issues with the pagan Greek who had defeated the great grandsires of Rome. But although Dante consigns Ulysses to eternal flames, one wonders if the intrepid sailor would not still have believed the voyage was worth it.

And this it seems is what so many of the great sailing fantasies are about. Reaching a goal or possessing a treasure is not as important as having discovered it was there.

From the beginning of time, people have looked at the ocean and contemplated what wonders might lie beyond and beneath its waters. Thus, having given us life, the sea lures us back with its mysteries. And the ensuing quests inform our lives, reminding us of the fluid nature of our transient endeavors, letting us know that an elusive sense of wonder can sometimes inform us better than a fully quantified understanding, which brings me to another literal encounter with literary truth.

———————⚓———————

A few summers ago, a sailing friend of mine equipped his boat with onboard sensors that he claimed took the mystery out of sailing. Now, at last, we could know from moment to moment and with absolute certainty exactly where we were on the surface and how deep the waters were beneath our keel. Technology had banished ambiguity.

To test the new sensors, we sailed east until the Maine shore sank beneath the horizon. It was a calm day: clear sky, sea like glass. With nothing in sight for miles, we sat in the cabin and watched the readouts.

Then, something incredible happened. Without warning, the ocean floor began rising, racing toward us so fast that the numbers blurred. Surely something was wrong with the sensors. And then we heard it, a shattering roar behind us, as if the glassy sea had broken open.

We turned toward the sound, looking astern to find the water ribbed with concentric waves, deep troughs spreading from a point fifty feet beyond the tiller. Something huge had come up beneath the boat, surfaced behind us, and plunged back into the depths.

"A whale," my friend said.

"You think?"

"What else could it be?"

The question remains.

———————⚓———————

Is it any wonder that the mysteries of the sea have figured so prominently in world literature? From the voyages of Gilgamesh and Ulysses to the twenty-eight stories you will find in this new collection of nautical quests and adventures, the sea continues to delight and confound us. And how could it be otherwise? The sea is as much in us as it is around us. To ponder its nature is to ponder ourselves. To explore it is to sound the depths of our existences. And since the latter is boundless, the sea's place in fantasy literature will certainly be secure for many generations to come.

I will leave you with a few lines from the great Irish poet William Butler Yeats, who, like so many writers from the Emerald Isle, seems keenly aware of the sea-centric position of human existence.

In "The Lake Isle of Innisfree," Yeats speaks of an inner longing, an attraction to a place that is at once as distant as a mythical shore and as close as the throbbing of a person's heart.

He writes:

> *I will arise and go now, for always night and day*
> *I hear lake water lapping with low sounds by the shore;*
> *While I stand on the roadway, or on the pavements grey,*
> *I hear it in the deep heart's core.*

Keep those words in mind as you read the stories in this wonderful book, and, if at times you feel yourself being transported, do not hold back. Sail with the tide.

Lawrence C. Connolly
Pittsburgh, Pennsylvania
12 July 2007

Return, My Heart, to the Sea

J. C. Hay

Ysabelet walked out onto the docks and watched the carefully orchestrated maelstrom of a ship's complement preparing for departure. Casks of fresh water were being loaded into the longboats, while goats milled impatiently around crates of clucking chickens. Men shouted taunts, boasts and curses at each other, though none dared to utter anything at the short, olive-skinned woman who had joined them on the docks. Even the dimmest among them was able to recognize the swirling blue and green robe that hung from her shoulders, and avoided drawing her eye.

For her part, she welcomed the solitude—it allowed her to hear the song. Even here, where men had beaten and tamed Onde with their piers and breakwaters she could find it. It was faint, compared to how it would sound in deep water, but the Goddess's call refused to be broken by the hands of mortals. She moved to the edge of the dock and closed her eyes, picked out the delicate points and counterpoints of the melody, until her whole body thrummed with the desire to join the song.

"You look like a little fish, ready to jump back in the sea." The voice behind her was filled with a rumbling bass that she felt in her ribs, a sound that seemed to soften the rounded accent and turned his vowels to honey and sweetcream.

She smiled without turning, the accent rich with memories of distant ports. "Cushar, correct? Maybe from Estaires?"

He laughed. "Too many years ago to remember now, but perhaps once, yes. Now tell Denisot what you are doing on his dock. He has boats to load, and a ship to supply. He cannot do this if the men need a free hand to point and whisper about you."

Ysabelet turned around and found herself staring directly at the man's chest. She resisted the urge to take a step back in order to see him better, knew that the step would put her off the edge of the pier and into the ocean, and that was not the sort of first impression she desired to make. She made do by craning her head back so she could see the Cusharan's mahogany face, and the laughter in his eyes. She paused a moment, unused to such a direct gaze from sailors, then cleared her throat before launching into her formal title. "I am the Lady Ysabelet, Beloved of Onde. I am here to meet Captain Gieffroy, of the *Mademoiselle a'L'Espee*."

"The new Windmaiden, yes. Denisot was told to expect you. You have your papers?" He reached out a hand that could hide a pint-glass with room to spare. She rummaged in the oilskin pouch at her waist and produced the sealed and signed documents from the temple that certified both her profession and her skill. He opened them and read through them quickly. "You did not bring anything with you? Where is your chest? Your sea-bag?"

"They are still at the temple, of course. You'll need to send men around to pick them up." She tried not to sound frustrated, but she knew she couldn't be the first Windmaiden they'd had on board. It was standard practice, after she had met with the captain of course. She still had to gauge the feel of the vessel before she agreed to the contract, and that could only happen on board. "When does the next longboat leave for the *Mademoiselle a'L'Espee*? I want to finish the negotiations as quickly as possible."

Denisot laughed again and handed the papers back to her. "You are so formal to Denisot. Not at all like the last one, like Perrette—she was a sailor's daughter born and bred. All the same, if you want to see Captain Gieffroy, how can Denisot deny you?"

She tucked the documents back into their waterproof pouch and smiled tightly. "Thank you."

"Don't thank me yet, Little Fish. It's a crowded trip." He walked with her to where the men were loading, and they instinctively opened a path for the giant and the priestess. Denisot shouted down to the longboat, "Hennequin! Clear a seat for the Lady and prepare to launch."

She watched as a man at the tiller handed a crate of chickens back up to the dock, then brushed feathers and straw off a small space for her. He kept his eyes studiously towards the bottom of the boat rather then look up, even when he finished and called out, "All clear, Mr. Denisot!"

The Cusharan smiled, and Ysabelet found herself staring into the network of ritual scars that crossed his face—she knew enough of Cushar's traditions to understand that his family lineage and their great deeds was written in those scars and wished for a moment that she could decipher them. "Thank you, Mr. Denisot." She stepped down the ladder and into the longboat.

As soon as she had settled herself onto the space that had been cleared for her, Denisot leaned down and placed the crate of chickens in her lap. "I apologize, Lady, but if the hens do not make the trip, then the men will not have eggs." He caught her gaze again, all smiles, and stood. "To Oars! Boat to Launch!"

Four more hands descended from the dock and settled in at the oarlocks, and with a few choice oaths to their comrades still on land they began to cross the bay towards the bright blue hull of the *Mademoiselle a'L'Espee*.

⚓

No ladder descended from the quarterdeck when the longboat arrived, but that could not be helped. After all, she had hardly done anything to announce her arrival to the ship. Hennequin, the hand at the tiller, offered to call up for a dignitary's ladder as custom dictated but Ysabelet waved him off. "I can take the crew's ladder just as easily, Mr. Hennequin. Just bring us alongside." The oarsmen steadied the boat against the hull and she quickly scrambled up the ladder to the deck.

Several sailors had rushed forward to help with the unloading, but they quickly moved away and cast their gazes down when they saw her climbing towards them. She smiled and pulled herself onto the deck, then stood and walked aft towards the quarterdeck. The spar deck was a bustle of activity as the crew stowed supplies, mended sail, coiled ropes, and scrubbed the deck planks with pumice-stone until the wood gleamed white. She threaded among the men and left a soft murmur of whispering voices in her wake; a beautiful harmony to the barely contained susurrus of Onde's song, which vibrated in the boards beneath her feet.

When she reached the stair to the quarterdeck a voice called down to her.

"Permission to approach, Lady. Come up."

She looked down as she placed her feet on the steps, and was glad her thick hair hid her expression. Six words, and she already had this man's measure. He demanded to be in charge, the king of his little wooden fiefdom. She turned her sigh into a slow exhale as she climbed—he was a far cry from Jehan, but then again that's what she wanted, otherwise she would never have left.

Captain Gieffroy waited with his back to her. A table had been brought onto the quarterdeck, and he took advantage of being at anchor by plotting his charts in the fresh air. When her foot first touched the quarterdeck, he spoke again. "It had to be our priestess, of course. From the moment you came on board, I heard the change in the men, and followed the muttering until it had approached close enough that I figured you were below. It is not a difficult trick when you know your vessel and your men. Had I known you were coming, I would have put down a ladder for you to board the quarter directly." He turned and offered a smile that didn't quite reach his eyes. "Welcome aboard the *Mademoiselle a'L'Espee*."

"Thank you, Captain Gieffroy. I have come to negotiate for the Temple of Onde, so that you may—"

"I know why you are here. You are listening to the Goddess's creation song, even now. You are feeling for weakness in the wood, for Onde's call that this ship be offered to her. And if you think it a cursed ship, you will return to shore and abandon us to our fate."

"Which may or may not come. Onde does not demand we sacrifice ships to Her, only that some vessels travel without the full extent of her protection." It was a common enough misunderstanding for the uninitiated, and fueled many of the superstitions held towards the Goddess's chosen. She enjoyed the protection such fears afforded her, as did most of her sisters, and did little to alter the notions that they could doom sailors with a glance, or call down storms on crews that had offended them. She handed over her papers again, and announced herself. "The temple accepts that the death of your previous priestess was brought on by disease, and not your fault. Your increased tithes, no doubt, have helped to sway that opinion."

He glanced at the papers and tossed them onto the table beside his charts. "I've laid out our course for you, feel free to examine it." He stepped to one side and gestured across the table with a sweep of his hand. When she approached, he added, "Perrette will be sorely missed. She was good luck to us, even when she barely had the strength to sing. And even the crew liked her. Not like most of the Windmaidens I've known."

Ysabelet smiled around her clenched teeth. She knew the term was common parlance among the sailors, had heard it a dozen times a day since her ordination. It mocked her vow of chastity and belittled her connection to Onde's song of creation. Shortly after her ordination she had tried to correct them, but she'd have faired better trying to hold back the wind.

She leaned over and pretended to study his charts while her senses rode the melody of Onde's song. She heard no ill portent in the notes that flowed around the hull of the ship, and the captain had chosen a decent course, in exactly the opposite waters of those Jehan traded in; a perfect arrangement. She nodded once, and pushed the thick curls of dark hair from her face. "Onde blesses your vessel, Captain Gieffroy. It will be my pleasure to sing the *Mademoiselle a'L'Espee* across Her waves."

———⚓———

Supplying the ship burned away the last of the daylight, and rather than set out at night— a risky proposition even with her help—she and Captain Gieffroy agreed to wait and sail at first light. Besides, Ysabelet wanted the time to study the ship before they were underway. Gieffroy invited her to join him for supper, but she declined, taking a simple meal that had been delivered with her things from the temple. The long journey would provide plenty of opportunities to eat in the captain's quarters; she felt no hurry to do so now.

She walked alongside the gunwale and trailed her fingertips over the whorls and cuts of the wood, her ears tuned to the quiet slap of water against the hull. The *Mademoiselle a'L'Espee* bobbed easily among a few other larger vessels, too big to approach the docks personally and risk being stranded, but still able to seek the shelter of the bay within the protective arms of the breakwater. When she reached the bow she leaned out and brushed her fingers over the carved arm of the figurehead.

So close to the open ocean, Ysabelet felt the constant refrain of Onde's song, stronger than it had been ashore, though not as strong, she knew, as it would be once they were at sail. Onde, the Mother of Oceans, began the song when She pulled aside the waters to reveal the first lands, a lullaby to creation that reached out to everything in and on the sea. Ysabelet let the Goddess's song fill her veins, listened to the strands of melody that dictated the ship's place, and found herself eager for daybreak.

Footsteps sounded on the deck behind her and she heard Denisot's basso whisper. "It is almost time for third watch, Little Fish. Get some sleep. You will see plenty of ocean in the morning."

She turned and smiled at the giant Cusharan in the dark, found him meeting her gaze with his own. "Why don't you look away from me, Denisot? Even your captain isn't willing to look me in the eye for long."

He laughed. "Denisot and Captain Gieffroy are of different minds. He leads by telling, and does not care to understand. He hopes that when his time comes, he can order it away. Not so, Denisot." He thumped one dark fist against the white canvas of his shirt. "Denisot will take your curse, if you want to bring it to him. Denisot wants to look death in the face, not let it creep up on him. You would do well to learn that lesson. Lotatu comes for us all, it is how we face him that matters."

Ysabelet could not hold back a melancholy smile. The words were different, but the sentiment was so like Jehan's, so full of fire and daring that it couldn't help but remind her of his flashing smile and the glint in his eye. When she realized who Denisot reminded her of, the pain that hitched her chest forced past her lips as a strangled choke.

She pushed her hair back behind her ears and smoothed her robe, time-gaining actions that allowed her to drop a wall of formality between herself and the Mate. "Thank you for the warning, Mr. Denisot. I'll retire to my quarters." She stepped around him and walked away.

———⚓———

The breeze lifted her hair around her face and made the edges of her robe dance like fabric waves while the sea spray crusted her lips and eyelashes with salt. Had her voice not been dedicated to its higher purpose, she would have laughed out loud. Ysabelet felt the song in every part of her body, her voice raised to sing in harmony with Onde's creation hymn in a protective charm that brought calm seas and fair winds. Her hands gripped the gunwales at the bow and she leaned out over the bowsprit, her heart racing for the joy of communion with the Goddess. At no point did she feel as alive as she did at these treasured moments, and the rest of the ship faded into obscurity around her until only wind, spray, and song remained.

She had just begun to notice a countercurrent in the song, signs of another vessel, when she heard it confirmed behind her. A voice—she thought it might be Jaquin but with only three days at sea she had not yet learned all of the men by voice—shouted from the tops. "Sail ho! For'd the lar' beam!" A flurry of activity swept the decks at the cry, and she heard the captain give orders to bleed wind from the sails and slow the *Mademoiselle a'L'Espee* as they approached. Onde's oceans were vast, and encountering another vessel this far from port was a chance for welcome news.

Hopes of an unexpected trade meeting were quickly dashed as they approached. Little stirred on the ship, and her only deployed sail flapped uselessly in the wind. When they were closer, Ysabelet saw a few bodies face-down on the deck. When Gieffroy gave the order to grapple and look for survivors and salvage, Ysabelet dropped her voice back out of the Oceansong. A skin of honeyed wine hung on the peg near her hand and she soothed her throat with a quick splash of the refreshing liquid.

While resting, she picked through Onde's melody for the notes that encompassed the dead ship, tried to pull the sad saga from what remained that had brought it to its current low state. Ysabelet closed her eyes and listened again—no notes of destruction could be found, only the clear, crystal sounds of a fast ship, unsung but in her prime. A chill wind filled her lungs and she dropped the wineskin and ran towards the quarterdeck to shout her warning.

She was almost halfway when the world exploded.

The detonation of point-blank cannon fire buckled the deck and tossed the *Mademoiselle a'L'Espee* onto her side. Ysabelet fell to the pitching wood and scrabbled her fingers across the planks in an effort to keep from sliding overboard. Below her palms, the hull resonated with the panicked screams of men who had fallen asleep in their hammocks only to wake with their bodies and comrades torn apart in the whirlwind of wooden splinters created by the attack.

Though the blue-grey gunpowder smoke made her eyes water, she saw other members of the ship's compliment running across the deck. Denisot's baritone was bellowing out "Repel Boarders!" but quickly disappeared beneath the feral howls of the men that charged over the gunwales and onto her ship. Pistols rang out in the chaos, adding their own haze to the man-made fog, and then were replaced by the unmistakable sounds of men fighting for their lives.

Ysabelet struggled to her feet and ran across the tilted wood towards the quarterdeck. The *Mademoiselle a'L'Espee's* deck, already cramped, seemed covered with ropes, blood and the dead or dying. Someone had broken open the livestock pen and the goats bleated in terror as they dashed blindly through the smoke. Somewhere, she heard the sounds of axes on wood—too short to be an attack on the masts themselves—and realized that at least some of the corsairs were attacking the rigging.

As if to confirm her thought, a wall of ivory cloth crashed to the deck in front of her and succeeded in ripping free the scream of terror she had been trying to hold back. She backpedaled to keep from getting trapped in the collapsing canvas. Although most sailors would not attack her out of fear of the Goddess's wrath, that didn't prevent it from happening accidentally—especially if she was just another shape under a fallen sail.

A shadow emerged from the fog and resolved into the blood-spattered image of Captain Gieffroy. He crossed the short expanse between them and raised his hand to cuff her. She stared, dumbfounded, but before the blow hit he changed his mind and grabbed her by the arm instead. "Damn you, witch! You assured us this trip would be safe!"

Ysabelet struggled in his calloused grip. "No! They hid themselves somehow, cloaked themselves from Onde's song! I couldn't see them!"

"I paid my tithes! I've paid for Perrette's death, and it wasn't even my fault! Why would you curse us?" He was panicked, screaming to be heard over the din of battle. Ysabelet tried to make him realize that she hadn't seen the trap that had been laid until it was too late. It was not unheard of for some priestesses to lose the gift, but never with something so large before. She struggled to think back through the notes of harmony before the attack, to see what she might have missed in the song that would have hinted of the attack but found nothing.

She wasted the effort; nothing could break through the terror and betrayal that ruled Gieffroy's mind. Nothing, except for the blood-streaked fist that drove into his jaw in the middle of her protests, at the behest of which he crumpled bonelessly to the deck. She looked over at a wild-looking man, his face splattered with blood and smudged with powder and soot. He only held her gaze long enough to be certain of her robe, then raised one calloused fist and drove it into Ysabelet's temple. She staggered and fell to the planks, her mind a-reel at the idea of being struck by a sailor. With effort, she blinked and turned back to look at her assailant, just in time for his hammer-like hands to descend again and steal consciousness away.

———⚓———

Awareness crept back slowly, though Ysabelet kept her eyes shut rather than risk another blow from her captors. Her head throbbed mercilessly, and she could feel the spreading tightness of blood drying on her cheek. Whomever had hit her knew what he was doing and made certain he wouldn't need a third punch. She took stock of her surroundings as well as she could without her vision—she lay in a bed, in a dimly lit room, and the whole structure moved fore and aft with familiar regularity. Shipbound. She forced herself to calm down and focused on the water beyond the wooden walls of her new prison. Onde's song waited there, and she sighed in relief and let the notes wash over her like a cooling bath.

Her heart counted in time with the slow elegance of Onde's song, the notes of the melody picked out on the strings of Ysabelet's body. When she was comfortable with her submersion into the all-encompassing music, she stretched out for the notes closest—surely some part of the vessel had to affect the Song. Even if it could not be seen, its presence would affect the other notes in the harmony. As she pushed herself deeper into the pelagic music, she finally found it. A familiar chorus that she remembered all too well, and realized that it hadn't been invisible at all, she had just blocked it out because it reminded her so much of . . . "Jehan!" She sat up suddenly, his name a gasp of horror on her lips.

He smiled at her from his seat behind the captain's table. Behind him, the open windows let in the sea breeze and a dim orange light from the setting sun. It would have left him in silhouette had he not kept a tallow lit on the table in front of him. "I see you've decided to be awake, dear."

She couldn't be certain if it was her near-concussion or the sudden thrill of seeing him again that made her heart throw itself against the cage of her chest—she splayed her fingers onto the bed to keep from succumbing to the dizziness. "You fool! What have you done?"

"Only what I said I would do. I promised you that I would find you, that we could never be parted. At the time, you agreed."

Ysabelet's cheeks stung at the memory. "But not for you to turn pirate! Worse than pirate! You've kidnapped one of Onde's Beloved, the Temple won't just hang you—they'll have you drawn and quartered. They'll ship parts of your body to every port in the world, just to serve as a warning, and they'll feed your burned entrails to Onde's wolves."

He chuckled, that same care-free laugh he always gave when she warned him of danger. The sound made her breath catch in her throat. She quickly found something interesting to look at on the floor.

He stood and crossed the room. "Same old Ysabelet—you should have been a prophet of Cielle. Your doomsaying would have fit in well with that dour lot."

His hand drifted lazily over her thick hair, warm when it brushed her scalp. Her eyes closed a moment, and she leaned into the touch. The near-eternity of the last two months receded like pack-ice and she whispered, "I've missed you."

Jehan sat on the mattress and folded his arms around her. "You won't have to, ever again. I promise."

"Don't make promises, my love. Even I can't see that far into the future. Just hold me." She leaned back against him, found herself lost in the warm smells of pipe tobacco and brine, tallow-smoke and tar. They were sailor's smells, and as comforting to her as the whisper of the waves against the hull or the quiet melody of Onde's song.

"Why did you leave?" he asked, at last. She had sung for his ship, the *Dame Chance*, for the better part of three years; all his moods were laid bare to her, and the hurt in his voice that might be invisible to another stood out for her like storm clouds on a clear day.

She sighed. "You know why. If I remained with you, I would break. My heart beats too strongly when you are near, and my will ebbs too shallow. Had I remained, it would only be a matter of time before I became another of your conquests."

"Never you, Ysabelet. Never just a conquest. I have risked execution and worse for you, as you so deftly pointed out. I would take you as my wife."

The tide of her pulse crashed in her ears and she found herself gripping the sheet in one clenched fist. Carefully, he pried her hand open and laced his fingers into hers, then reached up to turn her face towards his. He brushed his lips over hers with a tease that made her shiver before he kissed her fully and she was lost.

A knock sounded at the cabin door, followed by a discreet voice. "Captain, the men have spotted sea-wolves chasing the boat and are beginning to panic. A sign from their brave leader that Onde hasn't cursed us all for his folly might be a good idea."

Jehan broke the kiss and she gasped suddenly, her skin tingling like the ghostfires that sometimes enveloped a ship's spars in a storm. Despite her sigh of longing, he untangled from her arms and stood. "Not yet, however. You must stay a maiden a while longer, if you are to guide us to a safe hiding place. Come up when you feel ready, love."

He blew a kiss to her, then turned and hurried out of the room. She leaned against the hull and listened to the lullaby of water against wood but it couldn't calm her mind. There were so many questions—did he mean it? Was he only speaking what she wanted to hear, so she would succumb? Most sailors knew never to think of the Priestesses of Onde as anything more than another piece of ship's equipment. Superstition kept the crew from wanting to draw her attention, and the studied indifference most priestesses exuded did not weaken the stereotypes.

Jehan had ignored all that, had met her eyes, and talked to her as a man to a woman rather than a captain to his crew. He wanted to meet his fate head on, he'd told her once. Small men try and avoid what the Gods have in store for them, but the truly valiant know that death comes for every man, and it is how they live that matters. Even while her stomach churned at the blasphemy of his piracy, she could not help but smile at his carefree attitude.

The thought shook her from her reverie, and she pushed away from the wall and crossed to the aft windows. The heavily leaded glass had been thrown wide to keep the tiny space from feeling too stuffy, and she leaned out over the sill to gaze at the ocean below.

As soon as her head cleared the window, she smelled the blood in the water and it was easy enough to guess the source. In his desperate bid to return to her, Jehan had disregarded the costs that would be paid by his men. Though she couldn't hear the screams now, no doubt it had only been a short time since the ship's surgeon had finished the grisly work of amputating limbs too wounded to be saved. Ill luck came if you stored the living and dead parts of a man in the same place—a man's body wanted to be whole, and the missing parts had a way of calling out to be reunited with their owners. Should the two find themselves confined together, the madness that could result was the least of a ship's worries. So the limbs, like any other ship's refuse, were pitched over the side.

When the first sea-wolf broke through the edge of the ship's wake beneath her window, her heart paused in its steady tempo. More than twice the length of a man, Onde's Wolves were considered the purest expression of Her divine wrath. Ysabelet's time in the temple had taught her to accept the beasts as she would any other symbol of the Goddess, but it had not prepared her for seeing them in the wild. Their maws trailed dark water as they leapt and snapped their hunger in the ship's wake. Even in the rapidly fading light she could make out the thick, oil-slick hair that covered their upper bodies—at odds with the occasional glimpse of silvery-scaled flukes that drove them through the waves. She had to remind herself that they were as likely to be drawn by the stench of blood in the water as by divine command to punish those who had offended the Goddess. She doubted the crew cared to make any such distinction. To see the wolves was to look at death—a man in the water among them could measure his lifespan in heartbeats, for he stood little chance against the vicious predators.

Ysabelet pulled away from the window and sat down at Jehan's desk. Charts, some new and some familiar to her, were held in place by an assortment of makeshift weights. One in particular called out to her, and she opened the red-leather book carefully. The smell of sweat and tobacco wafted up from the pages, his smells, and she felt warmth flush in her cheeks. She flipped to the last pages of Jehan's rutter. The entries were encoded—every captain kept his navigations secret so they wouldn't fall into the hands of a rival—but he had once trusted her with the key. At the time, she was honored. Now she was thankful that she still remembered it, even after two months without using it.

What she read in the pages bordered on obsession. Details of his attempts to plunder other vessels in the region, his desperate search to find the one woman who had resisted him, even her own name repeated again and again, stared back from the pages of the ship's book. She pushed through one page after the next, her blood quick to cool at what she uncovered—this was not love, she could be certain. This was a man, wounded in his pride and desperate to control things in a way he would never be able. She snapped the book closed and shivered at the sudden chill in the breeze.

Her assignment to the *Dame Chance* had been longer than the temple preferred, but it was a lucrative arrangement so they chose to turn a blind eye to it. The constraint kept a priestess from becoming too familiar with a ship's crew, so she would not hesitate to alter a man's fate should a member of the compliment be taken by the Goddess. It also prevented Onde's Beloved from giving up their hearts to the rare captain who, like Jehan, could overcome superstition with dare and rakish charm.

Good reason reinforced the restriction—Onde's jealous nature could turn in an instant and consume those who betrayed Her. If Ysabelet took a man to bed, the Song would be lost to her. While many of the Beloved made that choice as they grew older, found husbands and settled down near one of the temples, the thought of losing her communion with the Goddess horrified her. No man could match the feeling that suffused her when she fully gave herself to the Creation Song. When she found herself dreaming that Jehan might be worth the loss after all, she ran rather than remain near him. At the *Dame Chance's* next port of call, she went ashore and disappeared.

That same cold sense of reason filled her limbs now, but she knew there was no port of call in her future. Not until it was too late—she knew she could not hold her heart at bay for long. The madness he had revealed in his logs gave her the excuse she needed; despite the way her body thrummed like a ship's shrouds at the smell of him in the room. He would not steal the Goddess from her.

She barred the door and returned to kneel on the chair by the window. The reflection of the ship's lanterns and the moon danced on the water and she watched them until her heart had calmed, and then Ysabelet reached out to feel for Onde's melody and let it cover her skin. The soft play of notes danced on her skin and filled her lungs and pushed the pain from her heart until nothing remained but measure and bar, octave and pitch, Song and Singer. When she knew the melody as intimately as if it were an extension of herself, she opened her mouth and began to sing.

Rather than blend harmonically into the motif, however, she cast her notes at odds with it. While all of Onde's chosen were taught the method, they avoided acting so openly—far better to let the sailors have their superstition than to act and confirm their fears.

The Song responded the only way it could to her disharmony—it added new lines of music to complete the threads Ysabelet began. It didn't take long for the effect to become noticeable. Barely a quarter-hour had passed when the first white spear of lightning lanced into the sea beyond the windows. The sea-wolves grew tired of their sport, or perhaps realized a greater feast was near at hand, and vanished beneath the waves.

The Song grew to encompass the storm, until it seemed to have always been part of the hymn, its resonant notes a natural extension of the new shape of the song. It swelled in power and importance until it became the main theme, driven by staccato bursts of lightning and the endless rataplan of the pouring rain. Men pounded at the door to the captain's quarters, shouted for her to stop. They could hear her voice, and hoped to appeal to her sense of mercy to call off the storm. Ysabelet smiled and sang louder, and then the cloudwall fell upon the vessel like a pall.

For all its spirit, the ship stood little chance in the face of Onde unleashed. Waves poured in through the holes in the ravaged hull and gave her a dangerous list. Wind and rain scoured the deck and sent men scrabbling to plunge into the black waters of the sea. Lightning lanced down and struck sea and ship until the spars exploded beneath the relentless fury. Ysabelet stumbled and gripped the window to keep her balance as the ship shuddered and bled under the merciless squall. A sickening crack, louder than any thunderclap, shivered through the whole vessel. The ship tilted violently, and she tumbled from the window into the frigid darkness of the sea.

She kicked to the surface quickly, though the heavy fabric of her robes became waterlogged and threatened to pull her down if she didn't work to tread water. From outside Jehan's quarters, the damage to the ship was much more obvious—flashes of lightning illuminated a ragged hole in the starboard wall that the waves worked feverishly to widen. A distant part of her concluded that Jehan had fired his cannon through the closed gunports in his own ship to better catch the *Mademoiselle a'L'Espee* by surprise. It had also doomed the little ship to sink in heavy waves.

The main mast had cracked in the violent winds, but they had yet to cut free the rigging so the whole sail dragged down into the water and threatened to capsize the boat completely. Above the howl of the storm she could hear the screams of men, barking orders, prayers, or just giving voice to their fear as the sea they based their lives on rose up to destroy them.

A piece of a thick spar bobbed nearby and Ysabelet pulled herself through the water to grab it. A jagged splinter of wood caught her palm and she screamed into the wind as her wet skin ripped open. Still the makeshift raft held her above the water—it wasn't much, but if Onde allowed it, she might survive the storm she had called down.

A wave splashed over her spar and swamped it. Her already sodden hair swirled briefly before she broke into the air once more and left the strands plastered over her face and mouth. Ysabelet sputtered weakly and tried to clear the hair from her mouth, but it seemed like an impossible task; every piece she spat out was replaced by two more, and she was afraid to release her grip on the boards simply to increase her comfort.

When she looked, Jehan's ship had disappeared. All that remained now were floating boards and the screams of panicked men lost in the water. She wondered if he had managed to survive, even now. He had a cat's luck, she knew, and he might have been able to make it to a johnboat before the ship went down. She hoped, still, that he had not—that he had looked at his coming death and taken it in stride as he had always talked of. Perhaps once he had been welcomed into Onde's embrace he would finally understand her choices.

In the white-hot flash of lightning she saw another crest and sealed her eyes and mouth against it. The water slammed her down again and her cheeks ached as she held her breath until her face found air again. There was a distant part of her that realized her palm bled freely, that her own salt-blood mixed with Onde's. If the Goddess's sea-wolves still patrolled the water, they would not be far off. They waited for a moment like this—a violent wreck made for an easy meal—and Ysabelet wondered how much longer it would be before she felt the telltale bump of fur and scale against her legs.

Another wave, and the wind seemed to rise up again in greater fury. The water weighed in her chemise and turned the cloth into Onde's own hand, pulling her ever downward. Ysabelet gulped the air into her lungs, eager to end the searing pain in her chest. She pushed down on the wood to get her head as high as possible, felt it sink slightly before the ocean buoyed it aloft again, and realized her problem.

She, the Priestess of Onde, fought against the Goddess's Divine Will. How many sailors had she just sent to Her embrace without a thought? If the ocean had no favorites, then she should trust in Onde to deliver or claim her as She saw fit. Ysabelet listened to the raging chaos of the Song, then stilled her mind and released her makeshift raft.

Almost immediately another wave swallowed her, but rather than fight she allowed herself to be born along. She could hear Onde's song in her veins, stronger with each thump of her heart, more pure than she had ever heard it before. When her lungs could wait no longer she opened her mouth to join the melody.

A hand grabbed her by the wrist.

Before she could break free, strong arms hauled her above the waves and into a johnboat. Denisot's smile shone like a beacon, and his laughter seemed a challenge to the churning seas. "When Captain Gieffroy see this storm, he knows you are the cause. Lucky for you, Little Fish, Denisot has good eyes. Tonight is not your night to walk with Lotatu."

Ysabelet nodded absently at the boatswain's amiable laughter and let his words flow over her like water. She turned on the floor of the boat until she could look out over the waves. The wind turned her wet skin to gooseflesh, but she barely registered the cold. Instead, as Denisot directed the oars to take the johnboat back to the *Mademoiselle a'L'Espee*, Ysabelet trailed her uninjured hand in the ocean and for the first time in her life felt homesick.

Sea of Madness
Jon Sprunk

"That is not dead which can eternal lie,
And with strange aeons even death may die."
—H.P. Lovecraft

Captain Pender's hand hovered over the sheet of parchment, the wet tip of the quill waiting for inspiration. On the desk before him sat a lithograph of his wife. Anna's gentle smile reached to him from across the leagues. Her latest letter, picked up in St. Croix, rested at his elbow. Its fine paper was creased from being opened and closed a score of times. The words leapt off the page to burn into his brain.

> *Beloved Michael,*
> *It has been seven long months since you have warmed our marriage bed. The days are cold and the nights unending since your departure. The children are well, but they miss their father sorely. . . .*

Feelings paraded through his mind, but he couldn't find the words to express them. How to explain to her the loneliness of a life spent at sea, a loneliness that seeped into the bones until he was certain he would never be rid of it. He had lost something out on the ocean tides, some piece of himself. He hadn't missed it at first, but as the years rolled on he had felt it more keenly each day, until it yawned like a gaping chasm inside him.

He clenched his left hand tighter around the quill. The fourth and fifth fingers of that hand were missing, and the third sheared off at the middle knuckle—a souvenir from a skirmish with Portuguese privateers off the coast of Barbary.

A cry from above decks interrupted his thoughts, the nets being brought up with the midday catch. Grateful for an excuse to leave off, he put Anna's picture away in his sea locker along with her letter and shrugged into his overcoat. He hoped there would be a swordfish today. It had been months since he'd tasted swordfish simmered in Cook's spicy sauces.

As he left his cabin a sprightly wind leavened with the taste of the sea struck him. He inhaled the scents of salt and foam, oiled canvas and fresh-scrubbed wood. The *Mariner* was a trading carrack owned by Tobias & Hutchings Mercantile. Launched from Boston in '46, she was his first command and he her first captain. They had seen many a strange sight together in their travels across the oceans of the world.

Crewmen straightened as he came on deck. Manck, his first mate, a big New Zealander, nodded respectfully and started to call all-hands. Captain Pender waved it off. They were in the middle of the Atlantic with nothing but the endless blue around them. Away from port he allowed discipline to lax somewhat. As long as the men performed their duties faithfully, he did not drive them hard. That earned him a jigger more loyalty than most captains received, enough that every hand jumped willingly to his call when need be.

"What's the catch today?" he asked.

Manck limped slightly as he came over. He had taken a musket ball to the knee in the same raid that had cost Captain Pender part of his hand. The experience had bonded them in a way that few captains ever allowed with their crew. "A goodly haul, Captain. We'll eat like kings tonight."

The first mate opened the nearest net to reveal a glistening pile of twitching fish, mostly sea bass and sturgeon. No swordfish. Clicking his tongue, Captain Pender headed starboard to the second net, but a cluster of sailors blocked his path. Several spat upon the deck and muttered to each other in low voices.

"Make way for the captain!" Manck shouted.

With startled glances, the sailors hopped away. Captain Pender stepped among them, scanning the familiar faces, and saw unease writ there as plain as day. He looked down into the net, and the breath hissed between his lips.

He had seen all manner of things in twenty-two years at sea. He had traded with the cannibal tribes of South America, all done up in their garish war-paint and costumes of human bones, fought off pirates in a dozen waters, and viewed the monolithic heads rising on Isla de Pascua, but he had never witnessed the like of what lay on the deck at his feet. His first instinct was to call it a fish, but it looked like no other fish he'd ever seen. Nearly as long as a man, it was covered not in scales, but a coat of slime like an eel. Instead of fins it had long stalks projecting from its body at the middle and end, each ending in a fluke-like fan too much like human hands for his liking. A tapered snout protruded from the head with a mass of whiskery feelers beneath. It was dead, or dying, as it did not move, not even when Manck prodded it with the tip of a billhook.

"What is it, Captain?" McKiernan said. The Irishman was a stout lad with a shock of fire-red hair tied back in a short queue.

"I don't know," Captain Pender said, unable to pull his gaze away from the large black eye staring at them. "Throw it overboard. Whatever it is, I don't want it on my ship a minute longer."

At Manck's order, the sailors grasped the net—each careful not to touch the strange fish—and heaved it over the side. Captain Pender watched it sink beneath the waves.

He turned to see three sailors hunched around the ship's cabin boy. The boy was examining something in his hand. Van Eyck, a stocky Dutchman with a cruel disposition, made to swipe it, until Captain Pender strode over.

"What have you got there, Nicholas? Give us a look."

Van Eyck stepped away as the lad held out his hand. In his palm sat a flat piece of metal, like a coin, but with five sides. There was some design stamped on its face, but he could not make it out. The metal's surface gleamed like burnished bronze, but when Captain Pender picked it up he saw a brighter shine beneath the tarnish.

"Gold!" van Eyck said, and the whisper carried through the crew.

"That fishy had gold in its gullet!"

"Snatched from some sunken treasure ship right beneath our keel, I wager!"

"A whole armada of Spanish galleons, all laden with the wealth of an empire."

"Be silent!" Manck roared.

The crew fell quiet, but the whispers continued. Captain Pender slipped the strange doubloon into his waistcoat pocket. "All right, Mister Manck. As we were."

"You heard the captain. Back to work!" Manck shouted as he waded among the crew. The sailors moved to obey, but a few cast long gazes at the captain's pocket even after he pulled his overcoat shut.

Holding his coat tighter, Captain Pender went aft. A cold wind had crept down from the north. Dark clouds lay on that horizon. He had loved the sea his whole life. His father had been a fisherman with his own boat and the memories of their long hours hauling nets still echoed in his heart. But time had changed that love. Now every time he put out, he found his eyes cast longingly back to land as if he might never see it again. It was a bad habit for a seaman.

After checking the helmsman's course and making a slight correction to the heading, he tromped back to his cabin. He feared he would not get much sleep this night.

⚓

The captain wiped his face with the sodden sleeve of his wool coat, but water ran free down his cheeks a moment later. Rain drenched him head to boot, dropped by the bucketful from the iron-gray sky. A squall had swept over them from the north, just as he had predicted. It was early in the season for a big storm, but this one looked to become a nasty bitch.

"Tie down those lines!" he shouted to be heard above the wind.

Manck struggled across the wet deck to seize the ropes that had come undone from the foremast. Sailors huddled at their posts, watching the storm rage around them. He had called down the crow's nest an hour ago for fear that the lookout would be tossed overboard by the high winds. Captain Pender stood beside the helm where he could see everything, one hand clutched to the rail as the ship bucked and jumped beneath his heels. A sound pricked at his ears. Glancing up into the rigging, he saw two sailors wrestling with a spar that had come loose.

"Secure that lanyard!" But neither man acknowledged his order over the howl of the storm.

Manck started aloft toward the men. Captain Pender's stomach knotted as one of the sailors slipped from his perch. The other caught him by the arm and they both dangled precariously over the raging sea. Manck reached the yard where they hung and began inching across the slippery beam. The captain's fingernails dug into the rail. A black shadow fell across his vision as a mighty wave towered off the bow. The ship tilted, barely clinging to her balance on the shifting waters. For a moment she stood poised like a bird on a branch while the sea receded beneath her hull. Then the wave crashed down onto the deck, swamping everything in foam. The water tried to carry him away, but he kept his grasp.

Getting his feet under him, he looked up and his heart sank. The yard was bare where three men had been just seconds ago.

"Manck!" he shouted, casting his gaze over the side of the vessel. "Men overboard!"

"There he be!" A hand shot into the air.

The captain followed the pointing finger to a drenched figure clinging to the main mast by a rope. At his orders three sailors jumped into the rigging, despite the danger, and reeled Manck to safety. Captain Pender went to the side and stared about for the other two, but there was no sign of them.

"The sea takes her due," Old Davry muttered at the helm. Sixty and three years of age, he was the ship's elder statesman, as hard as petrified oak and a repository for all manner of nautical lore.

"What was that?"

Old Davry spared a glance for the captain before turning his gaze back to the surging sea. "She takes her due from every man that dares to sail upon her bosom, captain. For some that's death and there's none that can deny her."

The captain nodded, though he didn't understand. Or, perhaps, he did and could not admit it to himself. Either way, two souls had been lost, with more to join them if this storm did not soon abate.

"Steer us north, helmsman," he said. "Into the gale."

Old Davry nodded as if this was a piece of great wisdom, too. "Aye, Captain. Due north."

Captain Pender's gaze swept the leaden sky as the ship swung around into the teeth of the storm.

———⚓———

A muted knock woke him. With a sigh he rolled over on his bunk and sat up. He was still wearing his salt-encrusted clothes from yesterday. The storm had finally broken just after midnight. Dead tired and soaked through, he had stumbled to his cabin and fallen into a deep and mercifully dreamless sleep.

He blinked against the harsh morning light streaming in from the three tall windows at the rear of the cabin. He could not make out any details through the frosted glass, but he was glad to see the sun was out. A good omen for sure.

"Captain?" Manck called from beyond the door.

"Come in. Are we underway?"

Manck ducked his head to enter beneath the low lintel. His eyes were red from lack of sleep, but the fatigue didn't show on the hard planes of his face. "The sails are set, sir, but we're not moving. The winds are gone."

Captain Pender heaved himself off the narrow bed. "Let me see."

He followed his first mate out on deck. The waist was quiet with only a skeleton crew on duty. Manck had sent everyone else below to catch their rest after last night's exertions. The few men on deck avoided his gaze, but he saw it in their faces, the same unease he had spied yesterday, a fear of something that had no name but only a feeling, the same fear every man who made his living on the sea held in his breast. He felt it, too, sometimes at night when the full moon shined its eerie light over endless leagues of ocean and the mind quailed at the thought of so much water beneath with not a speck of land in sight. The sailors called it the Deep, and they feared and hated it as much as they loved it.

He went amidships and peered over the bulwark. The sea stretched flat as a pane of glass for as far as he could see. Not a ghost of a breeze whistled over the waters. He had been becalmed once before off the coast of Sri Lanka on a late-season voyage back from the Indies. For seventeen days they had sat like a buoy on a still sea, until the first of the monsoons came through and gave them enough wind to make sail, but he never heard tell of a calm in these waters. At the least they should be moving with the ocean current. Yet, peer and listen as he would, he could not detect any motion. He ground his teeth together to stave off the tremor that wanted to take root in him.

"That's not all, Captain," Manck said. "Cook wants to see you."

The sound of wood tapping on wood echoed behind him. "Captain?"

Shaking off the memories of those seventeen harrowing days, Captain Pender forced himself to stand tall and turn. Cook stood in Manck's shadow. Dressed in a shabby smock over his breeches, the man looked almost abashed to be above decks during daylight hours. Cook ran the ship's galley single-handedly. He walked with a halting gait due to the stout peg where his right leg had been. Though he told the green-horns that he'd lost it in a fierce battle with a devilfish, the truth was his foot had been run over by a wagon wheel while on shore leave in Havana. It had turned black because he was too busy carousing to be bothered and eventually had to be amputated.

"What is it?" Captain Pender held up a hand to forestall the man. "And none of your stories about sea giants and ancient curses. I've enough worries without you adding nonsense to the pile."

"No, sir," Cook said in a subdued tone. "Would you come with me, Captain? There's something you ought to see with your own eyes."

With a sigh, Captain Pender nodded for the man to lead the way. When Manck made to follow, he said, "Go fetch a few winks. From the looks of things, we won't be going anywhere today."

He saw the look shared between two nearby crewmen and snapped his jaws shut, angry at himself. The events of the last day had been unfortunate enough without him adding ill-talk to it.

Manck nodded. "Aye, Captain. I'll be in my bunk if you need me."

Captain Pender followed Cook down into the ship's interior. The galley stood at the stern, directly below his cabin behind the crew quarters. It was a tight affair, a narrow corridor squeezed between the stoves and a bank of cupboards with racks of pots and utensils hanging by hooks from the ceiling. Cook led him to the back and opened the small door to the pantry.

Captain Pender almost gagged as the rank stench met his nose. Several of the meat barrels had burst, spilling long, oily strips covered in green mold onto the deck. Bundles of fruit were rotted black. "I'll have Mantuba's guts for this! He'll never sell another fig to any sea captain in this lifetime."

"Pardon, Captain, but it wasn't Mantuba," Cook said. "The food was good when we got it and I've been checking it everyday since we left San Juan, just like I always do. Captain, I swear it was good yesterday morning, on my mother's soul. Then this morning I went to fetch breakfast and I see everything's gone bad."

Captain Pender sagged against a counter. "Is there anything left that's edible?"

Cook kicked a barrel with his peg. "I've got a couple kegs of pickled ham, and pickled pickles, of course." He smiled at his own joke, but sobered at a glance from Captain Pender. "But everything else is rotted through and through, Captain. And there's another thing, too, even worse."

Captain Pender was afraid to ask.

"The water's gone bad."

"Gone . . . bad?"

"Aye, sir. I smelled it when I dipped into the open casks this morning. I broke into the sealed ones, too, just to be sure. They've all been fouled, sir. Not a one of them is fit to drink, not unless you want men falling down sick."

"Almighty God," Captain Pender whispered. "Why hast thou forsaken us?"

"Sir?"

Captain Pender pushed himself upright. Running a hand through his short-cropped beard, he blew out a long breath. "All right. Tell no one of this, not the food or water, none of it. And keep everyone out of here, by my orders. Is the rum still good?"

Cook grinned. "Aye, Captain. A little fermented, but it's still good enough for these swine."

"Then give them that for lunch and whatever food you can muster up, but ration it carefully. Understand?"

The man chortled. "You're sure to have the drunkest, smelliest crew in history, Captain."

"How long can we last?"

"A couple days, four maybe, if I stretch it."

"Stretch it, Cook, as best you can." Captain Pender turned to leave and paused. "I mean it. On your life, tell no one about what you found."

The man bobbed his head. "As you say, Captain."

From above decks came a cry. Wondering what else could go wrong, Captain Pender dashed up the companionway, only to be greeted by scattered cheers. He felt the reason at once, a faint zephyr that caressed his face as it puffed out the sails.

"The calm is lifted!" Gilman shouted from the forecastle.

Sighing at the first good news he had heard in twenty-four hours, the captain climbed up to the bridge. The ship was moving once more. The breeze gained strength steadily until it filled all the sails to capacity. Eager to take advantage of the weather while it lasted, Captain Pender sent a man below to rouse more hands. Manck came up with the rest, rubbing his sleepy eyes with the back of a hand.

"So we've had a turn of fortune?"

"Indeed, Mister Manck. It appears that way."

Lowering his voice, the first mate said, "Do you plan to sail direct for the Azores, or turn back and hope to reach the Antilles before the stores run out?"

Captain Pender cursed. "Damn Cook and his loose tongue!"

Manck shook his head. "Not his fault, Captain. He came to me first, not wanting to bother you after the calm struck."

"Still, if the crew finds out, we'll have a mutiny on our hands."

Manck crossed his massive arms. "No one will find out. And if anyone goes spreading rumors, I'll send them down to scrub the Devil. Don't worry, Captain. Now that the wind has returned, all will be well."

"Aye," he said, and wished he could believe it. "But we're smack in the middle of the deep. Even with the fairest wind since Noah, it's two weeks to landfall in either direction. Diverting to the Azores will cost us a sennight if not more, and we'll still run short of food before we reach them."

"Do we have any choice?"

"Damn me, but we do not," the captain muttered. "Helm! Change heading to north-by-northeast."

"Aye, Captain. North-by-northeast."

"Do you want me to say something to the crew?" Manck asked.

"No. I'll tell them over noon mess. They should hear it from me."

"As you will, Captain."

Captain Pender listened to the sounds of the ship, the straining of ropes and full sails, the songs hummed in the rigging, as the deck rolled beneath him to the motion of the sea.

"Middle watch!" the bosun called out and the watch bell rang.

Captain Pender turned his gaze northward toward the Azores and their salvation, before leaving the bridge in Manck's capable hands and heading back to his cabin. The feeling they were headed for a typhoon of trouble rumbled in his belly.

———————— ⚓ ————————

"Land ho!"

Captain Pender looked up from the charts scattered across his desk as the cry came down from above. He had stayed up all night, poring over his maps, updated this past April in Norfolk, trying to find some way to save his ship and crew, but it seemed hopeless. They were at least five hundred nautical miles from landfall. By his most forgiving calculation, they would be a week out of Sao Miguel when the rations ran out. A belt with two Navy pistols in tooled leather holsters hung from a wall peg. He had rummaged them from his locker, cleaned and loaded them. The crew had taken the news with sailors' typical aplomb, and resorted to furious whispers as soon as his back was turned. When the food was gone, things would become hairy. Now some fool was up in the crow's nest singing about land. There were no islands of note in this part of the Atlantic.

With a curse for slipshod cartographers and drunken watchmen, he pulled on his coat to lumber out the door. Several sailors lounged about the mid-deck as he emerged, but they clambered to their feet as they spotted him. Casting a sharp gaze about the ship, he went up to the bridge. Manck was waiting for him. Without a word, the first mate handed him the spyglass and pointed a sun-browned finger northward. Captain Pender looked through the instrument, and bit back another oath. A rocky spit of land rose amid the choppy waves. Gauging the distance, he estimated it at two miles across. It had no beach to speak of, only a stony shore rising to sharp gray-green cliffs all around. There was something about those cliffs that made him pause, like some distant memory nagging at the back of his mind, but he could not put his finger on it.

"What do you think, Captain?" Manck asked. "Do we put ashore?"

Captain Pender wanted to deny the request. He wanted to put the isle aft of his ship and never look back, but he dared not. Whatever malignant atmosphere hung over the isle, he would be derelict in his duty to not stop long enough to look for water. With a long exhalation, he ordered the course change.

"All hands!" Manck shouted as he strode from the bridge and men raced through the rigging.

Captain Pender kept his gaze fixed on the island as the *Mariner* came about. His hand slipped into his waistcoat pocket to touch the metal token. This voyage had experienced more than its fair share of bad luck. Perhaps things were looking up with the sighting of this island. Perhaps they would find water and reach the Azores in good condition, but something told him strange forces were at work.

⚓

The longboat rose and fell with the swell of the waves. Captain Pender sat on the bow. He had decided he would be the first to set foot on the isle. While many of the men were anxious to explore this new piece of land, he could not shake the disquiet that had settled over him. He was glad to have Manck at his side. The big New Zealander had a cutlass and a dirk strapped to his hips, and he held a thick-handled axe. The captain had seen him use the axe before and knew it for a deadly weapon in close quarters. For himself, he had worn his pistol belt. He felt peculiar wearing two guns with only one good hand, but no one looked askance at him out of respect. The rest of the landing party were stout men, although he wished Manck had left van Eyck back aboard the *Mariner*. The man knew his job and never failed to show the proper courtesies, but Captain Pender had never felt comfortable around the Dutchman.

As they drew near land, the foreboding in his chest grew stronger, as if they were rowing closer to some unseen danger, but he sat with his back rigid, face turned to their destination.

A quick circumspection had revealed that the cliffs surrounded the entire isle. They landed on a narrow stretch of shore on the east side of the island. The longboat's prow lifted with the surf and scudded on loose ground. Captain Pender jumped out with the others to pull the boat ashore. Cold seawater ran over the tops of his boots. His feet squished with every step as he fought the tide to climb the stony beach. Once the boat was secure, he turned to survey the lay of the land. A hundred paces past the shoreline, steep hills rose to the feet of the cliffs towering tall above them. From here he could make out a few breaks in the redoubtable stone wall. A powerful smell fouled the air like rotting carcasses.

"Spread out!" he said. "Find me a spring so we can get off this miserable spur."

Manck sidled up to him. "This place has a hellish stench, eh?"

Captain Pender clenched the finger and thumb of his left hand. "Water or no water, I want to be off this rock before sundown, Mister Manck."

"Aye, sir."

As Manck left to lead the search, Captain Pender stared up at the cliffs. He felt like he was being watched by unfriendly eyes. He wondered briefly if the island had any inhabitants, but discarded the notion. The only vegetation he saw were sickly brown vines clinging to the cliffs. He heard no birdcalls, no chattering monkeys. This place was as dead as a tomb.

Scuffing his boot heel in the gravel, he spotted a bloated fish higher up on the shore, likely washed up with the tide. It looked like a bonefish of some type. He paid it no mind until he heard an odd sound, like gentle suckling. He cocked his head and followed the sound to the fish corpse. He leaned over the body. The flesh was mainly intact. As he watched, the corpse rose and fell in a slow rhythm. Nudging it with his boot, he flipped the body over, and recoiled in horror. He reached to his belt for the sword hilt that was not there and pulled out one of the pistols. A huge, blood-red worm had been attached to the underside of the fish, its toothy maw slicing into the flesh while it fed, but it withdrew into a hole in the gravel with startling swiftness. He backed away.

"Captain?" Manck limped over to him, eyeing the pistol. "Is everything all right?"

"Yes," Captain Pender said. Feeling foolish, he slid the pistol back into its holster. It had only been a worm after all. Yet, something about it had triggered an instinctive response in him. He couldn't help thinking how it would feel to have the thing attached to him, sucking out his insides. "What have you found?"

"Nothing. There's no water source along the shore here. We'll have to go inland."

Captain Pender looked up to the cliffs. "Well, let's be about it then. Gather the men. We'll all go together."

Manck formed up the shore party and they marched deeper into the isle's interior. The hills were every bit as steep and difficult to navigate as they had looked. Captain Pender found himself slipping with every other step as his boots failed to find purchase on the bare rock. After much heaving and bemoaning, the party scaled the hills and stopped to consider the greater obstacle before them. The cliffs rose six hundred feet into the sky. The outer face was exceedingly flat. Gazing along the circumference, the captain noted long cuts in the cliff wall, too straight to be cracks.

"Strange," Manck said as he fingered a strand of vine with broad, round leaves. "Sea kelp, but what's it doing draped all over the island? I've never seen it growing out of water."

Van Eyck tugged on a vine and it came away easily in his hand. "It's not growing, sir. Look, it's not even attached. It's just laying there."

"Maybe the same storm that hit us threw the whole mess up here?" McKiernan said.

Captain Pender stared at the grooves in the cliffs, trying to follow them beneath the curtain of vines. Sudden realization struck him like a bolt from the heavens. The cliffs were not a natural formation. They were man-made, though he could not fathom the people who could have engineered such a feat. He tried to calculate the weight of the massive stone blocks and gave up. It was all too much to comprehend.

He could see in his first mate's eyes that Manck had realized it as well. They shared a glance. Then Manck shouted, "Someone find me a way through these cliffs!"

They soon found one of the breaks the captain had spied from below, a vertical crack in the wall wide enough for a man to squeeze through. Manck went first with the others trailing him. The captain glanced seaward to where the *Mariner* sat riding at anchor. This was a fool's errand. They should go back now while they still could. With a shake of his head, he followed his crew.

More kelp vines choked the craggy gap in the great wall. Clearing the way with their machetes, the sailors pressed through to the other side to find themselves at the edge of a vast, bowl-shaped gorge. The view was spectacular, but what drew the captain's attention were the monuments clustered on the floor of the basin. Made of the same gray-green stone as the island's mighty sea-wall, they ranged from simple obelisks and free-standing pillars to vast domes hundreds of feet wide, palatial buildings fit for any crowned head of Europe. Captain Pender's first impression was they had found the ruins of some ancient culture, but what culture that could be he had no clue. The structures were built in a bizarre style with odd angles and walls that extended into the air, only to stop for no apparent reason, as if the builders had planned on continued stages of construction that were never completed.

Captain Pender wanted nothing to do with the ruins below. He was about to order a retreat, but several of the crew were already filing down a narrow path to the floor of the gorge.

Manck spat over the side of the precipice. "Shall I call them back, Captain?"

Captain Pender's right palm rested on the handle of a pistol. With a shake of his head, he took his hand away. "No, we need that water. But keep them together. No wandering off. There's no telling what's lurking down there."

"Lurking, Captain? Begging your pardon, but it looks abandoned. Like as not there hasn't been a living soul on this island in a hundred years."

"Still, let's not tarry a moment longer than we have to. The sun's getting low."

As he followed Manck down the narrow trail, his gaze darted among the buildings, searching for the source of the mysterious presence he had felt on the beach, but his first mate was right. This city had been dead for centuries. But the feeling of dread still coiled in his stomach.

The sailors spread out as they reached the basin floor, wandering among the ruins. Captain Pender stayed with Manck. Side by side they walked down an ancient boulevard with strands of white mist swirling about their feet. Stern-faced eidolons frowned at them from bas-relief friezes carved around the rooftops of several structures, their elongated features only half-visible from the ground. A layer of gray slime covered everything. It sucked at their heels with every step. The stench here was worse than on the beach. It clogged in his nose until his head began to hurt.

Something chittered above and behind him, a bizarre sound that slid down his spine like a greasy finger. He turned to spot its origin, but there was nothing but gray stone and sky. A loud call grabbed his attention.

"Ho!"

Sparing a last glance to the rooftops, Captain Pender followed Manck to the doorway of a tall, narrow building where several sailors had gathered. McKiernan stood in their midst, holding something aloft to the light. Captain Pender caught a glimpse of gold.

"What have you found, Mister McKiernan?" Manck asked as he pushed through the throng.

Captain Pender got close enough to see the object in his crewman's hands, a golden statuette as long as his forearm, all adorned with sparkling jewels of blue and red.

"It must be worth a fortune!" someone said.

McKiernan grinned. "Enough to return to Ireland in style, I'll wager. Fine clothes and a big house, that's for me!"

Captain Pender bent close for a better look. The idol had a queer look to it. He couldn't discern whether it had been fashioned to resemble a man or a beast, for it had the features of both.

"There's got to be more where that came from!"

The sailors scattered through the streets in their search for booty. Captain Pender scratched under his beard as he gazed at the statue in the Irishman's hands. There was something wrong about it, about this entire place. They didn't belong here.

He was about to give the order to clear out when a garbled cry echoed across the stone facades of the strange city. Manck didn't wait, but ran to the next intersection, quick as a thought despite his limp, and disappeared around the corner. Captain Pender rushed after him. As he turned the corner, he saw Manck enter a long, squat building with three slanting minarets rising from its flat roof. He heard another cry and Manck emerged, the blade of his axe smeared with some blackish gore. The first mate's face was blanched like a new sail.

"What is it?"

Manck just shook his head and stared through the open doorway. Captain Pender tried to enter, but Manck seized him with a strong hand. "Don't! It's not right. A thing like that . . . it shouldn't be allowed to walk under God's sun!" He dropped the axe on the street and wiped his hands on his clothes, leaving gruesome streaks on his tunic.

Hearing the strangled tone of terror in his first mate's voice, Captain Pender didn't need any more convincing. "All right. Let's gather the lads and get out of here." Lifting his gaze to the buildings around them, he spoke up. "We're going! We don't want anything from this accursed place."

He aided Manck as they hurried away from the squat structure. Captain Pender shouted for his crew, but the mist had risen higher since their arrival and his voice echoed back to him. He thought he saw Samuel Cloister standing at the corner of a triangular obelisk, bent over something in his grasp, but a gray shadow passed between them and the man was gone.

"Where are they?"

"Gone," Manck whispered. "All of them gone."

"Nonsense!" Captain Pender said. "They're around here somewheres, poking around for golden statues. They've all gone treasure crazy."

He spotted a cluster of shapes lurking on some broad steps at the foot of a massive building. If the city had a center, this was surely it. Rising taller than the *Mariner's* main mast, its architecture seemed a combination of several civilizations: Greek, Egyptian, Aztec, and others he could not identify, but even older if that was possible, predating them all. Rhythmic pounding and the scratch of steel on rock echoed through the fog.

Captain Pender drew a pistol in his right hand. "Mister Manck! Produce your saber."

But his first mate stood as if stricken by an ague, his large body shuddering with awful tremors. Captain Pender squinted as he tried to peer through the cloying mist. The barrel of his pistol waved back and forth, tracking the figures, but his right hand had never been as accurate as the left.

Pressing forward, he saw a knot of his crewmen wrestling with a tall stone door at the building's entrance. They were trying to break open the massive valve using their machetes and the butts of their rifles. A symbol of some sort was inscribed on the door, but time and the elements had worn it indistinct. Still, peering through the gloom, Captain Pender thought he could almost recognize it.

Some years back he had bought a carving in Senegal said to have been taken from an ancient temple lost in the jungles. It was an ugly thing of some bestial pagan god, all horns and gnashing fangs. He'd meant it as a gift for Anna, but thought the better of it later and sold it to a trinket-trader in another port. Something about the symbol on the door reminded him of the strange letters carved around the base of the idol, written in

no language he had ever seen before or since.

Van Eyck spied him and beckoned. "We found it, Captain! It's the treasure trove! There's sure to be a mountain of gold and jewels inside."

Captain Pender stood with Manck's arm over his shoulders. "We're leaving, men. There's nothing for us here but an early grave."

The door lurched inward. The sailors stumbled to catch their balance as a cloud of noxious vapor billowed from the aperture. As the door shifted on its ancient hinges, beams of fading daylight struck the engraved image and Captain Pender shuddered. A pentagram stared at him. His left hand went to his waistcoat. Fumbling with the pocket, he pulled forth the bizarre doubloon Nicholas had rescued from the sea.

The street bucked beneath his feet, sending him and Manck reeling against a broken pillar. Captain Pender gritted his teeth as a sharp edge of stone gashed his leg above the knee. Exasperated, he pointed his pistol into the air and pulled the trigger. Its loud report echoed through the mist-shrouded boulevards. The sailors looked down, blinking as if they had emerged from a daze.

"To the ship!" Captain Pender shouted as a tremor ran under his heels.

The men raced down the steps in bounds, casting fearful gazes over their shoulders as they ran, all except van Eyck. He remained at the doorway, reaching an arm into the murky darkness.

"Mister van Eyck!"

The sailor turned and the captain saw his features, drained of blood. The sailor's mouth quivered. He lurched back against the door, his arm pulled deeper into the aperture. "Captain!" he cried.

Shrugging off Manck's arm, Captain Pender leapt up the broad stairs. His heart thudded in his chest as he watched his crewman being dragged into the shadowed doorway. Manck had said they weren't men, weren't human. He didn't waste time reloading the pistol, but thrust it back into the holster and reached across his waist for the second gun. He drew it with a trembling hand as his left thumb and forefinger gripped the crewman's shirt. He pointed his pistol into the doorway and pulled the trigger without aiming. Another shudder ran through the ground.

"Pull, man! Pull!" he shouted as he tried to pry the sailor free, but whatever had hold of van Eyck wouldn't let him loose.

Captain Pender's gaze followed his crewman's arm. In the darkness beyond the stone door he sensed a great mass looming. That which grasped van Eyck's arm was not a hand or a claw, but a slimy, twisting limb like a squid's tentacle. Blood-red and bloated, it expanded and constricted as it held the man fast. At its end a mouth-like sucker burrowed into the flesh of his forearm with sharp teeth. Captain Pender lifted his eyes and what he saw there made him stagger back, almost tripping down the steps. The discharged pistol dropped from his hand. Great eyes stared at him from that awful abyss, so many eyes, all huge and yellow with ancient malevolence. This place was not a treasure house. It was a crypt for something from another age. *Something which had never died!*

A sinuous appendage reached for him. Captain Pender lifted his arms before his face, trying to block out the image, and a golden light flashed. Icy pain shot through his left hand. He clamped his jaws tight to keep from calling out. The Thing withdrew, but the limb holding van Eyck pulled with renewed vigor. Captain Pender tried, but he could not bring himself to approach the doorway again. He closed his eyes as the sailor began to scream, high-pitched shrieks that cut through him. Flush with shame, the captain turned and ran for his life.

Manck staggered on the avenue as the isle shook, but the first mate looked to have recovered some of his wits. His gaze traveled to the stone door. "What—?"

Captain Pender seized the man by the arm and dragged him away without a word. Together they ran through the ruined city as the ground trembled beneath their strides. Cries echoed around them. More than once the captain saw horrid shapes darting through the misty alleys on either side of them, long-limbed shadows with large eyes like glowing lanterns. Patches of blood stained the entrances to those streets, but he and Manck did not pause to investigate. He prayed every man in the landing party would reach the shore safely, but a primal instinct for survival had risen up in him. He could face tribes of hostile natives and stare down the gullets of raging hurricanes with impassive stoicism, but he would not remain on this isle one moment longer to save his own sweet mother.

Up to the precipice they raced and through the gap in the wall. Seaweed clutched at his shoulders and looped around his ankles as if trying to slow his flight, but Manck's cutlass cleared a path for them through the clinging strands. They scampered down the hills on the far side without regard to their safety. Two sailors had reached the shore before them, struggling to launch the longboat. As he drew closer, he recognized McKiernan and Two-Thumbs Obed. Manck threw his shoulder in to help and Captain Pender watched the tall cliffs. No one else emerged.

"Captain, it's time to get off this rock!" Manck roared, up to his hips in the surf. He clung to the side of the boat as another tremor shook the ground.

The others had already clambered aboard and seized the oars. Captain Pender waded through the breakers and accepted a hand up. He settled in the bow as the sailors turned the longboat about and strained their backs pulling out to sea. The *Mariner* sat offshore where they had left her. The sight of his ship had never been so dear. His right hand clamped onto the side of the boat, silently urging the men to pull harder. In his left he grasped the strange doubloon.

As they drew up alongside the ship, ropes snaked down from above and strong hands heaved them up. "All hands!" Captain Pender shouted as soon as his boots touched deck. "Weigh anchor and raise the sails!"

Manck strode through the deck, pushing men into the rigging as his voice rose to echo the commands.

Young Nicholas ran over to meet them. "Where are the others?"

McKiernan shoved the boy out the way. "Be off and let grown men save your skinny hide from the beasts of the deep."

"Beasts of the deep?"

Captain Pender frowned at the boy. "Not now, Nicholas. Go fetch some rum from the galley."

As the cabin boy dashed off, he turned his attention to the running of the ship. As the sails lifted, he felt the *Mariner* move through the choppy waters, much too slowly for his liking. He counted the seconds as his gaze went out to the isle. With the motion of the sea, it looked as if the cliffs were shaking. It took him a moment to realize the island was sinking. The waters rushed over the shore and climbed the great wall until the isle vanished, swallowed by the sea.

"Back to the lightless hell you came from," he whispered.

A passing sailor glanced at him. "Did you say something, Captain?"

Captain Pender shook his head, but his gaze never left the spot where the isle had sunk beneath the foamy waves. A few cries called from the rigging as others noticed the isle's disappearance, but Manck kept the sailors too busy to make much of it.

The captain opened his left hand. The five-sided doubloon sat in his palm, glinting with an odd cast in the dwindling sunlight. Lifting back his arm, he hurled it over the side in the lost isle's direction. Then he retreated to his cabin, with the shades pulled tight and all the lamps lit to stave off the coming darkness.

───────⚓───────

He sat at his desk in the early morning hours, gazing at Anna's picture. Her letter lay folded on his lap. Sleep had evaded him, or he had avoided it, afraid of what he might see if he closed his eyes. A clean sheet of parchment rested on the desk before him. With an unsteady hand he lifted the pen from the inkwell. Its black tip shone like a raven's beak, wet with blood. He clenched his left hand and dispelled the image.

His hand moved of its own will, flowing over the parchment with neat letters. He wanted to go home, his true home, not this gypsy's wagon of wood and sailcloth. He wanted to be quit of the sea. Let her keep her mysteries hidden beneath wave and endless dark. There were things men should not know, should not see with their own eyes, ancient things from epochs before the first man had raised his head to consider a starry night.

Sealing the letter with a dollop of hot wax, he set it aside. The creak of the mastheads rumbled through the cabin. The winds had returned, but how long could they survive on rum and boiled leather? Days, perhaps a week. They would never make the Azores. He should have retired last year when Anna begged him. He could be living the life of a landed gentleman, enjoying his twilight years with his children before they got too old to care about him. He could take Anna to see Philadelphia like she had always wanted, and anywhere else she desired so long as they could travel by coach. If he survived this crossing, he vowed it would be the last time. Almighty willing, he would never set foot on another sailing vessel as long as he lived. But he knew it for an empty oath. They would die to a man on this ship, their rigged coffin.

With a heavy sigh, Captain Pender reached for his rum bottle. As the first rays of a new day broke through his window, he unholstered his pistol and considered the five-sided mark branded into the palm of his left hand. How long did it take for a man to starve to death? The answer whispered in the crack of the salt-stiff sails above and the slow roll of the deck beneath his feet.

Forever, forever, forever. . . .

Stillworld: Sailing to Noon
Chun Lee

I had a plan to save Stillworld. It was going to require a lot of magic, maybe more than I could produce, but I had to try. Stillworld couldn't limp on like this forever.

We hadn't always called it that. Those of us from the Black Star Academy had called the world Blue Three, on account of it having been the third blue planet in our system—we of the academy, too busy with our books, ancient scrolls, and abacuses, weren't the most poetic of sorts.

Other cultures and races had their own names for the planet. The Creblah of the southern lands of Leeva, with their four spider-like arms, had called it Vesnuen, a pretty name that translated to Old Mother. If you had ever spoken to the underground people of Urukan, they had a name for the planet that was impossible for a human like me to pronounce, but it translated to the Great Dirt Ball that Hides Us from the Light of the Sun. Orc had called it the Ground.

It no longer mattered which culture you were from; after the calamity, everyone on this planet called it Stillworld.

It was the third moon of our journey through the Shaded Road. Rena and I had a ship to get to. We were an odd pair because I had been quite young when I had graduated from the academy, and I had taken her as my apprentice soon after. She had been twelve and I had been seventeen. So our relationship was more like an older brother with his sister than master and apprentice.

Rena was now seventeen. She had made the right choice when she decided to be a Black Star mage. She was quite the bookhead. There were times I had to pry her from her books in order to do the daily chores.

Today she had tied her strawberry-blonde hair up in her usual ponytail but she wore a light blue travel outfit rather than the traditional black robes with a shining, dark violet star a Black Star mage should wear. I was lenient with her because she could have been a full mage by now. I hadn't told her this, but she had well enough talent to be one. I just needed a trusted assistant to help me with my mission to save Stillworld.

The Shaded Road was always dark, with a tinge of purple in the air. Dead black trees lined our way on either side of the trail. We occasionally came upon a starved corpse that had probably been desperate to get to Dusk. Rena's purple eyes turned away whenever we passed one. It could get cold on the fringe of the Ring of Dusk and Dawn but today the weather was mild.

"I'm getting tired of walking," I said to Rena, lowering my black hood to wipe a thin film of sweat from my brow. I pointed to our two large chests carrying our supplies and several mathematics texts. "I think we should just let these chests carry us the rest of the way."

"The mages at the Academy said to never use magic for day-to-day purposes. 'Only when necessary and only for emergencies.'" She blew a loose strand of hair out of her face and readjusted her spectacles after reciting the most repeated line at the Academy. "We've already balanced out the gravity of the chests so we can pull them with ease. Isn't that bad enough?"

"Rena, do you think those old bookheads from the Academy would walk this distance? If they took the same trip they would have balanced out the gravity of some large rug and taken every comfort of home with them. We teach humility at the Academy so some hothead doesn't get the idea to fly off the planet."

"I heard you were the biggest hot head the academy ever knew."

"Maybe I was." I lifted the bottom of my robe and straddled my chest so that I faced Rena and not the direction we were headed.

"Don't," she said, a warning in her eyes.

I waved goodbye to her and zoomed off down the trail. She turned into a small dot in an instant but I stayed close enough to keep an eye on her. The Shaded Road was not safe. There were desperate bandits everywhere.

I hoped she would get on her chest and follow me, but she was such a stickler for the rules. She continued to walk at her own pace, and I waited for her, floating on my chest. *She must learn that a good mage will know all the rules, but a master mage will know where the rules can be bent.* That was a hard lesson for someone like her.

She finally caught up, and she didn't have a word for me. We went on at our slow pace—I hovered with her while she walked the path. We'd reach the city of Agenmouth in two more moons.

—⚓—

Agenmouth was one of the few original cities to survive the planet's stop. If that wasn't lucky enough, it also neighbored a mountain, which fed the river that flowed into the city. Agenmouth was now the largest city on the Dusk side of the planet. The skies were always a bright orange flare. There were even some small farms, crops clinging to life, on the outskirts of the city. Guards stood watch around these small farms; the food was for those with the power to guard it. The poor and helpless still had to scrounge and beg.

Homes were packed in tightly with many buildings built atop older ones; they had to maximize what precious space was left. Gravity mages helped wooden towers of impossible design defy architectural limits. The largest of them was Jefro Landing, the skyport, standing like a giant white thorn jutting out of the ground. Ships of all sizes hung from the sides of the building, taking on supplies or unloading cargo. Some came from as far away as Dawnside.

Rena oohed and ahhed at all the sites; this was her first time in Agenmouth, and she had never seen wonders like a working fountain or the ancient marble statues of lost kings and queens.

We headed into Pennytown, a shantytown of brothels next to Jefro Landing. Blue scarves hung out of poorly crafted windows to signal that a room and a Penny was available for a few hours of enjoyment. A thick stink of poorly made perfume choked our nostrils. Females of all races called to me from their windows, soliciting me with vulgar invitations. I smiled and waved at them, enjoying their attentions. Rena lowered her head, her face reddening.

"Why did we have to come this way?" she asked.

"The brothels form a great ring around Jefro Landing. It can't be avoided. Sailing is a hard life, especially now that the oceans have dried up or frozen over, so don't ever get in the way of a sailor and his Miss Penny."

"Pennys," she said as if they were vermin. "Perez, have you ever used one?"

"Of course not. We of the Black Star Academy have a name to maintain."

A Miss Penny of the Lizard clans of Leesha told me from her window all the amazing tricks she could do with her tongue, then showed me four feet of her marvelous red and slimy appendage.

"I sometimes wonder what I've been missing out on though."

———————⚓———————

At the base of the skyport we found a crowd of people from several different cultures waiting to buy passage or meet their loved ones. Most of them looked ragged, but for a few landowners in silly bright colors and frumpy designs who waited with their servants. A band of travelers, each wearing a large red feather stuck in their hair, talked to one another in a circle. I covered the Black Star emblem on my chest by crossing my arms.

"Stay away from those men and don't let them know you're from the Academy," I said to Rena.

"The Red Feathers?"

"They don't teach this to you at the Academy but we do make mistakes from time to time."

Her purple eyes squinted at me, failing to understand.

"Fifty years ago, when the world was slowing down to a halt, the Black Star Academy calculated the rate of the planet's deceleration. Even then we knew that the Rings of Dusk and Dawn would be the only places left on the planet capable of holding life."

Rena nodded as if to say she assumed all that already. Bright girl.

"We calculated that the dusk side of the planet would be the eastern continent of Crognin."

Rena's mouth dropped open and her eyes widened.

"And we were right," I said, pointing at her nose. "The world *did* stop spinning like we had calculated. Except, we didn't expect something."

"When night and day ran backwards."

"Yup. You've read about it, I'm sure." People could get used to longer and longer days but when the Sun rose on the wrong side and day followed day and night followed night. . . .

I didn't want to think of what the calamity had been like. There were plenty of books on *that* event. I hadn't known an illustration in a book could have so much red.

"A lot of people trusted our calculations. Especially a small tribe on the eastern coast of Crognin."

"But that was fifty years ago. Why would they blame those of us who had nothing to do with the error?"

"They aren't the most logical of people. They have some kind of blood oath or something. That's actually why they wear the red feather. They want to kill the Black Star Academy. So just remember to stay away from them."

Rena shifted her eyes away from the Red Feathers, keeping her head down.

"Come now, we have a pirate friend to speak with," I said.

The uplift was operated by a boy with some gravity magic. He was impressed by the Black Star emblem and treated me as if I was nobility. I told him that math was the key to every good Black Star mage and he seemed to appreciate the knowledge I gave him.

The docking levels were a flurry of people loading and unloading supplies and goods. The thin air reminded me of my apprentice years when I had traveled under my own mage, Lyga the Puzzle King. We'd taken a few steps onto the walkway to the docks when Rena finally asked the question I was expecting. I guess the Red Feathers had really worried her.

"Did you say pirate?"

"Well, ex-pirate . . . kind of."

"What?"

"He doesn't go around trying to take cargo from other ships anymore—"

"You mean raid?"

"But he's also not going to pass an opportunity if it presents itself."

"His name?"

"Captain Kroodshect."

"That sounds like an Orc's name."

"Not all Orc are roving barbarians ready to kill anything that moves."

"He *is* an Orc?"

"He's from the Karshak clans. They are very social Orc. They like to speak and trade with people."

"And rob them when the opportunity arises?"

"He doesn't do that . . . well actually, he might do that, but he's also the most experienced captain there is. He's old enough to remember sailing on water."

I stopped in front of our ship. Made from the sun-bleached trees of Dayside, it was white as a pearl, was three masts fast, and carried broadsides of ten cannons. A fine ship.

"What's she called?" Rena asked.

"Officially, the captain named her the Jagged Wooden Spoon—something about how his mother would force food down his mouth when he was young—but everyone calls her the *Duchess* on account of how she looks like the white wedding dress the Duchess wore on the day of the calamity."

"That's horrible. I think history looks at her poorly. I don't see anything wrong with insisting your wedding proceed, even if the world is falling apart. Might be even more reason to insist on it."

A familiar and nauseating musk stung my nostrils.

"Yar, yer right, bonnie. But we call her the *Duchess* 'cause she's a stubborn bitch like her namesake. 'Tis a good name." It was our good captain. He tipped his tri-corn hat to us. The grin on his face had an added gaudy effect thanks to a gold-capped tusk. The wide cutlass at his side jangled against his squat, black boot. He didn't wear a shirt to cover his dark-green skin, but he did wear two gun belts over his chest and shoulders; each one held six pistols of polished red wood.

"Captain, it's good to see you again," I said. "You haven't changed at all."

"You sure have, matey. I figure you've grown a full foot since I've last seen you."

I presented Rena to the captain. "This is my apprentice, Rena."

"Nice to meet you, Captain Kroodshect," she said. Her small hand was engulfed by his large green sausage-like fingers.

"Please, bonnie. Don't be calling me that. The crew be calling me Captain Krood and that's how I like it." He had a smile that could either send shivers down your back or make you think of a fat child in a bakery.

"Krood?" she asked. The Orc's musk must have hit her because she started coughing.

"Yes." He turned his attention to me. "Now, Perez, I was expecting you two here much earlier. Gravity mage like you should be able to fly here in half a moon."

I gave Rena a stare. "Yes, well, we're here now and ready to shove off."

"Arrr, well that be the problem. Seems when you were late I decided to give the crew leave. They've been carousing with the Miss Pennys the last two moons."

"So I've been paying you and your men to drink and cavort with Pennys for two moons?"

"Yar, 'tis been a fine shore leave."

"You hear that, Rena? Seems I've been keeping half of Pennytown in business while we were taking our time getting here. I haven't even been able to visit a Miss Penny."

Rena gave me a tired expression.

---⚓---

Krood was able to find every member of his crew within half a moon. I kept track of each crewman and how much they weighed. I had to have a good idea of how much the ship would finally weigh in order to balance it out. I knew from memory exactly how much the *Duchess* weighed when empty of crew and supplies so that wouldn't be a problem.

We were finally ready to shove off when Captain Krood rested a large hand on my shoulder.

"Me crew thought me mad to send off my three gravity mages in exchange fer one Black Star master and his apprentice. But I knew. I know one of you was worth ten of them."

"Thanks," I said.

"Now, let's get this fat girl in the air. Me legs've been wobbly since we docked."

Normally a captain would give his orders to the first mate and the first mate would bellow out those orders, but Krood's first mate was a large mute Tug named Argen. He didn't speak because his tongue had been cut off when he was young. Krood preferred to yell out his orders anyway, and Krood's idea of a good first mate was a loyal man who kept the ship from mutiny. A large blue-furred Tug kept mutiny out of the minds of his crew just fine.

I concentrated on the *Duchess*, taking into account the crew of fifty-five. There were heavy stores of water packed and sealed with camel butter to keep them from leaking. We carried enough tack for twice the trip. Several packs of blood fruit to keep our teeth from rotting out, buckets of camel butter, and the usual amounts of tar and extra rigging rested in the ship's hold. The powder room held an unusual amount of shot, but that was expected from an Orc captain. A more than generous portion of rum to fuel the crew sat next to the cook's supply room. Something else weighed down the ship at the bottom, but I adjusted accordingly.

I searched for the point of equilibrium in the familiar place it was the last time I lifted the *Duchess*. Soon, the ship was balancing out and a stray wind shifted the ship a few inches. A pinch of my own energy and the ship was afloat.

Captain Krood bellowed out orders as soon as we were in the air. "Clear moorings. Lift sails. Helmsman, we be heading straight into that there ship. Hard to port and we better not be hittin' her or you'll be getting cut from stem to gudgeon."

After some tricky navigating, we finally left the bustle of flying ships from Jefro Landing. Several pigeons followed us in what looked like a mock tribute.

"Destination, Captain?" the helmsman asked.

"The Sun, lad." Captain Krood took in a lungful of high air. "Take her to the Sun and don't stop till we be right under that fiery bitch."

———⚓———

When your only job on a ship was to keep it afloat, you end up being incredibly bored. The constant sunlight drained us of morale and put most of us on edge; each moon was hotter than the last. We also had to keep ourselves covered in camel butter so we didn't lose any unnecessary moisture. It felt horrible and gunky but you needed it if you wanted to stay under the sun for so long. We even put some in our water. It made it taste bitter and greasy.

Even with our books, we often walked around the ship looking for something to do. There was nothing much to gaze at when we looked over the railing. The sun side of the planet was nothing but white desert as far as you could see.

We watched the sailors perform feats of acrobatics, hanging from the rigging. Or we watched them play their gambling games, calculating the odds of who would win and lose—they disliked us doing that. Sometimes a rousing air chantey raised our spirits, but even that was fleeting.

The rest of my free time was spent training Rena. I would let her take control of the ship for a few hours at a time so I could sneak in a nap or two, but it required a keen mind to keep a ship afloat. You had to always keep your mind on the object, making minor adjustments to the balancing point due to weight lost by moisture evaporation or regular degradation. Spending too much time finding the balancing point would drain you as well.

While we were training in our small quarters, Captain Krood grabbed me by the arm.

"Arrr, I figured I'd just be having to sit around and wait for you to tell me what your plan be, but I guess 'tis some humility you've learned since I last knew ye, lad."

"I suppose so," I said.

"Captain Krood?" Rena asked.

"Yes, bonnie?"

"Forgive the interruption but would you mind if I dabbed some of my rose oil on you? I don't wish to be rude but your scent has been repugnant since I met you."

Krood let out a rumbling laugh. "Aye. You can, just don't be telling any of me crew."

Rena dabbed generous amounts of rose oil on Krood's neck; I doubted if it would do any good.

The captain continued with his line of questioning. "Well, will you be telling me or are we to sit around with our hands in our pants when we reach Noon?"

I pointed at the Black Star emblem on my chest. "It all has to do with this."

"The Black Star?"

"Do you know much about Black Star history?"

"Not a bit, lad. Waste o' time, the past. I only be dealing with the present."

"The first grand mage, the one who started the Academy, was named Bernardo. He was the first to realize that there was a math to gravity magic. A math to everything in the world, actually. He had a talent for sensing the weight of everything around him—once again, the first to do so.

"While traveling the world, Bernardo sensed a great pull of gravity from the western continents. When he got there he found a small piece of dark material that weighed billions of times more than it should have."

"Yar, and how big is a billion?"

"Let's just say it's a lot," I said. Rena snickered but the captain didn't notice. "Through chemical tests, and a lot of calculations that I won't bore you with, he figured out that the rock was actually a piece of a dead star, a black star."

"Arrr."

"It's my theory that a much larger piece of black star is resting at the center of the great desert."

"You think that be what's made the world still?"

"I do. If something that heavy were to land on our planet, then the world would slow down till it was still. It even explains why the planet spun the other way for a bit. The planet was adjusting to the weight."

"Don't let him go on about this for long or he'll get too excited and never sleep," Rena said. She'd heard me go on and on about my theories.

"So yer planning on moving the heavy rock somewhere else when we get to it?" Captain Krood asked; his last words seemed to drift off. He turned his head to look over the side of the ship. His brow furrowed. Sometimes I forgot that Krood was alive when the world was still spinning. He must be missing the oceans more than living with fellow Orc.

"Ship at our stern sir," bellowed out the four-armed Creblah sitting in the crow's nest.

Krood ran to the poop deck with a telescope in hand. Rena and I followed after.

"She's flying no flags," the captain said. "But take a look at the figurehead."

Krood handed me his telescope and I pointed it at the figurehead. It was a mermaid like on almost every other ship but I noticed someone had tied a red feather to the back of her head. A jolly roger rose up their gaff.

"They'd raise that flag to me?" Krood asked in amused disbelief. "Mister Hills, raise our own."

The Black Star emblem that we flew was lowered and a jolly roger soon flew from our gaff.

I saw a glimmer of excitement from Krood's eyes and I had to admit to a bit of my own. A week of reading made me anxious for a diversion.

"They must've known we'd be fat with supplies, sailing to noon," I said. They were gaining on us.

Krood turned the ship around to face our attackers.

"Load cannons," he said.

The crew, although a motley group, were well trained, and worked with a method-ical speed, which reminded me of gears in a clock. The two ships faced one another. It was a strange feeling to face your enemy for so many beats of your heart. Eventually we were nearing range for our cannons. The captain ordered the ship hard to port.

"Rena, you'll have to take control of the ship," I said.

She nodded and adjusted her spectacles.

"Remember to change the balance every time we fire or take a cannonball. Just a minor adjustment but if you don't you'll be exhausted by the end of the moon."

"Just be careful," she said. "And remember not to over strain yourself." She was quoting more Blackstar rules.

"Don't worry about me."

Krood was never a patient Orc. As soon as we were in range, he ordered the cannons emptied. Several booms shook the *Duchess* and the enemy ship was peppered with black clouds of dust and debris. Some of our shots missed in the captain's haste but we did our damage.

"Hah. Enjoy the taste of splinters, you rusty amateur," Krood said.

The other ship waited till all their cannons were properly facing us before they fired. This was when I came into play. As soon as the cannons let fly, I concentrated to balance out the weight of the balls. You needed to do this as fast as possible since the cannon-balls moved in an instant. I tried my best but I only managed to balance out three of the cannonballs and three others smashed into the side of our hull. The ones I did balance bounced off our side. The *Duchess* rocked back and forth. I watched Rena concentrate as she stabilized the ship. She seemed drained for a moment but then she regained her bal-ance. Good. I was afraid the ship might have rolled over on her side from the force of the blow, but Rena was learning fast and she has a larger source of life energy than she knew.

"Arrr. Give her another volley," Krood said. He pulled out his cutlass and pointed at the other ship.

But the crew was unable to reload in time. Our pursuers were faster than us and flew by our stern. We were about to take a near-point-blank volley.

"Perez," Krood said and I knew what to do.

Rena gave a startled grunt as I took control of the *Duchess* and raised her sixty feet.

The Red Feather ship emptied into air and our crew cheered because of the brilliant escape.

"Yar, you can tell they have an inexperienced captain. They don't know that we can go up and down as well," Krood said.

"But you did, didn't you?" I asked the captain. He lived for these kinds of moments and I was happy to oblige.

"You could be betting your mother's pearls on them." He screamed into the lower levels with a childish grin. "Bottom hull cannons."

The extra weight at the bottom level I had noted earlier was a line of cannons facing keelward, four strong. They were hard to aim and reload but Krood knew how effective they could be.

He waited until we were right above them, our hull scraping against the top point of their main mast. "Fire, and add some of yer hate to it."

Two solid shots on their main sail shattered their mast into a spike of splinters. The large white sheet fell and covered half the crew on their deck.

Captain Krood let out a loud guffaw that rang my ears.

Now that they had lost their main mast we could have left them be. They would limp home minus a sail, and if they were smart about provisions they would have enough water for the rest of the journey. But Krood wasn't one to take pity on weakened prey, not with the smell of shot in the air.

"Grappling hooks," he said. Now the real fun started.

"Rena, I'll be stepping off for a moment." I gave her my most charming smile. "Please keep the ship steady."

"What?" She did a good job at controlling her shriek.

I didn't answer. Pausing to give her a slight salute, I leapt over the railing; air rushed all around. Pure exhilaration.

I think I heard a frustrated "PEREZ" from above but I couldn't be sure. I lightened my body and landed on the Red Feather ship's poop deck. I balanced out the weight of three men and pushed them over the side of their ship. Now there was enough room for my comrades.

Captain Krood jumped over the side of the *Duchess* with rope in one hand and a pistol in the other. Several others followed him, including his mute first mate.

I pushed away two more sailors and Krood shot one pistol, dropped it, and then shot another. His crew took on the rest of them and chaos spread on the deck. I threw off anyone that was still in the rigging, waiting to jump upon us. I loved a good melee. And I could tell from Krood's great smile that he was enjoying it as well.

When the sounds of battle died down to a murmur, we decided to go below deck to find their captain. Most of the crew donned the red feathers but none of them wore the High Eagle beak around their necks.

Krood ran down below, firing off two more pistols; I followed him. He had a nose for fighting; the tusks probably helped too. The Red Feather crew left Krood alone—who wants to confront a heavily armed Orc? Some charged at me but I pushed them aside easily.

Captain Krood found a cabin in the center of the ship. There was nothing there except for one man meditating crossed legged, wearing the High Eagle's beak. Krood pointed the pistol at the man.

"Wait," I said.

Too late. It was hard to talk reason into an Orc when he was enjoying the heat of battle. Krood fired his pistol right into the man's head.

"Bad," I said. The ship lost stability, rolled to one side, and went into freefall.

"She's sinking," yelled Krood, who grabbed onto the frame of the doorway, his feet floating in the air.

I reached out my mind to balance out the weight of the ship but found resistance. There was another gravity mage somewhere, forcing the ship down. I could fight with him to take control of the ship but we had no time and he seemed to be using all he had to force the ship downward; guess he didn't care if he used up all of his life energy now.

I used my own energy to push myself and Krood downward so we had some semblance of gravity. Essentially, we were falling slightly faster than the ship, and that didn't put my mind at ease. "We have to find the rest of the boarding party," I said.

"Aye," Krood said with a heavy nod. He stepped gingerly, as if one bad move could trigger an explosion.

I spotted two more of our crewmen and Argen the mute first mate and gave them a push down so they could walk in the freefall.

"To the top deck," I said. We ran up to the main deck and I found two other crew members but I had no time to search out any more.

I pointed at the dinghy hanging from the side of the Red Feather ship and moved everyone into it. I concentrated on balancing out the weight of the small boat and Krood cut off the lines holding the dinghy to the main ship.

Our descent finally stopped and the big ship wooshed down without us. Everyone in the dinghy, including me, leaned over the side to watch the ship hit the desert floor and shatter into an explosion of shrapnel and splinters. Cheers and smiles filled the dinghy.

"Arrr, that was a might too close," Captain Krood said as he punched and grabbed at his fellow crewmen.

⚓

The battle with the Red Feather ship had been a fine diversion but we soon realized we lost more than a few crew members.

I heard the snap of a whip up on deck and ran up to see what the matter was.

Two Orc were tied to the mast taking a heavy flogging.

"What happened?" I asked one of the onlookers.

"Those two raided our most precious resource."

"Our freshwater?"

The sailor looked at me with his brow lowered. "No, man, are ye mad? They took the rum!"

It seemed that two Orc brothers, who had lost a third brother in the battle, snuck below deck on their shift and raided the rum. I didn't know they could drink so much. Only a few half-empty barrels remained.

Although the quartermaster tried his best to add in an extra sting to his floggings, the two orcs were so drunk that I don't think they even felt it. I had enough experience from my sailing days to know that rum was the grease that kept sailors working together when any normal man would go mad from the close quarters.

It didn't help that as the air grew drier and hotter, most of us had to stay below deck near the barrels of water to stay cool. I wished we had an ice mage. Not that any of them would have been willing to sail to Noon.

Fights broke out with regularity now. The crew lost all efficiency and some even gave me angry looks now. They must have all thought we'd gone too far and that we should turn back. Luckily they needed me alive and well to keep the ship up in the air or I might have been tossed over the side a long time ago.

The Sun was now over us, constantly dumping its rays of bright light, seemingly weighing us down. We were close.

One strange moon, the Creblah in the crow's nest announced that he saw something in the distance, something black. I went up to look at the object, only to be confused. We were floating above what used to be an ocean but I saw a great black structure on the horizon. It was as tall as Jefro Landing and twice as big.

"Who could have built such a thing?" asked Rena.

"We're going to find out," I said.

Krood ordered us closer to the building.

Large horns and spikes jutted out of the sides of the structure like twisted rose vines. It seemed to be covered in a black armor. Maybe some type of new iron. The plates of the armor reminded me of a great black beetle.

"I don't see any windows," Rena said.

"I don't even see any doors," I said. "I'll land us near the base, Captain."

"Arrr, something about this smells of fish," Krood said.

"I can agree with you there."

The *Duchess* couldn't fully land on the ground or the hull might shatter, but it could rest on it with my help.

"Do you feel that pull of gravity, Perez?" Rena asked.

"Yes, and I have to adjust the ship with some of my life energy."

"Want help?"

"No, it isn't a problem for now."

When we got off the *Duchess*, or "come ashore," as Krood said it, the sting of the heat burned our eyes and skin. I felt as if my robes would catch on fire from the strength of the burning sands. There was no shade here, our shadows hiding under our feet.

We had to be careful when we stepped on the floor of the great sand ocean. Most of us wore leather boots, but even if one grain of sand touched our skin it burned horribly.

"So what is it, me matey?" Krood asked. He took off his tri-corn hat to wipe the sweat forming on his brow.

"I don't know," I said. "It wasn't made by us."

We were sixty feet from it but as we walked towards it the gravity pull got stronger; it felt as if I were walking with a great wind pushing me along. I would have toppled over if it wasn't for more gravity magic keeping me and everyone else steady.

"I can hardly breathe, lad," Captain Krood said. "The air, it stings me lungs."

"We just have to figure out what's causing this gravity pull. Then we can head back to the ship."

We were much closer to the black structure and I could see the curves of the tower. It was very intricate work. Some of it seemed to be impossible to forge.

It was then that I noticed the beats, one every few minutes. It was so loud now that I was shocked I hadn't noticed it before. A cold realization struck me.

"Back to the ship," I said. I couldn't hide the panic in my voice. I grabbed Rena by the arm and pulled her back.

The captain and his crew stopped. "Matey, something be a problem?"

"Come back to the ship."

Rena was reluctant but she let her feet point back towards the ship.

Walking away from the building strained my legs like I was climbing a hill.

"Are you nuts?" one of the crewmen asked. "We just got here and I'm not turning back for nothing. Besides a big black building like that's got to have some treasure in it."

"I'll move you myself if I . . ."

A great rumbling began. Some of the crew fell to the ground and screamed as the sand burned their flesh.

"The tower's going to collapse," Rena screamed. It swayed one way and then shifted to the other. The top point of it, ugly spikes and all, must have shifted a hundred feet. Then the entire thing froze then shivered, releasing a cloud of sand that had collected in the nooks and crannies of the black armor.

"Enough of this," I said. I lifted everyone up and flew us back to the *Duchess*.

"That's not a building, is it?" Rena said when we were safely aboard the ship.

"Not even close," I said. I lifted the ship up high, still fighting that strange gravity pull, until we were level with the black and twisted spires of the great thing.

"Those things there," Krood said, pointing with such emphasis that he was almost over the railings. "Could they be eyes?"

"Yes," I said. There were no creatures in all of Stillworld this large and yet I was staring at one now.

"Should we just leave then?" Rena asked.

I had no answer for her. I had expected a piece of a black star, not a creature like this.

"I'll be damned if'n we run away from this thing now that we be here," Krood said. "I say it needs a good killing." Another one of his crazy ideas.

The crew cheered to that idea, but they cheered anytime the idea of firing our cannons was brought up. I wasn't one to suffer from indecision but I had to be careful. If we killed this creature then we might be able to save Stillword but on the other hand we were probably going to fail and die in the attempt and I really did enjoy living.

"What do you think?" I asked Rena.

"Me?"

"I'm not sure if any action will be a good one. For all we know we could break Stillworld into a thousand pieces if this thing dies."

"Well, I don't think that's likely." Rena took a moment to watch the creature. I enjoyed watching her think. "We have to do something don't we?"

I nodded to the captain.

Krood let loose a volley aimed at the head of the—what I decided to name—Star Wyrm. Even though they all hit, one right on the eye of the thing, they only bounced off its tough armor as if they were made of paper.

Krood tilted his head in confusion. I doubted his cannons had ever failed him like this.

"Try it again," I said.

Rena knew what I intended to do. "Are you sure about this? You've been using a lot of magic and this gravity pull must be draining."

"I've got plenty left," I said. "You've never seen me reach my limit. I'm not one to brag, but there is a reason I was the youngest graduate of the Black Star Academy."

"I thought it was because you were so aggravating they had to graduate you so you would leave them alone."

I laughed. "Was that a quip? From *Rena* of all people?"

"Just be careful," she said.

They fired the cannons again and this time I concentrated on the one ball that was pointed at the Star Wyrm's eye. This time, right before the ball hit, I increased the weight of the ball drastically. The back of my head began to pound from the use of life magic but I must have multiplied the weight of the ball a thousand times.

The armor of the creature cracked when the ball landed. I had hoped it would have shot clean through. The great big eyelids of the Star Wyrm opened and I felt a chill run down my back. All we did was wake the thing up.

Many thousands of legs sprung loose from the underbelly of the creature, each of which emitted a loud chitinous crack with the motion. The Star Wyrm spied us then swung at us with its head. I dropped the ship to avoid the blow but the damage had already been done. The wind of the mighty blow was enough to tear our sails. We were dead in the air.

I didn't see things getting this desperate so quickly. "Rena, I'm going to do something crazy."

"No, don't."

"We don't have a choice. I'm going to try to balance out the weight of this creature."

She looked at me funny but I thought she understood this was our only way. "Doing something like that is against one of the Black Star rules. You can't use that much life energy. It could kill you."

I only stared at her.

She sighed in defeat. "Do you want me to take control of the ship?"

"Not at all. I'll still hold the ship. I need you to increase the mass of half that thing—the head or tail half, your choice—as I lift it up."

Her eyes widened at the idea and she bowed her head, shaking it no. "I can't. I can't Perez. The Academy taught us not to strain ourselves that much. It's one of the most important rules they have."

I lifted her chin so I could look into her purple eyes. "We don't have a choice. Not every rule has to be listened to, Rena. You have the talent for it. I've seen the strength in you."

She continued to shake her head.

"She's coming for another swing," yelled a crewman.

I dropped the ship again till we were on the ground. The ship tilted and rested on its side. I leaned on the main mast to not fall to the sand and Rena and the crew did similarly.

"Well, at least I don't have to worry about the ship anymore. It's now or never," I said. I didn't wait for Rena's reply.

I concentrated on the Star Wyrm. I don't think anyone had ever balanced out something this large, but the math would still have been the same. I also had to take into account the strange gravity field by making some quick computations in my mind. Math was a Black Star mage's strength.

My first attempt failed. I tried to guess at the wyrm's weight and knew I was off the minute I tried. A wave of dizziness hit me and a drizzle of blood came out of my nose.

The black beast was almost over us when I tried for the second time. I sensed

that half of it was still in the sand so I knew how big it was but not how heavy. The material it was covered in was nothing anyone had ever seen before. I made a guess as to how much its armor must weigh and I was close enough to move the creature slightly out of its hole.

Krood said, "Perez, if you manage this one I'll be calling you the greatest mage ever known."

"Shut up," Rena said. "He has to concentrate."

I put more of my life energy into the magic; more than I thought was safe but I had no choice. A wave of pain started in the base of my head and I felt I would pass out from the thunder storm in my head but I held it. The creature began to lift up and out of its hole.

It writhed and spun, trying to drop, but I used more of my life energy to maintain control. Once the creature was out of its nest, I tilted it so its great length was parallel with the ground. I thought I heard the cheering of the crew. Nice to be back on their good side; they must have thought we'd won. Not yet.

"Rena," I said with my teeth clenched.

"I can't. We were never trained for this."

"Rena." Blood was pouring out my nose and I tasted it down the back of my throat.

"I'll try."

I felt a great push from Rena's magic and the pain in my head turned numb. It sounds crazy but the numbing actually helped me concentrate. The Star Wyrm snapped at us, realizing what was happening.

"Rena, more," I said.

"I can't."

"You can." I turned to her. A small stream of blood was coming out of her nose; what a funny pair we made. "Do the math. It's no different than anything else."

Rena convulsed. Her head shook, loosening some hair from her ponytail and her eyes rolled.

The pressure on the creature increased. I heard loud groaning noises as the Star Wyrm's armor bent and cracked. The creature's head pulled away from the rest of its body, a flood of thick white fluid rushing out of the two halves. Both Rena and I let go of the balance.

I collapsed, falling on my back and Rena fell on top of me.

"Good, very good." I kissed the top of her head and the world turned black.

The bang of a pistol firing snapped me awake. Then a loud ringing. Krood was trying to talk to me but I couldn't hear him.

"What?"

"I said, I be sorry to do that to you but I be needing you awake now."

"What's the matter?" The creature was dead. I was sure of it; we had taken its head off.

Krood helped me and Rena to our feet and I saw what the problem was. Even though the creature was dead, it seemed that its gravity magic was still active. The *Duchess* was slowly being dragged towards the Star Wrym. I reestablished my control of the ship and felt a slight pain at the base of my neck. I was nearly drained of life energy.

The ship righted itself and we could finally take a breath. I moved the *Duchess* farther away and we got off the ship to examine the Star Wyrm. It had a clear, thick fluid for blood which the sand was greedily drinking up. Even though it was dead, the gravity magic was as strong as ever. Something tingling at the back of my mind made me doubt the creature was generating this magic.

"What is this thing?" Rena asked.

"I think it must have come from the stars," I said. "The Black Star Academy has a pretty complete list of all the living creatures on Stillworld and this is most definitely not from this world. I'm thinking of calling it a Star Wrym. What do you think?"

"Maybe it be a lost god," Krood said. He dipped his finger in the blood and stuck it in his mouth. "Tastes like the grubs me mother fed me."

Something was still tingling at the back of my mind. "This way," I said. I led them to the large hole the creature had been in. I felt drawn to it and I didn't mean the gravity pull. The large cavernous hole the Star Wyrm had been hiding in was collapsing on itself. We had to be careful where we treaded or we would have fallen into the creature's nest.

"Do you notice that the pull is not coming from the Star Wyrm?" I asked.

"How can you tell?" Rena said. She adjusted her spectacles and tried to tie her hair back into a ponytail but it was too much of a mess.

On the ledge of the hole rested one black, round, rock, three times as large as I was. Too round.

"This is it," I said.

The closer I got to the object the greater the pull became. Sand and smaller objects would get drawn and absorbed by it. I had to constantly change our balance or we would be absorbed into this black ball.

"This be a black star, mate?" Krood asked.

It was nothing like the black star fragment we had at the main academy. And then it dawned on me. "This thing is an egg."

Eyes widened as they gawked at me. Krood looked like he'd swallowed a rock.

"And this egg be stopping the planet from its spin?"

"I think so. It'll take me about a year of meditation to generate enough energy to lift it off the planet, but once it's gone, the planet should start spinning again."

A grin spread amongst the group. It was probably the first time they were told that their planet had a future.

"I'll want to set up camp here. I'll be—"

The ledge collapsed. I was foolish to think this patch of sand could hold all of us. Rena balanced herself out before I had to. I balanced out myself and the remainders and we hovered for a few moments till we climbed back to steady ground.

"Look," Rena said, pointing into the crevasse.

"Yar, 'tis a big hole. We all would've been dead if not for you two."

"No," she said. "Look."

As the merciless sun cast light into the cavern I saw thousands upon thousands of eggs. Of course the creature couldn't have just laid one. There were just too many.

"I can't move all these," I said. "Maybe one or two in my lifetime. All the gravity mages in the world would take a hundred years to move them all, and we'd probably be dead for our efforts."

The frustration was boiling inside me. To come this far and realize nothing could be done about it. I felt I would blow up until Rena's hand rested on my shoulder. Then I felt Krood's giant hand rest on me and soon the others were patting my back.

————— ⚓ —————

We used the spare sheets to patch up our sails. We had saved enough water and if we took generous portions of camel butter with our water rations then we would be able to make it back to Jefro Landing without dying of thirst.

I was in a grouchy mood through the repairs and everyone left me alone to sulk.

Captain Krood gently opened the door to my quarters. "We'll be ready to shove off in a few hours, matey."

"Alright," I said.

He didn't seem to like the way I spoke. "Listen, lad. At least you tried. And at least people know now why the Ground stopped spinning. They'll know you killed the creature that started it. They'll be glad to have that."

"I've always had this talent, and I thought I was given my gifts to help everyone. I was so sure I would save Stillworld."

"Not everything can be saved. 'Tis a harsh truth. Even this Star Wrym, with all its power, couldn't protect her own eggs."

The answer was so obvious.

I left Krood in mid thought, threw open the door to my cabin, and walked up to Rena, who was learning how to tie knots under the main mast. "Rena, you'll have to take the *Duchess* back to Jefro Landing on your own. I'll be staying here." After she had shown me what she could do with the Star Wyrm, I was confident she could float the *Duchess* back home by herself.

Rena adjusted her spectacles and took a moment to see if I was kidding or not. I flashed her my smile.

"What are you planning?"

I balanced out the weight of my trunk and threw it overboard. I also balanced out some tack and a few water barrels. "This will do for now but I'll need you to come back with more supplies; enough for me to last months or longer. And also go to the main Academy and bring back as many texts as you can on eggs. Speak with Professor Ingrid, she knows plenty about the subject."

She watched me, my excitement spreading to her wonderful purple eyes. "You're staying?"

"I'm staying. I think I can devise some kind of shelter using the carcass of that Star Wyrm. I'll have plenty of material to work with. When they're out, they may try to eat up the planet, but I'd rather risk it than let the planet stay the way it is."

"What are you talking about? Don't tell me you're going to try to balance out those things. You'll die."

"The eggs, Rena. The Star Wyrm didn't have any gravity magic, only the eggs. We can still save Stillworld. I just need to figure out how to hatch them."

Female Rambling Sailor
Murray J. D. Leeder

They call me Sweet William, Bard of Renown. At least, that's what I call myself. This isn't precisely my story, so I'll gloss over the situation that led to my taking up residence aboard the ill-fated ship *Lady Harriet*. It involved Lord Draymond catching me in his bedchamber alongside his lovely wife, and challenging me to a duel of honor. Knowing that he was certainly a far better duelist than I, I thought it was time to take my leave of my homeland. From there, it was to a tavern in Sandbourne, where the crew of the merchant galleon *Harriet* was reveling. They were shortly for a trip to the Far Colonies, a journey of months at best. A perfect opportunity to take my leave of this land, I thought.

The tavern was charmingly called the Dirty Oar, and for an hour or two it belonged to me—I held the lot of the drunken sailors under my spell with my voice and lute, stirred them into revelry with songs of the romance of the waves, or brought them to tears with songs of lost loved ones. A burst of flash powder or two added a touch of magic; I projected myself as an able conjurer, though this was my only spell. I humble myself, it was a command performance.

It was well past midnight when a man in a spotless blue and white uniform stepped in, a tall-crested blue hat atop his head. Barrel-chested and imperious, he was the captain of the ship whose crew I was entertaining. Standing next to him was another man, gaunt and bird-featured, his velvet red outfit combining aspects of magician and sailor.

"We sail at dawn!" the captain said to his crew. "Mere hours now. You'd best find yourself some scrap of sleep before the waves beckon." At his authority the sailors scurried or staggered away to their beds. "As for you," he said, walking up to me, "allow me to introduce myself. I am Captain Bryce Makar of the *Lady Harriet*. This at my right is my ship's wizard, name of Urlano Tystar."

"They call me Sweet William," I said with an exaggerated bow, "Balladeer of Note, Bard of Renown."

"A man of modesty." His smile was warm. "I must respect any man who can so hold my crew in thrall."

"I have long desired to place the entire crew under a magical trance," Urlano said. He had an accent of the eastern kingdoms, perhaps Hajin, where people of his talents were more common. I'd spent a few seasons there over the years, picked up a bit of the language and just enough of their magic to enliven my act. "Or perhaps even replace them with the walking dead. They who never mutiny nor disobey." I assumed he was joking, but I found it very hard to tell for sure with any Hajinian.

"What I'm asking is," Captain Makar said, "would it please you to ship with us? We sail for Regentia Colony. It is farther away than the moon, and we shall be months at sea, and you should also know—"

"Yes," I said, knowing that Lord Draymond was currently combing the land for me. Only later did I learn that the *Harriet*'s last minstrel died shipboard of the withering pox.

So my new home became the *Harriet*—or the *Harlot*, as I quickly became accustomed to calling her, an affectionate crew nickname—and it was on that floating coffin that I began to fathom something of the true magic of the sea that I sang about in old ballads. I myself did not much enjoy looking out at the rolling blue, once no land was in sight any which way. I felt so dwarfed by the immensity of the ocean. My ego will not stand being reminded of my insignificance. I knew that all the ocean could, on a whim, swell up and swallow us all in its bottomless, shapeless depths.

So, where I could, I kept my eyes on deck, to the ship and its crew, lest my mind stray and be boggled.

For all my travels, I had never been to sea for an extensive voyage before. I may not have been a sailor, but I lived like one, and that meant bad food, mere inches of sleeping space and a hold where stinking male bodies were piled high, and the monotony of the endless sea. And for a man of such *inclusive* appetites as myself, I found it endlessly amusing to witness the atmosphere that unfolded among the sailors. No doubt there were some of an inverted bent among this mass of men, but certainly if their inclinations became obvious they would be ostracized, tormented, possibly even killed. Yet I quickly discovered that a popular prank, one from which I was fortunately excluded, was to tie a man to his bunk and whack his face with one's mighty genitals, while shipmates stand on and cheer. A strange thing, this shipboard life.

And that was not the least of my examples. This mass of men, months from port and from women, slaked off their urges in the only way acceptable to them. And the entire spirit of their sailorly camaraderie, it seemed, that which made for a *crew* and not just a collection of rabble, depended on it.

I stayed clear of it, observing it like a writer of penny dreadfuls stands clear of a murder scene but takes it in all the same. Truth, I had little in common with this mass of manly men at the apex of their manliness, all tattoos and arm muscles larger than their heads—they, unlike me, were required to actually do physical things around deck, something I could never allow my valuable fingers to be subjected to. I could entertain them, laugh with them, but never be one of them. So I sought whatever time I could find alone.

It was late one night when I was on deck, a carpet of stars seeming alarmingly close to the topsail, I reflected on the figurehead that jutted from the ship's prow, rolling with the waves and guiding us across the lonesome sea. It was a splendid carving of the female form, nude and pure, large breasts tipped with rosy-hued nipples. Her face was stately and impassive, revealing no emotion. There was something very primal about her; she spoke of sleeping power. I liked her very much.

Who was she, I wondered? The Lady or the Harlot?

Both in one?

"Sailors' lore speaks of faeries who live inside figureheads," came a voice.

I turned to see a sailor standing before me at the prow. I must have been so lost in thought that I did not hear his approach. He was a lean man of youngish looks, slight by sailor's standards, rather a similar build to my own. I knew his name to be Jack Summergild, and that he was considered one of those sailors set for an officer's rank, quite apart from those more interested in fleeing the law or paying their bar bills. He was quieter than some, and only for that reason had I not taken much notice of him; I realized now that he was quite handsome in his blue uniform, the wind tousling his raven-toned hair.

"I believe they call them water mannikins," Jack went on. "They're some breed of the fey race, nature spirits that guard the ship in times of stress, help it to avoid rocks, foul winds, storms and the like. And they guide sailors' souls on to the final provenance. There are even those among the most suspicious lot of seamen who hold that if a ship goes down without a mannikin watching it, its crew will wander the lightless wet forever, and never find peace."

"What do you believe?" I asked him.

"Well," he said with a slight smile. "I'm not a superstitious sort by nature, but I'm still glad we have her."

After that conversation I came to consider Jack the most fascinating person on the ship, or at least the most agreeably fascinating person. The overall prize would have to go to wild-eyed Urlano. I occasionally dined in the captain's mess, and had ample opportunity to observe this curious creature. He would sit there like a vulture pecking at his food, mostly silent but occasionally tossing in epically odd contributions to the discussion at hand. I had to choke back laughter several times as I watched the officers try to contain their reactions to Urlano's bizarre comments. A request that he pass the potatoes was more than likely to be answered by a homily on the potato's mystical properties or its dietary importance to the wild men of the Untamed World.

I wondered about Urlano's function, myself. All claimed that his magic helped to ensure favourable winds, and while we had our share of those, we had plenty of cruel ones as well. Who was to say that Urlano's supposed spells did anything? But whenever I doubted his powers, I reminded myself that I'd never seen him fend off one of those Bandirite privateers or kept a cruel storm at bay. From the tales I'd heard, he'd saved the *Harriet* more times than I had toes. "Worth a dozen cannons, that mage," a seasoned sailor told me. I heard stories of him personally navigating the ship through impossible storms, and reducing enemy ships to floating cinders. Nevertheless, I couldn't shake the feeling that there was something of a fraud to him. I recognized a fellow performer when I saw one.

Once at dinner, shortly after my conversation with Jack at the ship's prow, I brought up the subject of the figurehead. "Is there anything to this talk of water mannikins?" I asked.

"A common sailor's superstition," the captain said, "one with which I will not tamper. But Urlano has something to say about our figurehead, I'm sure."

All other conversation at the table silenced

"Our Lady of the Bulging Protuberance," said Urlano, chuckling. It always bothered me when he laughed. His kind of joy seemed alien to me. "The Klaboutermannikins, no, sailor talk and nothing more. But that oaken tart is special, make no mistake. You, balladeer, would surely have heard of Dunan Forest."

I had indeed, for there was a song about it, though I confessed I knew it only in passing. It was an ancient, reputedly magical wood on Fair Sunward Isle. But it was long since gone, torn up to build the king's navy. It occurred to me that probably much of this ship was made from wood culled from that famous forest.

Urlano smiled with a perverse relish. "The figurehead is carved from what had been the oldest, thickest tree of that forest."

"Does that make her magical?"

"It makes her a tribute," Urlano said. "The forest sacrificed itself so that we may strive to tame the waves."

I sneered. The ballad I recalled was rather a lament for the beautiful ancient wood torn up by heartless industry—far from the forest willingly laying itself down for the betterment of man.

"There is a lot more water on this orb of ours than there is land," I said "Taming the sea seems like a losing game."

Though the officers around us looked puzzled and bored, Urlano seemed to like my line of thought. "Perhaps the sea will yet conquer us, rising up to drown us all. But we shall go down fighting."

"So that is to say," I said "that the figurehead is a reminder of man's dominion over the earth, and heralds man's extension of his dominion over the oceans as well?"

Urlano's smile showed teeth glinting with saliva. "I couldn't have put it better myself."

———⚓———

Urlano's words were still running through my head days later when we made harbor at a small green island that emerged on the horizon like a piece of driftwood. We were there to take on fresh water and fell a few trees to repair some damage to the *Harlot*'s hull. It was scrap of green paradise, untouched by man, but I wondered: how long till this island was as bare as the ruins of Dunan Forest?

While the repairs proceeded, I took to wandering the beaches, strumming my lute. "Do not wander too far, William," Captain Makar said as I went ashore. "You might regain your taste for firmness 'neath your feet and refuse to come aboard again." I understood what he meant, as little as I relished being marooned in even so lovely a spot as this.

I sat at a little cove where a stream trickled to the sea, resting under the shade of a strange tropical tree with exotic palm leaves and warbled a ballad to nobody. Jack Summergild came to me. He smiled shyly, and I welcomed his company.

"Have you come to fetch me?"

"Not yet," he said. "We shall not be underway till late tonight. For now, there is nothing to do but relax."

"Which I intend to do wholeheartedly," I said. "It's rather nice not to have a rolling infinity beneath me."

"True, true," he said, standing there awkwardly. Something was on his mind, that was plain.

"Is there something I may do for you, Jack?"

"I wonder if you might favor me with a tune," he said, taking a seat next to me.

I smiled wildly. "That's what I like to hear. Any specific requests?"

"I remember having heard some songs about a woman going to sea dressed as a man."

He spoke his request plainly, too plainly, and I already guessed the truth, or part of it at least.

"Yes, there are plenty of those," I said. "I know a couple. I've not played them for the crew; I figured such material might cause offense among some. It is my understanding that a woman about ship is a terrible taboo."

"'Tis true, 'tis true," said Jack, anguish burning quietly behind his brown eyes. "Save for the figurehead, that is. She is woman enough for all our men." He laughed. "But let us hear these songs."

I knew three well enough, and I played them each for Jack as we sat on this desert stretch of beach on a nameless island. The first was the lovely romantic ballad concerning a woman whose lover has gone to sea. She resolves to follow, disguising herself in sailor's clothes, and signing up on a ship headed for the Far Colonies. Curiously, the song never reveals what became of her lover. Rather, she is found out by her fellow sailors, who threaten to throw her overboard. But the captain flies into a rage and rescues her from his own men, and when they reach their destination they are married. The song ends with her as the finest lady of the colony, the envy of all other women.

The second tells of a merchant's daughter who spurns her wealthy suitors to marry a young sailor. He is called away to fight in a war to the east, and she follows him in man's dress. Proving an extremely valiant fighter, she is undeterred by all the battlefield carnage she witnesses and eventually finds her lover wounded and dying. She carries him to a physician, and the song ends with the knowledge that they are married. Though I did not voice this to Jack, it's always been unclear to me whether they live happily ever after or if this wedding is conducted on his deathbed.

In the last, perhaps my favourite one to sing, the situation is somewhat different. Rather than following a young man to sea, this time we're told that her love is dead before the song begins, pressed away and drowned in a faraway sea. She goes off to sea only afterwards and loves it as she never loved her life as a woman, proving to be an astonishingly successful sailor, noted for her valor and wits, and she saves her ship many a time. But then a gale comes that claims her life, and only then is her true identity discovered. She is buried with honor nonetheless, and laurels grow 'round her grave, becoming a beacon for fair maids who long for the sea.

This, too, was a command performance. Normally I would wish there had been more of an audience, but now it seemed so right to make this my private gift to Jack. My fingers strummed dexterously on the lute, trying my damnedest to evoke a rattlesome sea voyage with each pluck. Jack sat quiet and blank faced, absorbing every word of the ballads. "So these are the fates for the female sailor," he spoke as I concluded. "Death or domesticity."

"I suppose," I said. "It's in the eye of the beholder which is the greater tragedy."

Jack laughed, but joylessly. "The woman's motivation is different each of the songs you've sung, but every time it's tied to a man. But in the last song, her man is already dead. She is off to sea not to find him, not to be with him, but to . . . replace him?" His expression grew blank and faraway. "To resurrect him?"

That was fascinating. I had never thought of it that way.

"Why did I go to sea?" He was speaking to himself in my presence, his mind faraway. "I do not remember. When I doffed my dresses and donned the blue and white, just what did I have in mind?"

"You mean to say . . ." The words stuck in my throat. "You mean to say that you are a woman?"

"No," Jack said. "I am not a woman. But I was."

I wandered back onto the *Harriet*, my head swirling with the story. My first instinct was to doubt Jack, to think him—her, I now insisted on thinking—a liar. I passed the captain as I paced the deck.

"This island has no name known to us," he said. "It's to us to give it one. I'm thinking of having our cartographer label it 'Sweet William's Isle.'"

I didn't have time for a moment's acknowledgment. "Call it what you will," I said, and vanished into the hold. Alongside teetering boxes of cargo I crouched in the darkness and let Jack's words ferment in my teeming brain. "I don't know what I am not—not a man, not a woman," she told me. "A mysterious change came over me, Will. I've spent many years on the ocean, on this ship and others—dry land has not been home for so long that I do not miss it."

I didn't know what to think. I scanned the contours of her face for anything, anything that identified her as either male or female, and I could find nothing.

The acrid taste of vomit rose in my throat but I bid it back down.

Urlano. It had to be Urlano—did it not? He did this to her. How? Why?

My heart overflowed with sympathy for her, but I needed to get away from her. I turned away, ran, back into the ship, deep into the dark.

I thought of the *Harriet*'s bounteous-breasted figurehead, who led our way across the sea.

And I thought of the sea itself. The terrifying *eternalness* of it. "I feel shapeless as the sea," Jack had said, turning from me to look on the rolling waves. "When I look onto the face of the deep, I see myself."

She was a monster. Like those with head of one beast and the hind of another. A freak. Abomination. Something intolerable. Vile. Anathema.

I wept.

Then another feeling set in, a fascination tinged with perversity. My sense of disgust stayed but it shifted targets—I was disgusted with myself now. This felt wrong, wrong, wrong, as my mind charted the imaginary contours of her flesh.

I sat in the darkness of the hold until the ship sailed again, and when I emerged I did not know what to make of the burden she'd given me.

Days went by before I would speak to her again. I would see her on deck and we would avoid each other; our eyes never met. But then I cornered Jack in the galley, clutching her arm to keep her in place even as her fiery eyes burned into me. With seamen all around us, I said as calmly as I could, "I am on your side."

Her expression was even. "Do you mean it?"

I nodded. "We need to talk."

"I need a true ally," she said.

"You have one." So seldom was I ever constant at anything, but for once in my life, I was committed even to the grave.

Watery grave, as the case may be.

———————⚓———————

I detected a scent of brimstone from under the door at Urlano's cabin as I stopped outside it to inspect the lock. I heard movement inside and I tried to look natural.

The door opened and shut so quickly that I barely caught a glimpse of what was inside, shelves of books and curios. The incense smell almost overwhelmed me for a moment.

Urlano's hawk nose all but grazed my cheek. "What do you need, bard?" If he was happy to see me, he was hiding it well.

"I hoped we might talk," I said. "As men of magic."

"Pah." He grimaced. "Is that what we are?"

"Don't misunderstand me, Urlano. I'm not pretending to be your equal. I'd never do that. But as you know, I have a bit of magic."

"Little more than flash tricks, lest you've been keeping something from me," Urlano said.

"More than that," I said, "but not so very much. There's still a long journey ahead of us and I wondered if this might be an opportunity to learn more. That's if you're willing to take on a lowly pupil."

Urlano sniffed. "I don't know if I can believe you're serious about this. I have no time for dilettantes. But that being said, I will think about it."

"Even if you don't, I'd appreciate the opportunity to study a few of your books."

Urlano laughed at that. "Sure hope you speak Hajinian!"

"Just enough," I said. "Just enough to ask: which way to the festival?"

He walked away unsmiling, off to the deck and his duties. I reached down and felt the doorknob on his cabin and turned it just enough to confirm that it was locked. Never thought I'd have use for my lockpick set at sea, but that might well be. I just needed a proper diversion.

———————⚓———————

"So you think it was Urlano," Jack said as we met by night in the first place we talked, under the figurehead. We spoke in hushed tones as moonlight rippled across the black water before us.

"You say it happened on this ship, while at sea? I suspect him because there's no one else to suspect. Have you ever had any dealings with him?"

"None that I can recall," she said. "I don't think I've ever talked to the man, save for in passing. What reason would he have to . . ." an awkward hand ran over her body ". . . change me?"

"Who knows with a wizard? Who knows with a Hajinian? Could be that he sees it as a punishment for your transgression. But the opposite might be true too, it might be that he's trying to protect you. Is it not true that, had you been discovered as a woman, you would have been in grave danger from the crew and captain?"

Jack nodded sadly.

"Then maybe in his mind, Urlano is helping you."

"Some help."

"I don't understand, though," I said. I asked what I had been meaning to all along. "You donned a man's clothes, you went off to do a man's duty. And now you have become a man, and are so unhappy."

Her face flushed with anger. "To want one is not to want the other."

"I'm not saying that." I placed a hand on her shoulder but pulled it away quickly. "I just want to understand."

Tears flowed from her eyes. She turned to the sea to keep the lookout from seeing her from his perch so high above.

"You must think me pathetic. I did not cry while I was a woman, not on this ship. I was the bravest, the boldest of them all. I personally killed three Bandirite officers when they boarded us in the Sun Sea last year. I took nary a scratch. I fenced with them, and I bested them. That was a good day." Her voice was full of pride and regret. "Have you ever killed, Will?"

"Only musically."

She chuckled through her tears. "They fell under my rapier like kindling. I protected my ship, my friends, and no one could get in my way."

"You can remember that day," I said, "but you can't remember why you went to sea?"

"I can't explain. I can remember who I was: a gallant sailor, born for the sea. Man or woman did not matter. But then the change came. Before, I knew who I was. A misfit, a fraud perhaps, but I was who I was. And now I haven't a clue. You want to understand? So do I."

I wrapped my arms around her. Damnation to whoever might be looking! A wave of revulsion swept through me for an instant but then it vanished and it all felt normal.

"You are under a curse," I said. "Curses can be undone." I wonder if my words convinced her as a little as they convinced me.

———⚓———

My opportunity came about two days later. A storm gathered before us, spreading black and gray menace all across the horizon. Prongs of lightning danced in its heights and fat raindrops battered the deck. The storm rushed to meet us. The waves came up and rocked the *Harriet* till she felt no more substantial than a leaf caught on a draft. Exciting material worthy of balladry, but I had other things on my mind.

Urlano was up on the deck, along with most of the crew. He was at the prow, his hair flying crazily in the wind and rain, but he stood perfectly still, his arms outstretched and straight, pointing all around like a human sundial. Occasionally he would bark instructions to the wheelman. I didn't understand his technique and I still wondered if it was all pure hokum, but it sure made for impressive showmanship, which I admired. Supposedly, he was dowsing for a safe path through the storm, navigating the gales. Good luck to him.

And the best part for me was that, from the looks of things, it would keep him on deck.

I came to his doorway, my shoes filled with water. It was not easy picking a lock with the floor rolling side to side beneath me, but in time I managed it. I vanished into the cabin and shut the door firm behind me. Incense filled my senses. The only light were a pair of knotholes on the wall that burst with whiteness as lightning crackled through the clouds.

There were books all around. I wondered, not for the first time, where I was supposed to go from here. This was a long shot; I knew it all along. Where to begin? I did not know much Hajinian—and for all the gods' love, I only knew one magic spell! Just what was I doing here?

I heard footsteps outside the door and crouched in the darkness, but they passed by.

When all the light was gone, though, I noticed a strange glow coming from a dark corner of Urlano's cabin. Attracted as I am to shiny objects, I investigated. It was a small wooden chest resting underneath Urlano's hard bed; a bead of light shone through its keyhole. I picked it up. It felt warm to the touch. I held it up and peered through the hole.

For an instant, I felt a wash of emotion over me, equal parts pain and rage. I cried out and dropped the chest, which landed on the bed with a dull thud.

I saw nothing inside, only light, but there was something in there all the same. Something invisible, something powerful. Its energy crackled before me. And I knew that there was more mystery on this ship than Jack's transformation.

"What are you?" I said, though I suspected I knew the answer. "Can you speak to me?" I picked up the chest.

Images flew through my mind. Perhaps it could not speak, but it could make itself known all the same. I saw a forest, ancient and magisterial, clogged with magic and mystery. Only when the axes came did I realize my perspective was that of a tree, one that stood for a thousand years only to fall in an instant. And I was cut into boards, and sewn into a ship. Carved, made female, breasts protruding, lacquered and fitted on a ship's prow.

The *Harriet*'s prow. I felt a lifetime of sea breezes on my brow and foam across my face. I remembered dozens of trips through the lightless depths with substanceless sailors wrapped in my hand. These were the deceased, those who died at sea, mere wisps of formless light. I guided them home, to their final rest.

Only impressions in my mind, they shaped into a story with a terrible ending. The intensity of the rage shocked me, terrified me.

Ripped away from my perch and caged in a box of my own flesh. Such anger, epic anger. Anger against the *Harriet*, craving her destruction. Shorn of my power, all that sucked away by a jealous magician. By. . . .

Urlano Tystar. He stood before the open door, and my knuckles whitened on the chest.

"Shouldn't you be on deck?" I said. A lightning flash bathed the room in white, showing the grim look on his sharp Hajinian features. "Shouldn't you be up there, saving our lives as usual?"

"A greater threat is down here," he said. I expected to hear anger, whatever Hajinian anger sounded like, for breaching his sanctuary and learning his terrible secret. But instead his voice was calm and measured, sounding for all the world he was talking down a man from a ledge. "You could doom us all if you were to tamper with that creature much more."

"It's a water mannikin," I said. "It's the *Harriet*'s mannikin, in fact. You took it out of the figurehead and imprisoned it in here. Why?"

"For the ship's sake," Urlano said. "It's raw power, power that humbles mine. With its power channeled through me, I can battle the elements and our enemies as I never could without it. The fey is an insular creature. It does not care if the *Harriet* floats or sinks. In fact, it would rather prefer the latter. Free it now, and you would see the true depths of its rage—and we would all become very well-acquainted with the bottom of the ocean."

So my instincts were right, I thought. Urlano was a phony, after a fashion.

"You had no right to make it a slave like this!" I said. "And what of its role in taking sailors to the afterlife? That's no myth—I know it's true, I felt it! Does that mean nothing to you?"

"No!" Urlano said, hands flying up to pull at his hair. "I feel it every time a sailor dies under my protection. Their souls will have to find another way, if there is another way. But listen to me and hear well, bard: I can still justify my choice. This ship would have sunk and drowned a half-dozen times now, all crew lost, if I didn't have the power to protect it. We've lost a few dozen men, true, but their souls swimming the sea for all time is a small tradeoff for the rest of us still drawing breath."

"And just what," I said, "does any of this have to do with Jack Summergild?"

If I needed any further certainty that Urlano was behind everything, I had it now, as his face tightened and his eyes fell. It may simply have been anger at being found out, but I read it as guilt.

"I know what you know," Urlano said. "I know of your schemes with her. It's very hard to keep secrets from me on this ship of mine. But she managed it." He sighed heavily. "Only after she was dead did a lily white breast come into view, and I realized the truth."

"Dead!" My heart sank. What could this mean? I ran through all of our time together, and I remembered my singing of the ballad where the woman sailor went to sea in tribute to her dead lover. "To *resurrect* him," she said, as if the word had a meaning to her that she wasn't even aware of herself.

"Yes, it's true." Urlano frowned. "Last year, a Bandirite privateer attacked us in the Sun Sea, just outside of the free port of Riggscar. They had a wizard of their own and the *Harriet* was boarded while I dueled him. He was far more powerful than me, but I had the mannikin's power as my trump card. I slaughtered the wizard, and we watched then the sloop beneath burn, but we lost many fine sailors to the Bandirites that day. Jack had just as much role in saving the *Harriet* as I did. She fought with a bravery of few men I've ever seen."

"And no man was she," I said.

"No. I don't know who she was, her real name. I don't know what brought her to sea. But I'm glad she did. She saved us all that day, and paid for it with her life."

"And so you brought her back," I said. "But you brought her back *changed*."

"Not just I," Urlano said. "The mannikin and I both. I did not know if its power would let me resurrect her and I'm next to certain that I could not have bent it to that task, but I petitioned it and it *agreed*. Why, I have no idea; its motivations are unknown to me. Understand me, bard: I was no slave master at that moment. If it did not want her back, it could have withheld the power."

"But which of you chose to change her sex? Or to scuttle her memories, so she has no idea of who she is?"

"Not I," Urlano said. "If it was an act of provenance, it was the mannikin's, not mine."

Those were the magician's last words. She came up to him suddenly, sleek as a shadow, and before I knew it a slim blade jutted through Urlano's chest from behind. A flash of lightning illuminated a look of utter surprise on his features. Jack was standing behind him, sliding the rapier home, the open door swaying behind her. She pulled it free and Urlano barely managed to spin about and look her in the eye as he slumped to the deck.

"For what it's worth, I believe you," Jack said as Urlano rattled in death. Stepping over the mage's body, Jack walked over to me. She held up the sword, gore clinging to its blade.

"Free it," she said

"Are you mad?" I said, my fingers turning white as I clutched tighter onto the chest. "You slaughtered the ship's mage—how on earth are we supposed to get off this ship alive?"

"We're not. You heard the magician. The *Harriet* belongs at the bottom of the sea. Only by Urlano's tampering with the way of things are we still aloft. *We must go down*." She spoke with mad conviction and nary a hint of sadness or reluctance. Something had changed in her. Even in the low light I could see a hardness in her face unlike any I'd known.

"What are you saying? You would drown yourself, and all your shipmates?"

"What has one of them done for me?" she said. "Would they not have killed me themselves if they had known the truth?"

"And what about me then?" I said. I felt a wave of despair as my words had no effect on her. "The 'way of things?'" I said, repeating her words. "Were you not transgressing the way of things when you donned men's clothes and went to sea?"

"Or when men cut down the Dunan Wood to build his vessels?"

In that line I understood everything. The being before me was not truly Jack Summergild, or whatever her real name had been before her death on the Sun Sea. The water mannikin brought her back to life but left a piece of itself in her. It maneuvered her so that she would eventually turn on Urlano and serve its agenda, to free the mannikin from its prison.

I realized in that moment that the creature in the chest I held, wronged though it was, was more diabolical than Urlano. It could have brought her back properly with its magic, but it tampered with her, altered her, made sure she would be so miserable and lacking in identity so that she would come to play properly her role in its plan. Jack was nothing but a pawn to it, and would certainly be doomed along with the rest of us, but she would kill to free it all the same. *Had killed*, I corrected myself, looking down at the Hajinian wizard's lifeless body on the floor.

"We cannot free the mannikin," I said, pleading with her. "Jack, you have to think this through."

If she heard me she showed no sign, but raised her sword to my neck. "Free it," she said, "or I shall."

Pulling the chest close to my breast, I dropped to my knees and rolled forward, rolling under her sword and past her. I was glad at that moment I did some tumbling in my act. I rolled past Urlano's body on the floor of the dark cabin as I heard a sword-stroke behind me and felt the wind of the blade.

Hopping to my feet just before the swaying door, I turned back on her for a second. I shut my eyes tight and extended a hand even as I held the chest tight, setting off a magical fire-flare of brilliant yellow. The room lit up brighter than the sun for an instant, invading even my tightly-shut eyelids, and I heard Jack shriek and stumble against a bookshelf dazzled, books tumbling to the floor. Not pausing a moment more than I had to, I left the room and ran onto the deck.

The storm was battering the *Harriet* hard. The winds tore holes in her sails and the deck was slick with water. Sailors worked like the devil, pumping and bailing.

I spotted Captain Makar at the wheel, looking less like a captain than a badly-drenched ship rat. A gale nearly took me from my feet as I dashed towards him.

For a moment my attention went to the figurehead, which bobbed up and down on the waves, a figurehead bare of the mannikin it needed. How bravely she bore the torment of the ocean.

"William!" he shouted when he saw me. "Where the hell is Urlano? Whatever possessed my wizard quit the deck just when he's most needed?"

"He's dead." The words came in a gulp. "We all will be soon too, if we can't stop Jack."

"Jack? Whatever are you talking about, William?"

I just didn't know where to begin.

Then she was standing there in the rainy gloom of the deck. Her soaked hair clung to the sides of her head, framing a mask of rage. A lightning bolt cast the whole deck in its sepulchral white and for an instant rendered her hollow to my eyes, a puppet of bones and little else. Not man, not woman, but something that transcended them all. The mannikin had taken her and shaped into something beyond.

Was she even human any longer? I wondered as she raced forward, her rapier carving a delicate path through the raindrops even as the thunderclap shook the deck.

The stunned Captain Makar abandoned the wheel and barely had the time to pull out his own cutlass and parry when Jack reached him. With inhuman speed, her sword reared back and thrust. The two of them tangled and twisted in a deadly dance, even as the wind and rain pounded and the deck shifted beneath their feet. The clang of steel was barely audible amid the noise of the storm.

Watching this swordfight unfold, I took a few steps backwards and found the rail of the ship and a wind against my back. The wild churning sea crashed against the side of the ship below me. I looked down at the little chest in my hands. To my surprise, I felt some sympathy for the water mannikin within it. Twice ripped from its home, it had every right to anger. But it was no friend to this vessel any more.

The angry waves rose. The sea wanted the mannikin, and it the sea. I knew what to do.

I judged the captain as probably the better swordsman, but Jack was propelled by something inhuman, and sure enough, she won the day. She slashed Makar's wrist and he dropped his rapier; she kicked him to the ground and sliced his belly open with one cruel swipe. A slosh of salt water filled his wound; his scream reverberated in my bones.

Jack raised her sword and stepped towards me.

"The chest, Sweet William, Bard of Renown." As she came closer, I saw nothing in her eyes I recognized of the person I had known.

So I had no regrets as I lifted the chest and tossed it overboard. Chiseled on my memory for all time will be the sublime look of shock on her face, though I only saw it for a second. Dropping to the floor, I rolled out the way as she sprung from her place, up and over the railing and plunged down to the sea. I peeked over the edge of the ship to see her form vanish into the raging brine.

"Are we safe?" Captain Makar said, summoning the last of his energy as he lay dying on the deck of his ship.

I had my answer as I saw a flash of light from within a black wave. The light started as little more than a pinpoint and I wondered if I was just imagining it, but it grew and pulsed, a beautiful flower of crystal white. Jack had reached the chest, or perhaps the chest had struck the hull and broken open. It didn't matter; either way the mannikin was free.

And that meant doom for us all.

A bolt of lightning leapt down from the heavens, deafening us all and turning the whole mast into a tree of flame, the sails reduced to nothing but charred wings of smoke around it. The mast fell, cracking through the deck, tempest winds fanning the flames as they raced all around.

Sailors caught aflame and leaped overboard; others were trapped or cornered. They screamed, they yelled for help, but no help was coming.

The *Harriet* was dying.

A maelstrom settled underneath her, twisted her sideways and spun her. Sailors screamed in terror as their ship ripped apart. Huge waves rose up and crashed to the deck, clearing men away with its power. I gripped a rope and held tight, as Captain Makar's body was swept from the deck and vanished into a fissure that cracked its way through the *Harriet*'s middle.

We were going down. *Lady Harriet* would soon rest on the ocean's floor as a twisted wreck because that's what the mannikin thought she deserved.

Regarding the walls of water on every side, I released my grip on the rope. I didn't see what good it would do to hold on.

At least the sailor's souls would presumably be guided to the afterlife, even if it was by the same force that killed them. Did that make this any better?

But I was no sailor—did the same rules apply to me?

These were the questions I wondered about as the envelope of water closed upon us and we were all gone.

———⚓———

It is a strange thing to wake up when you never expected to wake again. I gulped a lungful of salt water, but pulled myself the surface. Coughing, vomiting viciously, I took in air, every gasp of it like it was my first, just as desperate and just as precious. A thick piece of wood bobbed on the ocean and I clung to it.

The *Harriet* was gone, but I was still alive. How? Why?

The sun shone bright, and not a single cloud marred a blue sky. The fatal storm was long gone. I ached desperately and could barely keep my eyes open, and it was all I could do to pull myself up higher onto the piece of driftwood. I was floating towards an island, green palm leaves swaying in a warm breeze.

I knew the place. I had been there before. This was "Sweet William's Isle," though I had no idea if Captain Makar had formally named it thus. Even if he had, his charts would never reach anyone now. Still, no reason for it to be called anything else, if I was to be marooned there.

The piece of wood spun beneath me and I found myself looking into staring wooden eyes, those of the figurehead. I steadied myself by placing my hands over her protruding (and remarkably sharp) breasts. Some of her lacquered sheen was lost to the ocean, but she was beautiful anyway.

The mannikin spared me, and I guessed me alone. There was no sign of any other debris from the *Harriet* anywhere. This island was days away from where the ship went down; no random waves brought me here. Why?

Urlano had saved the ship using the mannikin's power, but never when I was on board. Perhaps that was the reason. Perhaps I was not part of the ledger it sought to even up.

Or maybe it was even an act of mercy.

When we up washed on shore, the figurehead and I, I pulled myself up. I could barely walk but I stumbled around the beaches, looking up at the trees. I decided that I'd have to erect the figurehead among them. Dunan Wood was long gone, but perhaps this place would do just as well.

What did this island have to offer? Could I feed myself here? Did other ships stop here—would I be rescued in mere weeks or months, or would it be where I would live out the rest of my life? Would I be grateful for having been spared, or would I prefer to have gone down with the rest? All that remained to be seen.

I found the shaded cove where I had sung for Jack those three ballads, and there

I fell to my knees in the sand and sobbed my life out for her. Death or domesticity, those were the fates they promised for the woman who goes to sea, choices she found so unsatisfying. The horrible thing, I thought, was that she never truly had a choice. Urlano and the water mannikin both pulled her strings, denied Jack her own path. That was her tragedy.

I wished it could have been different. Did there need to be an ending, a fate at all? Does a song need to end? Could she not have just continued on forever, a female rambling sailor so bold and brave, sailing the seas she loved and fighting her enemies for all time?

I wondered what kind of instrument I could make in this place. Hopefully I would manage to come up with something. I had a ballad to write.

The Bokor
Jens Rushing

Miles Redmond, Governor of Green Turtle Cay, sliced open the yellow envelope. It was light, which was puzzling, and it was from Bartholomew Nolan, which was damned bewildering. He had not heard from Nolan in twenty or twenty-five years. "Let's see what this portends for our little corner of the Caribbean," he said, smiling wryly to his footman. The smile masked his trepidation well; no news from Nolan could be good news. Redmond extracted a single sheet of paper, and read it, murmuring to himself. His face went blank, then white, the color drained in an instant.

"Sir? Are you well?"

"Leave me," he croaked, waving at the door. The letter fell to the desk. The sum of the missive was two lines: *The bokor has returned. Perry is slain.* Redmond fumbled in his desk and produced a bottle of rum. He gulped two quick glasses and returned the bottle. He inhaled deeply, feeling the warmth of the liquor wash over him. He made a circuit of the room, locking both the doors and all the windows, pausing at each one and peering into the tropical night. When he was finished, Redmond returned to his desk and fumbled in the drawer again. His hand found the thing he wanted: a flintlock pistol. He primed and loaded it, his eyes darting from window to window. He finished and laid the pistol on the desk.

"O, God . . ." he said. "The Father of Heaven. Have mercy upon us miserable sinners. O, God, the Son, Redeemer of the World." His memory failed him. "I have never prayed as I ought to," he said, lifted the pistol to his temple, and fired.

———⚓———

In Port Royal, Henry Appleby took the same letter from Thomas Ashbury's trembling hand. Ashbury's daughter, unsettled by her father's sudden paleness, moved to Henry's side and read the letter over his shoulder. "What can it mean, father?" she asked, while Henry pored over the paper.

Ashbury produced a handkerchief and mopped his brow. "I don't know, Emma, darling," he said. "Some prank, I suppose. Ha!" He laughed feebly and grasped for a chair. Finding it, he collapsed and murmured to himself, speaking into his handkerchief. Henry puzzled over the letter, his brow creased, then returned it to Ashbury's desk.

"Who is Perry?" he asked.

"Ah, lad . . ." Ashbury, recovering, folded his handkerchief and replaced it in his pocket. Ashbury was stalling. Henry prickled; he may be engaged to the old man's daughter, but he disliked being lied to, and he had the distinct sensation that he was about to be misled. He often got this feeling from Ashbury, and it strained their relationship more than Henry might have liked. Ashbury finished with the handkerchief and waved dismissively. "A former colleague of mine. I haven't seen him in a number of years. I suppose this is Nolan's idea of a joke. He's an odd cove. It matters little."

"Little? Father, you're on the verge of fainting!" Emma said, and it was so. The old man dripped with sweat, and his hands trembled madly.

"I suppose the letter has disconcerted me somewhat."

"My good man," Henry said, studying the letter again, "I would be very inclined to construe this as . . ." He looked from Ashbury to Emma and smiled. "My dear, would you please grant us a moment of privacy? We would discuss worldly matters, and I am reluctant to bore you."

Emma gathered her skirts. "Of course, darling." She smiled reassuringly at her father and swept from the room.

"I would construe this as a *threat*!" Henry said, tossing the letter on Ashbury's desk.

Ashbury flashed with anger. "And you would be *right*!" he hissed in reply. "I have never attempted to hide my origins from you, dear Appleby–Henry," he said. "But in my days as a merchantman, before my present wealth as a plantation owner, I made a number of enemies."

"Enemies how?"

"It's a cutthroat business, lad, that's how. I won a contract from His Majesty's Navy, and put a rival in desperate straights—this Nolan. And Perry was a colleague of mine, as I said. Perry disappeared at sea some months ago, under circumstances still not known to me, and I wonder if this Nolan dealt him poorly. I know not." He began to sweat again, and fished out his handkerchief once more. "And now he may have turned his attentions to me."

"How is it that you think this man capable of murder?"

"He has murdered before." Ashbury blew his nose at length, turning aside politely.

"Say no more." Henry stood. "I will go to this Nolan, in my capacity as an officer of His Majesty's Navy, and have the truth of him, or see him imprisoned. Where can I find the rogue?"

"Montego Bay was the last I heard. If he still runs ships, inquire with the harbormaster." Ashbury bit his lip. "Look sharp, lad. He was a desperate sort then, and twenty years of poverty and bile cannot have improved him."

Henry tapped his belt, where his rapier would hang were he on duty. "I'm not concerned. As my future father-in-law, I must consider threats against *you* as I would against my own father," he said with a warmth that he did not feel. "It would serve the dog right if I laid him out."

"It may come to that, my boy." Ashbury leaned forward, suddenly very hawkish. "It may be best were it to come to that."

Henry repressed a shudder. "Your *sentiment* is noted," he said.

Ashbury nodded and, leaning forward, tugged on Henry's sleeve. "Stay a moment, my boy." He gestured at the opposite chair. "There's something I would tell you." Henry sat. Ashbury was not forthcoming by nature, and such moments were rare; in fact, Henry couldn't remember Ashbury ever bidding him stay for a confidential chat, not even when Henry had asked for his daughter's hand. He wondered what the old merchant could want. Ashbury, finally composed, adjusted his periwig, which had slipped slightly. He steepled his fingers and cleared his throat. "You must know, before you are wed—I apologize. I should have told you this long ago. Before you wed my daughter, you must know the truth of her heritage. She is adopted. She is not my own child. Emma does not know this herself." He stopped, studying the effect of these words. "I can assure you, though, that her parentage is of excellent quality. I am reluctant to disclose to you the identity of her true parents, though that is your right to demand . . ." He trailed off and waited for Henry to speak.

"I waive that right," Henry said. "Her parentage is of no concern, when her upbringing has been of such apparent quality. As far as I am concerned, good sir, you are her parent." But as he thought about this confession from the typically staid Ashbury, gratitude warmed the corners of Henry's consciousness. "But, sir, I thank you—*thank* you for seeing fit to share this confidence with me." He grasped Ashbury's hand and pressed it.

"No, no, my boy, only fit for you to know. You are going to be my *son*, after all." Ashbury beamed at him. "We should be more forthright with each other. I respect you, lad. I want you to know that."

Henry bowed low. "Fare thee well, sir. I will return tomorrow or the day after."

"Godspeed, my boy." Ashbury inclined his head graciously. Henry bowed again and swept from the room.

———————⚓———————

Emma walked slowly along the bougainvillea-roofed veranda, gazing at the dark harbor below. Henry watched her from the doorway. *Such a fair creature!* he thought. *Such refinement, such grace . . . regardless of her breeding.* He enjoyed a moment of exultation that, of all the men in the world, she should select *him*, that he should love her and she him. It seemed too wonderful to credit.

"Emma," he said suddenly.

She gasped, then blushed. "I had thought myself alone."

"Forgive me if I gave you fright," he said, taking her hand.

"You are forgiven."

Henry frowned. "My love, I cannot join you for the ball tomorrow. I depart on business for your father."

Displeasure clouded her countenance for a moment. "I see. And what business is this?"

"A trifling matter. It pertains to the letter he received today. I would hesitate to burden you with the details, my sweet." He kissed her pretty forehead.

"The matter lays outside my concern, I'm sure."

"You may go to the ball without me, of course," he said.

"I'm accustomed to making such journeys alone."

Henry stiffened. "My dear. I regret that my service to the King requires my frequent absence. But at this stage in my career, it is of great import that I distinguish myself and win distinction, by industry and loyalty. Would that I could accompany you to every governor's ball or soirée . . . but duty demands otherwise."

Emma turned away. "I know, I know!" She sighed, and Henry thought he detected resignation. A breeze wafted the heavy scent of the flowering vines across the veranda. Henry wrapped his arms around her from behind. She leaned back into his embrace. "But knowing it does not make your absence easier to bear. But I will wait, and celebrate your return. If I have forgiven you by then," she said, half-jesting. "What's this?" she said as Henry encircled her neck with a shimmering braid of gold. She fingered the necklace and examined the setting—a single sky-blue topaz in elaborately wrought chain.

Henry clasped the necklace in the back. "Does it please you?" He smiled and kissed her ear.

Emma hummed to herself, running her fingers along the chain. "You are forgiven."

Henry whirled her around and kissed her as she ought to be kissed.

———⚓———

Henry mounted his sorrel mare and rode through the streets of Port Royal. The city woke, shaking off the revelry of the previous night, shuddering back to life. Skippers and their crews carried chests and crates up gangplanks; lean and tawny slaves rolled barrels of molasses or rum across the cobblestones; the governor watched impassively as a black-hooded man kicked the stool from under a man accused of forgery, dropping him to his death; dogs tore at scraps in a refuse heap below a tavern's window; Henry Appleby parted the morning mist on his white charger as he left the city and began the overland route for Montego Bay.

The ride was a long one and he arrived just before dusk. The pestilential old harbormaster politely dissembled what little information he had, hoping perhaps for a bribe, but underestimating Henry's incorruptibility, finally sent him to the Green Dragon Inn to be rid of him.

Henry threw open the door and surveyed the crowd. A slaver from Brazil had arrived that afternoon, and the crew was carousing. *Desperate coves, every one of them, worn ragged and half-mad by the demands of their trade, now emboldened with drink,* Henry thought, his lip curling in disdain. He pushed his way through the clamoring men, ignoring the hostile looks, and rapped on the bar.

"Hallo, barkeep; I seek a man. Know you Bartholomew Nolan?"

The barkeep cupped his hand to his ear. Henry leaned forward and shouted his question. The man shook his head. Henry looked quickly about the bar as he spoke; a one-eared salt by the door had looked his way when Henry said Nolan's name, then quickly became interested in his ale. A sailor on the stairs played "Drunken Sailor" on a concertina; the reedy notes rattled around in Henry's weary head. The sailors, themselves largely besotted, picked up the chorus, someone joined with a mandolin, and some lost soul bellowed "Spanish Ladies" at the top of his lungs. Soon the whole house was a-roar with it; investigation became impossible.

Henry pushed away from the bar, frustrated, and shouldered through the sweat-smelling crowd to the door. "You," he said, kicking the reclining one-eared sailor. "On your feet." The sailor muttered an oath. "On your feet!" Henry said, and kicked him in the ribs. "Outside." A small shove was sufficient to herd the sailor outside, where he leaned against the opposite building and rubbed his ribs, glaring sullenly.

"I'm looking for a man called Bartholomew Nolan," Henry said.

"Are ye? An' why?"

"Never mind why. Tell me, or stand in the way of justice."

"That so?" The sailor rubbed his ribs. "What's he done that made you come after him?"

Throw the dog a bone, Henry thought, *and maybe he'll be more compliant.* "Very well. He's threatened a plantation owner. And is perhaps complicit in the murder of another shipper, name of Perry."

"Perry, eh?" The sailor snorted. "Shouldn't think so."

"Why not?"

"Well, they sailed together, he an' Perry. They were partners, an' friends. Five of 'em. Perry, Nolan, Ashbury, Redmond, one other. Can't remember his name—'s a Frog name, Duvall or something."

Henry bristled. "Do not mislead me. Nolan and Ashbury are enemies."

"Well, *now* they are, maybe. But fifteen or twenty years ago, they were close indeed. I worked for 'em meself. Ran sugar to Bristol an' slaves to Barbados."

"Ashbury never dealt in slaves."

The sailor laughed. "Sure, he didn't. An' that plantation he's got—that all came from sugar, roight?" He spat. "Hardly. Good money in sugar—not *that* good."

"You are mistaken."

"Think I'd know, sirrah, think I'd know!"

"Watch your tone! You address an officer."

"Apologies, guv'nor. I didn't mean any offense—not too hard a thing to say a man's sold slaves, when there's far worse charges on the docket."

Henry's blood froze. "What do you mean?"

"Sayin' that it's not bad to be called a slaver, when one might be called a pirate."

"You lie. 'Tis slander that you speak. Thomas Ashbury is a man of unimpeachable reputation."

"Think o' it. Henry Morgan died *Sir* Henry Morgan, didn't 'e, an' all the world knew him for a buccaneer. Killed more Spanish than the influenza, 'e did, and 'e's a man of 'unimpeachable reputation,' too. How much do you think a reputation costs?"

In a flash, Henry's dagger was out and he pinned the sailor to the wall with his left forearm, pressing the blade to his throat. "Slandering *dog!*" he hissed.

The sailor's lips peeled back in vicious sneer. "Take it or leave it," he said. "'s only the truth. I tender my 'umblest apologies if they upset ye." Henry released the man and he slumped to the ground, feeling his throat. "Anything else ye'd like to know?"

"Where is Bartholomew Nolan?"

"Last I heard, he had a shack out in the jungle. Shall I draw ye a map?"

———⚓———

Henry followed the worn goat-path through the jungle, hacking at obstructing vines with his saber. The sun had vanished over an hour ago, and darkness deluged the jungle completely. Henry emerged from the jungle; a shack sat on a little sand spit before him. Beside the shack was a rack strung with drying fish. The moon hung huge and low over the black water.

He heard a sound like the rattle of pebbles in a dry gourd, and a low chanting—but the chanting was soft and indistinct enough that it might easily be the wash of the waves on the sand. The rattling could be anything at all—the chitter of some forest insect. But its sudden appearance and cessation were curious, and set Henry's teeth on edge. He proceeded cautiously, scanning the trees ringing the beach for movement.

Ears alert, nerves a-quiver, he crept to the little hut, the soft sand masking his footfalls. He circled the windowless building, trying to divine something of its inhabitant. Except for the susurrus of the surf, all was quiet; not a sound came from the little wooden house. He tried the door and found it barred. He slid his knife in the crack and wiggled it about, trying to lift the bar. He eased it upward with difficulty; something pressed against the door from the other side and hindered the bar's movement. Finally it slipped from its place. Henry put his shoulder to the door, straining against the weight behind it, which yielded slowly. He struck a match and peered into the darkness of the shack.

Nolan? Dear—God! Something had mutilated the man beyond belief; his limbs were torn from his body by main force, leaving vessels and stringy sinews dangling from stumps ruddy with congealed blood; shattered bone fragments protruded from the human wreckage. Some bludgeoning force had demolished the face completely, crushing bone and mangling skin past recognition. An ingot of ice dropped into Henry's stomach as he turned to face the hut—there, on the lone cot, lay the victim's arm. Its companion hung over the firebox like a discarded stocking. A thick, uneven smear marked the demolishment of one leg, and of the other, nothing could be found. Henry was sick; dizziness overtook him, and he stumbled faintly in the sand. He clawed at the earth and fought back nausea. Nolan was slain, then, too . . . yet the door had been barred *from the inside.*

Henry stood, knees shaking. He must investigate . . . perhaps the remains would yield some clue as to Nolan's slayer. Then *that sound* reached his ears again, locking his muscles and freezing his thoughts. Slowly, he turned, sweeping the jungle for movement or signs of an enemy. The rattling increased in volume, swelling from the sound of one jungle insect to a hundred, and *there*, the trees parted and a form emerged.

He squinted in the moonlight, trying to pick out the details of the form as it approached. Then he glanced once more in the cabin—no place to hide. He was trapped out on the little sand spit as the thing drew near. He studied it again; it was tremendous in height and bulk, almost seven feet tall and perhaps four hundred pounds, with a barrel chest and massive hands. The head was squat and round as a rum-keg and the legs thick as tree trunks. It glistened in the moonlight. It reached the sand spit, walking slowly, massive legs plodding in the sand, and Henry convulsed in fright; it had the form of a man, but it was definitely not human.

Its facial features bunched together, crushed like those of a frog: a wide, flat mouth, drawn to the edges of its broad face, with slit eyes several inches across. The nose was flattened and almost nonexistent. The creature carried no intelligence in its expression. It shined in the moonlight, its skin an almost incandescent white. *It has six fingers*, Henry noted absently. Save for a canvas breechclout, it was entirely naked.

"I am an officer in the Royal Navy," Henry shouted, stepping forward. "I command you, in His Majesty's name, to halt your advance and stand down."

The creature made no reply. It continued its stumbling progression up the sand spit, now fifty, now forty-five feet away. "Should you continue, I will have no choice but to fire upon you," Henry barked. His voice grew taut and hoarse. He drew his pistol and displayed it. "If we fight, one of us will die." Forty feet, thirty-five feet.

"You have been warned," he shouted, and took aim, steadying the barrel on his left wrist. The pistol roared, the sound rising over the cacophonous rattling from the jungle. The thing halted, frozen in mid-step, and Henry saw the hole punched in its forehead by his shot. It stumbled and crashed face-first in the sand. The rattling stopped. Henry replaced his pistol and approached it, saber and dagger out.

He prodded the fallen behemoth with the tip of his sword; the blade made no puncture. He poked it again, with greater force, and the skin only dented where he jabbed—no puncture. He could not draw blood. Henry tried to roll the carcass over with his foot and could not. He jabbed it again, again without success, and was about to sheath his saber when he heard it groan.

It groaned slowly, the sound scraping up from the depths of its gargantuan mass, gaining momentum, erupting in a horrible rasping, muffled slightly by the sand. But the groan grew louder and louder. Henry backed away in horror; a long shuddering spasm passed over the creature. The hand moved; the fingers dug long furrows in the sand as the whole arm twitched, and groaning, it rose from the sand, swiveling to face Henry, its inhuman features contorted with mindless rage, the pistol wound now completely vanished. Henry swung at it, putting all his strength behind the blow. His blade glanced off the monster's skin and Henry stood in wonderment for a moment until a thunderous clout sent him sprawling. The blow from the creature felt like a cannonball slamming into his skull. Colors swam before his eyes, and he did all he could to gather his limbs and senses and sprint away with all possible haste. He staggered to his legs, stumbled, fell, staggered up again, and dashed for the trees as the thing plodded inscrutably, unstoppably behind him.

Henry dashed through the jungle, leaping over fallen logs, ducking under vines and tree branches. Creepers entangled him and he hacked maniacally with his dagger, struggling to get free to escape the *thing* that dogged him. He ran without ceasing until he saw the lights of Montego Bay, and heard the roar of shanties from the pubs, and was among men, in man's world, where his instincts told him that beast of nightmare would not follow. And only when he was safe in a room at the Green Dragon did he allow himself to think on what he had seen.

Bartholomew Nolan, torn apart like a rag doll by an inhuman creature, which could not be stopped or killed by mortal weapon . . . this same creature, now bound for Ashbury, his future father-in-law, whom he had sworn to protect as he would protect his own long-dead father. And perhaps bound to slay all those associated with Ashbury—he thought of Emma and panic gripped him. He recalled how useless his saber had been, and how even the pistol shot had only stunned the beast. His hands trembled; panic unspooled him, there, in his dingy room, and he lay shuddering for an hour or two.

Henry was a practical fellow; he had been raised in the Church of England, and by that upbringing he doubted the existence or power of witchcraft. But in India he had seen fakirs lie without breathing for hours; he had seen blank-eyed children bitten by snakes without suffering; and now he had seen an indestructible monster. He never doubted the evidence of his sense, and in not doubting his fear increased; there was no chance that he had imagined the events on the beach or been fooled in some way. The hulking giant was real, and it was *going to kill him*. He bolted his door. Then he remembered that Bartholomew Nolan had bolted his door, too—little good it had done him.

Sleep was impossible after that realization, so he made the best of his time by speculating as to Ashbury's possible past. It was true that Ashbury had never attempted to conceal his past from him, but Henry had never really pried into the matter. Ashbury had told him that he had made his fortune "on the sea," which, he reflected, could mean any number of things. Henry had no difficulty in suspecting Ashbury of these darker deeds; he had seen too much in the Navy to believe the best of anyone. Ashbury's implied command regarding Nolan's death came back to him, further strengthening his conviction. Henry would give him a chance to explain; he would lay it all out and listen to what Ashbury had to say. Hopefully the old man could divulge something that would help. Henry defeat the undefeatable monster and prevent death and dishonor to himself, Emma, and old Thomas Ashbury. Knowing then his duty, he dropped at last into a brief and awful sleep.

———⚓———

Henry rode back to Port Royal in broad daylight, urging his horse to reach the city before dusk fell. The mare needed little urging; it seemed just as fearful of the darkening jungle as Henry was. He reached the town as the sun drew down in the west, casting long golden shadows in the streets. Henry passed through town to Ashbury's mansion, left his horse at the stable, and marched directly to Ashbury's study, where he found the old man pouring over some documents. Ashbury set a stack of books on the documents as Henry approached, and Henry couldn't help but notice the subterfuge. Despite this, as he came into Ashbury's presence, and as the old man smiled so warmly upon him and rose to take his hand with such goodwill and loving-kindness, Henry's determination wavered, and he saw no way of broaching the subject of alleged piracy. So after exchanging greetings, Henry only sat, vexed, not bothering to hide the anxiety on his face.

Finally, Ashbury spoke. "Out with it, my boy. What have you discovered?"

"Where is Emma?" Henry said.

"At the governor's ball. I expect her return shortly. I don't care for these little fêtes myself, you know—gammy leg. But think me not distracted by this subterfuge—what have you learned?" Ashbury said it with a smile, but Henry detected a lean wolfishness in that smile. He looked away.

"That, good sir, perhaps though you never attempted to hide your past from me, it may be due to the fact that I have never sought full knowledge of it."

The smile evaporated and Ashbury was instantly cold, hard. "What do you mean, boy?"

"That Bartholomew Nolan could not have been responsible for Perry's death."

"How not responsible?"

"He is slain himself."

"How slain?"

"Horribly, sir, in a way not conceivable by man." Henry's face burned as he said it; it sounded ridiculous, and he knew it. But Ashbury gave his words credence, only nodding and considering what he had said; Ashbury plainly knew more than he allowed, Henry realized. "Torn limb from limb, mauled and mangled—inside a locked cottage."

"Foreboding."

"Aye, sir, especially as I laid eyes on and confronted his murderer."

"And?"

"An inhuman giant, of great size and strength. I laid iron between its eyes and only stunned it. It could not be killed."

Henry's words had an immediate effect on Ashbury; the color drained from his face and he collapsed in his chair, slumping against the back. Henry leapt to his side in alarm. "Dear God, sir, are you well?"

"The giant . . . it was white, with a misshapen countenance?"

"The very beast!"

"Then the bokor really *has* returned."

"What is this bokor?" Henry returned to his seat. "Some hideous dago word, I warrant."

"Correct. A bokor—a practitioner of the foul jungle craft known as vodun. Voodoo."

"Voodoo?" Henry's heart raced; he thought of the blank-eyed Indian fakirs, the serpents writhing 'round their arms; he thought of drums pounding in the jungle, and obscene dances in the firelight; a pierced and tattooed shaman drinking vast bowls of boiling blood; goats' heads hacked off with machetes . . . all the vile things he had been told by his fellows in the Navy or heard from Frenchmen in the free ports of the Caribbean. "But such a thing has no power over God-fearing men . . ." He trailed off.

"You have witnessed its power yourself. Think you not that Nolan feared God? Among other things."

Henry was silent; fear had gripped him indeed. There was no room for anything but the dread of that unstoppable giant with the enormous hands, plodding slowly but inevitably after him. . . .

After a long while he spoke. "I would know, then, the bond that tied you and Nolan together, and what it has to do with this bokor."

"I told you. Nolan was a competitor. We parted ways years ago."

"I met a man who told me differently. He claimed to have sailed under you—the *five* of you." Henry watched Ashbury carefully while he said this. "You, Nolan, Redmond, Perry, and a Frenchman. He said you were partners."

Ashbury reacted with an inclination of his head. "Did he disclose our enterprise?"

"He did, sir."

Ashbury's eyes narrowed to slits. "I see." He paused, biting his knuckles. "As I said, I have never attempted to hide my past from you, my boy."

"I have never attempted to pry."

"You may."

"He said you were involved in piracy."

Ashbury slapped his desk. "That is a slanderous lie!" he shouted.

"Yet . . ." Henry said heavily, "I believe him." And he really did. Ashbury's reaction rang false. "If I am to help you, sir, I must know all. Disclose to me the exact nature of your enterprise, and its relation to this bokor, or I will be powerless. Speak without worry of the legal consequences. I am your future son, after all," he said with a tight-lipped smile.

Ashbury heaved a great sigh. "Very well. But 'pirate' is not the most fitting appellation—'privateer' perhaps fit us more. For while we were not sanctioned by the King, we nonetheless struck only His enemies—the galleys of Spain and the Dutch. We *began*, in truth, on a Spanish galley—we were all of us slaves, prisoners of war, snatched from our ships by those Catholic dogs, and pressed into service in their Venezuelan mines. Four of us drew together because of our common defiance of our captors—I could remove my shirt, boy, and show you the ruddy marks of Spanish whips." Ashbury's face darkened with long-dormant resentment. "Every day more and more good men were carried out, feet first—mines are hell, lad, and Spanish mines the most charnel hells of all.

"Came a day when we were being transported, God knows why, but we loaded on a galley and were shipping north. We knew this was the best chance we'd ever have, so we began to plot. Desperate men, all of us, each feeling his life burning down to the quick under the Spanish, so we hatched a plan.

"We had no chance of seizing the ship by main force, but if we desired, we could draw blood. They would put us down at the cost of lives, and we would make them pay dearly. But I devised a way to put that sacrifice to use. Among us was a Frenchman. Gaston Duvall was his name. He had lived for years on the island of Hispaniola, among the Africans there, and learned their ways—the dark ways of vodun. He called himself a bokor, a sorcerer. He told us he could work a powerful magic that would guarantee our freedom, but that powerful sorcery required blood—great amounts of blood. We were prepared to spill it.

"Once a day they unchained us to walk the deck for a few moments. When they came for us on *that* day, we were ready. I took my fetters and laid to, slashing left and right with the heavy iron links . . ." Ashbury stared into the distance, his hands clenching, remembering the weight of the makeshift weapons. "Redmond and Perry and Nolan were with me, and we slaughtered the guards . . . of course, the alarm was raised, and soldiers were beating down the door, and we were dead in an instant if Duvall could not fulfill his end of the bargain. But he was up and dancing over the fallen soldiers, the bottoms of his bare feet stained with their blood, rattling a hollow gourd filled with pebbles." Henry thought of the sound he had heard on the beach. "And presently we heard . . ." He stopped.

"Heard what?"

"The sound of dying men, of bones snapping like sapling branches, of men screaming and praying in Spanish, breathing their last rattling breaths. When we opened that door—*God*. It was slaughter. Men mauled and mangled, torn limb from limb. The last of the soldiers, their officer among them, were crowded on the foredeck, firing down as a—being—moved up the stairs. A being just as you describe. All white, enormous, misshapen." He shuddered. "They emptied their harquebusses into the thing, and I could hear the balls smacking into its flesh from across the deck. No effect. It mounted to the foredeck. Then I closed the door.

"When we opened it later, the foredeck was the same slaughterhouse as the rest of the ship—littered with rent corpses, gory odds and ends of human beings. Jesus Christ, forgive me for what we unleashed upon the world." He passed his hand before his closed eyes. "O, merciful Father . . ."

"Come off it, man," Henry snapped. "Then what?"

"Then we claimed the ship for His Majesty and turned her guns against her former masters. We captured another galleon and sank it—we came to a tiny port on the Mosquito Coast and sacked and burned it, and each time Duvall and his witchcraft aided us. We shipped cargo, too. Aye, and slaves we seized from the ships of Spain, we sold in Barbados." He waved dismissively.

"But the Spaniards were after us, and we were afraid—afraid of them and afraid of Duvall. A man cannot live in communion with evil of that sort." He shuddered again. "So the four of us decided to get rid of him. We marooned him on a barren rock south of Jamaica, well outside the shipping lanes and with little hope of rescue. Were not for the evidence to the contrary, I would think him still there. Then we scuttled the galleon and parted ways with our booty, vowing never to speak of it again."

Henry steepled his fingers. "And he has returned to revenge himself on you," Henry said at length.

"Aye. A punishment, I think, far too severe for the offense."

Henry eyed Ashbury, studying him sharply. "Unless there is more to the offense that you have not told me."

"There is no more."

"There *is*!" Henry shouted, not meaning to. He calmed himself with a considerable effort. "I cannot express my disappointment in you, Ashbury," he snapped. "What I imagined sterling is instead reechy and rotted. But I will still endeavor to protect you, for the man you *are* somewhat compensates for the man you *were*. And the familial ties that bind us are too strong to be ignored. But *if* I am to protect you from your fate, I would have the whole truth from you. Now! No more lies."

Ashbury hung his head. He seemed entirely beaten. "Very well," he whispered. "Duvall begged us not to abandon him. On one principle—that he had a child. A daughter. Her name was Emma."

"Oh . . ." Henry could only groan. "No . . . no."

"Aye. Emma Duvall, whom you love so well, young man, daughter of this dread bokor! He who communes with devils!"

"Oh, God . . . Oh, Emma . . ." Henry rocked in his chair, head in hands.

"He had left the child in the care of an aged aunt some years before, when he had first gone a-roving, but he missed her dearly. 'A child needs a father,' he said. Then, beseeching me, he grabbed my wrist, just before we shoved off. 'Port-au-Prince,' he said, 'find her,' and then Redmond and Perry heaved at the oars and we were off, the mad Frog flailing behind us in the surf, shouting, 'Find her! Help her!' And I did."

"And your conscience is salved?"

"It is," Ashbury said softly.

Henry choked. He felt ill.

"I'm glad to hear that, Father!" Emma's voice was loud and clear in the study. "I would be *so* dismayed should you lie awake at night." She stepped into the doorway.

Henry realized the door had been ajar.

"How long have you been there?" Ashbury said, his voice raspy.

"Long enough," she said. "To learn for certain what I have always suspected."

"Suspected how?" Ashbury asked.

"I was four years old when you took me from my aunt, Father," she said. "Memories from that time survive. And the earliest memories, of my father, kind and laughing . . . you weren't him. I could tell." Her eyes glittered as she moved across the study. She lay a hand on Ashbury's cheek and tilted his face to hers. "But the intervening years of your kindness and your sustenance have more than supplanted him. You may not have sired me, but you alone are my father." She kissed his forehead. "Almighty Christ forgives you; how, then, could I not? The quality of mercy is not strained." She embraced him, and Ashbury, shaking with a grateful sob, returned her embrace.

"Thank you, my daughter. Thank you."

Henry's stomach churned violently. Ashbury's confession had thrown him into confusion; the whole stinking business was not finished. The bokor lurked with his monstrous creature, ready after twenty years to reap his vengeance.

"Ashbury," he said, "we have yet to deal with Duvall."

"What would you do?"

"While you remain here, you are not safe. Every citizen of Jamaica knows the Ashbury estate; Duvall will have no trouble finding you. And, my dear," he said to Emma, "I cannot imagine his ambitions regarding you."

She trembled. "I will not go back to him! Should he be responsible for these monstrous deeds, he has no claim over me."

"I agree. Then until this crisis passes, it would be better that you were concealed. Perhaps you might stay with the governor's daughter?"

"I will not." She lifted her chin. "I will not hide while my father is endangered."

"He will not be endangered. He will hide as well."

"If you think it best," Ashbury said. "I am totally dependent on you, my boy, until this is over."

"I would stay with my father," Emma said.

"Please, my sweet," Henry implored. "I beg that you heed my counsel on this. It is a matter of blood and iron—a matter for men, my dear."

Emma smiled. "I suppose you're right. Where will my father be sheltered?"

"I have not thought on it," Henry said. "But go make ready, Emma; prepare for several nights' stay." She hurried from the room.

"Where will I go?" Ashbury asked.

"For now, to the harbor, to hire me a ship. Then you will mark on a map the rock where you marooned Duvall. Afterwards, you may stay at my lodgings. Here is the address." He wrote it on a scrap of paper, and handed it to Ashbury, avoiding his eyes. Henry did not want to see the terror he knew must lurk there.

"I don't need to mention, my son, that this must be handled with the utmost discretion. My position and reputation cannot be jeopardized."

"Your *neck* cannot be jeopardized!" Henry hissed. "You fear you would swing for a pirate and a thief! But worry not. I would not have a known criminal for a father-in-law."

"Then we understand each other." A little of the old cunning crept back into Ashbury's eyes. "Good."

————————⚓————————

Henry sailed the next morning on a tiny cutter procured by Ashbury. The captain and crew were good men all, of an unquestioning disposition, and they assured Henry that the journey would be swift. Henry had seen Emma to her lodgings before departure, carefully avoiding mention of her father's whereabouts. Henry's experience of men was too vast for him to allow himself to reveal more than was necessary when at all possible, and this suspiciousness nagged him. He stood at the rail while the cutter plowed through the morning fog, then went to his cabin.

The captain summoned him to the deck just before dusk. "We're here, squire." He gave Henry a spyglass and pointed. "Ten degrees to starboard." Through the gloaming Henry could see the wave-beaten island—barely a rock, indeed. It was surely less than a quarter of a mile across, with a little peak in the center covered in thick foliage. He saw no signs of life.

"Lower a boat, captain," he said, collapsing the spyglass. "I'm going ashore, alone."

"Aye-aye."

————————⚓————————

Saber and pistol drawn, Henry scoured the island, searching desperately for some clue of Duvall's passage. The island scarcely seemed capable of sustaining life. A sulfurous spring provided the only fresh water, and Henry spotted little game: only a thickly muscled serpent coiled about a tree branch, and furtive scrabbles in the underbrush indicating rodents. Dark had fallen by the time he found the cottage.

It was a shack, really, scarcely larger than Nolan's own hut, and obviously built of improvised materials. Palm boughs thatched the roof, and bamboo formed the frame. Before it was a great ash-pit ringed by volcanic stones; Henry probed the ashes tentatively. In the center he found a few hot coals. Someone had used the pit recently, perhaps within the past few days. His hand found something else in the pit, an object of unexpected hardness, too light to be a stone. He withdrew it, shaking off the ashes and squinting to examine it in the moonlight—a ghastly demonic image, slanting diabolical shapes–wicked devil's horns! He gasped and dropped it, realizing as it rolled at his feet that it was no more than a goat's skull. But—

He probed in the ashes again, and found more and more of the hard, round objects—he swept the ashes away with his hand and beheld, one, two, a dozen of the grinning demonic skulls, illuminated horribly by the moonlight, and, among them, bones of a size and shape that made him wonder whether they belonged to goats at all. . . . He turned away from the ash-pit. The cottage held the answers he sought.

Around the ash-pit were numerous torches on decayed bamboo stands. He took one and lit it from the coals, and, pistol out, approached the cottage. The night was quiet, waves murmuring on the beach the only sound. Something rattled and fear lanced through him—no, a breeze had stirred some hanging gourds, that was all. He flung the door open and entered, pistol first. A human shape, barely visible, sprawled on a mat, surrounded by strange fetishes. Henry had to squint to determine their shapes in the torchlight: some root, twisted into human form; a squirrel or rabbit skull, bound with bark to twigs arranged in a mockery of arms and legs; hollowed gourds, filled with—he smashed one open and examined the contents—human teeth. Henry advanced on the recumbent shape, torch held high.

A skeleton, the flesh long since decayed and vanished in the Caribbean climate, the bones shrouded in tattered seaman's clothes. The bokor was dead, then; Duvall had expired ages ago. Rings decked the skeletal fingers, large gold bands studded with rubies and emeralds, and several bracelets of apparent value encircled its forearms. The carcass was covered all over with jewelry. Duvall, long dead, yet dressed like a king. Henry spied something that froze his blood; his heart plummeted in his chest. "It can't—can't," he said, nonsensically, knowing he was babbling. "If this is Thy will, O, Father—I reject it. I find it poisonous," he said, even as he snuffed the torch in the sand and raced back to the boat.

———⚓———

"All haste to Port Royal," he told the captain. "I believe Thomas Ashbury to be in danger."

"The wind favors us, squire," the captain shouted. "We can be back by daybreak."

Henry sent Ashbury a scrawled summons upon his return, and a similar note to Emma, and waited in Ashbury's study for their arrival. He paced to and fro in the study, not wanting to look at any one thing for too long, lest dizziness and horror overtake him. Finally Ashbury arrived, pale and haggard. He had clearly not slept the last few nights. Emma arrived not long after. She embraced Henry.

"My love," she breathed, "I am so relieved that you have returned safely."

"I am relieved to have returned, myself," Henry muttered. "Ashbury!" he cried, "Here is your bokor!" He opened his bag and withdrew Duvall's yellowed skull. Ashbury sat heavily; Henry glanced at Emma. She blanched, the color drained from her face, her lips parted in shock and fright. Henry tossed the skull at Ashbury's feet. "Duvall is long dead," he said, stiffly. "He poses you no threat."

"Then who?" Ashbury said. "Who summoned the creature you fought at Montego? Who slew Perry and Nolan?"

"Indeed." Henry swiveled, his gaze locked on Emma, who glanced from the skull to Ashbury to Henry, the same expression frozen on her face. "I wonder, my love, where is the necklace I gave you? The topaz, set in wrought gold?"

"I—it's in my room," Emma stammered. "I was afraid of *losing* it, it's so dear, so I locked it away . . ."

"Stop," Henry said. "Stop speaking. Your words are foul—they sicken me. They poison me." From his pocket he produced a gold chain, wound around his fingers, a flashing blue topaz dangling from his hand. "Here it is. I found it set on that *corpse*, looped about his neck lovingly . . . with all the devotion of a daughter."

Emma's paleness flushed to brilliant anger, her skin red with sudden fury. "Is it not *meet*?" she hissed. "Is it not fit that a daughter honor her father? Yes—my *father*, not this *fraud*, this *usurper!*" She snatched a paperweight from the desk and hurled it at Ashbury; he flinched away and it shattered on the wall. She was screaming now, the concealed anger and resentment twenty years in the making finally finding expression. "Over whom I must fawn for my bread, when my real father calls to me from across the sea and beyond the veil, clamoring for *justice* to his murderers!" She spat on Ashbury's face, and the spittle dribbled down his cheek; he was too stunned to wipe it away. "Yes, I call you *murderer*, for you left him to die, he who served you well! On whom you built your fortune, with whose blood you bought *this!*" She indicated the whole of the estate with a sweep of her arm. "But he came to me, and I *ate him*, swallowed his spirit and all his knowledge, and in turn grew more powerful than ever he was. And now, betrayer-father, it is your turn to follow Nolan, and Perry, and Redmond. . ."

Emma took a small gourd from her handbag and rattled it, and Henry felt the pebbles clatter as if they clattered within his own skull. "*Tonton Macout!*" she said. "*Tonton Macout moun la!*" She chanted louder and louder, rattling the gourd, and Henry, still frozen in shock, heard a groan, instantly familiar, from outside. It penetrated to his very bones; he was dead, he knew it. He was already dead, and there was no escaping; how could he escape when he was already in the grave?

He stirred his mortified flesh to action. "Emma—Emma, don't do this—for God's sake!" he cried, his own voice sounding weak and thin in his ears.

"*Separe sa ant nou!*" She glared at him, and took a letter opener from the desk. Emma splayed her hand, palm upward, on the wood and after a moment's hesitation plunged the letter opener into her flesh. She cried in pain even as she twisted the blade left and right, blood welling up from the wound; she held her injured hand high, and her maiden's blood poured down on her. "*Pa gen moun la!*" She rattled the gourd with her other hand.

The study door flew from its hinges in a great burst of splinters; most of the wall went with it, and on the other side stood the giant, its hideous features distorted horribly. Ashbury wailed, "O, merciful Father, deliver us!" Panic crushed Henry; Death, Death was here! He leapt to Emma, wrenching her arm. "Stop this madness!"

"*Tonton Macout moun la! Moun la!*" she replied, and he could see no trace of her personality in her eyes; her face was a perfect mask of unreckoning hate. The giant advanced, unstoppable and colossal, and Henry felt death's ineluctable talons at his throat—that awful weight! That blasphemous strength!

"Jesus, God in heaven, forgive me," he said, and he drew his dagger and sheathed it in Emma's throat. Blood gushed forth, a rubescent torrent, far too much blood, flowing across the floor; gurgling and choking, her eyes wide in disbelief, Emma dropped to the floor. The giant was gone.

———⚓———

Morning broke begrudgingly on the day of Henry's hanging. All the town turned out for it, hundreds of people, crowding the beach to see the madman who had slain Ashbury's lovely daughter. He'd protested his innocence to the last, despite the fact that his own blade had done the deed. He had been drenched in her blood, cradling her cooling corpse. Her father had seen the act with his own eyes, and bore witness against him. In answer to Ashbury's testimony, Henry had remained silent, giving

nothing to discredit the man, and when the judge asked if he had nothing to say in his own defense, he had muttered only, "Nothing that can be believed, milord."

The drums beat, and the hooded man approached the gallows where Henry stood, a noose around his neck.

"A moment with the condemned, please, sir!" Ashbury pushed his way through the crowd.

The executioner looked to the governor, who nodded.

"Thank you, thank you, sir." Ashbury bowed deferentially and approached Henry. He gazed upon the condemned man a long while, seeking something written on his face. "I have nothing because of you," he whispered. "You took my *daughter* from me."

"She was never your daughter. And you still have something—you still have your reputation."

Ashbury smiled grimly. "That I do, lad! I suppose I do have something. And from there, I can build."

"You will. In a year no one will remember this. The stench of death on you will have changed to the aroma of roses, I'm sure, once I'm gone."

"Aye. And I thank you for that, my son."

"Get away from me." Henry snarled. "I have few moments left as it is. I don't want them sullied by your lying, putrid presence. You excrement. You *waste*! I thank *God* I will not see you again!"

But Ashbury had already hobbled away on his cane, not turning to watch as the trapdoor opened and Henry dropped and kicked and strangled his last; he *did* see the ecstatic looks on the faces of the onlookers at the moment of death. *Ghastly*, he thought with a shudder. *To look on death with such satisfaction.* Soon he was home. He read a book for about an hour before lunch.

Albatross Dark
Jaleigh Johnson

If you fall from the ship, drink deep. Don't be afraid.

Kaari floated in the dark. Strands of her pale hair drifted up to kiss her cheeks like restless ghosts. She opened her mouth to heed the Matron's words. The light stopped her.

Distant, but hugely ovoid, she might have mistaken it for a Nera whale. The light drifted closer, and she recognized the Magus Taint.

Not a whale at all, Kaari thought, but a ship's hull—a ship protected by a Magus's shield. Perhaps she would not die after all.

The ship, a cutter class by her shape, was going to pass directly above her. Kaari forced her deadened limbs to swim. She propelled herself close enough to see the dying fish caught too close to the magic sealing the ship's hull.

Chest burning, she put her hand into the flowing current. She wondered, belatedly, if she would end up like the gasping, bleeding-eyed fish. Soril, the sea goddess, did not suffer magic kindly.

The red spell shield enveloped Kaari. A haze of pain fogged the novice Matron's mind. She tried to pull her hand away, but it was too late to give her body to the sea.

⚓

Cai cast a handful of flash powder into the fire elemental's mouth. The salamander's v-shaped jaw detached weirdly from its face to accept the tribute. The room flared brilliant orange for an instant, then darkened again.

Cai removed the black lenses from his eyes. "Tell your master the cutter ship *Grinmoir* requires passage through the Red Maw—*safe* passage."

"At great cost to the captain of the cutter ship *Grinmoir*," the salamander said, its mouth thick with burning powder.

"That's his problem."

A soft, grating wheeze drifted out of the corner of the cabin. The figure stretched out on Cai's bunk rolled onto his side. His skin had turned bone yellow in the past twenty-four hours. His bloodshot eyes fixed on the salamander. "Always knew . . . you worshipped the demons, Magus."

"You are delirious if you think a bit of flash powder is a sacrificial offering," Cai snorted. "I thought you'd be grateful for a little less pitch and roll on this leg of the journey." He nodded to the coil of bandages encasing the sailor's abdomen. "How are you feeling?"

The sailor spat on the floor. Cai saw blood mixed in the spittle. "The traders made a pact with Haeros when they brought you on board. Captain never would have stood for it. You'll bring the ship down into Soril's arms, you will."

"Oh, please." Cai fixed a martyred look on his face. "You could at least whisper a few sweet words in my ear while I change your dressing. Gods know the smell warrants a little distraction. Even the Sea Witch would be offended."

The sailor grabbed Cai's shirt when the Magus bent over him. Pain cinched his face into a weathered knot. "Will I be seeing the other side of the Maw?"

Sweat bloomed on the sailor's forehead. He was not ten years older than Cai, but the sea and his wounds had made his face an ancient, ravaged landscape. Stubble grew around knife scars at his lips. His nose twisted into a crooked hook shape between his eyes.

Cai resisted the urge to pull away from the smell of rot coming off the bandages. "You'll see the Maw," the Magus said.

He straightened and took a cup from his worktable. He filled it with water from a pitcher on the floor. Turning to the salamander, he lifted the cup and caught an end flame from the creature's tail. The water hissed.

Cai blew on the concoction, creating a tiny vortex of stirring. "Only the men I like seem to perish on this ship," he said idly. "The bloody nuisances who want the captain to string me up by my nether regions always seem to survive. Lucky me."

The sailor coughed up something that might have been a laugh, but the sound was too ugly for Cai to be that generous. "Arkeron. You liked him well enough."

"Yes, I did."

"And the captain had him executed." The sailor took the cup Cai offered, but his sharp eyes never left the Magus's.

"Yes, he did." Cai stared at the sailor without really seeing him. "Drink. The wound will do better if you sleep through the Maw."

The sailor gulped the water down. On the table, the salamander hissed and gurgled. Cai speared it with a look that had magic stirring from the corners of the room. The creature obediently went still.

"Feels . . . warm." The sailor took a steadying breath and turned his face to the wall. The cup slid from his nerveless fingers.

Cai caught it before it hit the floor. He put the cup back on the table.

"Poor, dumb creature," gurgled the salamander. "Doesn't know, does it? To drink a mix of Haeros's fire and Soril's water is death."

"Blame the gods for never getting along," Cai said. "Go. Take my message to your master."

The salamander snapped its orange tail, leaving scorch marks on the wooden table. He disappeared.

Cai spent a moment disposing of the poisoned water. When he'd finished, he glanced at the door to his cabin. The portal always stood slightly ajar from the listing of the ship. "What is it?" he said.

He heard no sound from without, but a female voice answered, "You'd better come. The captain's chased off some pirates in the midst of scavenging."

"Is the other ship intact?" Cai said, pulling on his coat. "Survivors?"

There was a pause. "One. You'd better come."

Cai paused in the act of buttoning the dark copper buttons. "You might tell the captain that Markus has succumbed to his wound."

"When?"

"Almost this moment—"

The explosion came from somewhere directly above Cai's head. The force hurled him against the door frame. Pain exploded down his shoulder. He hauled himself to his feet and pushed through the door to the ladder at the end of the hall.

Smoke and magic stink clouded his vision when he got to the deck. Pale silhouettes moved through the clouds.

The ship was running toward the horizon. In its wake were the remains of a second, much smaller vessel that had literally been blown apart by a Magus's fireball.

"Report!" Captain Hennedy pounded across the deck, stopping just out of reach of Cai's billowing coat. The thick crimson of the Magus garment stood out sharply against the trading company's royal blue colors. The captain thrust a spyglass into Cai's hands. "Who are they?"

Cai raised the glass to his eyes. The retreating vessel flew no colors, though that was hardly a surprise. Cai was looking for magic.

"She has fire-proof sails," he murmured. "Flame guards are wormed deep in the wood. Her figurehead is a Watcher."

The captain cursed mightily. "So she has eyes, and proof against your own fire. What good are the thousand coins a season the company pays you if the pirates have a Magus that can do one better than our own?" He snatched the spyglass back.

Cai blinked at the red-faced Hennedy. "Your hull has never been breached by cannon. If they've a Magus on board, we'll simply have to adjust our strategy. Will you continue pursuit?"

"By the Maw, no!" the captain shouted. "We've got larger problems. Have you seen the colors of the ship they razed?" The captain pointed amidships. "Of course you haven't, as she's wearing them."

"She?" Cai looked toward the center of the ship, where a crowd of curious sailors had gathered. He caught his breath.

The girl looked to be about twenty. Her smooth skin was blue from the cold water. Her hair was a white mass spread out on the sun-bleached wood of the deck. No color, not even the sun could touch her. Naked, she lay in a puddle of rags and seawater on the deck. The torn cloth had once been the defeated ship's colors: black, with a solid yellow line cutting the center.

Cai's jaw tightened. "They attacked a plague ship? Why, in the name of the gods?" He felt eyes upon him and looked up.

The first mate, Sira Dam, stood behind the captain. She had her cutlass in her hand.

"No," Cai murmured.

"Bind her hands and feet," the captain said.

Tilray, the helmsman, hurried to comply. He stopped, the rope dangling from his hands, when he caught Cai's eye.

"Don't you know the bad luck you engender when you refuse an offering from Soril's own hands?" Cai jumped to the rail, drawing the eyes of the crew to him. "The Sea Witch will not be pleased."

From his superior height, he could see that the girl would be tall. Her body was thin and underfed, but that hardly mattered.

She was still the most breathtakingly beautiful creature Cai had ever seen.

"You forget your place, Magus," the captain said, his voice soft but thick with menace. "I already suffer one albatross on this ship." He raised his voice so the crew could hear. "She is plague-ridden! For the safety of us all, she must go back to the sea."

Murmurs of agreement flew through the crowd. Cai was losing them. Sira Dam stepped forward with Tilray. Her cutlass flashed green from the jade veins running down the blade. She met Cai's gaze briefly, and hesitated.

Cai hissed something under his breath that sent a flash of heat across the deck. The sailors standing near him blinked their eyes and found them watering. When they looked up, they saw that Cai was no longer standing at the rail. He had disappeared, materializing on his knees between Sira Dam and the half-drowned plagueling.

The captain gasped and took a step forward, but Cai already had his hands on the girl's face. "By the Maw, Magus, if you've infected yourself—"

"I don't think so." Cai lifted one of the girl's eyelids. "There," he said.

As one, the crowd bent closer to see the blank, white irises, framed by slashes of stygian black. Gazing at her face only, one might have mistaken her for a sightless, deep-dwelling fish, Cai thought grimly.

"Gods," Sira Dam said, sheathing her sword. She ignored the captain's black look. "She's a Dark."

"Not plague-ridden," Cai said. He twisted her head so the crew could see. "She's a caretaker, a tender of the infected. Kill her and by order of the Pact, you commit murder." He lifted his gaze to challenge the captain. "Will you pursue?"

The captain said nothing for a long moment, simply staring at Cai with open hatred. Then he said, "I will honor the Pact. Get her out of my sight."

Cai clenched a fist. If she'd been among Magi, the plague caretaker would be treated with the greatest respect. Darks—men and women immune to the plague—were to be valued. But he nodded, deciding he'd tested Hennedy's will far enough.

Cai gathered the unconscious girl in his arms and strode to the ladder. He heard the captain's nasty chuckle behind him.

"That's it, Magus, take your new pet, but keep her out from underfoot. You don't want her going the way of Arkeron."

Cai opened his mouth to reply but felt a stirring in his arms. He looked down and saw the girl's eyes were open and staring at him intently. Cai felt a flutter of cold in his chest but dismissed it as the water from her body seeping into his clothes.

"Who is Arkeron?" she said. Her eyes drifted closed on the last syllable, and she clutched at his copper buttons in sleep.

Cai swallowed. He carried her to the ladder and spoke the word that would float them gently down the hatch.

The last thing he heard was Sira Dam speaking to the captain in low tones.

"We checked twice, sir. It's the damnest thing I ever saw. There are no other bodies. None."

———

Kaari smelled the blood before she opened her eyes. She was in a caretaker's cabin. People had died here. It was the same as on the island. Tresamare—the plague isle—her home.

It always smelled of death.

Kaari felt a puff of hot wind against her face. She opened her eyes and saw the salamander attached to the bunk above her head. It stared at her with twin, smoldering eyes.

Hissing fearfully, Kaari backed up against the corner of the bunk. She tucked her legs protectively against her chest. Two feet away, the salamander hissed back and flicked out its tongue. It seemed amused.

"Don't mind him. He's never seen a Dark before."

Kaari turned her head. The voice came from a man sitting with his back to her at a large worktable that was bolted to the floor. The man swiveled on a stool to look at her.

His face was colorless, like hers—she'd never seen a face to match her own so closely on someone who wasn't a Dark. His cheeks were hollow triangles; there was no hair on his face, and only a fine brown suggestion of it on his skull. His eyes, though, were not a Dark's eyes. They were sharp, amber points, like fire trying to thrive in snow.

"What is your name?" the man said.

But at that moment Kaari recognized him. *Magus.* Having touched his shield, she could now smell his magic curling around every object in the room. And around him—his body was soaked in it, yet they were still on the sea. She could feel the movement of the waves.

How could the man stand, his gait swaying gracefully with the ship, without screaming in terror?

"Are you a madman?" Kaari said. Her voice sounded harsh, scraped by salt water and fear.

The Magus poured water into a cup and handed it to her. "Am I mad for asking your name? I hope not. Why, is it a cursed name? Will speaking it aloud cause me to grow spines and a tail?"

"Soril does not suffer Magi in her domain," Kaari said, bewildered. "The plague—"

"Well, now I am reassured," the Magus said. "Your near-drowning hasn't relieved you of your grasp of the obvious." Seeing her expression, he seemed to take pity on her. "Yes, I am a Magus, and there are still a handful of us who will venture upon the sea, despite Soril's warnings. If you hadn't lived on that accursed isle all your life, you'd have known that. Now, your name?"

"Kaari," she said, against her better judgment. She couldn't tell whether the madman was laughing at her or not. He didn't smile, but the amber orbs sparkled. If he was mad, shouldn't she be afraid of him? Instead, she took a sip of water.

The Magus nodded. "Kaari, it is, though I rather like Dark," he said. "Did you know that's what outsiders call the caretakers?"

Kaari shook her head. "I'd never been off Tresamare until yesterday. I was born there."

"I see." The Magus nodded thoughtfully, as if she'd just revealed something very important. Kaari felt naked under his gaze, as if he could see right through her.

She looked down at herself, only then realizing she was wrapped in a thin cotton shift. "I thank you for rescuing me," she said. "Can you tell me what ship this is?"

"The cutter ship *Grinmoir*," he said. "You need to rest now."

"I feel fine. For what port are we bound?" She would not expect a trade ship to return her to the isle. Only the plague ships were allowed within sight of Tresamare. All others were warned away by the cannon mounts on the north side of the island.

"We are passing through the Red Maw as we speak," the Magus said. "Our ultimate destination is unknown to me."

"How can that be?"

This time the Magus did smile. It was not a pleasant thing to look at. "Because—perhaps wisely—the captain does not see fit to include me in his plans. I never know where we intend to dock until the anchor falls."

Kaari didn't know what to make of the man. "And you are content with this arrangement?"

He tilted his head, considering. "More than content."

"How can you stand to be on the water?" Kaari's voice rose involuntarily. Nothing around her made sense. The salamander's heat burned the top of her head. It moved above her with soft, undulating motions. "How can you be here?"

"I am here because the Alacor Trading Company engaged my services to protect this ship from pirates," the Magus said. "My name is Cai, and I do not fear Soril, so you can rest easy." He rose and headed for the door. "When you wake, I'll ask you some questions. I think you owe me a dozen, at least."

"Wait!"

Cai stopped at the door. "There were no other survivors," he said, as if reading her thoughts.

Kaari leaned back against the wall and closed her eyes. "Might I pray for them," she said, "before you commit their bodies to the sea?"

She opened her eyes then and caught the shudder that passed through the Magus's body. She might have remarked on it, but grief held her silent.

"Their bodies are gone," Cai said shortly. "You're too late."

He left the cabin, closing the door behind him.

Kaari stood up. She couldn't lie down any longer. She felt numb. She was used to the detachment that came with comforting the dying; it was part of her life, for good or ill. But she'd never lost a friend, and the Matrons, her teachers, had been the closest people she'd had to family.

She had nothing of value to tell the Magus. She remembered little of the attack, except seeing the glint of sails when the pirates appeared. A moment before, the horizon had been clear. She didn't know where the menacing doom had come from.

After the first wave of fire, Matron Sillian had ordered that the sick be executed, a mercy killing before they were burned alive. Kaari's hands had been shaking the whole time she held the knife. Then Sillian had pulled her aside and told her to drink deep of the sea if she was cast overboard. Kaari remembered the older woman's face, frozen as if carved from stone. She'd left Kaari then, alone with the dead plague victims. Kaari never saw her again.

Would Cai care to know those things? Would he care to hear how frightened she'd been? Being a Magus, he must know intimately the fear of the sea. The goddess Soril suffered no Magi in her domain.

Didn't he realize that if he fell into the water, he would be killed instantly by her wrath?

Cai knocked at the door

"Come." The crisp invitation came after a long silence.

Cai slipped inside the cabin, closing the door securely behind him.

Kaari crept up to the door. It was beyond foolishness to shadow the Magus, but she had to know if he was what he claimed, or if he was a madman. She found a gap in the door's crooked planks and pressed her milky eye to the hole.

Candlelight illuminated a sparsely furnished cabin. A desk stood directly across from the door, with a stack of books arranged meticulously, spine to spine, in the center. On the wall above the desk hung a sword. Veins of green ran down the hilt.

Kaari strained to see into the corners of the room, seeking the sword's owner.

A hand passed in front of her vision, slapping against the back wall of the cabin. Nails dug into the wood and veins stood out on the hand. Kaari's gaze followed the hand down a slender arm and a fall of straight, black hair.

The woman whose hand braced the wall sat astride the Magus, one naked leg on either side of his body. He clutched her shoulders and rocked back and forth. The woman let her head fall back, and a sigh of pleasure escaped her lips.

Kaari turned away from the door, her cheeks flaming, and turned into the hand that caught her by the throat.

Coarse skin forced her windpipe closed. She could not hope to scream. Flailing, she tried to kick the crooked door, but another pair of hands caught her ankles and pulled them up into the air.

They were men. Kaari could see their bearded faces in the shadows of the lamps on the walls. One carried a rope. The other covered her eyes with a stinking scrap of cloth.

"You'll sleep well in Soril's arms tonight, luvie," one of the men said, putting his lips against her ear in a wet kiss.

If you fall from the ship, drink deep.

Kaari remembered the Matron's words and the harsh, cold water. She couldn't do it. The water terrified her. Fear galvanized her limbs.

She kicked and bit and struggled until she felt a man's wrist between her teeth. She bore down, tearing flesh.

The man screamed and released her throat. Kaari kicked free, catching the other man in the chest. He grunted, and she hit the floor with a stinging pain to her backside.

Jumping up, Kaari charged blindly for the crooked door. One of the men caught her shift, tearing it, just as she ripped the blindfold from her eyes.

Cai leaped off the bunk when Kaari burst into the room. The black-haired woman went for her sword. Kaari's momentum brought her to the wall first, and she grabbed the glistening weapon. Whirling, she brandished it at the hall, but the sailors were already in retreat. They did not want their identities known.

"Cowards," she hissed, and broke into a run. She'd bury the steel down their throats.

Cai caught her at the door. Half-naked, her shift ruined, she felt the heat of his skin against her cold flesh. A thought drifted in the back of her mind: *he's just like the salamander, warm and strange with his amber eyes.*

"Let me go!"

"You're in no shape to take them both," Cai said calmly. He tried to take the sword from her, but she twisted it, brandishing the steel against his throat.

"Let. Me. Go."

Cai released her. "Sira Dam, meet Kaari the Dark," he said, when the black-haired woman came to stand next to him. "Sira Dam is first mate of the *Grinmoir*."

"Kaari." The woman inclined her head respectfully. "Lady, if you'll surrender my sword, I will pursue the men who attacked you."

The woman's voice was so formal, regal, almost. Kaari was suddenly ashamed of her nakedness, her pale skin next to the woman's dusky beauty. "Thank you," she said quietly, offering the blade.

Sira Dam nodded and took off down the hall, her sword flashing green in her wake.

When they were alone, Cai said, conversationally, "I seem to recall I left you sound asleep?"

Kaari looked at him and, finding nothing to say in her defense, blurted out the first thing that came to her mind.

"Who is Arkeron?"

His eyes changed, though she couldn't have said how, exactly.

"Come above with me."

She followed him up the ladder. The night was crisp and cold, the stars like brittle slashes in the sky. Kaari would have savored the view, but she was watching Cai.

"Arkeron was a sailor—the ship's doctor, in fact," the Magus said. "Captain Hennedy had him executed for being my friend."

Kaari stared at him, bewildered. "How can that be? A ship's doctor—"

"Ostensibly, his crime was letting the first mate die. Yes, Sira Dam is newly appointed to her position. The former first mate, Cochran, suffered from a rotting sickness of the brain. Arkeron couldn't save him. The captain called it murder and had the man executed." He stared at her with those odd eyes. "Now someone wants you dead, little Dark, for no crime to anyone."

"Because I'm an albatross," Kaari said, spreading her hands. "I bring bad luck."

Cai nodded. "You weren't quite as unconscious as you seemed, when they brought you up."

She didn't deny it. "You saved me. But I don't know if I can trust you."

"Most assuredly, you shouldn't."

He took her by the shoulders. Kaari was surprised at the heat emanating from his body. She thought it might be the clash of magic and sea creating a friction around him. How could he stand it?

"Did you see the ship that attacked you?" Cai said. "How many cannons did she have?"

"Ten that I could see, but she never fired a shot. It was all Magus fire. The Matrons stayed on board until the ship disintegrated out from under us. I swam through the debris, looking for Sillian, but I never found anyone. When I went under, I saw the glow of your ship."

"In all your time on the isle, have you ever heard of a ship carrying plague victims being attacked and scuttled?"

"You know I have not," Kaari said. "To do so is the act of a madman."

He actually laughed. "Yes, we must all seem mad to you out here, don't we? Tell me, Kaari, do you know why the Magi god and the Sea Witch are forever at each other's throats? Did they tell you that story?"

Transfixed by the glow of his eyes and his hands on her shoulders, Kaari nodded. She licked dry lips. "Haeros desired to make peace with Soril. He commanded his Magi to form a colony on Tresamare, a decade ago. He hoped, in time, to mollify the goddess by planting Magi in the middle of her garden."

Cai's lips twisted. "But it didn't work out that way, did it?"

"No. The goddess was not pleased. She saw Haeros's gesture as a poison to her domain. So she turned it back upon the Magi. She created the plague."

"All the Magi on the island were infected," Cai said, "and on Denale and Felores, continents to the north and south, Magi started falling ill. The god-curse had spread to all of Haeros's temples. The plague would have wiped all of us out had not Haeros intervened, confining the plague to the islands and his holy temples."

"And so all Magi who fall ill are taken to Tresamare by the Darks," Kaari said. "We were headed there when the attack came. I'd never been to the continent before."

"I'm sorry," Cai said. He looked like he meant it. "And you're right, of course. Only a madman would attack a plague ship. There's nothing to gain. But a sudden, brutal assault like you described tells me the pirates were after much larger prey. They remained invisible, waiting, and when their Magus brought them out, I'm guessing they were expecting a ship other than yours to be in their path."

"But there were no other ships nearby," Kaari said . . . and then it dawned on her. "They were after you," she whispered. "Gods, it was all a mistake." Her gaze flew to the horizon. "Are we in danger yet?"

"Yes. I'd wager they're in the invisible right now, bearing down on our position. They'll come back to finish what they started."

"What will you do?" Kaari said, hating the fear in her voice.

The Magus's mouth quirked, this time in a true smile, one that made him seem much younger. "I'll sink them, of course."

He strode away from her, to the helm. Heat trailed in his wake, and Kaari thought she saw a shimmer in the air. More magic, forever clashing with the sea goddess's power. But Kaari saw no force manifest itself.

"What are you doing?" she called out.

"Trying to make them show themselves."

Kaari started to ask how he would manage that, when her world erupted in fire.

The force of the spell blast threw her to the deck. Her jaw struck the wood painfully and she lay still a moment, her head spinning.

When she could move again, she saw the ring of Magus fire encircling the ship. Beyond it, she could see the outline of sails and rigging, like puppet strings against the dark.

The pirates had come.

———⚓———

Sira Dam was on deck almost instantly. Her hair hung in wild strings around her shoulders. Her uniform was askew. She crossed the deck to where Cai was helping Kaari to her feet. Cai knew what she would ask.

"Can you take her down?" The first mate nodded to Kaari, but her focus remained on the approaching ship.

"In a ship to ship battle, yes—if I can kill her Magus first. You'll have to do the rest." He lifted a mocking brow. "Will the captain give the word?"

"The word is given." Hennedy's voice came from the helm. "Go to your station," he ordered Sira Dam. "If he brings the ship down, we'll have a boarding party on our hands."

The first mate nodded and took off running. When she was gone, Hennedy approached Cai.

"So, was I the target all along, or did you sell out your entire crew to them?" Cai said. At his side, he felt Kaari stiffen.

"Just you," the captain said. "It took a long time to find another Magus willing to set foot on the sea. When I found out he was also a pirate, how could I resist the chance to be rid of you?"

"But we were delayed going through the Maw," Cai said. He braced Kaari as another explosion shook the deck. Soon the magic would penetrate his shields. "They must have been angry when you failed to put the ship where you said you would."

"Yes, I imagine it didn't sit well with the captain to find he was attacking a plague ship," Hennedy said. He glanced at the ring of fire encircling the ship. "Might have been a deal-breaker, in fact." He looked back at Cai. "So what will it be, Magus? Will you let us all die?" He pointed at Kaari. "Will you let her die, to revenge yourself on me?"

Cai shook his head. "Prepare for the boarding party, Captain," he said. "Tell the crew to brace themselves."

The captain nodded, a triumphant light in his eyes. He strode away, leaving Cai and Kaari at the rail.

"Time for you to go, little Dark," Cai said.

"Go where?" Kaari threw out a hand to the sea, to the doom sailing toward them.

"Home." He turned her, forcing her to face the water. "This is your home, Kaari. You just don't remember."

"You're talking madness again," the girl said. She backed up against him, and Cai closed his eyes, inhaling her scent for a moment. Then he forced her away from him.

"Look down," he hissed in her ear. "See the truth. See why there were no bodies for you to pray over. You don't know the rest of the story."

"What do you mean?" Kaari's voice shook.

"No good deed goes unpunished," Cai said. "Haeros stopped the spread of the plague, but he wasn't done with Soril. There had to be a reckoning."

Kaari stopped struggling and went very still. She looked up at Cai. "What did he do?"

"He solved two problems in one stroke. The plague-ridden needed tending.

Any human—Magus or not—who was exposed to the plague would be infected. So he summoned the Darks to Tresamare."

"Summoned?"

"From the sea," Cai said, and felt her shudder under his hands. "He summoned Soril's children from the deep and gave them a semblance of human form. But their blood was still Soril's, and so the plague could not touch them. They were bound to tend the sick and the dying until their own deaths, or until they were cast back into the sea."

"If you fall from the ship, drink deep," Kaari whispered. Cai almost didn't hear her. "The Matron told me that."

"The Matron must have rejoiced to see her ship sinking below the waves," Cai said. "You can't return to the sea by your own will, but I can send you there." He pushed her toward the rail.

She wobbled and grabbed his shoulder for balance. "Stop. I'm afraid."

"Of course you are! Haeros wanted it that way. All the newly born Darks would fear the sea, and so bind them more deeply to the isle and their servitude. You've forgotten what you were, but you will remember. You will thank me."

He grabbed her again, forcing her to stand on the rail.

She looked back at him, wild-eyed. "What about you? The captain wants you dead. He'll try again."

Cai smiled grimly. "He will fail."

She shook her head helplessly. "Why do you remain on the sea? Leave the ship." She squeezed his arm. "We could leave together. I could learn to live on land."

Cai shook his head. "I can't. My place is here, the blight in Soril's perfect garden."

"Is that why you stay? Why you did not avenge your friend?" She shook her head. "You *want* to be the albatross, don't you?"

"Yes," he said. "Until I fall and Soril is forced to kill me, I will stay and live and invite her hatred."

He started to push her, but she latched onto him. She pulled his face close and pressed her cold lips to his.

"Why do you help me, then?" she said. "A child of Soril—shouldn't you hate me?"

She tastes like the sea, Cai thought. He almost couldn't stand it. To wake with her, to kiss her every day, would be the worst pain and the greatest joy.

He pulled back, gazing into her strange, otherworldly eyes. "Drink deep," he said, "and remember. Don't worry about forgetting me. The sea will take care of that."

She nodded jerkily, and he pushed her.

She fell a long way, through the fire ring, into the cold sea. He saw her white form disappear beneath the waves.

Heat replaced the cold throb at Cai's lips. He called the magic and turned to face the approaching vessel.

"So much magic, clashing together," he said. He knew, without looking, that Sira Dam stood behind him. He laughed loudly. "Soril's going to love this."

———— ‡ ————

Kaari felt the water close over her head, but she was already swimming with all her strength. She swam away from the surface before she had time to be afraid. By the time she allowed herself to think, she was too deep. She would not make it back to the surface.

Thrashing, she let out a silent scream. The air rushed from her lungs. She drew in water to replace it. She expected pain, the horror of drowning, but instead she felt nothing. The cold and heaviness of the water did not trouble her lungs. She felt like she was floating in a cloud.

Her strength began to return, the power in her limbs greater than she remembered. She used it to propel herself downward, into the black.

She knew where she was going, though she could not have said how. Her form, when she spared a moment to look, was no longer anything human.

Above her, she felt a faint vibration that might have been an explosion. But the sound was far away, and she forgot about it as soon as it faded. Her thoughts were consumed with her destination. She'd been gone too long.

Soon, her mind was all the sea, and she was left with only the vaguest impression of copper buttons and warm, amber eyes.

The Sea in Silence
Gerard Houarner

The fish would not answer Jeloc's call.

The ship's creaking lingered in the salty air like a subtle accusation. He hadn't failed. The spell worked. He'd felt the connection to the sea, and then to its inhabitants, and had overwritten the native store of instincts with a single compulsion. But the fish ignored him.

The cook did not. He stared at Jeloc, blank-faced, as if he'd just been told he'd have to prepare ghost soup for a hundred dead men. The smell of fish guts filled the cabin, pepper pricking for attention through the stench.

It was the first trick he'd learned on this world, a fundamental element in its system of magic. A step toward mastering the water, itself. Pick the fruit, trim the branch, and soon enough the trunk and finally the roots would bend to one's will. A common path to power on his travels through worlds.

If you were skilled. And strong. And lucky.

But now the fish would not come. Jeloc did not know what that might mean on battle's eve. Standing in his cabin, the ship's cook before him, the answer to the problem eluded him. He had far larger fish to prepare.

"Break out the smoked stores," he said. "I don't have time to feed the crew, much less the fleet."

The sailor bowed and left without comment or attitude, uncommon for the wooden-legged old mate who'd been known to kill merchants if they delivered provisions below his standard. The crew, the entire fleet, had been spoiled by the conveniences of Jeloc's power. Providing creature comforts and an unerring ability to spy treasure ships and traps before they slid over the horizon had gained him the loyalty of a fleet of buccaneers that rivaled any empire's sea power.

But unlike the captains of ships belonging to this world's three empires, his ship masters held their fiercest loyalty only to themselves. It wouldn't take much pressure for alliances to crumble, for all to scurry like blade fish before the biting swarms back to their supposedly hidden islands and secret bays, back to the hard life of independent predation.

Thank the gods he still had the Ghijon forging ahead of the fleet, the occasional water spout and tentacle raised to taste the air visible at regular intervals to reassure his men that Jeloc was leading them to certain victory.

"Problem, Lord Jeloc?" Ketan asked, his mass squeezing through the cabin doorway. He cast a serious look back at the deck, where the crew was no doubt watching Jeloc's cabin, carefully searching for signs of weakness. Then he closed the door, faced Jeloc and crossed his eyes.

"Spring a leak, little one?" he asked, then burst out in his roaring laughter. "Are even the fish afraid of you now?" He lost himself in hysterical amusement.

It was a good sign to give the crew, and the rest of the fleet, which would hear of Ketan's laughter through clear-day signaling almost immediately. As long as the greatest warrior among them still had confidence in their wizard, the captains would stay the course.

It was when Ketan stopped laughing, with no enemy near, that Jeloc's allies would start to worry.

He waved the warrior to his usual seat, a throne taken from an emperor's barge early in their partnership. Ketan flopped into it, spread his legs out and wide, taking up half the cabin, and settled down. At least his musky odor chased off the fish stench.

Jeloc studied the charts laid out before him—charts not of stars, navigational currents or channels, but of spells and incantations. He didn't care about the damned fish. It was the empires arrayed against him—Otha from the West, Cimetrul to the East, the Poran due North—and their assembled sorceries that had him nervous. He would not have moved to gather the pirates and engage the empires if he hadn't felt ready. But in the back of his mind, there was always the doubt that he was too eager to prove himself ready to go back to Aum, face his mother the Matriarch, and force her to lift his banishment from his birthplace.

If he couldn't conquer a simple world and its lugubrious water, what chance did he have against the Matriarch?

Ketan reported on the readiness of his warriors, who had completed days of boarding rehearsals in conjunction with fleet maneuvers. Despite a few captains finding it necessary to break formations to showcase their daring, and the occasional stray cannon shot, the fleet was as ready as they were ever going to be.

Alone, the various alliances among the freebooters had no chance against any of the empires' disciplined forces. And even the simplest captain understood how much the world was shrinking with three empires spreading their might, with little interest in pirate allies. But with Jeloc, and his tricks and wisdom gained by mortal lifetimes of experience in Aum and the worlds connected to it by the Gates, the brigands had a chance at surviving. Perhaps even at carving a place in the new world that was rising around them.

"But what are we going to do with it all if we win?" Ketan asked, suddenly, frighteningly, sincere.

Ketan didn't have many moments of clarity outside of the realms he ruled with strength, fighting skills, and appetites. Jeloc had learned they represented clear signals of danger.

Jeloc took a deep breath. "We'll play with the world the way we play with the wind in our sails."

Ketan smiled. But not as broadly, or as eagerly, as he once did. Things might change after the coming battle.

Or not. Which was worse?

The spells on the scrolls and tomes before him swam through his mind like a school of fish dipping and turning as one through reefs, flashing colors one moment, blending into the background the next. He knew each one—their history, creators, uses and variations. He found no mystery in them, no reason for the fish he'd called to ignore him.

There was no mistaking the craft he'd mastered, or the dread gathering in his gut—cold, putrid, like a body thrown to shore after the sea had softened its bones.

It had taken Jeloc over a hundred years to master the water. In Aum, water came only as stinging Mist, or through a perpetually opened Gate to another world as sweet, fresh nectar at the start of the Aenchelos Canal. What it became as it collected Aum's waste to be deposited through another opened Gate was something no one had ever come close to controlling. On the day his exile came to an end, knowledge of water would be useful, and so he'd decided to remain on this world of countless islands to which humanity clung like insects on floating leaves, and learn what he could. He had time, if not patience, to spend. He'd studied, and tried his tricks, and felt the other masters of the sea acknowledge his presence. Even fear him. But he hadn't dared challenge those masters on his own. Even when he'd sensed them pass from their frail mortal bodies to make way for untested acolytes and apprentices.

Exile's sting still coursed through him like poison, fresh and potent, crippling confidence. Immortal memory was the cost of Aum's immortal blood, which had been cursed along with the city when exiled into the Mist between worlds. His hubris, and the Matriarch's response, was as fresh now as the day he'd been thrown out of his birthplace. His defeat could have happened yesterday, or millennia ago. It didn't mater. The work of his exile was to restore himself to what he had been, tempered by wisdom. He had many years of work left to do.

And there were other memories he couldn't forget, memories he escaped by filling his head with spells and strategies, as if they would some day tire of waiting for him to recall every last part of himself he'd lost.

But on this world, it was Ketan, in his prime, only twenty-three, who had finally inspired him to move out of the shadows. It was Ketan's rise to prominence among the brigands that had given Jeloc a path to power. It was Ketan who'd helped guide him through the political world of pirate captains and empires, merchants and sorcerers, women of the land, and of the sea.

Jeloc had learned to respect those moments when the pirate warrior raised a question. But he never thought, at so young an age, that Ketan would think beyond conquest. Apparently, with both water and men, he had more lessons coming.

At least with Ketan, he had another answer he wasn't ready to express: he didn't care what happened after they won. He'd give this entire mess of a world to Ketan or whoever stood in his place if he fell, and make arrangements to move on through Aum's Gates, daring capture and death, to find another world on which he'd continue preparing for a return to Aum and all the consequences that would follow.

The sea, however, with its tiny mystery of missing fish hinting at greater pitfalls, was not so easy a problem to resolve.

Jeloc swept aside compendiums and parchments. He wanted air. But going topside now might be seen as a sign of weakness.

Of course, so could hiding in his cabin.

The knot of dread in his belly turned into a pale, festering wound of uncertainty.

Ketan had found the grat, in skins hidden under a pile of furs in a corner, and was spraying the amber liquor straight into his mouth. He finished a skin in one long squeeze. He picked up another and offered it to Jeloc. "You look like you could use a pull."

"I need to keep a clear head."

"A clear head doesn't seem to be doing the trick. You should try a drunken one."

"Slurred words don't cast spells."

"Crisply spoken words apparently don't bring in the fish, either."

Ketan, a man of action, was provoking Jeloc to action. That was one of the many things he did well, and why Jeloc had chosen to work alongside him. But all the jab did was make Jeloc pace, arms crossed over his chest. He felt the bars of an invisible cage surround him, the boundaries of a trap ready to close.

No need to worry. This wasn't Aum. He wasn't facing the Matriarch and the assembled powers of Aum. At least for the crews and captains, the absence of fresh fish in calm seas could be forgiven. Even the cook understood the stakes of the fight ahead of them. The fleet would rather have their most powerful weapon gathering strength to use against the enemy than wasting itself on luxuries. It hadn't been so long since they'd left behind harder days of picking at stray threads of commerce left unprotected by empires.

Jeloc closed his eyes, breathed to the ship's swaying, sank into the rhythm of his beating heart. The sea murmured, its darkness and depths acquiescing to his presence. He was not alone. The wind still jumped at his command, but the reins of other sorcerers tugged it this way and that. He'd have to be careful. A rogue wave or an ill wind could run his ships into each other. But waves and winds could turn many ways.

"You look nervous, Jeloc, " Ketan said, his voice subdued so no one could hear them through the door. His eyes were clear, his gaze direct and alert, as if he'd just downed spiced tea instead of grat. "Has your challenge been answered?"

"It's the damn fish."

"To hell with the fish."

"What does it mean?"

"It means the enemy was hungry and got to them first. When we split their bellies, you'll find your fish."

Jeloc tried to lean on Ketan's bluster, but he still couldn't shake off his sense of unease. Though he'd borne the brunt of many desperate fights, against odds larger than the ones he faced now, there was still the sea to contend with. He'd harnessed gods and demons; fire, wind, earth and lesser waters. But a world blanketed in seas, with too much darkness and too many hidden depths to contain in his mind, was suddenly promising him more surprises.

"You're afraid the tide's changing on you," Ketan said.

"Tides don't matter out here. Neither do currents, when I can turn them."

"Can you? Are you?"

Jeloc stopped pacing. "What do you mean?"

"The wind's at our backs well enough, but the current's turned and those storm clouds on the horizon have been tracking us for a week. Didn't you tell me magic costs? I think the bill's come due."

"The current?" He'd been watching the clouds marking the fleet's progress for imperial sorcerers. Fighting the spell hadn't seemed worth the effort when everyone shared the same magical medium of the sea. But the current in these waters couldn't change so early in the season, and certainly not without his feeling the touch of the hand that made the shift. He'd just tested the ocean, how could—

But he saw the change reflected in Ketan's sailor's eye. A subtler hand than he'd anticipated had dipped its power in the water, costing the fleet perhaps a half hour a day. Hardly worth the effort, unless the trap being set against them required the timing of multiple elements.

Jeloc rubbed his temples, then the bridge of his nose. Sweat beaded along his forehead. "Our enemies struggle against my power, as I fight theirs."

"Is it the empires that work against you, or the sea?"

"Don't be ridiculous."

"I was raised on this water. You weren't. A strong threat makes strange allies."

Suddenly, the cabin walls pushed in on Jeloc. Nausea rolled in his belly, rose to choke him. He needed air. No matter what the men might think. Jeloc opened the door, stepped out.

The crisp, salted breeze cleared his head in an instant. He tapped his fingers against his lips and took a few tentative steps on the deck, as if counting all the directions his thoughts might take. The crew went on with their duties, but he felt each member check him with a glance. Ketan stayed inside, letting him play out his drama.

Jeloc put his hands behind his back, looked up at the sky. Took a deep breath. Smiled.

"Come on, Ketan. Do you give up?"

Ketan appeared in the cabin doorway, eyebrow arched as if he already knew where the story they were improvising was heading.

Jeloc nodded his head once and said, "Her name was Hija."

The punch line to a non-existent joke.

Ketan punched the cabin wall and laughed, loud and long, so he could be heard across the waves, and Jeloc joined him though the bigger man swallowed his voice whole. They slapped each other like relaxed comrades and climbed up to the quarter deck. After a cursory inspection of the watch, they stood by the railing looking ahead.

"Feel better?" Ketan asked.

"The horizon's lost."

"Haze. Want to laugh again? It's fair medicine for misery."

"The day is supposed to be clear."

"What's over the horizon?"

Jeloc didn't answer. Ketan didn't press the issue, knowing no answer was all the answer required.

"Do you have another one of those hidden in reserve?" Ketan asked, glancing at the Ghijon.

"No."

"Too bad. Now would have been a good time for another show of strength."

"Are you afraid?"

Ketan laughed, slow and guttural, a good-natured growl. "You really weren't born to these waters, were you?"

"I always thought that was a strength."

"Could be a weakness, as well."

"Regrets?"

"I've lived longer and seen more than I ever thought I would," Ketan said. "And the dreams! You've planted such possibilities in my head. A fine vintage, those dreams. Stronger than anything I ever swallowed, smoked or drank. I never regret a good drunk."

They stayed on deck through the rest of the day, taking their meal and ration of rum with the crew out in the open. The sun crossed clear sky, the steady wind cooled sweaty skin, the surging rhythm of the ship under sail marked the passing of the day into night. Officers reported in with signals from the fleet, and after consultations with Jeloc, Ketan gave out orders. There were no signs of concern in the requests and messages. The captains followed orders, still united under the banner of conquest.

Between routine tasks, Jeloc chased away the clouds on the horizon, then the haze ahead of them, working harder than he should have for such minor annoyances. He managed to restore the current's proper flow without letting the effort it required to show. He tried again to bring back the fish, but they wouldn't listen to him, even if they heard him.

They sailed steadily through the night, under the stars. Jeloc counted them, checking the major and minor arcana that could be traced by knowing eyes, making sure there were no surprises masquerading as signposts.

Ketan and Jeloc stayed up through the change of watch, like strong fathers watching over village children in case witches and goblins flew in. Lanterns swayed, tracing lines of flame in the darkness. The crew relaxed, exchanging occasional banter through the night. Someone in the rigging whistled a lonely ballad. The cook paced below, his peg leg tapping out a steady rhythm.

Phosphorescent whitecaps sprayed brilliant shapes of light that danced briefly in the air before falling back into the sea. Jeloc stared at them for too long, suspicious at first, then teased by memories when he found no danger.

She'd danced like spray kicked up from the waves. Her grace always took away his breath.

He caught himself, grunted at the heartache he hadn't felt in decades. He'd buried himself in his studies and work that well, losing himself in the discipline required for mastering the world's magic. But the length of time he could keep pain away was shortening. What would he do when he'd have to feel the loss every year? Every day?

He surrendered his senses to the sea's vastness, listening for the echo of enemies sounding from afar, the whisper of ancient voices trying to insinuate themselves into his thoughts. He filled himself with the sea, but this time, mastery gave him no comfort. The water was cold and dark inside him.

"What was her name?" Ketan asked, later.

Jeloc, still trying to probe beyond the horizon, was shaken by the question. "What?"

"The one you left behind when you had to leave your world. The one you've never talked about."

Irritation flashed at the intrusion. Others had pried, uncovered his secret pain, picked at the bleeding scars. Discovery had done none of them, or Jeloc, any good.

"It's not good, not being able to feel the loss," Ketan said, in his plain and innocent way. "It leaves you vulnerable."

"What loss have you ever felt?"

"I had a father. A mother. A pair of sisters, twins. Older. They thought I was a doll the gods gave them to play with."

Jeloc didn't know how to answer.

"I was the only one in the village who survived. I mean, even the ones who came for us were dead. After all these years, it's still the longest, hardest battle I ever fought."

Hours later, just before dawn, Jeloc whispered, "Ymel Shal-Ikah."

"A beautiful name."

"She's dead."

"Then I'm sure she's a beautiful ghost."

The truth of Ketan's observation gave him another shock. He had to work hard to hang on to the reality that Ketan could not possibly know anything about what had happened to him, to Ymel, in Aum. He wasn't his mother's spy, the agent of Court elders desperate to maintain the iron of tradition and the shine of wealth milked from a curse.

"Have you ever loved anyone?" Jeloc asked. "Since your family?"

The pause that followed made Jeloc think Ketan's answer would have been the same as his.

But then Ketan said, "Myself. Because no one else will." He took a long pull from a water skin. "And you."

It had been such a long time since he'd been offered anyone's love that Jeloc didn't know how to hold or look at it, whether to dismiss Ketan's words, keep what he needed and return the rest, or simply accept the feeling. Worse still, Jeloc had always assumed their relationship was rooted in a drive for power. And it was. But he'd never thought there might be more.

Ketan stood as he had the whole night, facing the main deck to track crew and ship. He was done talking. There was nothing left to say between them.

And then Jeloc understood he didn't have choices. Ketan had not offered him anything. He wasn't looking to satisfy a need for a father, brother, comrade, friend, or lover with Jeloc. He'd simply stated what he felt. He didn't care what that feeling meant, to himself or anyone else.

Jeloc retreated into their shared silence, stunned by the intimidation he felt in the presence of a mortal Aum's hierarchy would consider still fresh and bloody from the womb.

Dawn didn't break their peace, but the light stirred the watch as the crew scrambled under the deck master's direction to change sails to catch the sun-running wind. Orders were barked, officers came up to survey the sea, work songs broke out. The Ghijon bellowed.

The day came on bright and fresh, free of nagging clouds and crossed-currents. Jeloc embraced the new start, feeling in control and confident. Assembling a fleet of pirates to challenge the sea power of empires no longer seemed suicidal. The air, at last, had done him good.

They took their tea and biscuits outside, conferred with officers, gave out the day's orders. They were crossing into patrolled waters, and a gathering their size wouldn't be ignored for much longer. Officers smiled, thinking of victory as they glanced at Jeloc, and signals passed with unusual intensity between the ships. The fleet was ready.

When the morning rush had settled down, Jeloc turned to Ketan and said, "I wonder when they'll ask me for more fish."

Ketan smiled. But he didn't laugh.

Observers atop the mast cried out. A ship close by fired off a signal flare, warning of danger. Sails and flags flapped with greater urgency.

"I think they'll be asking for more than that," Ketan said, leaving Jeloc to go forward.

The Ghijon bellowed again, and sputtered.

Water churned all around the ship. For a moment, Jeloc thought the fish had answered his call, at last. And worse, they had all come, from all over the world, from every ocean. His enemies had tricked him, forcing him to continue calling them by concentrating on blockading his awareness of his magic's effect. Now his fleet would be overwhelmed.

But what could simple fish do? The largest could ram and even break wooden hulls, but Jeloc could put a stop to that. Was this the best they could do?

A skittering flurry of dark shapes scrambled over the railings. Sailors cursed, broke out swords and clubs and began smashing them down on the planks.

It wasn't the fish that had arrived, but rats, discharged from vessels over the horizon, and swimming over open water to the nearest dry land they could find. Jeloc's fleet.

He hadn't looked for rats. They weren't in the books he'd studied.

The rats were mad from their compulsion to swim, and from hunger, and whatever else the empires' sorcerers had done to them. They swarmed over sailors and officers, squealing and squeaking. Biting. Tearing. Shredding.

It didn't matter how many died. They teemed in living waves of soaked fur and rippling flesh over the sides of the ship, overwhelming the crew. They dripped sea water on the decks, and then blood.

Ketan yelled, giving all of his voice to the war cry. But the enemy was small and nearly infinite. His challenge had no effect on their madness. Already, Jeloc couldn't see his legs beneath slick-furred bodies.

The cook turned over the cooking fire pot. Others threw lanterns. Oil spilled. Rats burst into flame.

The ship caught fire in a dozen places. If the rats didn't get them, the flames would. A quick survey of nearby ships revealed they were all facing the same foe, and problems.

Jeloc assumed his warding spells had been ruptured, but when he dipped into the sea to repair them he found they were intact. Just irrelevant. The rats ignored them. Just like the fish refused to obey his call.

The rats came for him. He scrambled for higher ground, taking a step toward the main mast.

Popping sounds drew him to the railing, afraid of another weapon being drawn against them. As Jeloc harnessed fire along a line hook to clear a circle around his feet, he hoped the burning rats were leaping overboard and exploding from the heat as they reached the water. He conjured diversionary spells that lured waves of rats into walls or down scuppers, giving him a moment to appraise the situation.

The rats weren't exploding. The rolling sea surface had suddenly bloomed with thousands of floating white globules. Eggs. Jeloc traced their trajectories to the ocean bottom, where egg sacs had been planted, timed for release on this day, this sunrise.

What had grown in the eggs hatched suddenly, violently, bursting from their flexible shells starving, frightened, stalked eyes waving frantically, legs and pincers and tentacles all working to get them out of the water, where they were vulnerable newborns, and straight at the meat they needed to survive.

Camaracks.

Jeloc had found a nest of them the week before and fed the fleet for days on their carcasses. What was rising all around them was more than a single nest. And the young camaracks were also immune to his warding spells.

Propelled by desperation, Jeloc tried deflection rather than outright warding, treating the animals like currents and winds instead of living creatures capable of succumbing to his will.

He introduced the rats into the faint camarack minds as prey, and more, the only food they could consume to survive. And to the rats, he directed their rage and delusions against the camaracks.

The two species instantly turned on one another, leaving crews and officers half-eaten on the decks, nursing wounds, or hiding in the superstructure.

The battle was swift, and the decks cleared as the rats leapt back into the sea to take the war to the enemy. Jeloc concentrated on spreading his misdirection throughout the nearby water. As the sea churned and frothed blood red, the ship's crew slowly recovered, officers and masters falling back first into survival's discipline, and the rest quickly falling into line.

The fires were put out. The wounded quickly brought below to the cook and doctor to mend. The dead were tossed overboard even faster.

A number of ships were burning. Others had collided. Formations were broken. The fleet was ripe for an attack.

"Is that the best they can do?" Ketan roared, pushing away a mate trying to tend to his wounds. "That's all? They send mice and shrimp to stop us?" He gave them all his deepest laugh, long and hard, a hot wind blowing from the equator, full of life's promise.

The Ghijon cried out. Not all of the tentacles it waved in the air were whole.

Jeloc went forward, healing where he could without expending too much of his power.

"That last one was a good trick," Ketan said, clasping Jeloc's shoulder. "Glad you were able to do something that worked," he said, much lower, just for the two of them to hear.

Below, the rum casks burst into flame, sending jets of fire through hatches, and setting off the crew into another frenzy of activity.

Jeloc started calling up sea water to douse the flames, but Ketan checked him with a squeeze of the arm.

"Can you trust the water?" he asked, pointing to a smoking ship that was sinking much more quickly than the apparent damage would indicate.

Most of the ships carried their own spell maker, clumsy and even dangerous in battle, certainly not the equal of an imperial mage's apprentice, but useful in open sea for calling up winds and quick maneuvering to escape pursuit. Sometimes, they even summoned fish, if there were any very close by. And they were good for putting out fires with controlled streams of sea water. But only if the water could be trusted.

"I think that rum went off quicker than our enemies thought it would," Ketan said. "I would have broken the kegs first, let the stuff spread, then set it on fire. Of course, maybe that can't be done. Something to remember for the future, anyway."

Jeloc shook his head. He'd anticipated none of what had happened. The tactics, the spells, were all additions to the traditional lexicon he'd studied. They didn't depend on the usual means of controlling water, nor use the world's usual water-based monsters like the Ghijon or the biting swarms. Rats? Slowing ships down with currents so they'd sail into hatching camaracks? Outrageous. Fundamental elements of the reality of sorcery had been transformed, as if by an outside force.

But he was the outsider. It occurred to him that he should have done more than master the discipline of this world's magic. He should have subverted the rules, changed them, made the magic his own, as someone else had done.

But he wasn't sure he had the strength inside himself to go that far, to create instead of dominate or simply destroy.

He remembered the Matriarch's laughter as his rebellion collapsed.

Panic flowered. Had she sent someone from her court after him? Had he walked into another Aum trap?

Reason told him he didn't matter to that city, anymore. The Matriarch didn't care. The enemies he'd made were more than satisfied with his trial, humiliation and exile. He'd been put out of their way, and nobody wanted to waste the effort required to track him simply to indulge themselves in another round of humiliation, or to kill him. There was no profit, no reward for the work. And Aum valued reward.

In Aum, anything can be bought. For a price.

He wasn't in Aum. His defeat was long past, ancient history. He was smarter. Stronger. Better.

But his emotions, loose from the mooring of control and purpose, rocked him until he had to close his eyes and lock himself in a moment of darkness in order to see the day more clearly.

"Better open your eyes," Ketan said. "Something else is coming."

Jeloc looked beyond the ship's bow.

Mist.

The association was natural, but too quick. And wrong. The fog that had suddenly encircled the fleet, cutting off the horizon, blending into the sky, was brighter than Aum's Mist or any fog Jeloc had ever seen. It was an incandescent wall, piercing in its intensity, like the sunrise. And like the sunrise, it seemed to rise from the sea. Frowning, he looked to Ketan, who shook his head.

"I've never seen anything like it," the warrior said.

Dread, nearly forgotten in the excitement, seeped from his belly, spreading cold, numbing fear.

He wasn't ready for fire on a world of water.

The fog sped over the water like the sun rolling over waves, swallowing ships. Nearby sailors cried out, shielding their faces with hands and forearms. Tears stung Jeloc's eyes, but through slitted lids he tried to discern the nature of the assault. He conjured spells to control clouds and salt spray, real fog and driving rain. Nothing worked. He called on tricks to spill small ship fires out of their pits, and a lava flow incantation nearly forgotten by most. The fog came on, until all the surrounding ships were gone, and then the water, and then everything but the blinding light driving into Jeloc's head.

A roaring filled the air. Jeloc thought his men were screaming, dying. But then a sharp crackling split the roar, silencing it.

He waited for the fire, the pain, not believing he was going to die.

He'd never see Ymel, the ghost of her haunting Aum, ever again.

He felt like she'd died, once again. Aching. And then, for an instant, he welcomed obliteration.

An even brighter lance of jagged light flew down from above.

Gods. Throwing down wrath.

The ocean twitched. Waves surged to smash the hull. The ship bucked. Lightning singed the air.

He didn't burn.

Masts, spars and sails did. Lightning fell in a mad dance of spidery legs running through the fog. Dimmer than the fog, fire struggled to catch, as if intimidated by the air. Crew-members roused themselves from shock, falling back on their years at sea to forget terror, close their eyes to mystery, and simply cope with the flames and survive the moment.

The Ghijon screamed.

Jeloc forced himself to stare into the blazing light. At least there were no shadows, or figures, boarding the ship from out of the bright. Steadying himself on the foundations of his own training, Jeloc called up wind, and was thankful for its response. Something was working. He whirled the wind in tight circles, smothering fires first, then spread it wide over the sea, hoping to catch as many sails as possible to move the fleet's survivors, and to disperse the fog.

Moments stretched into a string of pearls too brilliant to see clearly. They left the lightning behind quick enough, telling him the enemy could no more see inside the shining haze and track him than he could reckon what lay beyond it. The fog refused to disperse, as if willfully riding the gusts, rising, dipping, circling in swirling inflamed ribbons. Jeloc passed his hand through a dense wisp curling close to him, examined the dimming moisture on his palm. The light died to reveal specks dotting his flesh. He was reminded of tiny sea gypsies that sometimes gathered in luminescent clouds just beneath the waves on clear, calm, windless nights, as if to send a signal to the stars so far above them. Their dispersal in air in a blinding mist shocked him, and provoked his curiosity. A new world of sorcery was blossoming all around him, and he wanted to explore its source and structure even as he tried with all his power to destroy it.

But the grinding noise of wood and metal colliding warned him he had no time for curiosity when his best counter was driving the ships of his own fleet into one another.

"I don't know if we can survive many more traps, or your tricks to escape them," said Ketan. "We need a plan to beat the enemy on our terms."

"I'm not even sure who the enemy is. Or where." Jeloc eased back on the drive of the winds, hoping the captains were getting their crews back to work.

Bells rang out, a few at first, then a steady clanging as ships signaled their position. The fog dampened the sound, made each ring seem as if it was coming from everywhere at once. But the old seamen caught the subtle nuances of tone and echo, called out to each other, and gave their pilots and captains warning when ships drifted too close to each other.

At last, the fog dissipated and the familiar blues of sky and sea filtered back through the fiery, fading wisps of cloud to define the true shape of their world.

"There they are," Ketan said, pointing at the line of sailing ships arrayed before them, gun ports opened, ready to unleash common cannon fire. Black, blue, and brown hulls marked the joining of the three empires in the cause of destroying the pirate fleet.

Ketan laughed. The crew took heart in his confidence. Jeloc saw an opportunity for victory against their opponents.

The empires preferred fat, heavy craft to protect their coastlines and trade routes. With even a brief victory in a duel of winds with the opposing sorcerers, his far more maneuverable ships should have been able to turn and cross the enemy line at both ends, spraying their ships with shot without having to take any fire in return.

They weren't broken, yet. They still had a chance. As long as he was alive, Ketan and his people always had a chance.

Ketan surveyed the battle line and his own jumbled force. "Do we have a chance?" he whispered.

"Yes."

"You were never a good liar." He laughed again.

Jeloc looked to the sea that had betrayed him. His sister had told him the same thing many times. The last, when he'd been sent into exile.

A wail, thin and high-pitched, cut through the air. The Ghijon, somehow, had survived the lightning and had found its way out of the fog. Jeloc imagined it might have navigated by the feel of the wind's direction on its tentacles. The monster responded to him, their bond untouched by whatever magic had blocked him from calling fish to the fleet. If he'd known about that trick, he would have summoned all the fish he would have needed for the trip before setting out.

The Ghijon was still a power. Jeloc sent it against the imperial ships while Ketan first brought his crew to order, then the rest of the fleet. Long range guns opened up on the creature. Jeloc did his best to deflect fire, and to submerge the leviathan and time its break back to the surface into the center of the imperial line.

Clouds gathered nearby, boiling angrily as they grew out of darkened air and water spouts, but Jeloc diverted the storm with the winds he still had in hand. After all that had happened, the dispersal seemed anticlimactic, until the winds returned suddenly like a mass of writhing, wrathful snakes to dart in every direction through the pirate fleet, once more pushing ships into each other.

"Get us into them before we lose any more," Ketan shouted.

Jeloc was already taming snake air by splitting and realigning gusts and breezes. He readied his next flurry of spells, relying, he knew, too heavily on air to protect the fleet while they tried to get their cannon shot true into the enemy. Then he checked on the Ghijon. The monster was laboring, leaving a dark trail in its wake as it swam at half its normal speed. The Imperial ships in its path were already breaking formation, apparently hoping they could out-maneuver a wounded Ghijon.

Jeloc's heart skipped. With luck, they might drive through the enemy's center instead of flanking them.

They hadn't lost their chance at victory, yet.

Then the wind died. And the water boiled.

Another play at fire by the enemy, perhaps the deadliest, rising up from a source below. He might have been allowed control of the wind simply to advance to a position over a volcano primed to explode.

Though the threat was not yet identified, Jeloc thought he was beginning to understand the pattern of magic deployed against him, and he dared to hope he could master it in the short time left before defeat. If he understood, he could anticipate. Counter. Use the same power in his own attack.

But again, a new trick turned to surprise him. It wasn't fire rising to the ocean's surface, but weeds. Kelp.

The ship slowed. Moaned. Lurched.

The fleet lay trapped like flies in webbing. There wasn't enough wind in the world to get them through. They were grounded in a floating bed of vegetation.

Ketan shouted orders, and sailors raced to secure the ship and brace for another attack. By Jeloc's count, they'd already lost half the men. Signal flares fired from the rest of the fleet, in a variety of colors to indicate the depth and density of the trap, leaving ribbon trails of smoke in the air. They were all caught. They had no choice but to sit in place, with no chance of using the advantage of their maneuverability in combat. They were waiting to be destroyed.

Jeloc stared at the Imperial line, trying to judge their next move. If they approached, their advance would indicate the boundary of the weeds, or even lanes for safe passage and bombardment and boarding of the pirate ships.

A sharp pain split Jeloc's head from ear to ear, and he hunched over.

The Ghijon screamed again, then did something Jeloc had never heard from such an enormous beast: it gurgled, drowning in the sea.

The ships of the Imperial line hadn't been falling back before the beast's assault. They'd been getting out of the way of their own trap.

No one had ever seen a Ghijon die. Great heroes from ancient epics and ballads were said to have defeated them, but the details of their demise were never specific. Jeloc, his bond with the monster from the deep intact, felt its panic and disorientation as it flailed, undulated, rolled, all in an effort to free itself from the mountain of weeds which had swallowed it from below. Unable to keep moving, the creature couldn't breathe.

Its dying screams echoed through the stillness, haunting, terrifying, as much for the pain that warned of the pirate fleet's fate as for the eerie vulnerability exposed in the greatest of the world's sea monsters.

The day wore on, and the imperial forces refused to approach, allowing the Ghijon's death to play out, until as the sun began to set, the monster's cries faded and it died.

The enemy showed them more weapons: embedded in the weeds, tiny larvae were hatching, releasing swarms of biting insects. Even Ketan couldn't resist swatting and scratching, a few sailors tore at their flesh until they were bloody.

Jeloc noted that hardly any of the larvae had hatched. Tomorrow, they'd be eaten alive.

A few long, sinewy lizards with low, elongated legs skittered across the ocean's surface, walking on the solid mass of weeds. They flicked their tongues, bared fangs. They were too few to in the assault to swarm the ships, and sharpshooters in the rigging killed them. At least one weapon in the enemy's sorcerous armory was not yet ready, but the warning was clear: there would be more, tomorrow.

And, at last, there was singing, like an assassin's blade to the heart, cold and sad, piercing in its sorrow and bitterness. Jeloc couldn't hang on to the tune, nor make out the words. But he'd heard of sirens—the shelled creatures haunting isolated islands, survivors of a primeval age using the wind and the holes and folds of the shells they constructed over their soft bodies to call to one another, and to anyone and anything who might be seduced by their song to crash into the reefs and rocks of their homeland and provide them with fresh meat.

There were only a few sirens singing, not a full choir. They were enough to let Jeloc feel his heart break over Ymel's loss once more, to make men weep and a few jump, including the cook, over the side, and to make Ketan grimace and shudder at a pain his entire body strained to contain.

It was the kind of song that would make men give themselves to the sea, not for lust or love, but to return to the comfort of their mothers, or to the arms of mothers they never knew.

Deep in the misery of his exile, stripped of his power, Jeloc understood there were no more chances for victory left when three glowing figures rose from ships along the imperial line and floated across the water, through the dusk, heading straight for Ketan's ship. There was no more room in him for fear. Despair was all he felt.

As they approached, the figures glistened with the water of their making, translucent like jelly fish. But each was detailed in appearance, more than enough to differentiate them from one another, and to source them to their various homelands. They were only sendings. The wizards did not trust their flesh to him, and that weakness sparked the courage, but not hope, to face what was to come.

Jeloc named them for the empires they represented: Otha, a thin, light-haired young man in black leggings and shirt who looked more like an apprentice than a master, with his smile and flashing eyes; Cimetrul, a matronly woman in a flowing earth-toned gown, her hair rising like a golden halo around her round and fleshy face; and Poran, sharp-featured, bald, with narrowed eyes and pursed lips, who looked ill-at-ease in his tunic nearly as blue as the sea in the last light of day. Otha appeared to be the most confident and happy; Cimetrul, tolerant and slightly bored; Poran, suspicious.

Ketan stood by his side while the surviving crew retreated to the lower decks to tend to their wounds and wait for death.

"I'm sorry, it's over," Jeloc whispered to him.

"No, it is not," Ketan said.

Jeloc glanced at his comrade and caught him laughing, silently, the fury coiled in his eyes greater than any storm this world had ever seen. Jeloc turned away from the clarity in Ketan's presence, feeling the blades of both friend and foe at his flesh.

"I'm the one you're looking for," Jeloc shouted, as loud as he could. The effort was a relief.

"Yes," said Cimetrul, vying to take the lead as the three figures lined up before Jeloc. She had to settle for remaining at the center of their line.

"Go ahead. Kill me. I should have died in my homeland, but my enemies left the task to the ones they knew would bring me and my pride down, again. You'll earn my mother's gratitude. Journey to Aum and she may reward you."

Or kill you. Jeloc couldn't resist setting a trap of his own, to mark his death. The old Matriarch might find the gesture amusing and, perhaps, even regret the death of her son.

"We came to thank you," Otha said.

Ketan tensed. Jeloc felt his unspoken accusation of betrayal. "For what?"

"For freeing us." He grinned as he bowed his head.

"From what?"

"Our fathers," Poran said, his voice grating, his tone rude, the least cultured of the three. "Our families. The old ways."

Jeloc followed the sense that he'd stumbled into something more complicated than an alliance of empires. "What are you?"

"The same as you," Cimetrul said. "Sorcerers."

"Magicians," Otha said.

"Killers," said Poran.

"You're better than me." Jeloc felt a touch of pride in being able to make the admission. His sister would have been shocked.

"Not better," Cimetrul said. "Different."

"You defeated me."

"We changed the rules," Otha said with a slight smirk.

Jeloc frowned. "How?"

Poran made a sharp, sweeping gesture in Jeloc's direction. "By following your inspiration. By being different."

"That's not an answer."

It was Cimetrul, her hair shimmering with captured sunset light, who offered an explanation: "We, and those we lead, were the lowest of our masters' apprentices. The sons and daughters of lesser sorcerers, the cast-offs of warrior, merchant, and royal families. The kind not favored to succeed or to marry well, but necessary for family pride to account for through scholarly careers, priesthood, crafts, arts. We were sent to sorcerers, never to take the place of the favored children of master magicians, not destined to become powerful, merely useful."

The culture of family and power was familiar to Jeloc.

"So we studied the grand traditions and ancient spells, like everyone else. And a few of us strayed, as others had done before us, and found and served secret masters who followed older paths in the hopes that one day, they might lead to a power that might overthrow the kind of magic that has ruled our world since the birth of empires."

Poran interrupted, with the hint of a sneer and a sidelong glance at Cimetrul. "Our glorious emperors allowed our transgressions, as their fathers had done, as long as we didn't actually threaten the foundations of their power. Conspiracies they could control were better than ones they didn't know about, and so couldn't shape and use. It's an old tradition, along with the sorcery of our masters, handed down from one generation to the other."

"Your world isn't the only one with such traditions," Jeloc said. He was finding himself drawn to the court politics, even as he waited for death. Again, it was familiar territory, almost like being home.

"Yes, well, revolution isn't revolution when it's a tradition," Poran said. "Revolution didn't come until you rendered all that our masters knew useless."

Jeloc's hands went up in self-defense. "I didn't try to change anything. I never even attacked you, until I was ready."

Cimetrul opened her mouth, and closed her eyes, as if drawing in a big breath to continue the effort to speak.

Otha gave her a glance, winked at Poran, who ignored them both as he scowled at Jeloc. Then he jumped in before Cimetrul could drag out her words, saying, "You didn't have to. The old sorcerers felt your power through the sea. They tried to find ways to stop you, but you became too strong, too quickly. You were better at their magic than they were. And you remained elusive, so imperial assassins couldn't find you. Our masters knew when the time came, they'd be no match for you."

Cimetrel straightened so she could look down on Otha, lips pressed together. Otha ignored her, stared through Jeloc. Ghostly threads drifted loose from his leggings.

"And worse for them, so did the emperors," Poran said. He pulled down on his tunic and rolled his shoulders.

Cimetrul jumped in quickly from her slightly higher ground, eyes narrowed in a way that made her look like a distant relative of Poran. "It was our emperors, and our priests and generals, who gave us their support, who joined our conspiracies, nurtured them, and gave them birth. Our secret schools were allowed to overthrow the old master magicians from within their sacred temples and towers. The traditional sources of power rooted in the elements, particularly wind and air, were set aside. New traditions, new ways of harnessing power were explored and mastered, building on knowledge banned, or half-forgotten, because it did not fit into philosophical or spiritual beliefs favored by those who ruled."

"Strange how beliefs change when confronted by the reality of a greater power," Poran said, this time with venom.

"Magic is magic to the uninitiated," Otha said, his smile wavering. He suddenly looked older than the young apprentice he'd appeared to be, as if the years and their sadness had suddenly caught up to him. "Few understood, or cared, that a great change had occurred in how power was raised and used. What confounded most citizens and other nations was the alliance of the world's three greatest empires. Our ways are . . . very different. None outside our ruling circles understood how severe a threat you presented. But we each have resources and strengths, and together, our emperors agreed, we could find a way to stop you from leading this ragged legion of cast-offs into civilized territories and bringing down all order and beauty."

Poran rolled his eyes. "Beauty? We're the new magic. The revolution. Reaching deeper into the sea, its meaning and purpose, than anyone before us. Deeper than you, who studied what our old masters knew. You only studied books. You never lived what that magic meant to us. You're not from this world, and you brought nothing new with you from wherever you came from."

"But what's new about this magic of yours?" Jeloc asked, willing to die just to know.

Otha and Cimetrul both started to speak, but Otha continued after Cimetrul choked on words that weren't hers. Her mouth hung open for an instant, as if she'd tried and failed to swallow Otha's refusal to defer to her. "You are the sea, but you don't know it. You control the sea, the wind, fire, earth, like a weapon, a stick you pick up and hit someone with. But the sea is inside you. All the elements. You can move the sea, and all that lives in it, like you move your body. But you don't know yourself well enough to do that."

"These are old ways," Poran said, "from before the time of emperors. To master them, you can't study scrolls and books. You have to go into yourself, into the source of all power."

"Politically," Cimetrul said, with an exaggerated display of forceful patience, "you must understand that it was also expedient for our rulers to develop schools and encourage books, and take the process of magic out of the hands of common people."

"But the cost," Poran said, "was to the magic. And the people. We all stopped evolving. There was no reason to change."

"Even among the rival empires," Cimetrul said, almost dueling with Poran for space to speak, "the emperors preferred protecting their own power and territories over the risk of fostering rivals within their own courts."

"We master our selves, our minds, bodies, spirit, and then the sea," Otha said, gently, as if to comfort Jeloc. He cocked his head, and hair fell over his forehead in loose curls. "We move the sea by moving the sea within ourselves, the wind with our breath, fire by the heat of our bodies, not by reaching out with will and strength and spells to change the course of nature. Calling to the fish, bonding with the Ghijon, these are the beginnings of that path, small tricks you gleaned from the texts. You did not go far enough down that path. You worked your spells, but we were already inside what you tried to control."

Jeloc felt foolish. He wasn't a stranger to the disciplines the new magicians had used, but had never considered them. Looking inward was not a conventional means of gaining power in Aum, or in most other places. Such a thread of wisdom might have served him well, if he'd had the chance to live long enough to weave something useful from it in his exile.

He looked to Ketan, shamed, full of sorrow. He'd led him and his people to their doom. But Ketan's face showed no emotion. It was as if he was already dead.

Of course. Jeloc understood. He'd felt the same way for hundreds of years.

"Do what you came here to do," Jeloc said. He put a hand on Ketan's shoulder, which was as much as he could give him.

"We are masters, here," Poran said, raising his voice. It carried far, over the water, to all the pirate ships.

Cimetrul continued, quieter, allowing her gaze to soften as Poran's assertion faded. "We offer you the freedom to return from where you came from, in thanks for clearing the way for our rise."

"We are so grateful," Otha said. "You're our savior." His cheer returned, and his thin frame seemed to shudder. Or perhaps the movement was just another illusion.

It took a few moments for Jeloc to understand. "You're setting me free?"

"We're letting you run away," Otha said, with a loose wave of the hand. "You delivered us from our bonds. Now we deliver you to freedom."

"What about Ketan? My allies?"

The last rays of the sun vanished. The stars glittered through the shimmering bodies of the three messengers. Screams drifted up to the stars from the pirate fleet. "We are all of the sea," Otha said.

"And we will all suffer like the sea in silence as your allies die." Poran closed his eyes. The hint of a smile peeked from the shadow of an upturned corner of his lips.

Cimetrul looked to Ketan and said, "But we'll let him live. As a living message for others who would challenge our power."

"While we finish the fight among ourselves," Poran said, beginning to fade, "to see which empire will rule over all."

The others disappeared into the night. The silence that followed swallowed even the sound of Jeloc's own breathing, and was more threatening than a knife's edge against his throat.

Jeloc turned to Ketan, who held his hand up to ward off words. Crewmen came up from below, and Ketan spoke to them, gently, quietly, singly and in small groups, until all had come up on deck to watch the stars and play games of fate from the constellations of major and minor arcana.

In the morning, a single-sail boat skimmed across the water between the two fleets, and over the weed-choked sea. Lizards circled each ship. Clouds of insects hovered between empty spars.

"I'm surprised you didn't kill me in the night," Jeloc said, standing at the side, still expecting a blade's point in his heart.

Ketan didn't laugh. He stood off in the cold distance that Jeloc had always feared from his ally. "It was a good journey," Ketan said, at last. "The only one worth taking."

When Jeloc was safely in the boat, it skimmed over the weeds and then over the sea, away from the fleets, back to the islands from which he'd come. Back there, he knew the Gates, and he'd quickly make his usual arrangements to use one to get back to Aum and then use another to get back out, to another world, before the Matriarch or anyone else knew he'd passed through. He had a feeling the mercy extended to him here would not last long.

He looked back to his old ship.

Ketan waved, as if waiting for Jeloc to see him. And then turned his blade on himself and cut his own throat.

Thunder rumbled from the imperial line. Clouds gathered. The lizards leapt aboard, the clouds of insects descended. Lightning flashed, but there was no thunder.

The sea, in its silence, taught Jeloc a final lesson.

There had been the opportunity for only one death. By killing Jeloc, Ketan would have been left to live with his defeat and the loss of his people. By taking his own life, he'd given himself peace, and denied his enemies the use of his imprisonment and humiliation. There hadn't been a choice at all, for Ketan.

Jeloc looked away, thinking of Aum, and of Ylem, and all that he had yet to endure. He wished he'd had the same courage when he'd faced that moment in his life. He wouldn't forget Ketan, his strength even in defeat. He couldn't.

There was too much blood on his hands. And he knew, with terrible certainty, that there would be more blood, and far more pain, for him and all who touched him, before he found his way through the darkness between exile and home.

Azieran: Distilling the Essence
Christopher Heath

e careful when we reach the island," Captain Silversten said, standing over Damon Maxx like a saint, the sunlight forming an aureole as it backlit her long, golden hair.

"Save your worries." The scholar looked up into her eyes as he sat on an overturned bucket. "I have read the myths; my master prepared me well before we left Philosopher's Hold."

"Oh?" she said, smiling slightly. "Then tell me, little one—"

"I am nearly sixteen winters old."

The captain nodded, lightheartedly. "Tell me, what do they know in your vast libraries of Pandemoor that our pirate tales have overlooked?"

Damon thought for a moment before answering. "There are said to be great flashes of emerald witch fire that erupt from the island, and that a faint afterglow appears some weeks later and lasts for several days."

"I know as much."

"But did you know that this event occurs at a regular interval, roughly once every two centuries?"

"This I did not realize." The clouds veiled the sun, and the corona faded from around her head. She leaned against the larboard rail of the two-mast ship.

"There is also said to be a vast horde of treasure that might be exhumed during this time."

"The Vault of the Ky'Branthians. I have heard mention of this, of course, by my greedy brothers-in-arms. But thus far, none have been brave enough to relieve Ky'Branthis of her fabled jewels."

"Is that what 'he' is going to pay you with . . . for transport, that is?" Damon motioned toward the red-cloaked sorcerer who stood ominous at the fore of the ship, his back to all others.

"He has already paid an absurd sum, and promised an equal amount when we reach Ky'Branthis, provided I do not pry into his business. So, I suppose the answer is 'yes.'"

"Do you know they say that those who venture onto the island never return?"

"I know that as well. What's that look? Do not fear for me, young one. And consider your own warnings. I will send some of my crew to collect payment. I have no intention of setting foot on that damned island." She shot him an accusing glare. "Some of us value our lives far too greatly."

"You do fear Vinn Kavilon, then?" Damon immediately thought of the lore surrounding the mage, how wise men all agreed that not even enruned steel of the mystics could harm the Ky'Branthian.

Captain Silversten's gaze fell to the front of the ship, upon the back of the sorcerer-king, but she did not speak. A cold breeze blew ripples along his ruby-red cloak, and it shimmered as if satin.

"You would be a fool not to," Damon said, sensing that it was pride that kept her words in check.

"If I truly feared the last Ky'Branthian, I would not have agreed to transport him back to his homeland."

"I think he terrifies you . . . but I think your greed outweighs that dread."

"And I think you think too much. Worry about yourself, Damon, for there is more than just a sorcerer to fear aboard this boat." She nodded toward a great brute of a pirate with yellow and black teeth, laceration scars criss-crossing his face, and burn marks along his fore-arms. "That's Balden. He enjoys the company of young men." Captain Silversten departed swiftly, but cast a glance over her shoulder. "Be sure to lock your cabin door at night."

Damon watched her disappear down the galley stairs, wishing she had stayed. Slowly, his thoughts and gaze turned to the sorcerer-king. He steeled his resolve and forced himself to stand.

As all young scholars in Philosopher's Hold, his lot was to travel abroad, unable to return until he collected valuable information pertaining to myths and legends. His hand sought out the crystal sphere deep within an inside pocket of his robe, a newly developed instrument of the arch-sages. He felt its magic against him, pricking his skin with minute energies and recording all that he experienced. The sphere would determine when he had uncovered enough mystic lore to return home. Damon hoped it would be soon.

He approached Vinn Kavilon slowly, his heart racing. He nearly turned and ran, but instead paused for another moment to collect himself, eyes fixed to the broad back of the tall king. Moments crept by before Damon found the courage to continue.

At his immediate approach, the scholar's mind filled with debilitating fog, and soon he was stumbling forward. His eyes shifted to the deck boards but for a second, and when he looked up, he was staring into the deep, dark hood of Vinn Kavilon.

Damon's heart nearly burst as he was confronted by an elongated face, almost bestial, with overly large eyes of vibrant amber and thick bovine lips. Upon his head sat a crown of twisted antlers, like those of a stag, though these were short-cropped, rising no more than a finger's length from the king's long black hair. Amid the tangled horns, saffron-colored petals were thickly layered, rife with slightly darker, crumb-like seeds.

The young scholar swallowed hard and stammered before steadying his voice and asking, "You are the king of the Ky'Branthians, the last of your kind?"

An abysmal hiss simply answered, "Yes."

"What killed your people?"

"Sorcery." The word was a deep, dry whisper, and the creature's eyes suddenly blazed, as if mere mention of the art had summoned some innate power that yearned to be released.

Damon's mind reeled as he tried to remember the series of questions he wished to ask. He could not fully remember, and blurted, "Why are you returning to your homeland?"

"For my people."

Vinn Kavilon turned his back on the scholar and stared out to a distant speck on the horizon, the island shores of Ky'Branthis. He would answer no further questions beyond the three.

———————— ⚓ ————————

Sheer rock walls formed the shoreline of Ky'Branthis, save for occasional patches of richly vegetated lowlands that steeply inclined toward the island's interior. Beech trees and water oaks loomed in abundance among other types of trees, overshadowing thick bracken and nettles entwined with black briars. The dangerous, churning waters and jutting rocks in the shallows prompted dire concerns, but with a subtle nod of the sorcerer-king's hooded head, the waters calmed.

Vinn Kavilon stood stoically, scarcely moving, a hand of bejeweled fingers resting on the bowsprit, long black nails filed to points. It was not until a rowboat was positioned to be lowered into the waters that the mage stirred to action, taking his seat at the prow, facing the oars, accompanied by six strong pirates.

Damon Maxx exited his cabin to join them, but Captain Silversten blocked his path. "You do not have to go, you know. This is dangerous business and I do not trust the mage. Once you are off my boat, I cannot protect you."

Damon gazed upon her, feeling her beauty and warmth, wishing he could touch her. She was dressed like any pirate captain, dark breeks and full-sleeved, white-frilled blouse under a heavy wool gray naval coat. On her head rested a black tricorne hat with silver trimmings and a cameo consisting of an ivory image portraying numerous weapons intersecting on an ebony background, the stems of three dark red feathers pinned beneath. Despite her attire, the scholar saw her as something more refined than a pirate; the way she moved with a pronounced grace, and certainly the elocution and refinement of her words—they were not pirate-speak. Her obvious display of compassion set her apart from the crewmen as well.

"How came you to be a pirate captain?" Damon asked, finally gathering the courage to pose the question that had weighed on his thoughts for quite some time.

She smiled, and if it was not such a somber occasion, might have laughed. "I wondered when you would ask me that," she said, her eyes becoming wistful as she considered her past. "My father was a minor noble and weapon master to King Everott of Pendath. One of the finest swordsmen in Sykis. My family was disgraced through a treasonous plot. I believe father had no involvement, but he and my family were hanged and the bodies desecrated." The captain paused, fighting back a tear; she took a deep breath, suddenly detached as she stoically resumed her story. "He trained his daughter well enough to handle a foil before he passed, however. I was also to be executed, but had the good fortune to escape Pendath on a merchant ship and soon found my way aboard a pirate vessel that accepted women who could hold their own in combat. It was only a matter of time and fortune before a skilled blade carved its way to the top to become captain of *The Silver Spray*, eh? Well, to be honest, I renamed the ship in honor of my family name. Still, I am very much the Lady Blair Silversten—but please don't tell the crew. It will be our secret."

Damon nodded. "I thought you had to be something more." He began to blush, wanting to tell her that he thought her stunning, but merely stood, dumbly. "I thank you for sharing your secret."

"I've kept it all inside for far too long. It felt good to speak of my family again. Stay here on the ship with me, Damon. It is not worth the risk."

"I must go. My master is expecting me to uncover the mystery of Ky'Branthis . . . I cannot disappoint him. I should be safe enough, he has sent a gift." Damon idly felt for the small crystal sphere inside his pea coat, but did not show it to her. Several moments crept by before his lips repeated the words, "I must go."

Damon crossed the deck and settled apprehensively into the boat among the loutish pirates, who themselves seemed anxious, all of them attempting to avoid the inhuman gaze of Vinn Kavilon. Slowly, they were lowered into the water, and each moment seemed an eternity for those caught in the close confines with the last Ky'Branthian. Audible sighs of relief escaped the lungs of several pirates as the boat finally hit the waters, for now they could exert that nervous energy in the task of rowing. The paddles sliced the water in strong, swift strokes.

Within the quarter hour they had hit the muddy banks of Ky'Branthis. A heavy-set pirate jumped into the shallows and pushed the boat till it was grounded on the shore. Vinn Kavilon stood abruptly, and his satin cloak swirled as he turned and stepped from the boat in one fluid motion. He immediately crossed a bank of mud and white stones, shambling toward the incline leading toward the island's interior. He left a trail of cloven hoof prints in his wake.

The crew—further unnerved by the prints—followed, noting how the thorny vines and underbrush seemed to part ways, clearing a path for the sorcerer-king. Occasional boulders littered the area, perhaps randomly, perhaps not. Damon tried to make sense of them, tried to discern if they had been juxtaposed against heavenly bodies or placed geometrically, but his observations were inconclusive. A white hart suddenly appeared, distracting him, and darted among the trees. It vanished as quickly as it had come.

Soon they were among plentiful cypresses and oaks and yews, their canopies shielding the forest floor from the already sparse sunlight. An arduous path took them through thick vegetation along a steep rise. Jagged cliff walls several hundred yards to either side gently corralled the escarpment to the right. In time, the company lost view of *The Silver Spray* far below as their direction changed to north, and Damon's eyes caught the glint of gold beyond distant tree and brush, forming a gilded parapet between two cliff walls, thick stone towers on opposite sides.

Moving closer, Damon noted portions of a grand scene embossed upon the golden surface, piquing his curiosity as he followed Vinn Kavilon, till the full wall could be viewed in all its glorious artistry. He studied what he believed to be the image of a robed mage with a crown of thorns upon its head—obviously a Ky'Branthian king, possibly even Vinn Kavilon himself—that took center, surrounded by wisps and smoky tendrils that curled to its feet. It held a large sphere over its head with odd shapes circumscribed. There appeared to be water drops—perhaps tears—falling from the head of the king, showering six smaller images of crowned Ky'Branthians, one-third the size of the central image, and at each of their feet, six more sleeping, crowned Ky'Branthians. The four corners of the gilded wall each displayed the portrait of a stag with a twenty-point rack, and three others centered atop and at the sides.

Vinn Kavilon walked forward, within arm's reach of the barrier, and brushed it lightly with his dark nails, speaking an arcane language. The gilded wall shimmered and moved, seeming to split at its center, opening forward till a ten-foot-wide gap allowed entrance to a natural cul-de-sac formed of steeply angled cliffs. A wide path led through tree and brush and large boulders to cave entrances beyond. The sorcerer-king strode forth, motioning for the others to follow.

Damon and the pirates hesitantly walked beyond the great gate. A gnawing sensation that something was surely wrong crept into the scholar's mind. Hands fingered hilts, and eyes scanned the shadows in speculation; the band subconsciously huddled closer together as they crept forth. A palpable sense of doom overshadowed them.

Damon spotted something white and gray amid a bush—a skeleton. He followed a bone down its length to discover that it ended in a hoof—the remains of a Ky'Branthian. He noted several other skeletons lying about, nearly wholly concealed by vegetation, and then his attentions were distracted by something entirely strange.

As Vinn Kavilon raised his hands to the sky and uttered an archaic invocation, a sudden azure glow threw its tint upon rock and foliage, emitted from no less than seven throbbing, mucus-laden sacks some four feet in diameter, now easily seen by their own luminescence despite being partially obscured by thick tree trunks or heavy brush. The pirates—confused as they were—stood motionless, unsure if they were in immediate danger or if the fabled treasure vault was somehow being summoned for their promised payment.

They spun rapidly around at the first sound of movement, drawing blades that gleamed with hints of the azure tincture. A small herd of deer entered the cul-de-sac and charged headlong into the band of pirates who scarcely had time to scatter, such was their amazement at being uncharacteristically attacked by an otherwise reticent and shy animal. The fire of hatred seemed to burn in their eyes, and they moved with a determination as if possessed.

Cries of agony filled the air as horns crashed against bone and tore into flesh. The harts released bestial wails whenever a pirate landed a blow, but the bucks were overtaken with hostile fury, spinning and kicking, dancing around the few pirates that remained standing. Damon was knocked aside from the sudden clash, finding himself prone between a large boulder and thick bush.

As the cacophony of battle continued, Damon stared into the orbits of a Ky'Branthian skull, and saw that from its pate issued forth a number of tiny horns, like those of a stag. It suddenly dawned on Damon that Vinn Kavilon was not a king at all, wearing a crown of horns, but that this was a natural trait of all Ky'Branthians. The revelation meant little to him as he shuddered at the death wails of more pirates. He wished sorely that he had heeded the warnings and stayed on-ship with Captain Silversten.

Damon arose slowly, as the din subsided, and he looked over the bush to see that but a single deer yet lived. Crimson vapor arose from the corpse of man and hart alike, then moved toward the pulsing mucus sacks. The mists settled upon them, and then were seemingly consumed, melding into the membranes.

A semi-tangible green tendril suddenly lashed out to grab the buck around the throat. Though Damon could not see the mystic appendage's point of origin, for his view was obscured by the boulder, he knew that Vinn Kavilon directed the attack. The hart wailed and kicked, then suddenly went limp; the tendril released it, a ring of blood around its broken neck.

Damon, horrified, crouched behind the boulder, gathering the courage to make a run, hoping to survive through subterfuge. He then heard the snap of a twig, saw the sway of a crimson cloak come into view, a cloven hoof beneath a hairy leg press into the ground beside him. The green tendril probed back and forth in the air, as if sniffing for a life force. The last Ky'Branthian was but a breath away from stealing his life.

"Vinn Kavilon!"

The captain had come.

Damon peered through the brush to catch sight of Silversten and a good number of her crew. His heart nearly burst with joy. They had slunk forward during the commotion.

The tendril lurched toward the band of pirates, latching onto the nearest throat—that of Balden—and wrenched the life from him in an instant. Blood formed a ring around his throat, and in unison with that of the recently slain hart, their blood moved in clouds to hover together for but an instant, then swift as a bat sought out a throbbing sack, to coat it and be consumed.

Captain Silversten rushed forward, unsheathing a dirk and sending it flying. Damon wanted to cry out, to warn her that surely no mere sliver of metal could possibly defeat the Ky'Branthian mage, but his words choked in his throat; he remained crouched dumbly in his horror. He thought that she would easily die by the mystic tendril, but was relieved when he saw the mage topple and fall to its knees, the crimson hood falling back to reveal horns amid saffron-colored leaves. A zephyr kicked up, and the black, crumb-like seeds amid the leaves took flight, scattering amidst the cul-de-sac. Where they touched upon the throbbing sacks of vibrant blue, they turned dull and gray, appearing as stone.

Vinn Kavilon fell face-forward to the rocky ground. A thick green mist expanded from beneath the crimson robe, and bone could be seen where once there was flesh. Damon stared on in shock, his mind reeling at the implications that the scholars had been wrong—apparently metal could affect the powerful Ky'Branthian mages. It somehow all seemed too easy.

Damon found himself suddenly encapsulated, as if in a globe of glass, as he arose into the air. It was the sphere gifted to him by his master; he had recorded enough, accomplished his mission, and would now be returned to Philosopher's Hold. He stared at Captain Silversten, gazed in her deep cerulean eyes, wished he could remain to thank her for her bravery. As it was, he sped across the ocean at incredible speed, looking back as the mythic emerald haze began to envelope the island.

———⚓———

Many days later, Damon Maxx sat in his tower study overlooking the ocean and the western sky, puzzling over the events that had transpired. He had shown his master the recordings through the very same sphere that had spirited him away from Ky'Branthis. The elder had made one puzzling observation that echoed Damon's own musings: it was reputed metal blades—magicked or otherwise—had no effect upon the sorcerer. The master took such ponderance a step further, and surmised that Vinn Kavilon had allowed himself to be slain, dropped his defenses through sheer force of will. This mode of thought offered more questions than it answered. Damon retired to his study to consider the matter.

Days later, the scholar retrieved a quill and scribbled in his log, recounting his adventure to Ky'Branthis. His dissertation ended thusly:

It has been well noted that Vinn Kavilon, last Ky'Branthian of his age and erroneously considered a king, could, if he wished, be impervious to metal weapons. He has allowed himself to be slain—but why? It is my summation, and supported by the images on the gilded Ky'Branthian monolith, that the ways of the Ky'Branthians are ceremonial and cyclical, repeating roughly every two centuries.

I shall begin describing the cycle with the birth of seven—seven Ky'Branthian sorcerers. They grow powerful in the ways of the mystic arts; soon they feel the instinctual need to wage war upon each other. Only the strongest one will survive. He will then birth seven embryonic sacks that must be ritually nourished by a mixture of man and hart blood, then seeded by the last Ky'Branthian. These sacks will then turn as if to stone, protecting the new Ky'Branthians within. In time, they will emerge, and the cycle will repeat.

As for the gilded image upon the monolith, it supports this claim; I now realize my error in originally thinking the prone images were sleeping, rather than having been slain, and that the central image was shedding tears, rather than seeding his race. One aspect of the image gives cause for great concern—for it suggests that as this cycle repeats, the essence of the Ky'Branthian mages is being distilled by evolutionary means, each generation more potent, more powerful, than those before. The image of the central mage (I assume this depicts when the essence is distilled to perfection, its most powerful form) is shown to hold the world in its hands, for one of the shapes circumscribed seems to relate to Liiendor, the known continent of Azieran. This is most frightening, for I believe this means that in time Ky'Branthian sorcery will enslave us all!

Damon stared out across the western ocean, wondering if he would ever see the beautiful Captain Silversten again, and if she came to exhume the fabled treasure that was said could only be obtained during the emerald afterglow. Surely, she had set foot on the island to plunder the full hoard, not to save his life. But more importantly, he wondered if he would have the courage to return to Ky'Branthis and attempt to disrupt the cycle that would ultimately spell the doom of all. Perhaps that would best be left for the arch-sages—but some inexplicable yearning drew his thoughts out over the waves, and his body wished to follow; for the first time in his life, he longed for adventure.

Thief of Hearts
William Ledbetter

Odd, that damage," Captain Mordecai Birch said as he examined the Dutch flute's splintered starboard hull.

"'Twas witchcraft, Capt'n," the first mate, Mr. McConnell said. "She slipped into that devilish cloud just at dawn and came out limping."

Birch lowered the glass and shook his head. "I've never seen storm damage the likes of that. It looks more like shot."

A good hundred rounds of grapeshot was the only thing Birch could imagine causing such holes and splintering. The *Sibylla* had been sound when she left port at Cartagena and the *Beholder* had not been more than ten leagues from her since. No one could have delivered such a barrage without Birch and his crew hearing the attack. It made him uneasy.

McConnell crossed his arms and leaned back to look up at Birch. "'Tis an ill wind, Capt'n."

The name Birch fit the captain well. At six feet four inches, he towered over most men and his mutilated face—scarred first by the pox and then by a cruel keelhauling—could easily be mistaken for tree bark. But the crew had elected him captain of the *Beholder* for his skill and cunning, not his looks.

"So you think we should not pick this ripe fruit?" If their spies in Cartagena were to be believed, the *Sibylla* was bound for Lyon with a hold filled with tobacco, coffee, and some smuggled Spanish silver.

McConnell raised an eyebrow. "Nay!"

"Nor I." Birch turned his attention to the young man at the whipstaff. "Steady at the helm, Davy."

"Steady helm! Steady as she goes," Mr. McConnell yelled from the captain's right elbow.

"Sink 'em Capt'n!" his nine-year old cabin boy, Apple, yelled from his left.

Birch was surrounded by unneeded help. He looked down and frowned. "Apple" was the first English word the little dark-skinned boy said when they rescued him from a sinking Portuguese merchantman the previous summer. He loved the fruit in any form and the crew had since made sure there were always some on board. They had also called him Apple ever since.

Birch put on a stern face. "I thought I told you to go below."

"But I'll miss . . ."

"Go!"

The boy disappeared and Birch raised the glass again.

Their prey limped along with only the top sail on her damaged foremast, a shredded lateen on her mizzen and her mainmast completely gone. She was a sluggard and many of the gun ports were empty of cannon, yet she'd refused to yield when they fired across her bow. Birch sighed. He'd given them a chance, but they chose the hard course. "Run up the red!"

"Run up the red!" McConnell yelled.

His crew cheered and raised the red flag as they pulled down their false Union Jack. "Ready all gunners."

The captain turned his glass and focused on his Dutch counterpart. The man looked too young to be a ship's master and the activity on deck broadcast his intentions. He was trying to move cannon from the port side to the damaged starboard side, expecting the raiders to attack his weakest point.

Birch bent over the rail and yelled at his gunner's mate.

"Bob, I want to take her without firing if we can. She's already taken a beating and I'd wager she could not stand a fight."

"Aye aye, Capt'n!"

"He's getting ready to cut," Birch said. "Turn on my mark, helm."

As the *Beholder* pulled close, the Dutch captain sent his vessel leaning hard to port. "Now!"

The quick little pirate sloop turned even sharper to port, across the larger ship's wake and closed the gap. She came abreast quickly, within ten yards of the *Sibylla*. Birch held his arm aloft until they crested the next swell, and saw their prey still had cannons manned on the port side. So much for not firing.

He dropped his arm, sending the signal. "Fire!"

The gunners echoed his command and eight four-pounders on his starboard side fired in a synchronicity that would have made even the British navy proud. At such close range every shot hit, sending wood, rope, canvas and men flying into the air in a gruesome and deadly cloud.

"Boarding party!"

The majority of his seventy-man crew massed near the gunwales as the sails were furled and the grapples thrown. Like the thoroughbred she was, the *Beholder* groaned as the ropes forced her to slow and pulled her hard alongside. A secondary explosion aboard the flute sent more debris into the air.

"She's afire on her aft quarter, Capt'n!" the lookout yelled.

McConnell waited with the boarding party for a decision. Tying alongside a burning ship was dangerous, but pulling away would lose the prize for certain.

Captain Birch grinned and raised his sword. "Heave to, laddies!"

Cheers arose and everyone with a gun fired, raking the defenders away from the rail. Ten men sailed across on ropes to secure the port side while the rest of the raiders scrambled up the side of the larger ship. The flute's crew met them with guns and swords, but Birch's men didn't slow, not even when young Davy Cooper took a ball through the chest and fell into the crevice between the grinding hulls.

Birch crawled up a rope and ducked just as a whistling sword sliced off the top of his hat. With an angry yell, the captain vaulted the rail, drawing his cutlass in mid-air. When he landed, ready for revenge, the gallant defender was already dying at the end of Mr. McConnell's sword. Birch glared at the first mate, who winked and then ran aft to join in the fray.

"Give them another chance to yield, Mr. McConnell," he yelled, but the first mate gave no indication he'd heard. The remaining defenders were backed against the aft railing, fighting for their lives. Once the red flag—or *joli rouge*—went up, all understood there would be no prisoners, so his giving them another chance would anger some of the pirate crew, but was it the sailors' fault their master had been so young and foolish?

The captain paused to survey the carnage. His men were nothing if not efficient. The deck was littered with the dead and dying, yet in the ten minutes since the attack started, they also managed to drop the sails and find water to throw on the fire. He tossed his wounded hat aside and picked up another from the deck.

As the last of the Dutch crew died or surrendered, McConnell returned, dragging an injured man and leaned in close to whisper. "He speaks English, Capt'n. Says there's a witch on board and that she brought the sky down on them this morning. I told yee that cloud was an evil thing."

Apple appeared from behind a coiled rope and posted himself between the captain and the prisoner. "A witch?"

Birch cursed. "Apple! Get back on the. . . . Never mind, just stay right next to me."

The captive's fine clothing—though ripped and bloody—revealed his status as a passenger or maybe the ship's doctor, but not of the *Sibylla's* working crew. "Where's your captain?"

The man glared and didn't speak until McConnell poked him with his foot. "Dead . . . in the storm this morning."

Birch glanced at McConnell. "Aye, we saw a strange cloud, but heard no thunder."

The man shivered. "From the depths of Hell, that storm."

"Who commands the *Sibylla* now?"

The man shook his head but didn't answer.

McConnell kicked him in the ribs.

"Oufh! No one! The first mate did, until your cannon blew him apart."

"Fool should have yielded," McConnell said.

The man glared up at them. "To filthy vermin? Become pirates or die? I think not."

Birch grabbed the man, lifted him so they were nose to nose and then grinned. "So what's yer name, mate?"

"Kenner."

"Well, Mr. Kenner, I'm not an evil man and may spare your life if you make it worthwhile. Are you a wealthy man with associates who would pay to get you back?"

The man's eyes narrowed. "Not an evil man? A priest once said that the evil in men—when strong enough—would seep out through their skin, making them as ugly on the outside as they were inside. If that be true, then yee must be the devil himself."

Birch roared, lifted the man above his head and carried him to the rail. He stood there for a second, then turned and threw him to the deck. The man may yet be valuable and money was the only cure for Birch's ugliness. He had to stay focused on his goal.

In his youth he'd known a landed lord who had been terribly scarred by fire, yet no one taunted him. Because he was rich, old Lord Clement had a pretty, well-bred wife and friends who invited him to grand balls. If Birch became one of the wealthiest men in the New World he could live like a normal man. His shares of *Sibylla* and her cargo, added to what he already had stashed away, would put him even closer to that goal.

Raucous shouts and whistles erupted from the captain's cabin.

McConnell grinned. "Sounds like they found yer witch, Capt'n!"

As Birch approached, the whoops and hollers faded.

He looked in to see a girl, barely of marrying age by the look of her, tied naked to a chair next to the Dutch captain's table. Birch had seen many things during his years on the ocean, but this kind of thing never failed to sicken him. He yanked a blanket from the bed, covered her and stepped outside the cabin. "Antonio! Get her some of Apple's clothes. And be quick about it! The rest of yee be about yer business!"

The men scattered, but watched from their stations aboard both ships and whispered among themselves. Birch pulled his knife and the girl's eyes widened until she realized he intended to cut her bonds. When she was free, Birch brushed aside silky brown hair and looked at her frightened face. "What's your name, child?"

She met his gaze but didn't answer.

McConnell bent close and whispered. "Take care, sir. It may looks human, but I be thinkin it's a selkie."

Captain Birch sighed and sat down next to the captive. "A selkie? A woman that can turn into a seal?"

"Aye, Capt'n. An enchanted creature of the sea. Mind now, it'll bewitch you and kill us all."

She was indeed a strange creature, with smooth, pale skin, deep black eyes and a tiny nose with narrow slit-like nostrils. Birch also noted four mysterious symbols tattooed in a vertical stack between her breasts. Odd as she looked, she was still human and Birch thought she was beautiful.

"Are you a selkie?" he asked, but received nothing but a stare in return. He smiled at her and pulled one of her hands from the blanket. She shivered but didn't yank it away. They were tiny for a girl of her age, with very long fingers. She flinched when he then took one of her feet, but again didn't pull away. They too were small, narrow and icy cold. Both told Birch what he needed to know.

"Well, dearie, you're much better than a sea monster. With feet and hands so soft and free of calluses, I'd wager you're of noble blood and your poppa will pay handsomely to get you back."

McConnell scowled and shook his head. "Look at her back, Capt'n."

He carefully pushed the girl's hair away from her neck and pulled the blanket back. What he saw sent a chill through him. Her rooted hair did not stop at the base of her head, but continued down her spine in a thick ridge that gradually diminished as it approached her waist. A narrow band of short, silky fur also spread across her upper back and paled to nearly invisible as it reached her arm pits.

Several of the crew had gathered again, peering through the door, murmuring among themselves.

"Yee have to throw 'er back, Capt'n," McConnell muttered.

Birch covered her again and took the clothes Antonio offered. "Throw her back?"

"She's a creature of the sea. That's where she belongs. Just look at this ship, sir. We'll end up same if she stays."

Nodded agreement from all around.

Old Ben, his quartermaster, bent forward and whispered. "I agree, Capt'n. Do yee know what *Sibylla* means? It's Dutch for *Prophet*. A bad omen."

Birch looked at her again. She offered a small, hopeful smile and he knew he would not throw her over the side. Of course, if he didn't play it right, the men may eventually do it for him.

Apple pushed through the crowd at the door, saw the girl and began dancing around her wearing a huge smile and singing in his native Malagasy tongue. He whooped, whistled and jabbered. Then to their amazement, the girl grabbed Apple in a big hug and started speaking to him in his own language.

———————

The *Beholder* did not like to go slow. With most of her canvas down, she still pulled ahead of the sluggish *Sibylla* and they had to lay to every few hours, to let her catch up.

Before getting underway, he had loaded Kenner and the other prisoners into a longboat, with a sail and enough food and water to last two weeks. If they were skillful and lucky enough, they might hit the Virginia or Carolina coast before they died.

Captain Birch had left half of his crew on the *Sibylla* with the much-trusted Beau Gaudreau in command and split the cargo between the two ships. Even though they didn't find any smuggled silver, the cargo and ship would fetch a good price in New York, so he wasn't about to let the prize out of sight until they reached harbor.

Crystalline female laughter drifted from his cabin's open door and most of the men turned to look. Their hard faces didn't betray if they had lust or fear in their hearts, but the strange girl was another prize Birch would have to watch closely.

He leaned into the cabin and saw Apple still trying to teach the girl English. Even stranger than this girl's odd appearance was the fact that she was white and spoke a savage language perfectly, yet didn't seem to know any of the European languages. Even if she'd been raised in a pirate port on Madagascar, which would explain her knowing Malagasy, she should have still spoken some French or English. When she saw the captain, she jumped to her feet and ran over to him.

"I need your ship!" she said, in almost a perfect imitation of Apple's musical accent.

"What?"

She grabbed the lapels of his waistcoat and pulled his face down closer to hers. "Take me home. In your ship!"

With her face inches from his, he felt an odd lack of breath. He remembered what McConnell said about her bewitching him and gently pulled away. "I . . . I don't know where you live."

Her face twisted in thought and she looked at Apple.

"She live on a Mother Island, Capt'n. It like a big beast and it swim around."

Birch smiled. "A swimming island? There are hundreds of islands in these waters and they are hard enough to find when they sit still."

Her little face hardened and she returned to sit next to Apple. "Take me home. I miss my children."

Birch raised an eyebrow. "Children? Does she mean her parents?"

Apple shook his head. "No sir, she misses her kids. She has three. She a grown up momma."

Birch looked at her again and chewed his lip. What a silly lie. Did she think it would keep her from being sold or ransomed? "How does she know your language, Apple?"

"She not a selkie. She a Vazimba. Very old people. They lived in our land before Malagasy came. We give them offering to help crop and get good luck."

Birch scratched his head. "Is she from the Port at Sainte Marie?"

Apple shook his head. "Her people lived on the big island, long, long time ago."

⚓

That evening Captain Birch watched the girl from across the cabin, but the soothing creaks and groans of the gently swaying ship soon forced his eyes closed. He next opened them when the ship jerked hard to starboard, nearly tossing him to the floor. The dim and flickering lamp light revealed a frightened Apple and a missing girl.

Yells from outside launched Birch to his feet, but opening the cabin door took great effort against the wind. Once outside, he beheld not a typical storm, but like the Dutchman had said, "something from the bowels of Hell." Toward each horizon the sea was calm, with stars and a near-full moon visible, but the waves under and around the *Beholder* lifted her on ten-foot crests and the sky above her was a swirling black mess.

The captain yelled orders but the roaring wind snatched them away, so he pulled himself along rails and ropes until he found men and sent them to their tasks. Then, as he looked toward the prow, the dim light silhouetted the strange girl standing with arms spread wide and hair whipping wildly around her face.

He'd been warned and didn't listen. The girl had seemed harmless yet now, due to his stubborn negligence, his ship may suffer the same fate as *Sibylla.*

"Stop!" he yelled into the maelstrom, but the girl ignored him and the storm strengthened. The air chilled suddenly and the clouds above them lightened in color, glowing green as a massive whirling column twisted its way down to the frothing waves. The vortex touched water just aft of the *Beholder* and then separated into three thinner tails.

The air between the three waterspouts crackled with blue light and for just a second Birch thought he saw two moons in a pale purple sky. The vision faded as the cyclones separated further, with one moving up the starboard side, another to port and one remained aft. They grew thick and hissed as they spun. The *Beholder's* only escape route was dead ahead.

Captain Birch had seen many of the delicate water twisters in his time on the sea, even been hit by one of them, but none ever looked or sounded like these. The hiss rose in volume until it drowned out the howling wind, then stinging bits of ice pelted him in wave after wave. He looked around and realized his men already knew what to do. They were trying to get the sails down, but the hail chunks were getting larger. Time was running out.

He crawled to the port side and, using the railing as a horizontal ladder, dragged himself forward. Ice had formed on the wood rails and the pounding hail broke it into glassy shards. It bit into his hands, freezing and gouging, but the girl stood just ahead on the bowsprit, defiant of the storm. When he reached her, he rose to his knees, grabbed her around the waist and pulled her down.

She fought like an angry cat and almost slipped his grasp several times, but he held tight and started dragging her back toward the cabin.

"My ship!" she screamed.

The hail now came in a constant torrent, splintering the wooden deck and pounding Birch, but never seeming to touch the girl. If the barrage continued, he knew he would never make it to his cabin.

"No, my ship!"

"I need the ship!" She pounded on his back, adding little to the drubbing hail.

"Then why are you sinking her?"

She stopped fighting and the hail lessened a little. The captain pushed his advantage. "How can I help you if I'm dead and the ship is on the bottom of the ocean?"

"Let go. I'll stop."

He released the girl and she scrambled to her feet. In turn, she faced each water spout, rattled off some incantation and made motions with her hands. The twisting columns on either side moved further away, but the one in the rear remained close enough that it still lashed the *Beholder* with occasional bouts of hail.

"Stay between the water spouts. They will take you to my home," the girl said. Then her eyes rolled into the back of her head and she collapsed to the surging deck.

Captain Birch stood up and surveyed the damage. The *Beholder* had tattered sails, her uppermost spar was broken and about half of her crew were bleeding from their hail beating, but his mainmast was still standing and none of his men had died. They got off far lighter than the *Sibylla*.

———⚓———

The crew was angry and rightly so. Their scowling faces, weapons and ropes left no doubt as to their intentions, but Birch didn't move from his place before the cabin door. They had elected him captain and could easily elect another. He tried to shift attention away from the crisis.

"Any sign of the *Sibylla* yet, Mr. McConnell?"

His first mate shuffled and shrugged. "Nay, but we can't see much past these blasted cyclones."

They had been blown steadily northward, far to the east of New York and had seen no sign of the *Sibylla* since the initial storm.

McConnell stepped closer. "We're doin' thirteen knots Capt'n. Hard to tell how long the mast can hold under such a strain."

"And the repairs?"

McConnell shrugged. "Best we can manage here. Conner is working on the mainsail while we're flying the storm canvas and the top spar is replaced, but Mikey still hasn't woke up. He took a hard hit to the noggin." McConnell glanced back at the crew. "'Tis time, Capt'n. Time to throw her back. While we still can."

"I agree," Birch said. "I'm ready to toss her over the side at any time."

McConnell raised his eyebrows and several of the men smiled and stepped forward.

"But we can't. As you said yourself, Mr. McConnell, she is a magical being. If she truly is a magic sea beast, then she'll be able to swim like one. Throwing her over the side would make her so mad that she'd follow and hound us like one of Hell's own demons."

McConnell glowered. "There are other ways."

For emphasis, one of the boatswains smacked his club into the railing.

"You men are not using your God-given sense. These whirlwinds are still herding us, even with the girl in a deep sleep. If we kill her, they may never go away and in time it would drive us onto some rocky shore. Do you want to take the risk?"

He paused to let that sink into their thick heads. "We have to wait and follow this thing through. If we take her home, maybe we'll get out of this with our skins. And who knows, maybe her daddy is rich and will give us a reward."

A couple of the younger men whooped, but most of them kept their sour countenance.

"Capt'n . . . Capt'n," Apple yelled from the door behind him. "She awake!"

The captain snapped orders and much to his relief the men dispersed and obeyed, then he slammed into his cabin. He intended to slap her and yell, hoping to scare her into calling off her cyclones, but when he saw her, he drew up short. Her eyes were sunken, she shivered violently and her teeth chattered.

"Her face and arms are hot, but her feets are so cold, five blankets can't keep 'em warm," Apple said with crossed arms and a concerned expression.

"What has she said since waking up?"

"She just want to talk to you."

Birch knelt next to the chair where he had tied her, just like the *Sibylla's* captain, and felt her feet under the blankets. They were like ice, much colder than human flesh should ever be, even in death. While he held them, her teeth stopped clacking and she sighed. "I'm so cold."

"How much longer can you go on like this?"

"It's not long now. We'll be there soon. When we get there, stay far from the shore until night. Then you will have to come across with me."

He dropped her feet when his hands started hurting from the cold. "If I leave the ship, the crew will leave me."

She started shaking again and through clenched teeth said, "No they won't."

———⚓———

The temperature grew colder and the sea rougher as they sailed north. An hour before sunset, the lookout sighted a fog-shrouded island. The girl, with her feet and legs wrapped in blankets and an arm over Apple's shoulder, hobbled out onto the deck. The crew gave her a wide berth and several clutched rosaries or other good luck charms. Two of the water spouts immediately dissolved and the third one moved a little further away. She stopped next to the captain, but turned toward the men.

"I'm sorry. I need Capt'n to come to my Mother. If you try to leave, the water spout will hit you."

Much to Birch's surprise, McConnell stepped forward. "Ye ain't taking the capt'n. Not without a fight."

The captain shook his head and looked at her. "I'll go with you, but if I'm not back by morning you'll let the ship go?"

"Yes," she said and then pointed at what looked like a natural cove. "Keep the ship away from that side of the Mother."

Birch looked at it through his glass and in the waning light could just make out a whirlpool spinning at the center of the little cove. He also heard a distant roar, like that made by a waterfall. "What is it?"

"The Mother's mouth."

About an hour after sunset, Apple and the girl came out onto deck. She pointed to the small boat. "We go."

Birch started to protest about Apple going along, but the boy had scrambled into the boat wearing a grin wider than the sea. He ordered the boat lowered. It was unseemly for the captain, even of a pirate band, to row his own boat, but she insisted he go and he wanted to get it over with. He checked to make sure he had his pistol, shot and his sword, then he took the oars. One last glance revealed the crew watching in silence. He hoped the *Beholder* would still be there when he and the boy returned.

The moon, just past full, lay low enough on the horizon to cast light beneath the clouds and gave everything an odd silver hue. Granules of icy snow pelted them as the wind gusted. It chilled Birch to the core, but the girl looked even more miserable, all wrapped up in blankets, with her jaw clenched to keep her teeth from chattering. He realized he didn't know what to call her.

"What's your name?"

She smiled, pushing the hair away from her face. A very human female gesture, maybe she wasn't a sea monster after all.

"Honna," she said and pointed toward a flat beach. "Go there."

As they neared the island, Apple started chattering in Malagasy and Birch turned to look over his shoulder. A crowd lined the beach. They were small and pale like Honna and they were as quiet as his men had been.

Honna must have read the unease in his face even in the faint light because she stroked his knee and said, "They won't hurt you. I told them we were here."

Before Birch could ask just *how* she had told them, the boat rasped to a stop against a shallow bottom and several of the men from her tribe rushed out to pull them ashore.

Apple leapt out of the boat and started jumping up and down on the shore. "See . . . it a live island!"

Birch had stood on many beaches during his life at sea, but none so strange. Like most shorelines, this one was strewn with flotsam, but instead of sand, he stepped out onto something that reminded him of a leather-covered divan. The surface gave beneath his weight, yet sprang back to shape after he moved on and it radiated enough heat that he immediately felt it through his pants and boots.

He considered for the first time that Apple might be right about the island being alive. A dozen ways to make money from such a beast sprang to mind. Leisurely cruises of the South Seas on a swimming island topped the list. The rich and royal in Europe would pay a fortune for such an opportunity. So would pirates looking for a base that was hard to find.

He realized the little people were still watching him with the same reserved silence. Apple stared back at them with a wide-eyed smile.

Honna tossed the blankets aside, peeled off the borrowed clothes and dropped to her knees on the shore. She laughed, squealed and pressed her face and widespread arms against the ground. Then she started to sing in a voice stolen from angels. The song vibrated through Birch and brought to mind tales of mermaids whose sweet songs doomed many a sailing man.

Obviously the song was part of some expected ritual and as soon as Honna stood, the people cheered and swamped them. Birch towered amid a sea of little faces that laughed, sang and swirled about him in waves and eddies. They hugged him and touched him and tugged at his clothes. They held wide-eyed children high above their heads for a better look at the strange giant. Apple laughed in unfettered glee as the pale children swung him around in a circular dance.

The little people produced green lights from somewhere and pulled a laughing Honna up the beach toward the tree line. They prodded Birch to do the same. In the weird light he saw a broad trail through the forest and the whole time his hosts darted and dodged around him like a pack of hungry puppies.

The trees were like nothing he'd encountered. Instead of growing out of the ground, they seemed to be a part of it, pulled up into what looked like melons stacked atop each other then crowned with tufts of fern. The rest of the foliage was equally as strange.

After a few minutes, they entered a village filed with odd, domed huts. There were hundreds of them, all different sizes, with warm smooth walls that, like the strange trees, grew directly out of the ground like a pox.

Though the little folk seemed innocent enough, by the time they reached the middle of the village, he realized his sword, pistol, and cabin boy had disappeared. Anger and a growing panic bloomed as he looked for the boy. How had he let this happen? Had he indeed been bewitched? He shoved his way through the little people, parting them like the sea before his sloop on a calm day. He stopped before Honna and yelled down at her. "I brought you home, now I want my sword and gun back! And where is Apple? We're leaving!"

Several of the people backed away, but Honna's smile never wavered. She said something to a woman behind her and within a couple of heartbeats, the woman produced Birch's weapons and the smiling, sweating Apple.

"See . . . we want nothing but your friendship and help."

Birch took a deep, steadying breath and understood with one glance at the boy, that he would most likely not return to the ship. And he needed to be careful until he found out how to move the island to where he wanted it. With a broad smile, he bowed to Honna. "Please accept my apologies for losing my temper. Pray tell, how might I further assist you?"

She gave him an odd look, took his big hand in both of hers and led him through the narrow walkways between the blister huts. The crowd followed until she stopped before a large one. When Honna pulled the leathery flap back and motioned Birch to enter, they all laughed and cheered. She pressed her mouth close to his ear. "I would like to talk to you in private, if you will allow my children to entertain Apple elsewhere."

Birch was no fool. Her expression and the gleeful crowd made her intentions clear. He didn't know if he was bewitched, but he didn't decline the offer. Apple obviously wanted to go, so he nodded and three of the pale folk stepped forward.

"These are my children," she said and touched them in turn. "This is Ima, Omer and Sinna." The first was a girl of her mother's height, the same who'd fetched Apple earlier. The boy, also apparently full grown, glared at Birch but didn't speak. The youngest was a girl, Sinna, and a full head shorter than Apple. She smiled sweetly as she took the dark boy's hand and tugged him away.

Birch followed Honna into the dimly lit hut. The heat inside stifled him as he bent under the low ceiling and tried to breathe. Honna knelt and pulled Birch down onto a sleeping pallet.

She slipped an arm around his neck and pulled his head down to whisper in his ear. "Until now, I've forced you to help me, but now I need to trust you with the fate of my people and our Mother. I need you to lead us to a place in the northern sea where we can cross over and be with the rest of our people. Our Mother is the last of her kind in this world and has been looking for the other Mothers and Fathers, but stubbornly refuses to go to the gate. If you do this for us, I have the power to give you what your heart truly desires."

Birch felt his anger returning as he realized Honna had either learned a complete understanding of the English language in the past few days, or had already known it and had for some reason been hiding the fact. But as her words sank in, his anger faded quickly.

"You're going to give me the power to lead your island across the sea?"

She nodded and moved her face closer to his, with their noses nearly touching. "I will give you her heart and she will follow it anywhere."

His own heart pounded in his chest. "And you can grant wishes?"

"No . . . not really, but I can read your heart and give you what you need to fulfill your desires."

Women had offered to grant his heart's desire before, in trade for a handful of silver, but she said she would give him the power to lead her huge living island and *that* would give him what he desired.

"Done. Just tell me what I need to do."

"We aren't ready yet," she whispered into his cheek and then took his face in her hands. "I need to read you. Hold still for just a little while."

She pressed her face against his and the already warm hut grew steadily hotter. He felt dizzy from the heat and her closeness. He suspected she was bewitching him, but he didn't care. Then, just as he began to lose the ability to control himself, she stopped, pulled slightly away and looked at him as if seeing him for the first time.

Her hands stroked his face, touching the holes and tracing the scars, yanking him out of the soft cocoon she had previously wrapped around him and forcing him to remember he was a fearsome freak.

"You poor man," she said as tears filled her eyes.

"I don't need your pity!" He tried to turn away, but her tiny hands held his face like a vise.

"No, but you do need me," she said and turned his face to hers. "And I need you." Then she kissed him long and hard.

⚓

They lay together, sweating and tangled in bedding on the hot floor. She dominated their frenzied lovemaking—as she had controlled everything since their meeting—but he liked it.

She knew more about pleasing a man than even Greta, the most expensive whore he had ever encountered, but he worried he might pay a much higher price if she had bewitched him. His crew already suspected he had come under her spell. They would kill him if he tried to help her again with no gain for the crew, but he didn't care. He felt so good he never wanted to leave.

Honna straddled him, took his finger, and used it to trace one of the tattoos between her breasts. "Mother," she said. The next one was Sun, the third was Moon. She opened his hand and laid his palm against the fourth symbol. "Father," she said with a smile and then kissed him again.

His hand tingled and he had a faint outline of the symbol on his palm, but before he could ask the ritual's meaning, she rolled off of him and stood up. "We have to hurry, it will be light soon."

"What? We have to do it now?"

"Yes, but we have to be swift and quiet. Even though I'm the Mother's ward, my people would never understand my giving her heart to a stranger, no matter how much we need the help. They would rather wait and hope the Mother eventually moves to the gate on her own. I know she will die soon if we do nothing."

Birch fought his disappointment and sat up.

She picked up a small jar, peeked out the door and turned back. "Wait until I return for you," she whispered and then slipped outside.

———⚓———

When Honna returned a few minutes later, she made a gesture of silence and pulled him out of the hut. They stepped over two sleeping men, before darting into the dark woods beyond the faint village lights. Birch saw little, but Honna drew him through the blackness, unerringly dodging trees and other invisible obstacles.

When they finally broke out of the thick woods and stopped running, the sky had lightened and they were surrounded by a swirling fog. Birch took a deep breath of the cool, salty sea air and heard the faint, alluring sound of the surf breaking on the strange beach. He also heard a dull, nearly imperceptible roar. He'd heard the sound before, from the massive whirlpool Honna called the Mother's mouth.

Honna led him a few steps forward then stopped, knelt and pulled Birch down with her. What he saw made his heart nearly burst from his chest. The ground, or skin, or whatever covered this island-beast had been formed into a deep pocket. The depression was filled with gems of every conceivable size and shape. Some were perfectly cut, others were in their raw form and still others were set in gold rings. Honna started scooping them out and tossing them aside like excavated dirt.

Birch gasped and scrambled around on all fours gathering up all he saw in the dim light. "What are you doing?"

"Shhhh . . . we have to be quiet. We don't need the offerings, leave them. We have to get the heart."

Birch couldn't believe his ears. He gathered up all he could find and then helped her empty the rest from the hole, but kept the gems and jewelry all in a neat pile. When they finished, she took his hand and pressed it to the bottom of the hole.

"You have to cut here."

"Cut?"

"Yes, with your big knife. The heart is inside. It is hard and the size of your fist."

He pulled his saber and shoved it into the soft spot until it hit something solid. The entire island rumbled. He cut the slit wider and a milky fluid oozed out.

"Quickly. Pull it out."

He pulled up his sleeve and thrust his hand inside. It was hot and Birch couldn't help but think of human entrails as he pushed his hand deeper. Then he felt a solid knot and without pause grabbed it and pulled with all his might. The heart came out with a sucking sound, but instead of some fleshy beating organ like a human heart, he held a diamond as big as a four-pound cannon ball.

Honna stiffened and whipped around toward the woods. "No Omer!"

Birch saw nothing. Then a second later Honna's son stormed out of the woods. "Arrrgh!"

Honna stepped between them.

With a face contorted by rage, Omer shoved his mother aside and lunged forward, grabbing Birch's arm that still held the slimy heart.

Seeing Honna land hard on her back enraged Birch. He raised his cutlass high and brought the flat down hard on the back of the boy's neck, but the attacker held tight and started biting Birch's gooey fist. Fighting the urge to run his cutlass through the fool's heart, Birch instead rolled backward, lifting the young man high on his booted feet. Then with all his strength, he kicked. The boy sailed backward into the fog. Instead of hearing the expected thud, Birch heard a much-delayed splash.

He and Honna both scrambled to an edge that was barely visible in the mist and started yelling, but heard only the surf and the Mother's roaring maw in return. Honna let out a strangled cry and clutched her head. "He's gone."

"Steady," Captain Birch said to the helmsman and raised the glass to scan the strange ice formation. The huge berg was just as Honna described it—a ragged arch soaring high above the other ice mountains—like a god's white ring dipped halfway into the northern sea.

"Steady helm! Steady as she goes," Mr. McConnell yelled from the captain's right elbow.

Birch growled at his first mate through his foggy breath and turned to look behind them. The huge living island still kept up. Wind from the waterspouts had driven them steadily north for three days and the island followed her heart.

Some of the men grumbled about the task, but most were satisfied with their share of the jewels. When Birch emptied them out of the shirt he'd made into a makeshift bag, they nearly filled a two-gallon bucket. Of course the cyclones helped to keep them in line as well.

As they neared the icy arch, the waterspouts died. Birch ordered the sails furled and a cask of rum opened to help warm the men. Then, with the crew busy drinking, he went to his cabin and retrieved the Mother's heart.

At first he'd thought it was a huge uncut diamond, but upon closer examination discovered it was some kind of crystal, with odd fractures radiating outward from the center to the edges. It looked very fragile and it throbbed almost like the real thing. Honna said that through her heart, the Mother spoke to other Mothers and Fathers but hadn't done so since the last of them crossed over to the other world.

She also said she would grant his heart's desire, yet if he let the island leave this world, he would probably never be rich enough to live like a normal man. He closed his eyes and saw his life as a rich land owner, with servants, a carriage and six, a wife and a big house. It was what he always wanted and would be his if he kept the heart stone.

He wrapped the heart in a scarf, shoved it into the thick clothing beneath his coat and went out onto the icy deck. The mark on his palm, the mirror image of the tattoo on Honna's chest, tingled. The Mother had arrived and Honna stood on the beach waiting.

He leaned on the rail. It was time to decide. If he ran, she wouldn't try to sink them as long as he had the stone. If he threatened to throw the stone overboard, she wouldn't even send her cyclones. So he *could* run.

She just stood there, waiting. Against her people's wishes she had trusted him. Even after he'd killed her son, she still let him take the stone. She had not bewitched him, he knew he had the power to make his dream come true, but he crawled down the rope into the boat and ordered his two men to row.

When he stepped ashore, she didn't run to him with the girlish exuberance she had shown before, but she did smile. "Thank you," she said. "Once I replace the heart and open the gate, the Mother will hear her kin and enter. You have saved us and I can never repay that kindness."

"Did . . . you find Omer?"

She shook her head. "No . . . he's gone to feed the Mother."

"I'm sorry, Honna. I didn't . . ."

She held up a hand. "It was his choice. He didn't understand and didn't trust me. He would have killed us both to stop us."

Birch didn't know what to say, so he pulled the wrapped bundle from his coat and handed it over just as Apple came running out of the misty woods, followed by four men carrying a large chest.

"They givin' you treasure Capt'n!" Apple said as he jumped up and down between Birch and Honna. The men sat the chest down and backed away, eyeing Birch and the *Beholder* with suspicion.

Honna smiled. "Apple said you like these kinds of things."

It was a very old chest, made of wood with rusted iron bindings. He opened the lid and his heart skipped a beat. It was filled more than halfway with gold cobs. He picked up a piece and clearly saw the stamp of Philip IV and the Spanish Santa Fe de Bogotá mint. Scattered amid the gold were more jewels, much like those he had recovered from the depression above the Mother's heart.

The two men who had rowed Birch to shore dropped to their knees next to him and touched the gold with shaking hands. Then they rose and yelled to the crew watching from the *Beholder*. Birch was committed. He looked at Honna.

She nodded, but with a sad expression. "It's yours. We have no need of it. Does it make you happy?"

William Ledbetter

"Get this chest on the boat. Quickly!" The men snapped to. He bent close to her. "I need to get this gold aboard and you need to go as soon as you can. Greed will make my men crazy and they will insist on searching every inch of the Mother for more treasure like this. If you are going to leave, you have to go now."

She looked at the gold, then at the *Beholder* where the crew was already preparing to lower another boat. She pulled Birch's face down and kissed him and then with the wrapped heart stone still in her hand, she turned and ran into the fog-shrouded woods.

Birch helped the struggling men lift the chest into the boat and much to his surprise Apple jumped in beside him. They pushed off into the cold, choppy waves and started back to the *Beholder,* just as the men finished lowering the second boat.

He looked back in time to see a shudder pass through the Mother, shaking all of her trees and rippling her shoreline. At almost the same time, the pale clouds above the ice arch turned dark and began to swirl.

When they neared the second longboat, Birch took a gamble. "You had better get back to the ship," he yelled. "She is getting ready to call those wicked waterspouts."

As if on queue, a massive column of swirling darkness dipped out of the clouds at the opening of the arch and the men in both boats began rowing as hard as they could. In a familiar pattern, the fat cyclone touched the surface and took on more mass and shape. The roaring hiss drowned out the wind and they felt the sting of sleet on their faces.

As they pulled aside the *Beholder* and struggled to hoist the chest up to the deck, the roar grew louder and the massive spinning column split in half. When the two waterspouts moved apart, the huge ice arch crackled with blue lightning and inside the hole, they saw a purplish sky, a black sea and two pale crescent moons hanging low in the sky.

The Mother moved quickly, faster than Birch would have believed possible and within minutes she had slipped through the hole. The cyclones slowly merged and rose into the clouds, leaving nothing but the ice arch in a choppy, gray sea. The Mother, along with Honna, was gone into another world and out of his life.

As Birch helped Apple climb the rope into the ship, he asked why he'd not stayed with Honna's people.

"I wanted to be with you and Honna said you would come back to her soon anyway."

Birch liked the fact that Apple had wanted to be with him, but he glanced at the icy archway and wondered how long it would take the poor lad to realize the truth about his friends.

Captain Birch paced the *Swan's* deck and smiled. He had missed the feel of wood and waves beneath his boots these past five years. The new Bermuda style sloop, built to his exact specifications was a fast and sturdy ship. He itched to be under way.

Apple dropped from the rigging and landed next to Birch with a thump and broad smile. Though still a head shorter than Birch, the boy had grown into a fine man and sailor. He had proved an invaluable leader and asset for McConnell when they went to Madagascar to recruit the all-Malagasy crew.

Birch slapped the boy on the shoulder. "Do you think we're about ready?"

"Aye, Capt'n. The cargo is stowed and the men are eager."

"So am I, Apple. Go make sure that they get the last of the water on board before the tide comes in."

"Aye, aye," he said and ran down the gangway as Birch heard the coach and six clattering recklessly along the Richmond waterfront. He took a deep breath, straightened his coat and strode down the gangway just as his wife's gaudily painted carriage stopped at the edge of the quay.

The coach door swung open with a bang before the footman could jump down to assist and out hopped Penelope's music teacher, a young man named Thorp. He lowered the step and held out his hand. Birch's wife of three years took the man's hand and gingerly stepped to the ground.

Birch gave her a slight bow, but did not kiss her hand. The town gossips who'd gathered to watch his departure surely noticed the slight. "I'm surprised you tore yourself away from your lessons long enough to see me off."

She glanced at the gathering crowd and gave him a cold smile and slight curtsey. She was, after all, a slave to appearances. "I would never let my beloved husband depart on such a long and dangerous journey without a proper farewell. Do take care, Mordecai. I would be inconsolable and emotionally destitute should you perish."

"I'm sure you would. But never fear for your welfare. I've left exacting instructions with my attorney, Mr. Peel. Should I not return, you'll be cared for in proper fashion."

Her tight expression revealed that she understood all too well what that meant. She would get to keep the house and receive a small allowance. Not nearly enough to support her many dalliances.

"Now if you'll excuse me, I must make ready to leave with the tide." Birch gave another small bow and returned to his ship.

⚓

"Can you see it?" Apple asked, his breath creating a fog around his head.

The captain raised the glass and scanned the ice field. The large arch was still there. "Aye Apple, I see it."

The boy whooped and yelled to the crew in Malagasy. They cheered and started singing. Birch smiled as the symbol on his hand tingled. At first he'd only felt another's presence when the Father mark woke him at night, then one day his son had spoken to him. In English.

During the last year he got to know his new son and realized that Honna had indeed given him what his heart desired. He just had to find a way to get back to them.

Are you close, Father?

"Aye, Mordi, I can see the arch. I'm coming."

I told Mother. She is very happy.

"I'm very happy too, son. I can't wait to see her and to meet you."

As they neared the arch, a thick swirling tail emerged from the clouds and the wind picked up.

"Steady at the helm," Birch said as the *Swan* fought her way through the ice, rising and falling in the white-laced swells.

"Steady helm! Steady as she goes," Apple yelled from the captain's right elbow.

Beneath the Sea of Tears
Patrick Thomas

"Feeding the fish again, Terrorbelle?" Saraid said. The roane wasn't bothering to hide her laughter. The corner of her right eye crinkled up under her eye patch. I debated about tweaking the patch, but worried she might push me overboard. Being half ogre, I sink quite nicely.

"They looked hungry," I managed to say before my stomach betrayed me again by heaving what little it still carried into the water.

"I would have figured you'd have got your sea legs by now."

"My legs are fine," I said. "I need a sea stomach. Ogres don't go to sea much. Too many swim like stones."

"You're only half ogre."

She was right. "My pixie half gives me my wings." The ogre blood made them tough and razor sharp. "Pixies swim all right in ponds, but waves tend to overwhelm them. We haven't all been raised in underwater sea caves. And being able to turn into a seal gives you a significant advantage on a water mission. It makes sense that Mab would send you. But picking me may have been a tactical error. Not that I'm questioning orders."

Mab took me into her army, trained me. Gave me a way to get back at the soldiers who killed my mother and raped me when I was eleven. Eventually I earned my way into the elite all-female Daemor. Not bad for a sixteen-year-old halfbreed.

Mab is the only person I'll take orders from easily.

"Mab doesn't make mistakes. Just ask her. Besides, maybe the fact that you can fly and probably lift my ship over your head are factors," the roane said.

I started to say I could only get airborne for short distances and might only be able to get one end of the ship up, but had to stop to make more fish food.

Saraid rolled her eyes and grabbed my hand. "Here, let me help." She pressed hard in the web between my thumb and index finger. The nausea started to lessen.

"You couldn't have done that earlier?"

"If I did, you wouldn't have had a chance to bond with the native sea life. Having you landies on *Tintreach* is a chore. Watch your aim. I don't want stomach flotsam on my decks."

"Don't you mean Mab's decks?"

"Nope. Old Lightning has been mine since I was a kid. Rescued her from the man who had chopped her down and made her a ship." Sentient trees don't take kindly to that, but their slavery is common. "She came with me when I enlisted to fight Thandau." Saraid scratched at her eye patch. "He destroyed my home, killed lots of my family. Damaged my skin."

Roane and selkie are very protective of their seal skins. They've been blackmailed into marriage by people holding the skins hostage. A roane without her skin would be as crippled as a pixie with no wings. Other Daemor have similar tales although Saraid told hers with more flair than most. I can't say for sure she was posing as she looked out over the sea, but she put one foot up, her right hand on her hip and the other on the sword that was strapped around her small waist. It certainly looked like she was waiting for someone to paint her portrait.

"*Tintreach* and I will build a new home when Thandau and his Destroyers are wiped from the face of Faerie. Until then we serve at Mab's pleasure."

And Mab's pleasure had sent us out to sea.

There are those in Faerie who consider women less than equals. Ironically, that thinking has saved many of our lives. Soldiers tend to slaughter the men and spare the women. The success of the Daemor has proved the folly of that attitude, but that doesn't mean it's been eliminated. We still have difficulty gaining allies, which is why we were heading for the underwater city, Cathair Uisce. They had managed to stay free, no small feat in these dark days.

I leaned over the side of the small ship and noticed the water was churning. "Saraid, are the fish looking for more?"

The roane looked over the bow and her face went pale. "*Tintreach*, move!" she screamed, drawing her sword. The ship obeyed her mistress, but it was too little too late.

Before her warning was finished, a serpentine head broke the water. It had jaws that could swallow me whole and I was no small fry. Saraid held her sword in front of her, but it was going to do as much good as a toothpick. The sea serpent lunged toward my fellow Daemor. The ship moved to protect her mistress, smacking the serpent with its hull.

I threw a bucket at the beast. "Over here, sea worm!"

The giant head snapped, locking its eyes on me. I had the monster's attention and I held no weapon. It thought I was the easier target and the tremendous jaws plunged straight at me. I dove flat on my stomach, just beneath its lower jaw. My wings shot up and bit into the soft flesh of the beast's throat. Next I moved to my feet, careful that my wings didn't pull away from the serpent's neck as I flipped over its back. At the peak of my jump I put my feet straight up. My weight helped my downward dive as my wings finished slicing a circle around the serpent's throat.

I landed on my hands, tucking and rolling away from the serpent's snapping jaws. When I spun to my feet I was facing the thing. Saraid had pulled a spear from an arsenal laid out along the sides of the deck. She leapt into the air and came down spear first onto the beast's snout, skewering the wood through the entire mouth and into the deck. The monster maw was pinned shut.

The serpent was dying and trying to take us with it. The body was thrashing in a last ditch attempt to sink *Tintreach*, but if we removed the spear the jaws might still get us. The little ship was fighting the monster, but the struggle could go either way.

The beast's head still held on to the rest of the scaly body by the spine. My wings hadn't been long enough to cut through the bone. Only our eyes spoke as we came up with a plan. Each of us grabbed a battleaxe from the onboard arsenal and took turns chopping. My swings caused more damage, but I packed more muscle.

When only a small piece of gristle was holding the serpent together, I grabbed hold of the upper part of the spine and put my boots on the lower. I pulled and was rewarded with a snap. I landed on my rear, but the serpent's body fell over the side and into the dark depths.

There were several moments of silence, the time after battle where you realize you're still alive and the rush leaves you tired and drained. It's one of the best feelings in the world.

"And I thought a sea voyage would be dull," I said. Saraid was inspecting the damage to the deck. Given time, the ship would actually heal herself. "Think it was eating my fish food?"

"Maybe it was attracted by the feeding fish, but I doubt it. Thandau has wizards who can control the serpents and send them out to destroy any ships that are without a protective amulet. This is the first I've encountered in these waters. Maybe our meeting in Cathair Uisce is worrying him."

"All the more reason to get there," I said. "Want me to throw the head over and feed the bigger fish?"

Saraid grinned. "I've got a much better idea. Something that'll make Thandau's ships think twice before attacking us." She told me her plan.

"I like it," I said. *Tintreach* seemed to as well, as the ship was rocking playfully. "At least until it starts to rot."

The roane ran below to the galley, returning with a preservative capsule. She slapped it on the beast's forehead and the liquid quickly enveloped the thing. "The meat will keep now."

We mounted the head on the bow, face out with the jaws propped open.

I took to the air and hovered in front. "It looks good."

Saraid stood on top of the beast's head and looked down. "It does, doesn't it?"

"Sends a message."

"Don't mess with me," she said.

"Most impressive," said a voice from within the waves. Below us a man floated, his torso suspended just above the water. "I trust you are the Daemor I was sent to meet?"

Saraid and I both pointed to the silver medallion with the black raven head that we each wore, then the matching emblem that flew on *Tintreach*'s flag. The badges were traditionally worn on the chest at the point directly below a Daemor's cleavage. It helped distract some men. The underwater city's emissary appeared to be one of them.

"Anyone could just wear a raven emblem," he said.

We both laughed. "Not if they wanted to keep on living," Saraid said. Mab has a death edict against anyone who falsely claims to be a Daemor. Otherwise, it would be far too easy for the enemy to discredit us through impersonation. Keeps the Daemor assassin Daye busy. "How do we know you are who you claim to be?"

"Mab's messenger said I was to show you this," he said, holding up a water-proof parchment.

I dove down and plucked it out of his hand, then flew back to the deck. It held Mab's seal. "It's good."

"May I come aboard?" he said.

Saraid leapt from the head to the deck. "You may for now." *Tintreach* was Saraid's home. Always best not to issue strangers unlimited visiting privileges. It can come back to bite you in most unpleasant places.

The waves rose in a miniature spout, lifting the man until he could walk directly onto the rail. "I am Stagnan."

"Nice trick with the waves," I said.

"I am an irragant, a water mage. There are many in my city who share my powers. It is what allows Cathair Uisce to prosper under the waves. Other than some small amounts of trade, we have remained safe because of our isolation and neutrality. Thandau's attacks on our trade ships and attempts to find us have caused us to reevaluate that policy."

"The enemy of my enemy . . ." Saraid said.

"You'll still have to convince King Trefor. I will bring you to my city, but there are certain conditions." Stagnan waved his hands from our heads to our boots, then pointed to a metal band on the roane's wrist. "No tracking charms."

"It's so I can find my ship," she said, leaving out that the ship could use it to find her as well.

"You will have to leave it onboard."

Saraid was not happy, but complied.

The irragant handed us a strip of fabric that had suckers similar to those of a squid. "You will both put these over your eyes."

"You want us to blindfold ourselves? That is an awful lot of trust you are asking us for," I said.

"And you wish to visit the hidden city. Trusting yourselves to me only puts the pair of you at risk. By allowing you into Cathair Uisce we risk the entire city. Our location must remain unknown to all outsiders, even those who would be our allies. It is non-negotiable."

Saraid and I looked at each other.

"Sorry, then I guess our trip was wasted," I said.

"Excuse me?" Stagnan's jaw actually dropped and I had to fight the urge to push it back up with my finger.

"With both of us blindfolded, we will be at your mercy. It is an unacceptable risk," Saraid said.

Stagnan was chewing his upper lip. "I was told to bring you."

Saraid grinned and slapped the mage on the shoulder, a gesture of familiarity his expression let us know he was not pleased with. "I have a solution. During the trip, we alternate being blindfolded. You choose the intervals at which we switch and the path we take. For a mage of your obvious skills, making sure we cannot find our way back should be child's play."

"I suppose that would be acceptable," he said with a sigh.

One thing was still bothering me. "What about an air supply?"

The mage reached into his bag and pulled out a bulbous creature with a single fleshy orifice. "This should suffice."

"What am I supposed to do with that?"

"You slip the symbiote over your mouth and nose. It will create a seal and take the air you exhale and make it breathable again."

"It looks disgusting," I said.

"But efficient. Unless you can hold your breath for a few hours?" Stagnan's grin was a trifle too sadistic for my tastes when he asked that.

"Fine," I said begrudgingly.

"Just be sure not to use one for more than half a day," he said.

"Why?"

"They have a tendency to start sucking out your life force with your breath after that amount of time."

"Wonderful," I said.

Stagnan offered one to Saraid.

"No thanks. I can handle my own air," she said. Part of the roane magic allowed them to stay underwater for almost a day on a single deep breath. Saraid opened an armored and locked utility pouch on her belt. The seal skin she pulled out looked too big to have come out of such a small pocket, but she had paid a mage handsomely to have the inside made larger than the outside. The roane slipped the hide on. Slipped on didn't quite cover it. The hide had no openings. It simply parted as her body touched it, melting onto her as if welcoming her home until she was transformed entirely into a seal. Except for her right arm. That stayed human from the damage Thandau's soldiers had done to her pelt. Her seal form had two eyes because her eye had been lost in human form.

"Why . . ." Stagnan said, staring at the human appendage.

I waved him to silence. "Best not to ask. Which of us gets the blindfold first?"

"The selkie."

Saraid barked at him and made an obscene hand gesture.

Stagnan looked at her. "Is there a problem?"

"She prefers roane," I said.

"Is there a difference?" he said as if answering yes would make us idiots.

It was a personal thing with Saraid. Roane are minor mages and can do much more than the average selkie, such as holding their breath so long.

I didn't like his attitude, and I tend to give attitude back. "Well, if your studies haven't told you the answer to that, I'm not about to explain it."

"You seek to lecture me?"

"Nope. I seek to help broker an agreement," I said, slipping on a pair of eyeglasses Mab had given to me. They molded to the skin around my eyes and were supposed to allow me to see well under water.

Next I put the symbiote creature over my mouth and nose. It practically sucked the air right out of my lungs. I was grateful I wasn't the first one with the blindfold. The breather was bad enough. With those suckers on my face, I would have felt like someone was attacking me.

Stagnan gestured with his hand. A wave rose and stood still next to the boat. The irragant stepped out onto it. "If you two are ready to join me, I will use my powers to take you to the city. I will also protect you from the pressure of the ocean depths."

Saraid barked, saying goodbye to her ship. *Tintreach* moved slightly as if acknowledging the farewell. The roane then jumped overboard.

"What did she say?" the mage said, his tone demanding.

I shrugged my shoulders. "I don't speak seal."

Mab had also given me a special belt that was designed to help buoy my density. Before I had gotten onboard *Tintreach*, I had put it at the level that would allow me to move through the water with the same ease as a fey with no ogre blood. I hadn't had a chance to test it, so I stepped out onto the water with more than a bit of trepidation.

The wave enveloped the three of us, pulling us beneath the surface of the ocean.

All my equipment seemed to be working well. Never having been this far under-water before, everything was new–light acted differently. When I wasn't blindfolded, my glasses allowed me to view all the wonders. I rarely saw fish, except on a plate. I never imagined they could move so gracefully, like dancers. I thought I was an expert in moving in three dimensions but most of the things beneath the waves had me beat.

Not everything down there qualified as fish, nor were they all friendly. While she was blindfolded, Saraid caught the scent of something that was stalking us. Ripping the suckers off her eyes, the roane ignored Stagnan's yells to cover. A moment later her human hand pointed at something easily the size of a dragon swimming toward us. Even with the glasses, the creature was so black it was hard to see except for the giant tentacles that it swam with.

My mind raced to come up with a way to fight a thing like that under the waves. Saraid raced toward me. With her small size, she could only swim with one passenger and she chose me, grabbing my hand with hers. She got us out of its path, then circled back to try to come up beneath it. Before we could try anything suicidal, Stagnan's hands glowed and the water in front of him spun like a liquid tornado. The monstrosity swirled so fast that when it stopped it couldn't even swim straight. The irragant waved his arms and the current caught the creature and smashed it into the ocean floor. It didn't move.

We swam back toward the water mage.

"Nicely done," I said, my voice muffled by both the symbiote and water.

Stagnan stared at me as if he wasn't used to getting compliments, but he managed to say "Thank you."

Over the following hours, the irragant switched the blindfold between us several times. I was wearing it when I thought the pressure was making me hear ringing in my ears, but the sound became louder as vibrations resounded through my body. The bells distracted me so I wasn't expecting it when Stagnan ripped the blindfold off my face, the sucker pealing nicely from the lens. From my skin, not so much. The salt water stung the hickey marks it left behind. I could hear the teasing now if they weren't gone by the time I had to report back.

We came over a sea floor hill and suddenly the city was there, huge silver towers springing out of the depths. I was expecting a small settlement. This was one of the largest cities I had ever seen. The main section was surrounded by a giant bubble filled with air. On the outskirts, there were farms with kelp and other vegetables, as well as hundreds of beds of clams and oysters being raised for food. There were several fishing parties hard at work, swimming with nets.

We were spotted as soon as we cleared the rise. A dozen armed troops came to meet us. Amongst them, were several land-breathers with symbiotes and two selkies. Introductions were made. They were led by a merman named Strongfin. The selkies began to whisper and laugh among themselves when they saw Saraid. I may not have spoken seal, but my fellow Daemor did. I didn't need to understand the words to know what was being said. Saraid's human hand opened and closed into a fist, but she remained silent.

I didn't. Two quick strokes of my wings brought me face-to-face with the merman. "Excuse me, Strongfin." I was practically shouting to make sure I was heard through the breather and ocean between us. "You are the leader of these guards?"

"Yes I am, pretty wing," the merman said, hitting on me for the benefit of his men. Things must be hard for the underwater set. I noticed his gills stopped moving when he spoke, probably using that air for the words.

"You are unable to control those under your command?" I said.

His scales darkened. "What makes you say that?"

"Those two selkie—" the pair did not appear offended so I assumed they were not roane "—are mocking my companion. So either you cannot control them or you do not value their lives very highly."

The selkies stopped and stared. The merman's head tilted in confusion.

"Saraid is a Daemor. I assume even under here you know what that means."

The merman began to look nervous. "Yes."

"Excellent. So when can we schedule the death match?"

"Excuse me?" Strongfin said. The selkie began franticly thrashing their tails.

"Her injury was earned fighting the tyrant Thandau. They mock a badge of honor, therefore they mock her honor. I command this mission and I cannot let such an insult go unanswered," I said. "We'll allow enough time for them to get their personal affairs in order. We can arrange for her to fight them individually or together. I'd recommend together because after the first death, the second would be allowed to beg for her mercy. She might leave you with the one."

"I'm sure no such insult was meant," the merman said.

"Nevertheless it was given," I said, extending my wings to their fullest. It was impossible to miss the sharp edges, even underwater.

Strongfin leaned in and smiled rather weakly. "Perhaps if they apologized?"

"It would have to be a very impressive apology."

Suddenly the smile was gone, replaced with a snarl. With a single snap of his tail, Strongfin was in the seals' faces screaming at them to apologize to Saraid as if their lives depended on it. The seal soldiers saluted and swam toward the roane and proceeded to do much groveling.

"Is that acceptable?" Strongfin said.

I looked at Saraid. She looked at the two males at her feet and held their eyes. They whimpered. She turned back to me and nodded.

"I return their lives to you. I trust you will have your troops exercise more respect," I said.

"It will not be an issue," Strongfin promised.

Stagnan rolled his eyes as if he was being forced to tolerate unruly children. "If the posturing is done, can we go inside?"

The troops escorted us to the edge of the bubble, but we were a good twenty feet from the ground. Nobody seemed inclined to mention to us that we should be lower, Stagnan included. He went in first, a bridge of sea water carrying him through the wall and inside the dome. Saraid and I exchanged a look. The roane swam to me, grasped her right hand in mine. She swam us through the remainder of the water at increased speed so we hit the air moving fast. Then I took over with my wings, lowering us slowly to the ground. When we were a few feet from touching, Saraid slipped out of her skin, and her human feet touched the ground. I ripped the symbiote off my face. Air never tasted so sweet. We turned to the guards that had escorted us, still on the water side. We each gave a showy bow and turned to follow Stagnan. No mention was made of his failure to warn us of the drop. Diplomacy at work.

Stagnan showed us to our rooms, perplexed by our desire to share quarters. The idiot actually asked if we were a couple, not bothering to think we did it for safety's sake. Too many people have had their throats slit when sleeping comfortably in guest quarters.

Once we were alone, Saraid spoke up. "Razorwing . . ." My nickname for obvious reasons. "Thanks for earlier."

"My pleasure. I've been through it." Being half pixie, half ogre, I didn't fit in either culture, although I tried in both. I'd endured more than my share of cruelty. "I wasn't going to stand idly by while it was done to you."

"The groveling was a great touch," she said. I agreed.

Our audience was scheduled for the next morning. They brought us trays of food, but we played it safe and ate the field rations we had brought with us. The bells never stopped ringing the entire night.

I took first watch, which meant I was sleeping when they came to announce it was almost time for our audience.

The palace was as impressive as any I'd ever seen. Twenty armed men escorted us under the pretense of an honor guard, but we knew we had simply made them nervous yesterday. We were ushered right into the throne room to a standing room only crowd. On the dais were three thrones. In the center was the largest, where King Trefor sat. To his left, Queen Gleda. The smallest throne was next over. In it sat Princess Dylane, a young woman a few years older than me.

To the King's right on the dais sat a line of mages, clothed in various shades of blue and green. Each wore the image of a whirlpool—including the royal family—marking them as irragants. Stagnan was third from the King. High ranking, but not top fish.

There were scores of others who could have been royalty, merchants, or party crashers.

King Trefor spoke as soon as he saw us. "Honored Daemor, please approach."

The man didn't bother with a herald. Spoke well of him. We walked to the base of the dais, then saluted by pressing our fist unto our chests where we wore our badges.

We got a half smile from Trefor, but a scowl from his wife.

"Tradition dictates bowing before royalty," Queen Gleda said.

"Tradition also rarely allows for woman warriors," I said. "Daemor bow before no one. We honor your majesties with a salute."

Gleda's scowl darkened. "I think—"

"That is acceptable," Trefor said. "You are here to discuss an alliance between the Gwragedd Annwn of Cathair Uisce and Queen Mab."

"We are, Your Majesty," Saraid said.

"What are you hoping to gain from us?" the King said.

"Troops, food, and perhaps even a safe haven to house the survivors of many of the rulings houses the tyrant has displaced," I said.

"Even if those troops are unruly, needing constant challenges to death matches?" the King said with a sly grin.

"I can assure you that after a very short time in Mab's army, control will not be an issue," I said. "Nor will there be any issue of soldiers insulting visiting dignitaries or causing a diplomatic rift."

"I'm glad to hear that," Trefor said.

"What would you like from us?" Saraid said.

"Training for our troops in Mab's fighting techniques, but done here, not on land. Escorts for our trading vessels. Favored trading status with Mab and her other allies. That is for a start."

"I think all of that is well within our power to negotiate, depending on what numbers you were thinking of for your favored status," I said.

"Excellent. There is one other matter. I would like Mab to take my daughter Dylane into her army and train her." The room filled with murmurs.

"My baby?" Gleda screamed. "I won't hear of it."

"Mother, I already told father it was fine. I would like to be a Daemor," Dylane said, sticking out her chest. If I was a male, I might be impressed.

"Becoming a Daemor is something earned, not given. I'm sure in time there is a chance of you becoming a Daemor," I said.

"I don't think you understand." The princess pointed her finger at me and it wagged with each syllable. "My father is making my being made a Daemor a condition of this alliance." Finished setting lowly me straight, she tossed her long hair over her shoulder and turned away. I was not even worthy of her.

Before I could explain that this would never be an option, the king spoke again. "Taking Dylane into the regular army will be acceptable."

"Daddy!"

"Trefor!"

The King lifted a hand for silence and got it. "The rest of what I have to say will be done in private, between them and I. Ladies, if you will please join me." Trefor stood and motioned us toward a door behind the thrones.

One of a pair of guards who stood by the door became agitated. "Your Majesty, I must protest. To take outsiders in there alone without protection—"

"Nonsense. In there I am more powerful than any other place in the city."

"Your Majesty." The guard bowed and opened the door.

I expected a gilded room. Instead there was the largest spell gem I have ever seen. It was wide at the bottom, and rose to a point, much like the spires in the city. And it was active. A beam of energy shot up toward an opening in the ceiling, becoming invisible before it reached the clear sky inside the bubble.

"Wow," I said.

"Impressive, isn't it?"

"Very." Saraid said. "This is the source of the bubble surrounding the city?"

"Yes, and it keeps us beneath the water. Cathair Uisce is able to be moved, but when Thandau began his attacks, we found the most inhospitable place within the oceans to hide ourselves."

"Then why the constant bell ringing?" I said. "It seems to announce your presence."

"To keep away the *shoryobuni*."

Saraid gasped. "Soul ships? You hid your city in the north of the Sea of Tears?"

"Very good, roane. Yes, we did. Our city cannot be reached above the waves by boat or air. The shoryobuni see to that. Of course, without the bells to drive them away, we would not be able to surface to our fleet. In fact, they would all be sunk. Each ship has a single bell which is charged from the power of the gem and allows them to ward off the soul ships. Only the captain can activate it, so even if they are taken, they cannot be used against us."

"I must confess to an ignorance of shoryobuni," I said.

Saraid smiled and slapped me on the shoulder. "Nice to hear a landie admit her ignorance. Shoryobuni are the reason even Thandau's navy is afraid of coming here: soul ships traveling through the worlds collecting spirits of the dead. Many take up residence in the north-most reaches of the Sea of Tears. They sink any ship they can catch. The only way to get away is to flee while they attack another ship or to distract them with gifts. The best is a token of contradiction, a bucket without a bottom or a candle without a wick. For some reason it confounds them. But each gift only stops one attack and they will not accept two of the same gifts during the same assault."

"And so far," the King said, "Thandau hasn't been willing to sacrifice the number of ships he'd lose if he tried to gain our spell gem. Not that it would do him much good. It's keyed to my bloodline, so he'd have to sacrifice most of its power to be able to use it. We have many underwater traps to prevent submerged attacks, which is why I sent Stagnan to bring you in."

"Your trust in sharing this shall be noted to Mab," Saraid said.

"I believe one has to give trust to get it in return, so I will tell you the reason why I wish Dylane to join Mab's army. My daughter has the potential to become as powerful an irragant as I and an even better ruler. Sadly, her mother has overindulged her and I have allowed it. I had assumed I would be able to undo the influence, but was wrong. The next ruler of Cathair Uisce is a spoiled brat and that will spell destruction for the city I love. I have heard tales of the Daemor and I think that the training will make a woman out of her."

I opened my mouth to speak, but he waved me to silence.

"I already knew that Dylane would have to earn a place as a Daemor, assuming she can. I would have it no other way. Either she will rise to the challenge or I shall have to be sure to never die. I may try anyway." In Faerie it was not uncommon to live hundreds of years, if not longer. Those with power seem to go the longer route. "Can you speak for Mab in this?"

"We can," I said.

"Excellent. Please let her know I want my daughter accorded no special treatment. In fact, Mab may have to be harder on her than those who don't assume they're entitled to be given everything on a pearl platter."

"It won't be an issue," Saraid said.

We spent the better part of the next week negotiating the finer parts of the treaty. In our off time, we began running drills with the local troops. They did well. I handled

the land-based exercises and Saraid the water ones. The pair of selkie who had originally mocked Saraid took well to her training once they saw what she could do, as did
the other aquatic soldiers. They soon saw the advantages of a seal having a human hand
when it came to combat and weapons training.

Unfortunately, some idiot came up with the bright idea of beginning the princess's training early. That idiot's name happened to be Terrorbelle. The princess may
have filled out a gown well enough to make men stare, but that hardly meant she
was in good shape. Within the first twenty minutes of calisthenics she was breathing
heavy and whining hard.

"I don't see why I have to do this. I'm a princess." Dylane cocked her head to one
side and put both hands on her hips, pouting. It may have worked on her parents, but
it only annoyed me. "Princesses don't fight."

"When you are on the battleline, I'm sure you can tell the enemy that and they will
just give you a free pass instead of running you through."

"You don't have to be snippy about it," the princess said with a roll of her eyes
and a smirk.

I wanted to wipe the expression off her face.

"You read the fine print and still signed your name on the dotted line. It doesn't
matter if you were a princess or a peasant before, soldier. From the moment the
ink dried you've been a tyro, a lowly grunt who I have the poor luck to have under
my command. You disobey me and I'll make your life so miserable you'll hate your
mamma for not having a headache on the night you were conceived."

"You think I'm going to take this sort of treatment? I'm telling Mab on you. I'm
going to tell my Daddy." she smiled as if she had won something.

"Drop and give me fifty," I said.

"And if I refuse?" she said, trying for snide. She might have pulled it off if her voice
hadn't cracked.

I moved my face close enough to hers that the tips of our noses nearly touched. My
smile was dark and I hoped scary. "I'm sure you'll be able to walk again in a week or so."

Dylane tried to outstare me but she never had to stand up to someone who wasn't
subservient to her, including her parents. I've been beaten, stabbed, and worse. It wasn't
much of a contest. I ended it by yelling "Boo!"

Dylane fell over backwards and landed on her padded rump. I stepped forward
as the princess walked backwards like a crab, a terrified look on her face. Dylane
had finally figured out this wasn't a game. I probably shouldn't have laughed at the
girl's fear, but I did.

Princesses don't get laughed at. Anger joined with fear and desperation. Her hands
waved, causing the water from two nearby fountains to spout into the air. The floating pools took up positions on either side of me. The penalties for attacking a Daemor
were severe, and usually left up to the Daemor's discretion.

My body never twitched but my wings moved faster than Dylane could follow.
My upper set was at her throat and my lower at her wrists.

"That water goes anywhere but back in those fountains, and I'll move some fluids of my own. Attacking a superior officer in times of war is punishable by death," I said, watching her eyes widen. "Don't make me hurt you. Am I clear, Tyro Dylane?"

"Yeah," she said and the water returned to the fountains.

"That's yes, Daemor."

"Yes, Daemor."

"You could have not joined." I had stressed that option before I let her sign the contract. "Now it's two hundred. Get going." Princess collapsed after eight. I got in her face and she did indeed finish the two hundred pushups, whining about how much her arms hurt. I told her if I heard another complaint, she'd regret it. Sure enough, a few moments later she complained.

I took her to the palace kitchens. They were preparing a large meal and had a pile of some sort of underwater tuber. I informed the princess she now had to peal the entire lot. I told the head chef that she was to have no help and left the kitchens. I didn't go far. I had spent more than my share of time doing KP, a military tactic Mab learned during her brief exile on Earth. I knew that if left alone, a soldier will do their best to get out of it. And when I made her mop floors the day before, I caught her using her powers. I wanted to see what Princess Dylane would try this time.

A few moments later I snuck back in. Every girl in the kitchen was pealing tubers furiously. Every one that is, except the princess who was sitting in a chair. The head chef was doting on her, plying her favor with pastries and a cold drink.

I smiled, then put on my angry face. "What in the seven hells is happening here?" All of the girls jumped. Several dropped their knives. "All of you, move away from those vegetables, now."

The girls obeyed, but the chef put his hands on the sides of his ample belly and stormed over toward me "Now see here, this is my kitchen and I told those girls to do that."

"You did, did you?" I said.

"You have no right to be ordering the princess around," the chef said, getting up in my face. It was a mistake.

I yelled loud enough to make plates shake. "Is that so?" I turned to the assistants. "Hear this. Every last one of you now has the day off. Any one returning here will be locked up. Now get out!"

"Anyone who leaves is fired. And I will make sure you do not work again," the chef said. The staff stood still and the chef smirked at me. "As I said, this is my kitchen and I am in charge here."

There was a fish on a counter that would have come up to my chin if it could stand. I stepped toward it and moved my upper wings over my shoulders. They buzzed faster than any cook could hope to move a knife. In seconds, I reduced the entire thing to bite-sized pieces.

"Correction—you were in charge until you interfered with a military matter. Now everyone here answers to me. Anybody still here by the time I count five will have me personally take them into custody. I'm not gentle by nature. One . . ." The last staffer was gone by four.

"You can't do that!" The chef's face was crimson.

"I guess you weren't paying attention because I already did it. You interfered with the training of my tyro and I can't permit that."

"I'll tell the King!"

I shrugged. "King Trefor has told me I have his full support. How do you think he will react when I tell him what you've done?"

"He'll thank me?"

At my chuckle, his shoulders slumped and his belly sank down. "More likely you'll be the one fired," I said.

"I doubt he'll be happy when his noon meal is not ready in time."

"That's your problem, not mine. And don't forget his evening dinner with all those guests."

"It's impossible. You sent away more than a dozen people. I can't do all that work myself!"

"You don't have to," I said, "you have Tyro Dylane."

"The princess?"

"No, the tyro. Have her do everything you need." I leaned in close to whisper in his ear. "You don't strike me as a kind boss. You will treat my tyro the same way you would the lowest of your staff. If I even suspect you are going the slightest bit easy on her . . ."

I'm not a violent person by nature, but by the end of that conversation the chef was convinced I was. It took him a while, but he started ordering the princess around like she was the hired help. I stayed and made sure she did everything she was told. A couple of times the chef whispered in her ear and Dylane responded with a giggle as they tried not to look in my direction. A glare was enough to put a stop to it.

In the last hours, it looked like dinner wasn't going to be done in time, so I pitched in. We made it, but barely. When it was done, Dylane was exhausted. "What now?" she said, assuming I had more for her to do, but there was already the smallest change in her.

"How do you feel?" I said.

"Tired."

"Anything else?"

Dylane looked at me, her brow creased. She looked back across all the food that was ready to be served. "Good I guess."

I smiled. "Amazing the satisfaction a little hard work will give you. You have a dinner to attend so you best go get dressed. Hurry, you don't have much time," I said. Dylane turned to go. "One more thing Tyro."

"Yes, Daemor?"

"You did well."

"Thank you, Daemor," she said and actually saluted me before she ran off. I waved to the chef before I left, but he glared and started chopping up something that didn't need to be cut. Odd, considering everything for the meal was already prepared.

At the dinner, Dylane was seated to one side of her father, Saraid and I on the other. The Queen was down the table seated next to Stagnan.

The King was very interested in his daughter's progress and asked her how things were going. The princess blanched since I was seated near enough to contradict her on any untruths.

"Well, I suppose things are going fairly," Dylane started, staring down at her plate which the chef had just put in front of her. Next came Trefor's, mine, then Saraid's. The roane started to eat, but I caught her hand and shook my head. I had a sneaking suspicion the chef made something special and unpleasant for me.

I spoke up. "Nonsense." Dylane's pale face went crimson and she glared at me. "Your daughter did quite well today. In fact, she is in large part responsible for this feast."

"And how does preparing a meal help one become a soldier?"

"Discipline and versatility," I said. "Your daughter shows great promise. We gave the entire kitchen staff the day off and your daughter did the work of a dozen people. Not an easy task for someone who knows their way around the kitchen. Dylane did not. Which makes her accomplishment all the more impressive."

"Then I shall have to try everything." The King smiled at his daughter whose eyes beamed with obvious pride.

I offered him my plate. "Please start with mine."

The chef practically tripped over himself pulling the food away from his king.

Trefor gave him a look.

"Sorry, Your Majesty. I brought the wrong plate for the Daemor. I'll get the correct one right away."

I picked up Saraid's plate and handed it to the chef and let my wings buzz slightly. Our eyes met and I knew we had an understanding. There would be nothing bad in the food he brought back.

The rest of the meal went well. It was during the after-dinner entertainment that things got interesting. There were musicians playing when Stagnan approached the King. "Majesty, might I speak to you in private for a moment?"

"Of course, Stagnan. If you will excuse me."

Saraid and I stood as the pair withdrew to the gem room.

"Why didn't you tell my father about my behavior?" Dylane whispered.

"You're in Mab's army, same as us," I said. "We take care of our own. If there is a problem, we will deal with it, not go running to tattle about it."

The princess began to nod just as her father's screams eminated from the gem room.

The guards at the door got inside before Saraid and me, but only barely. Dylane was right on our heels. Things were bad. Trefor had been stabbed in the gut. Two guards were encased in water and couldn't move. Fortunately, they were both water breathers and wouldn't drown, but they couldn't help us. Stagnan stood, holding the giant spell gem in his hands, a bloody dagger by his feet.

"You're too late Daemor," Stagnan said. "Thandau will have his spell gem."

"Stagnan, it's useless to you. Only one of the bloodline can use it," Dylane said.

Saraid cradled the King and slapped a battlepatch on him. It would help stop the bleeding and seal the wound until a healer could get to him.

"Oh, I found a way around that," Stagnan said, lifting one hand off the gem. It was sticky with the King's blood. "A simple spell brought his blood into my hands and bonded it there forever."

I darted through the air toward the traitor. The fountain's contents rose up, wrapping itself around my head in a liquid helmet, holding me in the air, my feet dangling. I had managed to take a deep breath first, but I didn't know how long it would be before I had to inhale water. Saraid was in a similar predicament

We hadn't been allowed weapons sitting so near the King, but we hadn't worried over much. I would have killed to have brought a table knife or even a fork with me. I could have ended the irragant with a single throw. I tried to use my wings to fly myself closer, but one wave of his hand stopped me cold.

"Let them go," the princess said, her fists balled up and her jaw clenched. Every inch of her demanded to be obeyed, but the traitor was having none of it.

"I think not," said Stagnan. "Dylane, you do not have to share their fate. Marrying you would help legitimize my claim to the throne."

"I won't consider it unless you spare my parents," she said.

"I can't leave anyone alive that could have a claim on my throne, so your parents are as good as dead. If you refuse my offer, I'll have no choice but to kill you as well. Certainly marriage to me is hardly a fate worse than death?"

There was a moment of silence and contemplation before Dylane spoke and moved toward him. "I don't want to die and I've always thought you were a handsome man, but I won't be some figurehead queen. I want real power too."

"If you are willing to go out there right now and announce our betrothal, we can discuss matters later." Stagnan extended a hand. "Agreed?"

Dylane took his hand. I can't begin to express my disappointment with the princess at that moment, but it was short lived. Her other hand reached out and grabbed the point at the top of the crystal. A moment later, the water released us and we tumbled to the ground.

I wheezed, gasped for air. Saraid wasn't even winded and rushed Stagnan as soon as she hit the floor, but he maneuvered the princess between her and him.

"You dare betray me?" Stagnan shouted, trying to put the spell gem away, but Dylane had too good a grip. She tried to pull it back, but wasn't as strong as the bigger man, so she kneed him in the crotch. The mage crumbled to the floor, cursing. A second later pressure made my ears pop. I looked up through the open ceiling to see the entire ocean crashing down over our heads.

I flew at Stagnan, but he stood and smashed me in the head with the gem. I saw stars for a moment, but people always say I have a hard head. The spell gem split where it hit me. Stagnan got the larger piece, Dylane the smaller spire-shaped one. The traitor enveloped himself with water from the fountain before floating out through the roof.

Dylane dropped to her knees, muttering a spell and clutching the fragment of the gem that remained. I was still stunned, but Saraid pulled out the fresh symbiote that was in a pouch on my belt and put it over my face, all the while changing into her seal skin.

Moments later the water came crashing into the room, smashing me against a wall. This time my head wasn't hard enough and I blacked out.

⚓

When I came to, I was still in the gem room, but I could see sky through the ceiling. The symbiote was no longer on my face. I blinked my eyes and muttered, "How?"

"Dylane raised the entire city," Saraid said, back in her human form. "Are you okay?"

"I've been better," I said, pulling myself to my feet. "You?"

"You took most of the impact. I'm fine."

"That explains why I'm extra sore. The King and Dylane?"

"Turns out the immersion in water helped him. The surgeons and healers are with him now. Dylane's over there." The roane pointed to the other side of the room.

I moved toward the princess who was pale, but conscious. "Dylane, are you all right?"

"Yes," she said, but when she tried to stand she tumbled back down. I caught her before she hit the floor.

"How'd you mange to move the entire city?"

"My father has let me adjust the bubble and move the city ever since I was little. He wanted to make sure I could do it when my time came. The air rushed to the surface and there wasn't enough power to hold back the water and draw more air down so I had to raise the city," she said. "I can barely move."

"You did good," I said. "I'm proud of you."

The princess practically beamed. Then I noticed the quiet.

"What happened to the bells?"

"Stagnan must have used the gem to stop them," Dylane said, trying to take some steps. She failed. Twice. "We have to stop him. Otherwise the shoryobuni will attack and sink the city. Without an air bubble, thousands will die."

"We will Dylane. What I need you to do is rest. We're probably going to need an irragant and with the King down, you're the strongest. I need you to rest and gather as much power as you can and be ready."

"Yes, Daemor," she said.

I couldn't help but smile. I picked up Saraid and flew toward the opening. I turned in midair. "And Tyro, if you keep doing what you did here today, someday you will make a damn fine Daemor and an even better queen."

I headed out into the city. Wounded were everywhere. There were hundreds of bodies floating on the surface. Not all of them were dead, but the shoryobuni were closing in from all directions. The masts were made from bones and the sails looked like ragged, leathery flesh. Dark mist swirled around the ships like tangible shadows. Each shoryobuni carried a skull on its bow, the eyes of which glowed, cutting through the gloom. I could barely make out figures on the decks, glad that mist obscured the details. I wanted nothing more than to curl up into a ball and hide. I didn't need to feel the warmth pouring out from the protection amulet in my Daemor badge to realize dark magic was at work.

"Get me over the water. I'll gather the survivors," Saraid said.

"By yourself? Even you can't swim that fast or carry that many."

"I won't be by myself. I sent for reinforcements." She pointed to the horizon where a small ship with a sea serpent head on its bow was moving like lightning toward us.

"Is that *Tintreach*?"

"Yep."

"How'd you signal her? Stagnan searched you."

"As a woman, not as a seal," she said. "I have amulets in both skins."

"You have bottomless buckets and wickless candles?"

"Nope, but the soul ships can't sink what they can't catch," Saraid said, pulling out her second skin. "Drop me in that open water there."

By the time I flew to where she had indicated, she was already a seal. Saraid dove out of my arms and into the water. Within moments, she had a survivor in her human hand and was swimming toward *Tintreach*.

I hovered, looking for Stagnan or something to use against the soul ships. The city's ships were secured to a series of floating docks. Alone, I'd never be able to get one of them sailing, let alone all of them. And without tokens of contradiction they'd only get sunk. Except I realized they traveled the Sea of Tears safely all the time. Suddenly I had a plan. I dove down onto one of the ships and tore its silver bell, along with its tiny belfry, from its mast and flew back to Dylane.

"Can you activate this bell?" I said, figuring the royal bloodline could do what a ship's captain could.

"Yes," she said touching it. It began to toll of its own accord.

"Come with me. I need you to start the bells on all the ships and use them to surround the city," I said. Moments later, I had the princess on the deck of the largest ship and she had its bell ringing a second after she touched it.

Strongfin and the two selkie joined us on deck.

"Strongfin, I need you to get this to Saraid's ship," I said, holding the bell I had ripped free.

"Daemor, I must protect the princess and I do not take orders from you," the merman said.

"Excuse me, guardsman?" the princess yelled, doing a pretty good imitation of me. "You will obey the Daemor Terrorbelle in all things. With my father unconscious, I am in charge and I turn over command of our military to her leadership. Am I clear?"

The merman bowed, practically groveling. "Yes, Princess."

"Get up," I said. "There will be plenty of time later to bow if Thandau comes to take your city. Get this bell to Daemor Saraid's ship and then obey and assist her in her rescue mission. Understood?"

"Yes, maim," he barked.

I handed him the bell. "Then go."

I turned to the selkie pair. "Who's faster?" The seal on the left pointed to the seal on the right. "Fine, you are to go back to the city and get enough crews for these ships. Bring any captains you find to help get the bells ringing. Then move them around the city to hold off the soul ships. Pick up any survivors along the way. Go!" I shouted. He dove overboard. I turned to the remaining seal. "You will escort the princess as she goes from ship to ship. Keep her safe or you will answer to me, understood?"

The selkie became an armed man holding a seal skin. "Yes, maim."

I turned to Dylane. "I'm going after Stagnan. Any suggestions where he'd be?"

"He would be with the remaining spell gem," the princess said, closing her eyes and holding the gem fragment close to her chest. "It's in there," she said, pointing to the tallest tower in the city, "the university where irrigants are trained." She looked at me. "Let me go with you. He's powerful even without the gem."

"Against one Daemor, he'll need it to even things out," I said with a bravado I didn't feel. I armed myself with three spears, an axe, as many daggers as I could stash in my uniform, and a sword from the ship's armory. "If I can't stop him, it will be up to you, Dylane. Rest as long as you can."

"Good luck," she said.

"You too," I said and took off into the sky. On the way, I fastened my water glasses and the symbiote. Stagnan would be hitting me with water-based attacks and I wanted to limit my vulnerability. My enemy had the high ground and the gem, which gave him two advantages. I was a Daemor. It had been enough in the past, hopefully it would be enough now.

A sneak attack was doubtful, even if I came up through the building. If he was watching, he'd know I was coming. Best to get in quick.

I wasn't fast enough. The traitor came out to greet me, kept aloft on a pool of water. I threw my first spear, followed quickly by my second. The water he commanded moved like it was a living thing, blocking both spears. Hoping to overwhelm the irragant I sent three daggers at his heart. The water deflected all three but not well enough to stop them all. The third bit into the flesh in his leg.

The irragant had stopped moving. I hadn't. Being stationary in most battles is bad, in an airborne one even more so. I used my last spear as a lance and got the mage in the side. He cried out in pain and engulfed me in water, the liquid pulling the spear from my hands. The fluid stopped me from flying. Stagnan dragged me out over open water. I started beating my wings. At first it felt as if I was struggling through a pool of honey, but I kept at it and my wings moved faster. Slowly, I began to toss off the water, giving me more maneuverability. I got closer, planning to use the axe. Stagnan used the opportunity to put his hand on my symbiote. Suddenly it was withering and draining the air from my lungs.

Stagnan held the spell gem between his left elbow and side. I chopped the axe toward his face. He reacted as I expected, thickening the water there to stop the blade, but it was just a feint. My real attack had been to bring my feet up and kick as hard as I could. The blow knocked the gem free of his grip. A second and a third kick sent it out of the water cocoon around us, plummeting toward the ocean below. Without the extra power, he couldn't stop the next axe swing that took him at the neck. The water quickly turned red. Before I passed out, I realized we were falling, following the gem into the Sea of Tears. My watery world went black.

———————⚓———————

I woke this time in a bed. Things had gone well. The ships' bells had held off the shoryobuni and allowed Saraid and the others time to rescue the water-logged survivors. My fellow Daemor and Strongfin had recovered the spell gem after the merman had saved me. Dylane used it to restart the tower bells. The King would recover in time, as would the city, with some aid from Mab.

There was no sign of Stagnan anywhere. If he survived he'd be hiding from both sides. Thandau doesn't like those who fail him.

Once Trefor was able, we left with Dylane to a heroes' sendoff. We also received commendations from Mab. Dylane got thrown into training. She told me her new commander is much nicer than me. All things considered, I can live with that.

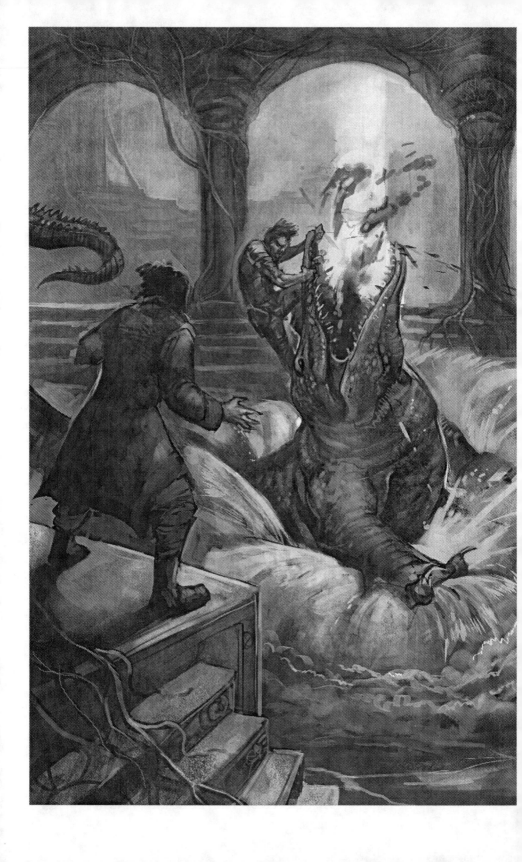

The Second Voyage of the Stormreaver's Blade
Jordan Lapp

It is the Year of Our Lord 1690. I am an officer on the *Stormreaver's Blade*. The captain has bid me join him on the bridge, and though I've detested him for every moment of the three years that I've laboured under this curse, I dare not disobey. Outside, the Eternal Storm rages; but every churning wave, every howling wind, is but the palest reflection of the anger that lurks in the depths of its master's cold blue eyes. Only one glimmer of hope remains in me: that we might one day regain the Bag of Winds and at last find the rest that has been so long denied us. I pray the Lord this might one day be so.

---⚓---

I shall begin my story on the beaches of Mud Shark Atoll. I stood with Captain Mastiff under the boughs of a palm, though its use as shelter was cast in doubt by the great runnels of rainwater that ran between its leaves. There wasn't a man amongst us whose jerkin wasn't clinging to his chest.

My man Duncan waited with Mastiff's crew on the shores for the jolly boat to beach. Our own longboat was already pulled well beyond the tide's reach, but Mastiff had ordered nearly half his crew ashore. He trusted neither my assurances, nor Duncan's honour pledge, that no treachery should befall his men whilst young Lady Chelsea remained unharmed.

Ah, Duncan! Now there was a man! I can see him still, moving amongst Mastiff's crew like a hound amongst mongrels and mutts. I found him on the docks of Havana, in the days when that town still built walls to keep the natives out at night. He was dressed in the beaded necklaces and feathered earrings of the island people though his pale skin and European name marked him as Anglo Saxon. Even in the ridiculous raiment of the heathens, he radiated menace. What kind of life must he have led to so reek of violence? Not a man on the docks would challenge him, though he stood still as a rock amidst all their crates and barrels.

I knew at once that our fates were intertwined, this killer and I, and he knew it also. When I offered him a job, he nodded as if he had known to wait on that precise spot for my arrival.

He worked with Mastiff's men to pull the jolly boat ashore, slinging a length of hemp as thick as his wrist over his shoulder and pulling with the pirates until it lay next to the longboat.

I wonder now, as I tell my story, if I shouldn't have started it with the girl who stepped out of the jolly boat and into the arms of a dozen men who'd commit atrocities upon her body that you or I could no more conceive of than we could bite off our own arm. Pirates all, they had slavered cross the bosoms of finer women than she. Though she must have known it, she descended into their midst like a Lady receiving suitors. Her regal demeanour was her defence against fear.

When I first laid eyes on the youngest daughter of Franklin, Lord Chelsea, Governor of Surinam, I am ashamed to admit that I saw only gold. Lord Chelsea had offered reward enough for the rescue of his kidnapped daughter to send every sea captain in the Caribbean after Mastiff's accursed ship, but only I had found it.

What Duncan saw I cannot say, save that when he pushed his way through the crowd of men and looked upon her, it struck him dumb. He stood before her, unmoving, heedless of the driving rain that ran in rivulets down his cheeks. An ordinary woman would have wilted under the stare he gave her, but something unspoken passed between them that my scientific mind cannot grasp. Suffice it to say that for the rest of the time I knew them they were never more than an arm's length apart, save for when we battled the Guardian of the Well of Winds.

Mastiff grunted, interrupting my thoughts. "I had thought that opening the Bag of Winds would make me Lord of the Caribbean, but now that we are so close to gathering the winds back into its leathery folds, I find I cannot wait to be rid of this storm. It granted me life eternal, but I find myself yearning for sight of the sun. "

"What good is immortality if you must spend it soaking wet?" I asked.

He laughed and slapped me on the back. "Truly. Had I known that snatching Lord Chelsea's whelp would bring you to my ship I would have done it twenty years ago. In my youth, I thought the Eternal Storm a small price to pay for eternal life, but eighty years of foul weather begins to grate."

He turned to the jungle. In the distance, lightning illuminated twin mountain peaks in bursts of white light. In the cleft between those giants lay the Well of Winds, the only place where the winds could be recaptured. "It will take twenty men two days to cut their way to the Well. I haven't seen jungles this thick since I sailed the Yucatan coast as a boy."

After the first day I began to curse whatever nameless cartographer had labelled the island "Mud Shark Atoll." It wasn't an atoll at all. It was a mass of twisted vines and stunted jungle trees that clung to the sides of the two great mountains at its center. A hell the like of which would make the darkest Congo jungle look like the fields of Elysium.

We lost two men on the trek, one to a snake bite and another simply disappeared while we were hip-deep in the stagnant waters of a swamp. There was no scream and no one saw him vanish. He simply ceased to be. Were it in any other place I would suspect desertion, but not there. Not there.

On the second day, we caught sight of the temple. We stood on the crest of a rise, surveying the valley below from under the hoods of the oilskin cloaks that Mastiff's men wore to keep out the rain. I knew at once that it was a place of unnatural magic. Much of the temple was covered in a thick yellow mist that eddied and pooled between massive columns. The smell of sulphur lay heavy in the air and we wondered what hidden bog was the cause of that awful odour. Through the mist, we saw a low structure, made all of a sickly greenish stone. It looked very much like an amphitheatre, except that its builders had followed a different kind of geometry than the Greeks. Great pillars lay at alien angles, joining the masonry in ways that my eyes have never before seen, despite my extensive travels. The dizzying building played with the mind, even from that distance.

Even Mastiff, who'd pillaged the waters of the Caribbean for a hundred years, was uneasy in the presence of that sick temple. He stood at the front of the column of men with his two trusted lieutenants, Long Turk (who was neither tall nor Turkish) and John Belly (who was as fat as a Swedish chef). "I feel the evil of this place in my bones, Kessler," he said to me. He sheltered his eyes against the driving rain of the Eternal Storm, looking at the boiling clouds above. "I've never seen a mist so tenacious that it could resist rains as fierce as these. I could be marching my men into the midst of an army and we would know not until they rose out of the fog."

"Any army foolish enough to hide in that would long have been devoured by the temple's guardian, Captain," I said. "We must be careful to avoid the same fate."

Two weeks before, when I'd first told Mastiff of the Guardian of the Well of Winds he'd laughed heartily, and several of his pirates had laughed with him. "A fifty-foot-long alligator!" he'd said. "You've got guts coming to me with that tale, scholar. A great beast like that would need to consume a horse a day simply to feed its enormous bulk. What would it eat on an atoll? Fish? You've fallen victim to a sailor's fable, my good man. That beast is no more than fifteen foot from snout to tail, mark my words!" Still, despite all his bluster, he'd brought half his crew into the jungle and armed them to the teeth besides.

I too had laughed at the sailor who told me of the temple's guardian. I'd dismissed his fear-struck tale as the type of exaggeration that makes cartographers write "Here there be dragons" on empty stretches of their charts. But I had stopped my jeering when he'd produced a jagged tooth the size of my dagger. I now bore that same tooth in my belt pouch, and it weighed heavily on me as I descended the slope towards the temple. So focused was I on watching the temple grounds for a glimpse of this beast that I was halfway down the slopes before I realized that I was alone.

"I've twenty men here that will slit your gullet from chin to belly if you fail to obey me!" Mastiff bellowed.

My man Duncan stood before him, surrounded by a handful of pirates. Four of them had drawn their sabres, surrounding him in a ring of steel. Duncan had refused to take the Lady Chelsea down to the temple. He would rather defy Mastiff and risk death at the end of a sword than endanger the life of a woman he'd met only two days before. I did not then comprehend the speed at which their connection had developed. Not being a believer in true love, my anger got the better of me.

"Duncan!" I said, rushing over to the group. "What the devil are you doing? Your sole duty on this voyage is to safeguard me in the temple grounds. Not to play escort to our charge." The Lady Chelsea's safety was of grave importance, but pleasing Mastiff was paramount. While we were on the atoll, we were at his mercy. He could slay us all at any time. Only the fact that I, and I alone, knew the words that would seal this tempest in the Bag of Winds kept us alive. Were I not on my guard, Mastiff might have plied me with rum, in the same way that I had the drunken wretch who'd given me the bag.

I'd found Tom Bellows in an alley behind a decaying tavern in Port-Au-Prince.

I was led to understand, by the rumourmonger who'd sold me the information, that Bellows had once been a member of Mastiff's crew, in the days just after the captain unleashed the Eternal Storm. Ambitious and immoral both, Bellows had stolen from Mastiff's quarters the Bag of Winds and the scrap of parchment bearing commands to recapture the winds, then fled into the jungle.

But what, after all, had he stolen? An empty bag that held value only to Mastiff, and at that time the pirate lord was perfectly content to sail in the embrace of the storm until Hell froze over. He hadn't even read the words to reclaim the winds, so sure was he of his decision. Bellows could not sell or pawn it, and so, penniless, he'd ended up where I'd found him. Covered in sores and reeking of urine, glad of the two bits I gave him to drown his sorrows. I felt no pity for the man.

With the bag in my possession and Mastiff growing tired of the constant storm, I'd been able to negotiate an agreement. His release from the curse in return for the Governor's daughter. Yet, despite our agreement, Mastiff was notoriously mercurial. He'd laboured under his curse for eighty years. I had no doubt he could last another two hundred should he feel the need to drop our corpses in the nearest sinkhole. Whatever provocation Mastiff had offered my man, Duncan would have to mind himself at least until we were safely on the beach.

"Look," I said before Duncan could set his mind against me. "Save your quarrels for after we leave these unhallowed grounds." And then, under my breath, "He'll get his due in time." Duncan glared at Mastiff with fire in his eyes for a long while before wrenching his gaze away. Mastiff would get his due, if the plan we'd concocted worked.

Any good sailor knew that whilst the Eternal Storm raged, the *Stormreaver's Blade* was the fastest ship on the seven seas. Reinforced double mast, deep keel—say what you will about Mastiff's crew, but in the eight decades they'd been plying the Caribbean, they'd mastered the art of harnessing the storm's power. Lord Chelsea had offered me the use of two of his finest frigates to chase down the *Blade*, but knowing this, I'd given them special orders to circle the edge of the storm. Once we managed to seal the tempest back into the Bag of Winds, they were to make sail for Mud Shark Atoll with all speed. Fast as she was in the Eternal Storm, in clear weather, the *Stormreaver's Blade* would wallow like a sow. Easy pickings for a couple of finely trained Captains of the King's Fleet.

Once reminded of the eventual fate that awaited Mastiff, Duncan stood down. I noticed with a smirk that the four pirates that had drawn naked steel against him lowered their swords with sighs of relief. Drawing a blade on a man like Duncan was like poking a sleeping lion with a stick and they knew it.

The Lady Chelsea, standing just behind her man, held her tongue in the face of Duncan's apparent cowing. A lesser woman might have squawked indignantly at this humiliation, but she merely glared daggers at Mastiff before retreating to the shelter of a date palm. I resolved then that if Duncan had not informed her of our plan, I would at the earliest opportunity. She deserved to know that she would not long remain at the mercy of that tyrant.

As Duncan retreated, Mastiff turned his wrath on me. "Keep your dog on a shorter leash than that, Kessler, or I'll string you up by your testicles and let this blasted rain rot your corpse."

I withered under Mastiff's fury. Damn Duncan and damn him again for good measure! He needed only to bide his time until we were off the island, but instead he had challenged the wolf in front of his pack. "My Lord Captain," I said, "I offer my deepest apologies. A man used to dealing with the Eternal Storm can sympathize with my difficulties in harnessing a servant of Duncan's primitive bearing."

Mastiff ignored my apology. "Walk with me, Kessler," he said in a tone that brooked no argument. He put his hand over my shoulder rather more forcefully than he might have and began walking me down the hill to the temple. "I had a dog once, a brawler with a torn ear and a scarred eye. Found him behind a pile of damp cargo netting he'd had for shelter. He followed me on board my ship, and I was feeling tender-hearted that day so I kept him. Well, he proved his worth quick as lightning. There was a mutiny 'board ship that night, and I'd have hung from a yardarm for sure if he hadn't barked a warning as the men came below decks. Well, after that we were like rum and whoring. He followed me from ship to ship; curled in the end of my hammock every night.

"It was eighty miles out of Lordsmouth where I lost him. The seas were as flat as a dinner plate for three weeks if it were a day; not a breath of wind in all that time. Stores were running low, and there weren't a man among us weren't wondering about his next meal. There was a commotion on deck and I found him at the center of a tangle of men, barking and gnashing his teeth at any man what came too close. They'd meant to eat him! Well, I laid about me with the flat of my blade, cursing them, and condemning the next man what set his hand on my mutt to the depths. The crew were more afeared of me than the rumblings in their bellies, and they scurried away like rats. When they were back at their stations, with not a man left with the courage to look me in the eye—then, I turned back to me mutt. And do you know what he did then?" Mastiff's hand tightened painfully on my shoulder, and I shook my head.

"He bit me," Mastiff said, "hard, on the hand. I suppose he must have been so worked up he mistook my intent. But he'd gotten the taste of my blood. So I shot him. We ate him later that night." He paused, perhaps feeling me trembling in fear. "If your dog ever bites me again . . . we'll eat him."

I winced. My stomach felt sick. I'd known at the start of this journey that the pirate captain was merciless, but I hadn't known how dangerous he truly was. I had gambled my life on his sense of honour, forgetting that evil has no honour at all. Now I was trapped. If I didn't seal the Eternal Storm back in the Bag of Winds they'd kill us all, but the bag was the only reason we were still alive. Once I'd fulfilled my part of the bargain, could I rely on this monster to keep his side? My only hope was that such a sense of elation would follow the lifting of the curse that Mastiff and his crew would feel magnanimous and let us go. Faint hope indeed.

One of the pirates, the helmsman I think, called Mastiff and he strode off into the darkness, ducking smoothly under a hanging vine. His story had lasted down the slope, and I now stood before the entrance to the temple. The whole building was overgrown with thick vegetation, like the jungle had formed in the shape of a leafy hand and was now trying to pull the temple into the marsh. Huge marble columns, stained green by floods, held up the remains of a crumbling roof. And a truly useless roof it was at that.

Instead of offering protection from the rain, deep cracks sent ice-cold water pouring down in a dozen freezing waterfalls.

Here and there were blocks of marble carved with scenes of battle and witchery that chilled my spine. Whatever race had built the temple cared not for the gods of the civilized world, and the foul reek of their dark deities lay heavily on the place.

Though the temple proper was huge, I felt hemmed in by the creepers and vines that had invaded the space. I could see only a few feet through the mist ahead, and the driving rain added to my misery. There were pirates all about me, but I heard rather than saw them. Sounds echoed; the crew could have been on the other side of the temple and I would not have known it. I proceeded cautiously, careful of my footing, for the yellow mist made it impossible to know if your next step would be into a hidden sinkhole. Already, I had heard a scream and a splash from one of Mastiff's crew.

Duncan had completely abandoned me at that point, preferring the company of his lady love. She followed close behind him, gripping his hand tightly and setting her jaw defiantly whenever a pirate came too close. If her glares didn't convince the offending sailor to keep his distance, Duncan would rise up before him and glower wordlessly. Perhaps they sensed a little of the wild man that I had seen on the docks of Havana, for no one would dare tempt Duncan's ire and the pair of them were given a wide berth.

Finally, a pirate emerged from out of the vines and mist. It was Long Turk. "Mastiff's found the platform—"

"The dais?"

"Yeah, that's it! The dais! After me then."

The floor of the temple sloped downwards quite sharply and was slick with mud. I looked frantically for a handrail—to no avail. Even Long Turk looked unsteady on the steep incline. The mist at the bottom of the slope was especially dark, and I heard water lapping against marble. I was certain that a misplaced step would mean a dunking. To my surprise, I kept my footing and no one slid past me into oblivion.

Soon, we came to a marble bridge that jutted out over the underground lake to a floating dais. The dais itself was nothing more than a raised circular platform not unlike a massive sundial.

"We're to cross this?" I asked, staring at the narrow bridge. The marble was rent with cavities; it looked ready to crumble away beneath my feet. Mastiff and those pirates that weren't guarding Duncan waited on the dais, but there wasn't a railing in sight and mist swirled about the edge of the bridge. It was difficult to discern where it left off and water began. Though we'd not seen a single sign of a massive croc, I was not yet convinced that the temple's guardian wasn't simply biding its time.

"Kessler," Mastiff called from the dais. "We've arrived and there's no sign of your beastie. Come along and do your part before we rot in this accursed damp!" His gruff voice echoed off the rafters before being swallowed up by the mists. "Turk! Bring them across!"

Long Turk eyed Duncan uneasily and motioned for the men to surround him. Once again, Duncan drew himself up and set his jaw, every muscle tensing like a cat. I was afraid it would come to bloodshed, but I hadn't counted on the bullheadedness of the Lady Chelsea.

"Your men simply needed time to cease their trembling. We certainly didn't want to paint them with a coward's brush by having a woman cross where grown men balked." And then, because she had said it, the three of us had to cross and mask our fear, simply to show up the crew. Near the midpoint, I felt the stone beneath me begin to crumbled, but Duncan's strong hand seized me and kept me from the fall. It does me proud to say that despite that predicament, I kept all decorum, never once betraying my fear.

When we arrived on the dais, I retrieved the Bag of Winds from my pack and mounted the platform directly. Wanting nothing more than to leave that place as speedily as possible, I began the ritual that would lift the curse of the Eternal Storm. A force welled up within me, stroking my soul like waves caress a drowning man. My lungs began to heave, drawing in air in great gulps and expelling it in mighty sighs. I could feel the power of the elements gather over the temple, nature closing its outstretched hand above me. A great howl pierced the air, and the bag leaped towards the sky, nearly jerking loose from my grip. Power surged through me and the skies above began to crumple like paper, collapsing towards the opening of the bag.

Through all this, I somehow managed to see the beast before Mastiff's crew.

It rose out of the mists like a breaching whale, uttering a throaty growl so low in tone that you felt it shake your bones rather than heard it. A crocodile the size of the jolly boat? Nay, I say, the size of the *Blade*! As tall as a man at the shoulder, those enormous jaws could have swallowed a stallion whole. Greasy scales covered it from head to foot, clustering into great ridges that protected its beady yellow eyes. Worst of all, was the gleam of intelligence that graced those baleful orbs. Fear seized me, and my chant faltered. Lady Clara Chelsea was the first to notice, and when her eyes followed mine and alighted on the beast she screamed in terror.

"My God!" a pirate gasped.

Quick as lightning, the Guardian of the Well of Winds took two steps forward and launched its enormous bulk into the crew. Three men disappeared under that scaly belly with nothing more than startled yells to remind the world that they had lived. One man, braver than the rest, drew his blade, but the beast's eyes locked on him and he was gone, swallowed whole.

"It's the guardian!" Mastiff said. "Fight! Damn you, fight!" His sword leapt into his hand and he made for the creature, shoving aside men who were in his way. His presence seemed to galvanize the crew and they regrouped, drawing their own weapons. Blades hacked at the beast's hide, but together they were not more than an annoyance. It roared again and lashed out; its claws parted flesh from bone like a shepherd shears his sheep.

A break opened in the crowd of men and I saw Mastiff, standing like St. George before the dragon, stabbing down into the guardian's snout with all his might. A great bloody geyser poured from the wound and the beast bellowed in pain. It lashed out and caught him a glancing blow below the ribs that hurled him back near ten feet.

In all this time, Duncan had not lifted a finger. Now, I swear to you that Duncan could feel no fear—he was incapable of that emotion perhaps. In this case, he simply chose not to get involved. He stood with Clara Chelsea on the lip of the dais furthest from the guardian, watching the battle impassively.

Mastiff climbed to his feet. "Do you cower under the skirts of a woman, dog? Fight!"

Duncan shrugged. Mastiff was no more his master than I was. He could not be baited. Perhaps that was what angered Mastiff most.

"Fine. If you will not fight for me . . . perhaps you will fight for her!" In a flash, he seized Clara's sleeve and yanked her off her feet. With a twist, he hurled her, screaming, into the crowd of men surging around the feet of the guardian. Her cries of terror focused the beast's attention and a yellowed eye turned towards her.

Many men might have been stunned by such a betrayal, but Duncan was not one to let the thoughts of civilized men cloud his judgment. He was a creature of instinct, dealing with fate rather than bemoaning it. Without even looking at Mastiff, he charged the massive croc. In three great strides he was in the crowd of men, passing amongst them like a ghost. Arms outstretched, he hurled himself into the air. The mighty beast saw him coming too late; great jaws snapped shut on empty air, and then he was upon it. He landed hard on the beast's upper jaw, collapsing it under his weight. Arms like steel wrapped around that great maw and tightened, denying the beast the use of its teeth.

I dared not stop my chanting; the bag twisted and bucked in my grip. The rain had stopped, but the elemental force of the storm still howled through the hole in the roof with the power of a cannon. It was all I could do to continue, but the conflict on the dais held my attention; I could not look away.

"Duncan!" Clara screamed from within the melee. The croc bucked, heaving its jaws into the air, meaning to crush Duncan against the marble roof. Duncan hurled himself aside, but it was too late. The beast's muzzle impacted hard into the ceiling, spraying dust and rock fragments everywhere.

There was no sign of Duncan. No body had dropped to the floor. The crew held its collective breath. Had he been crushed to jelly under that enormous force?

"I see him!" Jim Belly cried. A shadowy figure hung from the end of the creature's snout, his legs flailing against the guardian's thrashing body. Good lad! But, he was now in worse trouble than before; he'd lost his grip on the beast's bottom jaw. With a roar, the croc opened its maw and lunged forwards, hoping to trap the tiny man that hung from its snout.

There was a crack like thunder and green ichor spewed out of the guardian's eye. The croc howled and whipped its head from side to side, nearly throwing Duncan off. Of all Mastiff's crew, only Long Turk had kept his head. The crafty pirate had used the guardian's distraction to take careful aim at one of its beady yellow eyes with his rifle. The hit re-energized the crew and they took to the creature again, hewing against its scales with heavy axes.

Duncan had a blade in his hand now. He'd hooked his other hand under the edge of a scale on top of the crocodile's snout and swung wildly at the beast's tongue and teeth—whatever he could reach. But the guardian was not finished yet. With one tiny human hanging from its snout and a dozen strong men at its flanks, it focused its one good eye on Mastiff's crew. A thirty-foot spined tail lashed out like a whip, sweeping men into the water, snapping ribcages and sawing men in half. Bubbling screams erupted as blood poured from crushed chests and punctured lungs. One of those struck was Jim Belly, his enormous frame distorted and broken like a punctured balloon.

For a nightmarish minute, I could not see Lady Chelsea. Had she too been killed by the creature? Had this whole journey been for naught?

"Back! Back, you foolish girl," said Mastiff as he pulled her away from the carnage. Her skirts were bloody, but I prayed it wasn't her own. She looked dazed, allowing the captain to pull her away from the fight. Bless Mastiff! His first selfless act—I was sure of it.

Perhaps the hope of lifting the curse had been enough to restore some flame of humanity to the cold hearth that was his soul? But then Clara seemed to come to her senses. She yanked Mastiff to a stop. I could not hear what she said next, but she slapped him hard across the face and turned back to the battle. The fool woman wouldn't leave her new love, though it might cost her life! I pitied Mastiff, with his slack jaw and uncomprehending eyes. He'd stood on the edge of greatness and Clara's slap had shown him how foolish it was to risk himself for another. What might have been, had she stayed her hand? The world will never know.

Back at the water's edge, the croc snarled. The sound was terrible, like a ship crashing into a dock. Duncan had flung himself back on top of its jaws and was raining down blow after blow on its sensitive snout. It was bleeding freely from a dozen axe wounds around its shoulders and its eye still dripped ichor. Still snapping futilely at Duncan, the massive croc took a few unsteady steps backwards into the muck. It had had its fill of pain; the petty morsels of meat that lay before it bit harder than it had expected. A cry rose up from the remaining pirates as they sensed their victory, but the creature paid them no heed. Duncan was like an animal, hacking away huge chunks of scale and flesh with the ferocity of a wolverine.

As the animal retreated, Clara became more frantic. Had she seen something I hadn't? She was screaming at Duncan, nearly incoherent with fear. The beast was ten feet out into the lake and rapidly sinking below the surface. And then it finally occurred to me that Duncan had no way to let go. If he let his guard down even for a moment to leap for the shore it would snap him up in a heartbeat. He didn't seem to realize the danger, even when the lake began lapping at his boots.

Poor Clara. It took three pirates to restrain her, and still she tore at them. I swear to you now, she would have hurled herself into the lake had we not held her back. When the water reached his waist, Duncan stopped hacking. He shook his head as if to clear it, and looked back towards the shore and his lady love. The look that passed between them was physical, binding them together. It was filled with hope and despair, and love . . . and at the end, something that I can only describe as determination, but far more than that. I may never again see such a look from a man, nor, I think, do I wish to. Duncan raised his blade one more time before he plunged beneath the waves.

Only then did I remember the Bag of Winds. I held it before me, my hands wringing its edges like an old woman wrings her wash towel. I had been so absorbed by the fight, the drama playing out before me that I had completed the ritual without conscious thought. Sunlight streamed in above me, but I swear I was the only one that noticed. All eyes were on the lake's glassy surface.

Not a man breathed. Even Clara was silent. She stood like a statue, sure that he would break the surface, and none of us had the heart to tell her different. The crew began to turn away. Those who still had hats removed them solemnly. No one could hold their breath for that long.

"There!" Clara said. But it wasn't Duncan. Instead, a huge thing of yellow scales and blood breeched the surface, rolling gently.

"Is that . . ." Mastiff muttered numbly.

I grinned in triumph. "The guardian. Yes. He's killed it." Duncan broke the surface a few seconds later.

The trip back through the jungle to the beach took twice as long as before, for the simple reason that no one would watch where they stepped. Not a man in Mastiff's crew had seen the sun for eighty years. They stared at the open blue skies like children, pointing in awe at the solitary white cloud that clung lazily to the horizon.

By the time we caught sight of the black sails of the *Stormreaver's Blade*, most of them were burnt as red as a fine French wine, and the rest nearly half blind from staring at the sun.

"I suppose this is where we part company," I said to Mastiff as his men put shoulder to the jolly boat.

"What? And leave you stranded on a deserted island? I wouldn't dream of it! I'm in a good mood, Kessler. A sunny day will do that to a man." He slapped me on the back and grinned—an expression I'd not seen on him before. It looked unnatural, a wolf in a pink collar. "You may yet get out of this alive."

I faked a smile, but inside I felt sick. Who could have believed that the terror of the Caribbean, plunderer of a thousand ports, could have felt generous? Somewhere out there, two British frigates were rushing towards us at full sail. I'd counted on Mastiff leaving us behind. Without the power of the storm behind her, the *Blade* was a floating brick. The plan had been for the British ships to make quick work of her and then turn round and pick us up. I shuddered to think of what Mastiff would do to us if he realized we'd betrayed him while we were at sea.

"I thank you for your generosity," I said, struggling to keep my voice calm. "But this island lies within twenty miles of several trade routes. We'll be picked up well inside a week, I assure you."

He looked me in the eyes for a long while and my heart sank. I was transparent under that gaze.

"No. I could not in good conscience leave you on this island. You and your friends will be my *guests* until we reach Havana." His tone turned my blood to ice.

Duncan frowned when I told him, but didn't say a word. Instead, he smiled grimly at Clara and left to help the crew with the jolly boat.

"Is something amiss?" Clara asked.

Mastiff watched us carefully.

"M'lady. We are nearly home. You have performed admirably so far." I tried to calm her, but she was too clever by far.

"So far?" She raised an eyebrow. I had not the heart to answer, instead I turned away and busied myself with my pocket watch.

⚓

"I would have let you go," Mastiff said as he watched the second frigate round the point. Only his white knuckles on the railing gave away his anger. "The curse is lifted, my men and I were free to live our lives the way we chose. What interest could we have in your petty affairs? Once we reached Havana, I would have let you go."

He turned and paced the deck, stopping next to the *Blade's* double mast. A hand reached out and patted it affectionately, but he knew as well as I did that his ship was turning on him. He'd been master of the Caribbean for eighty years, but without the power of the storm, he was the captain of the slowest ship on the seas.

The crew was silent. The men on the rigging had seen the other ship and word had passed among them that they were outnumbered two to one. After so many years of despair, the sight of the sun had brought them hope for a new life. Now that hope had been snatched away. Though they were murderers all, I felt a twinge of sympathy for them.

Mastiff took offence to their fatalism. "What's wrong with you? This is the toughest crew on the Caribbean! We don't need the storm to fight!" His eyes caught sight of Clara, nestled under Duncan's protective arm. "We have the girl! She's Lord Chelsea's whelp! They'll not dare harm us while she's aboard." He lunged at her, but Duncan was too quick. He lashed out with his fist and sent Mastiff tumbling to the deck.

For a moment, no one moved. The deck of the ship was eerily silent. Then the crew's shock turned to anger. As a man, they stormed across the deck towards Duncan. Even he could not stand against so many.

"Stop!" Mastiff rolled to his feet and rubbed a trickle of blood away from his nose. "That's the second time you've bitten me." With a supernatural calm, he rose and turned to his crew. "Run a flag of parley up. They'll listen to us. They don't dare put her ladyship in danger."

"What can you hope to gain?" I said. "Do you plan to trade Clara's life for your ship? I dare say, you'll get no more than a league in this bucket once they have her, deal or no. You've wreaked destruction on these seas for far too long. They simply cannot let you sail away. Surrender now, I beg you, and I'll see that you do less than swing for your crimes. Hard labour perhaps, exile God willing." I felt sorry for him. He was thoroughly trapped. But a penned animal is at its most dangerous. "If you harm us, they'll have you in two days flat. His Majesty's frigates are the fastest on the seven seas."

Of course, threats would never cow Mastiff. An evil gleam crept into his eyes and he turned to his crew. "Gentlemen! This is a new day! A new sun shines down upon us! It's time for a new ship! How would you feel about sailing an English frigate?"

⚓

I should have known that a rat like Mastiff could free himself from any trap. He knew I was right about the *Blade*. He ran up a flag of parley and, when Captain

Wallace came aboard, demanded the *Eagle's Nest* as the price of Lady Clara's life. He threw in the *Blade* for good measure.

Rare is the captain who willingly gives up his ship, and for a long while I feared Wallace would simply blow us out of the water. But Lord Chelsea is a powerful man in these parts, powerful enough to revoke Wallace's commission should he hear that the captain was responsible for the death of his daughter. The reward for Clara's safe return must also have weighed heavily on Wallace. Perhaps he thought that he could claim the reward and Mastiff's ship, then recapture the *Eagle's Nest* at a later date. The frigate would not be easy to hide.

I watched the last pirate cross the plank to the *Eagle's Nest* with something akin to joy. My mission was accomplished. Captain Wallace would take us back to Havana on the *Blade* while the other frigate chased down Mastiff. I had little hope they'd catch the wily pirate. The *Eagle's Nest* was the fastest ship in the fleet. I'd never see Mastiff again and was damn glad of it.

"Mission accomplished, Master Kessler," Clara said. Even Duncan was smiling.

"Not quite," I said, my hand falling to my side. "There's still this to dispose of." The Bag of Winds looked small and pathetic in my grasp. I'd expected it to writhe with the power of the winds in my hand, but it felt inert. Still, I tied a double weight around the end, just to be sure. I was about to throw it into the ocean where it could do no further harm when I caught Duncan's eye.

He was grinning from ear to ear.

It was that grin that made me finally realize that we'd won. Mastiff's boat was turning to catch the wind, the Lady Chelsea was safe, and I was a very rich man. Looking at Duncan standing before me, my only thought was to wonder what Lord Chelsea would say when he found that he very likely had a new son-in-law in his future.

"Here," I said, handing him the bag. "You do the honours."

I was proud of him. Without Duncan, our mission might have ended in the belly of the Guardian of the Well of Winds. He had earned the honour of hurling the bag into the ocean. Whatever happened in the future, we would be fast friends from now on. I couldn't imagine a better man to have at my side.

He leaned back to throw when a voice yelled over the water. It was Mastiff on the *Eagle's Nest*. "Duncan! This is what I do to dogs that bite!"

There was a crack and a cloud of smoke . . . then nothing. Long Turk brought his rifle down and rested it against the deck. Behind me I heard a gasp.

The Lady Chelsea stumbled backwards, a plume of blood brightening her chest. With one shot and two of us, Mastiff had chosen a target that would hurt us both. Duncan stared at her with open mouth, watching her fall, powerless for the first time in his life. She was dead before she hit the deck.

He fell to his knees slowly, mouth still open for a howl that never came. I could not imagine his loss. He had known Clara for only five days, but to an elemental man like Duncan, to love was to give over his soul to another. Their souls were joined, and with her death, his was torn away from him.

"Duncan, I . . . I . . ." How can you console the inconsolable? How could I, having never loved in such a way, understand the pain he felt now? There was nothing I could say.

Duncan's mouth snapped shut, finally, without a single sound ever escaping. His eyes grew clear and still, like the surface of a mountain lake. There was no longer any fire behind the marble blue. In a fluid motion he turned and faced the retreating British frigate. The muscles of his jaw clenched, twisting his face. His breathing grew deep and powerful, readying for the chase as if he were a wolf and the retreating ship a ewe.

"You can't catch him," I said, but he ignored me. "The *Eagle's Nest* is the fastest ship in the fleet. The *Blade*'s no good without the power of the Eternal Storm to propel her."

Duncan looked at the *Blade*'s double masts, then back at the frigate and his hands clenched on leather.

It was only then that I realized what he intended.

My heart leapt into my throat. How could I have been so careless? I had to get it away from him before it was too late. He'd doom every man on the ship for the sake of revenge!

"No . . . Duncan. Don't do it."

But Duncan's hatred had already consumed him. Rage was an aura around him, terrible to behold. He hungered for Mastiff and nothing I could say would deter him. His anger was as unstoppable as a flood.

Mindless with fear, I turned and reached towards the setting sun. . . .

The Drum of the Sea
Gerri Leen

Sir Francis Drake sat in the moonlight, watching as the movement of the *Defiance* made his claret roll back and forth in the exquisitely chased silver goblet he'd stolen years ago from the Spaniards. He'd tried to get more treasure this trip, tried to take it from the Dons at San Juan harbor. What a fiasco that had proved.

A cannonball had nearly ended him. But his infamous luck had held out. He hadn't been in bed when the great ball of iron tore through the hull and landed where he should have been lying. His luck was still good, but despite that, he wasn't the man he'd been. Wasn't the man who'd sailed into Cadiz harbor for the sole pleasure of singeing King Philip's beard on behalf of his queen. By the Lady, what a day that was. Occupying the harbor for three days, destroying nearly three score of ships. He'd pushed back the Armada's invasion of England by a year or more.

Of course, they had just come later. But he'd pushed them back then, too.

He'd always push them back. Always.

Even if now he was doing it on the run. But that was good. He was back here, lying just off Nombre de Dios. The invasion of Puerto Bello hadn't gone any better than San Juan. Baskerville had returned in defeat. But there was time. Drake would lead the next attempt himself.

Giving up was not something he knew how to do. He'd take Panama for England once and for all. It was time. And he was ready for it.

He heard the low strike of a drum, then the more distant echo back on land. The sound of oars dipping into water and coming up again carried to him, then another drumbeat.

"Davey," he said with a smile, calling to the boy who insisted on hovering nearby like some damned manservant instead of doing the chores he'd been hired to do. "Davey, go fetch more claret. And some bread, too." He turned back to the water, to his beloved sea. "We have guests coming."

Reaching down, he touched the head of the drum he'd carried up with him for no good reason other than that it had felt right. He'd lived his life doing what felt right and had never been the worse for it.

A drum sounded again, an intricate story coming out of it, and it wasn't the cadence of Pedro's large hands he was hearing. It had the subtleness of *her*.

It had been years since he'd seen her. Would she still be as beautiful?

Would she still be as unknowable?

He picked up the drum, grabbed the drumsticks from where he'd shoved them in his coat. He started the slow roll that changed into something more like the song that was emanating from the Cimarron drum in the pinnace so quickly approaching. He played with his eyes closed, his ears hearing a music that only lived in lands southern and hot.

Music that could tell a tale. That could carry news for miles.

He heard an answering drumming from the pinnace. He tried to read it, caught only a small portion of it.

She was happy he was back.

She was sad he was back.

It was the last time he'd be back.

Drake swallowed hard, feeling as if the moonlight was burning into him the way the sun had that day so many years ago, when a coal-black Cimarron priestess had taken his drum from him and held it to her belly, dancing with it as if it was a lover. Changing it—the drum had been different ever since. It seemed . . . alive.

The woman had been wild and the most beautiful thing he'd ever seen—even if technically she hadn't been a woman any longer. Pedro had tried to explain it to him. How a loa— one of the deities his people managed to worship along with Drake's God—could possess anyone, gender be damned. This gorgeous woman was no longer a female to her people.

She was Papa Ogun. Named after the loa who'd possessed her. The god of iron, and war . . . and drums.

There was a slight bump as the pinnace nudged the side of the *Defiance*. Then Drake saw the rope ladder stretch tight, and a moment later, Pedro crawled over. His smile was huge, lighting his dark face.

Drake held his goblet up to him in a mock toast, and Pedro smiled at it, as if in memory of that first raid, when they'd stolen more than they could carry. They'd buried the silver in the sand, had left it there because Pedro's people hadn't valued it the way they had the iron. Drake had escaped with the gold. Enough to make a queen smile. Enough to earn him a knighthood—even if his queen had been forced to wait years to do it, until his voyage around the world.

"El Draco returns." Pedro's voice was soft and lilting, at odds with his imposing physique and scarred black face.

Drake shook his head. "El Draco comes back with his tail between his legs."

"But a fine tail it is," a huskier voice said, and *she* crawled over the rail.

She was older. Her hair streaked with gray, just as his was. But she stood straight and tall, and her white clothes hung easily on her curvaceous frame. She wore her hair short, cut like a man's, and it accentuated the sharp bite of her cheekbones and the silver earrings he'd given her once after a successful raid. She landed easily on the deck, bare feet clean despite the dirt she must have walked through to get to the shore. A loa didn't walk the same way a human did. Even when it was inside the body of one.

"Papa Ogun."

"Draqui." She smiled, her teeth still white and gleaming despite her age.

He'd never known her as a true woman. Never known her when she wasn't possessed by the god of war.

That fact hadn't stopped him from falling a little in love with her. He'd never told his first wife Mary about it since his infatuation with Papa Ogun hadn't changed how he'd felt about her—and he'd never touched the Cimarron woman despite his desire.

He suspected touching Papa Ogun would have been his last earthly act, even if she did like to play at seducing him.

He'd also neglected to mention the Cimarron priestess to his new wife Elizabeth, the spoiled young woman who'd married him only because, even at his age, he was famous and exciting. The charmed man—but not, he knew, a charming one, and he thought Elizabeth wished she'd chosen differently.

Each time he'd sailed away from Mary, he'd had a leaden feeling as if he was leaving half his soul behind. But he'd said goodbye to Elizabeth easily, knowing she'd probably be happier alone with their combined riches than having to deal with him puttering around Buckland Abbey and getting in the way of her teas.

His manners were rough. He was a seaman, by God, and Elizabeth had known that when she married him. He could afford to buy the finest things. That didn't mean he was at ease with such luxury.

Davey came bustling out with more stolen goblets and a decanter of claret. He had rolls, too, tied up in a cloth, and Drake took them from him and put them out on the table he'd had set up on deck even though there'd been no reason for it.

Had he known Pedro and Papa Ogun would come tonight?

He'd known something was going to happen. He'd been restless and thought he'd heard his drum vibrate with the sound of a dying drum roll just before he'd come on deck to drink. It was why he'd brought it with him. Why he'd jammed the drumsticks into his coat.

Pedro sat down on the chair Davey pulled forward. Papa Ogun ignored the proffered seat, leaning against the rail, one leg hitched up. She pulled out a cigar, snapped her fingers, and stared at Davey.

"She wants a light."

"But . . . she's a woman, and they don't—"

"Give her a light, Davey, if you value your life." Drake nodded at the boy.

Davey lit a taper from a lantern, held it to her cigar until it began to glow. Papa Ogun inhaled deeply, then blew the smoke in his face.

Davey coughed, but he didn't move, seemed to be frozen by her amber eyes and the low tap-tapping she was drumming with her free hand.

Shaking his head, Drake took the sticks to his drum, raising a tight, fast roll; Davey jumped back as if struck. "Don't you have chores to do, lad?"

The boy fled.

Papa Ogun stared up at the full moon and laughed. "You never let me have any fun, Draqui."

"He's one of mine."

"Maybe so. But have a care how you take on the god of drums. Especially tonight." She let her foot drop, took a deep puff from the cigar, then walked to the chair between him and Pedro and sat.

Drake noticed that Pedro shifted, so he was leaning on the arm that wasn't right next to her. Drake felt a moment of rebellion, and leaned in, almost getting lost in the scents that wafted off her skin: tobacco, musk, and some spice that he thought grew only in Africa.

"What are you trying to do here, Draqui?"

"I'm going to take Nombre de Dios. Once and for all."

"There's nothing to take, Englishman." She laughed, and Pedro fidgeted in his chair.

Drake frowned, then he looked at Pedro.

"It's true, Francis. Everything has been moved to Puerto Bello, and it's heavily fortified. There is no taking that."

"As you found out." Papa Ogun leaned in. "You could go back and try to take San Juan, maybe?" She laughed softly at his expression. "Oh, yes. I have heard how well that battle went."

"How could you have possibly heard?" Then he felt the drum vibrate against him. "Oh."

"Wherever my drums are, I have ears and a voice."

It was why the Spaniards had tried to forbid slaves any access to their traditional drums. As long as the slaves could talk to each other, some part of them remained free. And free meant dangerous. Just ask anyone who'd met the wrong end of a Cimarron iron arrow.

"I will take San Juan, then." He wished his voice was more certain.

"Will you?" Her smile was almost sweet.

Pedro couldn't seem to meet his eyes. He held his goblet out for more wine, said nothing as Drake filled it for him.

"You seem to think I won't?"

"You will not take San Juan. You will not take Nombre de Dios. You will not take Puerto Bello. In fact, you will not take another journey for a very, very long time." Papa Ogun stared at him, and he remembered a time in his youth, on a ship much younger than his beloved *Defiance*.

On a ship filled with slaves. Slaves he'd sold. Slaves like her and Pedro. Only he wasn't sure any of his had broken free.

Unlike his brethren in the trade, he hadn't been able to stomach it. He'd refused to continue to transport humans. His guilt over having done it at all had led him to do reckless things. He remembered an African boy in Santo Domingo—his messenger, killed by the Spaniards for no good reason other than that they could. Drake had demanded the killer's execution. When the Spaniards refused, he'd killed friar after friar until they had brought the bastard to him. He'd made the man's captors kill him.

He'd earned censure for that. Such trouble and risk for one ex-slave. One of his detractors had said it wasn't for the boy, at all. That it was only another way to play naughty with the Dons. Would he have gone after an Englishman or the Portuguese so relentlessly for killing a former slave?

"What are you thinking?" Pedro asked, but Drake could tell that Papa Ogun knew. He could practically feel her inside him, crawling around like some kind of snake.

She did not smile. "He is thinking that helping us wiped his slate clean."

"I don't understand," Pedro said, and Drake realized his friend didn't know what he'd done. "I transported slaves."

Pedro looked as if he'd been punched in the stomach. He put his goblet down on the deck, stared at his feet for a long moment. "We fight for our freedom. We kill those who enslaved us."

Papa Ogun tapped her drum lightly; the sound seemed to echo into eternity.

Pedro exhaled, the breath lasting longer than was humanly possible. As if he was letting go of much more than air. "I have fought next to you. I do not like this, but you are my friend, and I must accept it." Then he met Drake's eyes. "I have never known why you hate the Spaniards so much."

"He does not know, himself." Papa Ogun nodded, then smiled as if at a great secret. She flicked her cigar into the air, over the rail, away from where the pinnace waited tethered. The cigar flared, then it exploded into a shower of sparks, leaving only tiny cinders to float down to the water. "This is nothing compared to what is coming."

Drake looked at her, white afterimages of the explosion playing on his eyes. "What can we do?"

She laughed, and the *Defiance* seemed to shake with her laughter. "Steal more treasure from the Spaniards? Sink more ships? No. That will not be helpful."

"Then what?" Drake felt the snake inside him move again. He was suddenly wracked with pain. Clutching at his belly, he stared at her. "Have you poisoned me?"

"No." She called for Davey, pointed at Drake as she and Pedro backed away. "He is sick."

Davey ran for him as another twisting cramp in Drake's belly made him fall to his knees out of the chair.

"Goodbye, my friend," Pedro said, then he disappeared down the rope ladder.

Papa Ogun seemed to follow him, but then Drake felt her hand on his arm, her soft voice whispering in his ear. He heard the sound of oars, the pounding of a drum that seemed to throb in time with the cramps that wracked him. A pounding that grew softer as the pinnace traveled away from them.

Yet she was still kneeling by him. How could that be?

"Help me."

"I cannot help you any longer," his version of Papa Ogun said.

"You're a ghost."

"Ain't no ghost, sir," Davey said through clenched teeth as he tried to wrestle Drake to his bedchamber.

"Can't you see her?"

"No one here, sir. No one 'cept us."

"Only you can see me, Draqui." She'd lit another cigar, blew the smoke into his face, and suddenly he was in the middle of a firefight—he couldn't tell which one, but he heard sailors yelling, felt the deck roll beneath his feet as whatever ship he was suddenly on rode a swell. Cannon crashed in the blackness, an explosion like her cigar as it had blown up, lighting the night.

"We'll take Puerto Bello," he murmured to Davey. "Baskerville will do it."

But Baskerville hadn't done it. Baskerville was back and there would be no taking Panama for queen and country.

"Your battles are done," Papa Ogun said. "For now." She began to chant, her voice soft and low. It wasn't Spanish she murmured, nor English. It sounded like the language slaves spoke. It sounded like the murmur of souls wishing for freedom.

"My soul will never be free, will it?"

"What do you think, Draqui?"

He'd spent his life locked in hatred. Driven by guilt. He'd done what he'd done, warred on his enemies because—

Her laughter broke his concentration. She was bent over, holding her belly the way he was holding his, only she was doing it to contain amusement, not gut-wrenching pain.

"What a liar you are. Even to yourself." She leaned in, kissed him for the first time, her lips blazing fire on his own. "You did it because you wanted to. You did it because you liked to."

He felt truth roaring through him, running wild from where her lips had touched his. He was . . . hers. He had always been hers. "I did it because I could."

"Yes. Because this is what you were made for. Do you think the god of war attends a common seaman's death?"

As Davey manhandled him into bed, Drake looked up at Papa Ogun. Shimmering around the body of the woman he knew, was the shape of a man. Tall, slender, dressed in a short, kilt-like thing. Holding a spear in one hand, a sword in the other. He exhaled smoke, only he had no cigar.

The god of war.

Drake's god.

He struggled to sit up.

"Sir, no." Davey tried to push him back.

"Get my armor, lad. Get it now." He laughed, but then his insides twisted again, and he had to heave his guts into the chamber pot.

The boy stared at him.

"Now!" The word came out as a roar, even as his strength deserted him. He lay back on the bed, felt Papa Ogun's warm fingers on his brow.

"Soon, my faithful one. Soon."

"Death will finally find me?"

"I can only keep him away so long."

And Drake knew Ogun had kept death away. So many times he should have died. So many wounds that had felled lesser men, and he'd walked away from them. So many shots that had missed, cannonballs that had fallen where he'd just been standing, reefs that had let his ship go when he should have been grounded forever.

Uncanny luck. The Devil's luck, some had said.

He supposed Papa Ogun might seem the Devil to some.

But tonight her fingers on his skin felt like home. Like hearth. His Elizabeth would not have done this for him, although he thought his Mary would have held him no matter how bad it got.

"If you could have one wish, what would it be?" Papa Ogun asked, her breath blowing warm breezes over his skin. He could feel the sun on his face, smell spice on the air, mingling with the smell of human fear.

God help him, why had he done it?

Because he could. Because he wanted to. Because back then, he hadn't known the price it would exact to do it.

Despite what she'd said, his life since then had never been about the gold or the silver. Or about rubbing Spain's face in it. He'd enjoyed harassing the Spaniards, but the raids and battles had been about redeeming a part of himself lost on those voyages from Africa to New Spain. They'd been about fighting for his lost honor—and never winning it back, because sometimes such things could not be regained.

"I'm sorry," he whispered to Papa Ogun.

"I forgive you."

A profound peace settled over him. And the smell of sweaty fear faded away.

"Davey, where's that armor? I'll meet Death well dressed. *Defiance* and her dragon, going to the Devil under protest."

"One wish?" She smiled at him the way any woman who wanted to prod a secret from him would. But her eyes shone with a light that held no womanly softness.

"To not go to the Devil?"

She laughed. "Don't worry so about that."

"To protect England." He saw that his drum was sitting on the table, even though he knew he'd left it on deck.

"I brought it in." She smiled, and tapped her own drum, and his drum answered it all on its own.

Davey stopped, turning slowly to stare at the table.

"If England ever needs me, Davey, beat the drum." He smiled at the boy. "I'll run the Dons straight back to Hell."

"It won't be the Spaniards," Papa Ogun murmured.

"Whoever. Whenever. I'll come."

"That's your wish, then." She leaned down, laying her head on his chest. He imagined his heart sounded like one of her drums. That she could hear the language of what was left of his life as she listened.

"Is it a good tale?"

"It's a very good tale, my dragon."

Then she was gone, and the weight on his chest wasn't from her, but from the armor Davey lifted onto him.

"Take the drum back to England. You make sure they know it will protect them."

"I will, sir."

"Now, help me onto deck."

"Sir, no."

Drake tried to get up, vomited twice before he could force himself to stand. He could tell he'd stained his breeches, felt his face color with shame. To die like this. With his body bleeding out of him and no war wound to point to as culprit.

"I'll meet death as a soldier." Even if he wouldn't. Even if he'd die of the bloody flux as any common lout might.

"Aye, sir." He saw that Davey was breathing through his mouth as they struggled out to the deck.

He'd die stinking.

"Go away now, boy." And he pushed Davey gently, knowing he'd run for the others.

From far away in the jungle, Drake heard the drums. He wished he had his drum to answer them with, then felt something in his hands. He looked down; the drum vibrated, held fast against him as if by straps. Lifting the sticks that appeared in his hands, he beat a slow cadence, heard the sound echoed by hands on a drum far different.

His strength gave out and he fell. He worried for the drum, but it and the sticks faded away as he watched. Slumped against the rail, he stared out at his beloved sea, and as the *Defiance* rolled easily in the mild swells, Drake closed his eyes and let go, the thrumming of drums guiding him just as gently to his next battle.

Cassia's Song
T. Borregaard

*S*omething is wrong. Cassia Aquila's eyes flew open. She stared into the darkness. The smell of sweat and leather assaulted her. No movement disturbed the hostelry room; the twenty or so supine bodies around her remained perfectly still.

Cassia adjusted her senses, straining for some noise that might have woken her. Nothing but a heavy, oily silence.

Exactly, said her brain. *Even this late the Plaza Publico outside should be loud with sailors and whores.*

Cassia was instantly and completely awake. She slept in her stola, partly so she could leave quickly, but mostly because it was the only clothing she had. She sat, strapped on her sandals, and was standing in seconds.

I'm getting better and better at running away, she thought. Moving as quickly as possible around the sleeping bodies, she tied her belt about her waist and adjusted her cloak as she went.

In the hallway she began to run: across the atrium, through the courtyard, and under a peristyle. Only then did she hear shouts and cries behind her. *Father's ill will catches up with me again.*

The bleary-eyed horse boy looked up from a pile of straw as she ran through the stables and out the back door. Very few way-stations in Ostia had more than one exit. It had taken her half the day to find this one. *Worth the hunting*, she thought.

She leaped over a pile of fur and bones that might have been (and possibly still was) a cat. Landing badly, she stumbled, catching herself with one hand against the wall. Something sharp bit into her palm. She held back a cry of pain.

Behind Cassia, port guards poured through the hostelry and into its courtyard. *Father must have sent runners to all the major cities, and Ostia must have magi on the payroll to have found me so fast.* She was more impressed by Mercator Aquila's efficiency than annoyed at being found.

Cassia emerged from the back alley onto the Plaza Publico. Fortuna was with her, for the guards had left no one at the front. She touched her injured hand with her good one, feeling for blood. Wet stickiness welled from the cut in her palm. She cursed and wrapped her hand in her stola to stop the bleeding. Perhaps Fortuna was not so kind. *No time to deal with it now, just don't drip. Don't know what the blood will do if it drips.*

Cassia put her head down determinedly and charged across the open space of the Plaza. On the run for weeks with little food and less rest, she had just enough speed left for one mad dash. Panting hard, she dove down a small side alley and took off through the dark city.

There was no moon, and the high buildings, looming monoliths of shadow, blocked any light from the stars above. Here and there a lone lamp-lit window cast a rude orange slash into the black, so bright against the darkness it did more harm than good, momentarily blinding her with its glare. Cassia ran further and further into the dingy back streets of Ostia, away from the docks and prized monuments of Rome's greatest port.

Eventually she slowed to a trot, and then to a walk, as it became clear no one followed.

Magi are probably tracking me, Cassia thought. *Best to keep moving.*

She felt her wounded hand. The blood flow had slowed. *Thank the gods.* She was more frightened of touching someone than she was of being caught. Her blood could do strange things.

She walked the far reaches of Ostia for the rest of the night. By morning, she was slumping forward over her feet, eyes sandy and half-lidded with exhaustion. She'd never seen anything so beautiful as the grey light of pre-dawn. Cassia turned down Horrea Street towards the port.

Horrea was the dingiest street in Ostia, and that was quite an achievement. Trash was piled in the gutters. People worse off than Cassia slept curled amongst the refuse. Transport crates and huge delivery urns were propped against brick walls. Rats scampered to-and-fro. But for all its flaws, Horrea Street led to the water.

Ostia's main dock was a hive of activity. Cassia straightened, using the last of her energy for the sake of appearances, and walked confidently along the front edge of the five-sided port. To her right, hundreds of ships were tethered, mostly fat, deep-keeled merchant vessels. Off to one side sat a small provincial fleet of *liburnia*. Each warship, a long galley with two banks of oars on either side, looked like a floating centipede.

Cassia tapped a young sailor on the arm. "Anyone hiring?"

He looked at her, stunned. "You have the most beautiful voice I've ever heard."

Cassia knew the refrain. Her voice was musically stunning. It hit most men somewhere in the gut.

She tried again. "Is anyone hiring?"

The sailor shook himself as though to clear his head. "You don't look much for the sea." He gestured to her skinny arms.

Cassia nodded. "Merchant-born," she said by way of explanation.

The sailor grinned in delight. "Just happens the *Oneraria* might be looking for a new purser." His smile turned malicious. "Captain Marinus should be finding that out right about now." He pointed. "He's the one that looks like he just ate the bottom of a boot."

Cassia thanked him and walked in the direction he'd pointed.

Captain Marinus was shouting at a smallish man who bore a striking resemblance to a red ground-squirrel.

"What do you mean Rufus is in jail?"

The squirrel rubbed his hands together in a worried way and chattered, "Well you see, Captain, there was this prime piece, all smiles, turned out she weren't whoring though, and her father—"

Captain Marinus slapped his forehead with the heel of his hand. "Stop there, I don't want to know. What now? We can't bloody sail without a purser!"

Cassia cleared her throat.

Captain Marinus whirled around and glared at her. "What do you want?"

"Merchant Cassia Aquila," she said. "I'm under the impression you need a purser?"

Captain Marinus took a moment to adjust to her voice. "How is it everyone on the docks knows my business before I do?"

"It was a very public sort of jailing," Squirrel said. "And you know Purser Rufus—

not much liked in Ostia."

Captain Marinus raised his hand to cut off any further explanation. He glared at Cassia. "Aquila? Really? Any relation to the Mercator?"

Cassia figured she was safe for the moment, but her voice was cold, betraying a little disdain. "He's my father."

Captain Marinus laughed. "Jupiter's own pain to work with, your father, but his product's good. It's part Aquila stock we're carrying now. Any experience with wool?"

Cassia gave him the benefit of her smile. "I handled all my father's sheep, wool, and textile production accounts, including herd tallies, shearing numbers, and transport. Aquila family holds over fifty herds in the northern region alone. That's eight boat-loads of raw material per year. *And* I have *grammaticus* schooling as well as *litterator*."

The captain's deep-set eyes lit. *Grammaticus* meant advanced mathematics, philosophy, and natural sciences, as well as reading, writing, and general accounting—rare in a woman and very useful.

"Letters of introduction?"

Cassia shrugged. There were no agents of the Aquila family in Ostia. Not that any would provide a recommendation for her. *Just lie*, she thought. "I've only recently arrived. You could contact my father if you'd like." She knew runners would be expensive and require more time than the captain could afford if he wanted to sail with the tide.

"Twenty denarii a day, with meals. You'll keep track of ship's stores and cargo, plus conduct transactions at each port." Marinus was clearly a man of decision.

Cassia shook her head. *I'm merchant stock when all is said and done. The captain won't respect me if I don't barter.* "Thirty denarii and my employment terminates at Leptis Magna or in two months time, whichever comes first. Also you'll not ask me to sing."

The captain looked a little confused by her final addendum, but pleased with the terms. "Twenty-five denarii and if your work is satisfactory, *Oneraria* has first right to rehire."

Cassia nodded. "We have a deal," she said, her voice bell-like with triumph. She was selling herself cheap. Farm laborers and donkey drivers made twenty-five a day, and she was fully educated. But it would keep her moving.

"Right then, onboard with you." Captain Marinus gestured, and Cassia trotted up the gangplank.

The *Oneraria* proved itself a neat little tub of a boat: almost round with a deep keel, pointed fore and aft, a single tall mast, and a cheerful yellow sail. Apparently, lack of a purser was all that had been holding her back, because as soon as the captain climbed after Cassia he yelled, "Roll'er out!"

In a matter of moments the gangplank was pulled in and the lashings untied. The crew rigged out the sail and steered the potbellied craft away from the pier.

Several ship-lengths out, Cassia looked back and saw a disturbance on shore. A contingent of port guards, leather armor and heavy boots distinguishing them from the collected sailors, pushed through the crowd to the edge of the pier. They were gesticulating with their long spears and yelling after the *Oneraria*.

"Those heavies wanting us?" the squirrelly man asked. "Should we turn back?"

Marinus looked at his gubernator, a hugely muscled sailor fighting the tiller attached to the ship's one massive steering oar. The gubernator shook his bald head.

"Too late," said the captain. "We've caught the tide. It'll have to wait until we're back up this way in three month's time."

Cassia let out a sigh of relief.

Squirrel, who clearly had little liking for guards, guffawed and went forward to have a conversation with the sailors tying down the brails.

The captain squinted back at the shore. There were a number of loud splashes as guards tussled with sailors and were shoved off the pier. "Really, this kind of spectacle is too much for an old man first thing in the morning," he said.

Cassia didn't respond.

"Friends of yours?" asked a deep voice behind her.

Cassia whirled about. *That's the biggest dog I've ever seen,* was her first thought. It wasn't the dog that had spoken, of course. But Cassia was momentarily hypnotized by the sheer size of the animal. It had a mottled brown coat, floppy ears, and impressive jowls. When she tore her gaze away, it was only to be hypnotized further by the size of the man standing next to it.

"Purser," said Captain Marinus, his craggy face split by a grin that did nothing to improve its looks, "meet our weathervane: Galinn Snorrason. Weathervane, meet our purser: Cassia Aquila."

"Captain! Yard's misbehaving, should I send a boy up?" the gubernator's yell interrupted them.

"Neptune's nipples," Marinus said, and marched off to deal with the problem.

Cassia barely saw him leave. She suspected she was supposed to say something to the weathervane at this juncture.

"Norseman," she stuttered. She'd never met one before, but she knew Norsemen had yellow hair like this man. Also his eyes weren't brown, but the most amazing pale blue color. Those eyes blinked at her.

The huge dog broke the silence by bounding up to Cassia, placing both massive paws on her shoulders and licking her entire face in one slurp.

Cassia patted its head tentatively. "Uh. Your dog is very . . . friendly," she said. She wondered what would possess the captain to allow such an animal on board. Having to feed it alone must be quite costly.

The Norseman said, "Your voice sounds like mead, all honeyed and potent."

Well, thought Cassia, *that's more poetic than most.* Then she remembered what Marinus had said: this man was the ship's weathervane.

"You're a magus?" she asked.

"Magus? Uh. Yes. That embarrassing beastie is my familiar, Hopp." The Norseman glared at the dog. "Leave the nice lady alone, Hopp." Looking back at Cassia, he said, "Welcome on board the *Oneraria*. Have you ever sailed before?"

Cassia shrugged. "Not much, but I think I'll like it."

Galinn Snorrason looked about, then said, "Those guards were after you, weren't they?"

Cassia was so surprised, she nearly told him her story, but then she rediscovered her backbone. *His eyes aren't that beautiful!* She snapped her mouth shut and tried not to look worried.

The weathervane grinned at her, his eyes crinkling. "It's OK. I'm not particularly friendly with guards myself."

Cassia remained silent.

"You always this chatty?"

Cassia cocked her head to one side. "Perhaps it's just you're asking the wrong questions."

"Right then. Care to lie? Start our relationship off on the right foot."

"Uh." Cassia chewed her lower lip. "We have a relationship?"

The pale blue eyes twinkled at her. "Now then, no need to rush things, you just came on board."

Cassia was saved from further conversation by the captain's return.

"There's cargo and supply inventories to be done," he said, slapping her on the back, "and I'd like you to go over the figures for the past four sales and catch any mistakes Rufus may have made. And you, weathervane," he rounded on the huge man. "We'll be clear of the harbor soon, we could use some running wind."

Marinus led Cassia across the deck towards the cabin.

The weathervane watched them the entire way. Then he turned and walked towards the prow of the ship, whistling softly.

———⚓———

Cassia spent most of her first week on board undoing the mess Rufus had made of the *Oneraria's* accounts. Then she did a full inventory of the ship's stores and cargo. Captain Marinus was impressed with her efficiency.

Once she'd sorted that all out, there wasn't much left to do. The *Oneraria's* business wasn't like the Aquila family's, with its constant flow of sheep-related calculations. Here, while at sea, purser's duties were moderate.

In the evenings, Cassia ate with the captain and his crew, most of whom developed a brotherly affection towards her. They generally thought of her as too quiet, and spent a good deal of time trying to tease her into speaking. They found her voice delightful and wished to hear it as much as possible. They even tried to get her to sing, but such requests were guaranteed to silence her completely or worse, bring the captain down on them for breach of employee agreement.

The weathervane, Galinn, had a much more demanding role on board. He spent all day, every day, in the prow of the ship commanding the winds. It obviously sapped a lot of his energy. He ate while he worked and went straight to sleep at sunset. Cassia felt neglected after his initial pointed flirtation but she couldn't help being fascinated by the Norseman. She noticed that the sailors tended to avoid him.

"Why are they so nice to me, when I'm new on board, and so indifferent to him?" Cassia asked the captain late one afternoon.

"He's not as pretty as you."

Cassia glared at him.

"Magi don't mix with regular folk, and regular folk don't mix with magi," Marinus said, "or that's what most of my men believe."

"Why bother hiring a weathervane then? It's expensive." She'd just spent three hours reviewing the ship's pay packets.

Captain Marinus turned and leaned his back against the deck railing. "Well, you can do the calculations better than I, but running ahead of the wind with sail at full cuts travel time by half. That doubles the number of journeys we can make in a year."

Cassia leaned next to him. "Twice the profit."

"Not to mention the insurance that comes with having a magus on board. More shipments arrive safely into port, protected from storm and pirate attack. That saves a lot more denarii than the cost of one magus employee."

Cassia nodded. *It's probably a sweet deal for Galinn as well. Good money plus endurance training.* "It has its benefits," she said.

She looked over at the Norseman. It was getting on towards evening, but the day was very hot. Galinn, who wore a Norse tunic and baggy trousers, had clearly reached his limit. As they watched, he stripped out of his tunic leaving his chest bare.

Cassia nearly swallowed her tongue.

"One more benefit?" the captain said, looking at her rapt expression.

One of the crew came up and tapped Marinus on the shoulder. "Food's up."

The captain turned towards the galley, where the cook was serving bread, cheese, olives, and dried figs. Cassia trailed along behind.

After they'd eaten, the captain handed her an extra portion. "Take this up to the weathervane, would you? Cook hates to do it."

Cassia hesitated. She might be attracted to the Norseman, but he was still a magus by profession. Magi tended to want her dead. *There's no reason he should know what I really am or be able to find out.*

She took a deep breath and walked across the deck.

Galinn greeted her with a gleam in his blue eyes, suggesting that the tunic might have come off with her in mind.

"Hel-lo," Cassia said, passing him the food. His familiar gave her a paw in greeting. Cassia hesitated, then shook it for lack of anything else to do. Hopp appeared to approve of this and wagged her skinny tail so hard it knocked over a nearby stack of coiled rope.

"Thank you, purser," Galinn said.

Cassia paused for a moment and then turned away.

The weathervane stopped her with his free hand. "Stay and talk a while?"

The winds slowed slightly. "I won't disturb your work?"

Galinn shook his head. "I can carry on the magic, eat, and listen all at the same time. Wind is easy for me."

"But you're so tired every night."

"Nice of you to notice." Galinn popped an olive into his mouth. Spitting the pit overboard he said, "Magi only have a limited amount of sorcery. Gets a little much, using it all day every day. That's all."

"Doesn't it, um," Cassia searched for the right word, coming up with a merchant one, "restock?"

Galinn took a bite of bread. "Takes a good night's sleep."

"How does it work?" Cassia asked, curious as to how different his magic was from her own power.

"You ask a lot of questions."

Cassia smiled a slow smile. "I'm interested in things," she said softly.

Galinn looked slightly bowled over, and nearly choked on a fig.

"Think of it this way. The sorcery of each magus is stored in a kind of cistern, filled by the currents of magic swirling around all of us. When we're not using it, it replenishes, but when we are, we can only access what's available in the cistern."

Cassia thought of her own abilities. *I never get tired and I never run out.* "So why do you get so exhausted?"

"Using it up is taxing. It's not a physical or mental fatigue, it's more like when you're sick and have no energy."

"That's too bad. It'd be nice to talk together some night." Cassia startled herself with her own boldness.

"We're talking now."

Cassia blushed. "I mean properly, sitting down, with the captain and the others."

"I'd prefer if it were just you."

Cassia's blush deepened. *I'm terrible at this flirting thing.*

Galinn grinned at her red face.

"I guess I'd prefer that too," Cassia said, opting for honesty.

Galinn reached out one enormous hand and caught her small fingers with it. Cassia could tell he was trying to be non-threatening. *Hard for someone his size.*

"We go into port tomorrow afternoon. Would you like to spend shore leave together?"

Cassia was nodding before he even finished asking the question.

"Good, that's settled." He let go of her hand and went back to eating. "So." His blue eyes were sharp. "What kind of trouble are you in?"

Cassia pretended not to know what he was talking about.

"Ostia port guards were after you."

"There are a few accounts I should deal with before bed," Cassia said.

Galinn swore softly. "It's all right," he said, "you don't have to talk about it."

Cassia turned away from him and hurried towards the cabin. Despite her obvious avoidance, she knew he followed her.

Once inside, she sat down at the small table and look pointedly past the Norseman. She watched as out on deck Hopp lay down for a nap.

Galinn closed the door to the cabin. "I'm sorry. It's none of my business," he said.

From the tone in his voice Cassia knew he wanted to help.

"I'd like to tell you," she said.

"Then go ahead."

"It's not that easy." Cassia picked up a papyrus roll and began checking the tallies written on it. She didn't really see the numbers. She saw her father's face: full of hatred and disgust. After the funeral he'd been all accusations—fear of what she had in her blood. He'd called for his pet magus and that was when she first learned how to run away.

Galinn was a magus. Magi were more likely than anyone to hate her. They saw her power as a corruption of their own even though, so far as Cassia could tell from Galinn's description, the two were nothing alike.

"Shouldn't you be enchanting the winds?" Cassia asked, feeling the ship slow dramatically.

"It's close enough to the end of the workday. Captain won't mind if I stop early for once," he said.

Cassia had no idea what she would have said next. She never had a chance because there came a heavy creaking thud and the *Oneraria* rocked wildly. Hopp burst into the cabin.

"Hopp, this is not the time," Galinn said severely. The huge dog whined at him.

Through the open door came a cacophony of sudden sound: screaming, clanging metal, yells, and thuds. It wasn't normal deck noise. Hopp bounded over to Galinn and barked one low loud command.

"What's going on?" Cassia asked.

"We must have company," the Norseman said grimly, quieting his familiar with a hand on her head.

"We're in the middle of the sea. Who's going to pay us a social visit?"

"Unfriendly company."

"Pirates?" Cassia sucked in a breath.

"Pirates."

Cassia moved toward the door.

Galinn stopped her. "Captain would want us here, protecting the cargo. From the sound of things, we're already boarded."

Cassia nodded and went looking for something to brace the door with, but all the furniture in the cabin was bolted down against the rocking of the water.

Galinn stuck his head out the door for a moment, and then slammed it firmly shut.

"What'd you see?"

"Mmm. It's more what didn't I see."

"Huh?"

"They started out with an invisible galley, that's why we never saw their ship approach. Now there's a large empty space in their attack line that the *Oneraria's* sailors can't break through. They must have a magus on their side using invisibility enchantments." He moved to stand over the hatch that was the only way into the main cargo-hold. "Dog's bollix, I hate counter magic."

A faraway look settled on his face. It was the same look he got right before he acted as weathervane. It meant he was reaching into what he called his cistern of sorcery.

He's been enchanting the wind all day, Cassia thought. She touched his shoulder, but got no response. "You don't have much magic left."

Galinn didn't even register her *voice*.

Cassia drew a long knife out from behind the accounting table. Captain Marinus kept it there for emergencies. She figured this qualified.

Galinn came back from wherever he'd been and blinked at her dully, noting the knife.

"Can you use that?"

"Better than I ought," Cassia said, hearing the sadness in her own voice.

The first of the pirates burst in through the cabin door. Cassia leaped forward to protect Galinn. He'd need to concentrate on his magic. She dispatched the man easily: a clean backhanded slice. He died lying to one side of the doorway with a new red smile across his throat.

Another pirate came through. Cassia's blade snaked forward. This one was better prepared: he had his long, thin, curved sword up and ready. There was a clang as Cassia's short blade slammed against it. Without pause, her left fist shot into the man's stomach, up beneath the ribs. The pirate doubled over and Cassia whacked him across the temple with the pommel of her knife. He too fell. Cassia kicked his body out of her way.

Galinn gaped at her, and then went back to his enchantments.

Cassia did pretty well, with the pirates coming in one at a time. But when a handful all charged into the cabin together, the tide turned. Two went for her at once, back and front, striking high and low at the same time. Cassia turned into a whirling dervish of steel, shifting where she stood so one attacker got in the way of the other. The other pirates closed on Galinn. They clearly had instructions to find the ship's weathervane and kill him at all costs.

The Norseman was looking pale, leaning up against the accounting table. His beautiful blue eyes didn't even see the invaders. The counter magic was taking all of his attention.

Cassia sliced one of her attackers in the stomach. The other lashed out, and while she saw him do so, she had no chance to dodge.

"No," came a cry from across the room.

Cassia's attacker burst into flames before his sword could touch her. He fell screaming to the floor. Galinn had turned his attention into the cabin. But he was running out of magic fast.

Another pirate caught fire but there were still several left alive and Cassia couldn't stop them from reaching him. The Norseman was unarmed, and a magus wouldn't know how to use a sword even if he had one.

Hopp came to her master's defense. The familiar leaped forward and bit into the thigh of the nearest pirate. She must have gone straight through the man's femoral artery, for blood ran everywhere. The massive dog spat out the leg and sneezed in disgust, shaking blood off of her muzzle.

Cassia let out a sort of strangled holler and hurled herself at the back of one of the remaining pirates. Hopp turned her attention to another. Galinn staggered to one side in exhaustion.

Then two more pirates entered the cabin.

Won't they ever stop?

They launched themselves at the weathervane.

The world turned into a mess of knives and blood and flesh and confused yells. Hopp's long yellow teeth snapped. But the whole messy group just kept inching closer and closer to Galinn, who was now slumped on the floor.

I'm going to have to do something.

Cassia turned her long knife on herself, nicking the palm of her left hand. Then she opened her mouth and began to sing.

Everyone in the cabin stilled in wonder.

Cassia's voice was haunting when she spoke, but it was magic when she sang. It rippled through the room, depositing warm drops of sound that slid down the listener's spine.

She looked at Galinn, wondering if he was even awake enough to hear or see what she did. She put him firmly out of her mind and bent down to squeeze her bloody hand onto the man she'd just killed . . . then the man before that, and before that, and before that. All the while she hummed softly, tying the blood into her song, braiding the two together with each note.

She'd never done it intentionally, but it was easier than by accident. Then again, perhaps it was the subject matter. She'd loved her mother. She hated pirates. Did hatred make it easier?

Then Cassia began to sing words. No need for her to reach out to a cistern of sorcery, the magic was in her blood, vibrating through her voice, making words and melody dance together.

Move, urged her song. *Rise. Move again.*

She felt her voice stretch. Her magic sent out tiny questing tunes, dancing down the supernatural path made by her blood, mixing with the blood of each dead pirate.

Cassia called them all to fight their former colleagues. She turned her song into a command, moving the magic about inside the corpses, so that it showed them how to reanimate. They obeyed: they stood, they walked, and then they fought.

The last pirates still attacking Galinn were quickly dead at the hands of their compatriots. Cassia walked over to these new bodies and squeezed her bleeding hand over them as well. With each drop, new notes were added to her song, new depth to the melody. Drip. Drip. Drip. Three more corpses danced to her commands.

All those in the cabin were now Cassia's.

Galinn was far away again, back to working counter enchantments. Cassia had never seen him so pale.

He'll kill himself protecting us. Cassia looked at him a long, sad, lonely moment. Then she sent her corpses off to find the enemy magus.

They rushed out the cabin door and onto the deck. Behind them, over them, urging them on came Cassia's song.

Suddenly the fighting on the deck changed in the *Oneraria's* favor. Captain Marinus' crew was joined by an unbeatably persistent group of bloodied pirates, fighting for the merchant sailors rather than against them.

And someone was singing.

Until then, *Oneraria* had been skirmishing hopelessly against invisible opponents. Galinn's counter magic made them visible from time to time, but it never lasted long. The pirates' magus was fresh while their weathervane was exhausted.

But now, someone was singing.

Cassia's corpses converged on the invisible magus and cut him down. No sorcery could fool the eyes of the dead. The magus became visible, screaming, partly in pain, partly at the shock of being seen and attacked by his own men. He knew his invisibility enchantments hadn't failed, but wasn't alive long enough to figure out what had gone wrong.

Galinn stumbled out onto the deck a short while later. He stopped one of the pirates roughly, turning the man to face him. There was nothing of life in those eyes, nothing but liquid bubbles of song. The man's head lolled in the wrong direction. Both tendons in his neck were sliced through. He wasn't a pirate anymore. He wasn't even a man. He was dead, but moving. Galinn let him go in revulsion and watched, in disgusted horror, as Cassia's corpses finished off the last of their former crewmates.

Cassia walked over and stood next to him, looking out at the deck, still singing. Her voice carried across the prow of the enemy ship and over the wide green of the sea.

"Will you raise up the corpses of dead mariners as well?" Galinn asked, his voice tinged with fear.

Cassia could picture them: dripping seaweed and skin. She could tell Galinn didn't want to believe what she was doing, but horrified realization was behind his question.

Cassia held her left hand cradled in her right. The bleeding had slowed. Her face was pale and haunted.

She was right there next to him. It would be so easy for Galinn to reach out to her, pull her close, comfort her. Or break her neck. Something in those beautiful eyes of his told her he wanted desperately to do both.

"You've siren blood in you," the weathervane said instead, as though by talking he could stop himself from doing either.

Cassia nodded, not pausing her song.

"Mother?" he asked.

Cassia nodded again. Then she sang out one piercing note. Her army of corpses ran and jumped over the edge of *Oneraria's* deck to land back inside their own ship, a many-oared *liburnian* built for speed and war. As she ended her song, they collapsed to lie limp in between the banks of oars.

Cassia looked at Galinn, eyes pleading. "What will you do, now that you know?" Her voice was calm, no sorcery in it anymore, just the sweet intoxication of honey mead.

Galinn's blue eyes narrowed. He didn't deign to glance at her, turning away to look at the sea. "You're stronger than I'll ever be. I can't stop you. Especially not as exhausted as I am now."

Cassia looked at her bloody hand. "My magic doesn't work the way yours does. It's in my blood, you see? It's all in the blood and the voice."

The weathervane shuddered.

"My mother's name was Raidne," Cassia said. "Father found her on an island all alone. He brought her as far inland as he could get and gave up ships for sheep. She never spoke, you know? Not one word. The priests asked me to do the blood rite at her funeral. I didn't know then that I wasn't supposed to sing and bleed at the same time."

"What happened?" Galinn asked. His mouth was drawn down in horror but his eyes stared in fascination.

"She walked right out of her grave and headed towards the coast. I couldn't control *her* corpse. I've no power over a full siren, not even a dead one. I think she missed the sea."

"Gods," the weathervane said.

Around them, sailors were recovering from the fight and murmuring suspiciously amongst themselves. Cassia could feel their eyes on the back of her neck.

Right now they were content to let the magus deal with her. But their reticence wouldn't last. It never did. There was something about necromancy that made the living want to kill. Cassia knew the sound of that blood murmur all too well. It was a hunter's song. It had once bayed after her in her father's voice. Now it would be Galinn's. She touched the Norseman briefly on the arm. He skittered away, repelled.

Cassia dashed across the open deck and leapt, just as her corpses had, over the edge of the *Oneraria*, landing in the pirate's blue-grey *liburnian* below.

Galinn didn't try to prevent her. He stayed with his back to her, staring out over the sea, not wanting to look, unable to stop himself from listening.

Her siren song swelled up out of the galley ship, not sweet like mead but salty as the ocean. Or blood. It called once more for the fallen to rise and do her bidding.

Only then did the weathervane turn to watch the dead row Cassia away.

The Duel
James M. Ward

His Majesty's Articles of War: Article Twenty-Five
Such punishment as a court-martial may adjudge may be inflicted on any person in the Navy
who is guilty of sending or accepting a challenge to fight a duel or acts as a second in a duel.

eep in the red-marbled labyrinth of the building known as the Arcania Admiralty, Carl Bassler, Lord High Protector of the Oceans surrounding Arcania, just finished reading a challenge delivered from the capital city's docks to the north.

"By the gods, has the entire world gone mad?" he said to the empty room. The worried leader started pacing to the wall and back, behind his desk. At sixty, he still had a younger officer's more muscled build. His large, calloused hands spoke of hours spent on the fencing strip every week, keeping himself honed for battle. His thick head of dark hair didn't show any gray. His clean-shaven face presented no wrinkles. He kept glancing at the crumpled piece of parchment in his hand, not believing what he held from the Maleen enemy. "Throckmorton, to me, man!"

Janek, a commander in the Marines, was the Admiral's orderly. Proud of his position, he'd already put several things in place that morning to speed things along for the Admiral. He walked into the office already knowing at least half of what the Admiral would be requesting that day.

"Have you read this?" Bassler said, knowing full well his aide opened and read everything that made it to his desk. Papers that weren't of the utmost importance weren't allowed to even come close to the Lord Admiral's office.

"Yes I have, Lord Bassler, nasty business that. What are you going to do about it, if I may ask?" Janek said.

"Summon John Blithe at once. I'm not going to ask any man to risk his life on such foolishness until I've established this is a real offer," Bassler said. "John is this lad's uncle and will have an opinion on the matter."

"I have him waiting for you in the antechamber. I'll bring him to you at once," Janek said.

Lord Bassler sat, once again marveling at the efficiency of his aide. Bassler had only received the ridiculous missive ten minutes ago and already Janek had managed to summon one of the busiest officers in the navy.

Bassler reviewed what he knew of John Blithe. The navel Master of the Exchequer for all of Arcania, John was in charge of paying the crews of the Arcanian fleets as well as commissioning new ships to be built. He had many brothers and nephews serving in the Arcanian Navy. In fact, the family of Blithe had been serving with distinction in the King's Navy for more than eight generations. Bassler had served under John's grandfather in a dragonship-of-the-line twenty years ago. Most importantly, he was the uncle of Halcyon Blithe, who was the subject matter of the parchment in Bassler's hand. While Lord Bassler routinely sent thousands off to die, he wanted John's opinion on sending just one young nephew out to encounter a possible death trap.

John Blithe walked into the chamber. Tall, like all the Blithes, he looked much younger than his fifty years. His white hair bespoke of his being an Arcanian wizard. All wizards from the island nation developed white hair overnight, when they came into their magic. The naval saber at his hip sported a well-used grip. It wasn't a fancy lord's toy; it was a killing weapon.

"Sit and read this, John. I find myself not amused by what it details."

The Arcanian Admiral watched the older Blithe's face change from calm to angry. The parchment's text was inflammatory and clearly a breach of protocol between countries and gentlemen. Bassler wasn't surprised.

> *This challenge has been posted in both the press of Arcania and the press on the continent.*
>
> *I, Duval Kingmaker, Maleen Admiral of the Western Fleets, publicly call First Lieutenant Halcyon Blithe a coward and a liar. His false reports of my actions have unjustly stained my family's name and my honor. This is my official statement calling him out for a duel to the death.*
>
> *Realizing our two countries are at war, I still require satisfaction. If the coward Halcyon Blithe accepts the duel, I will immediately turn over three captured Arcanian ships-of-the-line with their surviving crews.*
>
> *My second, Lord Garnt, stands ready to discuss the terms of the duel. The shape changer's warship waits off the shore of the Arcanian capital of Ilumin, under a flag of truce.*
>
> *I remain,*
> *Duval Kingmaker*

"John, three ships-of-the-line, lost to the enemy and now possibly returned. I'd be a fool not to want them back," Bassler said. "Even if they fought until they were almost destroyed, there could be as many as a thousand sailors still on those ships. The Maleens, in twenty years of warfare, have never been willing to trade prisoners of war. Will your nephew accept the challenge, allowing our men to come back?"

"If this were a normal call to battle," John said, "my nephew would take the order to fight and leap onto a deck of any Maleen first-rater. On the other hand, Article Twenty-Five is very clear on dueling. He will say no, no matter how much he wants to fight. Know this, there's no fear in my nephew. I've heard of this Kingmaker, and he's a nasty opponent, but Halcyon Blithe is a by-the-book officer, and the book says he can't duel."

"This is important enough to get the King to wave that article, if we can believe what Kingmaker says," Bassler said. "John, your nephew is a seventh son of a seventh son, why don't we have him in the Dragon Air Corps?"

"Halcyon spent a year shipwrecked on the Elese coast," John said. "He had amnesia and recovery from that took time. When he regained his memory and got back to Arcania, he requested a berth on another Dragonship. The Admiralty, at my urging, thought a little more work with sea dragons would help him when he went to deal with air dragons."

"A dashed good thing, he's the best Dragon Speaker I've ever seen. Shame to lose him to the Air Corps," Bassler said. "Throckmorton get in here!"

Janek walked in with a heavy parchment scroll, covered in the King's seals. "Here, my Lords, is a missive from the King allowing all officers and enlisted men the ability to duel in the King's name. After I realized that it would take men standing as seconds, a referee, and doctors to be part of a normal duel, as well as a ship and crew to transport them, I requested everything from the King. He's fully informed on the situation, and these were his exact words on the affair, 'Get our men home as soon as possible.'"

Both men examined the King's signature, equally stunned at Janek's efficiency.

"Well, yes, uh, excellent work, Throckmorton," Lord Bassler said. "Please show Halcyon Blithe in to my chamber."

Now Janek looked surprised. He couldn't help but wonder how the Admiral knew Halcyon Blithe was already available. "Immediately, my Lord."

———⚓———

Halcyon Blithe strode into the chamber, ramrod straight. Not looking left or right, he marched to the desk and saluted Lord Bassler. His face didn't show the joy he felt at seeing his Uncle John. Blithes didn't get together often, and each occasion was one of celebration. The six remaining uncles and all six brothers served in the Arcanian Navy and their duties rarely allowed them time at their castle on the Lankshire county shore.

Halcyon was extremely nervous. He'd traded blast-tube shots with the enemy and remained calm and rock solid, but being ordered to come to Lord Bassler's office put him on edge. He had been magically whisked off the deck of his DragonFrigate when Janek summoned him for this meeting.

At eighteen, Halcyon was an exceptionally talented young officer, clearly on his way up in the ranks of the Navy. His chest was filled with battle decorations, some of them given to him from kings of other nations. Standing six-feet-two-inches, he had the long white hair of an Arcanian wizard. The enchanted naval saber at his hip was designed especially to kill demons, and its well-worn bell-guard testified to a great deal of use. Seeing more than his share of blood and war, he still had the boyish good looks that made the court ladies swoon.

"First Lieutenant Halcyon Blithe reporting as ordered, Lord Admiral Bassler."

"Stand at ease, Lieutenant," Bassler said.

"Thank you, sir." Halcyon took a moment to hug his uncle. "It's good to see you again, Uncle John."

"What do you know of a Maleen fleet officer, named Duval Kingmaker?" Bassler said.

"Sir, I've given several reports on Kingmaker to the Admiralty. I first met him on the mission to seek help from the dwarves. He kidnapped the Arcanian ambassador we were escorting to Crystal City, and I was part of the group that won our man's freedom.

"Duval was the one who shot a DragonFrigate out from under me as we sailed back to Arcania from that same mission," Halcyon said. "I was shipwrecked on the coast of Elese. I'd smashed my head and had amnesia for a time. I wandered to Anatol, the Elesean capital. I met and battled with Duval again in that city. He's an expert swordsman and wizard. From things he's said, I gather he's some sort of royalty among the Maleen people. That's all I know."

"Please read this missive from the scoundrel and tell me what you think," Bassler said.

Halcyon picked up the parchment. As he read through the message his hand clinched tighter on the paper, but he controlled his expression. When he was finished, he came to attention once more.

"I am not a liar or a coward," Halcyon said. "If it weren't for his Majesty's Article of War, Number Twenty-Five, I would fight and kill this man for what he has said. I hope some day to meet him on the deck of his ship."

"You might be getting your chance, sooner than you expected," Uncle John said. "Now read this interesting order from our King."

"How can this be?" Halcyon said. "Dueling an enemy captain at his pleasure would bring chaos in the ranks of the entire Navy. We can't let this fool change the way the entire Navy operates, can we?"

"This affair and that parchment are going to stay in your hands," Lord Bassler said. "That order from the King is not becoming a general order of the Navy. It only applies to this one situation. Send a man you can trust to act as your second and meet with this shape changer. Establish the terms of the duel. I will be sending a war wizard I can trust to act as the referee for the bloody affair. Nothing happens until we receive the three ships and crews as promised. Since I see your desire in this affair, I'll put you and your seconds in the fastest DragonFrigate we've got. You'll sword this Duval and be back before the next full moon. Do you understand me, Lieutenant?"

"Aye, aye sir, I do." Halcyon saluted his uncle and the Lord Admiral. The thought of getting another chance to come to grips with Duval pleased him to no end. *Liar indeed*, he thought.

"Nephew, do not forget this is some vicious Maleen trap," Uncle John said. "This is not a normal affair of honor. Be the gentleman and officer I know you are, but expect foul tricks at every corner."

"Of course it's some sort of trick," Bassler said. "And make no mistake, we will take every measure we can think of to carefully inspect the returning crews and ships when they come to us. I'm sure this Duval wants you dead, but this isn't the only reason they're sending back our crews. You, Lieutenant, will caution your second to expect deceptions from the other side. The war wizard I send to be your referee will help watch your back. Take a day to get your affairs settled. Throckmorton!"

Janek walked into the chamber with a set of orders. He handed them to the Lord Admiral to sign. "This order puts the DragonFrigate *Leviathan* at the Lieutenant's disposal to sail wherever he needs. This order allows Halcyon to bring whom he wills into this duel. This final order frees up War Wizard Bite to act as the Lieutenant's referee for the duel."

"Bite is an excellent choice, well done Janek," Bassler said.

"I didn't know the *Leviathan* was back in port," Uncle John said.

"It's just coming into the bay now from its three weeks of trials," Janek said.

Uncle John looked pleased. "It's our latest and fastest DragonFrigate. The sea dragon used as the keel is unusually large and aggressive. The crew is experienced and you'll find Captain Gygax a sound officer with excellent skills."

"Well, Halcyon," Bassler said. "I'm used to sending fleets off into deadly danger, but I've never sent a single man to fight for his life and the lives of a thousand Arcanian sailors." Smiling for the first time, he filled four chalices with Arcanian Red wine. He handed the chalices out and raised his. "Confusion to our enemies, and especially yours, Halcyon. Drink up."

"Here, here!" they all said, drinking deeply.

———— ⚓ ————

Two days later, the *Leviathan* floated at anchor a mile away from the Maleen ship. The enemy second-rater had obviously seen a lot of hard use. The ship sported patches of new wood all over its hull, at odds with the darkened, sea-stained sections. Fifty closed blast-tube ports per side defined the ship as a killer of enemy vessels.

Two Arcanian first-raters floated a half mile off the prow and another two were off the stern of the enemy vessel.

"He's been there more than two hours. It shouldn't take that long for a second to agree to the terms of a duel," Halcyon said.

"Ashe will be fine," Deena said. Half troll and half human, she stood almost six feet, with long blue hair and olive-colored skin. A recently promoted lieutenant in the Marines, she sported thirty-seven tiny glass skulls in her braided hair, one for every Maleen officer she'd killed in hand to hand combat. Deena and Halcyon had been friends and fought in many actions together.

"I can sense he's finished with the negotiations and will come back shortly," Wizard Bite said. He stood almost seven feet. His flesh appeared bleached-white and tight to his bones, giving him a skeletal look. He had the white hair of all Arcanian wizards. A sunken look to his eyes spoke of some horror encountered earlier in his life. "You'll be happy to know my scans revealed your Ashe Fallow unnerved the shape changer just as much as that creature worried our Chief Petty Officer. They've never seen a changeling like Fallow. When you have time I would like to know about the magics that are currently transforming him into a dwarf."

"It's no secret," Halcyon said. "I foolishly used an enchantment to kill an enemy, but it burnt Ashe's hands in the process. Later, I was able to gain a dwarven wish, and I used that spell weaving to heal him. Unknown to all of us, using that wish began a transformation that is slowly changing him into a dwarf."

"An amazing story. I should like to study him a bit, after this affair is over," Bite said.

"Supply a few bottles of Lankshire Green, and you can study him all you want," Deena said.

In the distance, a red-haired sailor got into the jolly boat and its crew started rowing back to the DragonFrigate.

A plume of purple smoke rose from the center of the Maleen ship. The security teams of marines rowed their jolly boats out from the prow and stern, rowing toward the pairs of guarding Arcanian warships.

Ashe Fallow was soon on board the *Leviathan* and they all adjourned to the captain's cabin.

Ashe was a broad-shouldered sailor standing five feet six inches. He'd shrunk a bit under the dwarven wish. He sported bushy, long red hair, but kept his face clean-shaven even though he had to shave twice a day to keep back the growth. There was a sparkle to his eyes, and he looked thirty though his true age was fifty-seven.

"A nasty bit of business, that meeting," Ashe said. Downing a tankard of Alm Black wine, he appeared to relax. "That plume of smoke is summoning the three Arcanian ships they are turning over to our fleet. I told them we wouldn't budge until we had the ships in our control.

"Captain Gygax, we're to set course for Bone Island for the duel. It's about three day's sail west of here. It's a pirate's watering hole. There are two large volcanoes, and between them is a mass of sand dunes. There isn't much there, which is why they picked the spot. We'll need to signal the four warships to let the Maleen ship sail away, at your command of course, Lieutenant Blithe. We're allowed to follow after sunset."

"What are the terms of the duel?" Bite said.

"The shape shifter didn't ask for anything unusual," Ashe said. "We're to post our ship on the south end of the island, and he'll post his on the north. At sunrise we're to meet his people at the center of the island.

"I inspected the blade Kingmaker will use just as his second inspected Hal's. His is enchanted with red death runes and a demon has been bound to the pommel. I think it's the weapon he used when you fought him on the stairs, that day in Crystal City. I'll be inspecting Kingmaker and the shape changer will be inspecting you, Hal, just before the duel begins. Neither party can have magical fields of force established before the duel. I insisted we place his dragon familiar in a silver cage. Wizard Bite, you'll have to fashion one of those."

"He has a familiar?" Bite said. "The creature will be able to lend him some powers during the duel no matter what type of cage I put it in, but I can make sure it cannot cast spells."

"I'm sure you'll do your best, Wizard," Halcyon said.

"They didn't like the fact that I insisted your saber would be dipped in Tannin oil," Ashe continued. "We're giving them a barrel of it before they ship off. They wanted to test its properties. You are to have no other weapons or armor except for your saber. I couldn't get them to agree to your bracers, I'm sorry Hal."

"Not to worry, what about my luck ring?"

"You can wear it. He isn't allowed any other magic but his saber," Ashe said. "I was able to insist on that. Neither side can bring doctors. The shape changer made it very clear that this was to be a duel to the death. I made all attempts to stop the duel by asking Kingmaker to apologize, but that isn't going to happen. He wants you dead Hal, make no mistake about it."

"That's all right. I feel the same way."

"The Wizard Bite can have any spells he wishes activated before and during the duel," Ashe said. "There shouldn't be any of us thinking they aren't plotting some trick. We'll be as prepared for it as possible. I'll have my blast-pike at the ready. The shape changer is allowed his own weapon and equipment. That's it, does anyone have any questions?"

"Sails ho!" came the shout from above deck.

Everyone went topside to see three badly battered Arcanian ships on the horizon—a first-rater and two second-raters.

"They're from the southern fleet," Bite said.

The ships had their masts shot away. They were using freshly patched-together jibs to make way on the calm seas. Their bilge pumps were working hard, throwing tons of water off the sides of each ship. Their blast-tubes were all gone and the ships rode high out of the water.

"The Maleen love our blast-tubes," Deena said. "They stripped them all off the ships before they let them go."

"By the way those pumps are working, there's a lot of damage under the water line, but that's not our concern," Captain Gygax said. "The four ships guarding the Maleen have their orders. Wizards and healers will be all over those vessels to inspect them and their crews for Maleen tricks. We'll set sail when the sun sets, and with any luck, easily beat that shape changer's ship to Bone Island. Better get some rest, all of you. Your work starts in three days."

THUMPT

THUMPT

The loud noise from above decks woke Halcyon from a restless sleep the second day out. He leapt out of his hammock, pulled on his boots and jacket and went to investigate.

THUMPT

Deena was handling a huge crossbow. The weapon was almost as wide as she was tall. She used a claw device to pull back the wire, which bent the two metal bows of the weapon. Even her considerable muscles bulged under the strain. Far in the distance, off the stern of the ship, was a floating wooden target. It must have been almost five hundred yards away in their wake.

THUMPT and a foot-long wedge of iron flew from the moving deck of the DragonFrigate to strike the target.

THUMPT and another bolt flew towards the target.

Ashe held a far-looker in his hand. "High and to the right on that one, and it hit the outer ring."

After each firing, she ran to another section of the ship, arming the crossbow as she moved to the new firing position. Once cocked, she would turn and take another shot at the target.

THUMPT

She never missed entirely, but rarely hit the center. The look on her face told everyone she was getting more and more angry.

"Winds picking up, north by northwest," Ashe said. "That last one was low, but in the second ring. Good shot."

"I thought it took two men to use that type of crossbow," Halcyon said. "Even then, I've only seen it used on the forecastle of a sloop."

"One of us needs to be watching your back from a distance," Ashe said. There was a bit of sadness in his voice.

Halcyon knew his chief wanted to be the one in the action, eliminating hidden interference. If Halcyon were in his place, he wouldn't have wanted to be the one standing on the sidelines as a second, watching the duel, but not participating.

"It turns out she's way better at shooting than I am," Ashe said. "Deena's strong enough to handle that heavy crossbow like a personal toy. She's going to be able to stand off on a rise and pick off any unwelcome friends Duval brings to the party."

"This is supposed to be a duel, not a crossbow contest," Halcyon said.

THUMPT

"Bull's-eye!" Ashe said. "That's enough for today. Oil that thing and sharpen the bolts. You know what, Deena, dip them in Tannin oil. You never know when you're going to deal with magical foes."

Halcyon was going to tell them that this was his duel and he wouldn't need their help. Then, realizing whom he was dealing with, he kept his thoughts to himself. Duval Kingmaker was not a gentleman in any sense of the word. Halcyon also doubted he could keep his friends away, even with a direct order. Ashe, a fellow Lankshire countryman, had been giving him good advice since the first day Halcyon set foot on a dragon-ship-of-the-line.

"Deena and I are your seconds," Ashe said. "We have your back in case something evil happens. If all goes fairly and honestly, you won't even see her. I suggest you go and find some likely officers, and bout with them a bit. We want that sword arm nice and limber in a day or two when the quickness of your hand and sharpness of your eye are all that's protecting your heart."

— ⚓ —

The *Leviathan* reached Bone Island when the moon was high in the sky. Halcyon couldn't sleep and was roaming the upper deck.

Ashe came to stand with him. "I can't sleep either."

"Where's the jolly boat going?" Halcyon said.

"The Wizard Bite and Deena are getting to the dueling sight early," Ashe said. "They want to make sure there are no hidden or magical surprises when you two start dueling. You know Duval is going to find some way to cheat, don't you?"

"I've fought the man three times now," Hal said. "I know his true nature. With you at my back, I'm not concerned about his tricks. We Blithes are men of war. I've practiced with my saber for ten years. I grew up hearing war stories and listening to the brave exploits of my uncles and brothers. When the dawn's light strikes the sand dunes, I'll be there and ready to fight for my King and my honor. If fate takes me, I'll go down swinging, spitting in Duval's eye."

"That's the spirit, Hal," Ashe said. "We Lankshire men know how to deal with success or failure. You're going to have a long life, and the likes of Duval Kingmaker won't be taking your measure. Get a good meal in you now. You'll need the energy for later."

———⚓———

When the sun's rays moved above the horizon, Halcyon and Ashe climbed the last dune to stand in the middle of the island. Three sand dunes formed a small depression, with the sea lapping the fourth side. The entire area wasn't more than two hundred yards long and a hundred yards wide. The Wizard Bite and the shape changer were there at the edge of the sea, as well as Duval Kingmaker.

He stood a bit over six feet, with short dark hair, and a keen look to his dark eyes. Dressed in a fencing shirt, dark pants, and black fencing boots, he cut a stylish figure. His weapon was already drawn, and the red runes on the demon blade glowed like embers.

A small dragon flew above his shoulder. Duval's familiar. Bite motioned for Duval to send his creature into a glowing silver cage which he had prepared beforehand. The creature whined, but did what it was ordered. More arcane energies flashed purple on the bars and around the cage as Bite locked it in. The tiny dragon smashed itself against the bars, drawing purple sparks. It cried out in pain and anger, but kept away from the bars.

"Ah, Lieutenant Halcyon Blithe, so good of you to make it," Duval said. "A pity my small pet must be caged, but I quite understand."

"You will not talk to your opponent until the duel begins," Wizard Bite said. "We will observe the strict rules of dueling here. Lieutenant, stand on your mark while you hear what I have to say. Chief Fallow, you will stand on my left while Lord Garnt stands on my right."

The seven foot tall monster was in its true form with its four eyes and tusked maw. Its warty green skin and four massive arms testified to its power. Halcyon shivered briefly, remembering the life and death fight he had on his first ship with another shape changer.

The wizard raised his staff and it flared briefly with a blinding radiance.

Bite walked to the middle of the fencing area and turned to face the two seconds.

"We are here because of a dispute of honor of the third degree," the wizard said. "Seconds, have you talked to your primaries about settling this without bloodshed?"

Both Ashe Fallow and Lord Garnt replied that their primaries weren't interested in peaceably settling the affair.

Bite turned toward Duval. "By the dueling code, I'm required to ask you to put aside your differences. Will you settle this affair in a peaceful way?"

"It is my intention to kill Blithe to avenge my honor, and nothing less than his death will suit me," Duval said.

"Lieutenant Blithe, is it your wish to continue this matter to the death?"

Halcyon fought to keep his face neutral, not wanting to give Duval anything. "I'm at the Maleen's service in this matter."

The Wizard Bite took his post and raised his staff. "I am to act as the neutral referee. I take my duties very seriously. During the course of the duel, if either man displays dishonorable character, I will kill that duelist without mercy. If the seconds interfere, I will kill them too."

He narrowed his gaze. "The duel is not to move outside the limits of this depression. If either of you move over a sand dune, you will be marked as a coward and I will kill you. If one of you moves into the sea or uses myself or the seconds as impediments to the battle, I will kill you. Doubting my abilities would be a mistake."

The wizard raised his staff and a lightning bolt struck the sand dune on the opposite side of the dueling area. A huge pool of melted sand bubbled where the bolt struck.

"Seconds, please submit your primary's weapons for my inspection."

Garnt and Fallow brought the blades to the wizard.

"It is my understanding," the wizard said, "that Admiral Kingmaker is aware of the Tannin oil placed on Lieutenant Blithe's blade?"

"Yes, that's correct," the shape changer said.

"It is also my understanding that Lieutenant Blithe is aware of the enchanted death runes on Admiral Kingmaker's blade?"

"He knows about the bloody things," Ashe said. "But Lankshire men don't care about trifles, if you get my meaning."

"Return the blades to your primaries," the wizard said. "We will begin at once. Gentlemen, come enguarde with your saber tips almost touching."

Halcyon looked into the sky for a moment, taking the time to breathe in the fresh sea air. The sun's rays warmed his heart and settled his nerves. He'd had a good life, but wanted more years to avenge his father's death at the hands of four Maleen warships. Holding his blade in the loose grip of a master fencer, he took one more deep breath. He was as ready as he'd ever be for the duel.

"By the dueling code both countries recognize," Bite said, "I must ask you one last time, is there a way to settle your differences in a peaceful manner?" Bite said.

"Let's get on with this, I have a fleet to command," Duval said.

"To the death then," Halcyon said.

"Seconds, if your primary suffers a wound, you may not go to his aid," Bite said. "This is a duel to the death, and one primary must be killed."

Halcyon watched his opponent closely. Expecting tricks, he planned on fencing carefully in the first heartbeats of the duel.

"Allie!"

With that shout, the death duel began.

For Halcyon's part, he took a close guard stance with his knees lowered and his saber pulled in low and close to his hip with the tip aimed squarely at Duval's chest.

THUMPT

Duval ducked when he heard the noise, stepping back out of lunging range.

Halcyon knew exactly what just happened, and never flinched. "Ignore the noise, it won't effect what happens between us."

Duval shifted to an open ward stance with his blade held high between them, ready to slash down or parry across an attack.

The two of them tested each other by circling with the tips of their blades barely touching. Each blade wove a tight circle around the other.

"As you know, Kingmaker, my blade is covered with Tannin oil," Halcyon said, "which is excellent for allowing weapons to get past arcane barriers."

THUMPT

"Imagine if you will—"

Duval made a half lunge, and Halcyon countered with a perfect master cut that deflected the incoming blow and struck at his opponent at the same time. Both combatants stepped back out of range.

"If I may continue," Halcyon said. "Imagine a wizard with magical protections up, positioning himself on the edge of one of these sand dunes. He plans to cast hindering spells on me."

Their blades flashed back and forth in a dizzying display of attacks and parries, and still no blood was drawn.

"Our good referee would not detect that magic," Halcyon said. "Naturally, such an attack would be dishonorable and cowardly. You also wouldn't want the rest of the world to know you had arranged such a trick."

THUMPT

Duval grimaced, but didn't duck this time.

"Imagine those wizards and their surprise when a twelve-inch-long crossbow bolt punches through each of their skulls," Halcyon said. "A bolt coated in Tannin oil, of course."

Duval's face clouded over in anger. "I call you juggler and unworthy of the blade you use." He backed away and went into a purely defensive stance with his saber in a middle guard position close to his hip and pointing at Halcyon's face. "Now, permit me a story."

Halcyon stepped back out of lunging range. He held his weapon to the side and bowed, his eyes locked on Duval's face.

"Imagine three battle-worn ships filled with sailors. Those poor crewmen find themselves taken back to the capital city of a pitiful, struggling island nation. These same crews are wined and dined; finding themselves treated as the heroes they surely are. After all, the Maleen Empire has never traded prisoners in all its years of war. Those same sailors travel to their homes all over the island. They would be warmly welcomed by adoring family and friends."

Duval shifted forward ever so slightly. Halcyon moved back a step with a stop thrust to let Duval know forward motion was out of the question. Duval's brow was blotted with sweat, but his face broke into a grin.

"Then imagine the surprise as each of the rescued sailors erupts with a terrible plague of blisters and deadly fever. One could easily imagine most of the people of the island dying from that plague. Couldn't one?"

With killing intent, Halcyon rushed his foe. He raged at the thought that his personal duel could allow a devastating plague attack to his beloved island nation. He could only hope that the wizards would discover the plague. Halcyon used a throwing-the-point attack where he feinted a cut at Duval's head and turned the slash into a straight thrust to his foe's throat.

Duval was able to use a mollinet, twisting his saber in a circle to drive Halcyon's blade away and at the same time slashing at his forearm. The blade bit into flesh, drawing a line of blood.

Duval expected his blade to end his foe's life with just a touch, just as it had hundreds of times before. He gloated, and did not move back enguarde.

Halcyon's ring squeezed on his finger, letting him know it had just blocked a harmful enchantment. Halcyon twisted his saber along the line of Duval's attack.

His sword thrust straight into Duval's heart.

An amazed look filled his face as he sank to the sands. His weapon howled its rage, falling from lifeless fingers. Halcyon retrieved the deadly weapon, snapped it in two over his knee, and threw the pieces into the ocean. It screamed in pain and horror as it hit the water.

The dragon familiar screeched and suddenly burst into flame. In a heartbeat, all that was left of the creature were ashes at the bottom of the cage.

Garnt screamed and took a step toward Halcyon as if to attack.

The Wizard Bite raised his staff as he turned toward the shape changer. "Don't even think to move into the fencing strip. You'll report that your primary fought well and died today. We won't dishonor his name or this duel by mentioning the three wizards sent to help him. Take the body and go."

Halcyon turned away from the body, walked a few steps, and fell to his knees.

Ashe cheered for joy. Deena echoed his cry as she came running from the dunes.

Bite watched the shape changer as the creature easily slung the body of Duval over its shoulder and trudged out of sight.

"Lieutenant Blithe," Bite said, "as the neutral referee in this affair, I want to say you handled yourself very well. When other enemy admirals and generals come calling for a duel, please allow me to stand as referee again."

Halcyon could only watch the waves rolling in, glad to be alive.

Dryad in the Mast
Leslie Brown

Captain Jeptha Simms contemplated his mizzenmast from the vantage of his quarter deck. He was not yet worried, but he *was* mildly concerned. He had paid good money for that mast, funds that he could ill afford, having had to stay in port for the last month for fear of pirates and privateers. The High Seat had sent several war ships to clear the shipping lanes and, on its word that those routes were now safe, Jeptha had left port and was making his belated run to the Northern Spice Islands in his barquentine, the *Secret Wish*. It was good to feel the salt spray in his face and hear the familiar creak of the rigging.

The mizzenmast was a replacement for the last one, splintered into kindling by a privateer they had met. Jeptha had mourned Thyia as he would a good friend but he had been consoled by the sight of her soul in the shape of a white bird, winging its way to heaven. As upsetting as the loss of Thyia, was the decimation of his crew by the same attack. Half had been killed or maimed. The rest had decided to seek their livelihoods on land. Unlike Jeptha, they weren't willing to trust the High Seat's word, so a new crew had to be hired. They seemed to be working out well under the sharp eye of the first mate, and now all Jeptha needed was for the newest of his three dryads to put in an appearance.

Almost in response to his thoughts, there was a shimmer at the base of the foremast and Semele stepped out of the wood onto the pumice-polished deck. She looked around for Jeptha and smiled when she saw him standing above her. She made her way gracefully across the deck, deliberately oblivious to the looks of suppressed lust in the eyes of the sailors. Jeptha had promised that any man who touched one of the tree spirits would hang gutted from the crossbeam of the offended dryad's mast. He knew of many ships whose dryads never left their wood, only forming lips on the surface of their mast to answer questions. He was proud that his girls trusted him enough to sit and take honey water with him at the captain's table. He extended his hand to Semele, still amazed after all these years at her grace and the proud carriage of her slim shoulders. He knew better than to expect her walnut-brown hair to go gray or for wrinkles to appear around her leaf-green eyes but it still seemed odd that, after all they had been through together, she did not reflect the years as he did. Although she looked like a woman in her twenties, Jeptha always thought of her as the oldest, most mature of his dryads.

"May I offer you something, Semele? Dates? Honey water?"

The dryad shook her head. "No, I am fine, Jeptha. Please excuse Pherusa's absence, but she is fatigued."

Jeptha frowned at his mainmast. He had never known one of his dryads to admit to being tired. "Is she well?"

"Oh yes, but she was up all the night trying to talk some sense into the mizzenmast dryad."

Jeptha perked up at this. "Oh, so there really is one in there? I thought Timon at the shipyards might have sold me empty wood."

"She's in there all right," Semele said, tossing her hair back over her shoulders, a sign of irritation. "Her name's Aethre and I swear there's some rowan or ash in her."

Jeptha frowned in puzzlement. "But she's a pine mast."

Semele patted his arm. "It's just a saying, Jeptha. It means she's not placid and enduring, but rather, stubborn and a slight bit fey."

Jeptha did not understand any of this so he went to the root of his concerns.

"Can she tell the weather?"

"I don't know what she told Pherusa but you can probably be confident that she can. Catyd may be getting old but she hasn't lost her touch with bell-string spells."

"If that dryad won't talk to me, I'll have to invoke her through her bells."

Semele looked alarmed. "No, please don't do that: it would be very traumatic for her. Let Pherusa and me talk to her this night when it's quiet and the men are not around. We can explain what is required of her."

"Fine, fine," Jeptha said, grumpily. After all, he had paid good money for her. "Just remember, she's the one I need the most. I don't need Pherusa to tell me who's lying until we trade, and your clairvoyance is limited at best." Oh. He could have bitten his tongue. Semele turned her face away from him.

"I'm sorry, Semele. It's not as if I'm not pleased with you. I am, very." He had known Semele longer than he had his wife. He had brought his two infant daughters on board to show to her, only days after they had been born. It wasn't the dryad's fault that the spell of viewing distant events was fading thirty years after it had been cast. Eventually it would vanish and he would be faced with the possibility of having to cut the silver rope that kept the bells tied to Semele's mast and her soul imprisoned in the dead wood of her tree. Then her soul would fly up and away like Thyia's and he would have to buy a new foremast. Or he could keep Semele the way she was, forever. He didn't want to ask Semele what she wanted: he was afraid of the answer. Yes, best not to ask.

Semele nodded respectfully to him and made her elegant way to Pherusa's mast. She laid a hand on the wood and soon the other dryad's blonde head emerged. The two dryads conversed and Jeptha noticed he was tapping his fingers impatiently on the rail. If he had known that breaking in a new dryad was going to be so difficult, he might have bought a dead mast instead. Yet the spell that came with his mizzenmast dryad was the most vital to his business. She could let him know over which horizon the storms lurked, where the sea was becalmed and the safest way between all these hazards. A dryad could carry only one spell and it was entirely at the whim of the spellmistress as to which of the ten or so spells at her command she used. He had been lucky that a mizzenmast with storm-detecting abilities had come on the market so soon after losing Thyia.

"The men are afraid of them, you know," said the first mate, who had quietly stepped behind Jeptha.

"And what do you mean by that, Kincaid?" Jeptha asked, bristling at the implied criticism of his dryads.

"Nothing, Sir. It's just that sailors are a superstitious lot. They don't see or hear of mast dryads much these days: few shipbuilders bother putting special masts in their ships anymore."

"My family has sailed ships on the trading routes for two hundred years, Kincaid. Every single ship had dryad masts and every single ship prospered. Dryads are tradition for us."

"If they've done so well for you, Sir, why do you only have one ship left to your family's name and a season spent at dock?"

Jeptha spun on his first mate, hands balled into fists.

"The same bad luck that's kept everyone in port, dryads or no dryads. And that changed for the good when the High Seat finally started earning the taxes we pay to it by hunting down the pirates!"

Kincaid smirked at him and Jeptha realized that all the man wanted was a rise out of his captain. The man was a fine seaman and a natural leader which was why Jeptha tolerated his thinly veiled insolence, but now he wondered if he had made a mistake in doing so.

"If you don't like what's on this ship, Kincaid, you can leave and find one more to your liking at Vanad Port."

Kincaid, his bluff called, touched his forehead with his knuckle.

"No, Sir, I like it fine here. I'm just telling you what the men think."

"It's your job as mate to change their thinking and not bother me with it," Jeptha said, pointedly turning his back on the man. First a stubborn dryad and then a back-talking first mate. What an ill-luck run this had been, so far.

They made good time, running before the wind, and were on schedule by night-fall. Jeptha dined alone in his cabin and then went up to the quarter deck to watch the progress of his fore- and mainmast dryads. They stood close to the mizzenmast, heads bent close to the wood, but he could not hear what they were saying. He waited until the night watch had rung two sets of bells and then marched over to the mizzenmast.

"Any progress, ladies?" he asked and saw, with disbelief, both dryads position themselves between him and the mast. "What's this? What don't you want me to see?"

"Nothing, Jeptha," Semele said soothingly, "it's just that she's terrified of humans. We haven't been able to get past that yet. We need more time."

"She was in an isolated grove, far up a mountain," Pherusa said, her voice like honey. "She had never seen a human until one tied the bells around her and chopped her down."

"Ladies, I am a businessman. I can't afford to waste time coddling this girl. Step aside."

"Don't do this, Jeptha," Semele pleaded.

He looked at her with astonishment.

"Are you telling me what to do, Semele?"

"It's wrong," she whispered.

"Not at all," he said, still shocked at her resistance. "I'll be very gentle. If this upsets you ladies, I suggest you go back to your masts. Now."

The two dryads glided away, casting troubled glances over their shoulders. How dare they second-guess him? Who was captain of this ship?

Jeptha tapped lightly on the mizzenmast's bells, in the sequence taught to him by the spellmistress, to make the dryad extrude her face from her mast. He was not going to make her emerge entirely. He shielded what he was doing from the night watch with the bulk of his body. It would not do to have anyone else with the knowledge of how to summon one of his dryads.

A face appeared on the surface of the mast. It was wild-eyed, and the teeth were bared in fear. Through the distortion of the features, Jeptha could discern a young woman with the first flush of newly-discovered beauty upon her.

"Shhh, sweet one, little girl, it's all right," he crooned. After ten minutes of listening to his murmured nonsense, the panting gasps of the dryad slowed until finally the frightened eyes fixed themselves upon his face.

"Man!" It was an accusation.

"Yes, I am a man. I am captain of this ship. Her name is the *Secret Wish* and she is my pride and joy." He kept his voice low and soft, trying to lull her as he had his firstborn. Elisha's colic had been a terrible trial.

"I am cut! I am not a tree anymore." Her voice caught on sobs. "You have done this."

"It's the way of the world, my lamb. I did not cut you, but I did buy you to be a mast on my ship. On the *Secret Wish*, you will travel and see wonders, things you would never see if you stayed rooted to the ground."

"Take me back!"

"I can't, sweeting. You will see: things will be better when you stop being so upset." He ordered the watch to bring him a chair from his cabin and he sat beside the mast, talking to her about anything and everything. By four bells, she had calmed and seemed to be listening. He kept talking even though his voice was starting to crack. His father had done this with Semele and Pherusa although they seemed to have forgotten it.

Finally his voice gave out and he stood.

"I'm going to release you from the summoning now so you can go back inside your mast. I want you to think about how to use the power the bells have given you. You can sense the weather for many miles around the ship. I want you to try and look for storms. Will you do that for me, Aethre?"

Her eyes dulled with fatigue, the dryad nodded and Jeptha tapped the release sequence on the bells, allowing her to pull her face back inside the mast. Eventually, when he could trust her, he would tap in the sequence that he had done for Semele and Pherusa, which would allow Aethre to leave her mast whenever she wanted. He couldn't do this, however, until he knew she had accepted her fate. There had been cases of dryads throwing themselves overboard and getting too far from their masts. Those dryads, instead of turning into white birds and ascending, evaporated into a salt mist. Sailors claimed that these doomed dryads haunted the rigging of cursed ships as phosphorescent balls of corpse light.

Tiredly, Jeptha made his way towards his cabin. As he passed her mast, Semele stuck her face part way out.

"Jeptha, I'm sorry," she whispered.

He ignored her and went to his bed.

He was still tired the next morning but he rose at his usual time. He didn't want to seem weak in front of the men, especially Kincaid. He walked straight to the mizzenmast and bowed his head to it.

"Good morning, Aethre," he said to it and waited. Finally, just as he was about to tap her bells, the lovely face emerged from the wood.

"Good morning, Jeptha, Captain," she said, ducking her head away from his gaze.

"You may call Jeptha, my dear. Have you had any luck using your power?"

"I . . . feel things, dark knotted things, but I don't know what they are."

"They may be storms. Thyia called them headaches. When she faced in the direction of the storm, the headache got worse. Can you feel which direction these dark knotted things are in?"

The dryad was silent for a moment, thinking. Then she nodded towards the north. "There. It's there."

"Very good, my dear. We'll skirt a course in that direction just to see if you're right." He called commands to the steersman and got a shouted acknowledgment. The dryad had retreated back into her mast and he let her be.

He turned to his other two masts. "Semele, Pherusa, will you take breakfast with me?"

Two subdued dryads emerged and glided towards him. Semele parted her lips to speak, but Jeptha held up a finger to stop her.

"Today is a brand new day, my dears. Let us treat it as so." The dryads humbly went by him and entered his cabin. He followed smugly, satisfied that he had made his point. A captain was not to be questioned on his own ship.

A few hours later, the crow's-nest called a storm sighting. Jeptha trained his telescope on the horizon. The storm rolled and boiled in the sky.

"Hard starboard, helm," Jeptha said. "We don't want it to notice us." The ship heeled obediently and Jeptha kept an eye on the storm to make sure it did not move in their direction. It was a risk, coming close enough to see it, even through his powerful telescope, but he needed to know if he could trust his mizzenmast to steer him clear of the semi-sentient clouds, a remnant of the wizard wars of two thousand years past.

"Good job, Aethre," he said to his mast. She didn't emerge but he knew she could hear him. "Let me know if you sense any more storms, day or night. You come and tell me. I am tapping out the sequence on your bells that permits you to leave your mast of your own free will. If you are too afraid to do so now, tell Semele and she'll come and get me."

Later that afternoon, he took his chair and sat beside the mizzenmast again. This time, he asked Semele and Pherusa to join him. He could tell Pherusa wasn't happy to be out in the brisk breeze because it tangled her fine blond hair into a mess of knots, but he knew she was too chastised to complain. They chatted casually about ports they had visited and rich cargos they had sold. Enthralled by the conversation, Aethre slowly emerged from her mast until Semele stopped her.

"Aethre, dear, let me show you how to make clothing." She showed the young dryad how to fashion the salt spray and the sunlight into a white, gauzy robe, identical to the ones that she and Pherusa wore. Distracted by the novelty of forming a dress from the air, Aethre even laughed, a charming giggle. Jeptha beamed paternally on the scene and congratulated himself even further when Aethre, unselfconsciously, stepped out onto the deck. She quickly realized where she was and jumped back into the mast. Jeptha and the other dryads pretended they hadn't noticed.

"Aethre, would you like to see something interesting?" Jeptha asked.

The dryad nodded shyly.

"Semele, call the tiburi."

"Jeptha, I don't really like to . . ." Semele trailed off when she saw his face. Mutely she rose and stepped to the rail. The sailors noticed and nudged each other. Throwing her head back, she uttered a wailing cry that rose in pitch until it was inaudible. She gave several of these until one of the sailors at the rail shouted.

"There's one!"

Aethre stepped out of her mast to see better and Jeptha gently took her arm. She flinched and stared at him.

"I'm just keeping you safe, sweeting," he murmured and she let him guide her to the rail. Below them, the water started to churn. A sleek white body was turning in tight figure eights, making the sea foam. Semele gave one last cry and the creature raised its head from the waves.

"Look at its face," Jeptha said. She peered downwards and he tightened his grip surreptitiously. The tibur's face was that of a man's, except the mouth was wide and gaping, a slit that ran from ear to ear. Sharp rows of teeth glinted from the gaping orifice.

"Is it a man?" Aethre asked, frowning in puzzlement and completely forgetting that she was outside of her mast and vulnerable.

"They say it used to be," Jeptha said. "Many years ago, when the wizards fought sea battles, they cast spells on the ocean itself so any sailor falling into it would change into a tibur, ready to do the bidding of the wizard who had changed him."

"Can they speak?"

"I have never heard one do so. They come to ships when there is blood in the water or when a dryad calls them. Otherwise, you never see them. It is considered bad luck to kill one but good luck to be the first to see one. That's why that sailor at the railing is so happy." Aethre looked at the sailor who happened to be leering at her and suddenly remembered where she was. With a squeak, she fled back to her mast and vanished inside.

In less than two weeks, Aethre was joining Jeptha and the other dryads for dinner every night. She had to be shown how to pantomime eating. The dates and honey water were not necessary for the dryads, they were nourished by the sun and rain, but Jeptha liked to think they wanted to dine as humans did. He gave her trade trinkets to wear and she was fascinated by the sparkle. She danced around in the silken skirts he lent her until she was dizzy and giggling. Jeptha noticed that Semele's smile was forced at these antics and he turned to her.

"You're not jealous, are you, pet?"

"No, not at all," Semele said quickly. Pherusa looked away and pretended to be interested in a green glass necklace.

"Then what's the matter?"

"It's just that Aethre's seen so little of the world of men. In the ports, for example, she may observe things that will shock and terrify her. I just wish there was some way to prepare her, to protect her."

"Ah, always the mother hen, eh, Semele? I remember how you were with my daughters on that trip to Breesis. Always worried they were too near the edge. And then when Elisha did fall overboard, I thought you would evaporate into spray right then and there!"

"It was frightening," Semele said. Jeptha caught the edge of a dark glance thrown to Semele by Pherusa, one that gave him pause. Yet, the wine was excellent and it put a golden haze over everything. It must have been his imagination.

The next day trouble appeared on the horizon. The crow's-nest sounded the warning and Jeptha raised his expensive telescope to his eye.

"Pirate," he said to Kincaid. "The High Seat lied to us. Full sails. We'll outrun him."

Kincaid relayed the commands and politely asked for the telescope. He scrutinized the distant ship.

"She's got more canvas than us and is coming fast. She stands a good chance of catching us."

"Nonsense." Jeptha snatched back his telescope to look again at their pursuer. After a few moments, he lowered it.

"You're right, Kincaid," he said, the words tasting like bile. "I'll ask Aethre if there's a storm nearby. We can lead the pirates to it; it will spare us its full force because of the dryads." The storms seemed to not vent their full power on dryad-mast ships, as if they recognized the magic in the masts.

"We should depend on good seamanship," Kincaid said, "not magic!"

Jeptha spun on him, hand on his pistol butt. Kincaid stared back, daring him to draw it.

"We will have words when this is done, Kincaid. Now, you demonstrate the seamanship that you are so proud of, and I will summon magic to help us." Jeptha marched over to the mizzenmast, his back itching where he felt Kincaid's stare.

"Aethre, my poppet. I need you to help us." He kept his tone calm, even though his palms were sweating.

Her youthful face emerged. "Is something wrong, Jeptha?"

"We've got a bit of pirate trouble, my love. Can you spot any of those nasty storms nearby? I'd like to let one give those pirates some trouble." His palms sweated some more while Aethre closed her eyes. He resisted the urge to shake her into a speedy answer. Finally, her amber eyes opened.

"I cannot find any, Jeptha, I'm sorry."

"No matter, love. Go back inside your mast and stay there until I say it is safe to come out." Pale, she obeyed him. Semele and Pherusa were hiding as well.

He went to the poop deck and watched the pirate get closer and closer. He wanted to scream at his crew, make them speed the *Secret Wish* along, but Kincaid was doing that well enough.

"Kincaid," Jeptha said finally.

"Sir?" The word was laden with sarcasm. Jeptha wished he could shoot the man on the spot.

"Get the long guns ready. Fire when they are in range."

"Aye, Captain."

"And break out the small arms and axes now," Jeptha said. "They will probably get close enough to board us."

"Aye, Sir." The storage lockers were opened and the men tucked weapons into their belts.

There was a flash from a bow gun on the pirate and then a boom. The cannon ball sailed over the deck, smashing several men to pulp before it exited through the railing. One sailor, his arm a red, sodden mass, sagged against the mizzenmast, moaning. Aethre stuck her head out and, looking down at him, started screaming.

"Get that wounded man below," Jeptha bellowed. "Back in your mast, Aethre!" The other ship was closing fast. The men on the stern guns fired off a round and holes appeared in the sails of the pirate.

"Watch your elevation," Kincaid yelled from the deck below.

Jeptha was trembling but held his ground on the quarter deck. He remembered his father admonishing him never to show fear in front of the men. But his father had never had to endure this: his time had been a peaceful one. There was a second boom. With a crash, the ball sank itself into the foremast, a foot above the deck. A groan rose above the shrieks of the men hit by the splinters and the foremast slowly toppled, to rest tangled with the sails of the mainmast.

"Axes, men," Kincaid shouted, "Cut 'er free and over the side with 'er!"

"No, belay that," Jeptha called, running down the stairs to the main deck. Kincaid grabbed his arm.

"Captain, we've got to get that tangle over the side or we have no hope of escaping that son of a bitch."

"Semele's in there. We can't toss her over, trapped inside."

Kincaid slapped him across the mouth and Jeptha tasted blood.

"You're about to lose your ship, man. You can't be worrying about a dryad doxy." Jeptha fumbled at his belt for his pistol.

"This is mutiny," he sputtered, spraying blood across the front of Kincaid's jacket. Kincaid slapped Jeptha's hand away from his pistol butt and took the weapon. He tucked it in his own belt.

"Saul, take the captain below. You there, cut that mast free." The axes rose and fell. Saul stepped up behind Jeptha and wrapped a thick arm across his chest. With a crash, the foremast hit the deck and the sailors grabbed its butt and started dragging it towards the rail. Jeptha remembered Thyia, smashed to kindling before his eyes. Semele was still alive and throwing her overboard would condemn her to a lingering death, lying on the bottom of the ocean waiting for the cord of her bells to rot off.

He couldn't leave her to that, he just couldn't.

Jeptha smashed the back of his head into Saul's face. He felt cartilage give and the imprisoning arm fell away. Hurling himself after the mast as it slipped over the side, he heard Aethre scream his name. He thought briefly of his wife and daughters and what would happen to them if he died. Still, they were safe on land. Semele was in danger, here and now.

The cold of the ocean drove the breath out of his lungs. He splashed around weakly, alarmed by how heavy his clothes were. They seemed determined to drag him down. He trod water and was able to strip off his frock coat. He kicked up and caught a glimpse of the foremast, bobbing in the *Wish's* wake. He heard wails and looked back at the *Wish*. Aethre was hanging over the rail, arms outstretched toward him. Then she was pulled away. He flailed until he finally reached the foremast. When he tried to pull himself up upon it, it spun in the water, preventing him from gaining purchase.

"Semele," he said, "get out of there and give me a hand!"

Two arms reached out of the mast and pulled the rest of the dryad up until she was exposed from the waist up. She was sobbing wildly.

"Semmy, here, grab on to me."

She looked around and saw Jeptha. With surprising strength, she grabbed the back of his shirt and pulled him across the mast.

"Oh, what has happened, Jeptha?"

"A cannon ball cut you off, dear, but don't worry, I'm with you now." He squirmed a bit so he could see her face. She didn't look reassured.

"They've left us," she said desolately, looking at the two ships, still firing at each other, as they receded into the distance.

"They'll be back," Jeptha said.

Semele looked down at him through her tears with a familiar crooked smile. "No, they won't, Jeptha. Kincaid will say you died in battle and take the *Secret Wish* as his own. As long as he continues to haul cargo and give your family a cut, there will be no complaints because you have no son to follow you. We're doomed out here. It's time to let me go."

"Semele, don't give up so soon. We're in a shipping lane. Someone will come and I will offer them a good deal of money to take you on board."

"No, they'll rescue you but I'll float on the ocean until I become water-logged and sink to the bottom. How many years will it be until the cord rots off? Do not condemn me to such an existence. At least Thyia had a quick ending."

"I'll do it, Semele, if no one comes, but you're waxing hysterical. Where is the calm, steady Semele I've known all these years?"

"That's just it, Jeptha, it's been thirty years. Let me go."

"You *want* to go," he said, hurt.

"It's time, cut me free. Please. I have never asked you for anything before."

His penknife was in the pocket of his breeches. He pulled it out awkwardly and opened it up. He glanced up to catch an avid look on Semele's face. The spell prevented her from freeing herself but any human could do it with a quick slice of the cord.

"Are you sure, Semmy?" he asked, hoping her answer would be different.

"Cut it, Jeptha."

He didn't look at Semele again, he didn't want to see that eager look. He sliced through the cord and the bells fell away, heading towards the bottom of the ocean. He looked back to Semele with a fond smile.

The blow took him across his already sore mouth and he almost lost his grip on the mast.

"Semele?"

She leaned over him like an avenging angel. Already her outline was growing dim. Her face was terrifying in its rage.

"Goddess-damned slaver! Thirty years listening to your whining. I begged every sailor who would listen to cut my cord, but they were all cowards! I had to watch Thyia die and then you calmly go and buy another slave to replace her. I almost had my revenge when I pushed your spawn overboard but then you jumped into the ocean and saved her. How ironic that you have done the same for me and given me the vengeance I've craved all these endless years!" She threw her head back and gave an ululating cry, the one she used to summon the tiburi for their amusement.

"No, Semele, no, don't do this. I've treated you like family. You've never *said* anything."

"You never listened unless it was what you wanted to hear. And no one should treat family the way you treated me and Thyia and Pherusa. I hate you, Jeptha, rot in hell." Her face faded away, whitened and twisted into the form of a dove. It flew upwards into the sun and all that was left was a searing white afterimage in his retina.

Thirty years playing the role of the devoted companion, all the while hating him. The smiles, the concern for his well-being had all been false. She had tried to kill his child! No, that could not be true. The shock had deranged her. She meant none of it. He would remember Semele as that laughing summer creature, sipping honey water on the quarterdeck, tossing her hair in the sea wind. That Semele he knew.

Jeptha pulled himself up on the mast until he straddled it. He scanned the horizon, looking for a ship. The sea was calm. He could make do quite well for at least a day. By then, Kincaid would have escaped the pirate and turned around to pick him up. Then he saw a white vee heading rapidly towards him from the south. He swallowed convulsively and gripped his penknife tightly in a trembling hand. At least it would be quick: the tiburi did not play with their prey.

He said prayers for his wife and two girls, that they would not have hardship after his death. He hoped that Semele was right: that Kincaid would captain the *Secret Wish* and give them a share of the proceeds. Perhaps Kincaid would make a much better captain, not mislead by sentimentality as his predecessor had been.

Jeptha's death was close now. A sleek brown head was parting the waves.

The tibur stopped in front of him and raised its grinning face out of the water.

"Mercy?" Jeptha said.

The tibur lunged at him. As it arched in the air, a shrill ululating cry came over the waves. The tibur hit Jeptha hard on the shoulder, knocking him off the mast. Jeptha turned to face its attack but it was swimming towards a ship.

There was the *Secret Wish*, a bit tattered and missing a mast. Pherusa hung over the side, calling the tibur to her. The men were lowering a boat. Numbly, he let them pull him aboard and then haul him ungracefully up the *Wish's* side in the bosun's chair. Kincaid met him at the rail and helped him aboard. Pherusa and Aethre were behind the first mate and tried to run to him but Jeptha halted their rush with a raised hand.

"Keep them away from me," Jeptha said dully. Two sailors placed themselves between Jeptha and the dryads who looked hurt and puzzled.

"How did you get away?" Jeptha asked Kincaid, looking over the first mate's shoulder, not willing to meet his eyes.

"Let them get close, hove-to and broadsided them. They didn't expect us to have the guns we did."

"Good work, Kincaid. You and I must have a talk about the future of the *Wish*. I'm thinking of retiring. I need to spend more time with my family." He finally met his first mate's eyes and was surprised to see sympathy there.

"Now, Sir, you're a bit off. Close calls do that to a man. You'll feel differently in the morning."

"No, Kincaid, I will not. I am a poor captain for times like these and none of your men should trust their lives to me. It's time I went home." He started for his cabin and then paused, not turning around. "One favor, Kincaid?"

"Sir?"

"Cut the strings on those masts, please."

"Are you sure, Sir?"

"Perfectly, thank you."

Pherusa called his name softly and then more urgently as he walked to his cabin. Aethre's piercing voice rose above the slap of the waves and cries of the birds. "Jeptha! You promised you would show me the world!"

He paused, a hand on the knob of his cabin door, but he still did not look around.

"The world isn't what I thought it was," he said quietly and went into his cabin.

Balaam's Bones: A Tale of the Barbarian Kabar of El Hazzar
Angeline Hawkes

eneas brushed his wet hair from his eyes, and held to the rail, surveying the churning sea. They were closing in on the ship flying a purple flag, marking it as a Zaratanian vessel.

Fortune smiled upon him and Ninsu, his wife and fellow freebooter. The Zaratanian ship was unarmed, that was apparent. At this distance the ship would have fired at least one volley if they could. *Fools!* Aeneas thought. *Who crosses these waters with no cannons?* Lucky for him, but terrible for the wretch who captained the ship about to be boarded.

"We're coming alongside!" Ninsu called from the crow's nest of the *Black Lily*. Her nimble body scaled the ropes, and then dropped to the deck beside him. Her golden tresses hung in thick braids, black breeches revealing the curves of her hips.

"Prepare to board!" Aeneas called as they pulled beside the other ship. The crew brandished swords. He waited, and then called, "Be quick about it, dogs! Take it all and spare no mercy!"

Grappling hooks flew and the ragged seadogs leapt between decks, silver streaks flashing in the sun revealing slashing swords. Aeneas jumped decks and strode to the captain's quarters, the path cut clean by his fighting crew. He shoved the door, surprised that it yielded easily. Inside a chart lay unfurled, knives pinning it to the table beneath.

Aeneas leaned over it, when a cough sounded in the corner. Sword in the air, Aeneas took a cautious step forward. "Show yourself!"

A series of rattling coughs followed. A figure huddled beside a sea chest, and Aeneas latched onto the garment of the hapless sailor. Yanking the man into the beam of sunlight filtering through the dirty cabin window, Aeneas saw an old man in tattered robes.

"Who are you?" he asked.

The man coughed violently.

Aeneas raised his sword. "Never mind. It seems I've been sent by the gods to end your misery. A cough like that can't have death too far behind."

The man threw his hands up. "Strike me not, good sailor!"

"*Good* sailor, is it?" Aeneas laughed. "I'm Aeneas of El Hazzar. And *who* are *you?*"

"I'm called Marduk of Zaratan."

"Why does that name sound familiar?"

"I'm sorcerer to the king of Zaratan," the man said, coughing again. He wiped a hand over his long mustache, and then dried it upon his robe.

"Sorcerer? You should fetch a handsome ransom then."

Marduk shook his head and gestured to the chart. "I have something of more value than the mere gold you'd have to wait for from my king. Look here!"

"What has more value than gold?" Aeneas looked at the chart again.

"I can take you *here*." The old man poked a skeletal finger at the parchment.

"Where would *here* be? What is there that I would be interested in, old one?"

"Treasure like none you've ever heard existed. On this island."

Ninsu burst into the room, exhilaration writ upon her face. "The ship is ours!"

Marduk reeled to face her. "A woman? Aboard your ship? Among your crew?"

"My wife, worth ten men if not more!"

Ninsu squinted in the room as her eyes adjusted to the lack of light. "Who's this?"

"Marduk, sorcerer to the King of Zaratan."

She raised her eyebrows. "A great ransom he'll bring!"

Aeneas smiled. "As thought I, but Marduk was just telling me of a magnificent treasure on an island and I'm wagering that some negotiating is about to begin."

"We don't negotiate with captives," Ninsu said, thrusting her blade into the table.

Yanking the knife from the table, Aeneas handed it back to his wife, hilt first. "We negotiate with Hel herself if the price is right."

"Hear me out," Marduk said, tugging on his beard.

Ninsu sat on a bench and eyed the ragtag man. "Well, get on with it then."

Marduk stared at Ninsu hungrily. "I'll lead you to *this* island." He touched the chart. "You'll take the treasure and leave me behind."

"Maroon you?" Aeneas asked. "How will you return to Zaratan?"

"How I return is no concern of yours. Do you want the treasure or not?"

"What's to stop us from killing you once we get our hands on the treasure?" Ninsu asked, studying the chart. It had no writing on it, only landmasses and oceans.

"Nothing, except your word."

"You'd trust the word of a pirate?" Aeneas laughed.

Marduk looked Aeneas in the eyes, unflinching. "I would."

"That means you either can see what the future holds, or you're a fool," Aeneas said. "Which is it, sorcerer?"

Marduk laughed this time, and then coughed. "Are we for the treasure?"

Casting a glance at a shrugging Ninsu, Aeneas then looked at Marduk. "Take me to the treasure and you'll have it as you've asked."

One by one, Marduk pulled the knives from corners of the chart, and then rolled the parchment.

"We'll take my ship. It's faster and armed." Aeneas led Marduk and Ninsu onto the deck where the crew was transferring the bounty of Marduk's ship to their own. Red ran thick over the deck from the sprawled and lifeless bodies.

With an expression of suspicion, Marduk looked around the crimson-splattered deck, paused as if reluctant to leave the security of his own vessel, but sighed and followed Aeneas to the other ship.

⚓

The waters chopped with the wind as the island surfaced on the horizon. Marduk, robes billowing, stood in the bow, watching. Land inched closer.

"I'll lead you, Ninsu, and a few men to the cave that hides the treasure," Marduk said. "Have your men prepare food and water for my stay."

Aeneas gave the orders. He chose five men to row the boat ashore, and the ship dropped anchor.

Ninsu sat in the front of the dinghy with Marduk as they rowed to the island. It was a desolate, gray hunk of rock—barren, lifeless. Craggy mountains outlined the blue sky, an inhospitable landmass if ever there was one.

"You're certain this is where you wish to remain?" Aeneas said as the boat ran onto the sloping beach.

Marduk nodded, a slight smile curling his thin lips. He fell forward, and Ninsu grasped his arm to steady him. He slipped his frail limb around her strong one and leaned on her for support. They disembarked and started up the rocky beach. Aeneas stood still, the solidness of the island steadying his sea legs. A pungent odor permeated the air, stinging his nostrils. The others winced too.

"This place stinks of death," he said, pulling his tunic over his nose.

"Are you here for perfume or for treasure?" Marduk said, laughing.

"Show the way then, old man." Aeneas drew his sword. "I want to be aboard ship before sundown."

Marduk trudged towards the hills, the band of pirates trailing behind. A tremor rippled beneath their feet. Ninsu held fast to the old sorcerer as Aeneas thrust his hands outward, legs akimbo, to compensate for the budge.

"What the devil be that?" one of the men asked.

"A small quake," Marduk said. "The island is less than stable."

Murmurs trickled between the pirates. The path was stony, uneven, a rough walk for even the most stalwart of the crew. "Not only does this place reek of death," Aeneas said, "nothing grows here either. What cursed place have you brought us to, Marduk?"

The old man smiled. "Come," he said. "Let us save our breath for the trek and for carrying treasure once we get there."

The pirates grumbled behind him.

"Your men are restless, barbarian."

"Why do you call him that?" Ninsu asked.

"Is he not from El Hazzar? Was there ever a more wild and primitive place? If he isn't a barbarian, then what is he?"

"He's a *pirate*!" she said, with fierce pride.

Marduk cackled, and abruptly crouched. With a solitary punch he whacked the ground and a wicked smile curled under his moustache. "He's a *fool*!"

The ground quaked fiercely, not a vibration like the initial tremor, but a violent jolt that sent the men sprawling. Ninsu careened into Marduk who thrust his arms around her waist. She struggled against his embrace, surprised at his strength.

Aeneas attempted to stand, only to be dashed against the ground again. "By Shar! You've led us to our deaths!"

Marduk conjured a blade from the air and pressed it to Ninsu's neck. He backed towards a rocky mound, Ninsu kicking and clawing the entire time. As the island continued to shake, stones fell away from the great hill, slowly revealing a buried ship.

Aeneas struggled to follow but could barely manage to crawl behind the old man. "Marduk! Where are you going with my wife?"

With each heave of the island, the pirates were tossed around. They clasped onto each other for support. A few began to crawl towards the ship.

Aeneas saw them fleeing. "You dogs! You'll leave Ninsu behind?"

"She's your woman!" a black-toothed freebooter said. "Nothing but bad luck on the sea!"

"She wasn't bad luck when you needed her sword, you yellow dog!" Aeneas hurled a rock at the defector, and then was thrown onto his face.

Marduk cackled the entire way to the half-concealed ship. He alone was able to walk upright as the barren wasteland of an island rocked and twisted. The sea sloshed inland, washing all in the path of the waves out to sea—with nothing to hold to, the pirates found themselves scrabbling for purchase. Aeneas half swam, half crawled toward Ninsu, but stopped when a thought crept into his anguished mind.

"Make for the ship!" he shouted above the din of the waves. The men who could swim beat against the swirling water. The men who couldn't, fought for their last breath.

"Aeneas!" Panic filled Ninsu's voice. She didn't understand why he was abandoning her to the sorcerer.

His heart breaking with every stroke, Aeneas swam hard towards the *Black Lily*. He cast a look backwards in time to see Marduk pull Ninsu aboard his ship, cut anchor, and drift away from the island on the first wave big enough to take the ship.

Aeneas grabbed the anchor chain and shimmied up link by link, until he was able to heave himself over the railing, landing with a wet thud on the deck. "Raise the anchor!" he choked.

"But there are still men coming!" the helmsman said. "It'll mean their deaths!"

"It'll mean all of our deaths if we don't cut anchor! Look!"

Before them, the *island* rocked and swayed, and then twisted upwards, a massive head rising from the dark ocean waters.

"By Shar! What is it?" the helmsman said.

"A creature of Marduk's, no doubt! A giant devil-whale!" Aeneas held to a spar as the waves crashed.

"Myths and legends!" the helmsman said.

Aeneas pointed to the hulking whale. "Is that a *myth*, pirate? Or do my eyes show me things that you don't see?"

Another wave slammed the ship, lifting it like a child's toy and plunging it into the sea. The helmsman lost his hold and was carried screeching overboard into the black waters.

Aeneas caught the wheel and, using his belt, lashed himself to it as the beast moaned a deafening protest, spurting a geyser into the air. An immense wave carried the ship farther away as the lumbering giant descended into the ocean once again. The water churned as Aeneas searched the horizon for Marduk's ship, realizing now that the sorcerer had a sinister plan: no cannon, easy boarding, the chart, the island, the ship. All of it was a devious scheme. Marduk had been after a prize all along. He was a pirate in a sorcerer's robe. He had come for Ninsu.

Aeneas guided the ship towards Sardiel. His brother Kabar, the Barbarian King of Woldenstag, was there. Together they'd get Ninsu back.

———————⚓———————

The journey was long, but with less than a full crew, the provisions managed to hold. All the same, the sailors were elated to cast eyes upon the port town of Sardiel. Aeneas doubted any of his crew would return to his ship when it was time to cast off. He'd have to get new men before sailing again.

When he touched land, Aeneas wasted no time seeking his brother, Kabar. He found him drinking in the Red Dog Inn, a buxom wench on each knee. When he approached, Kabar jumped to his feet, catching each woman by the waist to keep from hurling them to the floor. He stood them on their feet and rushed to crush his brother in a hug. "Brother!"

Aeneas laughed. "Kabar! I always know where to find you!"

Kabar released him, indicating that he should sit. "What brings you to Sardiel?" he asked.

Aeneas recounted the tale of Ninsu's abduction. Kabar drank his mug dry and then stood.

"Where are you going?" Aeneas asked.

"To get your wife back!"

"But we don't know where Marduk sailed, and I'm not sure I still have a crew."

"I know a seer," Kabar said.

"Hmm."

"Have you gold?"

Aeneas nodded. "Our loot was safe below deck when the devil-whale lashed our ship. I lost many men but not a piece of gold or silver." He put a bag of coins on the table. "There's more."

Kabar picked up the bag, weighing the heft of it in his hand, and slipped it inside of his tunic. "Come, the seer will tell us where the bastard has taken your wife."

———————⚓———————

The old man was blind, his hair silver. White soupy eyes darted in his wrinkled face. He felt the bag of gold in his hand and undid the leather cord. After biting a coin, he dropped it against the others and drew the cord tight. Satisfied, he waved an arm in front of him. "Sit. I'll tell you what I see."

Kabar and Aeneas sat upon the dusty cushions that surrounded the velvet couch the seer lay upon.

"Who's this sorcerer that has absconded with your mate?" the seer asked.

"Marduk," Aeneas said, "sorcerer to the king of Zaratan."

The old seer sucked in a breath.

"What is it?" Kabar said. "What do you know?"

"Marduk of Zaratan is a man most foul—diabolically wicked. He has no living equals and he *cannot* be defeated."

Kabar scowled. "You said, no *living* equals. Is there one that has *died*?"

The seer laughed. "Are you Shar? Have you the power to raise the dead?"

Kabar grunted and looked away.

"*But*, what you ask cuts to the heart of the matter." The blind man shifted on the couch. "Balaam, once a king of Edom, and a powerful sorcerer, counted Marduk of Zaratan among his enemies. Only Balaam had the power to curse Marduk."

Aeneas leaned in closer.

"Balaam's power is so great, that even now, beyond death, he can still defeat Marduk of Zaratan."

"Maybe you are Shar, then, and can raise this Balaam from his grave!" Kabar laughed.

"No!" the seer said. "Balaam's bones hold his power. Find his bones and you'll find the power to rescue your wife!"

"Where are these bones?" Aeneas asked.

The seer chuckled. "That's the impossible feat, I'm afraid. Balaam's bones lie in the ancient temple of Chemosh in Moab—across the Sea of Medea, and beyond the Wilderness of Zin. Even if you survive the journey, the ruined temple is guarded by beasts most foul!"

"More ensorcelled creatures?" Aeneas said with a shudder.

"From the very pits of Hel," the seer whispered.

"Enough of the fear and doom!" Kabar said. "When I get these bones, how do they serve me?"

"*When*, Kabar? *If* Shar smiles upon you, all you have to do is take the bones to the sorcerer. When they hear his name, the curse will be bestowed and Marduk of Zaratan will fall."

Kabar stood.

"Where are you going?" the seer asked, flinching at the sudden movement in the room.

"We have bones to fetch and a woman to save."

"Ah, the woman! Marduk foresaw your ship, pirate," the old one said to Aeneas, "and claimed your mate as his booty. The gods only know what evil intentions he has in store for your fair wife."

Aeneas leapt to his feet, glowering. "Then we must make haste! Marduk has already had Ninsu too long!"

The old seer rested his head on his silk pillows, exhausted, as Kabar and Aeneas left the room.

It took a week for Aeneas to find a crew. Each day that passed tore at his heart. Misery turned to rage as he discovered that his former crew was spreading the story of their last voyage through the port and town, ruining his reputation. Risking life and limb for treasure on the high seas was a pirate's life for sure; scrambling half way across the ocean for a woman who wasn't theirs wasn't a wise man's idea of an adventure. The tale of the sorcerer and the devil-whale spread fear into even the most hardened of men. No one had any wish to have dealings with sorcery. Aeneas found himself making all sorts of promises to ensure he had an adequate, sea-worthy crew. In the end all that mattered was Ninsu.

Weeks rolled into months over the green-blue waves of the Sea of Medea. The men knew that even after the perilous sea voyage, they'd have to trek through the Wilderness of Zin to reach the Temple of Chemosh in Moab. They had been promised riches beyond imagination, all a crock of lies. The old seer had said nothing of treasure. Maybe they'd get lucky and find jewels in the temple along with Balaam's bones. It was a risk Aeneas was willing to take.

Thunder roared over the oceans. A storm raged across the sky turning the sapphire blueness of the waves into murky black. Great billows of smoke-gray clouds piled over each other. The men were skittish, busying themselves with tying things down as the waves grew. It wouldn't be long until the seas let loose their power and pummeled the ship with fury.

Kabar held to the rail, observing the turmoiled waters.

"Storm's coming," Aeneas said, coming up behind him.

"Looks like a big one." Kabar said without looking at his brother.

Aeneas leaned against the rail. "Do you think this is Marduk's doing?"

Kabar shook his head. "No. I've dealt with sorcerers before. Marduk would send a monster, a ghoul from the deep. Something dire, not an ordinary storm. Sailors expect storms; they don't expect ensorcelled creatures."

Aeneas eyed the cresting waves. "Perhaps you're right."

"I am."

Aeneas laughed—an unfamiliar feeling in the past months "Well, I hope you're just as confident that we'll sail through this unscathed as you are that it's Shar's storm and not Marduk's."

Kabar smiled. "Time will tell, brother."

Aeneas clapped him on the back and left to tend to the crew. Kabar surveyed the angry waves a moment more before taking up his position near the helmsman.

The storm blew the ship from side to side; at times, the deck touched water, threatening to capsize. Dark clouds covered the sun and as the hours passed, the men didn't know if it was day or night.

At last, the storm waned and blue skies crept from behind the ebony, the sun illuminating the waters again. Off to starboard was an uncharted island. It wasn't particularly large, but it reached high into the sky: the remnant of some volcanic eruption. It bore trees, and perhaps, fruit and fresh water.

"We'll go ashore and check the ship for damage," Aeneas said, "and replenish our stocks."

They neared the island, careful to avoid running aground on a high sandbar. They dropped anchor and went ashore in a dinghy, leaving men aboard ship in case of trouble. Kabar studied the beach, eager to stretch his legs. His brother was the pirate; he preferred land to waves. They rowed the boat into a beautiful lagoon. Trees with lush vines dipped into the emerald waters surrounded by rocky cliffs. Exotic birds cawed overhead in the trees, echoing against the mountains.

Leaping onto the ground, Kabar grabbed the rope Aeneas tossed him. He tied it around a tree and waited for his brother and the other men to disembark. They started along the shoreline, gathering coconuts and fruit, while Kabar and Aeneas went in search of fresh water to fill the empty barrels they'd brought. Sword in hand, Kabar hacked a path through the jungle.

"If we don't find water before nightfall, I say we return to the ship," Aeneas said, repeatedly glancing toward the ship bobbing cork-like in the waves.

"Not *all* islands are devil whales, brother."

Aeneas grunted. "We don't know how far the eyes of Marduk see."

"You speak the truth," Kabar said. "Perhaps it's wiser to stay the night aboard the ship. We can return at dawn." He swung his sword down on a branch, cutting it from the path. The distant sound of falling water suddenly filled their ears.

"Ho! What's that?" Aeneas said, peering forward. "Is that water?"

Kabar hacked his way forward until they came upon a bubbling pool, refreshed by a waterfall tumbling from a cliff. "By Shar it is!" Kabar broke into a smile. "Enough water to fill the barrels and more!"

Aeneas laughed and walked to the edge. Kabar set aside his sword and leapt into the water, ducking under, coming up shaking hair from his eyes. Aeneas followed him, swimming out to the center, just out of reach of the swirling wake of the fall.

Kabar floated on his back, soaking in the serenity of the pool. He gazed at the gentle fall of the water over the rocks. "It's really peaceful here," he said, his words echoing.

Aeneas swam to a large rock and heaved himself onto it. A swathe of sunlight bathed the shore in a golden light. "Yes, it is. Untouched by man."

A giggle cut the silence. The brothers were instantly alert, searching for the origin of the feminine sound, scouring the waters, the cliffs, the shore for the owner of the musical laughter.

"Who's there?" Kabar shouted, making his way to the shore toward his sword.

Another giggle.

"It's coming from over there," Aeneas said, pointing to an alcove. He dove into the water, swimming to the laughter.

"Aeneas!" Kabar yelled. "Wait!"

But Aeneas had already disappeared. Cursing, Kabar strapped his sword to his back and plunged into the pool again.

Aeneas swam to a rock, and began climbing the cliff until he reached the woman responsible for the lilting laughter. She stood calmly, naked, showing no sign of fear. "Who are you?" he asked, hesitant to move closer lest the woman misconstrue his intentions.

"I'm Scylla." Her voice was young and crisp. "What do they call you?"

"Aeneas." He studied the nude woman, not sure what to make of her. It wasn't everyday one stumbled upon a naked bathing beauty on a deserted island. "Why is it that you're here, naked?"

"You've interrupted my bath. Usually there are no others here. I've never bothered with robes." She reached for a large brush made from a shell and ran it through her hair.

"Do you live alone on the isle?"

"Yes. For a long time now." The woman looked to be little more than a girl.

Kabar emerged from the water, climbing the rocky cliff.

"And who is *that*?" she asked, moving closer.

Kabar seated himself on a rock, watching the scene closely.

"My brother, Kabar," Aeneas said. "Why are you here?" *Maybe a shipwreck? A sole survivor.*

"Where else would I be, silly man?" she said. Her laughter tinkled from the cliffs like a silver spoon against crystal.

"Certainly somewhere besides here, I'd imagine." Aeneas sat on a rocky protrusion. "You're both a long way from home?"

"Yes, we seek the Temple of Chemosh in Moab."

"This isn't Moab," she said, sidling closer, looking at him intently.

"You're right," Aeneas said. "We got blown off course by a storm and when we spotted this island we decided to come ashore to try to stock fresh fruit and water. Where are you from; where is home?"

Scylla laughed, sighed, and reached out to touch Aeneas's face. "This *is* home." She brushed her hand over the outline of his jaw, ran her hand along the definitions of his thews. He shuddered at her touch.

Kabar broke his silence. "We're sailing to Zaratan to save Aeneas's *wife* from a sorcerer."

Scylla frowned. "What of the temple in Moab?" Her hand rested on Aeneas's belt, delicately toying with the strap of leather.

"Our first destination," Kabar said.

Scylla kissed Aeneas on the lips, her full breasts pushing against the bareness of his chest. Her blue eyes entranced him, lulling him with their calmness.

Kabar's hand inched toward the sword on his back—ever so slowly.

Scylla pulled Aeneas to her, wiggling a long leg around his waist. She smoldered with raw, primal sensuality as her intent became clear. Leaning back against the stone of the cliff wall, she groped him, loosening his breeches. Aeneas moved like a man drugged; his rigid member pressed against her nubile flesh, seeking the soft well of her womanhood. His arms entwined around her, holding her tight. Her fingers curled through his hair, her tongue probing the depths of his mouth.

In a fluid motion, he was buried within her, his hands holding her against his hips. Her gasps of pleasure were loud, rushing with the tempo of the falling water. A flurry of motion erupted around them as a hoard of barking, serpentine creatures sprang from her waist, her legs vanishing beneath the coiling, undulating mass. Her long golden hair parted every way as five other heads on elongated necks protruded, her arms still clinging to Aeneas's strong back.

Kabar leapt to another rock, moving closer. Aeneas let out a whimper of surprise as Scylla's mouth drew back, revealing rows of sharp fangs that snapped for him like a rabid dog.

"The gods!" he shouted, struggling to get free from her writhing coils.

Scylla held tight. "It's been far too long since I've felt the strong sword of a man within me. Far too long since I've nursed young at my breasts. I'll grow a brood from your seed, Aeneas!" she said as though he'd be happy about it.

He pushed against her in revulsion.

"And I'll satiate my thirst upon the wine in your veins!" She sank her teeth into Aeneas's shoulder.

Kabar was upon her, his sword hacking at the serpents. They had wrapped around

his brother, pinning his limbs while Scylla ravaged the flesh on his shoulder. Down came Kabar's sword, over and over and over again. The creature opened her crimson maw and howled a torturous wail, rage boiling in her eyes. One of the serpents went limp, severed at her waist. She threw Aeneas to the side. He crashed to the stone and lay still.

"Try *my* sword, you monstrous bitch!" Kabar lunged at her with his blade, severing another barking serpent head, much to Scylla's fury.

With a rustle and slither, she swiped at him, serpents roiling in a cacophony of hissing rage. He was faster and with a mighty slice, took off two of her growling heads and partially severed a third. Scylla reeled against the craggy cliff, stretching an ivory arm towards Aeneas, who was regaining his feet. "Aeneas! Save me, lover!"

Though unbalanced and weak, Aeneas charged his brother. Kabar scowled and knocked him out of his way, sending him plunging into the pool.

Scylla howled in outrage, but grew visibly weaker. Another tremendous whack of his sword and Kabar took the fifth head from Scylla's shoulders; the wiggling cluster of serpents around her waist shrank as she collapsed.

"Aeneas!" she called raspily, blood seeping from her lips—and Kabar brought his sword down once more, sending her golden-haired skull flying into the blue of the pool, under the white foaming waterfall.

Aeneas clung to a rock, gasping for breath as Kabar kicked Scylla's body into the water, where it splashed and sank.

Kabar stood there for a moment, beholding his brother heaving for air, and then climbed from the ledge, swam to the rock and helped him to shore. He dumped Aeneas unceremoniously on the rocks. "Fool!" he said, and turning his back, trudged to the beach to tell the men about the water.

Aeneas lay panting on the rocks, watching Kabar go.

———————— ⚓ ————————

Crossing the Sea of Medea soon turned into trekking across the Wilderness of Zin. The purchase of camels helped ease the sun-baked journey, until at last they crossed into Moab, and made their way to where the ancient Temple of Chemosh was rumored to be. It was said that, at one time, it had been surrounded by a refreshing oasis and a bustling city, but legends are based on facts that shift like sand, so the brothers expected some things to be not as they'd been told.

After weeks of searching, Aeneas began to lose hope of finding the lost temple, and subsequently was losing hope of seeing Ninsu again. Kabar trudged on, determined to find the temple, not willing to give Ninsu up to the permanent possession of any sorcerer, especially not Marduk of Zaratan.

Discouraged, Aeneas called the men to a halt. They'd come to a small oasis and he told them to fill their waterskins and allow the camels to drink. They might as well take advantage of the water and take a needed rest.

Beneath the shelter of a palm tree, Kabar spread his cloak on the sand and sat upon it, sharpening his sword. Aeneas leaned against the palm, arms crossed, a frown etched into his haggard face. "We should go home," he said.

"We've come this far. There's no turning back now, brother."

Aeneas shook his head. "No. It's useless. This desert goes on forever. All that's here are bones and sand."

"Bones are what we're looking for, remember?"

Aeneas's scowl deepened.

"We should camp here. You're tired. In the morning you'll feel better about the search. We can't be far now."

"And how do you know this? Do you have the sight? We could hunt for a lifetime and still come up empty-handed," Aeneas said.

"Wouldn't you hunt for a lifetime for Ninsu?"

Aeneas was quiet, silenced by his brother's words. "You know I would."

"Then, what's this talk about giving up and going home?" Kabar held his blade up, turning it in the sunlight, watching diamond-gleaming rays burst from the steel. "Go to sleep. Your brain's hot and not thinking properly."

Aeneas sighed and pulled his sleeping blanket from the pack on his camel. He lay under the shade of the tree, and did as his brother bid him.

Kabar watched the men making camp, and then went to explore the area. When the camels had come upon the small oasis, he'd caught sight of something scintillating in the distance. Only metal could make a reflection like that. His curiosity needed to be quenched, so he set off in the direction alone.

The sandy hills sparkled like jewels under the burning sun. Careful not to lose sight of the camp, Kabar scoured the sandy dunes looking for the origin of the gleam. He began to jab at the ground, haphazardly at first, and then in a uniform pattern. A square here. A square there. Until he covered each dune like a grid, determined to find the source of the reflection he'd seen earlier.

He sunk his sword into the sand. *Clang!*

He struck it once more. *Clang!*

Kabar dropped to his knees and scooped handfuls of sand from the spot, slinging the grains over his shoulder in a frenzy. For every two handfuls he took out, another slid into place, but he finally uncovered enough of what looked to be a brass platter. He felt for the edges. It was oval. Gripping it tight, Kabar yanked, revealing the bones of a camel underneath the sheet of metal.

Examining the relic, he realized that it wasn't a platter at all, but a map etched upon brass. Kabar put his finger on the oasis that must be the one they were camped around. Nearby was a single palm tree, just like the one that Aeneas slept beneath. Kabar looked towards the tree and then back at the map. He smiled.

Tracing his finger from the oasis, to the tree, to the dunes where he sat now, he noticed a straight path beneath a bright star. The map was tied to the stars. The Temple of Chemosh lay directly beneath the brightest etched star on the map. Kabar leapt to his feet and rushed back to his sleeping brother. Tonight, he would reveal the location of the temple. He knew the other pirates would rush the spot where he'd uncovered the map. Let them look for buried treasure in the sand. Maybe they'd get lucky.

When night fell and the stars came out, glistening in the black velvet of the night sky, Kabar sat with his brass map, Aeneas at his elbow. They searched for the star that corresponded with the one etched in the brass, examining the constellations until they were confident they'd found the one. Together with a band of the more trustworthy pirates, they mounted their camels and rushed to the location revealed beneath the star on the map. Over sand dunes they traveled, farther and farther from the security of camp, until at last they came to an oasis, larger than the first. This was flanked by remnants of an ancient city, mostly stones peeking from sandy mounds, but in the center stood a tawny stone temple, falling in on itself, collapsing a little piece at a time in the harsh winds and heat of the Wilderness of Zin.

Kabar slid from his camel, handed the reins to a nearby pirate, and asked for a torch from one of the men. Together, he and Aeneas entered the cavernous temple. Iron sconces holding unlit torches lined the way. One by one, they lit them, illuminating the empty halls for the first time in the gods knew how long. Through the labyrinth of corridors they walked, seeking the inner sanctum that they prayed would hold the bones of Balaam.

"These tunnels go on forever," Aeneas said, exasperated. "What are all these rooms?"

"Maybe their priests lived here. Most of the rooms are small, simple."

"Maybe. At this rate we can search forever and not find the chamber we're looking for." Aeneas thrust his torch into the room on his left, finding nothing but dust.

"All of the corridors connect to this main hall. We should split up," Kabar said, lighting another torch. It sputtered and gasped, idle for so long, but at last burned bright. "As long as we come back to this central corridor we can't get lost. We can cover more ground that way."

"I'll take this side, you take that one," Aeneas said.

"Shout if you run into trouble. This stone will echo your words wherever I am." Kabar hit the wall, causing bits of ancient mortar to crumble and rain to the floor, then turned and tramped in the opposite direction of his brother.

The hall took Kabar through a straight channel that opened into a large chamber. A short shaft led to yet another room—a room filled with objects. Kabar felt the closest wall for a sconce, his hand landing upon an ancient torch. He lit it and the resulting fires illuminated the room in a sputtering glow. A heap of satin and brocade pillows filled a corner draped with gauzy curtains hanging from heavy brass rings. Tables with silver goblets and platters lined the walls. Sweet incense wafted throughout the lavish chamber. Nothing he had encountered so far had been so luxurious.

This room wasn't covered in the dust of a thousand years, but looked as if it had been tended regularly, as if someone still lived there. The hairs on Kabar's arms prickled at the thought and he quickly scanned the room for other entrances. When he turned back toward the main door, he found a woman standing there, half in the shadow.

"By Shar, woman you startled me!" Kabar said, holding his torch towards her. "Who are you?"

She smiled. "I am Siduri." She said it as if Kabar should already know who she was and why she might be there.

"I'm Kabar of El Hazzar. Are you the keeper of this temple?"

She walked gracefully, her hips swaying, a filmy swath of silk doing nothing to conceal the treasures the gods had bestowed upon her. "Does every temple have a keeper, Kabar of El Hazzar?"

"The ones I've scrabbled about in do, yes." Kabar's mind raced with unpleasant images of monsters of all hideous sorts, all encountered in various temples where man ought not to tread.

"Well then, I live here. I suppose that must make me the keeper." She laughed. "Why do you have a sword? Do you expect much trouble in a crumbling temple abandoned since ancient times? Will you fight age itself here in these dark tunnels?"

Kabar frowned. "Just because men have abandoned the temple, doesn't mean they haven't left the halls unguarded."

"Come," she said, crossing to a cabinet and removing a silver pitcher. "Have some bread and wine with me. I've been praying at the altar and now, I'm famished."

Kabar watched her every movement. Siduri waved a hand to a chair beside the table, and he sat in it. She put a platter of bread and fruit before him and poured wine into a silver chalice. Kabar watched her eat and partake of the wine before deciding it was safe for him to do so as well.

"I don't get many visitors, as you can imagine."

"Why do you stay here?" Kabar asked.

"It's the task I was born to do. The altar needs refreshed, prayers must be given." She reached over and touched his hand, turning it palm up, studying it. "Ah! What a hand you've been dealt!"

"Sorcery! My mother's a sorceress! Always she goes on about my hand!"

"It's wise to listen to one's mother." She ran her hand up his muscular arm, caressing every ripple. "I'm not, *fortunately*, your mother, Kabar." She stood and came around behind him, still massaging his thews with her soft hands. She let her hand slide down the front of his chest, to his middle until she found a sword of another sort.

"Ha! Woman, what *are* you doing?"

"You don't know?" she asked, feigning surprise, as she pushed the table back, faced him, and wrapped her long legs around his waist, straddling him. "I'm a lonely, lonely woman, not undesirable to men, as you see." Her dark eyes never left his. "I've given you food and wine, and you've eaten, now I ask for this small favor in return."

He kissed her.

Her response was full of aggressive passion as he carried her to the mound of pillows in the corner. He tossed the swathe of silk that passed for her gown into the shadows as he explored her smooth flesh.

She moaned beneath him, thrusting her hips against his, her fingernails raking his back.

"Kabar! I've found them!" Aeneas burst into the room, then stopped, transfixed, a large brass urn clasped tight against his chest. "What the—"

Siduri pushed up on her elbows and looked over Kabar's shoulder. "Balaam's urn!"

In an instant, she shoved Kabar away and sprang to her feet. As she did so, the flesh on her back stretched and split, dark fur protruding from the renting skin. Kabar fumbled near the cushions for his sword, watching in horror as

Siduri's pink lips transformed into a black, slobbering maw—fangs snapping. A deep growl emanated from her gullet, as the huge wolfish creature that had been Siduri lunged for Aeneas.

Kabar's fingers touched the hilt of his sword and he snatched it up. Aeneas clutched the urn, not willing to part with it. Dropping his torch, he went for his sword. The werebeast plucked the urn from Aeneas's hands almost gingerly and set it by the wall. Yellow eyes flashing scorn, the beast then cocked its head and growled at him again. In a flash she had him pinned against the wall, her deadly teeth tearing into his shoulder near Scylla's wound. Aeneas screamed in pain.

Kabar jumped on the beast's hairy back, slipping an arm around its thick neck. Locked in a stranglehold, Siduri fought furiously as Kabar pulled her away from his brother. He slashed with his sword, angered at the realization that Siduri had, in fact, been the temple guardian all along. He'd been beguiled by her beauty. Bleeding, Aeneas found his sword and thrust it deep into the heart of the beast.

She howled and fell to her knees, clawing at the blade buried in her heart. But, Kabar knew something of werebeasts, and he knew a mere steel blade wouldn't be sufficient. His eyes fell upon the silver pitcher of wine on the table. While Aeneas watched Siduri struggle against the sword, Kabar seized the pitcher, banging it against the stone until the handle broke away, jagged, in his hand.

The werebeast's eyes grew wide with fright and she scrambled to her feet, attempting to flee through the corridor, but Kabar was too fast. He yanked his brother's sword from her breast, and shoved the sharp silver into the gaping wound.

She panted and snapped, howled and writhed, until the fur began to subside, the flesh returned, and with her dying breath, Siduri looked upon Kabar with her own, human eyes. With one final attempt to pull the silver from her chest, she heaved a bloody gasp, and collapsed.

Aeneas braced himself against the wall, observing the pulpy bite on his shoulder. Blood trickled over his arm.

"She got you," Kabar said, stating the obvious, and grabbed Siduri's silk gown from the floor. He tied it around Aeneas's shoulder, lessening the bleeding.

"I'm as good as dead now, brother."

"No. We'll finish this, get Ninsu back, and then take you back to Mother. Surely she has something that can stave off the infection of the werebeast." Kabar picked up the urn that contained Balaam's bones. "You're sure these are the bones of the Edomite king?"

"I am. They were clearly marked, on a gold dais. I don't think the guardian of the temple ever expected anyone to come for them." Aeneas clutched his silk-wrapped shoulder.

"Good. Now, let us return to the ship, sail to Zaratan, and pray to Shar there's something of your wife left to save." Kabar thrust a torch at Aeneas, and holding Balaam's urn in one arm, and his sword ready in the other, he followed his brother out of the temple.

Aeneas would owe his men an explanation and the treasure they expected. Later.

———————— ⚓ ————————

Shar smiled upon the brothers as they made their way through the Wilderness of

Zin, and back to the *Black Lily*. They set off to the rocky cliffs of Zaratan, the wind strong at their backs.

The days turned into weeks, and finally months, before they saw the gray crags of their destination. Aeneas was exhausted. The full moon had been upon them the last week and Kabar had kept him locked in an iron cage. He'd fought against the bars continuously until the moon passed. Kabar knew no other way to keep the wolf at bay.

Aeneas peered over the railing, towards the cliffs of Zaratan.

"Are you unsure, brother?" Kabar said, coming up behind.

"Of saving Ninsu?" he asked. "No. I'm a pirate. That's what pirates do. We steal things. I'm going to steal my wife back from the clutches of that devil if it's the last thing I do. Maybe the wolf within me will prove useful afterall."

"Perhaps. But can you control the wolf if you unleash it? Can you make Aeneas return and the wolf subside?"

"I don't know. I pray to Shar I don't have to find out. I'm relying on your biting steel over my biting muzzle."

The brothers shared a laugh as the ship drew closer to land and the crew prepared to disembark.

"Drop anchor!" Aeneas shouted above the buzz of activity erupting on the deck. The clanging chains jerked into the water, and the ship came to an abrupt halt as the anchor grabbed bottom. He stood there, staring into the cliffs. Somewhere on those rocks, his wife was captive. He only hoped she was still alive.

"There!" the pirate in the crow's nest called out. Aeneas followed the man's outstretched arm and saw, high on the cliff, a fortress. It was ancient, chiseled from rock that had witnessed all manner of foul deeds. Around the jagged precipices of stone, a foreboding mist curled like deathly fingers.

Kabar scowled. "The fortress of Marduk of Zaratan."

"There," Aeneas said. "There's a cave in the cliff. We'll sail as close as we dare, and make our way from there. We should go at night, but if we have to climb the cliff, the stars may not be enough to light our ascent."

"I'm sure the old bastard knows we're coming. I say we make haste and act now."

Aeneas shrugged, then nodded. "We'll leave our jacks behind then, and you and I will make the climb. Your sword is stronger than any five of those seadogs put together anyway." He called to the men, "Pull up the anchor, make a path for that cave you see before us!"

There was grumbling among the hands as they had just anchored, but the ship started moving forward. Kabar returned to his and Aeneas's cabin and dumped Balaam's bones into a leather bag. He strapped his sword and the bag around his shoulders, and waited for the ship to make anchor once again.

⚓

Once the ship was near the cliffs, Aeneas and Kabar were lowered in a dinghy into the choppy waters. Rowing was difficult, but throwing their strong backs into it, they managed to guide the small boat into the cave. They searched the stalactites for a spot to rope the boat.

"Look, stairs!" Kabar pointed to a steep staircase chiseled into the stone of the cave that led forever upwards.

"This must be where Marduk docks. Those stairs probably go straight up inside of the mountain, right into the heart of his fortress."

Kabar smiled and leapt over the boat, and onto the ground of the cave. Aeneas followed. Up the stone steps they started.

They came to the lower floors of the fortress, and stealthily continued, amazed at the lack of inhabitants.

"Is there no one here but Marduk?" Aeneas whispered to his brother.

Kabar shrugged. "Who knows? Maybe he conjures the help he needs?" They continued up the stairs, the walls dripping with the wetness of the perpetual wind of the sea. A low archway led them into the fortress proper.

Floor after floor they searched. Doors locked. Not even a ghost to be seen.

"We should split up. This is going to take a lifetime," Kabar said.

"No. We did that back in Moab and look what it cost us. We stay together." Aeneas kept his eyes peeled for movement, his sword brandished before him as they neared an iron gate. He groaned. "The gods! You smell that?"

Kabar covered his nose with his hand. "Must be the dungeons." He kicked the aging metal sharply, and it swung open on rusty hinges. Before them lay dungeon cells boasting wood and iron doors, open for the most part, save a few at the end of the hall near a staircase of stone.

The brothers quickly made their way to the closed doors. Together they battered each down with their brute strength. The third one yielded the prize they sought.

Ninsu lay shivering on a heap of straw, a thin blanket drawn around her shoulders. A weaker woman would've died by now from the cold alone. Her hair was disheveled, her face gaunt as she stared unbelieving into the faces of Aeneas and Kabar. "You came!" she croaked, her voice cracked and hoarse.

"Did you think I wouldn't?" Aeneas said, scooping her into his arms. "Hel alone could not stop me from coming for you, my love."

Laughter echoed behind them. Standing in the shadow of the staircase was the sorcerer.

"You take Ninsu and get to the boat!" Kabar said. "Leave Marduk to me."

Aeneas began to protest.

"Do it. *Now.*" Kabar walked towards Marduk as Aeneas reconsidered and then ran back the way he and his brother had come, his wife over his shoulder. Kabar saw that there was no way past Marduk. He must cut him down or go back the other way.

Marduk continued laughing insanely, taunting Kabar with threats of torturous deaths and curses on his ill-bred birth. The sorcerer drew nearer, backing the barbarian through the hall, toward a stone archway, and onto an open balcony. The cliffs below were sharp and jagged. White bones glittered against the gray stone.

"You won't be the first to die on the crags of Zaratan!" Marduk said.

"And neither shall you, old man!"

Marduk laughed and raised his skinny arms above his head, shouting a string of magick to the cloudy sky. Bursts of fire rained upon them, Kabar scrambling for cover beneath the stone overhang. Chunks of stone and mortar fell, pelting him with flying debris. Sword in hand, he waited for his opportunity to punish the vile sorcerer.

Marduk stood invincible from his own magic. Cackling like a madman, he swept his arms toward the heavens, invoking the gods to continue their fiery blasts. Skeletons lay in a heap near the balcony railing, their battles long since over. His foot crunched upon brittle bones. A twisted grin crossed the old one's wrinkled face. With another shrill incantation, Marduk clapped his hands. Answering the command, a lone skeleton arose, sword in hand, shield ready.

With jerking movements, the gleaming bones came for Kabar, a rusty sword clasped in clacking fingers. Kabar fought back, as Marduk observed in gleeful exhilaration. Fire pounded the ground in blazing explosions, as swords clanged in a steel staccato. With his free hand, Kabar tugged the leather cord from the bag slung on his back, and the bones of Balaam tumbled out into a dusty heap.

Kabar swung his sword at the flailing skeleton, narrowly avoiding its rusty blade. Keeping the dancing bones at bay, he concentrated on Balaam's earthly remains at his feet, and summoning his loudest voice, shouted above the din of the fiery blasts: "Balaam! Hear me now! This foe I fight is your foe as well! Before me stands Marduk of Zaratan! Destroy this foul sorcerer! Destroy your enemy!"

Kabar felt stone behind him as the skeleton hacked ferociously. He had let himself get backed against a wall and had nowhere to flee. Frantically plunging with his sword into the hollow ribs of his attacker, Kabar waited, praying to Shar that the magick in old Balaam existed still. Otherwise, with an ensorcelled skeleton in front and a spell-incanting sorcerer beside, he was a dead man.

A rushing wind came down from the skies, and up from the sea. All around it churned and swirled, enveloping the skeleton, and bending the body of the sorcerer like a wispy twig. A low rumble filled the air, drowning out the crashing of the waves and Marduk's foul cries.

Thunder clapped. The great rock walls of the fortress quaked in the resounding echoes. Kabar clung to the trembling wall, knuckles bared white with the force of his grip. The balcony swayed, threatening to collapse under the onslaught that Balaam wrought.

Marduk shrieked as a gust of blackness engulfed him; he erupted into flame, and his ashes blew away on the torrent of wind. Everything was suddenly very quiet.

Kabar bent over, panting, clutching his side. He scooped the bones of Balaam back into the bag and slung it over his shoulder again.

———❦———

The ship set sail for Sardiel with a grumbling crew of treasure-less pirates, a victorious Kabar, and a happy, reunited Aeneas and Ninsu. Kabar had promised hefty payments from his own coffers to still the mutinous atmosphere aboard the ship. If Shar smiled upon them, a sea storm would arise and wash a few of the hapless men from the boat, thus reducing the inevitable blow to Kabar's treasury. Guardedly anticipating their reward, the pirates continued in their duties, anxious to reach home. Their worries were far from over though, as Aeneas still suffered the werebeast's curse.

"Sardiel is not far off, brother," Kabar said, watching the turquoise waves lash the wood of the ship.

"I hope Mother can cure the bite of the wolf."

"As do I. If not her, perhaps another can." Kabar carved an image of a seagull idly into the wood of the railing. "A stronger woman than Ninsu, I've never seen, but she remains a woman still. How fares she?"

"She's sleeping. That dog-sorcerer abused her in manners most foul. His spellcasting called for the heart of a woman warrior, a sword-wielding woman. Ninsu seems to have made quite the impression at many of the ports we've set anchor. I imagine that's how Marduk heard tell of her. A lesser woman would have died under his barbarisms. And they call *you* the *barbarian*!"

"Sleep sounds like a good idea. Can you hold down the hatches for a few hours without me?"

"I'm a pirate, Kabar. I was born to sail these seas. A few hours with the wind and the waves are but child's play for a seadog like me. The gusts coughed up by the strength of your snores, are another matter entirely." He laughed.

Kabar cuffed Aeneas on the back of the head playfully. "See that you set your men upon them then, brother! I'm off to sleep!"

Aeneas watched his brother saunter towards their cabin, the shores of Sardiel not too far away.

The Pirate and the Peach
Robert E. Vardeman

Rockets! Fire the rockets!" Lai Choi San said. The woman stood in a bubble of clear air, unsullied by the choking gunpowder smoke or the soot from burning sails. The junk beneath her slippered feet heaved treacherously, throwing two of her pirate crew overboard. She never noticed. Her dark eyes fixed on the four junks blocking her path, their orange and black checkered sails marking them as the Lord Yama King's.

"Madam, there are no more rockets," Pao said. The Emperor's eunuch stood, eyes wide, his round face showing fear for the first time since they had left port three weeks earlier.

"Then a volley of fire arrows. Those landlubber pigs will not stop me." Lai Choi San caught sight of the passage where she had been heading before the ships sent by the Lord Yama King had intercepted her. She had no liking for the narrow transit between towering cliffs that protected the inner sea of Hell. The Lord Yama King ruled the First Law-Court with an iron fist and obviously had no desire to let anyone not selected by him personally for death and torture to enter. Who was she to fight the King of Hell himself?

"Helmsman, veer to the starboard. Hard to starboard!"

"Madam, if I might suggest," the eunuch said in his unctuous tones. She glared at him. He was an annoyance, but she had to put up with him and his meddlesome ways because he was the Emperor's right hand at court and his eyes and ears outside. She hated him with a passion that knew no bounds, yet she could do nothing. To harm Pao was to harm the Emperor himself.

Lai Choi San's hands clenched into fists and then relaxed. She had no love for the Emperor at this moment, either. Her dear husband Jin languished in the Emperor's prison and would die there slowly, painfully, unless she returned with suitable ransom. She was a pirate—she and her husband were feared from the China Sea to the edge of the world itself. Even the sea serpents writhing at the most remote edge feared them and their crew. It had been only stark bad luck that Pao had captured Jin and spirited him away to the Emperor's palace.

"What do you suggest, half-man?" Her insult did not cause even a flicker of emotion on Pao's impassive face. He stood with his feet far apart to steady him against the rolling of the junk in the heavy sea. His hands were hidden in the long sleeves of his padded jacket. Sometime during the fight with the Lord Yama King's vessels, he had lost his hat. His short queue whipped about in the brisk wind blowing across the sea from the direction of the other four ships. This was all the animation Pao showed.

"You cannot fight them," he said. "They are more heavily armed."

"So we abandon the search ordered by the Emperor?" she said sarcastically. Such a thing could never be considered. Jin would not rot in the Emperor's clutches if there was a breath of life left within her lungs.

"Use your superior speed. See how they lie heavy in the water? There will be only a brief instant where your maneuverability will provide the chance to go past them and through the Gates to Hell."

Lai Choi San barked orders to her helmsman, saw he did not respond quickly enough, and pushed him out of the way to seize the rudder herself. Pao gasped and tried to dissuade her, but she had seen the genius in his plan even if the eunuch had not. There had been too much caution. The eunuch was used to subtle intrigues in the Emperor's court, usually ending in lies or efficient poisons. She was a wild creature of the sea and proved it now. She steered directly for the center of the small fleet.

"The ships," Pao said. "They will ram us!"

"Not if we get between them. They can't turn quickly enough to stop us." Lai Choi San bent her strong back to the rudder, guiding her junk directly between the two largest of the Lord Yama King's ships. Two of the vessels on her starboard side collided, sending sailors tumbling into the sea. The two on the port side could not heave to quickly enough to stop her. Fire arrows rained down on her junk, but Lai Choi San bent her head, ignored the fires burning holes in the fine hull and saw that the small fleet would never catch her now.

"Fires. Put them out," she bellowed. She turned the rudder back to her uncharacteristically timid helmsman. Sweat dripped from his skin and his hands shook but he did not shirk his job. He knew the iron determination of his captain.

"There," Pao said, seemingly calm again. "Between the towering cliffs. There will be damned souls guarding the way. You must make all speed to pass them so their piteous cries do not affect you."

Lai Choi San stood like a statue on the deck, staring ahead. Her exquisite white robe was smudged with soot and blood, but the jade buttons and green silk slippers had escaped such indignities. Reaching out gracefully with her left hand caused the sun to glint off the half dozen plain gold rings she wore. She might have been a courtesan at the Emperor's court rather than a pirate captain. She spun on Pao and dispelled any hint of graciousness.

"What do we seek once we are through those straits?"

Pao bowed low. He slowly straightened but could not bear her hot gaze. She was more Mongolian devil than Chinese.

"P'an-T'ao," he said as if the mere name might burn his tongue. "Once every three thousand years, the Queen Mother Wang harvests the peaches of immortality. This year the August Personage of Jade decided that the Lord Yama King would not be given that peach."

"Why?" Lai Choi San chafed at the slow recitation. The gods were immortal only in comparison with a human. The P'an-T'ao was the August Personage of Jade's greatest gift to the other gods. The decision to withhold it from the King of Hell must have been made with great consideration of the likely backlash. Such demotion would create unrest among the gods for eons to come. The Lord Yama King would certainly vow retribution and all Hell would be in turmoil.

"He ordered a thief to steal the P'an-T'ao in exchange for no punishment in Hell. The August Personage of Jade chose to demote the Lord Yama King because of this and other thieves being given light punishment. The Lord Yama King thinks himself above the August Personage of Jade."

"He is, of course, wrong," Lai Choi San said. "Does the Lord Yama King have the peach of immortality now? If so, he will certainly have eaten it."

"That would be unfortunate," Pao said. "Your husband will never be ransomed. The Emperor wants to recover the peach and present it as his spring solstice offering to the August Personage of Jade to curry his favor."

"So the August Personage of Jade recovers the P'an-T'ao and the Emperor is showered with the blessings of Heaven."

"And your husband Jin is released." Pao bowed deeply.

"Will we be allowed to return to our ship?"

Pao looked directly at her, then smiled slightly. "The Emperor is not a duplicitous monarch."

"That's what he has you for," Lai Choi San said angrily. "Jin is freed and *we* sail together once more on a junk crewed by our sailors. That is my condition for retrieving the P'an-T'ao"

"The Emperor's blessing will protect you," Pao said.

"If you are lying, I'd threaten to cut off your balls, but it's too late for that." Lai Choi San turned her attention to the narrow channel they had to traverse. From all sides came the whines of tortured souls. One mistake and she would join them. The Lord Yama King was a cruel, vindictive god, as he should be to punish those who had transgressed in life.

"Captain, the current is too much for us," the helmsman said. He clung to the rudder with both arms, fighting it. "The flow from the other side is incredible."

Lai Choi San barked orders and got what sail remained deployed. The wind coming from the China Sea at her stern aided their forward glide across a sea so choppy that she feared being dashed on the passage walls.

The walls were closing in. Looking closer, Lai Choi San realized that faces were pressing against the rock from the inside, as if trying to get out. Tortured souls, all. Some pressed hands against their side of the rock, forcing it out as if it were made from the finest silk. Worst of all for her were the cries. She fought to keep from clapping her hands over her ears. That would be admitting defeat.

"Ahead, Captain, ahead! We made it!"

The helmsman's cry spun Lai Choi San around. She took a step in the direction of the glass-smooth sea onto which they sailed. Then the rocky walls were past, and she was surrounded by the strange water. Looking down, she saw the junk slowly rise until the vessel floated above the gleaming, green surface.

"Where are we, Captain?" the helmsman said, his voice pleading.

"We are in the Kingdom of Hell," Pao said uneasily.

"Where do we find the Lord Yama King?" Lai Choi San demanded of the eunuch. She saw nothing but endless sea unmarred by whitecaps in all directions.

"Navigator!" she called when Pao declined to answer. The man dutifully shuffled to her side, clutching charts and instruments.

"I have no chart for this region, Captain," he said with his head bowed.

"Make one. We must return to this exact spot." Lai Choi San looked to the stern and saw only twin spires of jagged rock, seemingly suspended in midair, showing the passage they had traversed. Curiously, all around it was nothing but mirrored sea. It would be far too simple to become lost in this Hell Kingdom.

Lai Choi San shivered. That might be the point.

"I can shoot the sun and take our bearing from that, Captain," the navigator said. She dismissed him to do his work and grabbed Pao's arm. She forced the eunuch to the bow of the junk so they had an unhindered view of the sea and the distant horizon.

"Where do we go?" She shook him until his teeth rattled. "Where?" The sea was featureless and the horizon a line slightly rounded, showing that it lay perhaps hundreds of li distant. Not a single ripple disturbed the expanse.

"I . . . I do not know. The thief with the P'an-T'ao has not reached the Lord Yama King yet. I was told that in strictest confidence."

"Who? Who knows such things?"

"I will only say it is one of the Lung-Wang."

"Why would a Dragon King dare the wrath of the Lord Yama King? Unless he wants favorable notice from the August Personage of Jade."

"His motives are far more devious, madam," Pao said. "Be sure he is not lying. There is nothing for any of the Dragon Kings to gain if the August Personage of Jade's decision to demote the Lord Yama King is thwarted."

Lai Choi San shrugged this off. Such machinations were not her province. Let the court eunuch worry about the gods and their collective anger, their intrigues and alliances. She had only to find a thief with a peach to free her dear husband. Only. Only! How could she find anyone in the endless Sea of Hell?

"We are becalmed," Lai Choi San said, looking at the limp sails. The places where they were not torn or burned should billow with even a hint of breeze. She closed her eyes and turned slowly, hunting for a touch of wind against her delicately boned face.

"No wind."

"Captain, there might not be wind but we move," said the navigator. "We make incredible speed."

"Where?" Lai Choi San asked, not bothering to open her eyes. She knew the look of the strange sea. The sky was clear save for a few storm clouds directly behind them where the passage from Hell led back to the China Sea.

"I cannot say. Ahead."

She opened her eyes to see if the navigator was mocking her. The frightened expression on his face told her this was not so.

"We speed toward . . . there?" She pointed ahead. The navigator's head bobbed. He backed away, leaving Lai Choi San with the eunuch.

"Do we go straight to Hell?" she asked.

"I know nothing of this. The Emperor commanded me to assist in gaining the P'an-T'ao. That is all I know."

Lai Choi San snorted in contempt. Pao knew far more than he revealed. She gripped the railing and leaned forward, as if this would speed the trip. Returning with the peach would be more difficult by far, but she would form plans only after she had recovered the Queen Mother Wang's peach. What would that garden be like? Cultivating peaches for three thousand years to present to the August Personage of Jade to dispense as he saw fit. Such devotion the Queen Mother Wang had for her husband. Lai Choi San hoped the August Personage of Jade appreciated her.

She looked up and squinted at the sun. It moved visibly in the sky, telling her that the navigator had performed his observations accurately. Such speed was impossible along the China Sea even at its most peaceful.

"Repair the ship," Lai Choi San called to what few of her crew had survived. The battle with the Lord Yama King's guardian ships had taken a toll on her junk, but she knew the worst was likely to come.

"What plan do you have, madam?" Pao asked, following three paces behind her as she made her way along the burned, broken decking.

"None. I want everything in working order when I must make such decisions."

The words had barely escaped Lai Choi San's mouth when the lookout high on the main mast put hands to his mouth and shouted, "Whirlpool! Ahead! Whirlpool!"

"Full rudder starboard," Lai Choi San ordered. She saw immediately that the helmsman was unable to move the huge sweep. Three more of the crew lent their strength to augment that of the helmsman, to no avail. Lai Choi San ordered them back to their posts. Fighting against the pull was foolish and would only tire them. They would need all their strength later.

Like a monkey she scrambled up the rigging to hang over a yardarm next to the lookout. He pointed. Ahead rose a cloud of mist. Churning around it she caught sight of the edge of a fiercely swirling vortex. Such a hole in the ocean could suck down the Emperor's entire fleet and never come close to being filled.

"Should we abandon ship, Captain?" the lookout asked nervously.

"If the ship cannot survive, how could a lone man swimming? We have entered the Sea of Hell. Why do you think there are no fish jumping or fins cutting the water?"

"Serpents?" The lookout was more fearful of sea monsters than the deadness Lai Choi San saw.

"We stay with the ship until it goes to the bottom. And even then, a junk might be safer than any other place in Hell."

The lookout dropped down the mast and busied himself while Lai Choi San remained aloft. The whirlpool took on more definition. She swallowed hard when she saw the far downward curving side of the vortex. Dozens of ships were caught and whirling about, on their way to the utter bottom of the vortex where the Lord Yama King undoubtedly awaited them.

"So many ships and their crews," she said in awe. Squinting against the bright sunlight, she made out one ship after another. When she recognized the ship that had been commanded by Jin before being sent to the bottom, she released her hold and fell directly downward, deftly catching herself on a rope at the last moment. She swung forward and dropped to the deck beside Pao.

"Many years of ships are caught in that vortex. They fight the inevitable. I recognize my husband's ship."

"It was sunk, but he was rescued," Pao said.

"It was sent to Hell and you sent him to the Emperor's prison," Lai Choi San said. "Jin escaped that fate, for the moment. We are being sucked down onto the spiralling current."

"We are doomed," Pao said, sweat on his broad face his only sign of fear.

"If the ships enter the vortex in the order they are sunk, that means the thief has to be on a ship only a few spirals down the vortex wall. Perhaps the ship ahead of us."

Lai Choi San let out a startled cry as the junk tipped forward and began its inexorable trip to the bottom of the vortex.

"Keep us as high on the side as possible," she called to her helmsman. That tactic would work for only so long. The men would tire. The pull of the whirlpool would never slacken until they were crushed at the bottom. In spite of herself, Lai Choi San had to stare downward to see what Hell looked like. The mist veiled the bottom. The unimaginative would never know what came and those of more inventiveness would drive themselves insane with fear at their fate.

"That ship," Pao said. "That carries the marking of the Lord Yama King."

Lai Choi San looked across the broad vortex. Through the mist she saw the orange and black chess board pattern on the sails—the same as the four ships that had tried to prevent her entry into the Kingdom of Hell.

"They tried to stop us," Lai Choi San said slowly.

"What? What are you saying?" Pao was beside himself.

"Why would the Lord Yama King try to keep us from reaching this vortex?"

"He did not want you to retrieve the P'an-T'ao. I don't understand."

"That, Pao, is apparent. Yours is a world of intrigue. Apply your cunning. Why keep us from becoming trapped in the Lord Yama King's own domain? Unless there was a chance of my success, he would welcome my crew and me with open arms. He would try to prevent our passage only if we might regain the peach."

"Yes, there is something to what you say," Pao said. "But this is a trap we cannot escape! All these ships are destined to wreck at the bottom in Hell."

"No, they are not," Lai Choi San said, her mind racing. "If I am correct in my chronology and that is Jin's ship, the others have been wrecked since. That means your estimation of the ship directly across from us is accurate. It carries the thief with the peach of immortality. He spirals downward and will present it to the Lord Yama King."

"Yes, what you say is possible," Pao said.

"Then all we need to do is board that ship and get back the peach."

"It is on the far side of the vortex!"

"Every trip around the spiral is shorter. The ships speed up as they go lower and lower," Lai Choi San said. Her heart beat faster at the audacity of her scheme—and its danger. "They fight by trying to keep away from their fate."

"Even the thief?"

"The Lord Yama King must have rules he follows. Entry to Hell must be permitted only in certain ways."

"I do not understand how this helps us," said Pao.

He spoke to empty air. Lai Choi San dashed back to the helmsman, who fought to keep the junk's prow as high up on the side of the vortex as possible. For a moment, the man fought Lai Choi San, but she prevailed. With steady pressure, she altered the junk's course so the prow was aimed toward Hell directly down the side of the vortex.

The crew shrieked in fear as the junk sped up. They raced downward at a dizzying pace, but Lai Choi San was not insane. She dug her slippered feet into crevices in the deck and applied all the pressure she could to pull the sweep back. The ship creaked and groaned like a thing alive as it changed from a straight downward course to one again following the curve of the vortex.

"I've erased a month of spiraling," she announced to the crew. "Prepare to board that ship. Prepare to fight!"

There was a moment of uneasiness, then the crew fell into familiar patterns that allowed them to forget their fear. Broad-bladed swords and viciously sharp knives flashed in the sunlight.

"To victory!" Lai Choi San cried. A cheer went up that caused her to beam with pride. They were the most pox-ridden, despicable vermin in all the China Seas and they were hers to a man. "Grappling hooks! Bring the ship close for boarding!"

The crew aboard the checker-pattern-sailed ship pointed from the rail in surprise at their approach. Once in the vortex, they had not expected the pirates to catch them. They had undoubtedly been promised return to the world of the living in exchange for this passage—and the peach.

The junks clattered together, and wood splinters flew from the impact. The other ship travelled faster than hers and the ropes holding the two together strained. Lai Choi San had no time to contemplate the curiosities of magical travel. She was the first over the railing to board the other ship. Her blade lifted high, caught the sun and then slashed downward, expertly slicing off a hand. Her oppenent's sword clattered to the deck, and Lai Choi San stepped sprightly to avoid the slippery puddle of blood.

She fought with cold precision while others in her piratical crew summoned every last iota of fear and hatred to lend strength to their arms. Lai Choi San parried a cut to her legs, danced past and used her dagger to perform a half moon cut in the man's belly. He looked surprised, then his eyes went wide in fear as he recognized her.

"Lai Choi San," he muttered. "The pirate queen!"

Those were his final words. Lai Choi San heard nothing of his gasping recognition. She was already fighting toward the cabin where the P'an-T'ao must be secreted. Two more of the crew died under her blade before she flung open the cabin door.

Her eyes fixed on the peach. A small, unadorned thing, it simply sat in the center of a table. But she knew this was the P'an-T'ao. It radiated a power and sent tremors throughout her body simply being close to it. There was no questioning its vast power—or that it could grant immortality with a simple bite.

The mesmerizing sight of the P'an-T'ao almost brought her death. Spinning about from a hiding place inside the cabin came a small, wiry man, hardly tall enough to come to her chin. He was dressed entirely in black silks that snapped like a banner in the wind as he stabbed out with his dagger.

Only reactions born of long service at sea saved her. Lai Choi San shifted to the side, parried with her blade and still felt the sharp sting of steel sundering her flesh. Warmth billowed on her right side and ran down her hip to soak her white satin robe. She lashed out clumsily with the knife in her left hand but missed. The thief moved with twice the speed of any man she had ever seen.

"What manner of being are you?" she asked, trying not to show her pain.

"Damned," the man said. He moved back and forth because of the cramped quarters but always he kept himself positioned between Lai Choi San and the peach.

The nubs of horns protruded from the man's forehead. A demon brought from the depths of Hell?

He smirked when he saw her expression. "I am no demon. Only a damned spirit. My Lord Yama King has granted me pardon if I perform this task for him."

"You stole the peach from the Queen Mother Wang."

"Her husband would allow my master to become mortal. The Lord Yama King would be no more than I should that happen." He slid forward as if he moved on ice. His knife sought Lai Choi San's heart. She barely parried with her own knife. A nick on her breast turned warm and then burned like fire. The cut had seemed shallow, but from the flow down and across her belly, it had cut halfway to her heart.

"Stealing from the wife of the August Personage of Jade is punishable on the lowest level of Hell," she said.

"My master will never send me there," the thief said. "I will have granted him immortality for another three thousand years denied him by a fickle god."

"The August Personage of Jade is not fickle," Lai Choi San said, though she knew this to be untrue. She engaged the thief with his dexterous knife and quick movement.

"My knife is enchanted. My Lord Yama King gave it to me personally."

"Another affront. No mortal should use a weapon fashioned for a god." Lai Choi San blocked the door. Behind her she heard the sounds of the ship's dying crew. Her pirates were in control. But that was on the deck. It had nothing to do with this thief and the P'an-T'ao.

If she died on the thief's point, her crew would retreat and all would be lost. Depending on Pao to rally and carry the fight forward was a fantasy.

If she died, so did Jin.

That thought lent her strength to step forward as the thief launched another dazzling attack. Lai Choi San made no attempt to parry or avoid the thrust. The expression of surprise on the man's face as his blade drove home gave her hope.

Lai Choi San slashed with both sword and knife, scissors-like, at the thief's throat. His head was half severed and dangled by the spine to turn at a crazy angle. Lai Choi San lurched forward and continued drawing her weapons apart. The last ligament and nerve parted, sending the man's head bouncing across the deck. The look of surprise at what he thought was an easy victory remained etched on his face.

"May your soul be tortured forever," she grated out. Lai Choi San dropped her weapons and clutched her belly where the blade had sunk hilt deep. She started to remove it, then stopped. To do so would spill more of her blood. Steel within her, she stumbled to the table and picked up the P'an-T'ao.

A feeling of utter elation flowed through her. The pain remained in belly and breast and side, and the wounds continued to bleed, but she felt transcendent merely holding it. Would her wounds heal if she took a single bite from the peach of immortality?

"It will heal your wounds, now and for all time over the next three thousand years," Pao said. His voice trembled with emotion. "Will you eat what was meant for a god?"

"They were mortals once, too," Lai Choi San said. But something other than the cessation of pain and longevity kept her from taking the bite that would save her life.

Jin would die in the Emperor's prison if she saved herself with the merest of tastes.

"It's not my choice," she said, gasping for breath. "If the August Personage of Jade wants me to join the pantheon of the gods, he will tell me himself." She looked at Pao, hoping this insignificant little man would grow in stature and become the most powerful of the gods. He only looked more distressed.

"We must return the P'an-T'ao to the Emperor immediately," Lai Choi San said.

"You will not eat the peach?"

"I must find a way out of this accursed whirlpool now," Lai Choi San said. She moved in a shuffle. Her slippers almost betrayed her in the pools of blood slick under her feet. Not much of it was the thief's. Bent double, clinging to the peach for the potency it lent to her muscles, she motioned to Pao to get her back aboard her junk.

Two of her surviving crew, and there was a scant number of them after the fierce battle, helped her across.

"Allow me, madam," Pao said, once she was aboard her own ship. "I am skilled at surgery."

In a daze Lai Choi San allowed Pao to peel back the bloodstained fabric and then fashion bandages. But he stopped when he came to the dagger still protruding from her belly.

"What shall I do?"

"Remove it, then pour gunpowder into the wound and ignite it," Lai Choi San said in a low, firm voice. Pao did as he was told, using spilled gunpowder scrapped from the deck. The woman felt as if her guts exploded as the gunpowder cauterized her most dangerous injury. Head spinning, barely able to sit up, an idea came to Lai Choi San.

"Helmsman, steer directly downward."

"T-toward Hell itself?"

"Do it or we are lost." Clinging to the peach, Lai Choi San allowed Pao to help her to her feet. The eunuch's arm circled her and afforded substantial support as she made her way to the sweep that controlled the junk's course.

She almost fainted. The helmsman had already turned the ship from its spiral course to one that slid straight down the side of the whirlpool. They swept down with increasing speed until she had to order the sails struck to prevent them from being ripped away.

"Will you remember me in Hell, Captain?" The helmsman's voice was stronger now. She heard resignation in it.

"It won't be for many years," she said. "Turn slightly to port. More. More. Now hold this course or your soul will be damned!"

The junk gathered speed and arrowed downward with breathtaking speed. Pao was the first to understand her plan.

"We will bypass the pit of Hell and go up the far side of the vortex," he said. "But we cannot hope to reach the lip of the whirlpool. We can only go up as far as where we started. Then we will spiral back."

"Throw off everything that's not nailed down," Lai Choi San called as they hurtled down to the bottom of their course. "Everything overboard. We have the speed. We must make certain we do not carry all the weight back up."

"We have gathered speed with this weight," Pao said. "We keep the speed but will be lighter when we ascend. Will this work?"

As the eunuch pondered, the crew acted. Lai Choi San watched in dismay as they not only threw overboard all supplies but began tearing up the decking and heaving it out, too.

"Hold tight to the rudder," she said. "We are passing Hell now."

With a rush they tore past the bottom of the vortex. Lai Choi San caught sight of the Lord Yama King and his towering rage. He knew she held the P'an-T'ao and it was no longer his. But the junk flashed by so quickly the god could do nothing to them. And then the ship began the long climb up the far side of the vortex. Lai Choi San watched anxiously as they neared the level where they had attacked the thief's ship. And past. They went past!

She felt lightheaded as the junk began to slow. The lip of the whirlpool was above, not even a li distant. Then less. Then only a handbreadth. But they would not escape the pull of the vortex.

"The wind," she said. "The wind is freshening. Up sails! All sails unfurled!"

The crew scampered into the rigging and dropped the two remaining sails. Both were burned and torn but caught enough of the storm brewing to push the junk the final few feet up and out of the Lord Yama King's vortex.

"The Dragon King sends us a storm," Pao said. "He courts favor with the August Personage of Jade."

"We are free," Lai Choi San said, sinking to her knees on the deck. She held the P'an-T'ao close. Only its magical power imbued her with the strength to continue.

"How do we find the passage off this curious sea?" Pao asked.

Lai Choi San looked up. "The navigator. Get him. He plotted our course." Pao began to sob and shake with fear. "What happened to the navigator?"

"Dead, madam," Pao said. "He died at the point of an arrow fired from the thief's ship."

Hope fled and then returned to her like the ebb of the sea. She looked up at the heavy clouds above. Lung-wang the Dragon King summoned a terrible storm.

"More, my Lord Dragon King," she prayed. "Bring us all your bounty. All the rain you can deliver!"

"But we will be swamped!" Pao was beside himself.

Lai Choi San smiled wanly.

"Ride the wave. It will take us out of here," she said.

"But how?"

"Water of such magnitude will always seek to escape. Where else in this mirrored sea can such a wave escape?"

"But it will crush us in the passage." Pao moaned.

Lai Choi San knelt, head bowed. If she died, so did her husband. But she would die at sea, on her ship surrounded by the best pirate crew to ever sail the China Sea. She prayed as the storm began pelting her with rain. She prayed for life to the Dragon King and the August Personage of Jade and his wife, the Queen Mother Wang. And if that were not possible, then for death that would take her to Heaven.

"I see them. The cliffs. They . . . we're rushing toward them with immense speed!"

Lai Choi San looked up. Her eyes fought to focus. She finally saw what the helmsman had already. Dark rock cliffs rose out of the smooth surface of the sea. This was where they had entered. It would be where they exited. The strong current beneath and the powerful wave of the Dragon King propelled them smoothly between the cliffs and back down the narrow passage until they burst out into the China Sea once more.

"The Dragon King has saved us," she said. Lai Choi San blinked when she saw that the powerful wave continued to push the junk along at impossible speed. The remaining ships posted by the Lord Yama King were swamped and left behind in seconds.

"He speeds us on our way to the Emperor," Pao said, head bowed. "He is loyal to the August Personage of Jade."

"May he live forever," Lai Choi San said.

She clung to the P'an-T'ao all the way to the court of the Emperor, allowing Pao to take the peach only at the final presentation.

"Merchant ship," Lai Choi San said, lowering her telescope. "No, two of them. One might be an armed escort."

"What does it matter?" Jin asked. "Are we not beloved of the gods?"

She slid her arm around his waist and laid her head against his strong shoulder. For weeks they had been tended in the Emperor's court until they were both recovered enough to travel. And in the weeks beyond those, they had sailed the China Sea, pirating.

As it should be.

"If we capture both ships, we can bring them into our fleet. Three pirate ships will be far more profitable than one," she said.

"An ambitious plan befitting my wife," Jin said.

"Attack," Lai Choi San cried.

Hostage
Renee Stern

The *Osprey* shuddered in tight-packed ice that stretched as far as anyone could see. The blue-tinged ice growled louder and shoved harder against the ship, and the stiff-frozen sails rattled back. Sailors huddled against pellets of wind-driven snow in the lee of the wheelhouse raised their voices as they prayed.

Koros ignored the distraction—over the past four days the sounds had faded from notice as the creak of the rigging and the shrieks of long-absent gulls and skuas once had—and focused on the pale, lacy-barked sapwood in his hands. He didn't need the whole piece to strengthen the hull. They didn't have enough in the hold to waste even a finger-length, not when what he cut off would serve later to help heat the ship a little longer.

It took wood alive with sap to fuel his magic. Like any other wizard, he could do little, for good or ill, without it, and magicless folk used this weakness to bind wizards even tighter to their service. Good intentions or bad were little more than dreams without sapwood—and the *Osprey's* hold was empty of all but remnants and rejects past their prime, drying into deadwood that wouldn't spark his magic.

They'd counted on replenishing all their stores during their explorations, but hadn't reckoned on sailing so long without landfall. He no longer bothered to curse the storm that had blown floes and bergs into a maze that locked behind them. The ice that gripped them fast could kill them in too many ways: crush the ship, freeze the crew, starve them past endurance.

Koros rummaged for a saw in the carpenter's chest, then carefully cut away the extra length of sapwood with cold-clumsy fingers, catching every splinter and speck of dust in the wide-mouthed jar he kept for that purpose. Survival was too precarious now to waste anything. His wife's and children's faces floated through his memory as he stoppered the jar. Their survival rested on his return, hostages for his compliance and good behavior.

He gripped what remained firmly in each hand, the wood's cut ends prickly against his palms, each splinter a conduit between the sparks of his magic and the sap within. He walled away everything else—the noise, the lung-burning cold, the terrifying jolts of the deck beneath his feet—and concentrated on feeding those sparks into the wood.

The sap ignited in a blaze of magic, turning the wood into a shimmering line of golden force resting in his hands, controlled and contained by his will. Sweat beaded on the back of his neck from the effort, and he knew distantly that it was freezing into ice almost instantly, despite the high collars of his sweater and coat and the knit cap rolled down to meet them.

He didn't have time to worry about comfort. The magic in his hands fought for release, aching to be used. Koros aimed it like a lantern beam at the rail beside him, and drew it along the ice-rimed wood as he paced the length of the ship, down the port side from bow to stern, then back up the starboard rail until he returned to the drawn-up anchor just aft of the head.

Be strong, Koros willed. *Hold fast and keep us afloat.*

With every step and every hand-span of rail, he forced the magic deep into the wood of the hull, where it kissed the now-empty pockets that once had held sap before the builders' wizard had used its fuel to seal the ship's seams. Wood, even deadwood, was always the easiest substance to work with.

And then the magic in his hands sputtered and burned out, leaving the wood he carried dark gray and dead. He sagged against the rail, shivering from exertion—and an equal amount of relief. If he'd cut just that much shorter, the magic would have run out too soon, and the strength he'd raised in the hull would have unraveled and left them all prey to the implacable ice.

But it didn't, he reminded himself. He had to focus on what was.

Koros summoned enough strength to toss the deadwood into the carpenter's chest with other scrap. He bent his head and dragged one shuddering breath after another into his lungs until he coughed and gasped from the searing cold. Tears froze on his lashes and he fumbled his hands into his gloves.

"Are we safe now, wizard?"

Koros blinked up at Captain Wolof, who stood beside him looking out into the relentless fall of snow, one gloved hand braced on the fore stay. He hadn't heard the captain's approach, though he should have expected it.

He scrambled to his feet, cautious of showing weakness. He was no more than a tool to captain and crew, and even a desperately needed tool could be discarded if it broke. "For a short while longer," he said. "But I will find a permanent answer, I swear it."

If one exists. Koros didn't dare express any doubt.

"Or die trying, isn't that the traditional oath?" Wolof's lips twisted in an ugly smile. "Fail here and we'll all die. But I don't have to remind you of that."

Koros' fingernails bit deep into his palms, but he kept his face blank and shook his head. Six months forced together in the *Osprey's* tiny world, and still the gap between wizard and ordinary men remained as deep and broad as ever. He'd had hopes when they sailed from Port Malmy in the spring that successfully charting these unknown waters might even buy his wife and children their freedom, but instead he'd dragged them all still closer to death.

He *had* to find a way to escape the ice and return the expedition safely home. Damai's and their children's lives were bound for another year to the *Osprey's* fate. That was the span of their lives, should he never return.

He closed his eyes, calling up the image of his farewell, of proud, dark-eyed Damai, Noki with an easy laugh on his lips, Nijai with Damai's looks and magic already sparking in her fingers. Until now he'd saved his memories for the cold, weak hours of night, alone in his cramped berth, using them to rebuild his strength and defenses for the next day when he must once again appear aloof and impervious to slights, insults and pain.

Until now.

Koros was resigned to his own lot. It was the price of the magic the gods had gifted him at his birth. And Damai had joined her fate to his when he won her heart, against all odds. It was the prospect of seeing Nijai shackled as he was, sacrificing her youth and freedom, that had pushed him to gambling all on this journey to fill in the empty northern spaces of the charts.

"What are you waiting for then, wizard?" Wolof spat out each word as if it tasted foul, and Koros supposed it probably did.

"Have you discovered a new store of sapwood hidden in some dark corner of the hold, Captain?"

That was the heart of the problem. Before Wolof could answer, or show his displeasure through physical discipline for what might be judged impudence or rebellion, Koros continued in a more prudent tone. "I've strengthened the hull again. I needed a moment to recover my own strength before I returned to the main top."

A spark of suspicion flared in the captain's shadowed eyes. "What could you possibly need up there? And without my permission at that."

Koros clenched his fists hard enough for the bones to ache, but he forced a deep breath and said, as mildly as he could, "I asked the deck mate on duty, Captain, as you were in your cabin with orders to disturb you only in an emergency. He gave me leave, as I'm sure you'll find in the log."

Wolof looked over to the wheelhouse, where the mate was trying to shoot the sun one last time for the short day. Koros had overheard the men whispering that the readings showed them drifting slowly, but never in the same direction twice in a row. That had given him the idea for today's search.

"And your purpose in taking on the lookout's work as well as your own?" Wolof's suspicion was magic-bright now. He ran a strict ship, though he had a milder temper than most masters Koros had worked for, but even it had begun to splinter as the days passed and the ice piled thicker and thicker around them.

"Our survival, sir. I've thought of little else since the ice closed in around us. Isn't that my assignment on board?" Koros didn't wait for an answer that could as likely be a blow as a soft word, but quickly added, "I've been seeking in all directions since the dawn watch for a scent of sap on the wind, Captain."

"Since you didn't send for me, I assume you found nothing?" Wolof's eyes dulled once more.

Koros lowered his voice. "Alas, Captain, my nose must be too frozen to scent anything. Land must be out there, but I could do no more than guess in which direction to point the ship."

"And that would risk the last of your sapwood to drive us further into this icy wasteland." Wolof turned to stare at a towering wall of ice three ship-lengths away, the top edge glowing like ghost-fire in the last weak sunlight. It had crept closer, Koros thought, since the day before. Or they had drifted nearer. "We have a choice of sitting here with a few more days of the heat you call from the remaining sapwood before the ice crushes us, or striking out blindly and hoping to make landfall somewhere that grows trees before your magic fails and we freeze or founder."

Koros tensed to hear the familiar choices voiced so starkly. "I fear my skills have failed us, sir." With tingling fingers, he tugged his coat collar higher to block more of the persistent wind. *Damai, Noki, Nijai, I've failed you all.*

Wolof scowled and spat; the liquid froze into irregular clots as it hit the deck. "We're not dead yet, wizard. I refuse to let the ice win. What kind of a man are you to give up your hostages' lives so easily?"

Koros straightened and crossed his arms. "Hardly a man at all, if the fetters I've been bound in all my life are any sign." As if Wolof had broken down a locked door,

Koros' bitterness spilled out. "Am I a beast, to be goaded and curbed in my actions by threats and the rare reward? A man is given free rein to act or not act as he chooses, for his own good or the good of others, without a master to govern his every move."

The captain laughed, and the bitter edge silenced Koros. "Not one of us on board— nor any man alive—is completely free. I answer to my own masters, and they to theirs."

Koros looked away, allowing Wolof the argument without actually conceding. All men might be slaves to fortune, but wizards were bound by more than their own decisions and choices. The gods' gift of magic came wrapped in chains to allay the fears of the magicless folk wizards lived among.

It was a sign of their respect and awe for that gift, Koros had been taught as a child, and such gifts carried a heavy weight of responsibility to others. He hadn't believed those pretty words even then.

But he couldn't win such arguments any more than he could cut the magic out of himself; no one who hadn't lived a wizard's life could truly understand.

And Wolof was right in at least one thread of his argument: For his family's sake, Koros could not give up his fight to return home.

"I'll return to searching, Captain," he said. "Time is no friend to any of us now."

Wolof glared once more at the ice wall that cast a looming shadow over the *Osprey*. "Time catches us all in the end," he said softly. "Mind you use yours wisely."

Koros had taken only one step toward the mainmast. He stopped, shaken by the dark tone as much as the ominous words. "Sir?"

"No more than two hours aloft, wizard, same as any lookout, and then a break below to eat and warm up before you go up again. I can't have the ship's wizard weak or useless when the gods have put our lives in your hands."

A chill swept through Koros from the inside out. "Of course, sir. I'm at your orders."

He strode away, skimming one hand along the port rail as if for support. It was an excuse to avoid the crew at their prayers and the deck mate in the wheelhouse. Koros needed the isolation of the topcastle now.

Behind him Wolof shouted for the mate, then ordered the sailors to man their posts or go below. Whatever strange mood had touched him earlier was now gone, replaced by the brusque captain whose only concerns were ship and crew, wind and current.

Why does he bother? Koros wondered as he clambered stiffly up the main shrouds. *Surely he knows the tasks he's setting are pointless.*

Idleness bred fear, anger, perhaps even mutiny. But how many times could any sailor trim sails, tend rigging or polish metal fittings from bow to stern, when the ship was as good as grounded high and dry? The uselessness of normal sea duties would surely prove as dangerous as idleness. Standing weather watch, clearing ice and inspecting the hull for breaches were important tasks, more than distractions, but couldn't fill enough hours for the whole crew.

He hauled himself into the topcastle, and huddled into its meager shelter, tucking his hands tight into his armpits to warm them. He envied the crew below the long hours they struggled to fill, when he was stretched thin trying to accomplish the seemingly impossible.

Stop that, he chided himself. *If you expect defeat that's all you'll achieve.*

Koros pushed to his feet. Delay served no one. If the rest of the crew had a respite from their own work, well, that was no more than the balance correcting itself. They'd worked harder than he in the months before, when he had little to do beyond regular maintenance spells on the ship and preserving spells on the food stores, boosting the wind in the occasional calms, and healing the sailors' injuries. Light duties for a wizard, in his experience.

Now it was time to pay that reckoning.

The chill that swept him this time blew from hopeless despair. He might as easily figure out a way to grow wings on a pig or pull blood from a stone.

He clung to the topmast shroud and stared out past the bow at a line of ice tinted blood-red in the deepening dusk. *Blood magic.*

The solution can't be that easy, surely.

And it wouldn't be, not truly, he knew that. The ancient magic was forbidden, stamped out to keep the world safe. But the thought buzzed in his head, louder, insistent with the first hint of hope in days.

Koros straightened and focused outward, unwilling to overlook any possibility. He needed time to think through his idea, work out how to harness vague rumors and spotty history into workable magic, and plan how to sneak it past the rest of the crew, from Captain Wolof down to the galley boy. Their fear of magic would fall on him like a raging hurricane if they knew he even contemplated working with blood.

He took a deep breath, sifting the wind for a scent of sapwood, of living things, of land. His life would certainly be simpler if he could save them with familiar magic.

Blood magic, according to the stories parents scared their children with, left behind death and mayhem, and those who flouted the gods to attempt it reaped a terrible retribution.

Easier to keep wizards as slaves with such stories.

Certainly it needed more than blood alone, else every girl-wizard coming into her power at puberty would call up demons of destruction. But what would unlock that secret power and spark blood as if it were sap?

Koros stepped a quarter-turn around the topmast for a fresh lungful of air to filter and search. Still nothing. Live wood with its sap was the safe channel for magic—it was what he knew, it carried official blessing, within limits—but it left him drained after every working. *Perhaps that's why it's safer than blood magic.*

Which might mean that he could bend the magic to his will more easily if he filtered it through blood, once he discovered how to unlock it. What was sap but the lifeblood of a tree? Sapwood had once been as alive as any wizard, but a human mind would surely fathom the heart and soul of a dog or bird more easily than it could a tree's. Human blood ought to provide instant understanding and unlock magnitudes more power than even an entire trunk of ancient cedar.

Blood magic ought to shoot them through leagues of tight-packed ice as easily as a white-hot poker burned through bark.

But whose blood could he use? And how much would he need?

Koros shifted another quarter-turn around the topcastle and breathed deep. Still nothing but the sharp sting of salty snow. Only ice and emptiness in this direction as well.

He was flying ahead of himself. How much of whose blood was a pointless question without first learning how to spark blood—and control it.

He braced himself between the mast and the topcastle rail, then shut his eyes and focused inward, seeking the secret place within that nurtured his magic. The shrouds rattled in the wind that blew at his back, and his perch dipped and swayed in dizzying motions. Koros hunkered down, locking his arms around the mast behind him. He wouldn't think about falling. Snow hit his cheek and clung to his lashes, half-melted, and he buried his face into the shelter of his knees. Two hours suddenly seemed like an eternity.

He had no need to control wind or snow, he reminded himself. They were simply distractions he had to shove away along with the sense of passing time. He gnawed at his lip, falling into the sting of pain, letting it surround him and become a barrier to the outside world. What he wanted—what he needed—was that flat, gray, seemingly endless space where his heart, mind and will intersected.

Damai's face, and Noki's and Nijai's, flickered there a moment, then faded away. The ache for them anchored him, brought a pearly glow to the space around him.

It was enough. Koros recognized the jitter of anticipation, the faintest whiff of ozone as if a flint struck a spark off steel. His magic shimmered into view, rose-gold waves like dawn painting the sky, but motionless. Frozen.

He worried at his lip again, trying to understand why his magic appeared different now. He tasted salt and iron, bursting over his tongue like a bracing jolt of lemon juice. The frozen waves around him blew into motion, a startlingly frenzied dance that jerked him back to physical reality.

Sweat sprang up on the back of his neck. Sparks licked the inside of his mouth and bubbles seemed to fizz through his veins. Laughter tickled the back of his throat, but he held it in, clutching it as tight as the heady, joyous warmth that blanketed him.

His body itched to dance with his magic, to move, to burn off the force flooding through him. He clung tighter to the mast, resisting the urge. The snow had died, but the wind gusted, catching the sails and jerking at the ship. Still the ice kept its tight grip on the hull, but Koros knew if he could only break through that icy hold that the *Osprey* would harness the wind to soar back to Port Malmy.

Suddenly his mouth felt almost sticky, with a foul, bitter taste. He licked his bleeding lip, concentrating, trying to will himself back to where those rose-gold waves of magic had washed over him. But he gagged on the blood in his mouth, and his limbs trembled with exhaustion. Koros rolled his head back, staring up at the cloud-dimmed stars with tears freezing on his cheeks. The magic had burned out to no more than the faintest hint of ash on the wind. He sucked in deep lungfuls of air, desperate for another taste of power stronger and more vital than he'd ever imagined.

He smelled only sterile snow and hoarfrost, the same as before.

And still no sapwood, he reminded himself. He did not dare forget his original purpose up here.

Koros dragged himself upright, stamping his feet and rubbing his arms to recapture some warmth. Blood magic would free them, he knew it now with a soul-deep certainty. But he had no idea how he'd unlocked its power.

It had taken only a few drops of blood to fuel those brief moments. What could he do with a ladleful, or a jug of blood? His pulse pounded in his ears, and he sagged to his knees, wrapping his arms around his chest. The old stories that he'd scoffed at before suddenly seemed sickeningly possible: wizards leveling cities, calling up immense waves and sandstorms to smash fleets and bury armies, commanding packs of demons to hunt and devour their foes. They'd ruled from pools of blood, the stories said.

Visions of freedom tempted Koros. The *Osprey* was full of men without any hope of opposing his power. Their blood could free the ship, could swat away the troops guarding the wizards' compound, could unleash him and his fellow slaves and all their hostages. They could all escape, find a land where they might live free to use their magic as they chose.

They could rule.

And what of Damai and Noki and the others among their hostages without magic? Magic didn't always follow bloodlines, and the gods might as likely gift a wizard's family with none at all. Damai and Noki were no less precious to him than his wizard daughter—but if the magicless crew tempted him, his wife and son were as likely to tempt other wizards.

His stomach rolled. Who could be trusted with such power? He *had* to find enough sapwood to save the *Osprey*. Blood magic was too dangerous.

"Wizard!" Haral, the duty mate, called from the foot of the mast. Koros bent over the topcastle and waved acknowledgement. "Time's up! Captain's orders."

Koros waved again and worked himself into the shrouds. Had it been two hours already? His whole body creaked as he stretched and bent to clamber down the ratlines. A warm corner in the galley with a mug of soup thickened with ship's biscuit and spiked with a shot of grog would restore him as much as a night's rest in his berth.

His boots thudded against the deck and slid a little on a remnant of hard-packed snow. He tightened his grasp on the knotted lines to steady himself, then scuffed the snow up off the deck and kicked it toward the rail. He started to follow, to hurl it out onto the frozen sea, but a tap on his shoulder whirled him around.

"Report to the captain after you eat," Haral ordered. "Someone else will finish securing the deck."

Koros forced a weary smile, reading the mate's meaning clearly. Clearing snow and ice before it built to hazardous levels was a task suited to any sailor. The captain wanted him to focus his efforts on saving them all, on the skills no one else on board could muster. He saluted as neatly as he could and stumbled toward the hatch and the galley below. He had a report to compose, and decisions about his discovery to ponder.

⚓

Koros swiped his hands once more over his mouth to knock off any stray crumbs as he marched down the companionway between the galley and the captain's cabin. Six months on the *Osprey* and he'd never yet stepped into this forbidden territory. The wardroom and the cabin beyond were open only to officers.

And the occasional crewman called down for extraordinary discipline.

As a boy, isolated underground in the wizards' compound where their masters controlled their education and all practice of magic, he'd built elaborate, exotic pictures of the world above. Reality had both surpassed and fallen short of his imagination.

So he'd carefully avoided thinking of Wolof's cabin, leaving it as blank in his mind as the northern spaces on their maps. He'd have no call to see it—he'd intended to serve his duty with exemplary diligence so that none of the crew might complain of his behavior, so that he might return home with a spotless record, so that he might win additional freedoms for his family.

Yet here he was, staring at the varnished, close-grained oak of Wolof's door, polished to a shine that showed his wide eyes and bitten lip. He'd dawdled over his meal, wrestling with what to include in his report, and still he wasn't certain of his course. Koros swallowed hard and rubbed his clammy hands on his thighs. He'd almost rather he'd been summoned to account for some impudence or error. No lives rested on that.

But he couldn't delay here forever, much as he wished he might stop time or propel himself into the future, far beyond this moment.

The hull shivered and groaned around him. The ice must have shifted yet again, but his strengthening spell continued to hold.

He tugged off his knit cap and tucked it into his belt, then whispered his family's names under his breath before knocking.

"Enter!" Wolof's voice, muffled by the sturdy door, sounded almost angry.

Koros swallowed on a suddenly dry, gritty throat, and turned the gleaming brass knob as if it might become an adder beneath his fingers. *Damai*, he reminded himself again. *Noki, Nijai.*

He pushed open the door and stepped over the threshold, trying to catch details in the edges of his eyes: the chart table latched open under a shuttered window and strewn with new maps and old, a tidy bed beside it brightened with a red and yellow striped blanket. He focused everything else on the frowning man seated behind a leaf-carved table big enough to accommodate all six of the *Osprey's* officers, a bowl between his hands of the same biscuit-thickened soup Koros had eaten in the galley.

Wolof turned the bowl a quarter-circle with his fingertips, then looked up at Koros. "You've eaten, wizard?"

"Yes, sir." Courtesy demanded its return. "Thank you, sir."

The captain took up his spoon and dipped it in and out of the caramel-brown liquid. "I hope you've brought me better news than you had before."

Koros bit his lip. What was he to say? He'd hoped for some sign to guide him, and in its absence, hesitated too long.

Wolof dropped his spoon with a splash and pushed the bowl away. "Out with it, wizard. I've never yet killed the messenger for carrying unwelcome news. Every sailor knows the sea will get him in the end."

Koros opened his mouth, but words shied away from his tongue. Where was the fire that had burned so hot in the captain just hours before up on deck? The stubborn refusal to bow to fate and the determination to fight for his ship and all the lives within?

Wolof slapped the table, rattling the spoon in his bowl. "Out with it, wizard!"

Koros flinched, tried to mask it in a quick salute. "My apologies, sir. I feared I might have missed something. Has our situation changed since we last spoke?"

"Apart from being two hours closer to freezing to death or seeing the ship crushed in the ice?" Wolof pushed himself back in his chair and shook his head. "Isn't that enough?"

"Beyond enough." Koros pulled his hands behind his back, lacing his fingers tight.

This was it. No turning back now. "But I may have found a third choice, sir."

The captain straightened with a jerk, leaned closer, eyes burning once again. "You found a source of sapwood?"

The hope in his voice and determination in his face heartened Koros enough to say without hesitation, "No sign of any land at all, I'm sorry to report. But something else at least as powerful. Something long lost." Even now he didn't want to name it outright.

He didn't have to. He watched Wolof's face blank, then screw up as he chased Koros' meaning, and soon enough—too soon—take on a green-tinged pallor. He clasped his hands in one tight fist and his nose wrinkled as if Koros had poured a pot of rotting fish onto the table.

"Blood magic," Wolof choked out. It wasn't a question.

Koros nodded, wary of saying anything just now. The balance was too delicate; Wolof could tip either way.

The captain jerked a hand free and swept the bowl off the table to crash against the wall. Soup stained the white-painted wood down to the floor, where the bowl rolled in a noisy half-circle, spilling the rest of the liquid on the smooth-sanded planks. The spoon cartwheeled onto an inlaid chest with brass fittings, then slid off with a tinny clatter.

Somehow Koros stayed still, though all his instincts screamed to run and hide from the breaking hurricane. He conjured up the scent of sweet magnolia from memories of Damai, used it to force away the acrid stink of fear and anger that filled the cabin.

"Are you mad?" Wolof shouted. He jumped to his feet and pointed an accusing finger at Koros. "I'll hole the *Osprey* myself and scuttle her before I let you wash my decks in blood and call up your demons for that filthy magic."

Koros bowed his head. "That is your choice, of course, sir. I serve at your command as always, to the utmost reach of my skill."

The soft formality seemed to quench the worst of Wolof's fire. "Who taught you blood magic? How many of you know this secret, and how have you kept it hidden?"

Koros heard the unasked question: *Why haven't wizards used that power against us?*

"No one taught me," he said. "As far as I know, the secret otherwise remains buried in our past. I stumbled into it by accident, luck, and great need."

Wolof's knuckles whitened as his hands curled into fists. "Whose blood, and what damage have you done to my ship?"

"Only my own blood, sir, and little enough of that. It's easier to work with than sapwood in some ways." Koros pulled himself back before he pushed the captain's fears into action. "And no damage. In fact, I think you'll appreciate this, sir."

He pulled out of his pocket the round, milky stone Noki had given him and stepped forward to set it on the table. The heat he'd called into the stone while he ate— to convince himself his one feat in the main top was more than a fluke—still lingered.

The captain slanted a skeptical frown at the stone and then Koros. "You conjured a stone? How does that help?"

"Touch it, sir. I promise you, it won't harm you."

Wolof stretched out one finger, then plucked up the stone and cradled it in his palm. "It's warm." He shrugged. "Body heat, no more. There's no magic in that."

"I can do it again, with whatever object you choose." Koros summoned all his sincerity into his voice and expression. "It only needs a drop or three of blood."

The captain studied Koros as if he'd never seen the wizard before. "The warming pan," he said at last. "I'd be glad to sleep in comfort tonight. But we'll use my blood—if it's as safe as you say it is."

Koros nodded, glad he hadn't had to make the suggestion himself. It would ease the way when it came to tapping the crew's blood to break the *Osprey* free.

Wolof rolled Noki's stone onto the table, then turned to retrieve the warming pan from beside his bed. Koros scooped up the precious stone before it rolled onto the floor and returned it to his pocket.

"What should I do, wizard?"

"Place your blood on the center of the pan. I'll do the rest, sir. But I need to concentrate."

Wolof's lips pressed together and his hands shook, but he complied, cutting his thumb with the clasp-knife on his belt. Three drops of blood glistened on the pan's black metal and spread out in a wider circle as the captain curled his thumb into his fist and stepped back, almost against the bed.

Koros spread his hands out just above the blood and stared into it, through it, falling quickly into the not-quite-trance. But the empty plain remained dull gray. He pushed and pulled, called and pleaded and demanded, but the rose-gold waves of magic hid from him, refused to appear.

He shook his head. "No," he whispered. "Not this."

"What's wrong, wizard?" The alarm in the captain's voice pulled Koros back to the cabin.

"I don't understand. It worked before. What's different?" Koros gnawed at his tender lip. Metal? Wood *was* easiest to work with. But no, Noki's stone had seemed as easy as wood.

The blood. That's the difference.

Koros fell into a chair, heedless of the breach of protocol. *Wizard blood.* The implications terrified him. But he had to try one more test.

"Answer me, damn you, wizard! What's gone wrong now?"

"If I may borrow your knife, Captain? I seem to have found a flaw in my understanding."

Wolof stared at him a moment, then tossed the folded knife across the table; his expression demanded an answer soon.

Koros pricked the ball of his thumb with the knife tip, squeezed two drops of blood onto the pan and slid into the gray plain. Almost immediately the rose-gold waves shimmered into view, and he coaxed the magic into tendrils of heat that he threaded through the metal. He slumped in the chair, then skimmed the pan with his other hand. Set against the pan's warmth, the circle of the captain's blood seemed almost icy.

He closed his eyes and sucked on his lips, contemplating his death with a distance that surprised him. The dangerous secret to blood magic would die with him.

"The spell needs your blood?" Wolof asked gently.

Koros barked a dark laugh. "You and the crew are apparently no more than deadwood. Blood magic, it seems, is only potent when wizard blood is spilled." He looked up at the captain. "You and your crew are safe; the *Osprey's* decks can't run with blood when you have only one wizard on board."

"And will one wizard's blood be enough to free us? Why should I even consider letting you dabble in forbidden magic? You know better than I that you'll be condemned to a state execution when we reach home."

"My death is already assured, along with everyone else on board. We don't have enough sapwood, or any means of finding more. Not in time to do any good. We'll all die here and disappear beneath the ice, and a year from now, when the *Osprey* has not returned, my wife, my daughter, and my son all die as well."

"So you'd buy our lives and theirs with yours?"

Your lives are required to save theirs, Koros thought, but knew better than to say it. He tipped his head and shrugged.

Wolof stalked away to the row of shuttered windows above his bed, unlatched a shutter and stared out into the darkness. "You've thrown me into the crocodile's den, you know. I should have you executed right now just for making that suggestion."

The threat skimmed past like a summer breeze. Koros watched the stiff line of the captain's back, the way his fists knotted where they pressed against the teak framing. Wolof wouldn't kill him, not yet, not if he could save his crew and ship.

"I know, sir," he said when the silence in the cabin began to hum with too many unspoken words. "But I may as well die breaking us free of the ice. I want my death to accomplish something."

The captain didn't move, but continued staring out the window. "How old are your children?"

The unexpected question startled an answer out of Koros. "Noki is five. Nijai is seven."

"Both wizards? Or do you know yet?"

Sweat slicked Koros' body beneath his sweater and wool pants. Why was Wolof asking such personal questions? And did he dare answer with the truth? "Would it make a difference?" he asked softly.

Wolof turned around at last, his face as blank as the ice outside. Koros almost wished he'd remained facing away, with its pretense of anonymity. The captain shrugged, lips quirked. "I suppose not. They're only children, after all."

More ambiguity. Koros' nerves vibrated faster, sensing danger stalking closer to his family, and he knotted his fingers around Noki's stone tight enough to hurt. Welcome distraction. He didn't dare move, let alone speak.

The captain dropped onto his bed, bent over to rest his elbows on his knees, and rubbed at his temples. "I knew when I accepted command of the *Osprey* that charting new territory would be nothing like carrying cargo on even the farthest trade routes. I wanted the adventure and the honor. All of us did."

Not all of us, Koros thought. "You've certainly found adventure," he said, still keeping his voice soft.

"And honor enough to satisfy anyone. When we return."

When. Not if. Breath slid more easily in and out of Koros' lungs. But he had to ask: "Blood magic won't taint that honor? What I do to free the ship will come out. You won't be able to silence the entire crew. You might even suffer for permitting me."

Wolof snorted a harsh laugh. "What can any of that matter in the face of your sacrifice? If anyone receives recognition from this voyage, it should be you."

Koros choked on the irony. "The *Osprey* will sail on land before that happens. If anything, my name and all I've done will be stricken from memory. It doesn't matter. As long as my family is safe."

The captain rubbed at the deep crease in his brow, then nodded. "How do you want to proceed with this plan of yours?"

Koros almost smiled. His course was set, and his family would be safe. He felt suddenly lighter. Freer.

⚓

Haral rang the crew to their duty stations shortly after dawn. On his way below deck, Koros passed the cook and galley boy lugging up kettles of hot soup to fortify the men. He'd already eaten his on the foredeck, watching the sun rise.

The snow had stopped sometime during the long night while he slept, gathering his strength as he dreamed of playing foolish games with his son and daughter, Damai beside him. He could see their future in the children's faces, could see the grandchildren they would give her. That future was the only gift left he could offer.

A thin layer of ice and snow sparkled on the ship like fairy gilt in the bright sun still low on the horizon, and the ice walls around him scattered blinding rays. He breathed deep one last time before heading below. The cold still seared a path all the way down, but now he knew it meant he was still alive. Still fighting.

Wolof, a flickering candle-lantern in his hand, met him in the hold. "You're certain of this course?"

Koros found a true smile on his lips; the captain's concern warmed him as nothing else outside his family or working magic ever had. "This is the only way, you know that. You agreed last night, and I'm content with this last service to you and the *Osprey*."

"No one will ever call you or any wizard less than brave within my hearing." Wolof's eyes burned fierce in the dim shadows. "And I swear to tell your family myself, Koros."

His name sounded strange to his ears after so many months. Koros nodded tightly, unable to trust his voice to hold steady, but then forced out, "I wish my thanks were enough. But I have nothing else."

"That's because you've already promised us your life." Wolof started forward, picking a path through coiled rope, stacks of seasoned timbers, and mostly empty casks. "And some might say that's more than we deserve from you."

Koros shrugged, unseen, as he followed Wolof toward the bow. The air turned close and dank, and the hold narrowed. The captain pried open a half-hidden hatch in tightly angled confines and lowered his lantern partway down. Beside him, Koros wrinkled his nose at the reek, then winced at the thin shards of ice floating in the murky bilgewater and glistening on the ballast rocks.

"You said you needed to be as close to the heart of her as possible," Wolof said, apology in his tone. "You have access to the stempost and even some of the keelson if you stretch."

He swung the lantern a little side to side, and the shadows shifted enough to show Koros a thin ledge of sorts, bracing where the futtocks joined to the stempost and keelson. With care he ought to keep his feet dry. He snorted softly at the idea of worrying about a soaking now.

The captain slanted a questioning look at him.

Koros shook it aside. "A silly fancy, nothing more. This will suit."

He slid down through the hatch to crouch on the brace beam. Wolof shifted the lantern back to give him enough light, and Koros wanted to hug that tiny flame for every bit of heat it gave off. Seeing ice shards hadn't prepared him for how much colder the bilge was than topside. He was below the ice down here, surrounded by the frigid sea, separated from it by only a thin skin of deadwood.

But he could bring that deadwood to life, if only for a short span. He prayed he had the strength to hold it long enough.

Setting his jaw, he reached out for the knife in Wolof's other hand. The leather-wrapped handle retained the captain's body-warmth, and Koros nodded his thanks as he took it in a firm grip. It was a sturdy, utilitarian knife, the type all the sailors carried to cut and splice line—easily replaced if he dropped it in the bilge. No doubt it would wind up destroyed or deliberately lost for its taint from blood magic.

Koros shook those thoughts aside as well. He slashed his left palm lengthwise, ignoring the sting, then quickly switched hands and slashed the right palm. Twisting down, he wedged the knife into an out-of-the-way corner where the smeared blood on the handle might seep into the wood; from there he contorted himself to stretch as far as he could down along the keelson that ran lengthwise through the ship, smearing the rough oak with his blood and willing it deep into the wood.

The rose-gold waves of magic appeared instantly, before he'd shut his eyes or pictured the gray plain within. They stretched higher, sheened brighter and vibrated faster than he'd ever seen. The wood sucked up his blood as fast as it flowed out of him, making his head swim and pound. His magic felt eager—no, impatient, insistent.

Koros tried to pull away, escape back to his body, as his control frayed. *Too much power!* Sparks popped against his palms, heat scalding his hands, and steam slicked his face, hands, any exposed skin as the ice shards below him melted.

No! He fought back, struggled to impose his will. *Not fire!* He needed to wake the ship, strengthen it, push it into motion. A little warmth would melt the ice enough to provide maneuvering room. But he had to keep control. This much power could too easily turn to flame and burn the ship to the waterline—or beyond. Who could tell with blood magic?

The heat curled up his wrists, unfurled through his arms, swept over his torso—but the hull was safe. Koros panted as he began to sweat and burn as if fevered. How much of this could he stand? Rose-gold tendrils danced down the bilge toward the stern like marsh gas in the darkness, mocking him.

He clawed his fingers around the heavy square beam, ignoring splinters and gouges that drew more blood, and focused again on his family, his determination to save them, his need to free the *Osprey*.

He slowed his breathing, relaxed his straining muscles and pulled the gray plain around him. He was the master of his magic; he refused to let it master him. The lights dancing in the bilge winked out suddenly, and back in the gray plain they leaped around his feet like eager, unruly puppies.

Gently, he coaxed. *Build slowly, inexorably. We have time enough.*

A distant part of him hoped that was true, wondered if his body held enough blood and will.

"She's rocking," Wolof said, hope brightening his voice like lantern-light. "It doesn't feel like the ice shoving at us this time."

The *Osprey* bucked under Koros' hands like an untrained colt, shoving back at last at the ice. Now for the stempost. The keel gathered her force and showered it all on to the bow. The stempost would need his attention most, to strengthen it to cut through the ice without shattering under the stress.

He pulled himself back to a crouch, caressing the keelson one last time as he went. Beneath the heavy, constricting clothes, his body swam in sweat, and his head seemed to bob on his neck like a fishing float on the waves.

He blinked, seeing double: the shadowy bilge, the shimmering plain. Wolof was leaning head-down into the hatch, mouth moving in words that no doubt matched the near-panic in his eyes, but Koros couldn't hear him over the heartbeat that drummed in his ears and matched the rushing rhythm of the magic's flow.

"Don't interfere," Koros said, though he couldn't tell how clearly he formed the words.

He paid no further attention to the captain but focused instead on tightening his grip on the stempost where it joined the keelson. He stared into the wood, through the individual fibers and grains, imagining the empty sap channels wicking up his blood and the magic sparking within them. As he slid his hands slowly higher, the post seemed to take on an orange-gold glow, as if it contained living flame.

It was a deeper, brighter color than he achieved with sap. For a moment he thought it only a trick of the light and the blood loss, but then the *Osprey* surged forward.

And slammed to a stop that jolted Koros half-off his perch. His hands didn't budge from their position on the stempost, though, and he scrambled awkwardly back into place.

"It's working!" he shouted.

He pushed harder at the post, leaned into its heat as if it were a banked stove, sensed the ice shrinking away, hissing and steaming, from the *Osprey's* outer skin. *More heat. This is too slow.*

He thought he saw Damai shake a cautioning finger at him. *Too much, too fast, and I risk throwing away their only chance.* He'd almost lost control once. What if his strength gave out too soon, as if he'd cut a length of sapwood too short?

The *Osprey* surged again and this time kept moving, heeling a little as her sails caught the wind, then picking up speed. Her timbers thrummed with a force that had been absent for too many days.

"Home," Koros whispered. "We're heading home."

He slumped against the stempost, still gripping it tight and feeding it his magic. *They're heading home.* The bilge and the plain both vanished, replaced by a view from the prow, as if he'd stepped into the fierce-eyed bird carved there. A dark line snaked before him, ice splitting and splintering on either side of his hull as league after league slipped away.

They're heading home, he repeated. But it didn't matter. He conjured up his family's faces once again. *Damai, Noki, Nijai.*

Rum Runners
Jeff Houser

Captain Considine took a long look around the large jollyboat that held all that was left of his life.

It wasn't much: some meager rations, a few weapons, chests of miscellaneous artifacts, and four fellow survivors of the ill-fated *Peregrine*. They were an exploration team, sailing the waters of the New World to investigate all there was to be found; new islands, new cultures, anything and everything there was to collect and catalogue. Now they were five people in a rower, trying to figure out how to survive on open water.

There was one island in sight, maybe an hour to the southeast—the only problem: that island was where their attackers had sailed to after sinking the *Peregrine*.

"It's either that island, or we pick a random direction and try to make it to lands we already know are too far," the captain said to the remnants of his crew. "We can be scared and stupid, or we can make it to the land we can see, and go from there. I, for one, am more comfortable with the prospect of running or fighting on solid ground than dying of thirst, starvation or madness on open water in a little boat."

The crew uniformly agreed. They'd all seen evidence of castaway rowboats and the bodies of men who'd tried to survive at sea without the proper resources.

Silent as they stroked, the *Peregrine's* lifeboat made its way closer to land. Considine had more than enough time to survey his crew as they progressed, trying to discern their state of mind so he knew what he'd be working with when they came ashore.

To his immediate left, Deirdre Stone: aptly named Mistress of the Mine. She had a knack for caving and rock climbing, and was an expert miner. The woman seemed to have a nose for tunnels; namely ones rich in ore and gem deposits. She also had a gorgeous singing voice, and often regaled the crew with Irish folk songs on calm nights at sea. Her jaw was set hard, her eyes focused past Considine's elbow to the spot where the *Peregrine* had gone under. She had the taste of blood in her mouth, the captain could tell. She would have her revenge on the bloody pirates that had waylaid them, or else die trying. He couldn't blame her.

Behind Deirdre sat "Sureshot" Sean Morgan, young topsman and sail monkey. Although the boy wasn't sure of his own age, he was in the tail end of that stage of life where his voice sounded like a cat had gotten hold of it. While the crew liked to jibe him for his crackling speech, they knew where to draw the line because Sean was easily the best marksman of the entire crew. It was Sean who'd spotted the Rum Runners from the crow's nest, coming fast on their stern out of a nighttime fog bank, and given the crew of the *Peregrine* any chance at all of reacting. The boy was scared, that much was clear on his face. He'd do his duty until the grim end, but he didn't even bother with a façade of bravery now. The captain knew the young topsman would be looking to him to be brave enough for the lot of them.

To Considine's immediate right was a hulking, brooding form they called Tor. The man did anything that was asked of him. He was their cook, but there were only so many hours a day he could fill with that duty, so he filled in wherever needed, and his strength and size were great assets to the ship. The man rarely smiled, but he also rarely complained, even now with a musket ball lodged somewhere inside his ribcage. The captain thought he saw the glimmer of blood on the big Northman's lips as he rowed in silence, but he couldn't be sure in the dark, and he wouldn't challenge the man's pride by asking in front of the crew. Better just to let the big braid-bearded bear row in peace.

The last of the crew, rowing with what little arm strength he possessed, almost entirely eclipsed behind the bulky form of the cook, sat Nelson Terwilliger. The fine-boned, bespectacled, conservatively dressed man was the crew's number one scholar, and was still trembling in his boots from his near-death experience. The man was virtually useless in the many details of sailing a ship, so he was often excused to remain belowdecks to bury his nose in dusty books. Nelson was one of the foremost experts on New World islander cultures. He'd traveled with the *Peregrine* for years, studying and cataloging new civilizations. He was also a student of the occult, both of the old country and of all the wonderful variety of superstitions here among the newly discovered island tribes around the Caribbean. If you got him started, the man could go on for hours, babbling about the gods of this island tribe and how it affected their mating rituals and harvest cycles and what not.

"So what do we do if we run into those damned Rum Runners again, Captain?" Sean finally broke the silence. "Can't best them in a fight. With even numbers, it wasn't close. Now with just the five of us . . ."

"I'm working on that, Morgan. Just keep your mind on your paddle while I come up with something brilliant," Considine said with what little hint of a smirk he could muster under his tricorner hat, hoping it would calm the lad's nerves a bit. At the very least, the boy didn't ask any more questions.

Under cover of darkness and the rushing hiss of waves, the rowboat rode the tide to the island and beached in a tiny lagoon. The *Peregrine* survivors dragged the rower into tree cover and buried it with palm leaves as best they could before hunkering down to discuss their next move. To them, the answer was obvious.

"Well, at least we don't have to look hard for a secret hideout," Considine said, inclining his head in the direction of a distant silhouette further down the coastline of the small island. The Rum Runners' infamous ship, the *Tipsy Crimson*, bobbed lazily in the shallows where it had anchored. Not far inland from the ship, the tall palm trees reflected a dancing firelight. Even from a distance, the explorers could hear the braying echoes of revelry that could only come from victorious pirates. The *Peregrine* and most of her crew were dead, and these men were throwing a party to celebrate.

Sureshot Sean ran a nervous hand through his tangled, sea-soaked hair, a look of desperation spreading across his face. "Sir, there's no way we can win any kind of fight."

"A straight up fight against the lot of them? No," Deidre said, eyeing the silhouette of the pirates' ship. "But maybe we can see to it these bastards never ransack another ship."

Tor, a quiet, monstrous shadow, crouched against a palm trunk and grunted his assent.

Nelson Terwilliger squirmed in his boots, wringing out his sea-drenched shirt, but kept quiet.

Considine took a moment to scratch at the scruff developing on his chin as he weighed his options. "These bastards have to pay for what they've done. Not just to us, but to countless other crews. The Rum Runners have plagued these waters for an entire decade, and their legend grows with each raid. I've never heard of anyone ever stumbling across their home camp, but if this is it, then we may be closer to cracking them than anyone's ever been. Now any of you that want to stay here—"

"Not a chance, sir." Deirdre's eyes practically glowed in the dark with pent-up rage. "We're a crew. We stay together as a crew, ship or no ship."

"Where you go, I go, sir," Sean said, shouldering a trio of muskets he had snatched from their sinking vessel. The boy struggled to put a brave face on to match Deirdre's.

"Together," came Tor's baritone voice from the darkness. In one hand, he held a heavy butcher's knife from his pantry. He meant to use it.

"I . . . I'm with you all, of course. I'm just . . . not very—"

"We know, Nelson. It's OK. You'll stay in the rear, be our lookout."

Together, led by Sureshot Sean's sharp eyes, they picked their path cautiously across the landscape, closing on the firelight and the maddening sounds of drunken revelry. As they crept, each of them desperately tried to forget what a one-sided fight it had been on board the *Peregrine.* . . .

———————⚓———————

Sean spotted them and shouted down the warning. The captain called the men to quarters—something to which most of the crew were not accustomed. Only five had ever seen real combat before, and when the pursuing ship came close enough to recognize as the Tipsy Crimson, *they knew that there would be no fighting their way free. Instead, Considine ordered the crew to stand down and collect what few barrels of rum they had stored below. The majority of the* Peregrine's *crew were not heavy drinkers, so their stores were nothing impressive by most maritime standards. Still, everybody knew the stories: the dreaded Rum Runners always had one thing at the top of their list: rum, of course. They took food, riches, weapons as well, but rum was their stock and trade, as well as combat necessity, if the stories were accurate. They always fought while piss drunk, and somehow remained unbeatable, as if the booze somehow magically protected them.*

Even their bloody ship seemed drunk, bobbing and lurching unsteadily in it's approach, yet somehow defying logical sailing mechanics of wind and current, gaining quickly on the Peregrine. *More than once, it seemed the pirate ship might topple over and be swallowed by the waves entirely, when it would suddenly right itself again and seem none the worse for it.*

After being startled by a warning shot across their bow, the explorers drew to a halt as much as possible to try and give up their barrels of rum without a fight—so they hoped. It was not to be. The Rum Runners were in a bloody mood, it seemed, and the reek of their drink stretched across the span between ships even before boarding planks and hooks found their way onto the Peregrine's *deck. The bloodshed started immediately, without a chance for the captain to make any offers of surrender. The explorers tried to snatch up their arms and resist, but it was a losing effort from the start.*

The legends were true. These were no ordinary men. Some of them made fearless, miraculous leaps from the Tipsy Crimson's *rails to the* Peregrine's—*a distance no man should have been able to make. A pistoleer carried at least a half dozen pistols strapped to his body in haphazard fashion, firing wild shots off of masts and hinges and deck planks which always seemed to ricochet perfectly into one of the* Peregrine's *crew. One bald-headed man brandished a flagon in one hand and a torch in the other, taking deep swigs from his flask and spitting long, fearsome gouts of flame. A giant Moor covered in a latticework of tattoos, scars and piercings simply ran amok with fists like oversized coconuts, smashing and drubbing and stomping a bloody swath through the crew. His ogrish guffaws could be heard clearly across the cacophony of battle.*

And then there was the captain. Contrary to the assortment of wild fighters amongst the crew, the captain of the Rum Runners simply stood back to take in the sight, leaning against the starboard rail with his sword and main gauche still sheathed on his hips, smirking and commenting to himself as fights resolved around him. Like every member of his crew, the captain carried some kind of rum receptacle on his person. He drank from his bottle, occasionally saluting his men, who responded by pausing in the fight (when they could) to take a drink of their own. Here and there, pockets of rum-soaked pirates broke into drinking songs while fighting, as if it was all just some rowdy harbor party. All the while, the crew of the Peregrine *fell to the deck like mayflies.*

Captain Considine ordered the crew to abandon ship, but it was already too late. He found himself fighting back-to-back alongside one of the Peregrine's *few shield men, an athletic Italian called Florentine. His real name was Fiore, but the crew called him Florentine because that's how he fought: Florentine style, with a weapon in each hand, usually a matching pair of Spanish steel rapiers. The shield man shouldered his captain down the stairs, ordering a retreat to someplace more confined where they could bottleneck the pirates. He screamed for his crew to fall back to him, to retreat below. The number that responded was depressingly small.*

With Florentine holding rearguard behind two constantly flashing blades, the remnants of the crew made their way back to the captain's great cabin. The Italian sunk one blade up to the hilt right through the middle of the giant, scarred Moor, who howled in pain and rage, and brought both massive fists down on the swordsman's shoulders, driving him to his knees. The last thing they heard Florentine scream was, "Close the door! NOW!"

As much as it pained him, Considine slammed the cabin's thick oak door shut, locked it and slid the deadbolt into place. Muffled thumps and curses sounded from the hall outside, including one pistol shot to the door's lockplate, but the upper deadbolt still held. Hatchets and swords sunk repeatedly into the door until the pirates became frustrated enough to move on. They knew the last of the Peregrine's *crew weren't going anywhere. They were trapped.*

Considine had his people shore up the door with furniture, then had them take up points of cover as they rearmed themselves. Five. That was all the crew he had left, including himself. They waited for the inevitable attack as the sounds of battle died away. And they waited some more.

That's when an explosion rocked the ship.

Built for exploration, the Peregrine *was only a six-gun ship: three small cannons per side to scare off the occasional small-time sea bully. They were never equipped to handle a full pirate invasion. Like the rum, the barrels of powder on board were, by most standards, in short supply. From the sound of the explosion, the Rum Runners had gathered those few barrels together in the hold and lit them with a fuse. Considine knew at once that the ship was doomed. He could feel the vibrations of seawater rushing in through the hole that had just been blasted in the keel, and knew they hadn't much time to escape.*

"They're away, sir. Bastards are sailing off," Sean Morgan called as he peered out the cabin's windows.

Not wasting a moment, Considine snapped orders. "Tor, grab that locker—there's food and drink in it. Sean: weapons, as many as you can find. Deirdre, go with Nelson and save as many of our finds and records as possible. I'll prep the rowboat and look for survivors. Quickly!"

Minutes later, the last five warm bodies fled the dying Peregrine, *watching it roll over and sink. They spent a long moment in silence, solemnity and shock.*

———————⚓—

For the most part, the scene that Captain Considine and his crewmates discovered was exactly what they had expected; a broad clearing in the jungle with a massive bonfire in the center, around which more than two dozen pirates drank, sang, danced, played dice, drank, wrestled, joked, pissed, drank, and exchanged stories of their recent exploits—over a drink.

What they *weren't* expecting to see was the twenty-foot-tall, carved wooden totem pole that lorded silently, eerily over the proceedings. A tower of heads upon heads, carved in some exotic islander style, worn to a dull sheen by time and the elements. The uppermost head included a carved bottle jutting from its mouth.

"Well . . . that's different," Deirdre muttered under her breath.

The five explorers huddled in the cover of a dense cluster of vegetation as they surveyed the situation. Aside from the gargantuan totem pole, the most notable feature of the pirate camp was the enormous pyramid of barrels stacked at one edge of the clearing. Rum. A mountain of stolen rum. Three Rum Runners staggered over to the pile and refilled their mugs from one tapped barrel.

Deirdre stiffened in her crouch. "Wha—how the hell—sir, that man that just refilled his mug, the one with the long beard and the cheek scar—"

"I see. What about him?"

"He should be dead. I put a blade through his lung. He was gagging on his own blood when I moved on to the next fight. It was a mortal wound, sir, I know it was."

"I believe you."

All heads turned to Tor, lurking behind them, the firelight reflecting in his sky-blue eyes. He raised one thick-fingered hand to point towards the center of the pirate camp. "Look there. The dark man yet lives."

Sure enough, the explorers saw a familiar-looking Moor strolling out from around the far side of the bonfire. The man was shirtless, exposing a torso covered in scars and tattoos over a plane of rippling muscles.

"Not even bandaged. No open wound." Considine eyed the Moor closely, looking for any evidence of the grievous sword wound where Florentine had run him through.

"How is the man alive at all, let alone healed?"

"And there," said Sureshot Sean. "I recognize at least two or three more that I plugged. Look! They even have blood still on their clothes where I shot 'em! How . . ." He swallowed a lump in his throat.

Suddenly, Sean craned his head forward again, his eyes growing wide. "Captain! Far side of the clearing, in that bamboo cage—it's Florentine! He's alive!"

Considine squinted. "How about that. Good eye, lad. Hmmh. I'd heard the Rum Runners never took prisoners. We'll have to see about springing him, then. I won't leave him behind a second time."

"Nor will I, sir," Deidre said.

"Look. What the hell are they doing now?" Sureshot drew their attention back to the totem pole, where one barelegged pirate scrabbled up the rear of the sculpture until he sat atop the highest head. The Rum Runners paused in their revelry, and every man among them rose to their feet, faced the totem and raised their drinks in silent salute. The pirate atop the idol raised two wineskins, removed the stoppers, and began pouring their contents down over the top totem head's oversized bottle. "It's not spilling over," the young topsman said. "The bottle must have some kind of opening on the top, hollow inside. Why would—"

"*That's it. That's their secret.*"

It was the first time Nelson Terwilliger had spoken since they left the rowboat, and all eyes trained on him.

"Don't you see? The Rum Runners, all the legends, all the inhuman things they're capable of. The things we saw when they attacked us, and now we're seeing men who should be dead, walking around right as rain. This is how they do it! This is the source of their power! The rum, the idol . . ."

Captain Considine cocked an eyebrow at the scholar. "Nelson, are you saying what I think you're saying?"

Sean shot a sidelong glance back at the totem. "You're saying that thing is some sort of—"

"*Rum for the rum god!*"

The lone climber cried out first, and a deafening chorus crashed back like a tidal wave from every pirate in the clearing: "*RUM FOR THE RUM GOD!*"

A subtle but noticeable thrum rippled outward from the towering idol and washed across the landscape, including the explorers. They didn't *hear* the wave so much as *feel* it in their bones.

Nelson Terwilliger pointed meekly at the totem. "Yep. Rum God."

———⚓———

The explorers waited until the Rum Runners' revelry climbed back up to full volume before discussing their strategy further.

"So they, what, offer this stack of firewood a bottle of rum once every blue moon, dance around a fire, get piss drunk and they get these inhuman powers that make them unstoppable?"

"That would be my guess, Captain." Terwilliger shrugged. "I have countless chapters of notes on the various idols and deities of these islands. Almost every tribe has some sort of god or goddess that governs various aspects of their world; granting them good harvest, good weather, health, fortune, fertility, you name it. They appease the deity, play by whatever rules they have in place, and hope that the deity is pleased and plays nice. I suppose it's not out of the question that there's a Rum God."

"Well, this doesn't change the plan," Considine said. "They're still bloody murderers and thieves, and they have to be stopped, Rum God or no Rum—Wait. That's it. The rum. Nelson, if you're right, then their pact with this ugly stack of cordwood is dependent on one thing: rum. So we take their rum away. Maybe dead sober, they're just men. No more powers, no more healing—no more bloody legend on their side."

"Even so, sir," Sean said, "we're still outnumbered about twenty-five or thirty to our five."

Nelson shook his head nervously. "To our four, you mean. I'm not worth a cup of cold piddle in a fight. I can barely even fire a pistol."

"Six, then," Considine said with a wry smirk. "If we spring Florentine, he's worth two."

Deirdre leaned in, beginning to mirror her captain's confidence. "All right then, how do we pull this off?"

———————⚓———————

Lime Green Pete swayed across the sand and trampled jungle grass as if he was still on a moving ship. He had to piss. He also had to refill. He was on his way to do both, trying to be mindful not to do the wrong one into his empty mug. (It wouldn't have been the first time.) Setting aside his mug on a rum barrel while he relieved himself, the pirate hummed a sea shanty with a drunken, gap-toothed smile plastered across his face. He was still smiling and pissing when his head jerked sideways sharply and he fell to the ground, dead.

Several Rum Runners heard the gunshot and stood, their guard up as they looked around. One spotted Lime Green Pete lying flat on his back in front of the rum. That by itself would not normally have been cause for alarm, but for the smoking hole in Pete's temple and the spray of crimson dripping down several barrels. Seven pirates closed on Pete's body, still looking around for the source of the shot. Somewhere in the jungle, they heard a second shot crackle through the night. The musket ball missed the lot of them, punching a hole in one of the barrels.

Now the rum was pissing on Pete.

"There!" one man shouted, pointing towards where he had seen a muzzle flash. "Rum Runners! To arms!"

The third shot struck the powder horn strapped on the waist of a rum-soaked Lime Green Pete.

With a roar that rivaled any thunderclap the island had ever heard, the entire pyramid of pirated rum erupted in a rippling, rapid succession of explosions that obliterated every man within ten yards. The shockwave knocked the remaining pirates off their feet, leaving many on the dazed edge of consciousness. As the shock wore off, they rose in horror: *the rum!* As one voice, a terrible shriek of unbridled rage ripped through the island. The pirates charged into the jungle in the general direction they had seen their fallen comrades pointing before the explosion. Someone would pay dearly.

— ⚓ ——

Sureshot dove for cover behind a rock outcropping where his crewmates had moved to before the shooting. "That did it," he said, his voice cracking as he panted, laying down the three empty muskets. "They're mad as hell and headed that way," he signaled with a hand back in the direction he'd run from. "I think I took out eight of 'em, all told."

"Good work, Morgan." Considine clapped the topsman on the back heartily. "Outstanding. Did you see any of them stay behind to guard the camp?"

Sean nodded, gulping down air and wiping sweat from his brow. "Yeah, maybe a half dozen or so still down on their rears from the explosion. If we wanna take 'em, I say we move now while they're still out of it."

"Right. You heard the lad—let's go get our Italian back."

— ⚓ ——

"Quiet! You hear somethin'?"

Dirty Dan turned to question his companions, only to find them lying on their backs, run through with blades. He recognized the captain from the ship they'd ransacked earlier that night, the one who'd locked himself in his cabin with the last few crew members. The captain glared at him now, and whipped his arm forward. Before Dirty Dan could cry out an alarm to the rest of the Runners, he felt the quick, cold pinch of a knife in the heart.

Florentine waited patiently in his bamboo cage as Deirdre sawed through the thick ropes that tied it shut. "Thank God you survived," he said. "I didn't know if you'd gotten out in time or not. They knocked me out and I woke up here."

Once the ropes were cut, he pushed open the door and stumbled to a pile of weapons that had been left nearby, sorting through them until he found the belt with his twin Spanish rapiers still sheathed. Buckling them on, he turned to face his crewmates. "I heard them talking. They didn't bother watching their tongues around me because they told me I was 'to be converted to one of them soon enough.' They meant to put some kind of spell on me or something. It's *that* thing's doing," the Italian said, jabbing a finger accusingly up at the looming totem pole. "It's some kind of—"

Considine nodded. "Rum God. We figured that part out."

"Exactly. But with half of their rum gone, maybe we can—"

"Wait. Half? Where's the other—oh, sweet Christ on a clipper," Considine said. "Their ship. I should've thought of that." The captain kicked a sandy boot into the ribs of one of the corpses at his feet. "Dammit! We have to sink her. We can't let these bastards off the island to start their pirating again, and that ship's too big for the six of us to sail anyway."

"Six? Who are we missing?" Florentine did a quick head count to check his math.

The group took stock, and the answer was obvious. "Tor," said the captain, "where's Tor?"

Nelson poked his head back into the jungle, searching for the hulking Northman.

"The last I knew, he was right behind me when we left those rocks to come here. I never heard him slip away."

The captain swore again. "He was wounded. I knew I should've told him to stay back at the rower and rest, but his pride wouldn't have let him. He's probably passed out in the damned jungle somewhere."

———————⚓———————

Tor broke the surface of the water just long enough to gulp down a fresh mouthful of air, then disappeared again. He was only ten yards from the *Tipsy Crimson* now, swimming underwater to avoid detection by the two drunken guards he'd spotted on her deck. Each time he broke the water to breathe, he'd felt the lead musket ball sitting heavy in one of his lungs. His breaths were getting shorter as more blood leaked into places where it shouldn't have been. He was dying, and he knew it. He was the son of the White Bear, and he would not die skulking about in the jungle like some thief. He would find a better way to die.

———————⚓———————

"If we're going to have any hope of taking that ship with all the rest of the Rum Runners on or around it," Florentine said, "there's one thing we have to do: turn their secret against them."

Deirdre leaned over him as he crouched by the nearest corpse. "What are you doing?"

The swordsman turned and handed her the flagon from the dead pirate's belt. "We have to get drunk. Now."

She cocked an eyebrow at her shipmate. "Are you serious?"

"Absolutely. Look, we've all seen what they can do in a fight, right? When they were giving me their recruitment speech, they told me that the rum brought out their strengths, gave them abilities—like the ability to heal even the most serious wounds. And I'm betting that explosion has them sobered up some, not to mention all the running they're doing right now. If we can get three sheets to the wind and make it to that ship before they think to, we can hold them off, I'm sure of it." He went about liberating the remaining wineskins and bottles from the fallen Rum Runners, handing them out to his mates.

"As mad as that sounds," Considine said, eyeing his own filthy bottle by the firelight, "it might actually work. This has been a night full of strange things. But are you sure the rum trick will work on us? How do we know we won't just get normal drunk and sloppy and skewered like dinner meat?"

"I assume you were all watching when they paid tribute to that heathen idol?"
They nodded.

"And you felt that . . . that wave of power, coming from the pole?"
More nodding.

"From what they told me, that wave is what gives the rum power, gives *them* power. They give tribute at least once a month or so, and as long as that—" Florentine pointed at the giant carved bottle at the top of the totem, "—has someone pouring drink into it, keeping it from being empty, the spell continues, regardless of range. They could sail to Boston and back, and as long as there's one lackey here to keep filling the totem's bottle, the magic continues. But this time, we were all here to feel that wave—"

"And now we're all under that same spell," Considine said. "Wait—the rum has healing properties for all of us, then? That means if we can find Tor, we can get him fixed up. Let's start—"

"Captain!" Deirdre crashed into Considine as a loud pop sounded from nearby. A geyser of blood erupted from her left arm and she dropped to the sand with a sharp cry.

Sureshot drew a pistol and trained it on the source: one lone pirate who had woken on the far side of the bonfire. The Rum Runner reached for a nearby pistol from one of his fallen mates when Sean dropped him with a shot between the eyes.

The crew rushed to Deirdre's side to check the wound. It was a bad shot, right in the shoulder joint. Almost without thinking, the captain uncorked his bottle and held it over her. "I suppose we'll find out if you're right," he said to Florentine, then tipped the bottle and dribbled rum into the gushing wound.

Deirdre gritted her teeth and bore the pain as the alcohol hit her blood. The wound began to sizzle immediately, smoldering like a hot iron. Within seconds, the lead ball worked its way to the surface and spat itself out onto the ground. The skin melted together like wax, and all that was left behind was a round, light pink scar. She opened her mouth and poked a tentative finger at the scar. "Nothing. No pain. It's healed."

"Great, it works," Considine said. "But those shots are going to bring the Runners down on us in a hurry. Let's get pissed."

In unison, the crew unstopped their bottles, skins, and flasks, and they drank.

⚓

"We found this one on board, sir. He killed the two men on watch and was sneaking around down below."

Tor was driven to his knees in front of the captain of the Rum Runners, his face bloody, his right arm hanging awkwardly from a vicious sword blow. Beside the captain, the giant tattooed Moor cracked his knuckles. It sounded like the breaking of tree branches.

"Now I wonder," the captain said, scratching at his chin, "if this is our shooter, or if he has other friends on the island who survived that sinking ship—"

A pistol shot popped from somewhere not far inland. A second shot followed.

"Well I suppose that answers that question. Men, back to the camp! Hamza, I want you to stay behind and guard the ship's stores. And all you men, there. I want the dozen of you to stay as well. This is the last of our rum for the time being, so protect it with your lives! We'll sail out with the next tide and replenish what was taken from us tonight!"

The captain spun on a booted heel to leave when the Moor's deep baritone stopped him. "Captain, wot should we do with the prisoner?"

Without turning back to look, the Rum Runners' leader smirked. "Very bad things."

⚓

Hamza watched as his captain and the others disappeared into the jungle to hunt down the remaining intruders, then turned his attention back to his captive plaything, who was now clapped in irons and knocked on his side, coughing blood onto the deck. Crouching down, the Moor grabbed a handful of red-gold hair, matted and wet, and yanked it out of the man's face. With his other hand, he grabbed the prisoner's thick-braided beard and pulled down, watching the Northman's pained expression with morbid satisfaction.

A wet sound began to bubble its way up from the prisoner's throat. Hamza began to flash a pearl-white smile against his dark skin, as he did every time he made a grown man cry or beg for his life. Then he realized it was laughter.

"Wot so funny, fool? Do you not smell your death?" He yanked harder on the Northman's scalp.

Tor's mouth split into a bloody-toothed grin as he gazed up at his ancestors' stars. "I do. And I smell yours, too. Smells like . . . gunpowder."

Down in the *Tipsy Crimson's* hold, the last of a long fuse burnt away, igniting the first of 20 large powder kegs.

For the second time that night, a massive explosion rocked the island, and the sky lit up as if lightning had struck. The echoes rolled across the sky for miles around.

"What was *that*?" Nelson Terwilliger slurred, stumbling over his own shoes and falling backwards.

"That . . ." Captain Considine said, his voice solemn, "was Tor, I think."

The anguished chorus of cries that followed in the wake of the explosion told the remaining five explorers that the guess was accurate. Their cook had just single-handedly destroyed the legendary *Tipsy Crimson*.

The captain removed his tricorner hat, paying respects to yet another fallen friend. The others followed suit with a moment of silence. Sean raised his bottle high. "For that big Viking, and for every other soul we've lost tonight. It won't be for nothing."

"Here, here." The remaining five explorers hoisted their rum and toasted in memoriam. The first sound following the toast was a soft, delicate song on the air. Heads turned to Deirdre as she began to sing one of the *Peregrine's* most requested songs; an old folk song from the Emerald Isle, sung in Gaelic, so none of the crew ever really knew what it meant. It was a song they would ask for on cold, empty nights at sea when they tried not to think about the loved ones they'd left behind to go exploring, or about how far away they were from any land. The song's sound was at once comforting and inspiring on those nights, and this night it felt more so than ever.

Considine turned to his crew and saluted them, feeling the giddy effects of too much rum coursing through his bloodstream. It had been a long, long time since he'd indulged in so much drink. He felt . . . unstoppable. Deirdre's song helped bolster that feeling, and the captain started seeing it in the others as well. Before long, the sounds of approaching pirates could be heard crashing through the jungle, yet his people were smiling eagerly as they armed themselves from the Rum Runners' surplus weapon stores. All but Nelson. He just had the hiccups.

"So . . . what effects should we be looking for, Florentine? I mean, what—" The scholar hiccuped violently and rocked back on his heels. "What abilities is this rum-spell supposed to give us?"

Florentine shrugged. "From what I could tell, it's different for each person. It seems to bring out whatever strengths you already have. If you're a good jumper, you can suddenly jump incredible distances. If you're a good shot," he looked to Sean, "you become *really* good. They have one man like that—"

"I remember," Sureshot said, his eyes flashing in the firelight. "If he still lives—he's mine."

"But what if you don't have any strengths like that? I still don't feel like I'm going to be of any use in a brawl," came Nelson's muffled voice through his hand as he tried to stifle more hiccups. "I just feel . . . drunk."

"Then get yourself hidden, Terwilliger." Considine gestured to the thick tropical foliage beyond the clearing. "See if you can't think of a way to be useful."

Nelson didn't argue the point. He disappeared from sight the exact moment the remaining Rum Runners broke into the opposite side of the clearing. The two groups stared each other down. The four members of the *Peregrine* stood backlit by the bonfire as the grayish-pink hues of dawn began a slow bleed into the sky.

Captain Considine held his cutlass in one hand, a metal flask in his off-hand, and a stolen dirk jammed through his belt. His hat and coat were discarded, his shirt torn and filthy, his eyes wide and smiling. Marco "Florentine" Fiore had gone completely bare-chested at some point during the drinking phase, showing off his athletic musculature and the Andalusian stallion tattooed across his chest. He tipped back the last of his flagon of rum and tossed it aside, drawing his twin rapiers with a smile that was fifty percent genuine confidence, fifty percent liquid immortality. Deirdre had chosen a pair of daggers and stood with an uncharacteristic tilt to her hips, her hair torn loose of its usual neat ponytail and waving wildly behind her in the growing wind. Sean Morgan was strapped from head to heels with an ungodly number of pistols, a wineskin hanging from a cord around his neck, a long musket in his hands. For some reason, he couldn't seem to suppress a quiet, giddy laugh at what should have been a very tense situation.

Over a dozen remaining Rum Runners stood in a line across, huffing and sweating from their rampage across the island, and seething with rage at the unexpected losses they had suffered. The Rum Runners' sharpshooter was there, as was the fire-breather, and their captain.

In that moment, it would have been hard for a neutral onlooker to tell who the real pirates were.

"Mr. Flint," the Rum Runners' leader said, "take out their pistoleer. Dragon, fetch the woman. It's been too long since my island has had female company that attractive. Don't damage her too much if you can help it. Put her in the cage. The rest of you should be able to handle the Italian and the captain."

Someone screamed, and the basecamp erupted into chaos. Steel clanged against steel in a maelstrom of blades.

Deirdre dropped one pirate with a dagger to the chest. She whipped the second towards the bald fire breather, who angled the shaft of his torch, catching the blade in the wood. As he closed on her, he flashed a smile that Deirdre noted was full of sharpened teeth. The rum told her to run. She listened.

Sureshot locked eyes on his target, who was drawing a bead on him as well. Two gunshots popped, and somewhere in the air between the two marksmen, the air sparked.

Two musket balls dropped to the sand in one fused lump of lead. Both men blinked.

"Huh," Sean mumbled under his breath. "There's something you don't see every day."

They could have just as easily drawn more of their numerous pistols and began blasting away at the oppositions' other fighters, but the pistoleers recognized this as a matter of pride—a private contest between deadeyes. Sean sidestepped towards the tree line, dropping his musket in favor of drawing one pistol, and taking another swig of rum from the skin around his neck. 'Mr. Flint' mirrored his movements, and both men took off into the jungle, trying to outmaneuver each other.

Florentine spun and ducked, rolled and slashed, parried and thrusted. He was a blur of tanned skin and flashing steel against five men at once. Considine held his own against three more, using the metal flask to parry blows as he struck out with his cutlass. It was almost too easy, like they were playing a 'pirate theatre' of rehearsed choreography rather than a real fight. There should have been at least *some* fear in him, but there was none. He blamed—no, *credited*—the magic of the rum.

One by one, the Rum Runners fell under the captain and Florentine's blades. The Rum Runner's own captain sat back on a fallen palm tree and uncorked his own private stock, and he drank. And drank.

They found each other in a tightly packed grove of palm trees, and the shooting started.

Sean was trying to get a good line of sight on his adversary when he heard Mr. Flint's first shot ring out. Too late, he recognized the odd sound of a bullet ricocheting off of palm trees. The shot ripped through his left thigh, and he let out a yelp. A second shot sounded before he could regain his composure, and another ricocheting bullet found its mark. Something splattered across Sean's chest. Reaching to the sticky wetness he felt spreading across his shirt, his fingers came away with a mixture of blood and rum. Looking down at his chest, he saw the shot had gone right through the wineskin that hung around his neck. Moving the skin, he tore open his shredded, bloodstained shirt. There was no wound, only a wisp of dissipating smoke and a fresh, round patch of pale pink scar tissue. The rum saved his life—but now the rum was gone.

"Sonofabitch. Right—two can play the ricochet game." Sean reacquired his target, did some drunken math in his head, picked a palm tree and squeezed off a round. The shot deflected once, twice—and he heard a startled curse from behind cover. The two pistoleers traded shots in the labyrinth of trees, each scoring minor hits, but each managing to dodge death. Sean bled freely from four wounds in his legs and arms as he counted his remaining shots. He had three pistols left, and no extra powder or shot. He had to make them count.

Mr. Flint decided it was time to end the contest. He drew a long pistol with an engraved grip and a bluish tint to its steel. This was his favorite gun, and it never missed. Another shot rang out, ripping through the treetops. Flint looked up to see coconuts dropping towards him. They fell slowly, easy enough to dodge. Another shot cracked, and the last coconut exploded in a shower of milk and shrapnel. Flint dropped his pistol as splinters from the coconut's shell lanced into his eyes. He clawed at the pain and momentarily forgot about cover, stumbling one step sideways.

That was all Sureshot needed. He aimed with his last pistol, and Mr. Flint's head went the way of the coconut.

Deirdre remembered passing a giant outcropping of rock when they were skulking through the dark to free Florentine, and she raced there now with a fire-breathing drunkard hot on her heels. Recalling what Florentine has said about the magic of the rum playing to one's strengths, she decided her best chance of survival was not in a swordfight, but climbing up the rocks. Maybe she could lure the enemy into falling from a precarious height. Without pausing to look for solid handholds, Deirdre leapt onto the front face of the rocks and scrabbled upwards with alacrity that surprised even her. She found that her fingers and toes picked their own path, and up she went with more agility than a monkey.

Dragon clamped his sharpened teeth down around the shaft of his torch and climbed up after his quarry, hauling himself upwards with muffled growls. The woman was fast—too fast. He recognized the power of the rum coursing through her as she pulled out of sight. After another dozen yards, Dragon came to a ledge at the mouth of a cave where he unstoppered his flagon, about to refuel his own abilities when his sharp ears caught a sound from within the cave. He took a drink, held up his torch, and spat a gout of flame ten feet into the black tunnel. By the firelight, he saw a woman's wide-eyed face. He heard her scrabbling in the dark, trying to retreat as Dragon made his slow approach.

When he stopped hearing movement, Dragon took another swig and spat another flame. The cavern narrowed, and turned to the right, continuing out of sight. Then he heard singing. Poking his head around the bend, he saw his prey's silhouette against the dawn sky. The tunnel was open-ended, and came out at another cliff! Dragon snarled and began to slither around the tunnel's bend as the song grew louder. And louder.

Deirdre let loose her song as the magic begged to be set free. Her voice had never felt so strong, so clear. She all but screamed the chorus into the narrow cavern, and she watched as Dragon dropped his torch to clamp both hands over his assaulted ears, gnashing his pointed teeth in pain. Then came the rumble. It began as a light rain of dust and pebbles within the cavern. Dragon's eyes went wide in the torchlight and he let fly with an inhuman roar as the tunnel caved in on him.

The rum-magic was clearly the deciding factor.

After two explosions and several hundred yards' worth of running through the island, the Rum Runners had begun to sober up. The more they fought, the more the adrenaline wore off what little alcohol they had left in their systems. Florentine and his captain were only just now feeling their buzz begin to wear off, and the pirates were growing desperate. More than once, one made a grab at the explorers' stolen rum rather than paying enough attention to their swords, and it proved their undoing.

By the time the last of the lackeys was finished off, the two explorers had gotten so caught up in the fight that they had forgotten about the last remaining pirate.

"You've ruined everything," the Rum Runners' captain slurred, dropping an empty bottle to the ground as he drew his cutlass and main gauche. "Why couldn't you just die like everyone else?" The man made his drunken approach in a wobbling path across the clearing. He seemed barely capable of standing, let alone fighting. The smell of the rum coming off of him reached the men ten feet away.

No, not just rum, Considine realized. *Power.*

The drunken pirate king lunged, instantly sending both explorers on the defensive. As good as Florentine was, he couldn't find an opening in the pirate's erratic, unpredictable technique. He took a vicious slash to his left forearm, one sword dropping out of a numb hand. Considine felt the hot stab of a main gauche through his side, and his metal flask was sent spinning away by a follow-up strike. For as much as he and his shield man had outclassed the previous group of lackeys, they were now outclassed themselves by the leader of the ensorcelled pirates. Florentine tried to duck a sudden kick, but was too slow. Stars blasted across his vision as he fell to the ground. The sounds of ringing steel-on-steel kept him from passing out entirely, and he regained vision just in time to see his captain disarmed—and then pinned to the base of the totem pole by the pirate's cutlass. The victor left the sword in place and turned back to the Italian with only a main gauche, confident that it would be enough.

"No!" Florentine staggered to his feet as Considine coughed blood in a dribbling line down his chest, his eyes quickly growing dull.

The two remaining swordsmen danced and struck out with their blades until the more inebriated of the two made a spinning, lunging maneuver that never would have worked in a normal fight. Florentine found himself divested of his second rapier, scrabbling backwards on all fours until he stumbled over the bodies of fallen pirates. The last Rum Runner loomed over him, backlit by the dying bonfire. He raised his arm for the killing blow.

"*VOLO MARUMA SHI-SHE CON SE BIEMONO!*"

The voice, deep and reverberating, echoed across the clearing. The pirate captain turned his head slowly to the totem pole where Considine stood dying. The voice boomed again, originating from the top of the pole.

"*YOU HAVE VIOLATED MY IDOL. I DEMAND TRIBUTE TO MAKE AMENDS. NOW.*"

Wide-eyed and trembling, the pirate fell to his knees. "Wha-wh-what would you have me do, my God? I'll do anything! I meant you no disrespe—"

"*ENOUGH!*" the booming voice said. "*SWIM TO THE NEXT ISLAND TO THE EAST, AND RETURN WITH THE SACRED FRUIT THAT GROWS THERE. DO THIS, OR NEVER AGAIN RECEIVE MY BLESSINGS.*"

"The next island to the—but no man can swim that far, my Lord. What you ask—" The pirate captain frowned. "Wait a minute . . ."

Circling around to the back of the totem pole, he looked up to see a skinny man clinging to the back of the topmost carving, a giant palm frond curled into a funnel through which he boomed, "*YOU DARE REFUSE ME? I AM YOUR*—oh. Uh oh."

Nelson looked down and saw that his illusion was ruined. And he was trapped.

Below, the pirate captain folded his arms. "I can wait."

A shot rang out from the far side of the clearing. The captain of the Rum Runners flinched as he heard the bullet strike wood, but he felt no pain. Two figures walked out of the jungle as the shooter, still bleeding from multiple wounds, lowered a blue-tinged pistol with an engraved handle. Florentine leapt to his feet and rejoined his companions, still unarmed.

"Four to one, then," the pirate said. "Although I probably shouldn't bother counting your cowardly little seagull perching atop my totem there. No matter." He strode out from behind the pole to finish off the injured trio, and stopped in his tracks. He felt a curious sensation in the vicinity of his stomach. Hunger? No, that wasn't it. Looking down, he was surprised to see a good fourteen inches of his own cutlass poking through his shirt. Turning in a slow, dazed circle, he came face-to-face with the other captain, apparently alive and well.

Considine opened his ragged, bloodied shirt to reveal a fresh pink scar. From twenty feet above them, the totem's bottle dribbled a stream of rum, released by a fresh bullet hole in the bottom of the wood.

"Oh, that's just bloody brilliant," the pirate captain slurred. He coughed once, wobbled, snickered, and fell dead.

⚓

Morning was in its full glory across the island, but only two of the explorers were awake to see it.

Deirdre and Florentine had decided to spend the last of their drunken moments together in the privacy of the jungle, undoubtedly naked. Nelson had spent some time studying the totem pole and making mental notes to record in one of his journals later. For now, he had fallen asleep against the carved wood, not three feet from where his captain had been skewered and left for dead.

Considine and his topsman stood on the beachhead, looking out across the unbroken horizon of open sea as the sun danced across gentle waves. "That was pretty risky, using your last shot to break that bottle over me rather than taking out their last man. Could've gone badly for our side," the captain said.

Sean offered up a shrug and a roguish grin. "Blame the rum. It just didn't seem right, leavin' you stuck to that pole, dyin'. We would've all been lost without our captain." The young marksman adjusted his new clothing around him as the wind picked up. After the fight had ended, he'd shamelessly liberated the pirate captain's hat, coat and cutlass as trophies of their legendary victory. He stood on the beach wearing them now, with one foot planted on a barrel that had washed up on the beach from the wreckage of the *Tipsy Crimson*. It had somehow miraculously survived the explosion, still full of rum.

Considine took in the sight and laughed out loud. "Morgan, why do I get the sneaking suspicion that you're going to make a famous captain yourself some day?"

Rowing Near Hell
Jeffrey Lyman

Purgatory's swamps
are deeper than the River Lethe.
As Lethe takes your memory,
the swamps give back an imitation.
But sometimes Straylights lead you home,
and sing of what you are.

"Captain, the angel is coming," Lieutenant Terrion said.

Captain Richard Attain leaned against the railing of the wooden lookout platform they called the maintop, built high on the side of Purgatory's single mountain. He was a stout man, fat, others would have said, and gray—gray hair, gray beard, gray eyes. He had been fifty when he first died, and hadn't aged a day since arriving on Purgatory's shores. Today was the thirtieth anniversary of that landing. He had been killed five times since, during escape attempts.

"All right, Lieutenant," he said and turned away from the sunrise.

"Do you think he knows?" Lt. Terrion stood at the maintop's entry, looking down. Richard joined him.

"Of course he knows, or he wouldn't be coming all the way up here."

Sekeziel was indeed climbing the stairs. It had taken the carpenters nine years to finish those stairs, built from ship's beams as the trapped British and French ships sank one by one in the harbor below. The early morning sun reflected softly off the angel's white robes and proud left wing, a remnant of different days. The broken flag of his right wing jutted back from his bleeding and shattered shoulder, and hung like a limp banner. The great flight feathers were filthy and worn to quills from being dragged across the ground.

As Sekeziel strode up the final flight to the high redoubt, Richard stood and waited, irritated. The angel was inconsistent in his visits, but frequent enough to make the timing of escape attempts difficult.

"My Lord Sekeziel, what brings you up to our perch?"

"Captain Attain, I looked for you down in the town." Sekeziel walked across the floorbeams to the front-railing. His feathers rasped across the wood as he trailed his broken wing, threatening to disturb the black and white marker-stones on the calendar carved in the floor. Sekeziel pressed his eye to the brass spyglass mounted at the railing.

"I wanted to see the sun rise," Richard said. "Captain Dunwick holds his position well and does not need my help."

Sekeziel swung the spyglass down towards the harbor. Captain Dunwick's frigate, the *Dawn Rose*, had settled to the shallow bottom in the mouth of the harbor twelve years ago. Her port canons were pointed out at the ocean's horizon and her starboard cannons were under the blue water. The rest of the harbor was a forest of spars and masts, marking where each ship had settled over the years.

"You are planning an escape," Sekeziel said, sweeping the spyglass from left to right.

"Why would you think such a thing?"

"None of your little fishing boats are in the harbor this morning. You wouldn't be thinking of using them to attempt the swamps, would you?"

Richard's eyes were drawn to the swamps, partially visible over the eastern shoulder of the mountain. "That would be the height of foolishness, My Lord. One slip and we could fall into Hell."

Purgatory was a small tongue of land that extended out into the ocean from Hell-proper. It consisted of a single mountain overlooking a harbor, a lush tropical forest, and abundant fresh water, fruit, and wildlife. The shoals kept the two fleets trapped, though the open ocean seemed agonizingly close. A great cypress swamp crossed the neck of Purgatory, separating it from Hell. The dark clouds and burning fires were visible just beyond it. When the wind blew right, it carried the perfume of rot.

There was an obvious gap in the shoals right off the coast where Hell and Purgatory met, but the only way to get there was through the swamps. A few men had tried over the years. None had made it, or returned. Richard reasoned that if he took enough men and guns, they should be able to fight their way through.

Sekeziel turned and looked into Richard's eyes. Richard stared back and wondered why the angel always smelled faintly of bread mold.

"I walked to the edge of the swamp, Captain Attain, and saw your dinghies tied there. Isn't that, as you say, the height of foolishness?"

Richard nodded. "Yes, My Lord. It is."

"Then why attempt it?"

"You told me once there is a way out, if I can find it."

"And you thought that going down might be better than going up?"

"It is a possibility. Are you going to kill me now? If not, I'd like to go get some breakfast."

"Dying is painful, Captain, but I see you no longer fear it. You know that when you are killed you will be reborn, spat up by the mountain. But the swamps are not Purgatory, and my authority does not extend there. Should you die, who knows where you would end up?"

Lieutenant Terrion's face paled. Richard frowned. It was one thing to challenge the angel in Purgatory. Hell was another matter.

"So you aren't going to kill me?" he said.

"You are too fearless, so I will teach you a lesson. Go. Enter the swamps."

Richard chewed on his cheek. Sekeziel hated him, so it was obviously a trap. But maybe the angel was trying to intimidate him into backing down in front of one of his officers. "Lieutenant, gather the men."

"Yes, Captain." Terrion turned to leave.

"No, Lieutenant," Sekeziel said. "I didn't say your crew could go."

"I'm going alone?" Richard said. "I wouldn't last ten minutes in there."

"You don't know that, Captain Attain. It might be pleasant."

"I can see Hell from here, My Lord. I doubt the swamps are pleasant."

"I believe you have several men loading the dinghies? You may take them. And Lieutenant Terrion here. I would hurry, though. The sun won't remain in the sky forever. Purgatory has stars to light your night. Hell has her flames. I wonder what burns in the swamps?"

"You seem certain of our failure, Lord Sekeziel. Would you care to make a wager on it? Have a ship waiting for us outside of the shoals, and we'll meet it before sunset."

Sekeziel smiled, the first time Richard had seen him smile in thirty years. "All right. If you succeed, there will be a ship waiting for you, waiting to take you to Heaven, or home, or wherever you would like to go. If you fail, Captain, God have mercy." He turned back to the spyglass and swung it out to sea. A fresh drop of blood welled up from his shoulder and dropped onto the hem of his white robe.

"Let's go, Lieutenant," Richard said. They hurried down the long stairs that switched back and forth to the ground.

"Perhaps we should await another opportunity, Captain," Terrion said from behind.

"We are going, Lieutenant. He's just trying to scare us." Richard didn't expect a better opportunity than this one. A ship outside the shoals. Being trapped on land had been Richard's Hell for thirty years. He needed open ocean.

The path to the swamps led through tropical forest and terminated in brackish water and marsh-reeds. Forty dinghies, two-man rowboats, were tied there. All had been salvaged from sinking ships. Richard's brother, Master Stephen Attain, and a seaman, Alliester Balch, were dividing stores of munitions into forty caches.

"Captain?" They stood. "What's happened?"

"Where are the others?"

"They're fetching tree-gum to fix a few of the boats. They should be . . . here they are now."

Captain Chevalier, a stunted, ugly man who had been a ruthless adversary when alive, and Seaman Graux came down the path behind Richard and Terrion, both clutching broad banana leaves filled with clumps of gum.

"We're leaving," Richard said.

"Now, sir? We're not ready." Seaman Balch clutched his dirty shirtfront.

"Sekeziel found out about this and has made us a wager," Richard said. "He will permit the six of us to make the attempt. If we succeed, he will provide us with a ship. Are you willing, Captain?"

Captain Chevalier looked at the dinghies and crossed his arms over his chest. "A captain needs a ship. I have been the captain of a *petite bateau* long enough. *Oui*, I will come."

"Load up three dinghies with extra munitions and supplies," Richard said, "but don't overload. We don't know what's in there, and we may need to stay quick."

Stephen took Richard aside as the others began dividing up supplies. Richard kept sharp watch on Balch, who was eyeing the forest and obviously thinking of running for it. The man was a coward and lazy, and Richard had assigned him to boat-preparation duty as punishment. He would have preferred almost any other man, even the French, but he had what he had.

"Captain, the angel must be planning something," Stephen said. "Why else let us go? He's either trying to teach us a lesson, or he's bored and wants some amusement."

"I know, Stephen, but victory is achieved by engaging the enemy."

"I think we should wait." Stephen stood his ground until Richard raised an eyebrow. Finally Stephen saluted and returned to the boats.

Half an hour later, Richard and Lt. Terrion, side-by-side on the center bench of a dinghy, rowed out into the sluggish channel. Stephen and Seaman Balch came second, Captain Chevalier and Seaman Graux brought up the rear. They left shore in bright sunshine, but within a few oarstrokes they were under the canopy of black cypress trees. A parasitic gloom ate away the morning's light. Cypress boles, viscous mud and grassy hummocks spread out around them. A raucous flock of crows flew from tree to tree, keeping pace with them.

This is a drowned place, Richard thought. *All this water, and the fires of Hell so close.*

The first two hours passed without incident, and Richard's spirits were high. He was dreaming of the ship beyond the shoals. Then the second boat's keel hung up on a submerged tree. Balch swung his leg over the side to push off, lowering his foot into the black water.

"Use your oar, Seaman," Richard said, just as a hand reached up from the water and grabbed Balch's ankle.

Balch shrieked and tumbled backwards, rocking the dinghy so violently Stephen had to fight to keep from capsizing. Water sprayed as Stephen's oar came up.

Richard expected a demon to emerge from the water, some sort of sentinel whom Balch had disturbed. Instead, a perfect copy of Seaman Balch stood up. The thing grasped the gunwale of the dinghy and tried to clamber in.

The third boat had coasted in close and Graux jabbed the thing hard with his oar. It was unaffected. Richard drew his flintlock pistol and put a ball through its head. Echoes of the shot rolled through the cypress boles and across the water.

"Would you look at that," Captain Chevalier said, leaning over to look at the body bobbing at the surface.

"It looks like me," Balch said, horrified. He reached out to touch it.

"Withdraw your hand, Seaman," Richard said.

"Something's got into it," Lt. Terrion said as the body began to jerk and twitch. He thrust the head of his oar under the water near the body and tried to flip it. A small fish broke the surface and fell back again. "Piranha."

"Use your oar next time, Mr. Balch, not your foot," Richard said.

"Captain, another one," Stephen said.

Richard turned. This time it was a copy of himself standing in the ankle-deep, sucking mud of the shallows. It revealed incredible mimetic detail, down to the buttons on its wool uniform coat and britches. As the three boats began moving again, it leered.

"Should I shoot it, sir?" Lt. Terrion said.

"Just keep moving, Lieutenant. Save your ammunition."

From then on they rowed past increasing numbers of doppelgangers, first alone and then in pairs. Most kept to the hollow gloom and shadows amidst the trunks and hanging moss, or swam under the water, surfacing briefly like beavers only to disappear again. Captain Chevalier tested them. He and Graux slowed their boat almost to a stop and in fairly short order a double of Graux lifted its head from the water and reached for their boat. They quickly began rowing again.

"I warned you about entering the swamp," came Sekeziel's voice from the bow, behind Richard's straining back. Lt. Terrion's shoulder twitched, but that was his only indication of surprise.

"My Lord Sekeziel," Richard said, turning.

The angel sat on the bow, his feet on the seat. He held his good wing up, but his broken wing trailed in the water under the boat.

"We're making good progress. Does that bother you? Is that why you're here?"

"You are only half way across the swamp, and they are growing increasingly bold. You should think about going back while it is still safe to do so."

"What are they? Why do they take our faces?"

"Because they have forgotten their own. It is their damnation."

"Are they dangerous?"

Sekeziel looked at him for a moment and then vanished. Richard shook his head, lifting the oar and sweeping it forward. The doppelgangers were no match for an iron ball from a pistol. He had proved that.

"I see a light," Balch called a short time later. "Is that daylight? Have we reached the salt marshes?"

Everyone turned to look. Richard squinted. There was a brightening in the gloom. "It can't be. We haven't gone far enough."

"There's something there, Captain," Lt. Terrion said.

"I'll need to get higher to see what it is. Maybe climb a tree. There. That one." The tree he had spotted was a partially-fallen cypress rising from the murky water at a low angle.

"Is it wise to stop, sir?"

Richard looked around, but didn't see any doppelgangers. "Keep your pistols ready."

The tree had fallen against a neighbor, but it still rose about twenty feet into the air. It was thick with hanging gray moss, decorated enough to make it a treacherous perch. Richard threw the bowline around the trunk, which was almost as thick as his own ample waist, and secured the boat. The other two dinghies took up station to either side. The crows settled all around and cawed shrilly, tilting their shiny black heads to peer down.

"There's something under the water," Terrion said.

"I'll hurry," Richard said.

"Yes, sir." Terrion drew a ramrod, horns of powder, a handful of balls, and wadding out of the munitions pack. The men in the other boats did the same.

Richard unbuttoned his stiff, wool uniform coat and tossed it on the bow seat. The boat lurched as a pale hand grabbed the stern. A second hand joined the first. A copy of

Richard's head lifted into view, water streaming from its hair and thick, gray beard.

Richard winced as Lt. Terrion pulled the hammer back on his pistol to full-cock and fired. The pan flashed, his hand jerked, and the doppelganger-Richard fell back in a plume of blood and disintegrating face. Crows took off with thudding wing-beats. Another pale hand reached up and Lt. Terrion's head lifted from the murk. Terrion fired Richard's pistol and then began reloading the first gun, not stopping to watch the death spasms of his twin. Doppelgangers assaulted the other two boats.

Too many, Richard thought. *They're coming too soon.*

He stepped onto the fallen tree, praying it wouldn't roll under his weight. The ancient bark was eel-slippery. He placed one hand on each side of the trunk to steady himself, and began to walk out and up. Slime coated his palms. He tried to dig his nails into the smooth, swirled bark. A brazen crow casually made way for him as he climbed.

His boat thumped against the tree as something bumped it from below. A doppelganger surfaced and Richard gagged at its stench. He hadn't gotten the full effect before, but being directly above it. . . . It was a viscous stink, and it left an oily residue on his tongue when he breathed. The water was teaming with them. He could see ripples and trails of bubbles on all sides of the three boats. He had to move faster. Chevalier fired, then Stephen and Balch fired in rapid succession.

Richard reached the broken end of the tree, where it was wedged against the next tree's trunk. He stood up, leaning against the bole. A dismal vista unfolded around him: trees and ill grass rising from slow-flowing rivers and watery mud-flats, long tails of moss hanging limp above brackish murk. He tried to see if the distant light was sunlight on water. No, it was fire. Definitely fire. They had rowed close to Hell.

Below him, the firing and reloading continued. There was a feeding frenzy in the water as the piranhas assaulted the corpses of the doppelgangers, though they seemed to be leaving the living ones alone.

Richard backed down quickly and jumped into the boat, sending it bouncing and the balls on the bench seat rolling everywhere.

"Help me," Terrion shouted. He pushed the ball he was holding down the barrel with his ramrod as a Terrion-doppelganger flopped into the stern.

"Row," Richard shouted to the men in the other boats, pulling his oar out of the oarlock. He swung the flat blade like an ax into the neck of the doppelganger. It spat blood in a tendril of red, but straightened and appeared to be otherwise indifferent to its wound.

"Get back," Terrion cried and Richard lifted the oar. The pistol roared.

It took Richard three tries to jam his oar back in the oarlock while Terrion yanked the bowline free of the tree. New hands groped at the sides of the boat, followed by the stench of meat too long in the sun. Richard and Terrion rowed hard, dragging slippery things into deeper water.

"Keep rowing," Richard said, handing his oar to Terrion. The Lieutenant had trouble with the two-man oars, but Richard only needed a moment. He slipped to the stern and kicked hard against the grasping hands with his boot heel. To his surprise they didn't let go, even after several hard kicks that smashed fingers and stained the wood with blood.

They hung on until he had crushed enough fingers that they couldn't grasp anymore.

"That's something," he said, panting. Four heads, Terrions and Richards, lifted up from the water to watch the boat move away. The flock of crows followed noisily.

"Let's not stop again, shall we, Captain?" Captain Chevalier called back.

"That was a lot of them," Richard said. "More than I expected. I had no idea." What had he been thinking? He had allowed his contempt for the angel to lull him into complacency. He needed to be vigilant. They were not in Purgatory any longer. He couldn't afford to be casual about mortal danger.

"They must be waiting below the surface," Balch said, peering over the edge. The water of the channel was calm save for ripples from the dipping oars.

"What was the light, Captain?" Terrion said. "Could you see anything?"

"Hell. We've drifted too close. At the next opportunity, we need to move to starboard."

"You still think we can get through?" Stephen asked quietly. Seaman Balch rowed beside him with his eyes tightly shut.

"There hasn't been anything we couldn't handle," Richard said. "So long as we don't stop, the doppelgangers don't bother us." He said it more sharply than he intended, but he needed to keep them moving. They were too close to give up. A ship awaited them. All Richard had to do was keep them from mutiny. He sank into the slow and steady rhythm of the oars. Mist chilled him and mosquitoes descended on his bare arms with zeal.

"We're coming up on a turn," Terrion said, looking over his shoulder. "We should reload the pistols."

"Do it where the channels come together."

And so they pulled hard for twenty long strokes and then folded in the oars, gliding silently. The other boats did as well. Terrion snatched up two iron balls from the munitions pack and tossed one to Richard. They both loaded, concentrating. Their momentum carried them out into the clear space between trees where the confluence of three channels had dug a deep swath through the mud. Something bumped against the keel of the boat. Then again.

"Oars," Richard said, swinging his oar back out as Terrion did the same. He struck the water, trying not to scull the surface. Stephen and Balch barely got their oars out before a copy of Captain Chevalier surfaced.

"*Mon Dieu*, I am an ugly man," Chevalier said, looking at himself, and then he began to whistle.

"Captain, the angel," Balch called, pointing.

Sekeziel, radiant in the gloom, golden hair clean and combed, sat on a fallen log. His broken wing hung in the dirty water and ruined the effect. "Last chance to go back," he said. "It will get difficult from now on. Some of you will die."

"No thank you, My Lord Sekeziel," Richard said. He had never shown fear in the face of battle. He would not give the angel the satisfaction now.

"I warned you."

A Stephen-doppelganger leapt out of the channel from some submerged perch and grabbed Richard's brother around the neck. The dinghy rocked wildly. The two Stephen's tumbled over the side where more hands rose to grab the thrashing and punching man.

"Saint's blood!" Balch bellowed, hanging on as his bow rammed Richard's boat, knocking aside Terrion's oar. The water in the center of the channel rolled with the struggle, but Stephen didn't resurface.

"Stephen!" Richard aimed his pistol at nothing, searching the impenetrable water for his brother. "What did you do?"

Sekeziel stood. Water dripped from the broken tips of his feathers. "I did nothing. I hold no sway in this place."

"Where is he?"

"I don't know. This is not Purgatory, Captain. You are very close to Hell here. He could be anywhere."

"Seaman, get in!" Lt. Terrion said. He grabbed the edge of the drifting boat.

"But . . ." Balch was staring into the water. It rippled with the telltale signs of circling doppelgangers.

"Get in, damn you, or we leave you," Richard said. Stephen, his brother. Gone. What had he done?

Balch stood and shoved his pistol into his belt. He threw his munitions pack over and stepped across the gunwale.

Richard glared at Sekeziel. He knew the angel had caused this. The angel hated him. He aimed his pistol at Sekeziel's face and tightened his finger on the trigger. Then he lowered the pistol and prayed to see Stephen again.

The two remaining dinghies resumed course in silence. The afternoon passed slowly. Doppelganger attacks increased, but Balch made good use of his pistol and the large munitions packs. Sekeziel made no more visitations. The flock of crows kept up a loud call-and-reply, drowning out the slap of the oar-heads and creak of the oarlocks. Mosquitoes continued their torment. Tree after tree thrust up from the water in an unending vista that looked like the bars of a brig to Richard. He kept hearing his own voice in his head, refusing the angel just before Stephen died.

"Captain," Chevalier shouted.

Richard turned. Chevalier was pointing up. A line had been strung above them between two great cypress trees. Centered, hanging down from the line, was a flag: a golden lion, rearing up on a field of blue.

"That's the flag of the *Queen Anne*," Terrion said.

Richard shook his head. The *Queen Anne* was the first ship to make landfall in Purgatory. Captain Fannish's ship. She was long gone, stranded on the shoals in an early escape attempt. Her flag was followed by the white and red stripes of the *Dauphin d'Alois*, the first French ship to make landfall.

Five minutes later they passed a flag of three crowns on a crimson background. The flag of the *Marie Vellion*, sunk twenty-eight years ago. Then came the white stag banner of the *Green Season*. Both were sunk by the *Marquise de Lombria*, Captain Chevalier's ship. The battles between the English and French had been epic in those early years, before they realized it was wasteful and futile. Chevalier bowed his head as they passed his flag next.

The *Marquise de Lombria* had burned twenty-seven years ago after being driven aground by the *Shrive Lane*. The flag of the *Shrive Lane*, a ram's head with gold horns, followed. The *Shrive Lane* went down when her powder room blew. She rose again on a freezing night without a moon, the only ship ever to return, but she settled to the bottom once more two months later when her seams failed. The flags of all the ships followed one after the other, in order of their sinking. Richard's own ship, the *Southern Cross*, was one of the last. Every ship lost had been a blow, but the sinking of the *Southern Cross* had been a nail in his heart, stealing his dreams of open water.

"Who put these here?" Terrion said.

"Sekeziel must have."

"We should go back, Captain," Balch said.

"We go on," Richard said. "You think he'd let us go back now?" He was pleased Terrion continued to row without question. The Lieutenant understood. The Lieutenant understood that their duty to escape was more important than the threat of death.

"Ask him if I can go back," Balch whispered, his eyes wide. Richard turned.

Sekeziel stood in the water up to his waist, his white robes stained black. A doppelganger of Stephen stood on his right. Richard grew furious. How dare Sekeziel mock the effort Stephen had made to come this far?

"Let him rest in peace," he said.

"You led him in here, Captain Attain."

Dozens of doppelgangers gathered on both sides of the channel: Richards, Terrions, Balchs, Chevaliers, and Grauxs.

"I warned you," Sekeziel said.

"Are you afraid we'll make it?" Richard said. "Is God upset that you might have to give us a ship?"

"No," Sekeziel said. The doppelgangers surged forward with great heaving splashes.

"Row!" Balch screamed.

The boat lurched and shook as hands took hold of the sides, tipping it, pulling it down. Wild-eyed and shrieking, Balch fired down into the head of a copy of himself. Lt. Terrion pulled his pistol and thrust it, grip first, at Balch without missing a stroke in his rowing. Richard strained against the weight of the doppelgangers. Balch fired again, freeing the stern a little, and then began hammering at hands with the butt of Terrion's pistol. As happened earlier, the doppelgangers wouldn't let go, even with smashed and broken fingers. Balch tried to climb forward, to get away.

"Man your post," Richard commanded.

Balch raised the bloody pistol once more, and that was the last Richard saw of him as the seaman was yanked over the stern and into the water.

"Row harder!" Richard said. Arms reached over the sides and pulled rubbery, flaccid bodies after them.

"What do we do?"

"The shallows," Richard said. "Get to the shallows." He kicked a doppelganger that was almost in the boat. They dragged the rest of their attackers with them.

They reached the shallows in several strokes and Richard leapt out onto a wide, fallen log, taking his oar with him. He pulled his loaded pistol from his belt. Terrion tried to leap onto a hummock, but one foot slipped and he stepped into water up to his knee. He screamed as the piranha swarmed. He dragged his leg back out, torn and rent, and made his stand on the hummock's crest.

The attack didn't come. The Terrions surrounded Lieutenant Terrion; the Richards surrounded Richard. The crows landed noisily on branches. Terrion adjusted his feet on the uneven hummock. His leg was bleeding badly. Richard looked for the other boat, but didn't see it. It had gotten away.

"It didn't have to be this way," Sekeziel said, walking on the surface of the water. "You could have stayed on the mountain this morning."

"We would have gotten through if you hadn't interfered," Richard said.

"You would not. You got this far because I've been holding them back."

"Then you did it for your own amusement. You wanted us to suffer."

"Do you know the purpose of a swamp, Captain? It purifies. It scours away rot and leaches out the dross. Muddy water enters in, clean water leaves. Do you think the mountain is worse than the swamp? The mountain borders Heaven, the swamp borders Hell."

"You said we could escape! We will."

"You have never accepted that you are dead. You are here because of your own choices. Sometimes there are consequences of choices, even in Purgatory."

Richard raised his pistol and pointed it at Sekeziel. "You've wanted to break me since I shot you. I won't give up. Kill me, but I won't beg."

The Terrion-doppelgangers surged at the Lieutenant. Terrion swung his oar, thunking the blade against several skulls, but he couldn't bring it back for a second swing. They pulled it from his hands. Richard lifted his pistol to save his friend, but one shot wouldn't change the outcome, so he lowered the barrel. The doppelgangers dragged Terrion down.

Richard stood alone, his own oar held in one hand like a spear, with the blade-head up. His calves trembled as he tried to keep his balance. The Terrion-doppelgangers melted into Richards and joined their brothers around him. There must have been twenty of them.

Sekeziel smiled. "You are a proud man, Captain Attain. I think you wanted to best me almost as much as you wanted to escape. You have condemned five men to Hell because of your pride. Pride is your reason for being here. I tried to teach you this on the mountain, but you didn't hear. The swamp will teach you now. It is good at stripping away pride. This is a place where you can lose yourself." He swept his arm out, indicating the Richards around him.

Richard looked at Sekeziel's wing and remembered how this started. His fleet had engaged with the French off of Martinique, overpowering the smaller French frigates. Then a bird flew across the sky. An angel. For an instant, Richard saw it clearly. He lifted his musket and fired, not expecting to hit it. There came a shriek louder than the cannons. The angel's broad wing broke upward and inverted; his body dropped. Feathers fluttered against the sky. Then a French musket ball ended Richard's life. It wasn't his fault. He had mistaken an angel for a seagull.

"You're awfully quiet," Sekeziel said. "That is unlike you." His wing hung limp.

The doppelgangers trembled. They would attack soon—drag Richard down as they had the others. Richard shifted his weight. The fight was not done. The third dinghy was still out there. Maybe he could distract Sekeziel long enough to let the last two men escape.

"I have nothing to say." His words died in the humid air. He raised his pistol and squeezed the trigger. The hammer fell, the pan flashed, and a bloody hole opened in Sekeziel's chest to mark the path of the ball. The swamp shivered, like the tremble of a sail when the wind shifts.

Sekeziel touched the wound with his fingers. Red stained his robe. The doppelgangers advanced. Richard's oar was taken from him and he was pulled from the log. He was helpless against so many, but they were gentler than he expected.

The water was cold. They held him under. He kept his eyes open, but it was too murky to see light. The piranha fed. The little fish with their sharp teeth opened up his heart, but he held onto anger. This wasn't his fault. He should have gone to Heaven. He had served his country and king in wartime as a good Christian man. He shouldn't be here. The rest of his men shouldn't be here, or the French either. He had shot Sekeziel by mistake and the angel had punished them all.

His thoughts slowed as the fish devoured, but he resisted becoming a nameless, faceless thing like the doppelgangers. He would *not* run away from his duty to Chevalier and Graux. His mind and his will slipped free of the encumbrance of his dying body. He needed a new body and a new form. His soul swam through the swirling clots of rotting vegetation and surface slime and crawled into one of the doppelgangers. He took its body. The angel had said death might be different in the swamps. It was. It was liberating. Richard stood up in the shallow water and looked out of new eyes. Sekeziel, bloody tunic, shattered wing, turned towards him. The angel was not fooled and reached for him.

He abandoned the body he had borrowed and leapt into another Richard. This time he was more comfortable with the theft. He caught an echo of the life that had once worn this body. It had been Mr. Andrew Shain, His Majesty's Royal Navy, died 1778.

Sekeziel leapt after Richard with an awkward, single-wing beat. Richard jumped from doppelganger to doppelganger, sweeping across the swamp wearing the remnants of his fellow damned. He was desperate to find Captain Chevalier. He needed to do one thing right.

He took hold of a Richard leaning against a cypress tree: Mr. Ian Balken, who died of consumption, 1643. He took hold of a Richard swimming below the surface: Mrs. Patricia Geohagan, who died in childbirth, 1826. He took hold of a Richard perched on a sunken log, head and shoulders above the water: Captain Antonio Squilace, frozen to death, 1834. There were thousands of faceless souls, all who had lost their way in the swamps of life, and so lost their way in the swamps of Hell. Richard used them like stepping stones while the angel chased.

It took a little while, but he found a doppelganger watching Chevalier's dinghy row by. Chevalier and Graux pulled their oars in desperation. Richard leapt into the swimming body of a doppelganger below their boat. It had already assumed the visage of Seaman Graux. Richard forced it to become Richard. He would protect the last boat. Another doppelganger swam below him. He grabbed it by the arms and twisted it away. It came again and he grappled with it.

Another one swam past him in the black water. He couldn't see it, but he knew it was there, and he reached for it. He tried to fight. Several got past him and grabbed Captain Chevalier, dragging him into the water and the piranha.

Richard lifted his head above water. Seaman Graux had taken both oars and was trying to row the dinghy on his own. His face was twisted in a grimace. The angel stood behind him in the bow.

The ocean glistened in the afternoon sun beyond them, so close. The saltmarshes were all that stood between Graux and freedom. A schooner lay at anchor beyond the shoals, bathed in bright sunshine as the angel had promised.

"You still don't understand, do you?" Sekeziel said. Graux jerked around in the boat when the angel spoke. "Leaving is easy when it's time for you to go," Sekeziel continued. "There is no other way to leave." Two doppelgangers stood up from the water and grabbed the boat as it slipped by. Graux couldn't overcome them. The boat stopped.

"No, please," Richard said.

Graux, pleading as well, turned and tried to kneel in the space between the center seat and the bow seat. The doppelgangers pulled him screaming into the water.

Richard felt hollow. He had failed. In thirty years he hadn't managed to save one person from this place, and had even made things worse today. He looked at the beautiful ocean and the fluttering sails of the schooner with longing.

"You lose," Sekeziel said. He stepped onto a boggy patch of fen. His beautiful, left wing rustled as he moved. Behind him the ocean faded, replaced by endless swamp. The sunlight leached away. Richard looked around. The doppelgangers were still there, but they had assumed a formlessness, without eyes or noses or mouths or sex. For the first time he believed Purgatory could not be beaten.

The angel smiled. "Purgatory is vaster than you can imagine, and filled to the brim. Any one of them can leave, if they choose to. But I'm not here to do your work for you, and almost no one ever leaves."

"I wanted to go to Heaven," Richard said.

"You wanted to escape. That's not the same thing."

"I'm sorry I shot your wing, Lord Sekeziel. Is that what you want to hear? I'm sorry I didn't turn back when you offered. I'm sorry I caused my brother's death, and the deaths of five good men. I caused fifteen ships to be stranded here. Let them go. Is there anything I can do to save them? I'll go to Hell. I will. I'm sorry I broke your wing." Tears ran down his cheeks. He had known Sekeziel wasn't a seagull when he raised his musket. He had fired anyway.

"Do you really think you can shoot an angel, Captain Attain?" Sekeziel swelled and his broken wing became whole. "You damned none but yourself, and the Purgatory you knew was yours alone. Your crews, the ships, the French, they were all just the ways you were hanging on to the past. It took you thirty years to finally risk something irreplaceable. It took you thirty years to enter the swamps."

"I imagined it all?" Richard felt joy darkened by anger. He had not damned his brother and his crew, but on the other hand he had been played for a fool. "Stephen is safe?"

"No. He is here. Many of the men you lived with for the last thirty years are here, in their own purgatories because of their own choices. But the Stephen you saw die today was just an imitation."

"What about the mountain and the harbor?"

"Gone. That was yours alone, and they ended when you left."

"So I escaped after all," he said sadly.

"There's a way out, and perhaps you've started on the right path." Sekeziel vanished. Richard was alone.

In the back of his mind he could feel the swamp. Somewhere inside of it was the Purgatory he had known for so long. It was all a timeless lie. Richard had been here in the swamp the whole time. But he wasn't a doppelganger yet. He refused to forget who he was.

He climbed into Chevalier's dinghy and rowed down the channel aimlessly. Doppelgangers followed him, hoping to find themselves. He swung the oars forward and back, and whispered their names to help them remember. He began to search for his brother. He no longer sought escape.

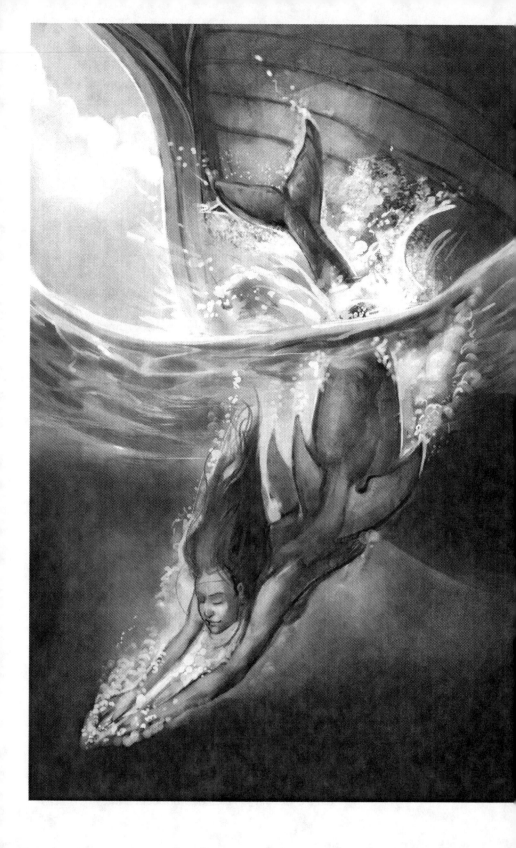

Currents and Clockwork
Lindsey Duncan

"Come on, Veli," Calais said to me in that tone, the one that promised headaches at twenty paces. "How much trouble could there be?"

I folded my arms and leaned on him with a look. The *Narwhal* was a wonderful ship, though the prow-spear that had given her the name was too damaged for use, and Calais Silverhand was an excellent captain when he didn't have his anchor in a crusade.

This was not one of those days.

I looked at our would-be passengers on the dock, a reedy man with gold hair the consistency of coral and a minnow of a child. They were homestead sorts, not travelers. They had never even walked the length of an island.

"How can I start?" I said.

Calais eased out a smile that twined around my guts and held. "Trust me."

"The last time you said that, the Farazi Ice Cabal set assassins on us when we put into port."

The harbor bustled, oblivious to the argument on the *Narwhal's* deck.

"That was only—"

"The time before," I said, "we ended up with sea dragon eggs, and not the sort you eat as a delicacy, the sort that hatches into a—"

"I remember that one turning out rather well financially once we found a fellow willing to train them." He brushed a hand through coldwater black hair. It brought my eye to the harsh scar that razored off the top third of his left ear and wandered like a lightning strike to the opposite side of his nose. "They want to come as far as Nevelia. We run the Iole, we'll make very good time through the isles."

Suspicion flitted through my mind. "What kind of toy did they promise you?"

"Not a toy, precisely," he said, "I might be able to salvage something of use from the workings."

"Calais . . ."

He heaved a sigh. "A clockwork bird. But the artistry! Absolutely astounding. If I could just have a chance to tinker with it."

The *Narwhal* currently had a variety of his inventions on board, some of them useful—we never had to drop a line to determine speed or worry about fresh water—and some of them not: the cook was still in a tizzy after a particularly violent altercation between his thumb and a mechanical device meant to chop vegetables.

I turned to watch them, nodded to the tight dark marks on their wrists. "Shardath slave-bands."

"We've transported escapees before."

"I can tell," I said in a pointed tone, "because of the diamond cross scars. That's where they embed syrillus into the workings of the slave bands. Done to ensure that tainted magic leaps to the slaves rather than the owners."

"I thought you'd have some fellow feeling." Calais twitched a smile, obscure, measured.

I drew my temper in with a breath and clenched it. "Let me Sight them," I said, vaulting over the ship's rail.

Calais darted around to the gang plank and joined me in a few rapid steps. "This is Vlisa Karhene, my first mate," he said, a hand resting comfortably on the small of my back. "She keeps us out of trouble on the trade routes."

I mouthed the words back at him. He had the grace to flush.

"Pleased to meet you, nel Karhene," the reedy man said, offering his hand. Another mark of one slave-born, he wore no gloves. Neither did I, but I had other reasons for the impropriety. "Arhenor. I'm a healer."

I clasped his hand. My mind seared with an image of the two of us locked close, his hand brushing gently down the side of my face. My body twitched with the effort of not jerking away. "Good to meet you," I managed, dry-mouthed.

It was not necessarily a foretelling. I found that sometimes I picked up strong thoughts on first contact, and I was no stranger to ardent attentions from even men who had no taste for wandering merchants. I tried not to size him up as I turned to the child. He didn't seem to be the type.

Her eyes were the color of lily pads. "Tyse," she said, placing a tiny hand in mine.

The world unfolded, and I felt surrounded by a sense of complete safety and contentment. There was no answer in the gentle light, and there did not need to be. I was peripherally aware of her hand falling away.

"Calais," I murmured, "she's a child of Aline."

He made an indefinite sound. Raised by the tribal Shie-lhir-narrin, he believed not in the goddess, but in a darker matriarch known as Pedara. We had danced about the idea that the two were one and the same, but who we were to decide theology?

"So?" His fingers curled along my spine.

"So I think it would be a bad idea if we left them behind." That was to say nothing of what might happen even with them, but what other choices did we have? I kissed him on the cheek. "You get your bird."

"Your magnanimity in deciding the fate of my ship overwhelms me," he said in my ear.

———⚓———

We sailed with the evening tide. I was left with the task of orienting our passengers, a role I dreaded. I couldn't even look at Arhenor.

"Land-gloves," I said as I paused by the bin. "Take a pair if we hit port during daylight hours. The *Narwhal* hasn't been detained on a decency complaint yet."

"Will we be stopping that long?" Arhenor's pale, slender fingers clutched the rail. "I was told it would only be two weeks to Nevelia."

I snorted, about to rip into him for presumption, then turned my head and saw the cool fixedness in his face. Something had him frightened. "We run fast," I said, "but we have a shipping schedule to follow. Two stops, three on the outside. You should disembark, take Tyse to see a theatre play. Spend a night on the town."

"I would like to see an old-world tragedy," Tyse said with a hopeful smile. "I've always loved opera songs, too."

On deck, I inundated them with technical terms in the hopes it would stun them into questionless quiet. Instead, I lost track of Tyse and found her on the navigation platform, studying the magic-sealed chart.

She was trying to compare the size of the islands with her fingers. "Everything looks so small."

I glared at Calais, who hadn't troubled to shoo her. He grinned back at me and pretended to be engrossed in a dialogue with the cook. "It does," I said. "If you study the coasts, you can almost see where they might have fitted together into one big block of land."

"There must be a word for that," Arhenor said.

I shrugged. "No sense in having words for things that don't exist."

"What are all the names for?" Tyse said. I tried to pick out her age—seven? Slave children grew up too fast.

"The Seventeen Seas," I said. "From the Icebow Sea north of Faraz down into the Tanduri Tide."

She frowned, fingers trailing along the blue illumination of the Iole. "But it's all one ocean."

"Try telling the traders that."

"Or the privateers," Calais said. "You'd be surprised how much business they do over boundary disputes. Needless to say, we stick to inner waters."

"I have every faith in your sailing," Arhenor said calmly.

Which meant, I thought, he was more worried about the authorities than pirates—not exactly a comforting notion. I drew him aside with one hand while Tyse played with the chart and Calais indulged her.

"What are you afraid of?" I asked.

His gaze slid over my face without connection. "I'm worried someone will come after Tyse."

"She's tainted, isn't she?"

He tensed despite the softness of my question. "It isn't her fault, and she's not dangerous—"

"Stop," I said. "So am I. But we're not equipped to fight off a hunter-ship, much less more than one." I didn't intend to tell him that my visions had promised only safe harbor. Right now, I was not sure I believed them.

"You don't have to worry about it." He leaned tentatively on the rail, watching the pitch of forest-tipped waves. "We covered our tracks. I would not endanger this vessel."

"I see." I wanted to snort at his overconfidence. "Magic is strong in the Shardath. If the seers want to find you, they will."

"When did they stop looking for you?" He turned his head to watch me.

"Too long ago to remember. They never knew to look." I shook my head. "Worry about yourselves, Arhenor. My life is in hand."

"It's been my experience, Vlisa," he said, "that no matter how content a person is, it warms the soul to be worried about."

I smiled wryly. "I don't need—"

"Ho, Veli!" Calais bounded across the deck and slung an arm around my waist, pecking my cheek. "You don't fancy a bit of swimming, do you?"

"Why is it," I made no effort to disentangle myself as he swung me about, "that you're only so cheerful when you want something?"

"I never stop being cheerful," he said with an arched brow. "How can you tell? Cook would love some fresh fish. Sure our guests would, as well."

I ruffled his hair. "Send your clockwork bird to do it."

He blinked at me with owlish hurt. "It might get water in the gears."

"Then what point was there taking it on a boat, precisely?" I twined out of his arms. "Don't gape," I said to Arhenor as I worked my shirt off. He was a gentleman, averting his eyes where the crew had stopped bothering years ago—but an unexpected blossom of heat started between my collarbones and wandered down.

The first dozen times I ship-dove, I didn't manage to finish the transformation until several bracing seconds after I hit the water. By now, I could take on a dolphin's shape in the fall and be swimming by the time I disappeared under the waves.

Calais had a good eye: there was a shoal of kerry carp within a few easy strokes, and they were swimming thick and sluggish. Easy pickings, though I was in no hurry to abandon the feel of cool water pouring down my flanks and an entire ocean before me. Here there were no worries, no muddied confusion about what the future might bring, no conventions or niceties to observe.

Once, when I was just experienced enough to stop thinking about it, I decided not to come back. It was Calais who rescued me from my adoptive pod. It took me weeks to get over the sea urge. We stayed at port in Shennevis all that time, and I've never forgotten it.

That memory was enough to bring me round when the catch was done. The crew threw a rope for me, and I climbed hand over hand back aboard as they pulled the net up separately.

The cook clapped me on one wet shoulder as he saw the contents; we joked, we laughed, and I would have taken my time sliding back into tunic and trousers, but for the eyes of the strangers on the whole scene.

Cursing them in my head, I retreated to my cabin.

———⚓———

The crow's nest turned out to be another place to escape from the pair. I spent a lot of time up there hunting storms and watching for trouble. Visions scuttled across the dome of my mind without definition, as wispy as shapes in the clouds.

The fourth day out was sticky and oppressive, and we were far enough away from land that the thought of it seemed like a dream. I imagined myself on a voyage that never ended, free from the complications that pockmarked the blue.

I should have seen the Pirie ship earlier, the white and silver outline crisp against the horizon. Wavy and diaphanous in a storm, prim and tidy on a clear day, I've always found the Pirieda navy to be somehow unreal.

I could just make out the blue and saffron weaving that served as a flag, standard of a southern Cascade. Foreboding punched through me, hard, raw and completely outside myself. I kicked to my feet, swung out of the crow's nest and descended with the reckless abandon of someone who could just as easily have flown.

"Ditch the current," I said. "We're on an intercept course with a Pirie guardship."

Calais studied me. "One of those feelings?"

I swallowed hard. "Yes."

"Do it." We had sailed together too long for him to play skeptic. Quiet orders swelled down the deck, taken up by each hand in turn. Some shot me peculiar looks, but they knew not to argue.

Tyse watched from a coil of rope near the prow, her tiny form bent like a figurehead in the heave and hustle. Her cheeks pink, hair tousled by a stiff wind, she had not caught the sense of urgency that played into our activities. No sign of Arhenor—down below studying Calais' texts, I thought. I frowned and started towards the girl.

Her eyes arrow-shot to mine. "Vlisa?"

"Come on," I said. "Below deck. Stay there."

"If something is wrong," she protested, "I can help."

I paused, for in that voice was perfect sincerity without an ounce of child's oblivion. What was her taint? But I had no time for the question.

"Not now. Better you're out of sight."

I came back on deck to find that the silver guardship had cut the distance in half, the sailors in their ice-white uniforms moving in easy formation. "Thought the plan was to avoid them."

"They're running faster than we are," Calais said. "Probably one of those experimental ship designs the Pirie are always churning out." His voice was high and bright, braced by hidden nerves. "We can't out sail them, and we'll just attract attention if we try. So we keep a steady course and we just see what happens, hmm?"

"Sure I'm wrong," I said.

Amazing how much silence there could be under slapping waves and the rhythm of sailing.

"They're tacking towards us," Calais said a few minutes later, his voice quiet. "You may want to sally up to the cannons, lads."

I paced to his side. "Do they even work?"

He grinned at me. "I don't think now is the best time to fire test volleys. I've made a few improvements . . ."

"We're doomed," I muttered.

"Your confidence in me remains a bulwark to my soul."

"Glad to help." They were close enough that I could make out the knots of sun-pale hair, the spotless livery, even the pistols worn by the officers.

Their first mate, a thickset man in his forties, called over to us. "Trader vessel, identify yourself and your destination!"

"The *Narwhal*, bound for Nevelia," Calais called back. "You're a bit far out of Pirie waters, sailor. Why question our itinerary? There's enough ocean for both of us."

"We were dispatched on behalf of the oligarchs of Shardath," the blonde said. "Word is you have one of their tainted."

I hate being right at times like these.

"Afraid you have the wrong boat, ner," Calais said. "We haven't gone near Shardath for years. Misers, them—make sure you read the fine print on whatever contract you signed."

The man's lips thinned. "Thank you for the advice." It came out sharp and snapped. "I advise you prepare to be boarded."

"Nope." Calais smiled genially. "Not going to happen."

I slid away from him, crouching down as if to tighten one of the ropes. My body coiled, readying the change. We had trained for this, kept it ready though it had been years since our last sea battle. Wasn't hard, I reminded myself.

"You have five minutes to reconsider, Captain."

"Sail on." His voice never wavered; he could be polite to a tribe of cannibals. "Hope you find what you're looking for." His eyes dropped to mine. "Think you still have it in you?"

"Always." I transformed, fluttering out of my clothes with insistent wings. It took me a moment to adjust to how vast the ship's deck had suddenly become. It was a veritable world to itself. I inclined my beak to him in acknowledgement, then hopped onto the rail and took flight.

The mammoth hulks of the ships surrounded me as I rode the winds in a lazy circle around the Pirie vessel. I made a perch of the mast and surveyed the scene. So many clipped heads promenading about their business, a sight that would have been comical if I hadn't been aware they were preparing to board.

The cook went below-deck—unlike ours, he probably had never studied the cleaver as a weapon of war—and I took the opportunity to follow. No one notices a swallow—tiny, dark, unremarkable—even when they invite themselves where they shouldn't be.

Below, the scent of close, dark wood and a touch of gunpowder. I grimaced as I winged into the shadows and watched the sailors load the cannons. They moved with fluid ease, no wasted step, no efficiency lost.

A slender youth started down the steps above me. I made the change, nearly cracking my head on the wood as I found my hiding place smaller than I had anticipated. Bracing my body to the beam, I waited until he passed and then yanked him around by the belt.

His eyes widened. He might have cried out, but there was something about being face to face with a naked woman that chokes a man's vocal chords. I bumped him over the back of the head and shimmied us out of sight.

I stripped the overgarments and didn't bother with the rest, counting seconds in my head. The first volley alone would be enough to rip the Narwhal's innards to shreds. I cursed under my breath as I tried to get buttons, ties and sashes settled so they at least looked authentic.

"Captain says the gunpowder is wet—whole supply is no good," I gasped as I bolted from the corner. I stumbled on the rough boards.

"Why that salt-tongued . . ." The speaker cleared his throat. "Well, don't expect much resistance from this rabble anyhow."

"There's good news," I said. "Brought on a stash of coria powder before we left Pirie waters." Coria was a substance more stable than gunpowder without the odor, and more the luck for me, the average soldier had never seen it.

To fit the rumors, his eyes twitched. "Saints! Come on, lads."

"I can roll it in for you," I said hastily. "Got to be a lot of work readying the cannons."

He nodded, and I scurried away. I knew exactly what I was going for: a bit of rooting around in the hold and I had the cook's prized flour on its side and rolled onto the cannon deck. With any luck, the confusion would be worth time enough for us to have the upper hand.

"Captain of the *Narwhal*," the first mate's voice thundered above me, "you have one minute to consent to be boarded or we will take you by force."

I courted the shadows again, waiting for an opportunity to change. To defend the Pirie sailors somewhat, working Coria powder was not a myth and Pirieda had perfected it. Unfortunately, where it mostly went was noble pistols so those notables didn't have to deal with the aroma of gunpowder. Calais had a small quantity of raw powder, but as far as I knew had never converted it.

"Crew of the *Narwhal*, prepare to be boarded! If any of you wish to surrender, merely kneel with your arms across your chest and you will not—"

"What's this, then?"

Hard arms caught me about the middle and threw me backwards. I hit the wall with a jarring crack as the man thrust my chin up.

"I've seen your face," he said.

Work with Calais long enough and you began to feel you could talk your way out of anything. It was infectious. "Of course you have," I said. "We work side by side on this ship. I joined up back in . . ."

He cuffed the side of my head so hard my ears rang, a sound that seemed to go on forever as staves clashed above us. "No, I don't think so." Voices poured in around his, animated, defiant, vigorous with the fight. "Came from the *Narwhal*, didn't you?"

Could he have seen my face from that distance? I slid my foot up against the board, trying to get leverage, but he thrust his knee into mine. "I don't know what you're—"

Cannons cracked to life—ours, not theirs. Wood sprayed like so much saltwater, and we dropped in tandem, sloshing, sliding. My head cracked hard on the floor.

By now, the Pirie sailors had found their Coria powder to be counterfeit and were working to correct the problem. I saw limbs flash past and tried to make sense of the chaos.

The soldier wrenched me upright before I knew which way that was, shook me hard. "You did this!" His fury spat blood droplets in my face; he had not come out of the tumble unscathed.

As long as he held onto me, I couldn't transform. I kicked only to have my knees knocked out from under me. Spitting expletives, he drew the cudgel at his side. "If you don't stop moving . . ."

The fact that the blow was meant to subdue, not incapacitate, made it no less painful. I cried out in the strobing darkness that followed, sensed more than saw his arm come back again.

A small wooden dart struck him in the upper arm. He glanced down at it in confusion—then twitched, his fingers spasming away from my shoulder as he clutched his arm.

I stumbled free, making it only halfway off my knees before the pitch of the ship sent me rolling. I straightened to stare through the broad hole in the side of the guardship and saw my rescuer: Arhenor, still on the *Narhwal*, his fingers shaky on the dart-tube.

On the deck above him, wood cracked and shattered, so much melee and no resolution. I jumped for the water and came up with a plan after. I saw a flash of silver and heard a wild ululation as Calais, pistol in hand, recited the questionable lineage of his opposite in a voice made for the stage.

At least someone was having fun.

Two transformations later and with an anxious hand from our gunning crew, I stood wet and shaking below deck. Arhenor wrapped a blanket about my shoulders and rubbed them. "Are you all right?"

"Fine." I was in no mood to point out the occasional spurt of red that ebbed across my vision. It wasn't as if being crimson made anything harder to see. "I need to get up there."

"They have it under control." He pulled me back, which left me wedged against him. "You'll get yourself hurt."

I bit back hoarse laughter. "I've been keeping myself out of trouble for almost a decade."

Calais would have pointed out that the practice didn't show. It was the lack of quips from Arhenor, the worried eyes and calm grip that left me without ammunition.

"How did you hurt him?"

"Spent some time in your kitchens." He guided me to a seat as the cannon crew labored into motion. "Mix two herbs in the right fashion and you come up with a poison. I told Tyse to stay in the cabin and did what I could."

I nodded, unvoiced gratitude for his interference. Silence on the deck above brought tension to my frame. "Is it over?"

"Cold-blooded Pirie are no match for a crew with profit in their hearts," the cook boomed from the head of the stairs. "We have the day, friends. They have venison aboard!"

Calais bound the crew, set their sails, and left them to find their own way, then called me into his cabin to redress matters.

"So what do you think now? And how is the head?"

"Been better, but I can live with it." I winced, trying not to dislodge the bandage Arhenor had wrapped around the back of my head. "As for the rest, it could be an isolated incident."

"I agree, but I'm surprised to hear you say it." He leaned back. "That healer has you in a bit of a muddle, does he?"

I had received a thorough drubbing, we had passengers that were more trouble than they looked—however much both Calais and I were willing to let the wind take us—and I was having enough trouble forgetting what I had seen in my vision. I snapped.

"What if he does? What do you have to say about it? You have your bird—"

"So you're entitled to the healer, is that it?" Cynical amusement in his voice, but he coiled, tense.

"Don't act wounded on me." I was conscious of tightening my claws in the anger when I should have let it go. "After everything I've gone through—"

"You need a toy?" One brow arched. "Does he know he's your designated booty?"

I stood in a rush, shoving the desk with my hands. It would have hit him in the stomach had it not been bolted down. The mocking words ran hot through my mind. "I'm off to tell him," I said. "Have a problem with that?"

"Why would I?" Calais leaned forward. "Do I own you, Vlisa? I don't recall signing any papers."

I slammed the door on him.

I found Arhenor in his cabin, playing a game of cards with Tyse. Discarded sevens and sixes lay in blossoms of color around them. The sight of them—she serene, he trying to keep a straight face while she teased him with a smile and innocent guesses—pulled me up short. Pure luck that they had stayed together for so long, and now the only thing that mattered was to make the most of it. I had never seen happiness so perfectly distilled.

Tyse looked up with those pale green eyes that seemed to peek past my guard. "Is something wrong, nel Karhene?"

"No. Nothing is wrong." Nothing I could explain in a few words, I amended in my head.

Arhenor smiled warmly. "Can I do anything for the hero of the hour?"

"Are you making fun of me?" Calais' sarcasm still stung.

"Never." He shook his head. "Do you want to join us? We could start a new game."

"He says this because he has a bad hand," Tyse said from behind her cards.

Arhenor tried to protest, but his expression was as ill-made for falsehood as it was for levity. I found it a relief, that straightforward ease: no wordplay, no jests laced with truth—a groundedness like the land I rarely walked.

"Deal me in," I said.

———————⚓———————

Two days later, Calais had me up sometime past midnight with a splash of milk to the face.

"Shardath war galleon," he said. "I need your eyes."

The bandage slung free as I jerked. "You don't need my help spotting something like that." I tried to tie the bandage back in place and only succeeded in looping it around my chin. "Have they sighted us?"

Calais opened his mouth to answer. A resounding thrum, a hundred times louder than whale-song underwater, echoed through the cabin. I kicked out of the bed to one side, he rolled to the other, and we collided shoulder to shoulder in my cabin door.

"Hunter horn," he said in a short voice.

I stood back to let him pass—even with my temper uncooled, this was more important than a quarrel. "Meant for someone else?" I said.

Questions rolled over us in a thick fog as sleepy crew wobbled to their feet. Calais flourished his hands in a helpless gesture and bounded for the stairs. "Not likely," he said over his shoulder. "We're the only ones on the waves."

"Options?" I mopped milk off my cheek with the tail of the bandage as I followed him. It was a dark night, suffocating hot, only a thimbleful of stars. Only one of the moons was past crescent, and it was fouled by smoky clouds. A night where horizon and ocean blended together and left a single void.

In that night without landmark, it was impossible to measure the speed of the galleon that closed in on our starboard side. Cold scarlet sails blended with the shadows, the Shardath crew moving aboard like so many ants.

"Run the rocks," he said.

I spun about. The reefs off the coast of Na'antira cut through the darkness in relief, so many gnarled fingers slick with seawater and faint moonlight.

The bandage fluttered off and landed in the water. I paid it no mind as I turned to watch the silhouette of the galleon again.

Silence. By now the crew had joined us, though lanterns remained covered and hands still. Waiting.

"Can we stay out of their range that long?" I said.

"No better ideas, hmm?" Calais managed a smile. "If we move now, yes—wind is running in our favor. You heard that, lads!" His voice was primed to carry now. "Cut us loose."

The flare of the lanterns, the creak of rope and mast, drove back the unending void. One voice, crusted with sleep, picked up the thread of a tune, and his neighbors pitched in. To the tale of a fairy sorceress who turned anyone who crossed her into an anemone, we turned for treacherous waters, the bulwark of the galleon. . . .

"Goddess," I said. "I didn't realize we had that much room to run."

"Eh, that's a good thing, right?" Calais leaned over the chart, adjusting a series of levers and dials. "Easier to outpace them."

I looked at him hard. "I didn't realize," I said, "just how enormous that thing is. If it were a fish, it would have swallowed us whole."

"If it were a fish, our cook would have us out there with harpoons."

"Do us both a favor and work." I dashed to the other end of the ship, partly to shut him out, and partly to strain my senses over the black water. I knew my visions weren't precise enough to pick up the maze of rocks below, but I could not tear myself away.

The hunter horn ripped through the night again, setting bone on edge. It brought my head snapping about. The blackwood flanks of the war galleon soaked up the ambient shadows so that it almost seemed that the sea itself was on sails in pursuit.

Without a word, Calais tossed me a spy-glass. I squinted, trying to find the opposing captain on the expanse. It was hunting for a minnow in a delta and I soon became lost. So many scarlet uniforms, burly arms, hair cut back in bristles–and here, then there, a figure with longer hair and slighter arms, one with a flute, others I could not see.

I threw the glass back to Calais. "Keep the distance," I said. "Mages on board." And more than enough time to light the creative spark and prepare what tunes and artistry they needed to work their art. "We don't stay out of range . . ."

One of the sailors let out a shout of dismay. "They have rowers!"

Calais' hand came down so hard the chart almost cracked. "Veli—"

"What do you want to me to do, get out and push?" My eyes were aching from trying to see beneath the waves.

There was, behind me, the kind of silence I've learned to dread. When black spots started to mar my vision, I turned to face him.

"That's not a bad idea," he said. "I remember you turning into a dolphin once—"

"Sea turtle," I said, reaching for a coil of rope. "Bind this fast."

"While I may not be an expert on marine life, I think I know the difference between a dolphin and a turtle," Calais pointed out.

"Turtle's a better bet," I said brusquely. I was already on the rail with my hands knotted in the bottom of my shirt. "More musculature by proportion, closer dimensions to the boat. I'm just warning you now, I've never tried to reach this size . . ."

"Can your heart take it?"

I paused. "As far as I know . . ."

The hunter horn boomed in the pit of my stomach—close, too close. There was no time to worry. I dove off the boat and surrendered to the blackness . . . and the cold! Saints, the sheer cold. I arranged the transformation in my head. I thought my skin would slough off and leave me defenseless to the black. I thought that perhaps it already had.

"Captain, the mages are mustering!"

Thick turtle hide swaddled me from the cold as my flippers cut through the water. I trumpeted, a short blast, and a massive knot—four ropes anchored on the ship and tied together—hit the water.

I gathered it up in my mouth, careful not to bite down, and pulled.

The *Narwhal* jerked with the first tug, and I heard a crash of glass and flesh as the boat rocked forward. Grimacing, I plowed through the water, knowing that the movement would smooth out as long as I kept swimming. The weight, focused on my jaw, sent a groan of pain through my frame, but it was dull enough. I could ignore it.

Raucous taunts from the deck told me that we had put distance between ourselves and our opponents . . . though not enough that such profanities were a waste of wind. I knew Calais would be calibrating his instruments, looking to steer the rocks by measurements and instinct.

The first stone fingers welcomed me, their curve a beckoning moon-bow. The usual human gestures—a grin, a nod of satisfaction—were impossible, so I settled for coursing into the darkness. The reef loomed, but night-eyes made it easy to follow.

"Brilliant, Veli!" From the sound of his voice, he leaned over the rail. "You dry off, I swear you can have my best wine."

My heart warmed at the words, but irritation filled in the hole behind it. As if he could buy me with the wine! I followed the channel I saw, confident of my progress. My shell was perhaps a few hands-span wider than the *Narwhal*. I had not intended to try and guide the ship through the maze, but it seemed our best chance.

"Is that. . . ?" Arhenor's voice, soft, wondering.

"She makes a pretty turtle, doesn't she?" Tyse said, as cheerful as if this happened every day. "Eep!"

That cry came as a sandbar made itself known and I jerked sideways to avoid it. My teeth came down on the rope and nearly cut it.

"Careful, would you?"

I ignored Calais as the labyrinth tightened. Twice I reconsidered a course because it looked too shallow, and the second time, I found myself doing a cautious full circle before I could find another way. Though there was a port this side of the isle of Na'antira, only native fishermen used it. I was beginning to wonder how even they could thread the maze.

A jagged spar reared up so abruptly I thought it was a living beast. Instinctively, I tried to roll away, a motion that body wasn't built for. I collided hard with the rock, a bruising shatter along soft underbelly. The rope broke under my teeth.

Dazed and smarting, I knew the *Narwhal* was next. I changed in the water, clinging to the spar. "Hard to port! Now!"

There was no telling if they had heard me, for the speed of the change and the bracing slap of the water made the world go numb. They fished me out a few minutes later, the cook draping a blanket around my shoulders.

I tried to say something clever. I ended up spitting water out my nose.

"Sorry you lads keep having to bail me out," I managed.

The cook clapped a hand on my back. "Usually you're sticking your neck out for us, nel."

"When you have a neck," one of the younger sailors said with a grin.

Out of the corner of my eye, I saw Calais standing rigid at the rail, his fingers turning by inches into a hold that could crack wood.

"We have to keep sailing," he said. "If you're hurt, Veli, get below deck and strap yourself to something. You—" his eyes darted to the two visitors, cold and hard "—below. Now. This will not be smooth sailing."

"I'm not going to be cooped up below like prize jewels," I said, knotting the blanket at the neck as I wobbled to my feet. "What about the Shardathi?"

The galleon had dropped anchor at the first finger-arch, but put down two longships loaded with men. Oars tapped the water in an unrelenting timpani.

"Calais?"

"We run the gauntlet," he said, "and hope they hit rocks." He bent over his instruments. "I don't like these readings."

We plied through the maze, the two longships sapping inches from our lead. I leaned into the rail with body braced, open to an enlightenment that would not come. I could almost feel the prickle up my spine of mustering magic.

One thing we had over their agility: Calais' instruments read the depths more accurately, and his calls came out quick and confident in the ever-dark. One of the other moons, a wan crescent, came out to inspect our progress. After casting a handful of flat grey rays over the deck, it surrendered us to our fate.

A lingering squeal rose up from the waters. I winced as Calais swore. "That, lads, was an inordinately close encounter with the rocks." I could see him running the situation over in his head, measuring. "Vlisa, could you find my sonic reflector?"

"The last time you tested it, it was spotty," I said even as I started towards the stairs. If I waited on finishing an argument with him, I would never do anything. "Spotty here could tear us on the rocks."

"I've made some improvements after studying a series of treatises on bats," he said, "but we don't have time to argue."

"Bats?" My head hurt just thinking about it. Rather than pursue it, I vaulted down and headed for his quarters. Memories slipped past me as I opened the chest where he kept the device, a spiraled horn attached by wires to a variety of cups and a notched wooden rod. He never seemed to age, a child with his toys.

"What do we do with this?" I risked a look towards the longships. They had split up, one arrowing in from the left, the other from the right. The air was thick with the crackle of potential; magic waited to be unleashed.

Tainted may have unique abilities, but nothing compares to the strength and expertise of a trained Shardathi mage. I could feel our borrowed time wither.

"The large one drops into the water—here," and I was nearly flattened by the rope Calais tossed in my direction. "The others fit here and . . . here . . . and . . ."

The man was mad, I decided in a fit of clarity, forgetting in the heat of the moment that I'd come to that conclusion at least ten times before.

The Shardath galleon blasted its horn again from the safety of the finger-arches. This time, the *Narwhal* answered with a soft pulse of sound directed into the waves. Calais frowned as the device attached to the other end of the wire quivered. "Deep waters hard to starboard . . . I hope." This last was muttered in a theatrical aside before he belted out orders.

The *Narwhal* shot through the waters blind, the winds licking eagerly at the sail. Rock hands tore at the ship's flanks, close and greedy, but did not connect. Then a terrible crack of wood—

Calais crowed. "Hold on tight," he called off the stern. "Water's cold!"

One of the longships had hit the very rock that scored my ribs. The smooth lines cracked and shattered at the point of impact.

"You are not the one who should be talking about the temperature of the water," I said.

He grinned at me, boyish, buoyant, and returned his attention to his invention. A steady series of melodious pings disappeared into the waves.

The crew, at first uncertain—they had almost as much experience with his on-and-off inventions as I did—now responded with enthusiasm. We cut the water smooth and easy, even through the claustrophobic labyrinth of rocks.

I saw the crew of the longship lean harder into the oars, heard the crack of a whip on the air, and knew it would not be enough. I glanced over at Calais, the scar hardened with the furrow of his brow. I tried to ignore the cringe in my head and readied myself for a fight. One ship, the odds would be close to even. . . .

"Fill the sails," he said, "let's put some speed on."

My stomach dropped with the words even as the crew moved to obey them. I suppressed the urge to shout, to tear ropes from their hands. "We can't cut through the rocks like this," I said, "no matter how well your instruments are running—"

But we were. Dark sea, dark sky, dark rocks, and we arrowed towards the shadows of nothing where Na'antira lay.

"If you can't take it, Veli," his voice was softer than rain, "go below."

I would sooner have cut out my tongue. "If you're trying to scare me, this is a bad way to do it."

"If this many years haven't frightened you, nothing will."

In cold silence, we watched the *Narwhal* cut the tide, sleek and easy—an ease that belied how quick we could go under. Then the waterway widened suddenly, two curled hands of stone to bid us farewell. We were free in one of Na'antira's broad bays.

Calais never changed expression. The mood passing between us was too bleak for that. "Find us a cove," he said. "We'll bury so deep the Shardathi will never find us."

Then and only then did I retire below deck, where I found Arhenor waiting for me.

"Tyse is sleeping," he said, "Are you all right?"

"Head hurts, back hurts, stomach hurts, mouth hurts," I said briskly. "Nothing out of the ordinary, though." I had to smile at the concern. "Thanks for asking."

"I should check your head." He stepped forward, reaching for the lock of hair that concealed the bruise. "Head wounds are tricky—"

The *Narwhal* lurched underneath us. Arhenor pitched into my arms, and I caught him for balance. His hand brushed the wound. . . .

I laughed even into my flinch as the ship steadied, then found I could not stop. The worries tangled in my stomach spilled out with the sound, for I recognized the scene. It was the one that had plagued me since he and Tyse boarded . . . one that was completely, entirely innocent.

"Vlisa?" His eyes were wide, confused.

Freed from fate, I pecked him on the cheek. "Never mind," I said. "Just an idle thought I had. What's the damage?"

"I should wrap it again," he said, "and you have to promise not to strain it . . ."

I thought of the past few days and our situation now. Who knew if we could sneak past the Shardath vessel to open waters?

"I promise," I said, and meant not a word of it.

———⚓———

Dawn watch meant I had space to think, a commodity more precious than our best cargo. I had spent only a few minutes on deck, however, when Calais burst up from below in a tsunami of motion.

"What if they put a bounty on our heads?" he said. "Not that I'm intimidated by that, but it could be bad for business."

"Give them what they want. If the Shardath wants one tainted this badly, it doesn't end when we put to port, not for them. So end it—our way."

Calais frowned. "What do you have in mind?" As I explained, his face eased. "Get them up. Let's do this."

An hour later, the *Narwhal* slipped from the cove in which we had hidden ourselves and made our presence known to the Shardathi vessel. Calais chivvied a messenger bird from the cages below deck and sent it winging away with a parchment missive.

"Now what?" Tyse sat anxiously on the deck, head back on Arhenor's shoulder.

"Now we see if they bite," I said, examining the rowboat. It was loaded down with two barrels of fish deboned and bleeding.

"Of course they'll bite," Calais said. "One thing Shardathi can't resist is a simple surrender."

"We are native Shardathi," Arhenor said mildly.

"Oh? My condolences."

I stamped about the deck to keep my nerves quiet. The pigeon returned a few minutes later, and Calais claimed the tube around its neck.

He grinned. "Game is on," he said. "They're letting us go for the tainted one, or so they think. Veli, hit the water."

I squeezed Tyse's shoulder as I passed them. "Remember that you have nothing to worry about. I'll thrash around you, stir up the blood—put on a good show—and then we'll swim to safety. Arhenor would never let anything happen to you."

Her smile seemed very small. "I know. I trust you."

I slid into the water as a shark, haunting the reefs. What had seemed treacherous now gave me ample room to avoid the fleet rafts steered by Na'antira fishermen. I paid them little mind as I tracked the rowboat. Arhenor had the oars, Tyse small and solemn in the fore with one hand on the barrels.

I circled around, thrashing foam as I went. Let them get close enough that the Shardathi were sure we had not played them false.

My vision grew cross-hatch as a net plummeted around me. Startled, I bit down to tear a hole and met what might as well have been iron. Magic!

The world went upside down and sideways as I was wrenched over the side of a boat and left sprawled on the deck. In panic, I registered Shardathi crimson. The six men shouted thick words amongst themselves, four heading for the oars.

It should have been simple to tip the boat and escape, but the net sapped all my strength. I jerk-twitched, trying to make sense of it. Maybe they knew who I was, and wanted to make sure the exchange would take place. . . .

They steered the boat behind the shelter of a large peak where one of the longships waited. My stomach seized, but I was not about to give myself away.

A Shardathi mage stepped into the boat and, with heavily scarred knuckles, rapped on the wood by my head. "Stop pretending, nel Karhene, we have you."

Because I could do even less as a netted shark, I transformed and struggled into a seated position. "She's a child," I said. "Whatever you want from her—"

Indulgent laughter interrupted me. "Her? The child Tyse? Useful, but we have no legal recourse to pursue her. You, on the other hand . . ."

My mind tracked sideways. "Me?"

"Do you know how rarely the taint provides a true seer? Untrained, of course, unreliable, but those things can be fixed." The mage turned on his heel. "Take us to the galleon before the estimable captain realizes what has happened."

I fought the net as they slung me from one boat to the other, but I might as well have been clawing out of a coffin. I kept talking; it was the only thing I could do. "How did you find me?"

The mage humored me as one would a child, an obscure smile on his lips. "An agent of ours had an enlightening conversation with a dragon-trainer. It took us some time to track your history, but we quickly confirmed our right."

Their right. My stomach knotted. They had the papers signed and sealed, and no one would challenge it–maybe not even Calais.

The longship slid into common waters. I heard a cry go up from the *Narwhal* and bit my lip. My grand plan had put me right in their hands.

The minutes trickled out from under me, too fast. The net kept me hard to the bottom of the boat: I couldn't see a thing.

A coarse murmur lapped over the longship. "What in the world is that?"

"Looks like some kind of bird—"

"It's clockwork." The words were tense. "I don't like the look of that thing—"

"Don't shoot it!" A flash of darkness as someone jumped between them. "It's got something strapped to it. It could blow up . . ."

"Told you these merchant captains were soft. We kidnap his first mate and the best he can respond with is doves?"

"They're a delicacy in Pirieda, you know."

A scornful snort. "We wouldn't eat a metal one, minimus."

They didn't know Calais like I did. I rolled onto all fours and inched as close to the far side of the boat as possible.

I managed to get my head up long enough to see the clockwork bird. Even with the

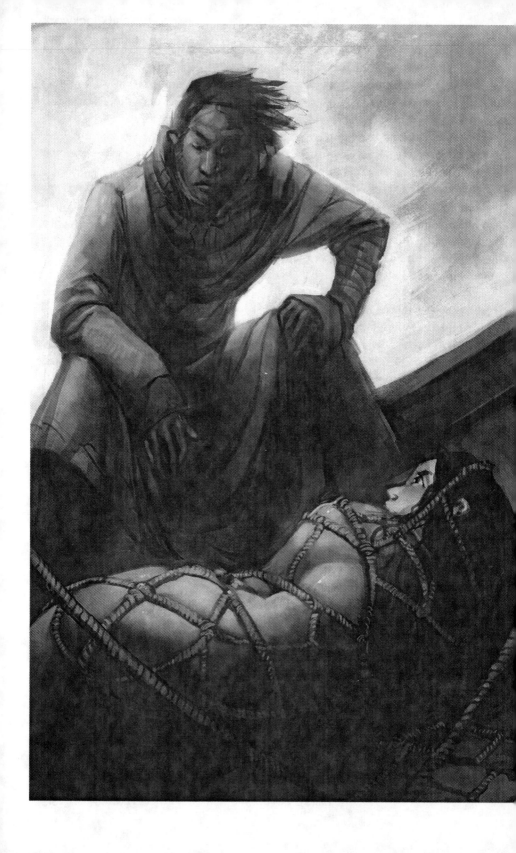

pouch strapped to its underside, it was a thing of beauty, with bright chartreuse wings and a ruby-encrusted head. Perfectly articulated wings, with the whirr of gears beneath, brought it to a graceful landing on the end of the longship.

Then it exploded.

The men threw themselves out of the way as the prow of the longship shattered. I cried out as I hit the back of the boat, then stopped as I found the tie of the net under my fingers. In the chaos, I was forgotten—

"Hold it right there, nel Karhene."

—almost.

I looked up with resignation into the face of the Shardathi mage. "What are you going to do?" I said. "You're stranded. The *Narwhal* will—"

He struck me across the face. "Your ship can't go anywhere without surrendering you. You can't win, woman. You can never win."

At first, I thought the tune was in my head. Then I realized that the ballad I was hearing was not a figment, its tones clarion and sweet. I heard a collective sigh around me, deep, slumberous. Even the mage swooned where he stood.

Though the sound encircled me, I was not moved by it. I only realized how complete it was when the mage started to snore.

In a second, I had the knot free, and once that was done, the net fell away. I wobbled to my feet, snatching for his cudgel and readying to defend myself.

The crew of the longship lay slumbering, one drifting face up in the water, others sprawled over the rocks. The *Narwhal's* rowboat approached, its passengers Calais, Arhenor and Tyse . . . Tyse who was singing with all the air in her tiny lungs, eyes closed, quiet to the world.

"Come aboard," Calais said, leaning out to offer me a hand. "Hurry."

I clasped it and swung aboard. "What did you load the bird with?"

Calais grinned, and had one word, "Coria." He gestured to the two oarsmen, and they put their backs into rowing.

When we were out of range, Arhenor laid a light hand on Tyse's shoulder. She jumped, the sound trailing off as she pulled in a breath. "Sorry we didn't use this earlier," he said, "but . . ."

But I saw it: a loss of height, a thinness, something less focused in the eyes. I shuddered with the truth of it. Every time Tyse sang, she became a little younger.

I drew a breath. "How old is—"

"She's my older sister. Every time, she forgets what she knew." His voice was quiet as Tyse curled up in his lap. "She won a civil war for them. Shardath gave us our freedom, but until I saw them net you, I thought they had reneged."

It was a loss immeasurable, and explained too well why he had been afraid. I stroked her hair as she fell to slumber, exhausted by her magics. She had brought us through—sometimes vision got the important parts right.

As we passed into the shadow of the *Narwhal*, Calais turned to me. With profound relief in his eyes, he said, "You owe me a clockwork bird."

Before I could respond, he crushed me in a hug. In the embrace were all the formalities we never said, the feelings we left to silence when words were so common.

"I'll make it up to you," I promised in his ear.

The Medusa
Chris Stout

When the storm struck our ship, I woke up to find myself alone in bed. Helena was sleeping with the captain again.

Between the crashing of thunder and waves, the flash of lightning, and my wife's infidelity I knew I would sleep no more. My stomach churned with the rolling of the ship. I needed air. I rose and tried to dress myself without flailing about the cabin like a child's spinning toy. I considered this to be no small feat. No one would ever accuse me of having been born a sailor. In truth, I hated the sea. But my father had vast acres of land in the New World, which he thought I was perfectly suited to run. And the adventure of the unknown would—we hoped—cure my wife of her wandering eye. Failing that, at least my father would no longer be burdened by the shame of a cuckolded son in his presence.

I put a tricorn hat on my head and made my way above-decks. If I could see the storm and the pounding waves, perhaps I could control the dual beasts of fear and sickness welling up inside me.

As I picked my way along the main deck I came upon the first officer. He was a tall and swarthy man, whose name had been given to me as Charlie and nothing more. The eye-patch covering what was left of his right eye was soaking wet and dropped below his eyelid. The awful scarring winked out at me with the flashes of lightning.

"Not a nice night for a stroll, Mister Percy." Charlie was shouting at the top of his lungs, but his voice came as whisper-soft through the roar of the surf.

"Is the captain on deck?"

Charlie looked away before he whisper-shouted his answer. "The captain has a bit of the stomach bug, sir."

I did not press the point further, nor did I ask if he had seen my wife wandering the ship. Maybe I would get lucky and the storm would wash her away as she stole back to our quarters.

The ship rolled again. The tang of salt-air mingled with the bile in my stomach. I reached for the rail and grabbed my middle, sure that I would empty my stomach on the spot.

"We should get you below decks, Mister Percy. Perhaps Agatha has a brew to cure what ails you."

I let the wave of nausea pass before I allowed Charlie to lead me out of the storm.

"Bad night to be on the sea," he said as we made our way down into the hold of the ship.

To me any night on the sea was a bad night, so I nodded my agreement.

"Especially in these waters." He produced a small flask and took a healthy swallow, then offered the drink to me.

"Why is that?" I took a mouthful and almost gagged. The liquid felt like fire coursing down my throat. My stomach lurched in protest.

"This is where the *Medusa* likes to hunt."

I managed again to keep my gurgling supper secure. "And what in God's name is the Medusa?"

Charlie shrugged. "An old sailor's tale. Just a myth, really."

I expected him to continue, but Charlie seemed content with the information he had already given. "So tell me the tale," I said.

"Not much to tell really. Some say she's a cursed ship, others that she's a vile sea creature. And some think she's both, changing form as it suits her. Apparently no one who's encountered her has ever survived."

"Well, then how did the tale get told?"

"Some sailors say they've seen her work. Scales stuck on bits of wreckage and that sort of thing. The First Mate on *Fearless* says he watched her destroy another ship on a clear day." The *Fearless* was the massive gunship leading our convoy of five vessels. If her crew worried about this ghostly ship. . . . "One of our cooks says he was on a ship that found some flotsam, and imbedded in the wood was a giant fang."

"Have you ever come across this *Medusa*?"

Charlie shrugged again. "Not personally. I've just heard about her. Like I said, it's an old sailor's myth. Nothing to worry yourself over." He opened a door and ushered me inside. "Here we are. And it looks like Agatha is up and about."

Agatha was old. Some called her a healer, others a midwife. Some said she was a witch. While I'm not overly superstitious, I tended to believe the last. Whatever the case, she liked me. While we were boarding the ship I caught her when she stumbled and nearly fell from the gangplank. She warmed to me immediately, and for the length of the voyage she and Charlie were the only ones I felt comfortable talking to.

She served as the ship's doctor. "Medicine Woman" was a term I'd heard some of the sailors say. Something that was popular among the natives of the New World. She was from somewhere in Eastern Europe, judging by her thick accent, but the term was appropriate enough. Her quarters were more menagerie than hospital room. All sorts of strange creatures slithered and crawled around and over the tables and beds that occupied her space. Cauldrons and pots boiled while vials and jars cooled the contents. Despite the macabre atmosphere, the place was clean and free of droppings. And truth be told, we had yet to lose a crewman or passenger to disease, something none of the other vessels could claim. We had witnessed several burials at sea from our sister ships.

Agatha greeted us with a dry cackle. "Ah, Charles! And Young Oliver with the pretty wife! What brings you to Agatha on this fine night?" Agatha was not one given to formalities or nicknames. Even though everyone—including my wife—called me by my surname, I didn't mind when Agatha used Oliver.

"The seas don't seem to agree with Mister Percy, madam. Perhaps you could provide a tonic?"

"Of course, of course. Come, both of you."

Charlie was clearly eager to get back topside. "I must beg your leave, madam. Have to see to the ship, you know."

"Nonsense. John is at the helm now." Even Captain John Howard did not warrant his rank with the witch.

"Our captain is . . ." Charlie caught himself and stole a glance my way, then looked at the floor when I caught him. "John is detained," he mumbled.

"No," Agatha purred. "My lovely Hector informs me that his visitation with Oliver's pretty young wife is concluded."

Charlie reeled in disgust. "You've let that slimy thing loose again?"

Agatha ignored his complaint. "Come. You both need protection. Tonight is a night for the *Medusa*." There was that name again. Somehow it had more gravity when voiced by Agatha.

She led us deeper into her lair. I stopped by a tub full of water. In it swam a strange looking serpent with a flattened, rudder-like tail. This was Agatha's lovely Hector. For a serpent, he really was magnificent. His scales gleamed an iridescent blue and gray. In truth, he looked more supple than slimy. Almost absently, I found myself reaching towards him.

"Watch yourself with Hector," Agatha said. "Outside of water he's as gentle as a lamb. But put him in the sea and his poison is the deadliest on earth."

I stayed my hand. Agatha gave me a curious smile and then turned away. As she did, Hector rose out of the water and nudged against my outstretched palm. I was right: he was very supple. Then he sank back into his lair. Neither of my companions noticed the strange encounter.

Agatha stopped at one of her vial-covered tables and began mixing liquids with strange crystals, powders and bits of animals. Charlie's firewater now seemed like a much better prospect. The old woman whistled. A raven fluttered across the room and perched on her shoulder, while a huge black cat slinked between her legs, hissing when it saw me staring. Agatha grabbed a tuft of fur from the cat and added it to the potion. Then she plucked several feathers from the raven, stirred the mixture with them, and pulled them back out. Charlie and I exchanged glances as she presented us each with a pair.

"Keep one in your hat and one by your heart. The raven and the lion are enemies of the serpent. The charms will offer protection if you fall into the *Medusa's* clutches."

I was grateful that we didn't have to ingest the feathers, and I'm sure Charlie shared my sentiment. So we obeyed her instructions with a flourish. The talismans gave off a strange heat, almost searing my fingers. When I put one in my breast pocket, I could feel it throbbing in time with my heartbeat.

Agatha turned back to her table and started work on a new mixture. "Now, Oliver, this one is for you. It will help you sleep the rest of the night." She turned, moved past me and reached into the tub where Hector was lazily floating. She pulled the beast from the water. Hector wound himself up her arm and settled across her shoulders. She walked back to her mixing table. Charlie took steps backwards as she passed us by. The witch picked up the jar she'd been mixing in and dribbled some of the liquid on the serpent's head. Hector responded by immediately lunging and biting down on the glass rim. I watched in fascination as rivulets of venom dribbled down the side of the jar and into the potion. The venom turned the mixture from a dark muddy brown into something more the color of strong tea. Agatha poured a bit of the potion into a glass half-full with water and then added something that smelled strangely like Charlie's rum. Still wearing the snake across her shoulders, she presented me with her concoction.

I accepted the glass. Charlie caught my eye and shook his head. "I wouldn't drink that." I shrugged in reply, took a deep breath and quaffed the potion in one long swallow. It was bitter and burned. I think I coughed, and then everything went black.

⚓

I woke up in my own bed, wondering for a moment if Charlie had put me there. I blinked the sleep out of my eyes and looked around the room. Though I couldn't see outside, I could tell from the relative quiet that the storm had subsided. I stretched mightily, feeling my muscles and tendons uncoil throughout my body. They seemed to go on forever. Perhaps I was still in that strange state between waking and sleeping. As I opened my mouth to yawn, I could taste the salt in the air, the musk of a ship full of cargo and sweat, and also the sappy sweetness of my wife's perfume. So she had returned at last.

"Dear Percy, are you all right?"

I looked over to my wife. Helena's voice was muffled, as if it came from a great distance. Her face was pale with dark, black circles under her eyes. She looked as if she hadn't slept in days. I nodded and sat up. "What is the time?"

"It's past midday. When Mister Charles carried you in, I thought you were dead. You were so pale."

I rolled my shoulders, twisted from side to side, stretched again. Remembering the strange tonic I'd drunk, I expected to feel a headache or other pains. But, as everything came back into focus, I felt good as gold. "I'm fine now, Love. I had a bit of a bug last night, is all. Agatha fixed me a cure. It certainly put my lights out, I must say."

Helena shuddered. "I don't like that old hag. She gives me the evil eye every time we pass. I wouldn't trust anything she gave me to drink."

"She's harmless, Love." Well, at least to me she was. "Her peasant potions have kept everyone on ship alive, haven't they? Maybe she's just jealous to no longer be the only woman on board." I smiled, hoping to elicit the same reaction from my wife, but as usual my jest fell flat. She looked away unhappily.

"Percy, something happened last night."

I sat up straighter. Was she actually going to admit her infidelities? Helena clutched the bed sheet like a frightened child, twisting it in her hands. "Go on," I said softly.

"We've lost sight of the convoy."

"What? How?"

"I don't know. The storm maybe. But the other ships are nowhere to be seen. And worse, there's a strange black vessel following us. Captain Howard doesn't think it means well."

I jumped out of bed. The feather in my breast pocket thumped against the beating of my heart.

The *Medusa*.

I changed my clothes. Helena protested, saying that we ought to stay out of sight below-decks, but I wasn't paying much attention. I strapped on my sword and pulled a pair of pistols from a case on my desk. Then I put the hat with the black feather on my head. Seeing it reminded me of the second in the pocket of my discarded shirt, and I retrieved that one as well, stuffing it away quickly to keep my fingers from being burned.

"Percy!"

I silenced my wife with a finger to her lips. "Stay here, Love. I'm sure everything will be fine." Then I kissed her cheek and rushed up to the main deck.

Crewmen were rushing about placing guns and securing anything loose. I made my way through the pandemonium of shouts and curses. Captain Howard stepped in front of me.

"Mister Percy, glad to see you're still with us." His voice dripped with displeasure at my presence. "Perhaps you should remain below with your wife."

I ignored his advice. "What's the situation?"

"We've lost contact with the convoy, but we seem to have picked up a new friend in their place." He nodded to the stern.

I followed his gaze. A dark mass followed in our wake, maybe two leagues off. As I peered harder at it, the mass took the form of a ship. "What colors are they flying?" I did my best to keep any tremor from my voice.

"Black," he said. "Remain topside if you must, but stay out of the way of my men." He looked over my sword and pistols. "I hope you know how to use those." Then he strode away.

I continued about the ship, stopping when I found Charlie inspecting a gun. He nodded to me, indicating that he would be but a moment. When he was satisfied, he waved me over. Like Captain Howard, he glanced at my sword and pistols as he addressed me. "I see you're ready for company."

"I suppose. Is it the *Medusa*?"

He didn't answer but motioned for me to follow him. We walked up to the captain's deck. Charlie handed me a spyglass. I put it to my eye and focused on the ship that was rapidly gaining on us. It looked normal as any other seafaring vessel, except for the black flag with the imprint of a skull that flew from its mast.

"Pirates?"

Charlie nodded. "Much preferable to the *Medusa*. Still wish we hadn't lost the convoy though. We could use *Fearless*'s guns. These chaps must have been pacing us, waiting for something to break our formation. Last night was what they'd been waiting for."

I looked through the glass again. The vessel was near enough now that I could see men swarming the deck and guns poking from the hull. "Are we a match for them?"

"We'll see."

I handed the glass back to him and brushed the hilt of my sword. Crossing blades with men seemed a much better prospect than engaging some strange sea-beast. As the son of a wealthy man, swordplay was something with which I was quite familiar.

"You staying topside, Mister Percy?"

I nodded. "I'll not be called a coward."

"Very well then. Stay close to me. Accidents can happen in these melees. We wouldn't want to make a widow of your wife, now would we?"

His gaze moved from the pirate ship to the figure of Captain Howard. He must have felt our gaze, for he turned and stared directly at me.

"No, we wouldn't want that at all."

Then we heard the first shot of cannon fire.

The cannonball sailed overhead and then slammed into the water just ahead of our vessel. "Checking for range," Charlie said. The rest of the crew watched the geyser with mute fascination, and then resumed scrambling as Captain Howard called for the men to draw muskets. I moved to join them, but Charlie caught me by the arm. "Muskets aren't much use here. After the cannonade they'll close fast, and then you'll be better off with your pistols and sword."

I nodded. "What should we do then?"

"Keep our heads low. Follow me."

We hurried back down to the deck. One of our own guns fired a ranging shot. Before the echo had died away there was a muffled roar as the pirate vessel unleashed a full volley. "Down!" Charlie yelled, but I was ahead of him and hugged the wood of the deck.

We heard a great crash and explosion. I glanced up to check the damage. One of the masts was splintered and a ball had crashed through the wheelhouse, crushing the helmsman.

"Nothing we can do here," Charlie said. "We'll move to the far side of the ship and wait out the barrage. They're going to try and cripple us, but if they sink us too soon then it's been a wasted effort for them. I'll wager the next rounds will be grape, so we should be safe as long as we have cover." As we moved, I felt our ship turning, preparing to unleash a full broadside on the pirate vessel. Our gunners wouldn't be worried about sinking the target too soon. They'd fire full round shot until the enemy was upon us.

We knelt on the starboard side of our ship, finding what cover we could in the stern. Our guns and those of the pirate ship fired at regular intervals. The shrieks of those shredded by grapeshot punctuated the roar of exploding powder and splintering wood. Crewmen armed with muskets rushed onto the deck. Coming towards us from their midst was the old witch Agatha.

"You both still have your feathers."

I nodded.

"You should go back below," Charlie said. "The pirates will be upon us soon."

From some hidden pocket, Agatha pulled a pair of vials. They had strange stoppers, with what looked like a hook protruding from the side. "Each of you, take one. Use these against your human adversaries. Pull the hook out to ignite a fire which even water cannot quench. Throw them at the feet of your enemy." She pressed a vial into each of our hands then disappeared as quickly as she had come.

I looked to Charlie. The pop of musket fire now punctuated the boom of cannons. "A fire that can't be quenched by water? Is that possible?"

"It was for the Greeks." He pocketed the vial and drew his pistol. "They're close now. God be with you."

The massive bulk of the pirate vessel loomed beside us. Both ships let off simultaneous broadsides into each other's bellies. The explosion lifted me from my feet. I landed on my back. The world went still for a few blessed seconds before hell came to our ship.

Using ropes, ladders, planks and anything that would bring them to us, the pirates swarmed over the side of our ship. Charlie charged into their midst. I saw him fire his pistol, draw his sword and hack into the onslaught of invaders. Then he was lost.

I took aim with my pistol, fired and was satisfied to see a pirate's head blossom red under the impact of my shot. Charging them looked to be suicide, so I moved towards the bow of our vessel, hoping to catch them in their flank. As I ran I reloaded my pistol, opting to keep my second as a reserve until the last possible moment. Shots dogged my heels and a group of the attackers rushed in pursuit.

The pirates were swarthy men: bearded, braided and dealing murder to the unfortunates who crossed their paths. But I did not despair. As soon as my pistol was loaded I put a shot between one of those pairs of hateful eyes and then drew my blade to deal with the rest. I knew the duels would not be classically fought—in truth, such choreographed engagements bored me—but my training served me well, giving me a quickness of foot far superior to their brutish means. My blade never touched one of theirs, and with a series of slashes and thrusts I gutted one and impaled two. The gutted man bled out quickly. I pithed the others with thrusts where their skulls met their spines.

Similar battles played out over the length and breadth of the ship. Fear should have consumed me, but I felt alive and vigorous in such a manner as I had never before experienced. The duels I'd fought in my youth were simple, almost bloodless affairs. None had been fatal. But this panorama of life and death, and me dealing out the latter, was thoroughly intoxicating. Gunpowder, sweat and blood mixed with the salt air. I drew it all in like a tonic.

I spied Captain Howard in distress, grimly fighting off three of the enemy brutes. Blood flowed freely from a gash along his cheek. I drew my remaining pistol and gunned one of the pirates down. His head erupted in a fountain of gore, splashing his companions and Captain Howard. I charged them with a great battle cry. I contented myself to stab one, but the other unfortunate wretch lost his head to a devastating cut from my blade. Captain Howard cowered before me in a state of fearful shock. Oh, if my lovely Helena could only see her bold champion now!

But there was no time to enjoy any of my victories. A group of at least a half-dozen killers bore down upon us. I feared even my own swift blade would not withstand the onslaught, but then I remembered Agatha's strange device. I stuck my sword into the deck and pulled the vial from my pocket. As per her instructions, I pulled the hook from the stopper. I saw a flash, such as a flint might produce, as the hook pulled free with a rasp. Then I threw the container at the oncoming marauders.

I grabbed my sword. For a moment I thought the strange weapon had failed, but then I saw a rush of flames that immediately reached for the pirates. Their sashes and kerchiefs ignited, and soon their clothes were aflame. The men shrieked and flailed as they roasted alive. Some jumped overboard. The others fell into smoldering heaps. The flames licked their bones.

I heard a shouted curse behind me. I turned and saw it came from Captain Howard. "By God, you are a madman!" He pointed his sword at my chest. "Stay back from me!"

I considered Charlie's words about accidents happening, and thought how easy it would be to dispatch the rival who was intent on stealing away my wife. But before I could decide his fate, there was a monstrous crash, the splintering of a thousand timbers. Captain Howard and I turned from our confrontation and beheld a behemoth vessel ripping into the side of the pirate ship.

The new ship was all black. It bore no colors, no sails, and no crew. It must have been timber—for what ship is not made of wood? But in the light and smoke, its hull gleamed and flashed, glistening like the scales of some great beast. Its bowsprit was a mighty serpent's head with a forked tongue lashing out. A tremor rushed up my body and I understood what fear truly meant. The *Medusa* was upon us.

The battle died away as pirate and crewman alike gaped at the spectacle unfolding before us. Several of the attackers had sensed the tide turning against them and already retreated to their ship. Those that were still aboard our own were torn between surrendering to our mercies and fighting to save their comrades and vessel. But the *Medusa* had torn into the pirate ship with such force that it was clear the latter was doomed. Then the screaming began.

I could see the pirates flailing madly about, hacking and shooting at their own torn decks. Captain Howard flew into action, gathering our own survivors in a mad rush to disengage from the other two ships. Pirate and crewman worked side-by-side to put distance between us and their vessel. I, too, sheathed my blade and went to help drop a plank into the sea. As I struggled with the wood, I saw a serpent, the likes of which I had never before beheld, and could scarce believe a creature of such girth and length was even possible. It wound its way around the plank, creeping inexorably towards our ship, but then the wood dropped away and crashed into the sea, taking the monster with it. Free at last, we limped away, leaving the pirate ship and its hapless crew to be devoured by the *Medusa*.

When it finished with the slaughter, the *Medusa* turned her bow toward us. As crippled as our own vessel was, it wouldn't be long before we were overtaken. Captain Howard gave the command to load the cannons.

"It won't stop her!"

The few crewmen who were alive to heed the order turned to see Agatha striding towards them.

Captain Howard threw his tricorn to the deck. "Well then what would you suggest we do?"

"Feed her your dead."

"Never! These were good Christian men who gave their lives to protect us today."

"Then their deaths were in vain. Feed her, or become food yourself."

The choice was straightforward enough. Not waiting for the captain to issue any such order, the crew and I reached for the nearest corpses, intending to heave them overboard.

"Wait!" Howard said. We paused; for the tone of his voice indicated that he did not mean to oppose our efforts. "Not like that. If we send them out piecemeal she might pass them by. Load the bodies into the lifeboats."

For once the captain made sense, and we adjusted our labor accordingly. The pirates still on board threw in with the crew, perhaps hoping for mercy should we escape, or preferring the end of a rope to being devoured by a monster. Either way, we sacrificed their comrades first, and in a few moments the first boat full of pirate dead went over the side. We posted a lookout to inform us of the *Medusa's* progress, and cheered when he announced that she had slowed to retrieve our offering. Another boatload went over the side. We emptied the ship of the dead pirates and then began the grim task of bidding farewell to our own fallen comrades. It was during this that I came across Charlie's body.

He'd died hard. His sword-hand was missing, there were over a dozen stab wounds to his torso, and someone had seen fit to finish him off with a pistol shot through his good eye. His patch, however, remained pristine. I mourned for him briefly and then set him in the last of the boats. "Goodbye, my friend."

I heard the snap of a pistol being cocked by my ear. "You can go with him."

I tuned my head. More weapons announced their presence. Captain Howard held a pistol to my face, backed by half-a-dozen crewmen. "Take his sword and pistol," he said. One of the crewmen hastened to obey. I offered no resistance. "Now, get in the boat."

"Captain, what is the meaning of this?"

In answer to my query he struck me hard on the side of my head. The blow pushed me to my knees. "I saw the murder you intended for me. The penalty for mutiny is death, and I see no reason why your execution shouldn't serve a higher purpose."

Two of the crewmen heaved me to my feet and dragged me to the boat full of corpses. As my vision cleared, I saw Agatha come up, ready to protest on my behalf. I shook my head. No sense the both of us being murdered. She kept her peace but whistled softly. Her great black cat darted forward and leapt in the boat with me. There was no room for us to sit, so I held the beast in my arms. She hissed at me, but made no move to claw her way free. The crew lowered us over the side of the ship.

I looked up and saw Helena had joined Captain Howard. He put one arm across her shoulders. "You never deserved her, Mister Percy! Adieu!" He waved a mock salute and escorted her away.

My grisly little craft hit the water with a thump and drifted away in the wake of our ship. Behind me, the *Medusa* overtook another of the boats. I stroked the cat in my arms and watched the sinister vessel work her way through the offerings of the dead.

———— ⚓ ————

Another lifeboat disappeared. I turned for a last look at my own ship. It had put some distance between it and the *Medusa*. The decoys seemed to be working, for now anyway. But after my own craft was consumed there was nothing standing between the ship and the monster. I didn't think my old vessel would be able to escape, but for the time being I had other concerns.

The cat jumped from my arms and onto a stack of bodies. She arched her back, hissing at the water behind us. Rippling tendrils snaked towards us from the demon ship. The devil take Captain Howard for not leaving me so much as a dagger to defend myself! That thought spurred me into action. Perhaps one of the crewmen still had an unused weapon tucked away.

The body on top was Charlie. Not wanting to desecrate him further, I shifted him aside and dug deeper. The next corpse was empty, so I threw it over the side. The third body rewarded me with a boot knife and a belt dagger. To thank the chap for his troubles I dumped him overboard as well. I looked up at the sound of splashing and my stomach lurched when I saw some hideous beast coil around the first body and drag it underwater. The second vanished in similar fashion.

A serpent slithered aboard.

This creature was smaller than I thought it would be. It reared up and hissed at me, baring a set of fangs that dripped with some vile ooze. The cat leapt upon it, tearing the beast's head with a swipe of her claws. A second serpent came aboard.

I didn't wait to be introduced. With a slash of the belt dagger I lopped its head off. The cat engaged another serpent, and then I watched as a mighty coil reached up and plucked one of the bodies out of the boat. By now the water was churning with creatures. I slashed at scales and kicked at mouths. Another body splashed overboard. I impaled a beast that I took to be an asp, then let out a wail of despair as I saw a creature wrap itself around Charlie's body. Instead of dragging him overboard, the serpent reared back and flopped in the bottom of the boat. Its belly sizzled, and I remembered the feather in Charlie's pocket.

I threw the injured creature into the sea. The cat battled a mighty serpent, and yet another body pulled away from our craft. Just as the cat slew her foe, she was crushed by the coils of a huge monster that wrapped around her and pulled her down into the depths. I slashed at it, then jumped to avoid the bite of a hissing viper. I crushed the wretch underfoot, impaled another with the boot knife, and lost my dagger in the scales of a third beast. Without any other weapon at hand, I reached into my pocket and produced the enchanted feather. I pulled the second one from my hat then waved the talismans at the coiling snakes, shouting at the top of my lungs.

The charms worked. The beasts retreated. Those that tried to lunge found themselves seared where the feathers struck them. The roiling around the boat ceased, and the ripples made their way back to the *Medusa*. The demon ship was close. I was alone in the boat, with only Charlie's body for company.

I went to work.

I figured that I would need the feather more than my dead companion, so I patted his pockets for the talisman. My search also yielded the strange flaming device concocted by Agatha. I pocketed that as well as his charm. I could find no other weapons borne by my friend, so I gave him an unceremonious burial at sea.

The boat was slick with blood. That combined with the waves made for treacherous footing, so it was with difficulty that I kicked one of the benches apart. My work paid off, though, for I had two pointed shafts of wood that would do nicely as stakes. I tucked the weapons into my belt and splintered another bench. And that was all I could do, for by then the *Medusa* was upon me.

⚓

The demon ship stank of rot and decay. I still saw no sign of a crew, but a rope lowered down to my craft. I shuddered at the sight, for the line was not made of hemp. Rather it consisted of the bodies of dead serpents tied together. Seeing no other course of action open to me, I reached out in disgust, grabbed the leathery rope and pulled myself hand-over-hand to the deck above.

At the top, I stepped over the rail onto a roiling mass of slithering bodies. I had my feathers in the cuffs of my shirt and waved my hands at the beasts. They cleared away from me. I pulled two of the stakes from my belt and walked towards what I perceived to be the captain's quarters. The serpents parted before me, only to close again in my wake. I stopped when I saw a human shape emerge from the depths of the ship.

The serpents parted for this new figure, which was clad in a hooded black cloak, and soon there was an open path between the two of us. Clearly I was about to meet the captain of the ship, judging by the deference of the creatures. I was shocked to see that the figure was that of a woman.

Given the name of the ship, I shouldn't have been. But if this lady was a gorgon, then she was one who had resisted Athena's wrath. She was more beautiful than any creature I'd ever laid eyes upon. My hands trembled, and the stakes clattered uselessly to the deck. Hissing beasts lashed out and pulled them away. The woman stopped to regard me through infinitely black eyes. Dark coils of hair cascaded down her shoulders. She was dressed all in black: ruffled shirt, breeches, and high boots. She took another few steps forward. We stood face to face. I stared at her shimmering hair, which moved of its own accord. Those cascading locks writhed in a gentle rhythm, millions of tiny serpents moving back and forth across her shoulders. The woman opened her mouth as if to speak, but instead, a long, forked tongue issued forth, flicking against my cheek.

The serpent-lady pulled her tongue back in and smiled. "You taste like one of us," she said. Her voice was low and dry.

I stood rooted to my place. "My lady," I said, "how can I be like you? I am a man, whereas you—beautiful though you may be—are some strange creature."

She laughed. "Yes, I am. And I've been looking for one like you for years now. One who would complete me."

I couldn't imagine what she meant by her words. I took a step back, but then a heavy coil wrapped around my ankle, holding me fast. I swiped and it drew back, spitting venom as my feather burned its scales.

The lady hissed. The sound chilled me to the bones, but it was not meant for me. The mass of serpents forming at my feet pulled back. She moved another step closer. "You have no need of these weapons. The creatures will do you no harm."

I held my hands up before me. "Stay back, you monster!"

The lady laughed again. "I'm surprised these talismans haven't burned you. You must still be more of a man than I thought. But it matters not. You are here now. Come to me, so I can finish your transformation!" She reached out and pulled the feathers from my cuffs. They sizzled in her fingers. She winced in discomfort, but whatever

magic she possessed overwhelmed the charms, and they crumbled into ash and dust. "There," she said, "nothing can keep us apart now." And she reached for me with arms that stretched and wrapped around my torso.

I thrashed against her coils, but she drew me close to her bosom. I could barely breathe under the crushing weight that enveloped me. But my arms were still free, and before my body was completely wrapped I pulled the vial of fire from my pocket and waved it in front of the serpent-woman's face. Her coils stopped their envelopment. She hissed in anger, and this time the deathly sound was meant for me alone. "I could crush you into pieces!"

I grabbed for the hook protruding from the stopper of the vial. "You do, and we'll both burn."

We stood there for several long moments in our strange embrace. Her coils held fast, but did not press any deeper into me.

"I am not trying to destroy you," she said at last.

"What do you wish of me then?"

"For you to be my partner. My companion. My husband, if you will."

"I'm sorry to disappoint, my lady, but I am already married."

She threw her head back and laughed, then regarded me once more with those endless eyes. "What should we do about that then?"

My heart raced, but not from fear. As strange as she was, the beauty she possessed was intoxicating and even more powerful than the coils she had wrapped around me. A faint musky scent drifted in the air, sweeping away the stench of rot.

"Search inside yourself. You are more like me than you can possibly imagine. I can feel a serpent writhing inside you, yearning to be unleashed. He protects you more than those charms ever could."

"I don't know what you're talking about."

"Watch," she said, and indicated an asp that crawled up my body and down my arm. She nodded to the beast. Before I could protest, it sank its fangs into my flesh.

I knew I was done for. I almost armed my weapon, but the woman shook her head. For some strange reason, I obeyed. The asp withdrew and joined its fellows on the deck. I regarded the two small holes made by its fangs. They bled a bit, but other than that I could feel no poison burning my veins. The bite should have been fatal within a few moments, but as they passed I grew more certain that I was immune. I stared at my captor in wonder.

"You see?" she said. "You are one of us. You can complete me, if you allow yourself to." Her coils slipped from my waist and pulled themselves back into arms that hung innocently at her sides. I made no move to retreat.

"What must I do now?" I asked with a tremor in my voice.

"Kiss me."

I hesitated but a moment. Then I tossed the vial over the side of the ship and took the strange woman in my arms. Our lips met, and I felt her fangs pierce the skin of my mouth. This time the venom did burn, but it was a welcome, warming sensation, and I knew I was home at last.

———⚓———

Before we could fully enjoy our union, there was one last separation I had to complete. My serpent-lady understood. As night fell, she set me in my small boat and sent me back to Captain Howard's crippled ship. Then her vessel cloaked itself in the mist and disappeared from sight.

Her venom coursed through me. I could feel myself changing with every wave that pushed me closer to the lanterns. I called out as I pulled alongside the ship. My voice was raspy but still distinct. Someone threw down a rope, and I secured my craft. Netting dropped down to me, and a pair of crewmen helped pull me aboard. They both stared in shock.

"What should we do with him?" one asked. His voice sounded faint and far away.

"The captain's occupied with other affairs. Let's bring him to Agatha. He might be able to tell us how to defeat that beast the *Medusa*."

The other agreed, and together they helped me skirt my way around wreckage and debris down to Agatha's quarters. I could feel the sinew and muscle beneath their skin, and my stomach churned in hunger. The queerness of wanting to feast upon them instead of a hearty roast nearly caused me to faint. Someday this sensation would seem natural, and that thought restored my senses.

The two crewmen dropped me in front of the witch and retreated back to the main deck. Agatha looked me over in wonder, then shrieked in fear.

I saw her cry, but did not hear it in the traditional sense. I flicked my tongue out and tasted the air. This more than made up for lack of sound. I could discern between her, her serpents, rats and birds. I could even tell which parts of her body were the warmest and most life-giving. But I had no desire to feed on her either.

I stood shakily and smiled as best I could. She seemed to understand that I meant no harm and reached out to touch my face. I gave her a gentle flick of my tongue. She smiled in amazement at me. "I should have known," she said.

Her words came as vibrations I felt low in my chest. I could tell what they meant, and I nodded in reply. She motioned for me to follow and led me to the vat where Hector swam in lazy circles. "Take him," she said. "He belongs with you." I slid my fingers into the water.

I expected Hector to lunge for me. Instead, he calmly slipped around my wrist and up my forearm. He wrapped around my neck and brought his face up to mine. Agatha drew beside me. "It is almost finished," she said. "But he will need water to be a weapon. Take him into your mouth."

I couldn't imagine there would be room, but I opened my mouth nonetheless. Hector pushed his way inside. I opened wider, distending my jaw until he had wrapped himself inside. The sensation was queer beyond anything I'd ever felt, and grew even more so when I felt his tail drop down my gullet, giving him more room to maneuver. When he was seated to his comfort, I closed my mouth around him.

Agatha touched my cheek. "Is it bad over on that ship?"

I shook my head. The movement caused Hector's tail to flap gently within my chest. The old witch smiled. "Perhaps someday I will join you then. Now go to those you seek. They are where you expect them to be." Agatha patted my cheek affectionately, then drew away into the depths of her chambers. I saw her no more.

———————⚓———————

The ship was still. Exhausted crewmen lay draped about the deck. Agatha may have helped them to their slumber with some strange charm cast over the ship. But they lived still, and in the morning would be able to sail away.

I crept soundlessly across the deck. The dull colors of the world had been replaced by vibrant visions of heat and cold. It was far more beautiful than my old sense of vision had ever been. Hector shifted in my mouth, drawing his tail up in anticipation, anxious to be unleashed. "Patience my friend," I thought. Somehow I know he heard me.

I slipped down a flight of stairs. At the bottom, a crewman blocked the way to Captain Howard's quarters. He bolted upright when he saw me and raised a pistol. "Halt where you are!"

I raised my arms. Saliva pooled around my strange friend. It was almost time. The crewman cocked his weapon. I opened my mouth.

Hector burst forth as if he had been launched from a cannon and went straight for the crewman's neck. The poor wretch never stood a chance. He dropped his weapon in his haste to pry the beast loose, but his defense came far too late. The poison worked quickly. He slumped to the deck and Hector curled around his body.

"Wait here for me," I hissed. I stepped over the body and pushed open the door to Captain Howard's room.

Captain Howard and Helena lay naked, wrapped in each other's arms. I flicked my tongue out. The heat from their bodies was low, indicating that they were fast asleep. I moved to the side of their bed. If they wished to be joined forever, then I would help them in their union. I moved quickly, grabbing them both. My arms grew like tentacles and doubled around the sleeping couple. I flexed my muscles in a slow, methodical constriction.

They woke with a start and thrashed in shock against me. But I held fast. I looped a coil around Captain Howard's neck and swiftly crushed it. Helena tried to scream, but my weight against her lungs allowed only a raspy cough to escape. And it was breath that she could ill afford to lose. Her eyes bulged and she clawed at me with one free hand. I dropped the captain's useless body to the bed and used my free appendage to hold my dear wife fast. Her mouth opened and closed; whether she was beseeching me for mercy or cursing me I couldn't tell. Neither affected the final outcome. Her eyes rolled up in her head. Her swollen tongue lolled out of her mouth. She shuddered, and then was still. I pulled my arms back to my side and flicked my tongue out. Her body cooled quickly without life's blood flowing through it.

I slipped back through the door. Hector unwrapped himself from his kill. Together we went up the stairs and across the deck. I aimed to return to my boat, but Hector hissed and I knew he was saying: "Follow me. I will guide your way." He slid up and over the railing. Without hesitation I followed him into the black waters of the sea. It should have been a shock, but now the water felt natural and comforting. I flicked my tongue out once more, sensing the movement of my friend up ahead. He waited for me to draw close. Then we swam together easily, gliding through the water into the mist. The ship was close ahead. My lady, the Medusa, awaited me there, and I was anxious to return to her embrace.

The Islands of Hope
Heidi Ruby Miller

(W)here did he come from?" Finn said, pulling at the knots in his peppered beard. "Men just don't appear on a ship in the middle of the ocean."

Julian stared up at the crow's nest of the *Ixchel*. "His name's Kami. He came with the ship." He wiped his nose on his wet sleeve. "Or so says the captain."

"Over a month at sea and three weeks adrift in the Horse Latitudes, with barely a half ration each to last us until Sunday," Vernor said. "And yesterday another mouth appears on board?"

"Just where has this Chinaman been hiding since we left York Island?" Finn said.

Julian would give his left foot just so his right one could touch York Island again. With all its sabal palms and white sand. He never paid it much mind except as one half of the tobacco run to St. Clair. That run was never meant to take them so far north into these windless seas.

"He's been in the captain's cabin, I'll wager. Wearing frilly things and bending over the captain's chair." Vernor's raspy laugh and exaggerated hip thrusts pulled Kami's attention from his spot high on the mast.

Julian's old spot.

"Quiet. The captain won't take kindly to gossip," Julian said. "And Kami's no Chinaman. He's from islands farther out."

"I don't care where he's from. He's not eating any more of my share." Finn pulled a small knife from a sheath around his bulging waist. "I'll cut off that pretty black braid with the rest of his head."

"Put that away before you start a panic." Julian glanced around deck for prying eyes.

"Always the captain's lap dog. Maybe it's you who's bending over that chair."

"I'll bet he does at that." Vernor's smile revealed his three remaining teeth.

"Just watch yourselves." The small threat held enough weight to make Finn sheathe his knife and walk away.

Julian passed below deck to the captain's door. The smell of incense meant there'd be no meeting with the captain today, but Julian knocked anyway.

Shuffling filtered from under the weathered teak, but no other response followed.

Worthless. Knew you would be. Your uncle knew it too. Why he gave you the York Island run.

Julian pounded a second time, frustrating memories strengthening his blows. The *Ixchel* should have been his, but the fleet owner chose his incompetent nephew at the last minute. Julian suspected the man needed to flee York Island in a hurry, but never passed that along to the crew.

"Captain. I need to talk to you."

Glass shattered against the inside of the door.

"Two more islands gone! You hear me? Two more!"

"Fine," Julian yelled. "I'll just let them mutiny."

He shouldered his way to the galley to be sure the rations were distributed fairly. The captain's job, except the captain wasn't quite right any more. Not since those five days in the Yucatan when the *Ixchel* made her maiden voyage.

"He should have stuck with his merchant run. Pirating's not in his blood. Doesn't have the stomach for it." Julian spit.

Yet I followed him for the promise of my own ship.

Hungry crew met him, their stomachs grumbling louder than their complaints. A squabble broke out among three nearest Julian. One crewman shoved another onto the rations table. The downed man pulled a rusty dagger. Encouraging shouts reached deafening heights in the small area.

Julian cocked his pistol in the man's ear. "Back of the line for you! All three of you!"

To the rest of the crew he yelled, "Any more problems and no one eats." A little risky and impulsive, especially with this half-starved lot, but some type of authority had to be maintained in the captain's absence.

Each day the men pushed a little further. Each day they took longer to back down. One day they wouldn't at all, especially if they found out Julian had been holding back food for the captain and Kami.

He could let them starve, but even a rattled captain and a stowaway deserved to eat. And there was something about Kami, something that stirred a kinship in Julian.

Day and night in the crow's nest. Reminds me of me.

Julian shoved a sack with two rations of pickled beets and jerky into his coat. He jiggled the iron key in the galley's lock until it clicked. The lock was the captain's last sane order before he holed up in his cabin.

Just before Kami came.

Back on deck, the calm of a breezeless night renewed Julian's dread. A gibbous moon shone on a glass sea. The water looked like dark ice or obsidian, its surface so smooth and flawless. So dead.

Julian chanced a look up at the crow's nest. Kami wasn't there. Fingers of apprehension crawled up Julian's spine. He pictured an albatross flying away just before disaster struck.

Probably just with the captain's all. Nothing to worry about.

At least Julian would have his spot back for a bit. He grasped the rope ladder. It felt good to stretch his arms and legs, to rise above the blackness of the ship.

"You haven't been up here in a while."

The words stopped Julian at the top. Kami, speaking English and with a Derbyshire accent.

"You been watching me?" Julian said.

"Like you've been watching me." Kami sat cross-legged, a difficult feat in the confined wooden tub.

Julian held tight to the rope ladder. "Everyone's been watching you, seeing as how you just showed up and all."

Kami's black robe reflected the moon a thousand times over in all its folds and crinkles. He looked fresh and clean with gleaming white skin, the only one around the ship who did.

"You used to talk to the mast all the time. Now you don't." Kami never looked at Julian.

"You make me sound drunk or not right in the head." *Like the captain.* "I just talk out loud, to the wind, to the heavens, maybe." Julian's tongue became heavy and thick in his mouth. "Wait . . . how do you know that?"

"I've heard you. You like it up here because it reminds you of climbing trees during your childhood in Derbyshire. No sea there, just daydreams of one."

How many others had heard Julian's lonely ramblings? Could be why his authority waned recently. As though that lot cared about anything but food and fresh water right now.

"When the time comes, I'll take you to my home, my islands," Kami said, "if you wish. You won't be able to leave until the builders come for you, though. Like they came for me."

Goose bumps raised on Julian's arms.

"Sorry, mate, I'll not be going anywhere with you." He scampered down the ladder on trembling limbs, still carrying the rations.

———————⚓———————

Julian twisted in his hammock to get a better position, not that sleep would come anyway.

A scrape in the hallway made him hold his breath.

"Stupid. Be quiet." Finn's voice. "Do you want to wake the whole damn ship?"

"What if someone finds out?" Vernor's raspy baritone.

"We chuck the body overboard and no one's the wiser. And we'll have one less mouth around here."

"When?"

Finn's reply was lost as the two men moved away.

Julian grabbed his pistol and crept into the hallway. Empty. He headed to the captain's cabin. Smoke drifted from under the door. Banging got no response. Julian fumbled with the ring of keys he carried on him at all times.

I've respected your privacy, but it's time you did something.

The lock clicked and Julian shoved the captain's door open. Sweet smoke fogged the small cabin. In the middle of the floor sat the captain, his clothes ripped and soiled and hanging from his gaunt frame like the rags they used to swab the deck. A hodge podge of containers encircled him, a silver pitcher from Taxco, a jeweled goblet from England, several carved wooden bowls from St. Clair, all shoved full of burning incense.

"Captain."

The man sitting on the floor showed no signs of noticing his mate. He smacked his hand to his forehead repeatedly, then studied his palm as though divining his fortune.

I'll save you the trouble. It's bad.

Julian crouched beside him and coughed in the smoky haze. "Captain. It's Finn and Vernor—"

"Do you smell it?" the captain said.

"What?"

"The copal. The incense. It protects me." The captain grabbed a bowl, breathed deeply, then offered it to Julian.

He was further gone than Julian had imagined.

"Captain! Finn and Vernor are going to kill Kami. I don't know when, but soon."

"Kill Kami?" The captain laughed and offered the copal again. When Julian refused, the captain hurled the bowl across the cabin, spreading ash and smoldering incense over the wooden floor. "Ha! Can't kill Kami. We're the ones who'll be dead soon."

The captain shoved his bearded face close to Julian's. His breath smelled sweet like the copal. "When Kami comes, Death waits. That's what they told me."

"They who?"

The captain crawled past Julian and pulled himself up to his chart table. "Mayan shamans. They promised me the copal would keep Kami away from the *Ixchel*. Said the sap's sweetness would hide me from the builders."

Julian grew cold at the name. "Builders. You're talking nonsense." He made for the door.

Superstitious bastard. Julian would handle Finn and Vernor on his own. Something struck his shoulder from behind. The silver pitcher fell to the floor at his feet. He spun, ready to deflect any other objects.

"See this?" The captain stood behind him, stabbing a finger at a chart.

Julian took it and scanned the pale parchment. A lay out of their course snaked in black across the chart to open sea. Someone had scrawled *The Islands of Hope* at the line's end.

"What are these islands?" Julian said.

"They're the Islands of Hope. Kami's home."

"Are they nearby?" Julian hadn't heard of them before, but new islands were being discovered and added to the charts every year.

"Hope is always near." The captain flopped in his chair. "But it fades. Like the islands. When we first set sail, there were thirty. Now. . ."

Julian ran his hands over the smooth paper, trying to understand the captain's ravings. "There's only five here."

While Julian watched, another one faded until disappearing completely. He tossed the chart away from himself.

"It's coming," the captain said.

"What's com—"

The captain held his revolver to his head and pulled the trigger.

Julian jumped back as the body toppled out of the chair. His hands shook as he pushed the captain to his back. Half of his head decorated the wooden bed frame.

A sudden shift in the ship sent Julian sliding across the cabin. He slammed into the far wall, dislodging a candle sconce. The captain's body rolled toward him. He shoved his foot out to stop it from crashing into him.

Even then his gaze fell upon the chart, resting near his other foot. One island remained. And its edges were fading.

Shouts from the deck above charged his fear-numbed limbs.

A howling wind swept down the stairs. Wind!

Salt stung Julian's eyes as he shoved against the torrent of rain and sea spray on deck. Men shouted to one another to secure lines, or grappled with loose objects sliding along the teak surface.

A giant wave washed up on starboard. On its way back to the sea, it took four men with it. The winds battered the ship with a ferocity pent up after three weeks of waiting.

Julian put his weight into controlling the flapping mainsail. A gust jerked the rope from his burning hands. A piece of the rigging crashed to the deck, its pulley punching through to the floor below. Another pulley felled Finn.

Julian shielded his eyes and looked up in anticipation of more debris.

Kami looked down at him from the crow's nest. In the lightning, Julian glimpsed Kami's face, white and smiling . . . with hope.

"Take me." The thrashing ocean drowned Julian's words. "Take me!"

In the next lightning flash, Kami stood beside him.

"I'll wait for the builders," Julian yelled. "Please."

Kami placed a hand upon the mast. It sunk into the wood, as did his legs and chest, until his entire body melded into the mast. Lightning speared across the sky. With a thunderous crack, it struck the mast and split it down the middle. The half nearest Julian separated from the ship and toppled into the sea.

Julian dove in after it.

———————⚓———————

Sand coated the right side of Julian's face and body. He pushed to a sitting position and vomited up salt water and a green, slimy bile. It left a syrupy taste in his mouth.

Julian took in his surroundings, wondering where he was and how he got there. The sand on the beach reflected a blinding sun. It stretched for miles in either direction, framed by a forest. Then he remembered.

The storm. The sea. *The mast.*

"Kami!"

Julian struggled to his feet and shouted for Kami in every direction. His gaze rested on the forest. Something looked off about it, as though it were . . . fake. He thought he might wretch again when he realized the problem. Perfect rows of tall, straight trees, spaced exactly twenty feet apart. All types, from hickory to coconut to balsam firs.

A balsam fir. Here.

He staggered to the nearest pine and stroked its needles with a tentative finger. Its waxy softness sent chills through him.

"The Island of Hope. Kami's island."

Julian ran from the trees until his feet soaked in the calm sea. The effort had him heaving. What had he done? Made a pact with the devil himself?

You're still alive. Act like you want to live.

He breathed deeply and closed his eyes, secretly wishing once he opened them the nursery would be gone. Nursery? Thoughts of harvesting and cutting filled his mind. They soothed him, allowed him to think more clearly.

The fear he felt for the trees subsided. If he opened himself to them he could almost feel them, an awkward kinship.

Only friends I got since Kami. . . .

Julian allowed a distorted memory of Kami to flash into his mind. When Kami merged with the mast just before the lightning struck. Then it was gone, banished until a time he might better understand.

He flopped down at the edge of the nursery by an elm sapling.

———⚓———

Julian was content to sit, for hours, for days. His skin grew dark and scabby. He wasn't surprised when his feet disappeared into the sand, his toes spreading roots through the ground.

On cloudy days he became hungrier than when the sun shone brightly.

He felt the touch of his neighbor's roots after a few months, massing around his ankles and traveling up through his calves. After a few years, he stood as tall as the elm.

Then one day billowing sails appeared on the horizon. Four ships arrived; the builders had finally come.

Julian rejoiced at the first buzzing of their saw blades. As they harvested him, they told him how he would be going back to sea. And this time he'd have his own ship.

The Sound from the Deep
Jack MacKenzie

Sirtago's broadly muscled back stretched taut as he thrust his head over the side and heaved. Poet winced. He'd felt like that for the first couple of hours after they'd set sail but somehow he'd found an accommodation with the rolling deck. Sirtago hadn't. As was his habit, the large man chose to fight rather than to succumb, and he'd spent two days in abject misery.

Sirtago finished heaving his guts into the sea and lifted his head, giving Poet an unobstructed view of the scarred side of his face. An involuntary shudder ran through him at the sight of the affliction. They'd known each other since they were boys but the hideous visage and long, misshapen tooth that thrust out from between his lips like some kind of tusk still filled Poet with fear and dread.

Sirtago turned, showing him the smoother side of his features. That side of his face was handsome in its way, but now it looked drawn and pale. "Gwut curse this rolling ocean," he said.

Poet shook his head. "Can you never learn your pantheon? Gwut is only the allfather on the land. *Ciesfor* is Lord of the Ocean."

"Piss on Ciesfor," Sirtago said, sitting heavily on the deck, his back against the rail. His hand went to his sword, as if he would draw it out and fight what was causing him so much woe. Instead he coughed and slumped back.

Poet sat beside him, adjusting his ever-present twin daggers. "We're halfway through the passage. We'll be in Bradex in another couple of days . . ."

"Two more days?" Sirtago groaned.

". . . then we'll be in Kandra, the Golden City. There should be plenty of work there for two such as us, eh?"

Sirtago nodded and his one eye took on a dreamy, far away look. "And women," he said, managing a small smile. "And ale houses and . . ."

Poet could see that the thought of an ale house and the victuals that Sirtago usually partook of in such places had brought on another bout of his ocean malady. Poet thought that his friend would heave again, but Sirtago gained control and blew out a breath in bitter frustration.

"Were I in the Great After I would find Ciesfor, turn him round and tan his salty backside!"

Poet smiled halfheartedly at Sirtago's words, but before he could say anything there was a great cracking sound like distant thunder and the vessel shuddered. The deck moved under his rump, jarring him backwards and causing his head to smack the railing behind him.

Ignoring the pain in his skull, Poet leaped to his feet. So did Sirtago, who was suddenly sharp and alert. "What was that?" he shouted.

The sailors frantically climbed out of the ratlines, scrambled about the deck, and crowded the railing to look over the side.

"What's happening?" Poet said to an old sailor. "Did we strike something? Has the hull been breached?"

The sailor ignored him. Based on his wide-eyed look, Poet guessed that the man did not know the answers to his questions.

Poet and Sirtago looked over the side with the others. The sea was relatively calm, only churning in the wake of the wooden vessel. The sails were fully billowed. A strong wind pushed the vessel swiftly and surely across the surface of the ocean. Poet scanned the water again and saw no sign of anything that might have caused the ship to shudder so.

"Did we strike a rock?" Sirtago said. He turned away, steadying himself on the rail.

"The ocean's too deep," Poet said. He turned as well and spied one of the other passengers, the veiled woman, standing on the deck.

Poet had first seen her soon after he and Sirtago had boarded. She'd been lifted onto the ship in a litter, seemingly deathly afraid of the waters. A haunted, frightened look stole into her eyes whenever she looked upon the great, rolling sea. He sensed that she was taking this ocean voyage only out of sheer necessity. She rarely left her cabin, and when she did, she always stayed well away from the sides.

She was wrapped in a simple, dark traveling cloak, but Poet had caught glimpses of colorful and exotic cloths underneath it. Poet knew such rich clothing came from the Eastern Lands, the lands of the Tey'ei Vaus, whose rulers used dark sorcery to achieve their mastery over that region.

Her cloak could not hide the swell of her breasts or the lithesome curves of her hips. She wore a simple black hood and her face was veiled. Only her eyes showed above her veil and they were two of the most magnificent and hypnotic orbs that Poet had ever seen. He gazed at her, fascinated and drawn by those alluring dark eyes as they shone out from beneath their hood.

She stood in the midst of the panicked sailors, calm and defiantly regal. She turned and for a moment locked eyes with Poet. A thrill went through him with the sudden connection, but beneath her calm exterior, her eyes were filled with dread, as if she knew what had happened and was deathly afraid.

The moment passed and the veiled woman lowered her eyes and hurried back to her cabin.

"That's enough gawking, you dogs!" a rough voice cut over the babble on deck. "Back to your stations! There's work to be done on this boat. I'll not have ye all sky-larkin' on my ship!"

The captain was a tall man with a great belly, yet covered with muscle. He possessed huge, strong hands. Since the passage began, the master of the vessel had hurled a continuous stream of invective at his sailors. It was surprising that he had any voice left, but his bellows still rivaled the gale that currently pushed them towards their destination.

"Get back below, you!" he shouted to one sailor. "You, get your thrice-dammed behind back into those lines! An' the rest of you, who seem to think you can stand around being bone-idle, can swab this here deck 'til it's clean!"

Sirtago regarded the captain with barely hidden disdain. He'd taken an instant dislike to the man. This was not unexpected. Despite Sirtago's fierce and low appearance, his blood was noble and he did not take kindly to those who had authority over him—particularly those who used that authority capriciously. The captain appeared to enjoy the cruelty that his position allowed. He regarded Poet and Sirtago as mere mercenaries, barely worth common courtesy and that only because they'd paid for their passage in coin from the kingdom of Ruegeld.

The captain would be surprised that Sirtago was, in fact, a prince of the southern kingdom of Trigassa, and heir to the throne. As it was, Sirtago needed to travel inconspicuously, so he bore the man's disdain, but only just.

"What caused the ship to shudder so?" Sirtago said, his manner surly, as if accusing the captain of being responsible.

The captain clearly took umbrage at Sirtago's tone, but did not rise to his bait. "Go below, you two," he said, turning away.

Sirtago persisted. "Did we strike something?"

The captain rounded on them. Fear and confusion filled his eyes. "Go below," the captain said again.

Sirtago stared defiantly at the captain with his one good eye, his monstrous features rattling the portly man. The captain dropped his gaze. ". . . or stay on deck. It's all one to me," he said, starting to walk aft. "Just stay out of my men's way!" he called over his shoulder.

Sirtago glared after the captain's retreating back until the rolling of the deck caused his stomach to heave again. He thrust his head back over the side. Poet sighed, sincerely wishing that he could do something for his companion's affliction.

Through the entire passage, it had been warm enough for Poet and Sirtago to sleep on the open deck. It was convenient for Sirtago, since he spent half the night with his head over the rail. Poet tried for sleep but it was elusive, between Sirtago's heaving and the general noisiness of the ship. Poet stared up at the glittering panoply of stars above him, his thoughts vacillating between the strange thing that shook the ship and those alluring dark eyes above the silken veil.

Sirtago broke into his thoughts by angrily dropping himself to the deck. He blew out a great breath of frustration. "I've fought enemies both natural and unnatural," Sirtago said. "Why can I not defeat the rolling ocean?"

Poet closed his eyes. "You cannot defeat the ocean," he said. "You just accept it."

"I can't do that." Sirtago pulled his blanket over himself and rolled onto his side.

Poet knew—better than Sirtago himself, probably—that Sirtago was constantly fighting and could not give it up. He had always been at odds with the world around him, fighting anyone at any time at the slightest provocation, even if it were madness to do so. Somehow he had always managed to come out on top. Most of the time it was because Poet had known how to steer his friend's wrath to do the most good. Poet also knew how to duck and get out of the way when Sirtago was in his wrath.

It was not easy for his friend, despite being the heir to a kingdom. As prince, Sirtago lived a life of pleasure, satisfying his lusts for food, wine, and women whenever he felt like it. That would end on the day that his father died. Trigassan Monarchs live a life of austerity and seclusion in the sacred palace, only being seen in public during festivals and great holy days.

That fact of Sirtago's life had kept both of them wandering as mercenaries. Perhaps Sirtago thought that Trigassa would forget about him. More likely Sirtago did not think of it at all. He merely ran. But it was no good. Eventually his father would die and Sirtago would be King. The Trigassan court would be determined to track him down and drag him back to the kingdom. There was no one else to take the throne. Sirtago had only a sister, Jeswana.

Jeswana. Poet marveled at how the mere thought of her name stung him. The hurt flared, as fresh and as painful as always even after all these years. The thought of Jeswana bound to another—the sight of her belly swollen with another man's child—caused hot, salty tears to come to his eyes. It was at these moments that he envied Sirtago's simplicity. Sirtago did not reflect on past disappointments, living constantly in the here and now and was always looking to the next horizon.

Poet wiped away his futile tears and turned over, trying to find sleep. He was almost there when he was startled by a great crash like a clap of thunder. The vessel shuddered.

Instantly Poet and Sirtago were on their feet. Poet rushed to the side and looked down. In the light of the stars, the ocean was a great black mass. The crack like thunder sounded again and Poet could tell that it came from just below the surface of the water near the ship's hull. Once again the ship shuddered violently.

The deck was in chaos; sailors ran to and fro in the confusion. Feet pounded the wooden deck and a bell rang a shrill alarm.

Poet stared at the surface of the water for a moment longer, but he could see nothing. His gaze traveled to the point where the ocean and the night sky met, melting into each other like lovers in a passionate embrace. As he turned away, motion caught his eye.

He sensed more than saw a black shape moving out on the water, like a great round wave swelling up from the calm surface. Amidst the confusion on deck Poet thought he could hear water falling like a great and heavy curtain. Was it his imagination or was there some glistening thing breaking the surface?

A pressure struck him like a musical note that went so high one could feel it in one's head. It was there, between his ears and at the base of his skull, a tiny shattering tone that buzzed like an angry hornet. He covered his ears but that did nothing to stop it.

"Do you hear that?" Poet yelled over the buzzing.

Sirtago was glaring at the ocean with his one good eye. "Hear what?" he said. "I can hear nothing over the clamor of these oafs."

The sound assaulted Poet's ears for a moment more, then began to fade. The voices of the confused sailors recaptured his attention. The captain cajoled and threatened his men back to work. Despite his bluster, fear and confusion was writ plain upon him.

The night calmed and men slowly returned to their bunks. Poet tried to settle back to sleep. Sirtago tried as well, but the rocking of the boat soon had his empty stomach heaving again. Poet tried to ignore it. After a while Sirtago flopped back down onto the deck with a curse. With sleep elusive once again Poet sat up. He was about to say something to Sirtago when he saw a figure approaching them from across the deck.

It was the veiled woman, no doubt woken by all the noise. She moved lithely, gliding almost, towards them. Kneeling in front of Sirtago, she stared directly into his face without a hint of revulsion, not even an involuntary shudder. Sirtago stared back. Her hypnotic eyes had given him pause even in his misery.

From within the folds of her dark cloak the woman produced a small glass vial that contained a milky liquid. "This is a tincture," she said, her voice smooth and mellifluous despite her strong Tey'ei Vaus accent. "It will help you. It will stop your stomach from heaving." She held the bottle out to Sirtago.

Sirtago stared at it, his natural mistrust mingling with his desire to be free of his malady. As usual with Sirtago, the two sides warred fiercely.

"Who are you?" Poet asked. "You're Tey'ei, aren't you?"

The veiled woman's eyes flicked to meet Poet's, but only for an instant. They quickly darted back to Sirtago. "Yes. I am from Tey'ei Vaus. My name is Fayethima. Take it." She gestured again with the tincture.

The woman seemed sincere, despite being a Tey'ei. But, as a people, they were versed in many arts that were strange to those from Trigassa. It truly could be a cure.

"You might as well take it," Poet said. "It certainly can't make it any worse."

"It could kill me," Sirtago said.

"At least that would stop you from heaving over the side all night."

"I promise you," Fayethima said. "It will do you no harm." She unstoppered the tiny vial and offered it again. "A tiny drop. That is all that you will need."

Sirtago stared intently at the vial. "Why are you doing this?"

The woman's gaze did not waver. "Even the Tey'ei are not strangers to compassion."

Sirtago hesitated a fraction of a second more, then nodded. Too weak to grab for it himself, he opened his mouth and stuck out his tongue.

Fayethima tipped the vial carefully until a single drop splashed onto Sirtago's outthrust tongue. She tipped the vial back, stoppered it again and slipped it back into the folds of her cloak. "In a little while you will feel better. You will likely hunger. Come to my cabin—both of you—and I will feed you."

With that she stood up and glided back across the deck. Both Poet and Sirtago watched her depart, hypnotized by her lithesome retreat.

Once she was out of their sight Poet turned to his friend. "How do you feel?"

Sirtago merely grunted and lay back down on the deck. "In a few hours, I will feel better or I'll be dead. Either would be preferable at this point."

Poet laughed mirthlessly and lied down as well.

———⚓———

True to her word, Fayethima's tincture had its effect. The dawn was just rising, painting the clouds in the sky with a rosy glow and Sirtago was up and looking better. One of the hands drew up a bucket of seawater and Sirtago did his best to clean himself up before they went to Fayethima's cabin.

They knocked upon her door. As Fayethima ushered them in, the odor of rich foods assailed their nostrils and Sirtago's stomach growled alarmingly loud like a hungry beast. Poet was not surprised. Sirtago had been unable to keep anything down for two days and must have been ravenous.

The cabin was small and the ceiling was low. Sirtago had to duck to avoid braining himself on the timbers. There was a small table in the center of the room that was covered in the finest sweetmeats that Poet had ever seen. There were cured meats and exotic fruits. There were strange Tey'ei delicacies that gave off an aroma redolent of heady spices.

There was wine, too. Sirtago stared at the spread with rapt attention.

"Please, gentle sirs," Fayethima said, "do avail yourselves of my—"

Sirtago had not waited for her to finish, but had tucked in. He ate like a ravenous animal and Poet had to look away.

Fayethima stood away from the table. She doffed her black cloak and her veil. Poet's breath caught in his throat. She was as beautiful as her dark eyes had promised. Raven hair cascaded down to her waist in gentle curls. Her form was exquisite; her womanly curves were displayed openly, only a few pieces of fine silk allowing her modesty.

Poet could not help but stare at this vision of feminine loveliness, but Fayethima did not take her eyes from Sirtago. She stared at him while he noisily masticated the food she offered. Most fine women were as disgusted with his appearance as they were with his appalling lack of manners. Fayethima was not. Indeed, she stared at him intently, as if he were an object of tremendous interest to her, as if, Poet thought with a shudder, she were a cobra gazing hypnotically on its intended prey.

Poet was about to apologize for his companion's lack of decorum when the high, shattering tone assailed him between his ears and at the base of his skull. He covered his ears in alarm, to no avail.

"What's the matter?" Fayethima said, her attention suddenly dragged away from Sirtago by Poet's obvious distress.

"Do you not hear it?" Poet shook his head, trying to dislodge the sound. "The tone?"

"I hear nothing," Fayethima said, but Poet noticed a look of disquiet in her eyes. Sirtago had obviously heard nothing, or if he had it had not affected his ravenous appetite.

Poet squinted his eyes and tried to block out the noise, but it just seemed to get worse. "It's everywhere," he said.

Fayethima looked from Sirtago, who continued to eat blithely, and back to Poet, seemingly at a loss for what to do. Unable to stand the noise, Poet stood. "Please forgive me," he managed to say before leaving the cabin.

Out on the open deck, the tone began to drop in intensity. Poet staggered to the railing and looked out over the rolling ocean. The tone faded steadily. A great wave rose up, and Poet thought he saw a black shape within, but the wave rolled back into the bosom of the ocean before he could discern what it was.

The shattering tone finally disappeared and Poet shook his head in relief.

He had always been sensitive to certain pitches. He loved music and as a lad had often listened with rapturous delight as the many passing musicians played for the entertainment of Sirtago's mother, the Empress. Poet would often thrill to the sound of a well-played flute, laughing as its highest notes tickled the back of his head. But this was no delightful music. There were no notes; only the disquieting tone that overwhelmed all his other senses.

Poet stood up from the rail and looked around the ship. The sailors were busily going about their daily routine. From somewhere near the fore, a sailor played a lively tune on a small pipe. Had that been the instrument that had caused his distress?

It seemed unlikely. It was just a simple hornpipe, incapable of producing such an agonizing tone.

Poet walked across the deck, back towards Fayethima's cabin. He would make his apologies to her and perhaps be admitted back into her company. There might even be some victuals left over, providing that Sirtago had not consumed them all.

As he approached, he heard Fayethima shriek, and Sirtago let out a loud groan. Poet unsheathed one of his daggers from within his shirt and ran to the door, ready to burst in.

He stopped himself when he heard them laugh. Then he heard sounds that were instantly familiar. He had been with Sirtago far too long not to recognize noises made in ardor. It was clear that Sirtago had finished satisfying his appetite for food and had moved on to satisfying his *other* appetites. From the sounds that Fayethima made in response, it seemed that she was only too happy to provide for Sirtago's satisfaction.

Poet let out a defeated breath, returned his dagger to its place of rest, and moved away from the door. He wandered up the deck to find the sailor who played so lively a tune on his little hornpipe. Poet sat, listening to the sailor play. The foredeck was filled with sailors working or relaxing in the bright sunshine. A group of them had a huge white sail bunched between them and they were meticulously sewing, closing holes and rents in the white fabric. Some whittled on bits of wood while others swabbed and washed the various parts of the ship. One sailor, a younger man, got to his feet and began prancing about which encouraged the player to make his tune even livelier. Poet took it all in, smiling and content.

He had nearly forgotten his disquiet when he heard a dreadfully familiar sound from aft. Sirtago was once again heaving his guts over the side. Poet wandered back to console his friend. Obviously he had overdone satisfying his desires. Fayethima's tincture was not as effective as she'd claimed it would be. Either that, or. . . .

Poet stopped and looked at the deck. Sirtago had begun heaving before he made it to the side; Poet's nose wrinkled in disgust at the vomitous mass on the deck. He looked away to his friend who had finished heaving. Sirtago wiped his mouth with the back of his arm, leaving a streak of silver across his face.

Silver? Poet glanced back at the vomit on the deck. Amongst the food that Sirtago had thrown up was a silvery glint, like crushed pearls. *What has she fed to him?* Had she poisoned him? But why? Why cure him of his ocean sickness just to feed him poison?

Poet was about to speak when the air was split with a crack like thunder and the vessel shuddered mightily. A second crack sounded and the ship shook again; Poet almost lost his footing. Then a third crack and a third shudder.

Suddenly the waters behind Sirtago were boiling. Horrified, Poet watched a hideous black shape rise from the surface. Long limbs, sinuous and snake-like, stretched out towards the boat. A glistening black body followed. A huge eye rolled in a black socket and a horrible open maw issued a great scream, spewing flecks of silvery spittle onto the deck.

Chaos erupted. The sailors armed themselves, grabbing hooks and daggers and cutlasses. Sirtago turned to see the giant ocean creature looming over him.

"*Gwut's Balls*!" he shouted, drawing his mighty blade and hacking at one of the thing's limbs as it slithered close.

Long, sinewy arms were everywhere. Poet drew his daggers and, with a yell, flew at one of them, stabbing and slicing as it tried to grasp hold of him.

Sirtago was fighting wildly, his great sword lopping off the tips of the creature's probing limbs. He normally had the strength of three men, but his slashes and thrusts were becoming sloppy and less accurate. Poet feared that the days of sickness had drained Sirtago too much.

Still, he had the strength to sever any of the sinewy limbs that came too close. Poet watched in horrified fascination as the arms fell to the deck and moved about as if still possessed of life. They bled a sticky liquid, which contained glints of pearly silver just like the stuff that Sirtago had vomited onto the deck. How much more of it had he heaved over the side?

The creature uttered another angry bellow that seemed to drag up from the darkest of the sea's depths. The sound ripped through Poet's head. Then the high tone that had so overcome him earlier rang back.

The sound faded for a moment and Poet was able to strike out at another limb that came too close. He glanced up. The creature had dragged itself almost fully out of the water. It was monstrously huge. The maw could eat a man whole and the dreadful eye that rolled back and forth was as big as Poet's head.

The creature let out another horrendous shriek. Again the high tone sounded, stabbing its shrill intensity into his brain. It faded long enough for Poet to see the havoc around him. The creature's weight had caused the boat to list to one side. He had to scramble to maintain his footing. Sirtago was having similar trouble. He tried to retreat to the higher ground but the thing kept pursuing.

And that was when Poet noticed that the creature was ignoring almost everyone onboard, concentrating its wrath on Sirtago. Limbs would snake out and toss sailors aside, but the main force of the creature's attack was centered on his friend.

The thing let out another shriek. The high tone answered. Poet cradled his head in his hands. As the shattering sound faded from his skull, he realized that the tone was just that—an answer to the creature's dreaded shrieks.

But where was it coming from? Poet had heard the tone on the open deck, but he had heard it most strongly in . . .

. . . Fayethima's cabin!

Poet leaped over a writhing tentacle and ran towards the door of Fayethima's cabin. It was barred, so Poet put his shoulder to it. Sirtago could have broken it open with a single push. Though Poet was a slighter man, not possessed of half the strength of his companion, he was wiry and determined.

The creature shrieked again and the answering tone rang through Poet's head. He

tried to ignore it and kept thrusting himself at the locked door.

Finally the latch gave way. The door burst inwards and Poet spilled into the cabin.

The room was in a shambles. The remains of the meal that Sirtago had consumed were littered across the floor, spilled there after having slid from the table with the deck's slant. The table itself was close to tipping over and small items rolled across the floor, following the downward slope of the deck.

Fayethima was curled up on the bunk. She stared at Poet with wide-eyed terror. "Get out!" she said, an edge of hysteria in her voice.

From outside, the creature shrieked, and the answering tone sounded in Poet's head, louder and more intense than ever. He doubled over and cradled his head in his hands, afraid it would burst open and spill the contents of his skull over the deck.

The tone passed and Poet reached for the Tey'ei sorceress. "What have you done? What have you done to incur this creature's wrath?"

Fayethima leaped off the bunk and swung a hand toward Poet, her sharp, claw-like nails narrowly missing his cheek. Poet grabbed both her wrists, one in each hand. She fought him with surprising strength. Poet lost his balance and she twisted out of his grip.

The Tey'ei woman had a crazed look as she ran to a corner of her cabin. There was a pile of blankets and clothes that had slid down the deck and had stopped there. Fayethima leaped on the pile and wrapped herself around it.

When the creature shrieked again, the answering tone was so intense that he thought surely it would cause him to black out. It filled his eyes with a white-hot wash of pain no matter how hard he closed his lids against it.

The tone began to fade as Poet realized that Fayethima huddled on top of the clothing and blankets because there was something beneath them that she was trying to protect . . . or to silence.

Poet pulled her from the bundle. She uttered a cry of rage as she flew to the floor in the center of the cabin. Poet whisked aside the clothes and blankets. There, beneath the jumble was a glowing orb.

Perfectly round and almost as big as a man's head, it was milky white and it glinted with silvery flecks. The sphere was made of the same substance in Sirtago's vomit—the same substance that dripped and oozed from the attacking creature's severed limbs. Beside the sphere was a small dagger. The floor immediately around the orb was covered by tiny motes of silver that looked as if they'd been scraped from its surface.

It all made some kind of sense. The orb belonged to the creature. The Tey'ei sorceress had stolen it somehow. She had scraped some of its surface and put it in the food. Was that why the creature's attack was concentrated on Sirtago?

Poet had no time for more speculation. Fayethima let out an angry cry and was suddenly on top of him. They toppled to the deck, as she screamed and slashed at him with her razor-sharp nails. Poet held up his arms to cover his face, and her nails slashed through the skin of his forearms. He let out a yelp of pain and then rolled over, trying to dislodge the screaming, slashing woman.

She shrieked in fear. One of the creature's sinewy limbs had slithered through the cabin's broken door, groping blindly for something to latch onto. Fayethima leaped off

Poet and back onto her bunk, pressing herself tight against the cabin's rear wall, staring at the approaching limb with wide-eyed terror, screaming at the top of her lungs.

Poet's heart hammered in his chest. The limb's surface glistened wetly, covered with silvery flecks. Poet leaped up, ducking once to avoid the limb's probing swipe. He scooped up the silvery orb, retrieved one of his daggers, and slashed viciously at the limb.

The tentacle jerked back and the creature outside let out an angry shriek.

The orb responded and Poet felt the white hot pain slash through his head. His legs buckled underneath him and he slid to the deck, squeezing the orb, holding it closer despite the pain.

When the answering tone passed, Poet climbed unsteadily to his feet and headed for the door, following the retreating limb out into the daylight.

"No!" Fayethima screamed, launching herself at Poet, but he was too quick. Outside, the creature's black form took up most of the deck. Only a few of the sinewy limbs still trailed in the dark ocean. Its glistening body pulsed and quivered in the bright light of day.

The sailors were doing their best to fight off the monster, but it tossed them about, mere annoyances to its pursuit of its one quarry.

But where was Sirtago? Poet looked up and saw his companion climbing the ropes towards the mainmast's lookout. He climbed with one hand and with the other he slashed out with his sword when the creature's limbs came too close.

Poet ran towards the creature, holding up the orb. He tried to shout but his voice was drowned out by the cacophony of battle. Before he could call again, the creature let out another thunderous shriek. The orb responded. Poet doubled over in pain, nearly dropping it.

The creature paused, its limbs waving snakelike in the air. The creature's great black eye rolled around inside of its head. The answering tone faded and Poet stood up straight, holding the orb out for the creature to see. "Take it!" Poet shouted at the thing. "It's what you want! Take it!"

Something hit him from behind. The orb flew from his hands and he fell to the deck. The air escaped his lungs in a great *Whoof*! His face smashed against the sloping deck. Fayethima was on his back, scratching him and shrieking curses in Tey'ei.

Poet bucked and tried to roll her off, but she would not budge.

"Return it to me! I killed ten men to possess it, including two lovers! Give it back to me, now!"

Poet tried to speak but he could not draw enough breath; she was suffocating him.

The creature shrieked again and the orb answered. Poet gritted his teeth, managing to turn his head to see the orb. It had come to rest further down the tilted deck against a coiled length of rope.

Fayethima must have seen it as well—suddenly she was no longer on top of him. Poet saw a brief flash of her pale, silk-adorned legs running towards the orb, then the creature loomed over him, its great black maw open wide, dripping silvery drool. He rolled, but not fast enough. A glob of the foul stuff splashed over his head and shoulder. Poet scrambled to his feet, coughed at the foul smell, and wildly wiped at the sticky mess in his hair.

The creature shrieked again, releasing a fetid stench, like dead fish that had baked in the sun. The thing, so accustomed to the depths of the sea, was rotting in the open air.

Poet managed to gain control of his fear and revulsion. He was dimly aware of Fayethima running towards her cabin, her body hunched over the orb.

Poet moved to follow her, but one of the creature's sinewy limbs wrapped itself around his midsection. It squeezed, once again forcing the air from Poet's lungs. The creature tightened its grip, crushing him. He tried to scream but no sound came. At any moment his ribs would crack and his heart would burst.

The world dimmed. Poet thought he was being dragged into that frightful maw. Through the blackness Poet heard a mighty shout— the sound of Sirtago's berserker rage.

Poet was jarred once, twice, and then a third time. The darkness began to recede. Sirtago still yelled his battle cries. Poet struggled anew against the limb that held him in its crushing grip. He had room to draw air into his lungs and it never felt so sweet. There was another impact, and then he was falling. He had only a fraction of a second to panic before he crashed to the deck.

Poet lay stunned for a moment, before realizing that the limb was still wrapped around him. It had cushioned his fall. It ended in a ragged, milky-white, silver-flecked mess where it had been hacked from the beast.

The creature shrieked again, but this time its bellow was weaker. Pain and rage seemed to have expended much of its energy. Sirtago, on the other hand, found a new strength as the creature weakened. He was back on the deck, continuing his attack on the creature's limbs.

The orb's tone assailed Poet, but the pain was lessened. Fayethima was nowhere in sight. She must have made it back into her cabin. He assumed that she was smothering the orb with blankets and clothes, trying to dampen the sound that she could not hear but must know it emitted.

The creature dragged itself towards the cabin. A tentacle snaked around the wooden cabin while another poked itself through the broken door. Fayethima screamed as the creature's limb lashed out. The tentacle retreated from the cabin, the screaming sorceress in its grasp. She clung to a bundle of blankets and clothes. The tentacle coiled tighter, and lifted Fayethima toward the creature's mouth. Her wail strangled off as the maw opened wide.

Then Fayethima fell, resuming her scream as she tumbled into that pulsating, glistening mouth. To the end, she did not relinquish her grip on the orb.

The creature slowly crawled back down the side of the ship. It had been in the open air for too long. It was missing limbs, and bleeding silver from dozens of wounds. Poet felt a small pang of sympathy for the creature.

As the creature retreated, Sirtago attacked it afresh. With a great bellow, he hacked at the creature's limbs. The creature flicked out a tendril. It crashed into Sirtago and sent him flying across the deck. Then the creature finally rolled over the side, splashing back into the dark sea.

As the creature's weight was dislodged, the boat rolled the opposite way. Poet lost his balance and crashed to the deck, rolling along with coils of rope, abandoned weapons, and various bits of wood. He crashed into the opposite rail, his head connecting violently with the timbers. The world rolled and spun and blackness overtook him.

——————⚓——————

Poet woke to a familiar heaving sound. He opened one eye despite the pain it caused his head. Sirtago was hurling his guts into the sea. Poet opened his other eye and sat up, trying to ignore the pain and the shaking of his limbs. The deck around him was littered with broken planks and splintered spars. The crew was valiantly trying to clean it all up.

Sirtago flopped onto the deck next to him, and focused his one good eye on Poet. "You're still alive," he said.

"So are you, it seems."

Sirtago grunted. "Barely."

Silence settled over them and Poet closed his eyes, allowing the sounds of the boat and the ocean to lull him, but it no longer calmed him like before. He kept hearing that high tone in his head.

"She was comely enough," Sirtago said.

"She was using you as bait for that creature."

Sirtago gave a bit of a start. "Why?"

Why? That was a good question. Gwut alone knew how she got the orb. She must have known that if she crossed the ocean with it, the creature would come to claim it. Perhaps she thought that if the beast ate Sirtago it would be satisfied long enough to allow her to reach the mainland.

What the orb was, and what it was to the creature, Poet would never know.

"She was a sorceress," Poet said. "Who can fathom such a one as that?"

Sirtago considered that for a moment, then grunted, seemingly satisfied. "She wasn't that comely," he said, standing up and heading to the railing.

Poet dragged himself to his feet as Sirtago heaved again. In the distance, a narrow strip of brown crept into view between the dark sea and the bright sky. Land.

Poet nudged Sirtago. "Soon we will be away from Ciesfor's domain and back on dry land."

"Now, *that's* the comeliest sight I have ever seen."

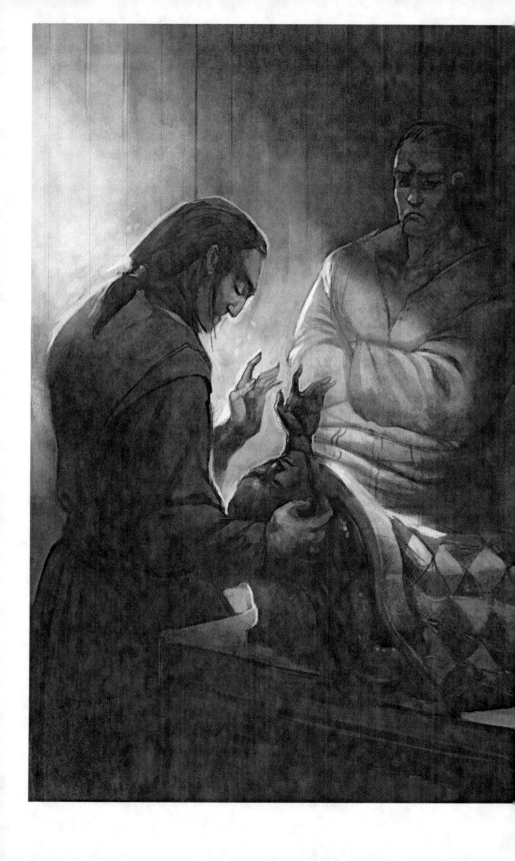

Dead Men Tell No Tales
Elaine Cunningham

The ship closing hard on our port side was a brigantine. Two masts, twenty canons, maybe a hundred men aboard. Pirates hereabouts favor the brig, so Cap'n Mayes sang out the make-ready long afore the black flag started climbing.

She come in fast and mean and sure, like a man raising a fist to an old Quaker, knowing all the while he'll only hold up his hands and say, "Whist now, Friend, there's no cause for brawling!"

If I was manning the brig, I'd be thinking much the same. The *Donkeybow* is Dutch flute, broad as a barrel and built to haul cargo, not to win sea battles. Her real name is *Donkerblauw*, which Natty says means "clear blue skies." A fine, good-omen name for a ship, if you can twist your tongue to it. Natty now, he can speak six different kinds of foreign, navigate by dead reckoning or with a sexton, make a wood flute sing like a meadow bird, and a half hundred other things I could no more hope to do than fly. Me, I can work and I can fight, and I don't mind telling you I was itching to get to it.

The Captain gave over the wheel to Mister Nichols and quick-footed his way to the rail. "Make ready the pinnace, Little John, then get you below decks." He reached up to clap me on the back. "One look at you, and they'll not believe we mean to give in without a fight!"

Why he calls me Little John, I couldn't say. I'm a head taller than any man aboard, broad and strong as any plow horse. And my name is Thomas. I asked Natty once, and he said the captain is powerful fond of old tales. That was no answer at all, so far as I could see, but most men find answers in what looks to me like a pile of more questions. So generally I just haul in the slack of my jaw and do as I'm bid.

"Aye, Cap'n Mayes."

"*Mister* Mayes," he said, correcting me. I'm ashamed to admit that it wasn't for the first time. When pirates are about to come aboard, he's "Mister." I forget that betimes. Being a gentleman, he don't often chide me for my lacks.

I hauled the pinnace into place and set the winches so it could be lowered quick and easy. Natty stood ready, three lads with him to help with the oars. The pirates will be expecting the captain to come aboard the brigantine to talk surrender. Instead, they'll be getting Cook, looking the very picture of a merchant captain in a fine, light blue coat and a fancy white wig. The cook's got a rich man's belly and a Dutchman's whey-colored face, and he does look the part but I don't mind telling you he's as dumb as a stump.

That don't much matter. Cook pretends he can only speak foreign and he mumbles something in Natty's ear for show; it's Natty who figures out what to tell the pirates that'll tempt them to empty the brigantine of men the better to carry loot off the *Donkeybow*. They're a mismatched pair, them two, what with Cook so big and round and pale, and Natty black as molasses, and scrawny besides. But it takes the pair of them to make a captain, and that's a fact.

Mister Surrey, the boatswain, bellowed out the call to strike colors. We harbor in Newport, and Rhode Island is an English colony, but the captain was flying the Dutch flag—a strip of orange atop, then white, then blue. As it come down, the men pulled out neck scarves in the same colors and tied them on. Some of them gave me hard looks as I passed by on my way below decks. I been known to cut down *Donkeybow* crew along with the pirates once I get to fighting. Even shot a shipmate once—shot him deader than salt cod. The crew's always changing, you see; I've no head for names and faces, and that's a fact. It helps considerable when they wear the colors, and I'm proud to say I never once killed a man wearing orange and blue.

The men in the hold—and most of the *Donkeybow's* men was in the hold—made ready for battle. A pair of nimble-fingered lads was loading flintlock pistols. I took two pistols and tucked them into my belt.

"Don't you be firing those in the hold again," Mister Sawyer said. Being a ship's carpenter, he has to think on these things. He was tugging at his fox-colored beard, which is what he does when he's riled up, so I promised him I would fight topside.

I checked the edge of my cutlass. The tang looked a mite rusted; I'd meant to have that mended.

Just then we heard the crash of grappling hooks and the screech of iron scraping across wood. Boarding planks slapped down, quicker than I could count them. Natty must have spun them some grand story about our cargo. Slaves, is what he mostly told pirates, and him being black as the devil himself and the slave trade at Newport's Brick Market being what it is, pirates generally lapped up this lie like cats on spilled cream.

The men blew out all the whale-oil lamps but a small, dim one and crawled into the wooden shelves meant to hold slaves left over from the Barbados. Before Cap'n Mayes took over *Donkeybow*, slaves was mostly what we carried, and I don't mind telling you it wasn't work I relished. The able-bodied slave men stayed in Barbados to work the sugar and beddable women had their own value; it was children we brought to Newport.

I ducked behind some barrels of hardtack, for there was no hope of me fitting into one of the slave-shelves. We hadn't long to wait until the pirates come down the ladders like a swarm of bilge rats. They roared into the hold, quick and happy, yelling insults at the one man in plain view.

He held up a ring of keys, which he spilled out over the broad plank that served us as a table. "Take any one of them, lads," he said in a quivery voice as he backed away. "The locks on them chains is all the same. Unhitch the end of the chains bolted just outside the shelves, then you can use them to haul the slaves out."

They set to. We waited until Mister Harris—a fine sailor and fighter, he is, next on the list to captain his own ship—sang out the attack. Cutlasses flashed out of the slave-shelves as the men slashed open whatever part of a pirate was closest to hand.

Some of them fell dead at once, big gaping grins on their throats to match their greedy smiles. Others stumbled away screaming, clutching at their opened bellies and tripping over more screaming men who'd been hamstrung.

While the crew rolled out of the shelves and finished the task, I hurried up to the deck to join in that bit. There was plenty of pirates topside, and I pulled my pistols and picked two of them to kill.

Small canons, that's what pistols are, and the flash of powder and the back-blowing smoke always blinded me for a heartbeat or two. That's all the time it takes to die, so I threw aside the pistols straight away and pulled my cutlass from my sash, slashing at the smoke as I charged.

My aim was good today and my luck better; one of the pirates I'd shot was flat on his back and twitching, the other slumped against the mast, holding himself up by the ropes and screaming as he stared at the blood pouring from what used to be his knee. I cut his throat quick and clean; I'd do the same kindness for a horse whose leg was broke.

I looked around for Cap'n Mayes, for he always finds the best of the fighting. He's not like most gentlemen; he does his own killing, and he's a good hand at it. It's a sight to see, him being a London man and gentry besides, brawling like a cornered badger. Once the fighting starts, he's another man altogether.

Cap'n Mayes stood near the wheel, fighting two men and holding them off handily. I started to push my way toward him through the noise and confusion of battle.

A big man come at me, cutlass held high and ready for a down-coming slash. I caught his blade just below the hilt of mine and swept his arm out wide as I drove my other fist into his face. Bone crunched like boots on gravel.

The pirate dropped his cutlass and set up a howl to beat the damned in hell. He was a sight, with his flattened nose and the blood pouring into his beard, and the noise he made set me back on my heels. When he charged at me, I saw that my blade had snapped clean off, leaving me holding a rusted hilt.

But I know how to fight the same way birds know to fly. It just comes to me, natural like. Afore my head could think of what to do, my hands grabbed Mister Bloody-beard and spun him toward another pirate. The second man's cutlass drove deep into Bloody-beard's gut. Before he could pull the weapon free I gave the dead man's head a good hard shove, slamming it into the face of the man who'd killed him. They fell together.

Bloody-beard's cutlass was a mite small for my hand, but it would serve for a single battle. I stepped over his body and grabbed ahold of a small man wearing the orange and blue neck rag. A quick shove sent him sprawling and put me face to face with the man he'd been fighting. The pirate looked surprised, and then he looked dead. I spun around and cut the throat of another man who was about to kick my fallen shipmate. I shouldered the dead man over the rail—the deck was getting as littered as a tavern ally—and then kicked the small man myself for not getting up quick enough. Some men, they'll take any way out of a fight they can find.

Not Natty, though. He come thundering over one of the boarding planks, hollering in some heathen tongue.

The captain looked over, startled-like, as a pair of pirates come over the side, daggers held between their teeth and blood in their eyes. Him being busy with the men in front of him, he hadn't much hope of dealing with two more. I'm surprising fast for a big man, but I stood too far away to get to him while the getting still mattered.

But Natty, he kept on running and he threw himself off the boarding plank, arms spread wide like he hoped to take wing. He slammed into both the new-come pirates and down they all went.

I killed three more men on my way to the captain's side, and by then he'd taken down his two. The fighting was mostly over by then and the second part of the killing well underway. This part, I didn't much care for, when the clang of steel gave way to moans and pleas for mercy. But that noise was almost over with, too, for aboard the *Donkeybow*, the louder a man begged, the quicker he died. Cap'n Mayes is a fair man, but he got no use for a coward.

The captain finished off Natty's two afore they had a chance to plead. He was crouched in a pool of their blood, his face grim as he gave study to Natty's small, dark form.

I don't mind telling you I was mighty happy to see Natty's eyes open. His loss would have been felt, and that's a fact. I done well enough for a man of my years and station, but Natty was a pure marvel. Slave children brought to Newport are sold to trade folk and they work at all the town's crafts: distilling rum, building fine furniture, casting silver, making tallow candles. Some of the Jews down on Touro Street bought Natty, and from them he learned to scribe and cipher so well they made a good profit selling him to a sea captain to learn map-making. The sea captain turned pirate and was caught and hanged and buried on Goat Island, but not afore he taught Natty all there was to know about seamanship. Cap'n Mayes often said Natty was the best of us all. He would have had his own ship years ago, except that most men wouldn't take orders from a freed slave no matter what his skills.

The captain looked up and saw me standing there. "Pick him up, carefully, and carry him to my cabin."

Something in his voice raised fear in me, and when I bent over Natty I saw what troubled the captain. In the close fighting, one of the pirates had got a knife between Natty's ribs. The wound was small, but the rough, wet sound of Natty's breathing told the tale. His lungs was filling up; he was drowning in his own blood. A slow and ugly death, that was. I wouldn't wish it on a poxed and thieving whore.

I lifted Natty up, gentle as I could, and followed the captain to his cabin. Cap'n Mayes didn't seem to mind Natty's blood on his quilt, though he'd paid good coin to an old Quaker dame to fashion him one in bright pieces of orange and blue. Money well spent, he'd said with a laugh, if it kept Little John from accidentally killing him while he slept.

The captain pulled the cabin's only chair up to the bed. He sat down and took Natty's thin, black hand in both of his. I don't think he noticed I was still in the room, or that he would have cared if he did.

I had no better place to be. Mister Harris would be busy claiming his new ship, choosing men to start his crew. He wouldn't choose me. No one ever did. Cap'n Mayes, gentleman that he was, told the men he kept me on because I was a fighter worth any three of them, but I suspect he wouldn't have me either, except that I come to him along with the ship.

What was happening topside was a tale often told. As far as the Court of Vice

Admiralty knew, Cap'n Mayes was one of theirs, an English gentleman following England law. And on the English king's say-so, pirates was no longer welcome in Newport. Not long ago, Newport loved pirates. When Cap'n Tew come ashore some years back, most of the town turned out to greet him. But after a time, too many pirates in the waters is like too many goats in the yard; after they eat up the weeds they start in on the gardens. Here's the long and short of it: the merchants complained, the king commanded, and Cap'n Mayes went pirate hunting.

Some of the ships we took he turned over to the Court and crown. As far as the captain's friends in Newport knew, the rest of those ships went down in battle. Now, that just wasn't so. Over the years, Cap'n Mayes built up his own fleet of pirate ships, crewing them with his own men and sending them to Madagascar and the Caribbean and suchlike. Not every man had it in him to become a captain, but every man who sailed with Cap'n Mayes had a chance to grow wealthy. Every man could expect to be treated fairly, for the captain was known as an honorable man, in his own fashion.

What he was saying now to Natty proved the truth in that tale. "You saved my life, lad. That's not a debt easily repaid."

"No need, Cap'n," Natty said. He was no fool; he knew he was dying.

"There *is* need," he said. "There's a great need for men of your caliber. So I want you to listen to a tale, and listen well. Do you mark me, lad?"

When Natty nodded, the captain started in. "Some years before I acquired the *Donkerblauw*, an ambitious young man came to Newport. He had been appointed as a judge in the Court of Vice Admiralty, and it was his intention to build a fine house for his bride, a young woman of good family who would join him the following spring. Do you know of whom I speak?"

Natty nodded.

"Have you heard this story?"

"Aye." It came as a gasp. "Or better said, part of it."

"Indeed. Well, spring came and summer followed, but no word of the judge's bride. He sent letters to England, and the last ships of autumn carried back an angry reply from her father. His daughter had set sail as scheduled, in good weather and calm seas. If she did not make port, he said, no doubt there were pirates at work, and the judge had no one but himself to blame for not doing his duty.

"At that, the judge went a little mad with grief and guilt, and in his fervor he hanged every pirate brought before him, even a privateer or two who carried letters of marque. After the fact, he learned that one of the pirates he hanged had worn a ring on a chain around his neck, a gold ring with a single ruby. This ring had belonged to the judge's young wife.

"The man became obsessed with learning her fate, but none could tell him. Had she been slain when her ship was boarded? Was she living unwilling in a New York brothel, or sold in some distant port where her golden hair would be a curiosity? If she'd come to disgrace, did she yet live? Since all the pirates who might answer these questions were dead, the judge went to certain wise men among the slaves and learned from them how to seek the spirits of the dead."

Now, I must have made a sound, because the captain looked over at me in time to see me cross myself. "Does this tale trouble you, Little John?"

"I'm not afeared of any man alive," I said, honestly enough, "but I don't like talk of spirits and haints and suchlike."

"Do you believe in such things?"

He asked this like my answer mattered to him, and I told him truly that I did believe. Many a man I'd sailed with over the years come from heathen lands. From what they told me, it seemed like their dead stayed close to hand, having no Christian heaven or hell to repair to. As for that, there was ghosts aplenty in the ruins near the village where I was born, even though people in that part of Ireland are Christian, or close enough.

The captain turned back to Natty and went on with his tale. "At first the judge sought the spirit of the pirate who'd had the ruby ring, and when that failed, the spirits of men who'd sailed with him. All efforts came to naught. Finally, in desperation, the judge purchased the home of a former sea captain and sometimes pirate, a man he'd previously hanged, who was said to haunt the premises. A man you knew well," the captain said, looking fiercely into Natty's eyes. "A man you know still. Do you mark me, my lad?"

A strange look come over Natty's face. "Aye, captain," he said in wondering tones.

"Then you might well guess what followed. On the night of a full moon, the judge entered the house alone. Come morning he left in time to catch the tides. He became a sea captain himself, and spoke no more of his lost love. Most men believed he had put aside his grief and found a new way to do his duty. Only one man—now two men—knew the truth:

"In that house a battle had been fought, a battle without swords or pistols. At the end of it, the living vessel set sail under new command. The house, they say, is haunted still. To this day, when the moon is full and high overhead, people who enter the house sometimes see the glint of a ruby and the ghostly shadow of a man, holding out a ring and pleading, 'What became of my bride? Tell me, have you seen her?'"

Natty's eyes drifted closed, and a smile curved his lips. "The better man won; the better man left that house."

The sound was faint and thick, and bloody foam gathered at the corners of his mouth. The captain wiped it away with his own lace-edged handkerchief.

"Aye, lad, that he did, and so he will again." He leaned in closer, and what he said next made little sense to me. "But before you do, *be sure to give Judge Mayes my regards.*"

— ⚓ —

We made port two days later, and Cap'n Mayes made report to the Vice-Admiralty court of the pirate ship we'd lured to our bait and burned to the waterline. Many men was killed in the fighting, he told them, and he added, all sad-like, that Mister Harris would never again be seen in this port. As I said afore, the captain is powerful fond of stories, and he has the knack of making a whale-sized lie out of two small truths. The men of the court believed him, as men generally do.

And they was all in a fine mood, being that the meeting was held in the White

Horse Tavern, and since the crown was paying for their dinner and their ale, they saw fit to add a small pension for Harris's widow to the bill. I knew the woman: she was a tiresome scold and ugly besides—as beaky and scrawny as a plucked hen. Harris wasn't likely to miss his home port.

I didn't sit with the captain, of course, but I had a good meal at the common table and afterwards a tumble with a big whore I favor. Her hair is red when it is clean, and she looks a little like the girls I remember from my village. She always seems pleased with me, as well—whether from her own liking or because the seeming of liking is part of her trade, I could not say. Nor did I care, so long as I had coin enough to pay her hire. The captain had been uncommon generous when he counted out my share of the brigantine's booty, so all in all it was a fine afternoon.

The sun was still high when I met the captain at the ship and carried Natty's mortal remains onto a small, quick sloop. He was to be buried on Goat Island, why I could not say, but the captain made it clear that I was to say nothing at all on this matter. As far as his friends at the Vice-Admiralty courts knew, the body wrapped in linen was a pirate captain who would be buried with others of his ilk.

Cap'n Mayes sailed the sloop himself, with only me along to carry Natty's body and dig the grave. He spent a long time saying heathen words over Natty. A strange, cold wind come up while he spoke, and I don't mind telling you I was glad to leave.

Seems like that wind stayed with us all the way to Newport, and by the time we tied the sloop to the Long Wharf, I felt chilled to the marrow of my soul. By then the sky and sea had faded to that tarnished-silver color that comes just short of full dark, and I was ready for a mug and a meal.

But the captain said he had one thing yet for me to do, and I went along with him willingly enough. We walked through the Brick Market, past the Quakers' meeting house and the fine houses merchants had built along Thames Street and Marlborough. After a time we turned down a narrow side street.

I did not like being here, though I could not say why. This place seemed uncommon dark even though the moon was full and high overhead, making the street better lit than most taverns.

A half-starved dog slunk out of the shadows and crawled forward on his belly, tail wagging like he knew us and hoped for a kind word and maybe even a bone. He stopped all of a sudden and his lip curled as if he meant to snarl. For some reason he thought better of it and lit out, running with his tail between his legs.

The captain shrugged and led me to a tall house surrounded by a fine iron fence. I'm not the most clever man you're likely to meet, but somehow I knew where he'd brought me.

"This house belonged to a man I once knew," he said. "He was a sea captain of considerable skill, and yes, a pirate as well. Still, in his own fashion, an honorable man. He rewarded men who deserved his favor and those who did not, each according to what he had earned."

Good words, those, but I didn't take any comfort from them. I scrubbed a hand across the back of my neck, where the hairs rose like the hackles on that spooked hound.

"Why have we come, Cap'n?"

He didn't answer me straight away. We stood there a while, the captain thinking his own thoughts and me wondering how much longer I could stand there until I tucked tail and ran, too.

"You could have your own command, Thomas Hale," he said suddenly.

The sound of his voice startled me, and so did his use of my true name, so a few moments passed afore the meaning of his words hit me. And even then, they didn't make much sense.

"Me, a captain?" I said in disbelief. "You'd trust me to command a crew, to sail one of your ships?"

"You've more natural talent for fighting than any man I know, and your size and strength could lend you a powerful air of command. Of these things, I have no doubt." He shook his head then, like he was thinking of all the things I done wrong over the years, things no sea captain could do and hope to hold a ship. "*Thomas Hale* could command a ship, but first you must battle what you fear most. And so we have come here."

I remembered then what he'd asked me about spirits and ghosts and haints. He must have caught wind of my fear, and decided this was the way to test my mettle.

But I did not want to go into that house, not even for my own ship. Not even for Cap'n Mayes.

"We part ways, Little John, whatever you decide. If you face your fears and spend the night in that house, then Thomas Hale will take command of the next ship we acquire. If you do not, well then, that is your choice to make, and I wish you well in whatever you do next."

That, I understood straight away. I was not a man who feared many things, but the loss of the *Donkeybow*, home to me since my twelfth summer, was foremost among them.

"I'll do it," I told him.

"Good man." He smiled at me then. "Did you listen well to the tale I told Natty?"

"Aye. There's said to be a spirit here, a man who holds a ruby ring and asks after his lost wife."

"In truth, I believe there are now *two* unquiet spirits hereabouts. If you see the judge's ghost, give it little heed and instead seek out the other."

This was ill tidings, but I saw no better choice than to do as I was bid. As I started through the gate, though, I was struck by a powerful fear. "If I go in that house, Cap'n, I'm not never coming out."

The captain, he reached up and clapped me on the back. "Take heart, lad. I expect to see that face of yours come morning," he said heartily. "And I've no doubt at all that a better man will leave that house than went in!"

Consigned to the Sea
Danielle Ackley-McPhail

"Blessed of the Divine Children
Cursed Immortal Soul
Call down a storm upon these shores
That nature may cry my tears."
Excerpt from *Sweet Liam Roanes*

Seven tears fell into the sea.

They spread my sorrow among the foam and surf, mingled it with the waves until it was destined to touch every shore upon the earth ere the water's wandering was done.

One tear for every year gone by since my husband went his way.

Seven tears fell into the sea.

'Tis said we all return to whence we began; why shouldn't they?

It was high tide. The ship that bore me away recklessly hugged the rocky shore off the Orkneys. At my back I heard a thudding tread, familiar and hated, measuring the length of the weathered deck, owning it. Louder with each step, closer with each tear. The rest turned to hot ash in my eyes as the devil drew near.

"Well, have you decided, poppet?"

I remained turned away and silent, my back stiff and straight and indignant. Captain Darian Gow merely laughed and wrenched me around; his large, thick fingers bruised my bare shoulder, his hard, shadowed jaw lowered inches from my face.

"Have. You. Decided?" His words were measured and deadly calm. Overhead, terns cried a strident warning as they hovered just past the rigging. Below, waves pounded the hull in a siege as old as seafaring ways. My voice rebelled against any answer.

I stood before him with my back pressed hard against the rail, shivering despite the sun, in a dress of crimson crushed velvet he'd flung at me earlier, replacement for the widow's weeds they'd torn from my body before they'd even brought me aboard. It was a whore's dress. Quite literally, in fact, I had no doubt. Blood rubies and rare black seed pearls crusted what bodice there was and the black-satin-lined skirts were indecently slit, fore and aft. A costly whore's dress, but one just the same. I'd been given no petticoats to serve my modesty.

Anger mingled with the fear in my heart. I smothered it for a time with slow, even breaths. I tried one final bid, begging freedom for my daughter. "Will ye na set her safe upon Eynhallow? An ye do, I'll gladly shew ye the way ye seek."

Captain Gow straightened. His eyelids lowered half-mast and his mouth curved but a degree at one corner. He looked back at the crew on the deck and in the rigging. He looked forward and pointedly scanned the shore as if the route he sought would magically appear to him; we both knew he had no hope of hiding his ship among the

Danielle Ackley-McPhail

islands to evade the King's Navy without a native such as myself to guide him along the safe paths. Finally, he leaned forward once more, the other corner of his mouth joining the first, as if he were amused.

I lifted my own chin and forced myself to ignore his massive hands settling on the hilts of his saber and cutlass. No expression at all did I allow upon my face.

He laughed as if delighted and came even closer by my ear.

"What a pretty package you make in my gift," he said, his breath stirring the fine ebon locks curled around my ear while the wind tugged at the rest of the tresses forcefully unbound at my capture. "You're lucky for the decency of even that dress, you know . . ." He turned away to swagger toward the stern, calling out over his shoulder when he was far enough amidships for his voice to carry to both myself and the crew. "Your bonnie lass . . . she has none."

Lust glimmered in every eye I could see, and none of it directed toward me. My gut clenched and my pulse tripped faster. I was driven by the need to rush for the hold where my daughter was imprisoned, but I knew I would not be let near it. I gasped and clutched the rail until a nail tore. The pain of my finger kept me anchored firm against my instinct. I remained still, the cold flow of the North Sea filling me up. The fires of Hell licked at my thoughts, sparked by his implicit threat. I could not hold back the growl as fury crept over my fear, burying it. The vile Gow heard. Heard and laughed once more.

"I've the charts laid out in my cabin, woman, if that will help you get your bearing."

I trembled such that the satin lining of the dress brushed my bare flesh in an obscene caress. My teeth clenched and every muscle flinched away from the sensation until I was a hard, tight effigy of myself. I spun around to stare out at the sea, battling both rage and despair. I closed my burning eyes and lifted my face to the constant breeze, letting it dry those tears that escaped the confines of my lashes. The wind whipping about me murmured empty comfort. Mingled with its fickle whisper I heard a call that haunted both my waking hours and my sleep. My fingers locked upon the rail and my body strained. To hear. . . . To leap. . . . I could not say.

The wind carried but the sounds of surf and gulls. I eyed the rocky islets and the choppy wake. Nowhere did I spy a trace of life not on the wing. Had I imagined that familiar call?

Hope bled away.

I turned my back upon the lure of the waves. The final freedom I could not claim. I worked my way across the ship toward the hold, deftly evading the crew bustling about the deck, keeping my gaze turned from those clambering like monkeys among the rigging. They ogled, they cast lewd comments, but they dared not touch. The dress I wore . . . the captain's mark upon me, sure as if he'd scrawled his name across my near-bare breast.

Heedless of that self-same dress, when I reached the hold I crouched upon the deck as if weary, pooling the hated skirts among the brine and slime cast up by the sea. None shouted me away; none laid their rough hands upon me. My head drooped forward to rest against the grate. I whistled a soft trill distinctly out of place upon the sea.

Scurrying sounded below. The slight thud of something—a hogshead or a crate—

banging against the hull timbers as my child hauled herself atop them. I peered down through false twilight, my face shielded from the pirates' sight by the tangled mass of my unbound curls. My daughter stared back. Her eyes—as dark and soulful as any seal cub's—met mine, large and glimmering and fearful. It was true! Her naked flesh shone pallid against the darkness; a sickly blue-white, as if she'd already been claimed by the sea.

A sob escaped me, and I lurched up, my slender arm thrust down through the gap.

"Mam!" Kate cried, both joyous and pleading. She reached for me, heedless of her precarious perch, stretching up until our fingers twined.

The deck creaked behind me. I barely heard. Why my arm did not snap, I do not know, but I tasted blood upon my lips as I jerked back from the jarring smack delivered by Captain Gow's hand. From below I heard my daughter yelp with pain as my torn nail caught at the delicate tissue of her webbed hand.

"The charts are in my cabin." His voice rumbled like the threat of thunder. "Not the hold. If I spy you near it again before you've shown me the course, you'll watch your whelp go to the crew."

Rage overcame my common sense.

"Ye devil! Ye bastard! Ye unwashed cock of a disease-ridden popinjay!" I hurled my fists as swiftly as my curses. My nails drew blood and my bare feet bruised themselves against his hard-muscled legs. So focused was my fury, I barely felt the hands of the first mate, McCray, as he pulled me off and restrained me.

The crew went still and silent. The air itself drew taut, and even the terns held their cries.

"Stand away from her," Gow said in a low, flat tone.

My eyes widened as sense came back to me. I trembled and hid my hands, scarcely believing what I'd done, though I could see the bloody welts that marred the captain's cheek. I opened my mouth to beg mercy for my daughter, but closed it without a word spoken. I dare not remind him he could strike me most fatally through her.

His arm lashed out once more, as swift and hard as a boom coming about on a schooner. I felt blood fly from my temple as I landed across the deck inches from a long drop and a watery death.

All traces of warmth left my body. Fear went the way of hope and darkness crept into the void. I fought that darkness off, waiting for rough hands to seize me, praying I would not hear the hold hatch lifted and my daughter pay for my folly. Only the muffled sound of the crew resuming their duties slipped past the ringing in my ears. As if from far off, I felt the boards tremble as Captain Gow strode away.

They left me there.

I dared not believe it. It was a struggle, but I raised my head. The effort was wasted: my eyes showed me naught but the blurred colors of the sea. I closed them again and surrendered to the darkness.

———————⚓———————

The ship was wreathed in twilight fog ere I woke again. I could hear the murmur of the men on watch, though I could not see them. My body ached and the mist-damp-ened velvet weighed me like an anchor. What purpose to rise? I did not bother, simply letting myself drift, staring at that little patch of sea before me. If not for Kate I might have crawled those last inches, cast myself into that final freedom I'd earlier refused. But I would not leave her to them by any choice of my own.

A sound drew me from the stupor: The sharp, sudden sound of something breaking the skin of the water. I edged closer to the railless gap meant for the gang plank. The sea was like a liquid jewel before me, rippling and flowing, all but where it sprouted a cluster of long, graceful whiskers. Raised just above the surface of the water, thick-fringed, black glossy eyes met my own. Did I imagine the anguish they held? Did I imagine a familiar glint? I strained my yet-blurred gaze looking for a collar of dapple spots strung like pearls about the seal's neck, but it was impossible to see. It didn't matter. I knew if this were not he, my charge would still reach him.

"A storm," I hissed to the creature. "A storm, Liam Roanes, ten thousand times as fierce as those ye've sent me before an' I'll ne'er curse yer name again!"

Naught but a lightening of the mists proclaimed the dawn, that and the calls of the crew going about the day's duties. My opening eyes burned, but they focused. I saw quite clearly the grey boards of the deck streaked red-black by my blood. I shifted myself—as much to avoid the sight as to determine that I could—and barely swallowed a groan as I did so. My stomach heaved and the ship seemed to tilt beneath me. Everywhere I ached, but I could not remain here. Slowly I fought off weakness and worked my way to my knees. The salty air stung my battered flesh and I swayed as my muscles rebelled. As I struggled to rise further, something disturbed the air behind me.

"Ah, perfect." Gow's mocking word drifted to my ears as a hard-bristled brush crashed down upon my fingers leaving the skin scored. "You can clean up your mess while you are so suitably poised. In fact, the whole deck could use a scrubbing."

"McCray," he called across the ship, "bring our lovely a pail and see she scrubs from aft to stern."

I could not help but flinch as a bucket of foul water landed before me. Half the content slopped out, soaking the front of my dress, molding it even more—if possible—to my body. I could feel both of them stare.

"When you're done, come to my cabin. I'll have the charts waiting for you." The captain paused a moment and a shiver ran from my neck to my toes. "And when I have my heading, we'll see about . . . cleaning . . . that dress."

My fingers were cracked and bleeding and my body trembled with fatigue as I dropped the brush into the bucket for the last time. Above, the weak sun crested the noon hour. No bit of blood or brine or salt marred the deck. The same could not be said for the dress. I sighed and slumped against the nearest crate, head lolling forward. My dull eyes drifted closed but a moment.

"To your feet, you lazy wench!"

I opened my eyes and slowly rolled my head back. Captain Gow stood over me, his expression as dark and dangerous as the depths of the sea. Weary and ill, I could not care. There was no strength in me to comply. His lips snarled as I remained where I was. His hand whipped out to grasp my arm. With no effort at all he hauled me up and whirled me against him.

I groaned and my stomach heaved once more, though it held naught.

The captain held me at the length of his arm and shook. "My patience is no more, wench! You were ordered to my cabin. I will have the heading. Now! Or be it on your soul the hell visited upon you and your brat . . . our ship holds a full complement, the end will be a long time coming."

My heart threatened to stop and were I not weak with injury and exhaustion, I know not which I would have done: fall upon my knees and beg him to spare my Katie, or summon my rage and again cast myself at him until all his face were bloody.

The crew turned their eyes upon us at Gow's threat. I could feel their anticipation. I smelled the rank odor of their lust. I drew myself up straight, my gaze sharpening and I made no effort to hide my hatred. I jerked my arm away and the captain let me; surely, only because it humored him. My dignity was a thin shell closed about me. Inside, my heart screamed. Screamed in fear and rage and bloodlust. That this man would treat us so, that he would threaten us and go unpunished. Worse yet, I had no doubt, whether I did as he bade me or not, in the end our fates would be the same. *A storm, Liam, now!* my soul whispered, low and lethal. *Now, if you'd ever a care for your daughter!*

A bark, deep and menacing, sounded off the port bow, from the rocky shore half a league ahead of us.

I darted my eyes in that direction and spied a massive bull seal with dark spots about his throat in sharp contrast to his light brown pelt. He was as slick as wet velvet from the sea. His pose both regal and aggressive. I imagined, could I see them, his eyes would be dark and hard as coal.

Tension poured away from me, leaving me limp with relief. I had to dip my head to shield the slight curve of my smile from the captain's gaze. I heard hundreds of seals break the surface of the water, the slap as they hauled sleek, wet muscle upon the spray-drenched rocks. In moments a mighty chorus welled up.

A sob popped upon my lips at the sound of answered prayer. Fear still tightened the flesh about my eyes at the thought of my daughter deep in the hold, but I forced it away. I had to have faith she'd be free before long.

The tone of the selkie-song shifted and changed, deepening as it crashed harshly upon all our ears. In moments the waters surrounding us went still as glass. Every bird winged away without even a cry. Far off, the clouds rumbled. The sound rolled closer and the grey sky took on an ominous yellowish tinge. Pirates cursed, their motions jerky and ill at ease. One in the rigging drew his pistol. There was a sharp click as the man cocked the weapon and took aim at the shore, though nothing short of maybe the cannons had that range.

"They're only beasts. Put up your weapon, you fool," Gow said, a tick at his jaw betraying his own doubt. "Secure the vessel for a squall." The men scrambled to comply. He then turned his eye upon me. "The course, woman, before we're caught in the blow."

I locked my gaze on Liam. He gave a short, sharp bark and a toss of his bewhiskered head toward the mouth of a nearby inlet. It was most decidedly not the one Gow sought.

Bobbing in agitation, Liam made the same motion again, followed by a prolonged roar. My eyes drifted closed and I gave a single nod.

Gow's fingers tightened upon my arm.

"There." I whimpered the lie, my hand waving limply in the direction Liam bid me. "There is the way ye seek."

The inlet seemed broad and opened, but hidden halfway through the passage, deep enough below the choppy waves that there was no sign, were treacherous rocks guaranteed to stove in any hull, no matter how shallow the draft. Combined with the coming storm, the ship and all aboard were doomed.

Better the embrace of the sea, I thought, *than the arms of the sailors.* In my heart, though, I prayed all the while that Liam would at least see his daughter safely to shore. I held no hope for his kindness toward me, not when my love—nor even my favors—had not been enough to hold him by my side.

With a triumphant laugh, Gow jerked me even more tightly against him and crashed his mouth down upon mine. His thick, foul tongue pierced my lips like a dagger before he shoved me away and hurried to the helm.

Trembling and nauseated, I slumped to the deck and crawled toward the hold, unnoticed among the frantic activity as the ship's course was altered and the vessel made fast. "Katie-Bug," I murmured through the grate, this time not daring to slip my arm through the gap as the increased chop of the waves made the ship buck and bob on the water. "Sweetling?" I cried just a touch louder when my daughter answered not. My heart gave a hard jolt as silence held sway. Then, from just below me, high up near the hatch, a pale flutter; my daughter's hand, not quite reaching the edge.

I scuttled to the far side, moving with care around barrels and coils of rope thicker than my thigh. I peered into the hold. Eyes as dark and stormy as her father's met mine. Her small, soft-edged jaw was hard set and thrust out, her body taut with waiting. My Kate, as ever attuned to the sea, had climbed up into the bracings and wedged herself into the cradle of the timbers. She'd lashed herself with a coil of rope in a loose knot. One tug upon the end line in either direction and she could tighten herself in place against any storm swell, or set herself free. Pride kindled within me nearly enough to overshadow my fear. I nodded and moved away, not wanting our captors to notice her precautions and wonder why.

"Come about, hard to port!" the captain called out, as I slid myself beneath the steps to the forecastle and braced for what was to come. In our wake I heard the selkies slide into the sea.

—⚓—

As we sailed down the inlet, the inexperienced aboard cheered at having outrun the storm. The old salts, however, were tense and edgy. Eyes flickered at the choppy water and back to the shore. Some crossed themselves; others rubbed at tokens they'd attached some superstition to. I prayed to God.

Just before we reached the hidden shoals, hundreds of whiskered faces lifted from the waves. Not one common seal was among their number now. In the distance, more selkies climbed from the sea to populate the rocks and islets we passed. Some retained their true form; others shed their skins and rose as men and women, unashamedly bare. They ringed the ship.

The crew paled. They moaned. The captain cursed. I held still and fast to the timbers of the stair, as with one voice, the selkies' invocation drowned out the mortal cries.

In the length of a breath the sky went black as soot. The sea reared up and slammed the ship forward. It crashed down against the rocks hidden by the swells. The sound of timbers giving way below was like a brutal hand wrapped around my throat, depriving me of breath. How long before the ship flooded high enough to reach my daughter's perch? Already we'd taken on enough water that buoyancy was lost. The winds grabbed hold of the vessel, tipped it and shook it, casting several of the men into the sea before once more thrusting the ship hard against the submerged rocks. There we stayed, foundered upon the shoal, listing slightly to starboard.

Katie was on the starboard side of the hold.

The echo of men's screams filled my ears, and the serenade rising from the surrounding rocks morphed from rousing and tumultuous to sensual and beckoning. Every sound melded masterfully: seal-like barks, the percussive slap of flippers upon the rocks, the rage of the storm, the shriek of tortured timbers, all sounding in dark harmony to the ethereal song lifting like a funnel about the ship. Even the jaggy sound of my breath was woven into the melody. What a compelling orchestration. It loosened my grip . . . tempted my will until I had to bite my lip to break the magic's hold, to remain steadfast. I was no unwitting fool, and yet even I nearly succumbed to the siren song.

I clung like a barnacle to my haven below the stairs and watched as my captors cast themselves into the sea. Some dashed upon the rocks until the foam was pink-tinged. Others hit the water and found themselves wrapped in welcoming embraces. Fae arms or flippers caressed the pirates' numbing limbs, locking them fast, as they spiraled down beneath the waves. Not even bubbles revealed their final resting place.

The sea was welcome to them . . . but not to me and mine. We were free of the pirates, now we'd only to escape the ship and the storm. My gaze darted toward the hold. With the hull breached I had to get Katie out before it flooded completely. We were not yet in danger of sinking, thanks to the shoal that held the ship fast, but the storm grew fierce and the vessel would be torn apart before long. Katie and I must get away before the waves were too much for the longboat. Crawling from beneath the risers, I turned toward the hatch.

Shivers wracked my body as waves cresting the side drenched me. The deck shook as the sea pounded against the hull timbers. I fought my way, crawling against the pitch of the deck when I could not keep my feet. Catching up the hook, as I had seen the pirates do, I braced myself against the deck and hauled upon the hatch covering the hold. My muscles cramped and my flesh burned against the friction of unyielding iron. Kate's cries rose like the mewing of a cub; an answering sob raged from my throat. My lips twisted with the strain and yet the grate remained cradled in its mooring. I screamed, cast the hook aside, and wound my fingers around the grate itself, unleashing my fury.

"Had I a full crew each as determined as you, no ship on the sea would stand against us." Laughter danced through the shouted words, but no mirth.

I whirled to catch up the hook once more, only to find it moved from where I'd dropped it. My gaze turned toward the helm. I'd known at the voice what I would see, and still the sight of Captain Gow lounging against the rail, the hook beside him, filled me with hatred more bitter than yarrow. I turned from him, scrambling across the hatch in the hope of finding another weapon to hand. Again the dress weighted me down. If I saw another day I would burn the hated thing. I was not even halfway across to the other side when the devil hauled me back, his hand locked about my ankle.

Not one to go easy to my death, I grabbed at the hatch, my arms snaking through the gaps. The smell of salt and pitch and fear were thick about me. Lashing out with my free leg, despite the water-soaked skirts, I caught Gow hard across the jaw. He growled and wrenched me fiercely until I felt the hatch lift from its grooves. I sent a prayer up to God and hugged the hatch tighter. I'd barely been able to lift it on my own, yet the strength of the captain it could not resist. Though my arms screamed with the strain, the hatch came up enough to cant sideways, no longer hardfast over the hold. When, with the next pull, it threatened to come up high enough to crush me, I let loose as it settled once more. With a quick tug, Gow pulled me flush against him.

"Tone deaf, poppet, I am tone deaf," he whispered in my ear, his voice a still and ominous counterpoint to the fury of the storm. "All of this . . ." he gestured to the continued song of the selkies, "naught but noise." His gaze assessed my body with offensive frankness. "But I imagine your screams will be music to my ears." He wrapped his fingers in my hair, jerking my head back until both neck and spine arched. My eyes rolled, but I forced myself to remain silent. No scream, no gasp, not even the sigh of a breath, as I watched him draw a dagger. His eyes alight with malice, he ran the point along my cheek, and down my throat, a tickling touch a thousand times worse than the bite of the blade would have been. With the tip he circled my breast above my heart and pressed just the slightest. I had seen the blade before, and knew its size. Yet it felt like no more than a pinprick piercing my skin. I was all the more chilled by that, as a spot of warmth welled from the wound. It trickled down along my neck until the salty sweet scent nigh overwhelmed me. My mouth gapped silently and I felt my eyes widen to the whites as I waited for Gow to sheath the full length through my heart.

He laughed nastily and stowed the knife. With a hard shove, he pushed me toward starboard. I stumbled and slid down the slick deck, nearly ended up over the side, but for the faithful rail I caught myself upon. I looked over the edge at the oddly canted longboat, before turning to look back at my captor.

"Yer mad an ye expect I'll leave my daughter."

"Have you a choice, faery's whore?"

"Faery's *wife.*" I snarled, for though forsaken, still I remained. "An nae better a man than he, certainly not the devil Gow."

"Ay, and God and Man sanctioned that marriage, did they?" He sneered back. "And that would be why you and your abomination lived alone on that cursed rock we found you on? Even your faery didn't want you, let alone good, decent folk."

As the words left his mouth, my hands flexed and fisted. I felt myself growl, though

I could not hear it. At the look of contempt upon his face, my rage broke loose of my control. I hurled myself at the man. He waited until I was close, then his booted foot came up to knock aside my legs, sending me to the deck at his feet. Then, gentle as a feather flutters down, he placed his foot upon my throat.

"A quick death I could give you, but you don't deserve it. You've cost me all but my life." His expression was dark and dangerous. "I think you must suffer long for all of that." With those words, his eyes slid toward the hold. An ugly little smile crept across his lips. I snarled and bucked, my hands clawing at his ankles. I had no hope against the thick leather of his boots, though, and most definitely not against the weight of him. A little harder he pressed down and the fight in me was for the moment done.

Before darkness could completely claim me, there came a thud from across the deck. Gow's head snapped round and his foot came down harder still. I bit back a gasp as a solitary twilight filled my vision.

A curse seemed to reach me from a distance and the weight left my throat. I gulped at the air though it pained me. The twilight receded, leaving in its place a pounding ache. With care I tilted my head to discover Gow at the ready, his saber in one hand and the other hidden in the folds of his coat. I tried to make out what he held but the folds were too full. Easing back, I peered past him, looking to port.

A bonny sight I beheld: Liam Roanes, in human form, crested the rail, his sealskin draped about his shoulders. I could feel his eyes upon me, large and dark and nary a white to be seen. When he spied my condition his jaw turned to granite. Then Katie cried out from below, and he roared with the voice of an enraged bull seal.

"Ah, come for your *wife*, have you?" Gow said, twisting the word in the same manner he'd said whore before. "Or perhaps your whelp? I'm afraid either way, you've come for naught."

I backed away from Gow and scrambled to my feet, clearing the way for Liam to charge. All the while, I eyed the hook still resting on the helm railing; longed for it such that I could feel its heavy weight in my grasp. Was the captain distracted enough that I could claim it?

My love shrugged off his fur cloak till it pooled on the deck, baring muscles more impressive than even Gow's. "I suggest you try your luck with the sea," Liam said, his voice dangerously even, though his eyes crackled and blazed. "It'll offer you more of a chance than you stand with me."

"So you say, faery . . . care to test your words against my steel?"

Gow tossed his saber at Liam, like a spear, in a reckless move I would not have understood were I not close behind him. I watched with dread as his hidden hand shifted. His finger curled and a sharp, familiar click reached my ears. My movement was swift for I had no care for silence or secrecy. As I dove for the hook the captain pivoted toward me. Before he could come completely about, I wrapped my fingers around the length of iron. He brought his pistol from its hiding place.

I did not wait to see where he'd take aim. The weapon belched smoke and I felt a burn along my side that left me cold. Letting loose a bellow, I swung for his head. The ship shivered and lurched, and Gow ducked aside. I staggered against the mast and whirled back around to come at him again. He tossed aside his spent pistol and drew his cutlass. The blade cut the air above my head, bit into timber, and caught fast. I scrambled away from the captain's reach as he wrenched the weapon free. Beneath me, the deck bucked and sheets of rain kept the boards slick. I came up against the rail close by the hoist holding the longboat aloft. Braced, I pivoted and brought my hook arcing up with all my strength just as the captain lunged. His cutlass sliced through the rope securing the longboat as he lashed down at me. The boat crashed into the waves as my weapon connected with Gow's head.

There was a spongy resistance that swiftly gave away, accompanied by a hot salty spray across my face and bosom. I gasped, my stomach heaving. Gow shrieked, and my weapon was wrenched from my hands. He staggered back, clutching at the curved length of iron imbedded deep in his eye. One step he took forward, and then another, before crumbling against me, tumbling us both down. The weight of him pinned me to the deck.

Numbly, I shoved at him to no avail. With a keen, I pushed harder until I could drag myself from beneath him and scramble to my feet. I trembled, scrubbing my hands hard across the wet velvet of my dress, flinching as my fingers brushed too near my side. My hands came away more red than before, yet I felt very little at the sight. Instead, images of my love, and Katie, and the past two days billowed through my thoughts, dampening the horror in me. Still, my gaze locked upon the man whose death I'd dealt and I could not draw it away. The only thought I had was that the longboat was gone, and with it our slender hope of reaching land.

"Mam!"

My daughter's cry called me back from Hell's edge. I shoved all thought of my deed to the recesses of my mind and turned toward the hatch, stumbling as the ache at my side grew sharper. I pushed the pain aside; there was no time for it. Liam no longer stood across the deck, though his sealskin was a rich, dark pool on the timbers. I staggered toward the hold, peering desperately at the nook where Katie had secured herself. Eyes dark and deep and unreadable met mine . . . another set, near identical but for the size and the uncertainty they held, stared up from just above the water. The level rose as I watched.

"A blade, Sionna . . . *now*."

Hardly the words of one lovelorn, I thought without bitterness. He had come for his daughter. 'Twas all I'd hoped for before he'd even appeared. And still despair took a tighter hold upon my heart. I forced it away as my mind conceived the reason for his demand. The rope that bound Katie would have swelled in the immersion, the knot locked tight. I turned without a word and dropped to the deck, my side screaming as I looked for the cutlass Gow had dropped. I was near tears when I could not find it.

Swallowing hard I turned toward the captain's corpse. Remembered with cold clarity the moments before Liam boarded the ship. I did not even flinch as I dove upon the body and shoved it over. Fresh blood marred my hands and face, my dress, but the dagger was clear. I snatched it from its sheath and rushed back to the hold.

Another selkie had appeared. Male or female, I could not tell, though it also was in human form. Its face was too young for the features to betray its gender. It must have come through the gash in the hull. I handed down the blade and watched as Liam slid it between the timber and the line. With one hard jerk he severed Katie's bonds and thrust the blade back into my hands.

Not knowing her father's face, Katie clung where she was, though the waterline lapped about her lips. I watched as Liam's expression softened and his eyes glowed like rich onyx. With a closed smile that did not bare his seal's teeth, my husband reached beneath the water for Katie's hand. She jerked back, but he was as firm as he was gentle. He pulled her hand toward him into the light. Holding his own so they were palm to palm, he spread both their fingers wide. Upon seeing her webbing mirrored by his, all fear and doubt fled Katie's face. Her smile was like sunshine upon the snow as she propelled herself out of the water and latched about his neck. I heard the echo of a seal's bark in Liam's laugh and savored the sweet pain of the memories it resurrected.

A smile lit my face as father and daughter at last met. It quickly fled as I watched Liam lower his face, pressing his lips upon Katie's. I saw her cheeks stretch as he forced open her mouth. Her eyes went wide. She started to pull back. He would not let her. Her hands came up and scratched at his face, and still he held her fast. The dagger fell forgotten from my grip.

"You vile devil!" I raged as I scrambled to pass through the hatch, only to double over with the effort, gasping from the pain I could no longer ignore. I groaned as fresh warmth spread down my side in sharp contrast to the chill that crept across the rest of me. Gow's ball had more than found its mark.

Liam's eyes slid toward mine. The look in them stilled me. Without a word they both ordered me to stay and begged me to trust. Though his mouth remained mated to our daughter's, there was no sign of passion. It was madness, but I could not move, whether by compulsion, or the stupidity of love, I cannot say. I watched in horror as he blew a deep, sharp breath into her lungs. Only then did he release her head and move his away. Dreamlike, his hand reached up to his own face, caressing a trail through the blood marring his cheek. He looked at the crimson on his fingertips then turned a solemn gaze on his daughter.

"Trust me . . ." he murmured, the words holding the ghost of pleading. She just stared at him, her eyes wide. And after a moment, perhaps under the same spell as I, she nodded. He swiftly hugged her to him, brushed across her brow a more fatherly kiss, and slid her into the other selkie's arms.

Before my eyes they disappeared below the water. They did not return. I shrieked and would have dove after but for Liam's arm locking fast about my waist. He had climbed from the hold swiftly, before I'd even realized. His grip tightened until agony drew a fog across my vision. I fought both it and him. He would not let me go any more than he had Katie.

Katie!

This . . . this is how love becomes hate.

"What? What?!" I snarled. "Was she too human for you?"

I twisted in his arms despite my growing pain and raked him as my daughter had. I bucked and thrashed and pummeled him as best I could, each effort weaker than the last. He simply took it, unmoving, anguish flooding his eyes.

Even fury could not sustain me long. Energy bled out of me. I went limp in his grasp and leaned as far out from him as I was able. I barely noticed the storm still raged about us. It was nothing compared to the one within my heart.

My daughter. My daughter was gone by her own father's doing. A weak keening broke free from my throat.

Liam's grip shifted until he cradled me in a mockery of our loving days. I held myself stiff but did not fight. Heedless of the danger of our situation, he lowered us to the deck and sat with me nestled in his lap. His hands traced a slow path along the length of me, as if he sought to relearn familiar ground. It seduced me to a calm quite at odds with our surroundings. It lulled me into a twilight place where there was no storm or death or doubt. With each breath my personal twilight crept deeper into night.

His hand stilled along my side. His head came up and his eyes looked hard into mine. Swiftly he caught up the blade I'd dropped to the deck. Carefully, he slit the whore's dress down the entire length and pushed it from my shoulders until it slid off my arms to the timbers. *Good riddin's*, I thought muzzily, glad to be freed from the hateful thing. No matter that I'd nothing to replace it with. No matter.

"'Od's Blood!" Liam cursed and it was as if the words were uttered far away and softly. He clutched me even closer and all I felt was a twinge. He muttered more but it was lost to me in the twilight. Again he caressed me, leaving a trail of warmth from one end to the other.

I almost felt loved once more as he sang a softer kind of selkie song into my ear. Not one of power and summoning, but one of comfort and entreaty. I took a step out of the twilight, struggled to conceive the anxiety in his words. I whimpered and my eyes drifted closed. With one hand he pulled his sealskin toward us.

He stopped his singing and I felt his fingers upon my chin, gently bearing up. I kept my eyes closed, comfortable in my illusion, wanting just a moment longer of feeling cherished. I did not want to see what he did or did not think of me, even more human than the daughter he betrayed.

"Look at me, my love." His tone was as pleading as his gaze had been. I could not hold on to why I should loath him. I wanted to see his bonny face once more. It was an effort, but I opened my eyes to find him peering intently at me. Worry etched his brow and wore grooves along his sinful mouth. I was puzzled by what I saw in his gaze. Dared not even try to give it name, but damn my soul if my heart did not pound with love for him still.

"Trust me," he said earnestly. My outrage tried to rise up with the memories as he mirrored the words he'd said to my daughter. My love ignored it. In a daze I nodded and watched as his hand pulled away. I gasped. His hand was painted red with blood, though I could see no sign of injury upon him beyond slight scrapes. He reached up and again smeared the fresh blood beading his marred cheek, mingling it with what already coated his hand. This time he brought the fingers to my closed lips. My eyes widened and I shook my head.

"You must trust me! We have no time to waste!"

Whether that were true or not, I was swayed by the desperation woven through his words. My lips trembled as I parted them. His fingers slid inside and brushed my tongue with his lifeblood. I swallowed reflexively. Liam smiled and withdrew his fingers, only to replace them with his lips. My entire body quivered as he breathed into me as he had Katie.

With his mouth still locked over mine, he reached over and hurriedly drew the sealskin around my bare shoulders, then shifted me to cloak my naked legs as well. Confused, I crushed the thick, rich fur between my fingers. Such power he gave into my hands. Eyes solemn, he nodded, as if I had spoken the realization aloud. He then drew a final fold up over my head, leaving only my face bare.

I heard him whisper into my thoughts, *Blood of my blood, breath of my breath, flesh of my flesh. Be reborn.*

I gasped and twitched and reluctantly reconnected with my sense of self. Leaving the twilight completely, I conceived at once the aches running the length of my body, moaned at the burning fire consuming my side. Just a shade short of overwhelmed, my head lolled back and I turned frightened eyes upon my love. I had no strength to voice the questions that came to mind.

This time the world disappeared in a golden haze and an electric tingle swept over my body, like a promise of lightning in the air. In its wake, the pain was chased away. Consciousness followed.

———⚓———

I woke to the sound of seals singing in triumph and joy. I woke to a small, furred body curled beside mine. I woke to the absence of pain. I woke to my own fur rippling in the warmth of a sun-baked rock. I woke to a dream: Liam's body nestled at my back, his flippers lazily caressing my side.

Seven years, my love, seven years I was bound by the curse of my kind to stay away, though I willed it not, Liam murmured sleepily into my thoughts. *But seven years have ended and nothing, not life nor death nor the devil Gow will keep me from your side e'er again.* Liam wrapped close about me as if he would be one with me forever.

Seven tears slid down to slick my fur and an unfamiliar bark escaped my throat, filled with both new joy and the remnants of sorrow.

The cub beside me stirred, arched its head back in the graceful, impossible way of seals, and peered into my face with the eyes of my daughter.

My voice joined the selkie chorus.

Tisarian's Treasure
J. M. Martin

e stood—most of us, that is—on a pebbled shore, each transfixed in his or her own combination of horror and dismay. We watched it burn. Little more than black shapes of so much flotsam along the mist-choked island coast; that was the doom of the *Decimus*, our gallant caravel. Soaked, frightened, some of us wounded to various extents, I knew it wasn't the fate of the ship that concerned us so much as our own.

I squinted, doing my best to peer through the black smoke and fog, beyond the burning wreckage. Whether it was my eyes or my panicked mind that illumined the silhouette, I cannot say, but there it came, a tall, black three-masted galleon, cleaving the choppy black sea. I knew a maligned figure stood on her deck, scowling and ferocious, examining the ruin of the *Decimus* with a critical eye.

Captain Thadieus Drake, bane of the West Tradesea.

He would not be fooled by our ploy. I had voiced as much, echoing despicable Oberon Teag. Much as I reviled to say it, we had something in common. We'd been pressed into the employ of that black-hearted demon, though but one of us took to it so eagerly.

"We should make inland," Teag said, an edge of desperation to his voice. "Be coming on, 'e will, wi'v a vengeance after 'e sorts it out, I daresay."

"What of the boat?" the cabin boy said—Dominy I believed his name.

"To the Hells wi' the boat! What about Cap'n Bellows?" Boatswain Marshall, like me, seemed to have been immersed in a cauldron of blood, none of it our own. His voice, much too loud for anyone's tastes, caromed off the cliffs above us. We winced as his echo rolled out to sea, and that's how I knew they suspected, as I did, our ordeals were far from over.

I noticed—since he was standing next to me—the Albiyan called Hamish impart a dark scowl to the boatswain, then glare out to sea. A bull-necked freebooter with a tow-headed shock of knife-cut hair, he stood carapaced in ash-coated, gore-smeared iron and leather, and, as I'd witnessed recently, was rather versed in the issue of bloodletting. My inquiries had led me to find he was once an officer in the Albiyan navy, forced into early retirement, discharged dishonorably it was said, but I could gather nothing more. Considering the man's usual manner, I was content to leave my curiosity unsated.

It would, perhaps, serve the reader best if I took a moment to shed light on the scene, and its players, in a bit more detail. Eight crewmembers of the erstwhile *Decimus* made it to shore in the ship's boat. This desperate flight came after Lieutenant Jeric Hensley, the ship's first mate, gave the order to fire the already-sinking caravel. You see, the pirate Thadieus Drake and his crew aboard the *skein*-galleon, the *Tatterdemalion*, had slithered out of a secluded inlet as we skimmed the coast of an island we believed was destined to make us wealthy beyond our imaginings. To a man—one being a lady actually—we felt our blood cool in our veins at the sight of that dreaded black flag with its laughing crimson skull.

The chase was brief. Drake was in no mood to bandy words. I was familiar enough with the *Tatterdemalion*, having been aboard her for the better part of three months, to know we stood nary a chance. Dark magic sailed her, and she bore fourteen culverins to each side, two sliding falconets at the bow, another three pointed aft, a long nine for bow or stern, and Drake at her helm. His voice thundered across the dark water: "Run 'em out, and send 'em all to the Nine!"

The Nine Hells, that is.

I'd like to say the fight was a valiant one, but how does the dove fare beneath the goshawk? Of course, that's putting it poetically. The *Tatterdemalion* blew the crew of the *Decimus* to who-knows-what level of hell; I suppose a deep, black, watery, dismal one. I'm certain there's a name for it, but it eludes me; which is precisely what those of us who remained alive hoped we'd done. Eluded Thadieus Drake.

Among those in flight: the unconscious captain, Laurens Bellows, freed of the anguish of witnessing his ship's consignment to the deep by a mess of shrapnel; his first mate, Lieutenant Jeric Hensley, fair, moderate, the very paragon of a naval officer; Boatswain Bartholomew Marshall, an ill-tempered chap with a thick walrus mustache and blind in one eye from a collision with a loose jib in his earlier sailing days; and young Master Dominy, a fledgling cabin boy of no more than ten. Also standing on the shore, the aforementioned Hamish, a mercenary bounty hunter and his captive, Oberon Teag, upon which this whole affair seemed to hinge, damn him; and a secret passenger, an intriguing Anturian who'd only deigned to share her first name, Katalin. Oh, and myself.

"Doctor Mallory? Haver look, will ye?"

Alexandre Mallory, that's me. A promising young doctor, born of an influential Berdainese family, studied at Nantyrr in Thansia, and just one year ago awarded my chirurgeon's license along with the Royal Doctorial Marque.

Lieutenant Hensley peered up from where he knelt next to the captain, who lay pale and sodden on the wet stones. All faces turned to me.

"Of course," I said.

"Now's not bein' the best time," the towering Hamish said, a mailed glove still gripping his claymore, the other suddenly lay heavy upon my shoulder. "We'd best get ourselves from sight."

"Aye, but the boy's got a point. They'll see the boat." The boatswain indicated the sloop where it pitched in the shallow surf.

"We move it, then. Behind yon boulders. Let's go." He gave Oberon a rough shove in the boat's direction. The boatswain, the bounty hunter, and the glaring prisoner all grasped the gunwales and heaved.

"Some help, Doctor?" Boatswain Marshall said.

I nodded and pulled my satchel's shoulder strap over my head, setting it down. I quickly moved to grab hold of the boat and together the four of us managed to drag it out of the sea several paces up the beach.

I'd venture to guess we were more than a good dozen staggering steps inland, when we heard that terrible, recurring thump, a noise strikingly familiar to the sailor's ear. A distant medium-pitched hiss suddenly became a keening wail.

Teag's stubbly chin dropped. "Bugger this," he said, then broke into a sprint. His wide-set, heavy-lidded eyes, short nose, and long upper lip had always conveyed a Chelonian air in my mind. Yet, ever swift and fleet of foot, the man was far from turtle-like in his actions. Hamish, the Albiyan, dashed after him with a rumbling snarl.

Two of its bearers having run off, the ship's boat thudded to the ground. I looked to the boatswain, whose head swiveled skyward, wide brow furrowed.

From several spans away, Lieutenant Hensley called "cover" an eye's blink before the beach around us and the cliffs above rained shards of rock and dust. We were too late. I pictured Drake watching through his spyglass, grinning as his 18-pounders spit bedlam and fear upon us.

I dropped to my hands and knees and pressed against the side of the boat, knowing it made flimsy protection but unable to do otherwise. The boatswain darted off toward the remainder of the crew, all in the wake of Teag and the Albiyan bounty hunter, who chased his fleeing prisoner toward the sheer cliffs some distance off.

A cannonball slammed the shoreline, and jets of gravel and sea spray pelted me. I would have clutched my knees, clenched my eyes, and prayed to the gods of my fathers' there and then if it were not for an odd sight suddenly commanding my interest.

Thin and long-limbed, auburn hair pulled loosely back so that wet-darkened ringlets framed her freckled face, Katalin walked toward the sea. Her hazel eyes fixed to mine with an undisturbed gaze as she bent down and retrieved my satchel from where it lay, while the *Tatterdemalion's* guns continued to powder the coast.

Pebbles and earth splattered us both as she approached in a casual woman's gait. She smiled and extended my leather bag down to me. "You will need this soon, Doctor."

How strange it seemed, that smile, barely crooked white teeth and dimpled cheeks displayed in a poise and surety amidst all the chaos. She offered her hand, as well. "You and I have nothing to fear. Leastways not yet. But we do need to leave the beach. Come."

I don't recall taking the satchel from her, but I do recall taking her hand, soft and long-boned like the rest of her, and feeling an immediate sense of calm and confidence. I didn't know anything about Katalin then, but in that moment I became her thrall.

We dashed toward the others, and though the beach exploded thrice more behind us, we caught up to Lieutenant Hensley and young Dominy as they grappled with the burden of their inert captain. The first mate yelled to Boatswain Marshall to lend a hand and the man rushed to grab the captain's ankles from the cabin boy. I bit my tongue, knowing it unwise to jostle the wounded man, but realizing, too, that Drake robbed us of any choice to the contrary.

"O'er here!" the Albiyan said in a gravelly bellow. He pointed after Teag, who was already scrambling around a corner in the cliff face.

We hurried over some shallow dunes, weaving amid patches of tall silt grass, into a cleft of sorts where a talus slope of earth ramped sharply upward. We scrabbled in bits of scree, but enough rocky outcrops were fixed to give purchase for a labored ascent, and I managed to scale to the high ground with little more than scuffed palms and a few other minor scrapes—a small price to pay for the corner we'd turned, removing us from the *Tatterdemalion's* barrage. The men hefting the motionless captain were the last to make it up. I saw, too, that Hamish had Oberon Teag well in hand, hard words shared between them.

The first mate and the boatswain plunked down beside the captain, and even young Dominy looked belabored, using his neck rag to wipe sweat from his brow. I bent, hands to knees, and took a breather, as well.

Lieutenant Hensley's voice snapped my attention from watching Katalin, who stood nearby, bosom rising and falling, accentuated by her tight-laced bodice. "We shan't tarry here, as I'm expecting Drake'll be making for land even now, but if'n ye please, Doctor?"

"Certainly," I said, rather embarrassed, fearing having been caught with a roving eye in that improper moment. "Of course."

I moved to the unconscious Captain Bellows and went to a knee, placing the side of my face near his colorless lips. Was it his breath or merely the sea air that barely draped my cheek? I could not tell, so I snaked two fingertips inside his high collar, placing them aside the distinct protrusion of his larynx. After a moment's hesitation, I found it; his pulse coursed weakly in the *carotis arturiolis*, a vital conduit for passage of blood and humors to the brain.

"His pulse is faint, his breathing extremely labored," I said to Hensley. "I fear I cannot help him unless I treat him straightaway, Lieutenant."

"Then we need to find shelter, a place to hide—"

"Every time he's moved we risk more damage. I need to treat him here, right now. For all I know, what's done is already beyond my ability to repair."

The first mate met my gaze and chewed the inside of his lip, unsure how to answer. He didn't need to voice his fear. The explosions on the beach had stopped and, even now, Drake and his roughest cutthroats likely rowed their way to shore. I recollected the evil eyes and ugly face of Aubrid the Myg Rothan, the one they called the Albatross, and I shivered; several weeks past I'd witnessed his pleasure in the disembowelment of a captive. Drake would most certainly have picked him as part of the landing party.

"That bein' the case, hardly matters if we move him some more," Teag said from where he stood next to the towering Albiyan.

Everyone watched expectantly. Lieutenant Hensley's jaw clenched once, then he sighed through his nose. His brown-eyed gaze met mine. "I'm loath to admit, but he's right. We need to keep moving. The captain would understand."

"Aye," Boatswain Marshall said, bobbing his head.

Prudence dictated our actions, and though my years of training urged further contention on the captain's behalf, I choked it down and nodded. We stood, and both Hensley and Marshall took up Bellows, his pallor that of a dead man's, and we moved hastily landward.

On the terrace, we traversed a short rock-strewn incline to a tangled mass of verdant, sharp-leafed palms, interspersed with other yellow-barked trees dangling thick strands of moss. The jungle extended both ways as far as we could tell, and away from the ocean. I became aware of the heat of the day with the sun beating down from the cloudless blue. The sounds of the sea, too, faded away and instead the jungle called out; tropical birds screeched and tittered from within its foliage.

The sea spray on my skin had since turned to sweat, and I found my gaze once more on Katalin, thanks to her décolleté garment. She stood quite near to me as we surveyed the jungle, sweating prettily, rivulets coursing down her exposed collarbone and over the tops of her breasts. I became aware that I wasn't the only one casting a lascivious eye. Oberon Teag's weathered face shared a brown-toothed smile, as if we were somehow bonded by virtue of maleness. I frowned and looked away.

"Now where to?" the boatswain said, his craggy features made all the more rough as he frowned and readjusted his grip on the captain.

"If shelter's our aim, seems not much choice but in," Hamish said, aiming his large chin at the trees.

Hensley peered with a grim eye at the jungle, his face dripping sweat, chest rising and falling, and mimicking Boatswain Marshall he, too, shifted the captain's weight.

As the first mate chewed on the decision, I chanced another glance at Katalin. Her expression was drained of all color, her gaze falling into some middle distance between Boatswain Marshall and herself. I touched her arm lightly. "Are you well, m'lady?"

She did not answer for such a while that I suspected she was in some sort of trance-like state, then her eyelids fluttered. Katalin suspired expressively, and she turned in my direction, leaning close. Something rippled in my chest as she did so. "For whatever good it's worth," she said in low tones, "don't let the boatswain near the water."

"Excuse me, m'lady?"

"Why I'm telling you this, I know not. My warnings fail to ever make a difference, but I'm telling you, Doctor, I've seen that man's end. It's not a good one . . . though they rarely are."

"I don't quite follow."

"No, I shouldn't think you would," she said.

The first mate had evidently came to a decision, and he barked something terse. The group began moving into the trees.

"Come, Doctor," Katalin said softly as she followed them.

If I felt trepidation before stepping into the shadowed forest, a few strides into its depths, my eyes struggling to pierce the darkness, and that foreboding turned to pure dread. The gravity of our predicament dawned on me. We no longer had a ship or a way to sail from this unmapped island, and we were walking into some nameless jungle where death lay in wait for fools. We had no food, no water, and no clear destination in mind, lugging our unconscious captain. And, of course, the most feared pirate from Harrahtun's Channel to the West Tradesea was hard on our heels with a band of cutthroats and freebooters at his beck and call.

"What is it, precisely, that we're doing here?" I said, shouting ahead to the first mate. "I mean, where exactly are we going?"

"Your guess be good as mine," Hensley replied. "I don't know where we're going,

Doctor, but we must find shelter for Captain Bellows. I don't know if we'll elude that vulture Drake, so we can only pray for a defensible position—or a miracle."

So we continued.

The jungle had no trails to speak of, so at Hensley's behest, Hamish moved to the fore and began using his claymore to scythe away at the tangled networks of vines, bushes, and small trees. His weapon proved no substitute for a machete, and we were often forced to turn back and find an alternate course. Every time we did so, I feared running into our pursuers. If someone with even a mote of tracking experience were among Drake's landing party, it would be a simple matter to uncover the broken limbs and trampled underbrush of our passage.

Despite my fears, we remained undiscovered, through what felt like leagues of foliage and webs of vines, often over treacherous footing, amidst spiders, snakes, large rodent-like creatures, and birds of every cry and color I could imagine. We finally came upon a clearing where grew a variety of flowers and weeds, and here we paused to rest.

I immediately saw to the poor captain, who'd remained clinging to life throughout the long day. His flesh was cold and bloodless, his pupils enlarged so that no evidence of his slate-gray eyes could be found. I palpated his wounds and was sorely dismayed to find part of his head above the ear puffed out and slick with blood. With a finger, I probed beneath the split skin to find his skull had all the fragility of a cracked bird's egg. Frowning, I removed some instruments from my chirurgeon's satchel. "I need water," I said softly to Hensley.

"He needs water," the first mate said to the others.

"We all do," Oberon Teag dryly grated in response.

The Albiyan shoved past Teag, evidently still in a foul way since having to misuse his weapon, and approached. "Here. A full skin," he said, taking out a waterskin from a weathered leather pouch at his left hip.

I accepted it with a nod and used the water to clean blood from the captain's scalp. Teag murmured something about "water damn wasted," obtaining several hard glares.

Once the blood was somewhat washed away, I proceeded to sew the wound with a needle and catgut, and bandaged his head with linen. It was the only treatment I could offer, and I harbored little hope. In a fog of exhaustion I conveyed as much to Lieutenant Hensley, with the boatswain and cabin boy looking on. Hensley merely nodded and tried pouring some of the water into the captain's mouth, but it dribbled out. After another try, the first mate shook his head and handed the skin back to Hamish with a word of thanks.

The Albiyan passed the skin around with a scrutinizing eye to ensure everyone took a liberal amount, then we all sat resting in morose silence for a spell.

"The day's fading," Hensley finally said. "No sense moving the captain more today. We'll rest here for the night."

No one issued a better idea and, in truth, all seemed quite leaden. Myself, I could no longer walk without my knees buckling, and Teag appeared already asleep, slouched at the base of a nearby tree. I looked to Katalin, who merely sat hugging her knees and gazing once more into that mysterious middle distance. Hensley, Marshall, and Hamish agreed to a watch order, then the lieutenant told the rest of us to get what sleep we could.

A chilly mist enshrouded us as night fell. I lay curled on a flat rock, fading in and out of awareness for the first hour or two, unable to sleep, fretting and fighting the urge to start at every night noise. In time, I rose to make relief, and managed to quietly find my way to a nearby tree, whereupon I heard whispering.

"We've got Teag and his bloody map, so we sail the course."

"Aye, 'cept what's the point, eh? Treasure's no good if we can't hie ourselves gone from this wretched place. I say we parlay wiv' Drake 'n' strike a deal." I recognized this as Boatswain Marshall's voice.

"Drake's got no honor," the other voice responded. Hensley's. "Nothing would stop him from killing every one of us and just taking Teag's map."

"You see dis map, den? 'Ow we know it even exists?"

"I haven't seen it, but the Albiyan says Teag has it."

"How come the Albiyan don't have it hisself? Why's 'e lettin' that rascal keep it? An' if we do find this thing, we still be stuck on the island, so what then, eh?"

If included in the exchange, I could bear out the details for them. I'd seen the map and knew beyond a shadow of a doubt Teag had it. I also knew how the 'rascal' managed to keep it in his possession. But Marshall had a point. Treasure or no, we were undeniably fixed in an ill predicament.

"Eavesdropping, Doctor?" a voice whispered in my ear. My head turned quickly. Katalin continued by softly saying, "Be at ease. It matters naught to me. I eavesdrop all the time, usually in spite of myself."

Her hand touched my shoulder, her nearness stirring my senses, but I managed to control myself somewhat. "You have a look about you sometimes," I whispered, "as if seeing something that's not there. Is—is that it? Is that what you mean?"

The moon shined down from high above, filtering through the leaves, tracing her silhouette in an eerie white glow. She imparted a brief smile, but a passing thing, it was, that swiftly fluttered and then was gone.

"You see things, m'lady?" I leaned in, carefully keeping my voice low, our faces mere inches apart. She seemed a ghost amid the twisted jungle silhouettes, and my pulse quickened even more.

"I've learned, Doctor . . . I've learned there's no sense in it, telling you what I see," she said. "It changes nothing. All comes to pass, whither I endeavor to stave it off or no, but I can tell you this: you will be there, at the end; you, me, the boy . . . and Drake. I foresaw it months ago. It's why I booked passage on the *Decimus*. 'Tis a strange thing, Doctor. It leads, I follow. My destiny lies ahead of us. Perhaps yours, too."

She paused briefly, head tilting slowly down, then looked back up at me. "Don't be startled. In a few seconds we'll be discovered." That said, she took my face in both slender hands and touched her full lips to mine. My eyes closed, my mind reeled—they were even softer than I imagined.

Lieutenant Hensley's voice suddenly wrecked the moment. Katalin pulled her lips from mine as he said, "Ah . . . um, pardon, Doctor, M'lady . . . but this is not the best milieu for a . . . rendezvous, if ye please? We shouldn't stray here, especially at night."

I wasn't sure just how to respond, my mind still reeling. Fortunately, Katalin spoke. "Apologies, Lieutenant. This is all just too much for me and I sought comfort from the good doctor." She looked at me. "I apologize, Doctor, for throwing myself at you."

"Uhm . . . quite all right," I managed to murmur, more breathily than intended.

Katalin turned and strode quietly back to where the others were asleep. I watched her fade from the silvery moonlight into the gloomy silhouettes, then turned my gaze to the lieutenant. He stoically motioned for me to return, as well. I managed a small embarrassed smile and nod, and did as he suggested. I idly rubbed my lips with my fingertips, recalling the taste and feel of Katalin's kiss, waiting for slumber to wash over me.

The next morning arrived much too soon. I sat up and stretched, still fatigued and shivering from the dampness of my garb. My eyes roved to Katalin, who sat several spans distant, working the snarls from her hair. Then, as the chilly mist that pervaded the night gave way to another day of sweltering heat, I checked Captain Bellows. He yet lived, but seemed to have worsened further—if that were at all possible.

Meanwhile, Dominy alerted Lieutenant Hensley to something in the near distance: a narrow dirt track—a trail. Whose was the question, but after everyone had roused and Marshall and Dominy had built a litter for the captain from fallen branches, we decided to follow it.

After two, perhaps three, hours of walking, the heat of the day gradually fell heavy upon us, the air practically suffocating. More than once an eerie feeling caused my flesh to crawl, and I would pause to glance about, searching the understory as best I could for some horrible brooding thing watching us. I looked for the dark shapes of men, but made out nothing. The uncertain feelings refused to fade, however.

We continued along and the trail eventually tapered to a tenuous shadow, lost among the wild plants. I peered up at the avenue of blue sky above, narrowed to a mere slit, then turned my gaze to Hensley and Marshall as they bore the captain on their makeshift litter. Both men looked done in, first whispering to one another with grim stares, then raising their voices into growls. Arguing, no doubt, and I wondered if it regarded their clandestine exchange I'd overheard last night. Were they deciding to give in and seek out Thadieus Drake?

"Shh!" Teag hissed. "Listen."

Then we all heard it: the beckoning sound of rushing water, somewhere just ahead. We stepped lively, rushing down the trail. A shaded clearing opened up to a long, thin, white rivulet of waterfall, flanked on each side by even thinner, trickling falls. The effusion cascaded perhaps twelve arm spans into a rippling green lagoon hemmed by large blooms of white and vermillion, then flowed onward, resuming its current some forty spans downstream.

Someone hooted and all at once we rushed down an escarpment of rock and large serpentine roots tangling and wending their way through the sediment. Being one of the first to emerge from the growth, I started when a dozen or more birds took wing mere yards away, launching from their baths in a sudden upsurge of cobalt-blue and brilliant turquoise.

At first, the water stung with its coolness, but after the initial shock I splashed my face, neck, and arms, thankful for the relief from the scores of fly bites I'd endured. Indeed, I started considering immersing myself entirely when a shadow fell over me.

"Here, Doctor," Master Dominy said, reaching into his kerchief and producing a plump, green, teardrop-shaped fruit. He tossed it to me.

I caught and considered it briefly. "Fig, is it?"

"Aye, trees full of 'em just over yon," he said with a wave of his hand toward the jungle. "You shouldn't be wandering away from the group, young master."

The boy shrugged, and strode away to dole out his findings to the others.

I watched him for a moment, then turned back to the water just in time to spy a ripple in the reddish algae where it gathered in places along the pool's edge. Boatswain Marshall kneeled quite near the movement, splashing water on his face. He paused and looked up, then I heard it, as well: an odd hissing noise that seemed to emanate from all around. Katalin's words came to mind, but too late. I opened my mouth to shout a warning to the boatswain, but the water erupted in a glittering shadow and a thing jettisoned forth, grabbing the man up.

The size of a large horse, armored in bumpy iridian plates from white to yellow to brown to orange, the beast seemed an arthropod of some sort. Its plated head bore a pair of hook-like legs—legs with which it held the screaming Marshall aloft. It scrabbled sidelong at the water's edge on a multitude of sharp appendages attached to its thoracic and abdominal segments. Mandibles and mouthparts snapped and scissored furiously in a terrifying din, conjuring in my mind the image of a thousand crows pecking against a single pane of glass.

The Albiyan sprang into action. He bellowed and brandished his claymore, leaping past me, and landing with one foot in the pool and one foot out. Hamish hacked savagely at the giant crustacean-creature, but his blade glanced off its chitinous armor. Marshall continued to scream. The thing twisted and swayed, backing further into the water.

With a grotesque cracking noise, the boatswain warped into a red nightmare. Blood and gore showered the Albiyan, yet he managed to shear off one of the creature's forelimbs before it submerged with what remained of Marshall. In the water to his knees, Hamish took one last thrust at where he thought the beast might be lurking just beneath the surface. Stabbing nothing, he growled and spouted a litany of curses in his native tongue.

Meanwhile, I searched for Katalin and found her standing alone on a moss-covered rise. She met my horrified gaze with a sad one of her own.

Don't let the boatswain near the water. . . .

My mind reeled as I realized she might be *skein*-touched.

"Where's bloody Teag?" Hamish rushed toward us, claymore in hand, a feral gleam yet in his eyes.

Oberon Teag had evidently decided to make the most of Marshall's death by fleeing into the jungle.

"There." Katalin pointed. "He ran that way."

"Wait!" Lieutenant Hensley yelled, but the Albiyan was already dashing off into the trees. The first mate turned to me and said imploringly, "We can't abandon the captain," as if he thought I, too, was planning to give chase—which I most assuredly was not; though I didn't relish staying near the monster in the lagoon either, lest it decided to surface again.

"No, of course not," I said, and strode over to where he and Dominy stood. I peered back at Katalin just as Hensley spoke again. "M'lady, please, come away from the water."

"As you please, Lieutenant," she said slowly.

"Gods, what was that . . . that *thing*?" Dominy asked, eyes still wide with fright.

"Not for sure, lad," Hensley placed his hand on the boy's shoulder, "but I've seen the like years ago on the Galleon Coast; all kinds of giant crabs and insects and other mutations. No way for a man to go. Poor Marshall. It's no way at all. May he rest in the morning tide with his lady love."

I assumed the first mate meant Marshall's deceased wife or some such, but dismissed the thought while joining them in a moment of silence for their fallen comrade. We stood quietly for several long breaths, a sullen mist rising in the sweltering heat as the tropical forest darkened. I felt the eyes again, and soon a commotion in the jungle drew up our heads. Something moved toward us through the underbrush.

Katalin looked at the ground beneath long-lashed drooping lids. She reached out and took my hand. Her words came fraught with a menace that stole my next breath: "*They* are here."

A crowd of shadows moved in the jungle, and Hamish stepped into view at the fore, his taut, suffused face set in a grim mask. Behind him came Thadieus Drake, tall and wide-shouldered, a crimson bandanna tied beneath his cocked hat, the brim of which partially shaded his grizzled face, yet not quite enough to hide those protean eyes, sometimes blue, sometimes gray, sometimes green, always deep-set and beaming. A broadsword with a gold basket-hilt hung in a scroll-worked baldric at his waist, and two gold-chased, burgundy pistols were housed in a cross belt over his ruffled silk tunic. He bore another pair of black silver-chased pistols, one cocked in each hand, pointing them at the Albiyan's broad back. Upon seeing us, his black-whiskered lips imparted a feral grin like that of a hungry leopard's. He swiveled one pistol in our direction.

"Ho, what fortune!" The pirate captain greeted us in his off-putting, self-possessed baritone. "Doubly so that we should renew our acquaintance, good Doctor." Then Drake smiled at Katalin. "Ah, an' a flower of womanhood, as well? Truly, the gods are fine."

He moved into the clearing, prodding Hamish ahead of him with a pistol barrel. The dimness of the jungle had grown thicker, the sky above no longer blue but the color of slate, gray and heavy. From the darkness of the undergrowth, more men came into view, some nine or ten of them, with Oberon Teag among their numbers. Pirates, they were, every steely eyed one, with metallic rings in their ears, noses, some even their lips, and armed to the teeth with blades and pistols of every sort, their very bearing threatening murder. Alongside Teag strode Aubrid, the Albatross, lean and scarred, with a hooked beak for a nose, black cavernous eyes, and a brass-hilted cutlass shoved through an orange sash about his slim waist. His tangled mess of iodine-stained hair and unshorn cheeks framed an evil, pockmarked face I'd come to fear, and his black gaze bored malignantly into mine.

"Sea Lord's salty balls on the Queen's chin, yer a game lot, aye!" Drake looked to Hensley. "Ye must be Lieutenant Hensley, then? Bellows' first mate? Bugger me if ye didn't lead a fine chase, lad. Slippin' off ta land in all that smoke—crafty, aye." He moved in close as he continued, and we clumped together as he directed Hamish with a wave of his pistol to stand among us. "But the chase ever ends sooner than later. Appears ta ha' taken its toll on poor Bellows. Now, I'm of a mind to make an accord, if ye will. Wha' do ye say, Lieutenant?"

"An accord?"

"Aye, that's wha' I said."

"Of what sort?"

"We seek the same merchandise, do we not? I have a ship, ye have a map."

What ruse is this? I wondered. My gaze darted to Teag, who shifted his feet. I realized then that Drake didn't know. Teag had never told him about the actual map.

Hensley began to answer. "I don't hav—"

"Lieutenant," I said, gripping the first mate by the elbow and giving it a hard—desperate—squeeze, thinking to myself a slim chance in hell was better than none at all. "It's our only option," I said to him, "for the lady, and the boy, if not for all of us. Please. We must make an accord."

Hensley paused to look at me. The implication of admitting we had no such map then dawned on him, and he gave a small nod. "Very well," he said, "but I'll have you know I memorized the way and burned the actual map."

"'Ee's lyin'," said Teag. "Troo 'is bloody teef."

"Belay, ye scab!" Aubrid said, clutching at the grip of his cutlass. "I'll cut yer tongue if ye spill any more muck."

"Before we begin, Captain Bellows needs tending," Hensley said, before Teag fouled up our last chance to live through the next few moments. "He's in a bad way, thanks to you. Doctor Mallory did what he could, but he needs further care. I suggest we transport him back—"

"Methinks we can tend ta yer captain easy enough," Drake said, stalking up to stand over the unconscious Bellows. He pointed the pistol in his left hand at the inert captain and pulled the trigger. The weapon spat a puff of white smoke and the resounding blast echoed throughout the deep dark jungle, shaking leaves from the canopy. Small shadows howled and screeched as they scattered or took flight from the topmost branches.

"Now he's jus' dead weight." Drake looked at us with a black stare.

My blood ran cold. Dazed, I found myself grasping Katalin's hand in a bone-crushing grip. In his febrile state, I could but pray that Bellows was mercifully oblivious to his cruel fate.

"Murderer!" Hensley's normally expressionless face purpled in rage. He rushed at Drake.

The pirate captain's right-hand pistol wheeled in the charging man's direction. "Perhaps ye'd care to join yer sorry captain, Lieutenant? Think again before ye take that next step, 'cause I can fair guarantee it'll be yer last. T'would be a shame for all o' us, no doubt, if indeed yer the only one who can find the loot."

Hensley stood stock still as two of Drake's cutthroats stepped forward and took hold of his arms. The first mate's furious gaze stabbed at the pirate captain with smoldering eyes. "Damn you, you devil."

Thunder murmured in the distance.

"Not the first time I've been called such, and worse. Doubtful the last. Disarm him," Drake said, scowling.

Aubrid strode over and relieved Hensley of his saber and also grabbed a knife from young Dominy's belt. He turned his smirk on Katalin. "I'll have ta search this 'un." He leered. "Weapons stowed in garters an' such."

"Stay yuir bloody hooks off'a the lady, you white-livered jackal," said a harsh voice. Hamish had spoken, taking a menacing step forward with an enviably reckless bravado. Several blades raised and halted him, as warm droplets began precipitating through the canopy.

"Or what, Albiyan?" Aubrid said, meeting Hamish's darkly pallid face with a resentful glare. "Yer threats 'r' empty as a crone's teat."

A faint smile came over Aubrid's malevolent face as he returned his attentions to Katalin. The fear and tension of the past two days curdled inside of me, and I relented to some firm hands taking hold of my upper arms from behind, pulling me a step back.

Katalin met Aubrid's wicked gaze defiantly, raising her small white chin, while a multitude of rain droplets pelted down, splattering the leafy foliage. The pirate used the tip of his cutlass to lift the hem of her skirt, revealing part of her smooth white leg.

"Relish your last few moments, Myg Rothan," she said, bestowing a crooked half-smile that never reached her eyes. "You'll not see another night."

Aubrid's sour grin faded. "Quit yer chatter, wench."

"You've terrorized, stolen, raped, and murdered your last. A whore's filthy urchin, you, taking vengeance on the world—and for what?" Katalin's lip curled. "Breathe it in, Myg Rothan. Your last few breaths. Suck the jungle air into your diseased lungs."

Aubrid raised the back of his fist and struck her across the mouth. She staggered back.

A sudden passion for violence roused up inside of me as the cutthroat hefted his cutlass and advanced. Brooking my typical sense of good judgment, I wrested away from the hands locked around my arms and stepped forward, placing myself between him and Katalin. I grabbed Aubrid's wrists.

The Myg Rothan's hot eyes burned into mine with a how-dare-ye expression. He pulled his sword arm from my grip and took a backwards step, giving himself more space to deliver a mortal strike. The warm rain descended in sheets as the treetops tossed and leaned above us. I tensed, steeling myself, reckoning my final moment had arrived, here in some unmapped jungle in a heavy rainfall. Not how I'd envisioned my demise,

I supposed. In that last intake of breath, I saw my bones lying amidst the dark soil and leafy vegetation, claimed by the earth beneath my feet, picked clean, forgotten.

"Avast now, Aubrey!" Captain Drake said. "Leave off the good doctor for a moment. He's a gentleman and, as such, protectin' the young lady's honor as a proper man should. Now, if'n ye want ta fight him, ye have ta do it proper-like. Is that not right, Doctor? A duel for privileges, says I!"

"I'm no duelist," I said, quite overcome by a conflicting muddle of incredulity and resignation.

"Ha! How unlike is a sword to a scalpel?" Drake grinned fiercely, still keeping a casual eye on the livid Hensley. "Both lots are a butcher's trade at any rate."

"We'll settle this matter, aye," Aubrid said. He leaned in at me, a savage grin on his ugly face. "Yer a dead man now."

"To the contrary," stated Katalin, presaging what happened next while touching her fingertips to her bloodied lips.

A horn-like blare heralded a white arc that whirred from the shadows. It made a *thwip* noise as it smacked the back of Aubrid's neck. His eyes widened, then quickly glazed. I managed to spy a thin bone-like spur no more than a hand's-breadth in length jutting from his flesh, just before he crumpled to the jungle floor.

Something whooshed mere inches from my face, so close I felt a puff of wind on my brow. I realized more wicked darts arced through the rain, followed immediately by large, leaping, howling shadows, and yet another hair-raising horn blast. A nearby pirate— mayhap the one who'd been grasping my arms—looked down at his own chest where three of the ivory darts suddenly appeared. He teetered headfirst, landing in a heap.

I heard Drake's pistol *fwash* and pop, as the jungle erupted in a hell-borne nightmare of fearful shapes and frenzied screams. A tide of enormous creatures surged out of the trees, something akin to hairless naked apes, their bronze skin glistening wet, with powerfully molded limbs and wide mouths filled with gnashing yellow teeth. If I thought Hamish a large man, these were indeed giants, easily a head taller than the Albiyan. They seemed to exude an intangible aura of something primeval and savage and borne of the early depths of a time before history. I had read accounts of early men in my various studies, barbarians who roamed the lands in a time when the Dwarrow empires and the Phaderi houses spanned from the Sunder Kingdoms to the Darkelands. *Isaurians*, they are called, the evolution of man in stasis, classified just above the order of birds and beasts, pushed into the wild places by the encroachment of one civilization after the next.

Are these such men? I wondered.

Katalin's hand found mine, or rather mine found hers. I drew her along with a steel grip as I dashed anywhere, as long as it was away from this fierce pandemonium where pirates and primitives clashed in a dark jungle storm. I chanced a look over my shoulder to see Lieutenant Hensley, having recovered a blade, stab one of the massive Isaurians through the throat. The giant collapsed, wrenching the sword from his grasp, and others rushed en masse upon him. He roared as he fell beneath their onslaught. I saw, too, Aubrid and several others slung over shoulders, their limp forms borne away into the shadows and rain.

J. M. Martin

I rushed recklessly through the jungle downpour, pulling Katalin along with me, while pistol blasts, screams, and barbaric howls split the darkness. We stumbled through the wet, twisted terrain for a hundred strides or more, around dozens of trees, through vines and branches, over fallen logs and brush, stopping just short of a sheer drop. Katalin ran into me and I teetered precariously, drawing one ragged breath as I glanced down at a deadly fall. She pulled me by my tunic, and we both tumbled to the ground, me landing atop her. We lay still, facing one another in the gloom, sucking great gulps of air. Our eyes locked for a long moment as I became aware of her closeness, her face upturned mere inches from mine. I looked at her pursed lips, her auburn locks in disarray, felt her bosom heaving beneath me; then the erratic snapping of movement through the brush came from our right, shattering the moment, thrusting us back to our dilemma.

Oberon Teag stumbled from the tree line mere spans away, nearly pitching over the same precipice. He panted and turned toward us, after a brief moment picking us out of the shadows with the horror-struck eyes of a man in flight. Realization dawned on his features, only for a half-breath, then he flung up his arms and screamed as his pursuer, one of the naked giants, sprang from the shadows.

The Isaurian grabbed Teag in its massive hands and heaved him up. I spied in Teag's hand a glint of metal, a long sliver, a dirk perhaps. He screamed unremittingly, kicking his legs and twisting his torso as he stabbed again and again into his assailant's neck and shoulders.

I lay aghast and gaping as the Isaurian uttered a bestial roar and squeezed with all its might. Teag ceased screaming and arched back, raising his pain-contorted face to the dark drizzling canopy. The dirk dropped from his fingers, and the giant gave a final wrenching motion, causing something inside of Oberon Teag—his vertebrae most likely—to make a loud sharp crack. The man's feet jerked spasmodically, then his entire body relaxed.

The damage wrought by Teag took its toll then. Its quarry now slain, the Isaurian wavered. Still holding the lifeless man in the crook of its elbow, the giant stepped clumsily to the side once, twice, and then enough for both of them to pitch over the cliff's edge.

After the span of no more than a breath or two, a grotesque *thwop* came up from the precipice. Katalin and I lay motionless, listening, slumped on our little wet mound of decayed earth. I know not how long we lay there, panting. I trembled, taking some little comfort in Katalin's presence as the gravity of our predicament pervaded my mind.

"We're doomed," I said.

A long moment passed in silence as the rain lessened.

"Yesterday, you said I'd be there at the end, you, me, Dominy, Drake . . . is this what you meant?"

"No," she said, then paused so long I thought it to be her only reply. I looked at her profile, and could tell she was trying to make sense of something. "No . . . something else, something more . . . something terrible . . . and unforeseen. I cannot skein it. It's peculiar."

"Well, can you skein us off this bloody island?"

She shook her head. "No. I'm not like that. I only see things, and I don't have power over . . ."

"Over what?"

She raised her long slender hand to shush me, then gave a subtle motion of her head. I turned to look where she indicated, spying two figures gliding through the dark. I feared the worst, that the savages had located us. Then I realized the taller of the two as Thadieus Drake, pulling along behind him the boy, Dominy, and bearing directly for us.

"I expect it rarely gets more inevitable than this," I said. "You certainly present a new view on the matter of one's destiny, m'lady. That, I have to admit."

We came to our feet as Drake strode up, gripping his red-stained broadsword in one hand, Dominy's skinny arm in the other. He pushed the boy at us and fixed me with a dark frown. It didn't escape my notice that three of his four pistols were missing, but the butt of one could be seen, the rest of it tucked in a dark sash around his waist.

"Ye don't want ta die, do ye, Doctor?" Drake said softly.

I shook my head.

"Then best ye tell me the truth about the map. See, I reckon Hensley lied. No fool, am I. By hook or by crook I'd cut ta the heart of it, except now the bastard's dead as dead, and yer thankfully not, so I'm turning my attentions to ye. Too bad yer little gesture ta him was fairly noted. I'm not blind, either, y'see. So, let's hear it, Doctor. Where's that fine little map?"

I knew the map, had seen it once, having treated Teag for the flux and a high fever aboard the *Tatterdemalion* a month prior. It mattered little now whether I told Drake or not.

I nodded. "Teag," I said. "He had it; though, he's dead."

"Dead?"

"Aye, slain by one of those . . . things. They pitched over the edge, just there." I indicated the spot where the Isaurian fell with Teag's corpse. I noticed for the first time, some ways in the distance through the break in the jungle, a craggy tree-blanketed mountain rising up from a white mist. It radiated something menacing, causing me to shiver.

Drake spared a glance in the direction I'd pointed, and returned a narrow-eyed gaze to mine. "He had the map then, ye say?"

I nodded again. "Tattooed on his back."

"Poxy little bilge rat." The pirate pursed his lips and thought for a moment. As he did so I realized the rain had ceased. Wispy vapors steamed from the ground in the rising heat. "I didn't come all this way ta lose the treasure o'er a damnable cliff," he said, then waved his blade. "Come. We're goin' ta get that map."

I hesitated, then, said, "How so?"

"Yer expertise, my grit, and a strong vine rope."

"I don't see how we could possibly—"

Drake's brow lowered, and he pointed the tip of his bloodied sword at me. "Evidently ye care fer the wench, so don't force me ta get ugly, Doctor. I've lost fair more than a dozen o' my crew ta this point on our little enterprise, so tryin' my patience right now is rather ill-advised."

"But more of those things are out there," I said.

"We risk that movin' forward 'r back. I'd quite prefer ta die strivin' fer a prize than tuckin' me tail and runnin' back, gainin' fer naught."

So by virtue of his sword and reputation, Drake held us captive. We spent the next few hours collecting vines and twisting them to fashion a makeshift rope, while the pirate kept one eye on the jungle and the other on us. At one point, as Drake took his attention away, cutting vines, I located Teag's fallen dirk, casually swept it up, and slipped it in my satchel.

"Good enough," Drake said, assessing the rope with a hard yank. He tossed the end to Dominy. "Knot it round the doctor, lad."

"Me?"

"Aye. Yer ta fetch the map."

"But, I can't carry him back up here!"

"Bah! I care not for Teag's mangy carcass. Yer a chirurgeon so jus' ya bring us that map now, eh?"

I imagine I paled at that, sparing a worrisome glance over the ravine's edge. Below, I could see the two twisted forms of Teag and the Isaurian among the jagged rocks and a slithering ribbon of dark water. The sheer drop, though not as deep as I had imagined, was nonetheless fatal even if one's back were not broken or they had been stabbed numerous times.

"If I help you with this," I said, "please do me just one thing."

"Ask," said Drake.

"Passage to the mainland . . . and if something should happen to me, your word that you'll deliver the lady and the boy to a safe berth, unmolested by your crew. We're at your mercy, Drake, but I'm asking just this one thing as my only recompense for helping you find this treasure."

"That's been my intent all along, Doctor." The pirate grinned through dark whiskers. "Ye have my word."

Despite the answer I did not believe the man. I felt both panicked and angered, but rather than show it, I looked at Dominy as he cinched the rope around my waist.

"I'm sorry, Doctor," the boy murmured softly.

I gave him a small nod, as Drake instructed him to tie the other end of the rope around a nearby tree. Katalin looked at me and smiled somewhat with a certitude that spoke: *Take heart. Remember what I have told you.*

I nodded, relying on her prophetic talent, as well as the tensile strength of our primitive rope, to hold true. Drake ordered Dominy and Katalin to take hold of it as I leaned a bit for leverage. I drew a long breath, and then lowered myself backward into the verge.

The rope gave some length at first, and I held my breath as I plummeted into space for a brief moment, but then my feet struck the precipice wall. The crude tether creaked ominously, but held firm. I steadied myself. The descent, though nerve-wracking, went quicker than I anticipated.

I touched the ravine floor a mere two spans from the Isaurian's broken body where it lay with its legs half-submerged in the gurgling black stream. The giant's head twisted at an extreme angle, its large maw gaping open in a silent bellow, two cold black eyes seemingly watching my approach. I assumed it dead, but gave as wide a berth as I could, while scrutinizing it. Naked and sun-bronzed, in addition to the nine or ten fresh stab wounds in its broad and once-powerful shoulders, the Isaurian's muscular body bore a myriad of scars, some of which appeared ceremonial. Black and gold war paint decorated its wide-boned face, and a large conch shell lay beside the massive head, having once apparently hung from the giant's neck on a tattered cord. I surmised this as the source of the earlier horn blasts, and attributed this particular Isaurian as a leader among its people.

Though brutish and heavy-browed, in truth, the giant appeared quite man-like. I suddenly felt the long-lost ages of a primeval world come over me, when such men as these, wild and vital, marched out of the mists and asserted their dominion among the elder races. But the age of the Isaurians had faded, and they receded into the dark places of the world from whence they had come, little more than painted primitives and savage man-eating marauders.

I looked beyond the Isaurian at Teag's shattered body. Though I'd known the man, and rarely felt even small pity for him, to see his corpse dashed face down upon the rocks, his lifeblood cooled in a seeping puddle, I breathed a silent prayer for his misguided soul. It was more than I would give for Aubrid, wondering if even now his body were being flensed and carved to fill Isaurian bellies.

I removed my satchel and set about the grisly task of skinning Oberon Teag.

Perhaps an hour later, I clambered over the cliff's edge and exhaustedly presented to Drake a bloody parchment. He looked at it briefly, stressing displeasure at its legibility. I began to explain the effects of saturation, but he waved me off with a curse.

After a few moments of silence, Drake waved his sword at us and we set off in the shimmering heat, back into the rank jungle. After an hour or more we came into an expanse of thorny understory. We pulled our way through it, the long needle-like barbs snagging clothes and flesh.

"Ow!" Dominy cried, from just a few spans behind. I turned as he lifted up his right foot and plucked out a needle. It hadn't occurred to me that the lad wore nothing on his feet. They were a mess of raw flesh and dozens of small cuts.

I walked back to him in my knee-high Pendaran leather boots. "Here, let's get you through this, young master."

"What's that, Doctor?" I could tell he wanted to be brave and cause no bother, but his lip quivered somewhat and tears formed in the corners of his eyes.

"Up with you," I said, and turned my shoulder so he could clamber onto my back. He paused. "Come on," I urged him. "It's alright, young master. Let's just get you through these blasted thorns now. Up. Besides, I never thanked you for the fig."

I'm no large man, but as far as doctors go, I'm rather fit. Besides that, I hailed from good stock, as my father and brothers were all hale men, none of us slouches, and tending more to a rangy physique. Mallory men made good soldiers and athletes and, for the nonce, good creatures of burden, as I hefted Dominy up onto my back.

"Move it, ye laggards!" Drake glared back at us.

After the days of hard travel, fear, and my travails in the ravine, fatigue clutched at me vigorously. Dominy wasn't heavy for a lad his age, perhaps no more than eight stone, but the uneven slope and patches of soft clumpy soil did little to relieve the matter. I staggered sideways into the bushes more than once, wicked barbs prickling my legs and forearms. I was covered with dozens of stinging welts and punctures, and beginning to wonder if I'd made a wise gesture, when suddenly, the trees thinned and the jungle opened up at the base of the ominous mountain. Drake halted us and peered at the map, and I eased Dominy to his feet.

From where he stood in the shadowy arch of the clearing's wooded entrance, the pirate captain turned to us and smiled. "I believe we have arrived," he said.

We warily advanced into the open. The sun tinted the sky a sickly yellow as it descended toward the mountain, while the thunderheads of the day's earlier storm darkened the entire horizon to our right. Here we observed the first signs of habitation on the island other than the brutish savages, though the mysterious inhabitants had evidently departed long since. Twin rows of six five-foot-high *stelae*, engraved with hundreds of worn sigils, flanked an overgrown pathway leading into the open. The ravages of time and jungle had taken their toll on this place. Once, several stone structures filled the clearing; these now existed as little more than piles of rubble, hemmed in by a crude wall of mud and stone mostly overtaken by low vegetation and thorny scrub. Directly ahead some eighty spans distant, a ziggurat in moderate repair somehow held off the jungle's grasp, holding silent dominion over the remains of an eerie, lost world.

"Ha! There we are," Drake said triumphantly, holding up the gruesome skin map, the tracings of the temple barely evident upon it. He gave an appraising look to the structure. "'Tis the only useful thing ye e'er done did, ol' Teagy."

"I feel so much death," Katalin whispered, moving close alongside me. "It's overwhelming."

"Drake, I don't like this," I said, taking Katalin's hand in mine. "Something's wrong here."

"Nay," the pirate captain said. "There be somethin' here, aye, but . . . it calls out." He paused as if listening for something, cocking his head slightly. "D'ye hear it?" He turned to look at us, a strange, covetous gleam in his eyes. "I hear it. Come."

When we paused, he sneered. He plucked the pistol from his sash, cocked it, and motioned with it toward the ziggurat. I sighed and relented, looking at Katalin and Dominy before striding past Drake and down the path amid the stelae. The rest followed and we picked our way precariously through the ruins. I feared something would lunge at us any moment, but soon enough the temple loomed large, its obscure carvings barely legible upon the decaying stonework. We stood at the base of a score of steps leading up to an entryway framed with carven lintels. Above it hung a moldering skeleton, limbs splayed, grinning skull warning us off.

The muzzle of Drake's pistol prodded the back of my neck. Mouth dry, unable to swallow, I ascended the crumbly steps, the others in my wake, to the gaping entryway.

Six niches to each side were inset with ancient skulls, the brow of each displaying the faint evidence of a runemark, doubtless some terrible curse or other ward of nefarious power.

"Captain, please . . ." I hesitated, feeling such dread in my heart it was nearly beating from my chest. My hair bristled at the thought of going into that forbidding-looking temple. If I had felt fear to this point, I knew not what sort of primal terror now had me in its grasp.

"Oh ho, captain now, am I?" Drake said; yet, this came without his usual barbed tone. Even so, the muzzle prodded me forward. "Go."

"But how are we to see?"

As if something had overheard my query, a pale luminescence emanated from the temple's depths. It did not flicker as fire did, but rather emitted a barely discernable aurulent glow; *skeinlight* I assumed.

The muzzle of Drake's pistol poked the back of my shoulder. I strode warily between the lintels, beneath the grinning skeleton, into the temple. My eyes were forced to adjust to the dark, finding the skeinlight's source still a ways off so that the passageway was but vaguely alight. Countless strands swept across my face and I turned my head, wiping away the sticky filaments. Drake prodded me and I used my hands to paw at the cobwebs.

Silently we strode, feet scraping the stone floor until we arrived at a small musty chamber. Skeinlight dimly lit the room from no apparent source, granting enough illumination for us to see murals all along the walls depicting rituals, domestic scenes, battles, and human sacrifices. Though faded, I found myself awed by what I could see, both by the meticulous brilliance and the spectacle of glimpsing life in some court long lost in the passage of time.

We moved onward, through a brief passageway into another mural-decorated chamber roughly the same size as the first, but with a roof that could not be seen and a choice of three passages: left, right, and straight ahead. A question froze on my lips when the golden light from the middle archway pulsed.

"That's it," Drake said. "That's the one. D'ye hear? That voice?" He looked at us, eyes agleam with a feral light like that of a ravenous wolf.

I shook my head.

He looked at the others, Katalin with her hand laid softly on Dominy's shoulder. They, too, responded quietly in the negative.

"How can ye not?" His excited voice reverberated in the chamber. "Bah! No matter. Forward!"

Though I would never accuse Drake of being the sanest man I knew, he seemed on the verge of sheer madness. I felt the need to draw him away from this recklessness and uttered the first thing that came to mind: "If the treasure lies beyond," I said, "you promised safe passage . . ."

Drake's arm outstretched, pointing the pistol at me with a fiendish look of purpose on his face. "I did. Now, go," he intoned, saying the last part with an angry-looking sneer.

I moved into the archway straight ahead, fearful over many things, the integrity of a murdering pirate's word of honor foremost among them. As I proceeded, I fought the need to fetch Teag's dirk from my satchel. The only chance for the three of us lay in my ability to surprise Drake and deliver a killing strike, but such a desperate lunge with the pirate's finger already on the trigger seemed unlikely. Fear and cowardice gripped me, drawing me into a wretched state of inaction in which I could only shuffle forward. There was still the matter of an inescapable island full of giant cannibals, which seemed a bit of a challenge. The *Tatterdemalion* was our only real chance. For that reason, Drake needed to live.

In the midst of my inner flurry of doubt and indecision, we entered a large, square chamber alight in a golden glow. Four pockmarked columns stretched into the oppressive darkness high above us. A shallow pit lay in the room's center, hemmed by obelisks little more than an arm span tall and incised with whorl-shaped, pulsating runemarks. Something small and spherical lay atop a blocky granite pedestal in the center of the depression. The short hairs on my neck bristled as I took a few more leery steps, the others moving slowly behind me, for the obelisks projected beams of light directly at the orb and I saw it for what it was: a cryptic, rune-covered skull.

We stood, the four of us, at the edge of the steps that led down into the pit. At first I thought it a trick of the light, how the eye sockets seemed to radiate, then realized the cavities housed golden crystalline orbs. It must have been the skull of a great king, or perhaps a deity of some sort.

Nio lurium vo su, sangre mih sangre, a foreign voice rasped unto our ears in a dialect both strange yet familiar. The words were plain in my mind: *A new day's light upon you, blood of my blood.*

Katalin, Dominy, and I glanced about, confused and looking for the source of that croaking voice.

"We've come fer a great treasure," Drake called out. "Reveal yerself and guide us ta what we seek."

Qua su atis? A treasure you seek, do you?

Drake peered about the chamber, eyes wild, his tongue nervously licking his bottom lip, and then a shuffling noise drew all our gazes toward the skull-topped pedestal. A figure entered the far side of the depression, draped in an ankle-length sleeveless white vestment, open down the middle and trimmed with gold. Beneath it the figure wore a plain black cassock; over it a black hooded mantle from which flowed his long snowy beard.

"Many might call it as such," said he, with a hoary voice that sounded weak and ghostly, yet in my mind suggested profound strength. "But what is housed in this place—this long-forgotten temple—is meant for the proper heir. Only they who may prove it through lineage are welcome here."

The figure had spoken as he strode slowly to the pedestal and paused beside it. He reached up and drew back his black hood to reveal a terribly gaunt face illumined by the skeinlight rays, pale and wrinkled, and a balding head of hair to match his stark white beard. Most striking, however: his eyes. The man fixed us with a pupil-less gaze, displaying orbs of pure gold, a perfect glimmering imitation of the skull on the pedestal to his right.

"Lineage?" Drake said. "What lineage?"

The head turned toward him. "The bloodline of Tisarian, of course."

"I'm not 'ere ta prove anything. Where's the bloody treasure, old man? I've lost all patience so best answer quickly 'r else I—"

A long finger stabbed at Thadieus Drake and halted him mid-sentence. "You have a rude manner about you. I like it not," said the golden-eyed man, a sudden frown on his wizened face.

Drake seemed to stiffen, standing awkwardly erect and frozen in place.

"What of the rest of you?" the man said, squinting at us. "Have you lost all patience, as well?"

Something palpable hummed in the air and my flesh crawled. In the gleam of those eyes it seemed to me that something very powerful roused.

"You are Tisarian the Skeinborn? Bringer of Light to the Darkelands?" Katalin said. I peered over to see her gazing in amazement at the man. "You are the Lord of the Crystal Arch? The wizard-priest of the Radiant Banner, who, in the presence of Avin the Prophet, ascended to become the Walking God?"

"Ah, Avin." The man's countenance lightened. "It has been long since I have known the Grace and Light of his company." He looked at Katalin and smiled. "You know of me. Can it be?" He narrowed his eyes at her and they flashed with an odd light, but then he frowned and shook his head. "Ah, no."

The man called Tisarian turned and caught my eye. Subtle warmth coursed through my body. He shook his head slightly, turned his coruscating gaze on Dominy for a brief moment, then finally on the motionless Drake, who relaxed and, able to move again, stepped back from the man.

The old man looked dismayed, then recovered quickly. "You? You're my heir?" His tangled brow lowered. "A murderous, Drear-tainted, whore's get?" The old man scratched his bearded chin, then he sighed. "Oh, how bothersome. Why am I not surprised?"

"Here is my vessel." Tisarian gestured at the skull on the pedestal. It rose into the air, emitting a faint glow. "My skull, in fact, which holds a measure of my essence, bestowing whoever claims it access to great knowledge of the skein. I have waited . . . I know not how long, for one of my descendants to be drawn here through an ages-old *geas*. It is with some disappointment that you have proven unworthy of this favor. Rather, I must now take the measure of these others in your company and decide who to gift with this great power."

Drake cursed. "No. If ye speak truth, then this is my birthright. I won't have it denied me!"

Tisarian's gold eyes narrowed on Drake. "You believe the choice is yours, do you?"

The pirate captain silently stalked forward, ignoring the ghostly Tisarian, and lunged to grab the hovering skull. Katalin rushed by me. She snatched Drake's tunic at the shoulder, tried to pull him away.

My blood ran cold as Drake whirled on her. He yanked his arm away, madness a'gleam in his eyes. A lone pistol shot clamored in the confines of the chamber. Wreathed in a plume of white smoke, Katalin dropped limp to the floor.

My vision ran red. "Nooo!" I screamed, puzzled in my haze to find it accompanied by some deep bellow from the steps to my right.

Something large leapt from behind a column. A few desperate blinks later I realized it was the Albiyan, Hamish, stripped to the waist, covered in mud and blood, and charging Drake with all speed. Seemingly having followed us and hidden behind a pillar, he now pounced at his prey like some ferocious tiger. He gave a great sweep of his blade at Drake, who barely managed to spring away, his tunic the worse for wear with a slash through the side.

The pirate captain's broadsword hissed from its scabbard and both he and Hamish looked fiercely into each other's eyes. The tall men circled, while the hovering skull emitted intense rays of light in every direction, causing their shadows to play about the chamber as if a score of men or more had arrived to give battle.

Dominy hunched over Katalin, worry and fright etched on his pale face. Tisarian seemed to have vanished, but I gave him little thought. In my satchel, my fingers wrapped about the grip of Oberon Teag's dirk. I glared at Drake as he and Hamish advanced and gave ground to one another, and my rage grew in my breast. I wanted desperately to strike at him. If I could but flank him to offset the Albiyan's pressing attacks . . . but then I shook, as if from a sudden chill.

My gaze turned to Katalin. Her face, bathed in the golden light from the floating skull, grimaced. *She yet lives.* I had presumed her dead, my ire so fixed on attacking the pirate, but without another moment's thought, I released the knife and rushed to her side.

I could see she was unconscious as I knelt beside her. I instructed Dominy to lay Katalin's head in his lap as I positioned her on her back and fished my toolkit from my satchel. I unrolled it and retrieved my scissors, using them to cut her tattered bodice and blouse to reveal an ominous blood-leaking wound roughly the size of a Berdainese penny in her abdomen just left and shy of her umbilicus. I rubbed my fingers across her flat belly, feeling for anything out of the ordinary, then examined her sides and back for an exit wound. Finding nothing, I steeled myself, clenching my jaws and reaching for one of my scalpels. The ball was inside.

"Doctor," Katalin said, suddenly roused. She looked at me through glazed eyes. Fear knotted inside my chest. "Don't make a . . . fuss. It is . . . meant to be. I have foreseen it. You mustn't—"

"Shush now," I said. "Save your strength."

The struggle between Drake and Hamish moved dangerously close, and Dominy flinched at the grating of steel as a shower of sparks fell over us. Drake grinned and lunged at Hamish, but the Albiyan deflected the broadsword and returned a lightning-quick slash aimed at the pirate captain's head. Drake danced away and thrust low at his enemy's groin, barely missing by a hair's breadth. This happened in the blink of an eye it seemed, a ferocious bear against a lean, darting wolf.

"Steady on," I urged Dominy. "Time's of the essence. Let's us help the lady. The Albiyan will deal with Drake."

"Aye, sir." The boy nodded.

Katalin winced and coughed as Dominy gently stroked her hair away from her brow.

"I'm sorry, m'lady," I said, "but I fear you're bleeding inside. I have to look and see what damage you've taken."

She shook her head slowly, a gesture of defeat. "It's no use . . . the skein sees all. My hour is . . . upon me."

"I can't believe that. You've predicted rightly since yesterday, I'll attest, but I refuse to sit here and let you die as long as I can do something. Now, please?" I looked at her imploringly.

She returned my gaze, coughed weakly. She licked her lips as if to say something; instead, her eyes rolled back and she shuddered. Katalin's head lolled in Dominy's lap.

I cursed.

"Doctor?" the boy said with an expression of wide-eyed panic.

I handed him a small strip of leather. "Here, put this between her teeth." Then I gave him some rags and said, "When I tell you, use these to wipe away the blood so I can see what I'm doing."

"Aye, sir. I've assisted on board before, sir," he said, taking the rags.

"Very good." I gripped my scalpel's handle. It can be difficult to know where to cut when blood pools in the abdomen, so I took a deep breath, then pressed the blade to Katalin's smooth white skin no more than a thumb's length above the wound. As I made the incision, blood immediately seeped through and a slight buzzing noise hummed in my ears. The golden light in the chamber brightened as I nodded for Dominy to wipe the blood away.

Hot sweat ran down my back beneath my tunic as I continued cutting through the layers of fat and abdominal membranes. *Here is the true test,* I thought, as the humming in the chamber reverberated and, in the depths of my mind, I swore I heard choral voices, but the roar and fury of battle assaulted me, drowning the voices out. My scalpel sliced cleanly through the serous membrane and, as suspected, dark blood geysered upward. Dominy used what was left of the rags to stem the flow, even frantically removing his tunic and using it, but Katalin's small bowel, the *eileos,* had been shredded. I pawed through the segments, but could find no way to mend the damage.

"She's right," I murmured, wiping sweat from my brow with a blood-spattered forearm. "There's nothing I—"

The golden light shined down from overhead and both Dominy and I squinted up at the sigil-etched skull. It floated a mere armspan above us, terete-shaped motes of bright light eddied about it, tracing argent patterns in the air.

"I lost a friend once," Tisarian's ghost said, suddenly behind Dominy. He placed an aged semi-translucent hand on the boy's shoulder. His golden eyes seemed oddly forlorn. "A drakhölve arrow, if I recall. The black tip festered in my friend's guts for days. He was a strong man. A hero, if you will. I arrived late. He'd already passed."

The man blinked, returning to the moment. "I've decided on the boy. I had wished to pass it on within my bloodline . . ." He glanced at Thadieus Drake, who was in the midst of a lunge at the Albiyan. Both men were bloodied. No victor seemed apparent. The old man shook his head. "Alas. Then, I intended to bestow it on the woman, her being skein-touched, but the boy will do. A halo surrounds you," he said, nodding his

head at me. "You're much too enveloped in the bonds of science. The boy has skein blood, mildly, though his abilities must be culled and tempered. Heed that; else he'll soon go mad—"

"Pardon me, m'lord," I said, "but Lady Katalin skeined her fate was to die here and now. If you pass on your power—"

"A measure."

"A measure, then. But even with that, can Dominy save her?"

"Her essence ebbs. It is moving from this world . . . but I suppose I could guide him."

"Begging your pardon then, but can we get on with it?"

"Indeed." He spoke softly. "Are you willing, boy?"

I looked at Dominy, urging his response with a desperate gaze. He glanced down at Katalin, glanced up at the man, and quietly nodded.

"Be it so," the man said and placed his long, withered hands on the sides of Dominy's head. The glowing skull moved slowly through the air until it transposed with the man's head. Merged together as one, the skull imbued the ancient man with a rictus grin, the etched sigils blazing into his flesh, which seemed to slough away from the bones of his face. The missiles of light accelerated frantically above us.

Across the chamber, Drake shouted at us, breaking from combat. He charged at the old man, Hamish on his heels.

"Now, boy. Place your hand into the woman's wound and will it healed," he said. "Quickly."

I held her flesh taut as Dominy plunged his thin right hand within Katalin's abdominal cavity.

Curia vitalasae, the words echoed in my mind. *Curia vitae.*

"Curia vitalasae," Dominy whispered.

Drake raised his broadsword to strike the old man just as the sundry motes converged into one spiraling ball of blinding light and the entire chamber vanished into pure nothingness. A loud crackle hummed, and I felt strangely weightless for a brief moment. A deafening chorus of a hundred voices rose from low to high in every range and pitch. Intense heat blasted at me from the old man's direction, or so I perceived. I shielded my face, squinting to see an arc of white skeinlight transfixing Dominy, limning his body in a nimbus of shimmering gold.

"Take away your hand, now!" the old man's voice pealed above the din.

He did. And the chamber fell silent and dark.

I blinked into the gloom, then heard Katalin gasp for air. I could see the outline of her body as it arced upward. I grabbed at her, pulling her to me, feeling her warm breath on my neck. In awe I stared past her tangled mess of hair at the shadowy figure of Dominy, who returned my gaze through eyes of gold.

"That is . . . quite interesting," murmured the old man. I peered up at him; he, after scrutinizing Dominy for the span of a breath or two, abruptly dissolved, garb and all, into dust.

A long moment of silence passed as the chamber darkened further. I heard the *plink* of Dominy dropping the lead shot to the stony floor as, with Tisarian's absence, the skeinlight continued to fade. I felt for Katalin's pulse in her neck as a shadow loomed over us. I glanced up to see Hamish. In one hand his naked blade glimmered dully, the other gripped the severed head of Thadieus Drake by the hair. He nodded down at me.

"I should think we'll want ta be leavin' this hole," he said. "But first . . ." The Albiyan strode over to the pedestal that had previously displayed the skull of Tisarian and unceremoniously plunked down the head of the wizard-priest's disdained heir.

"Thair's yuir bloody prize," he said, then crossed in the dark toward the pirate's fallen body, mere spans away from where Dominy and I knelt with the unconscious but steadily breathing Katalin. He bent and took up a selection of Drake's accoutrements: cocked hat, black pistol, cross belt, bejeweled rings of gold and silver, and ornate broadsword. He placed the hat on his head, draped the belt over his broad, naked shoulder, then said, "Dark's comin' fast in here. Let's be away."

I stood, hefted Katalin in my arms. "Dominy?" I looked to the boy.

Could he even see with those cryptic eyes? As if he'd heard me, his next utterance imparted an answer somewhat. "It's . . . peculiar . . . my vision is changed . . . light or dark, it doesn't appear to mean anything . . ." He reached out and grabbed my toolkit, placed it in my open satchel, and gathered it all up. He stood and nodded to me in the dimness, as the obelisks faded completely. "I can lead," he said. "Follow me." And we strode quickly from the temple, behind Dominy's vague shadow.

Once outside, the three of us paused at the top of the steps, transfixed in our own thoughts. I surveyed the spread of ruins throughout the clearing. The moon rode high and I could see some leagues beyond the treetops where the sea stretched toward the Orange Coast, toward the mainland, toward Dal Raedia, Anturia, and Berdain.

Katalin moaned and stirred in my arms, but did not waken. Under moonlight I could see that even the marks left by Aubrid's fist were absent. Her face was pristine, relaxed, and as lovely as ever.

"I can carry the lady, Doctor," Hamish said.

But I was not quite ready to relinquish her. "Not yet."

The Albiyan nodded in understanding.

"Where will we go?" Dominy said, his gold eyes glimmering in the moonlight. He seemed rapt with everything around him, and I watched intensely this bone-thin youthful inheritor of so much power. Tisarian's treasure had been sought by so many, yet an unlikely cabin boy unwittingly found it. What would become of him, I wondered. The skein exacted a heavy cost. It was well-known that some orders hunted unvarnished skeinwielders in order to guide them; some sought them so as to eliminate the threat before it did too much damage.

"Drake's ship be mine now, by right o' combat. I say let's make it known," Hamish said—now Captain Hamish—and truthfully enough. I wordlessly swept my gaze to the grim set on his strong face, whose keen blue eyes burned a path through the jungle. He rested his large hand on the pommel of Drake's broadsword. I imagined he fixed his sights somewhere down along the island coast where the *Tatterdemalion* and her crew unsuspectingly awaited us. That was Hamish's treasure: mastery over his own ship once again. A sea brigand's ship, of course, under the precepts of a pirate's code, yet I had a feeling the man was eager for it.

Katalin. What was her treasure? Another chance at life, I suppose, bearing with her the knowledge that the fates could be defied after all. Though, of course, that came by means of a legendary wizard-priest-turned-god, or at least some numinous manifestation thereof, and for what end? I could not say; perhaps as a guide to Dominy along the skein path? T'was the only guess I envisaged. Perchance if that were her treasure, I daresay I could imagine better . . . and worse, to be sure. At least she lived.

Mayhap that was my treasure. A chance to connect to someone. It was long since I had deigned to care for anyone but myself. Disavowed by my family for my decision to study medicine, I spent the next eight friendless years in a large city at a university rife with academic rivalry. Whatever belief in humanity, whatever innocence I had left—no, make that arrogance—was robbed mere weeks upon my embarkation from Nantyrr, taken by Thadieus Drake in those miserable months pressed into his dark service.

Aye. Katalin was my treasure. That's what Tisarian had given me. I shifted her weight and held her tight, then followed Dominy and Hamish down the temple steps.

A new man departed those dark ruins under faint moonlight, trailing behind Dominy and his new eyes. Somewhere among those broken stones and cryptic stelae, the hitherto Dr. Alexandre Mallory remained. A renewed Mallory entered the jungle, embarking with the thought that none of us left unchanged. In our own way, we had all found Tisarian's treasure.

The Spinner
Paul S. Kemp

Zhayim's stumps throbbed. Each beat of his heart sent a dull ache pulsing down his hand, his forearm. The pain kept company with the inexplicable sensation that his severed right thumb and left hand were still part of him. He thought it unfair that the ghosts of his amputated extremities haunted him only in moments of discomfort.

A storm was coming, a big one. Approaching storms always summoned pain and ghosts.

He stood and studied the sky over the aftcastle. The motion rattled the rusty iron chain around his ankle that bound him to the mid-mast.

A thunderhead as black as a rotten tooth benighted the western horizon. Flashes of lightning gave it veins. The distant rumble of thunder rolled over the sea.

The blow had come on fast. An hour earlier the sky had been clear in all directions.

Captain Holst stood near the steering pocket, beside the helmsman, and looked back at the sky through his spyglass. The crew, too, heard the angry sky and looked up from their duties in the rigging and on the deck. A few even gathered along the rails and pointed west. Some immediately cast suspicious glances back at Zhayim, and he took care to hold no eye contact. Others cast their dark looks at *Seahorse's* passengers, who sat together in a circle on the deck near their forecastle quarters, oblivious.

The Votaries of Jahlel wore the somber expressions and plain wool homespuns typical of their cult. Eight men, eight women, and a dozen or so children. They spoke little to the crew—mostly just thanking Neem the quartermaster for their meals—but often to their dead prophet and his God. They faced east and prayed as a group every day at dawn, noon, and sunset. Small wonder folks back in Dineen thought they trucked with spirits.

Zhayim assumed they must have paid Captain Holst a handsome sum to transport them to wherever it was that *Seahorse* was headed. Either that or the captain had been so stretched for treasure and passengers that he took whatever they offered.

Probably the latter, Zhayim decided. Holst could not even afford a decent ship's mage. *Seahorse* had no battle mage, no elementalist, not even a weather wielder. It had only paunchy Sestin, a third-rate diviner.

Zhayim sat back down on the deck and rested against the mast. The Votaries were praying. He enjoyed seeing children aboard but their presence reminded him of things he'd rather forget. And having little to do left him ample time to remember.

With effort, he wrenched his mind from the past, his eyes from the Votaries, and turned to his duty. *Seahorse* was three days out of port. Zhayim owed a story to the crew, the sea, and the temperamental sea god, old Korsin Foambeard.

He moved through the repertory he'd built over the years and soon settled on his tale. He would tell the tale of Dhost the sailor and Lissa the mermaid. It had satisfied the god before, and all sailors enjoyed the tale.

His mind made up, he stretched out his legs, endured the pain in his arms, and took his ease. The roll of the ship, the creak of its lines, and the familiar sounds of its crew as they worked soon lulled him to sleep.

The soft murmur of voices pulled him awake sometime later. He cocked open an eye and saw six Votaries, all of them children, standing in a semi-circle before him. Ranging in age from perhaps five summers to sixteen, they regarded him with unabashed curiosity.

He did not blame them. He knew how he must look to them, chained to the mast, mutilated, with only his copper pisspot and canvas sleeping blanket for company. Everyone always came to stare at the indentured spinner.

Seeing him awake, they whispered for a moment among themselves before a wide-eyed little girl finally said, "Viis wants to know how you eat?"

"Hush, Ysel," one of the older boys said.

Zhayim opened his eyes and sat up. "With my mouth, of course."

The children laughed. Zhayim enjoyed the sound. The two or three who did not laugh looked a bit green in the face. They were not accustomed to the sea.

"What happened to your hand?" said a thin boy. "And your thumb?"

"A shark, I would guess," said another.

"Not a shark," Ysel said. Her face looked as if the sky had rained freckles on it. "Father says he did something awful and was punished."

"What could be so awful?" said the boy, wide-eyed.

"That is a rude question to ask of an indentured old man," Zhayim said.

The tallest of the children, a young man with dark hair that hung almost to his waist, put a hand on the shoulder of the boy who'd asked the question.

"You are not an old man. And it is you who adopt a tone of rudeness."

The young man's directness surprised Zhayim. He had expected the Votaries—persecuted as they were—to be passive.

"What is your name, boy?"

The young man answered with dignity and without hesitation. "Nole ab Tolan."

"Do all Votaries speak their thoughts with such shamelessness, Nole ab Tolan?"

Nole's brow furrowed. "What shame is there in speaking one's thoughts?"

Zhayim smiled, winked. "That depends on the thoughts, I expect, yes?"

Nole did not smile, only cocked his head and looked confused.

"What does he mean, Nole?" Ysel said.

"Your faith does not foster laughter, I see," Zhayim said.

"We laugh," Nole said slowly, still perplexed. "When something is amusing. You intended a jest?"

Zhayim felt vaguely foolish, though Nole seemed to ask the question in good faith. He waved his hand, dismissing the children.

"You've had your look at the mutilated old slave. Go, now. I am composing a story for tonight's offering."

The Votaries murmured. "What kind of story?" a small boy with bright eyes said.

Zhayim opened his mouth to speak, but Ysel, the girl with all the answers and all the freckles, cut him off. "A sea story, Lorm. He's the ship's talespinner. Every ship has one, just as every ship has a weather mage or a diviner or an elementalist. His stories keep the sea god appeased."

"I do not like the sea," said another boy, one of those green in the cheeks.

Lorm seemed confused. "The sea god is a false god."

Zhayim chuckled.

"Whale's teeth, boy. Speaking thus is why you were forced to run away from New Dineen in the first place. More, it is certain to bring foul weather. And let someone on this crew other than me hear it and you'll find yourself swimming for shore."

The boy colored and looked as if he might cry. The other children, too, looked upset. All of them looked to Nole for comfort and Zhayim felt himself an ogre for scaring them. He had seen frightened children enough in his past and wanted to see no more.

"I did not mean that . . ."

"They are afraid of the sea," Nole said, patting the young boy's head.

"There is nothing to fear," Zhayim said.

Nole took a moment to calm the children, then looked into Zhayim's face. He nodded at the chain around his ankle.

"Are you a criminal?"

Zhayim had never been asked the question, not directly.

"I was. But I am no longer. Now, I just tell stories."

One of the crew strode by, a scarred, balding sailor with a reel of line over his shoulder. He regarded the lot of them with a sneer of contempt. "The wretched holding court with the wretched. You best have a good story for us, spinner. That squall is ugly."

Zhayim nodded, waited until the sailor had his back to him, then made an obscene gesture at the bastard with what was left of his hand. The children gasped and giggled.

"Come," Nole said to the children. "The spinner has a story to compose."

The children gave disappointed groans but obeyed. Nole shepherded them toward the forecastle but lingered after.

"We are not running away, you know."

"No?"

"No. We are on a pilgrimage."

Zhayim knew little of the Votaries but was aware of no holy sites across the sea. "To where?"

"To the new world, as foreseen by Jahlel. We will find it at the Far Shore."

Zhayim decided that Jahlel must have been an excellent spinner himself. The Far Shore was one long stretch of wild jungle, filled with dangerous beasts and disease. He thought of telling Nole as much but thought better of it.

"Mind what I said about loose tongues and false gods. I think there's space enough in the world for my gods and your Prophet. But they," he said, indicating the crew, "will not feel the same, especially if that storm catches us."

Thunder boomed in the distance, as if to make his point. Lightning ripped the western sky.

"I have not seen a storm like that in a long while," Zhayim said.

"That is not a storm," Nole said. "That is the end of the old world. And it was the reason we left New Dineen."

Nole said it all so simply, but with such conviction, that Zhayim could only stare at him, amazed. Nole looked as if he had said nothing more unusual than 'good eve.'

Finally Zhayim said, "Who is telling stories, now?"

Nole smiled, and walked back to his people.

———⚓———

The western sky devoured the setting sun, turning the sea from vivid blue to dull slate. Thunder rolled over the water like steady cannon fire. Captain Holst studied the storm through his spyglass until it grew too dark to see. Zhayim could not shake the echo of Nole's words from his mind, and he wondered what the captain saw.

As night settled on the ship, the Votaries made their prayers and the crew, despite the approaching storm, lowered the sails and prepared for the offering. Zhayim over-heard two crewmen as they worked above him on the mid-mast.

"That's a dark blow, and sure," the first said.

"Aye."

"It's these Votaries. Korsin don't like them on his sea."

"We oughta toss 'em over and see if that calms Foambeard," the second said.

"Can't," the first said, and grunted as he pulled a line taut. "Breaking oath on a berth always brings his wrath. Even more than carting these filth across the water."

"True," the other said thoughtfully.

The first studied the sky. "Capt'n thinks we'll outrun it, anyway."

The other grunted agreement. They noticed Zhayim watching them.

"What are you looking at, spinner?" the first said.

"Nothing." Zhayim looked away.

Soon the sails were down and *Seahorse* floated loose on the sea, temporarily at the mercy of Korsin and his currents. The crew lit the twelve shell lanterns that signified the god's twelve seas and arranged them in a circle around Zhayim. He sat in the center of the light and every member of the crew except those in the high nest gathered around him. Some sat cross-legged, others stood. Silence ruled the deck. Zhayim eyed the approaching storm and began.

"May my words please the ear of mighty Korsin the Old. Spare us from storms, Foambeard, and grace us with calm seas and strong winds."

As one, the sailors nodded and answered. "Hear the words, Lord of the Twelve Seas."

Zhayim spun his tale. He told of how Dhost the sailor fell in love with one of Korsin's daughters, the mermaid Lissa. Dhost's songs eventually won her heart, but Korsin refused to allow Lissa to love a man. Finally, a despairing Dhost cast himself from his ship and into the sea, to drown or be rescued by his love. Korsin prohibited Lissa from saving the doomed sailor and she watched as he drowned. After Dhost's death, the despondent mermaid won Korsin's permission for mermaids to rescue any sailors lost in the sea after that day.

"And so Dhost's death was not in vain," Zhayim said, concluding.

Satisfied nods from the crew greeted the end of the tale.

"That ought to hold the storm at bay," one of the crewmen said, looking west.

"Aye," said another.

Thunder boomed and lightning split the western sky. The crew's mood changed abruptly. They looked at one another, at Zhayim, then at the forecastle, where the Votaries berthed. Zhayim saw dark thoughts brewing behind their eyes.

"Thrice-damned Votaries," one of the men murmured.

Zhayim thought of the children and tried to placate the crew with his words, the same as he did Korsin with his tales.

"Captain says we'll outrun the storm. Isn't that so Captain Holst?"

Holst wore his perpetual frown behind his graying moustache. "We'd better," he said.

"By the gods," said a crewman.

"You'll go hungry if we don't, spinner," said yet another.

"Or you'll go over with them Votaries," another said.

Kleegan, the one-eyed first mate, started shoving men back to their duties. "We'll outrun nothing if you laggards don't get the sails back up. Offering's over and we're still dead in the water with Hellhole and the Pit coming up. Get a move on, dogs."

"Hellhole?" Zhayim said, but no one heard him, or no one bothered to answer him.

The crew snapped to, climbing rigging, tightening lines, getting up sails. Neem the quartermaster soon appeared from the galley and handed Zhayim a tin plate of pickled pork and stale bread.

"We're near Hellhole and the Pit already?"

Neem nodded. "You been too long chained to that mast, spinner. Lost your sense of the sea. We'll be between 'em with the morn."

There was fear in Neem's face. He was right to be afraid.

Zhayim knew Hellhole and the Pit. Both were lawless port towns built on islands beyond the easy reach of the Old Kingdom's navy. Pirates harbored there, and anything could be bought or sold in its markets—drugs, sex, violence, men, women . . . children. Zhayim had seen things in both of the holes that made Dineen's slave pens seem pleasant by comparison.

And the sea between the two towns was as pirate-infested a stretch of water as any man could sail.

Neem wandered back to the galley and Zhayim ate his meal. Afterward, he watched the storm gain ground on them. The clouds devoured stars and left a void in their wake. Zhayim had never seen anything like it and he wondered why Korsin had not looked with favor on his offering.

Presently the crew got the sails up. The canvas caught wind and *Seahorse* got back underway, soon holding its own against the storm.

"I enjoyed your story," Nole said from Zhayim's left. "We all did."

Zhayim turned to see Nole crouched on his haunches near the mast. The young man looked west past Zhayim, toward the storm.

"It seems Korsin did not."

"It was a sad story," Nole said.

Zhayim nodded. "Many good stories end with sadness."

"I had never heard it before."

"No? Dhost and the mermaid is an old sea tale. I don't remember where I picked it up. I have told it dozens of times. Sailors never tire of it. Gives them hope, I think."

"Hope for what?"

"Hope that if they go into the sea, a mermaid will help them get back out. And if she does not, hope that they will drown as peacefully as Dhost."

Nole nodded and echoed Zhayim's words in describing Dhost's death.

"Quiet and soft, like falling asleep."

"Aye," Zhayim said.

Thunder rumbled.

A crewman strode past, noticed Nole, and eyed both of them darkly. "We're floating in the water of your kith, now, spinner. And Korsin spat on your offering."

"Perhaps not," Zhayim said. "We're still running ahead of it."

The crewman grunted and continued on.

After he'd gone, Nole asked, "Why do they speak to you with such contempt?"

"Because of what I was," Zhayim said, and held up his stumps. "They take the left hand as punishment for past acts of piracy, the right thumb to prevent the holding of a blade. I was a pirate, Nole. I was caught, punished, and sold into indenture. I lied when I told you I was not a criminal. I am."

Zhayim expected shock or anger to greet his admission, but Nole continued to stare out at the dark western sky.

"Did you hear my words?"

Nole nodded. "I did. But you did not lie. You are no longer a criminal. So you said, and so it is."

The Votaries simplicity bothered Zhayim, challenged him. "How do you know that, Nole? We have only met this day."

"I do not know. I believe. Did you ever kill anyone?"

Zhayim shook his head quickly. "Never. I was the spinner. I just . . ."

He had just told stories to cutthroats and murderers, watched them do violence to others, partaken in stolen loot. And throughout it all, done nothing to stop any of it.

Nole stood up and smiled down at him. "I knew you had not. You are a kind-hearted man, despite your past. I would like to hear more of your stories, as would the children. The elders have approved it. Is that possible?"

Zhayim felt flattered and . . . strangely nervous.

"I know only sea stories, Nole. The children fear the sea."

"Perhaps your stories will ease their fears. In any event, they will help pass the time until we reach the Far Shore."

"Nole . . ." Zhayim started to tell him that the Far Shore was unsettled jungle but swallowed the words. "Bring the children around after your evening prayers tomorrow."

Nole thanked him, bade him good night, and took his leave.

Zhayim lay wrapped in his blanket, hand aching. When he finally slept, he dreamed that he was telling stories to the underfed, terrified children who lived in the filthy slave pens of Hellhole. They asked him to help them, to kill them. He refused. They told him the end of the world was coming and he believed them.

He awoke many hours later to the sound of laughter. He pulled his blanket from over his head and stared groggily about deck. Pre-dawn light cast it in grays and blacks.

Five of the Votary children stood gathered near the starboard rail not far from the forecastle, looking out on the sea. Zhayim heard a splash. He leaped to his feet, thinking someone had gone overboard. The children must have heard the rattle of his chain. They turned around, smiling and pointing at the water.

"Lissa!" Ysel said.

"What?" Zhayim said, his mind still sleep-addled.

"The mermaid," said a boy not older than ten summers. "Lissa the mermaid! We saw her!"

Before Zhayim could reply, Kleegan shouted down from the aftcastle, "Back to your quarters and your prayers or whatever it is you do, you whelps."

The children quailed before the big first mate's wrath. They lowered their heads and shuffled back to the forecastle.

Later, as the sun rose fully, the crewman in the high nest shouted.

"Dolphins to starboard!"

Zhayim climbed on a barrel used for rain-catching and saw a pod of dolphins cutting through the water abreast the ship. Dolphins were a good omen. Perhaps Korsin had favored his offering, after all.

They must have taken up station during the night. That explained Ysel and the other Votary children—they had mistaken a dolphin for a mermaid.

Zhayim sat on his barrel and watched the dolphins dart along and around the ship. They stayed beside *Seahorse* all day. Another pod joined them in the late morning. Another in the afternoon.

Man and dolphin ran ahead of the storm, which continued to draw on, slowly gaining ground. *Seahorse* had every sail out and skipped over the water as fast as she could. Her sails were as fat with wind as an ogre with ale.

Holst stationed a double watch in the high nest, and all of the crew eyed the sea with trepidation, fearing the appearance of sails on the horizon. The ship's mage, the portly diviner Sestin, cast his fish bones and shells, divined his portents, and spoke his tidings to Holst. The captain received them with a nod and studied the storm and surrounding sea through his spyglass. His red face was troubled.

After nightfall, the Votary children assembled around Zhayim. There was eagerness in their eyes.

"Do you think I will see Lissa again tonight?" Ysel said.

Zhayim looked at Nole, who only smiled.

"Perhaps," Zhayim said. "But she has her own affairs to mind. Would you like to hear another story?"

"About Lissa?"

"No. About someone else."

Ysel looked disappointed but the rest of the children nodded with excitement.

Zhayim told them the story of the albatross and the whale, their unlikely friendship, and how each saved the other from pirates. After he had finished, the younger children clapped. Nole asked an older boy to see the rest back to their rooms while he remained behind with Zhayim.

"That story did not end sadly," he said.

Zhayim smiled. "I changed the ending for the children. I did not want them to have difficult dreams. They seem . . . impressionable."

"Impressionable?"

"They believed Lissa's story to be real."

"Belief is a powerful thing," Nole said. "Belief makes truth, this the Prophet teaches."

Zhayim thought the Prophet a fool but did not say as much. "Beliefs are beliefs, Nole. Sometimes they are true, sometimes not. But they never change anything. You could not change seawater to drinking water through belief, could you?"

"If one's belief was strong enough. You think otherwise?"

Zhayim raised his eyebrows. "I live in the world, Nole. Of course I think otherwise."

"Then you are mistaken," Nole said with certainty. "And I pity you. You think the Far Shore a wilderness, yes?"

Zhayim nodded, surprised that Nole knew it to be jungle.

"Perhaps it was, but we are remaking it as we approach. That is why we gather in prayer. By the time we arrive, it will be the new world that was foreseen by Jahlel."

Zhayim could not fathom the assuredness in the young man's tone. He did not see any point in offending Nole, so he asked only, "And if it is not?"

Nole smiled indulgently, as if Zhayim were a child.

"It will be. Belief is transformative, so teaches the Prophet."

Zhayim shook his head, dumbfounded. "Nole, you know that Ysel did not see a mermaid last night, yes? She saw a dolphin."

Nole looked out over the sea.

"Possibly." He rose and smiled. "But she believes otherwise. Good eve, spinner."

"Good eve."

Zhayim turned Nole's words over in his mind and did not sleep for some hours. He watched the thunder and lightning in the west and marveled at the Votaries' credulity. They thought the world behind them ending, and the world before them being newly made.

When he finally slept, he dreamed that he could speak the language of dolphins. He learned that those beside *Seahorse* were led by a dolphin named Akka. They told him they were following the Votaries to the new world. He asked them about the storm in the west. They told him that it was not a storm, that it was the end of the old world and the Votaries had caused it.

Zhayim told the dolphins that they spun a good story.

He awoke after dawn, pleased that he had not been awakened by Ysel shouting during the night about seeing an albatross or a whale. He looked west and saw the storm had gained ground and intensity. The leading clouds roiled and churned violently, chewing up the sky. Lightning tore across the heavens.

The crew worked throughout the day in funereal silence, tense about the storm, the sea, pirates. Holst stared through his glass. The circles under his eyes could have been drawn in charcoal. The Votaries emerged from their quarters to face away from the storm, toward their new world, and pray.

Zhayim watched, and thought, and worried.

That night, Nole and the rest of the children came to him for another story. Kleegan and the captain watched them from the aftercastle, their mouths hard.

Zhayim looked into the faces of the children and put everything from his mind but the story. It would be his last to the Votaries before he had to make another offering to Korsin. He intended to make that offering something special and to convince Foambeard to quell the storm. If the storm hit them, he feared what the crew might do to the Votaries, to the children, and he had stood by too often in the past while children suffered.

He had intended to tell of the noble sea turtle and the evil shark but instead invented a new story inspired by his dolphin dream. He would tell it to the children and perfect it in the first telling, then offer it to Korsin on the morrow.

Improvising as he went, he told the children of Akka the talking dolphin and how he and his fellow dolphins, like the Votaries, were swimming over the sea to the new world. He told them how Akka outsmarted evil sharks, foiled the sea hag, and, in the end, found the new world.

The children listened, rapt, smiling. When he finished, they clapped. Many stood on their tip-toes to look out over the gunwales at the throng of dolphins that still trailed *Seahorse*.

"I see Akka!" Ysel said, and Zhayim smiled.

"Thank you," Nole said to him, and the Votaries returned to the forecastle.

The leading clouds of the storm caught them the next day. A drizzle wet the deck. Thunder rumbled, promising a heavier downfall to come. The seas furrowed and *Seahorse* rose and fell on the waves. The crew put safety lines across the deck.

The dolphins kept vigil to starboard, somberly chirping over the thunder from time to time. The Votary children waved to them, laughed at them, and seemed more comfortable on the sea.

Zhayim wrapped himself in his sodden canvas blanket, sheltered as best he could from the wind, and worked on his offering. He needed to make Korsin hear.

Members of the crew strode past throughout the day. Some only stared, but he saw the fear and anger behind their eyes.

By sunset the drizzle had turned to full-on rain and much of the sky was black. A noticeable border separated the stormfront from the otherwise clear skies before *Seahorse*. It was like the collision of two worlds.

Rumbles of thunder shook the deck and lightning tore through the sky. The crew gathered around him earnestly. Despite their contempt for him, they needed him now, needed Korsin to hear him.

"Tell a good one, spinner," they said.

Lighting the twelve shell candles took time, and keeping them stable in the rolling seas proved difficult, but eventually it was done.

Zhayim knew that he had to placate both man and god. He nodded to himself, spoke the opening invocation, and spun his story.

He told them of Akka the dolphin and his quest for a new world. Akka led his pod before the storm that would end the world, overcame sharks with his cleverness, waterspouts with his speed, and the evil sea hag Dirsila with his courage, to arrive, finally, safe in port at the new world.

"Built of belief, Akka's new world sheltered and sustained them in happiness for the rest of their lives."

When he pronounced the last word, the rain ceased.

Eyes widened. Men looked at one another in shock. Zhayim held his breath and remained perfectly still, afraid to move, afraid to break whatever spell he'd wrought.

The crew looked at him, at the sky. Smiles split their faces, despite the gray clouds that still roofed the sky. At least the storm had abated for the moment.

Zhayim exhaled. He could not contain his own grin.

"Well told, spinner!"

"Foambeard heard you and that's sure."

Even Captain Holst's perpetually somber face offered a hint of approval. Zhayim enjoyed the moment, the accomplishment.

The shouts of the crewmen in the high nest turned the mood on its head.

"Ship aft! She's got no colors!"

The smiles vanished and men whirled around to look aft.

The moment of peace Zhayim had crafted with his story ended with a roll of thunder. A vein of lightning split the sky and silhouetted a three-mast caravel bearing toward them across the waves. Zhayim saw what the spotter had already announced: no colors flew from her mast.

She was a pirate vessel.

"Get the sails up!" Kleegan shouted, and started shoving the men to their posts. "At it, dogs! At it for your lives!"

Zhayim stared, dumbfounded, his mood going from crest to trough in a heartbeat. Korsin had stopped the rain only to visit pirates upon them. The god must have been laughing at his joke in his weedy hell.

Zhayim clenched his feeble fist and cursed the god, loud and long, while the crew scrambled into the rigging and unfurled the sails. Neem the quartermaster and three others dashed into the aftcastle and emerged with three large wooden sea chests. They threw them open to reveal a pile of blades.

"Arm as you can!" Neem shouted.

Sailors dashed by as their duties allowed and received their cutlasses. Zhayim cursed his inability to grip a hilt. He knew how to use a sword well enough.

Nole, wide eyed, emerged from the forecastle and maneuvered his way through the activity on deck.

"What is happening?"

"Pirates out of Hellhole or the Pit," Zhayim said and pointed aft.

"Pirates?" Nole said.

"Yes."

Zhayim grabbed the young man's shoulder as best he could with his thumbless hand. "If they catch us, Nole, you must fight. Tell the rest of them. Do not be taken."

Nole shook his head, pulled back from Zhayim.

"No. No. We do not use force. The Prophet teaches only peace."

Nole slipped from Zhayim's grasp. Zhayim tried to clutch his shirt, failed.

"Dammit, boy! I know what they will do to you, to the children, to the girls. I have seen it. You must fight."

"We cannot. Our faith does not allow it."

Zhayim choked on his frustration.

"Then believe with all of your being that the pirates won't catch us! Because if they do . . ."

Nole stared at him for a moment, then spun around and ran back to the forecastle. Zhayim waited in vain for the adults among the Votaries to emerge from the forecastle and collect a weapon. They never did. He cursed them, shouted, "Fight, in the name of the gods!"

Thunder boomed and the rain fell anew, harder than before. His story had not even brought them much of a reprieve from the storm.

Holst and Kleegan moved among the crew, shouting orders, threats, and encouragement. Zhayim echoed the curses and threats, though it was not his place. He knew what would befall them if pirates took the ship.

"Move, you sons of whores! Tie that off! Cut it! Move, move!"

The pirate ship drew closer by the moment. Zhayim, unable to do anything other than shout, stayed out of the way and listened to his heart gong in his ears.

The sails unfurled, filled with wind, and *Seahorse* lurched into motion across the choppy sea.

She lost ground for a few moments more, then held her distance, then opened some space. A cheer went up from the crew. The dolphins echoed it with clicks and squeals. Zhayim let himself believe they would outpace the pirates.

A series of booms from the pirate vessel carried across the water and Kleegan shouted.

"Flamelings!"

Zhayim cursed.

Six thin lines of fire traced a glowing arc through the sky between the pirate vessel and *Seahorse*. At the front of the glowing trails flew half a dozen flamelings, shitting fire. The cackling of their mad laughter was audible even over the wind.

Zhayim knew, then.

The pirates had an elementalist aboard, and magical cannons.

Seahorse had only a diviner.

The ship was doomed.

The flamelings rode the propulsion of the cannons over the sea and steered a course for *Seahorse's* sails. All of them struck the canvas, giggling maniacally, and the mainsail, topsail, and spritsail went up in flames. The flamelings burned themselves out in an orgy of fire but they had done damage enough.

Men scrambled madly out of the rigging and down the mast. Two fell and hit the deck hard. Neither moved, and Zhayim did not know if they were unconscious or dead. The spotters in the high nest screamed, helpless, as the flames burned around them. The rain was not enough to put it out.

A shower of embers and flaming ropes fell around Zhayim. Trapped by his chain under the burning sails, he could do nothing but wait to die.

"Arms for every man!" Neem shouted, as *Seahorse* lost its wind and slowed.

---⚓---

Kleegan prowled the decks, a cutlass clutched in his hands.

"Now we're down to it, lads! Give them hell and fight for your lives! Your very lives!"

Zhayim knew *Seahorse*'s crew would fight. And he knew they would die. He had seen it before. Crossbow bolts would fall as thick as the rain. The pirates would lower a boarding ramp and storm aboard. Men would scream, shout, bleed, and die. And in the end, the pirates would have the ship.

Zhayim hoped the flames reached him before the pirates did.

Even as the thought crossed his mind, the rain turned to a downpour and quenched the flames.

Korsin was still laughing.

Zhayim stared at the forecastle doors, still closed. He imagined Nole and the Votaries within, praying, *believing* they would be safe.

He knew better. The world dealt harshly with belief. The Votaries would soon learn that.

---⚓---

The bolts dropped ten men before the grapnels hit the gunwales, the boarding ramp fell, and the pirates swarmed aboard. Blades, shouts, and screams rose into the night air. Blood slicked the decks. Zhayim tried to choke a passing pirate with his chain, lost his grip, and was knocked unconscious with the hilt of a cutlass.

Daylight, rain, and thunder awakened him some hours later. Ropes bound him at arms and elbows. He felt like a feast pig, trussed and waiting to die. The smell of smoke filled his nostrils. The sound of crying filled his ears. He opened his eyes to find himself aboard the pirate caravel.

Dark-eyed pirates moved purposefully about the deck. Their crimson sashes, swarthy skin, and high colored shirts told Zhayim they hailed originally from the Leenash Isles and harbored in Hellhole, told him, too, that they were killers. The corsairs of Leenash were notorious even among other pirates.

Barrels, crates, and sacks—the stores and cargo from aboard *Seahorse*—lay scattered in a disorganized heap over the deck. Crew worked in tandems to heave it and move it below.

"Get it below and out of the rain before the blow hits us full force," shouted a muscular, tanned pirate in a leather jack. A cutlass hung from his belt. Zhayim assumed him to be the first mate. He noticed that Zhayim was awake and leered at him.

The Votary children sat in a row beside Zhayim. Sobs shook Ysel and Lorm.

Others looked too dazed to cry. Nole sat immediately to Zhayim's right, his eyes on his feet. All the children had manacles about their ankles and a chain ran through all of their iron rings, linking them all together.

Zhayim's mouth went dry. He had told them to fight, hadn't he? Told them they should not be taken.

Black smoke poured into the sky from the remains of *Seahorse*. She burned a short crossbow shot to starboard. Zhayim knew the pirates would have executed every adult member of the crew and the children's parents. They had saved the children to sell in Hellhole's slave market. And they had saved Zhayim to provide them with sport. He knew what his fate would be.

"Nole . . ."

Black boots stopped before Zhayim. He looked up into the scarred, bearded face of the ship's captain. The man's eyes looked as hollow as empty barrels. He eyed Zhayim's hand, his severed wrist, and spat at his feet.

"You shoulda taken the gallows, yeah? Worse for you."

Some of the crew nearby, heaving boxes and hefting sacks, chuckled. Thunder rumbled and the first mate ordered the men to load the spoils more quickly.

"I was just the spinner," Zhayim said. "Bought out of the pens in Dineen."

The captain smiled coldly. One of his front teeth was gone.

"Well, you came a long way from Dineen just to breathe the sea. You know the way it goes, yeah?"

Zhayim did know the way it would go. Captured pirates were punished on land with amputation or death, their choice. Those who elected amputation and survived, if caught at sea by their fellows, were punished again by being weighted and dipped.

"Ain't got much time before the full force of that storm hits. You'll be breathin' Korsin's air ere that, yeah? You make it a good show for the men or I'll pull you back in and feed you to sharks. Yeah?"

Zhayim swallowed the fist forming in his throat. "Piss off."

The captain stared down at him a moment, turned, and walked away, chuckling.

"Get the swag below and set up for a dip," he shouted to the crew. "On the doublequick, now!"

The crew hooted and laughed.

A lifetime of regrets rushed through Zhayim's mind. He had done little of worth in forty summers. He'd had opportunities, lots of them, but let them all pass.

Beside him, Nole shifted.

"We prayed to the Prophet for safety, spinner. We *believed* we would be safe. I do not understand."

Zhayim could not look at him. "I know."

The crew hurried at their tasks. *Seahorse* sank below the waves. Zhayim swore he heard the dolphins chirping and clicking out in the water.

"What did he mean by 'dip?'" Nole asked.

Zhayim cleared his throat. "They will throw me overboard and gradually add weights to me until I go under for good. If I let myself drown easy, they will pull me back up and . . . do worse."

Nole said nothing for a time, then, "I am sorry, spinner."

Zhayim nodded, though he knew that his fate would be much more forgiving than Nole and the children's. He looked up from his despair, at Ysel, Lorm, the rest. They were sobbing. He made up his mind. He could not stand by again while children suffered.

He leaned in, speaking softly, so only Nole could hear.

"You cannot let them take you back to Hellhole, Nole."

Nole swallowed, looked around at the crew.

"They said they will not hurt us if we do as they say."

Zhayim seized Nole with his eyes.

"They are lying. They just want you to stay quiet until they can get you to port. They will sell you, all of you, and . . . I've seen what happens to children after that. Believe what I say, Nole."

Nole looked him in the face, his eyes red-rimmed, his long hair flattened against his scalp. Zhayim fought back his own tears.

"Please believe me, Nole."

Nole stared at him, blinked, looked away, looked back, nodded. "I do believe you."

Zhayim felt a hundredweight lifted off his back.

"Good. Very good. There is only one way to prevent them from taking you back. Do you understand?"

Nole looked at him, puzzled, his brow furrowed.

Zhayim looked at the children, at Nole. "Do you understand, Nole?"

Realization dawned. Nole's eyes widened. He looked to the children, crying, hurt, terrified. He chewed his lower lip. Zhayim saw the doubt in him.

"It is worse than you can imagine," he said. "Nole, it is worse. Did you see what they did to your parents? To the crew?"

Nole nodded. Zhayim knew the Leenash pirates would have cut throats and cast them over the side.

"It will be worse in Hellhole. It will be prolonged. Do not let it happen, Nole. You must not. I must not."

Nole looked at his hands, closed his eyes, opened them, looked at the children, inhaled.

Zhayim waited. He could do nothing else, but Nole and every child had to believe what he would tell them or it would not work. Surprise was their only hope. If anyone hesitated, even for a moment, it would fail.

Nole finally looked up at him and nodded. His voice was a whisper.

"I understand. But how?"

"The water. When they are all watching me. I will call to you, to them."

Nole shook his head and Zhayim saw the fear in his eyes. "They cannot swim. They are terrified of the sea."

"I know. But I will tell them a story."

"A story?"

Zhayim nodded. He did not have much time.

"Children, listen to me. Children. Make them hear me, Nole."

"Listen to him," Nole said.

Some of the older children comforted the younger and all of them looked up at him through tear-filled eyes. He felt a flutter in his gut. He was not sure he was doing the right thing. He believed he was, but how could he know?

He reminded himself of the tortures he had seen in Hellhole and steeled himself.

A low roll of thunder sounded and the patter of rain masked his tale from the crew. Korsin granted him that, at least. He did not waste words on the niceties of storytelling. He only needed them to believe the core of the tale.

"Do you remember how I told you of Akka the dolphin?" he asked.

A couple of the children nodded. The rest merely stared.

"I did not tell you everything about Akka," he said. "It is Akka and his kin who swam beside *Searhorse*, and Akka and his kin who swim out there right now."

Ysel and Lorm craned their necks and looked out over the water.

"Akka came to me in a dream and told me his purpose. He has not come to follow you to the new world. I misunderstood him. He said something else."

The children looked at him, anticipation in their eyes.

"What did he say?" Ysel asked.

Zhayim smiled. "He said he had come to *guide* you to the new world. He was sent by the Prophet, and he is waiting for you to come to him. The new world is not over the sea at the Far Shore. It is under the sea. Right here."

He almost told them their parents awaited them there, but could not bring himself to do it.

"In the water?" Lorm said, nervousness in his tone.

"Yes. It is not to be feared. He will lead you to the new world," Zhayim said. "This one is ending, children. We must hurry. Akka is waiting."

"How can we get to Akka, spinner?" Nole asked, playing his part.

"I will go into the water first," Zhayim said. "These pirates think to tie me with ropes and weights but Akka will chew them off of me. I will call for you when the new world is ready. When I do, you must stand together, run to the side of the ship, and jump into the water. All of you at once. Do you understand?"

He saw skepticism in some of the children's eyes.

The thunder died down, the rain slowed, and by all the gods he heard the dolphins clicking in the water. The children's eyes widened.

"There!" Zhayim said. "He is calling to us. Do you hear him?"

They nodded, wonder in their expressions.

"Remember, when I call for you, come running and jump straight in. Akka will take you to the next world."

"The new world," Lorm said. He looked past Zhayim with wide eyes, to the sea, to the sky.

"The new world." Zhayim agreed with a nod. He shared a look with Nole.

The pirates came for him, cut him loose from his bonds. They would replace them soon enough.

"Listen for the call," he said to the children.

"We will," said Nole, his voice tight.

"We believe you, spinner," said Ysel.

"Shut your hatches, all of you," one of the crewmen said, pulling Zhayim to his feet.

The pirates put their knives to his back and walked him to the rail at mid-ship where four lines of fine rope awaited him. Three were tied to rusty dinghy anchors; one, the retrieval line, was tied off to the railing.

Zhayim barely heard the chuckles, the taunts, the curses from the rest of the crew. He stared out onto the rough water. It looked as black as the sky. Thunder rumbled. A few dolphin fins broke the surface and he smiled.

"Hello, Akka," he whispered.

"Make it quick!" shouted the first mate. "Storm's coming in hard."

Zhayim looked up at the sky, knowing he was soon to see it no more. The roiling, black mass of clouds looked like nothing he had ever seen. The sky behind the front looked like a vat of pitch.

"It's not a storm," he said, and meant it.

"You say something, dead man?" the crewman tying ropes around his waist said.

Zhayim looked at the man, at all of them, and spoke loud enough for Nole and the children to hear.

"It is not a storm. It's the world's end and it's taking you down as sure as these weights will me."

The crewman attaching the weights sneered and punched him hard in the stomach. The rest laughed. Zhayim doubled over, coughing.

"Quick, now," said the first mate. "A dip for this dog!"

The pirates hooted.

The crewman beside Zhayim jerked him upright and finished tying the fourth line around his waist. He tested each line with a yank, pulling Zhayim off balance.

"All tight, Captain," the crewman shouted.

"Remember what I told you," the captain called to Zhayim. "Now, over with him."

The pirates cheered again as two crewmen seized him by his biceps and threw him without ceremony over the gunwale. When he hit the water, the impact and cold knocked the breath from him. He felt like a vise had closed on his chest. Instinct took over. He wanted air, needed it. He righted himself and came up, gasping.

The ship was a bobbing wall of wood before him. The sky a roof of black. The water stung his eyes.

The pirates, all of them gathered at the side or on the forecastle, jeered, laughed, and pointed.

"Swim, boy!"

The four lines attached to Zhayim's waist looked like umbilicals, stretching back up to the weights on the deck. The crew began to chant.

"A weight! A weight! A weight!"

A crewman hefted a weight, held it over his head to the cheers of his fellows, and cast it into the sea. It hit the water, sank below the waves, and jerked Zhayim under. It felt as if it were a hundredweight. He kicked his legs, swam for his life, and broached the surface.

"Huzzah!" shouted the crew.

The weight dragged on Zhayim. His arms burned. His legs felt like lead. He looked up at the grinning faces, the empty eyes. Something bumped into him and he gave a shout of surprise.

A dolphin. They were all around him.

He was losing strength. He gulped air, prepared to shout to the children, but the crewman lifted another anchor and the rest of the crew chanted:

"A weight! A weight!"

He would not be heard over the shouts. He imagined Nole readying the children, waiting for him to call.

The crewman threw the anchor into the water. Zhayim braced himself but it did no good. The weight pulled him under and took him down the full length of the slack in the rope still attached to the third anchor back on the boat.

He struggled to swim upward, kicked, pulled at the water with his arms. He could not make any progress. His lungs burned. Exhaustion ate at his muscles. He strained, blew out the little air left in his lungs, kicked, and moved up.

He broke the surface, gasping, his entire body on fire with fatigue.

The crew cheered.

Zhayim gasped, caught as much breath as he could, and shouted, "Now is the time! Now, children!"

He saw a few of the pirates turn around in surprise before the two anchors pulled him back under. He saw forms about him, dolphins, and waited for a splash that did not come.

Despair gripped him and he tried to swim up but his body would not answer. Thoughts raced through his mind, images from Hellhole, from his childhood, from the days of his life before he had ever taken to sea.

A dolphin bumped into him. He could hear them clicking, squealing, and chirping at one another all around him.

The children hit the water as one.

They sank like stones, legs kicking, arms flailing, all of them attached together by the chain that would drown them in the sea but save them from hell. The dolphins chirped and swam away from Zhayim, toward the children.

Spots filled the water, little flashes of orange like torches. He was dying.

The dolphins swam a circle around the sinking children and the manacles opened. The chain sank while each of the children, freed, took hold of a dolphin's dorsal fin.

The dolphins did not swim for the surface but down toward the depths.

Zhayim looked down and saw a glowing doorway shimmering below. Light poured out of it—sunlight. He thought at first that Akka and the dolphins were carrying the children to the new world but realized he was delusional. He was dying, seeing spots, inventing images.

He had just told them a story, only a story.

But he could not take his eyes from them.

The dolphins carried their riders ever deeper, away from Zhayim, away from the

pirates, away from the old world.

Zhayim, his lungs ablaze, could only watch. He would have swum for the bottom himself, but two lines still attached him to the pirate vessel.

Among the children he saw Nole in the lead, one hand on a dolphin, legs kicking him ever deeper into the sea, toward the light. Nole and the children swam down, down. Zhayim watched them go, more and more spots dotting his field of vision.

Words surfaced in his air-deprived brain.

Belief is transformative, so teaches the Prophet.

We believe you, spinner.

Zhayim wanted to believe, too.

Nole, on his dolphin, in the lead, near the lights, reached out a hand for the glowing doorway. He looked back, smiled, his eyes alight.

Zhayim returned the smile, then his burning lungs acted of their own accord, gulping for air.

Everything went quiet and soft, like falling asleep.

Afterword
Mark "Cap'n Slappy" Summers
& John "Ol' Chumbucket" Baur

T he sea has always been a subject for painters seduced by its ever-changing nature and its function as a metaphor for Life. But there has yet to be a painting that captures the enormity of the sea alone—without an element of the touch of human hands. Ships at sea, lighthouses, and even shorelines allow us to place ourselves within the world of the painting and breathe in, albeit vicariously through the artist's brush strokes, its world.

Storytellers also find the sea a fitting canvas for their creative works.

Tales of the sea are tales of Life itself in heroic proportions. The monsters and mythic creatures are metaphor for our hopes and horrors—the peril and the promise of the world around us. It is the work of the hero–pirate, sailor, survivor—to navigate his or her way through life while handling and harnessing these strange and unknowable forces. To that end, the storyteller's imagination becomes a seascape upon which the hero's voyage takes place. And as with Life itself, the outcome may remain in doubt while all of the characters—human and otherwise—seek to have their needs met in the mind of their creator.

We laugh at those points where the story presses closely to the life we are living. We also cry there—and feel fear.

It is in this world of imagination that we prepare ourselves for the twists and turns that fill the world of reality and practice finding the courage, the humor, and the will to continue on in our own adventure. This book is a collection of explorations by some very gifted storytellers. It's as if they've gathered in a darkened pub on the wharf of a bustling pirate town to lay their innermost hopes and fears bare before a crowd gathered in front of the fireplace and watch as we, wide-eyed, take in their tales.

———————⚓———————

The phone rings at the home of Mark "Cap'n Slappy" Summers, who answers it.

Mark: This is Mark.

John: Hi, it's John.

Mark: I know it's you. I've told you, I've got Caller ID. Every time you call you say it's you, and I always say 'I know it's you, John. I have Caller ID.'

(pause)

John: What's your point?

Mark: Just that you don't *have* to say it's you. I know it's you, and you KNOW I know it's you. So why do you say it?

John: It's the way I was taught, it's good phone etiquette. You identify yourself. Like back in the Edwardian Age when you'd send your card up before dropping in on someone.

Mark: But the Caller ID acts as your card! It's like a tiny little annoying butler who delivers your identification to me before I even pick it up and start speaking into it. It's not the Edwardian Age, it's the Computer Age, and it—

John: *(stiffly)* Are you criticizing the way my parents raised me?

Mark: What? No, I'm just—

John: My parents, as you know, raised eight children who grew up to be successful and happy adults—

Mark: No, I'm not criti—

John: And as you also know, both of my parents have passed away and their memory is very dear to me and I would hate—

Mark: I'M NOT talking about your parents, okay. Just tell me why you're calling.

John: Ha! Your super phone couldn't tell you that, could it? It may know who's calling, but it's no help in telling you *why* I called. The art of conversation isn't dead yet, is it?

Mark: No, but you will be if you don't shut up and tell me why you're calling!

John: How can I tell you why I'm calling if I shut up? That makes no sense.

(long pause)

Mark: *(with forced enthusiasm)* Hi John! What's up?

John: That's better. I got your opening for the afterword for *Sails & Sorcery: Tales of Nautical Fantasy*, and I like where you're going.

Mark: Thanks, I thought it was a good start.

John: You realize, of course, that a painted seascape featuring neither man, nor bird, nor ship, nor even a wave-battered coastline—just the ocean—would probably be the most boring painting ever committed to canvas.

Mark: I do. That's why I am betting that there is no such painting. It's a joke, a touch of levity. Get it?

John: Oh, sure. I get it. *(longish pause)* So do we want to say something about the connection between pirates and fantasy fiction? I mean, that's what the book is, a collection of pirate-fantasy fiction. Since they asked us to write an afterword for it, maybe we should address that, sort of sum the whole thing up.

Mark: Of course we should.

(another pause)

John: How?

Mark: Well, freedom, of course.

John: Freedom?

Mark: Sure! Think about it. Why did people become pirates?

John: To get rich and drink rum?

Mark: Okay, yeah, sure, to get rich and drink rum. But mostly for the freedom. They lived in a world where roles were defined, where they had no chance to improve their lot. They didn't like what life had to offer so they said to hell with the rules and created their own life.

John: Sure.

Mark: Well, it's the same with writers of fantasy and science fiction, isn't it? They don't want to settle for the rules of the world as it is. They embrace the freedom to create their own world. Their fictional heroes live lives unbounded by the rules of conventional reality.

John: Unbounded by the rules of conventional reality? Doesn't that sound kind of hoity toity, coming from us?

Mark: Yeah, well maybe. But you get the point. Who was that historian you're always quoting?

John: Marcus Rediker.

Mark: Right, Marcus Rediker. He said—

John: He said "Pirates were the freest people on Earth."

Mark: Right. And fantasy writers are the freest writers on Earth.

John: Because they can make up—

Mark: Create.

John: Yeah, right. I get it. Create. They can create whatever reality they need to tell their story.

Mark: Exactly! In fact, the reality *becomes* the story, in a way, just like the reality that pirates created for themselves became the story of their lives.

John: I get it. And it's good, a good point to make in a book that mixes fantasy and pirate fiction—sort of the best of both worlds.

Mark: I think so.

John: But how does it tie in with the whole thing about the boundless ocean and the lure of the sea?

Mark: We can get there. It shouldn't be too hard to connect them.

John: Okay. But you know, there's another connection between fantasy and freebooter fiction that we haven't even talked about.

Mark: What's that?

John: They're both cool. I mean, fantasy, magic, sci fi—that's all pretty cool. And pirates were cooler than anybody.

Mark: Except Samuel Jackson.

John: Of course, except Samuel Jackson, who is cooler than anybody. But Samuel Jackson aside, pirates, magic, sorcery, fantasy, that's all very cool. So besides the whole freedom thing, there's also just the fact that both subjects are cool, and that mixing them together might just be the coolest thing ever.

Mark: Okay, sure. I don't think that's as profound or as intelligent as the freedom thing, but it's something else to work with. So what do we have?

John: One, the boundless ocean, two, freedom and the idea that fantasy writers and pirates share the freedom to create their own world, and three, it's all extremely cool.

Mark: Okay, we can do that. How long is this supposed to be.

John: They asked for between 1,000 and 1,500 words.

Mark: I'm pretty sure we're there already.

John: Good. Then are we done?

Mark: Looks like.

John: Great! Then I'll talk to you later.

Mark: You have any plans for this evening?

John: Not really. Why?

Mark: I might head over to the Calapooia Brewing Company tonight. Care to join me?

John: Sure. Sounds good. Give me a call before you go. Just don't give me any grief on how I answer the phone.

About the Contributors

Julie Dillon is a freelance illustrator based in California. She earned her BA in Fine Arts at California State University, Sacramento, and is currently studying at Academy of Art University. Her previous clients include Paizo Publishing, Fantasy Flight Games, Great White Games, *Orson Scott Card's Intergalactic Medicine Show*, and USRPG. More of her work can be seen at www.jdillon.net.

Lawrence C. Connolly's stories have appeared in *Year's Best Horror*, *Best of Borderlands*, *Best of the Magazine of Fantasy and Science Fiction* (from Audible.com), and numerous magazines and anthologies of science fiction, fantasy, and horror. He also plays lead guitar with the Laughrey Connolly Band, a Celtic rock ensemble whose play lists include numerous songs of the sea.

His most recent fiction has appeared in *F&SF*, *Cemetery Dance*, and *Bash Down the Door and Slice Open the Badguy* (also from Fantasist Enterprises). His latest story "Die Angle" will be published later this year in *Darkness on the Edge: Tales Inspired by the Songs of Bruce Springsteen* (from PS Publishing). His novel *Veins* is scheduled for release in early 2008.

J.C. Hay lives a thousand miles from the nearest ocean, and so is forced to sublimate the desire to be a pirate into writing, knitting, and writing about knitting. When not cloistered behind the keyboard, or tangled up in yarn, J.C. is subservient to a pair of Papillon dogs—the dark masters—and a supportive, loving spouse. A part-time film snob and a full-time food snob, much of J.C.'s free time is spent trying to introduce friends to new experiences and tastes and not enough is spent updating the website, www.jchay.com. In addition to other publications, J.C. Hay's novella "Collar of Iron" will be included in the upcoming anthology *Blood and Devotion*.

Jon Sprunk lives in central Pennsylvania with his wife, Jenny, and their three enormous cats. Between his day job as a juvenile detention specialist and time spent with his family, he tries to squeeze in some time for writing. When not working on his latest novel, he enjoys traveling, collecting medieval weaponry, and pro football. "Sea of Madness" is his fifth story in publication. More of his works can be found at www.jonsprunk.com.

Chun Lee is dreaming of pirates more than ever now that he has moved near the Gulf Coast. He now resides in Lafayette, Louisiana, dodging gators and trying to survive in the humid heat. His short story "A Contained Inferno" is featured in the webzine *The Late Late Show*, and he is currently writing *The Fracture*, a comic book with Diana Dru Botsford for FE Comics. He is a graduate of the Writing Popular Fiction program at Seton Hill University and is currently trying to earn a PhD in English at the University of Louisiana at Lafayette.

Murray J.D. Leeder is the author of *Son of Thunder* and *Plague of Ice* for Wizards of the Coast as well as around twenty published short stories, four of them for Fantasist Enterprises' fine anthologies. He lives in Ottawa, pursuing a Ph.D. at Carleton University, and his academic writing has appeared in *The Canadian Journal of Film Studies*.

"Female Rambling Sailor" borrows the name of a traditional nautical ballad of at least 150-years vintage, an example of what's sometimes been called the "trouser song," the story of a woman going to sea disguised as a man. Two others, "Canadee-i-o" and "Jack-a-roe" are the basis for the other two songs Sweet William sings to Jack. All three have been done by Bob Dylan at some point and are available in many other versions.

Jens Rushing writes fiction of every stripe, with over a dozen stories published in the first half of 2007. Look for his work in *Out West* magazine, *Space Westerns*, and other fine publications. Visit www.jensrushing.com for a journal, some stories, and a complete list of publications. Jens plays the banjo. His wife is exceptionally beautiful.

Jaleigh Johnson lives and writes in the Champaign area of Illinois. Her first novel, *The Howling Delve*, was published in 2007 by Wizards of the Coast, and her short fiction has appeared in various small presses. In her spare time, Jaleigh likes to haunt movie theaters and garden in the wilderness of her backyard. Visit her online at http://jaleigh-johnson.livejournal.com.

Gerard Houarner is a product of the NYC school system who lives in the Bronx, was married at a New Orleans Voodoo Temple and works at a psychiatric institution. His latest novel, *Road From Hell*, as well as the collection *Dead Cat's Traveling Circus of Wonders and Miracle Medicine Show*, are available from your favorite bookseller or www.necropublications. com. Recent/upcoming appearances include *Weird Tales 344*, *Cemetery Dance 58*, *Alone on the Darkside*, *Dark Acts*, *Midnight Premiere*, *Blood and Devotion*, *High Seas Cthulu*, *Dueling Minds*, *Darkness On The Edge: Tales Inspired by the Songs of Bruce Springsteen*.

On better days, he sees himself standing at the crossroads of myth and nature, the psychological and the supernatural, the real and the surreal, the past, present and future, waiting for someone or something to come along, take his soul and leave him with the voice to tell anybody who will listen to the story of how it all happened. He continues to write whenever he can, mostly at night, about the dark. For the latest, visit www.cith.org/gerard or www.myspace.com/gerardhouarner.

Christopher Heath lives in Indiana and has been writing fantasy for over a decade, either as a role-playing game designer under the official *Dungeons and Dragons* logo or producing short stories and novels for his Azieran fantasy world, which have been published by such companies and publications as Fantasist Enterprises, Pitch-Black Books, Carnifex Press, Ricasso Press, ComStar Media, Kenzer and Company, Daybreak Press, *GrendelSong*, *Forgotten Worlds*, *Rogue Worlds*, R&R Endeavors, Heathen Oracle (co-founded by Christopher Heath and veteran fantasy artist V.Shane), and others. He also won Pitch-Black's Storn Cook writing contest, garnering a cash prize and publication in their *Sages and Swords* anthology appearing alongside works by such acclaimed writers as legendary pulp pioneer Harold Lamb and Tanith Lee.

William Ledbetter was born in Indiana, but now lives in northern Texas with his very understanding wife, two of his three kids and way too many animals. He is a long time space and technology junkie and an active member of the National Space Society. His fiction has also been published by *Jim Baen's Universe*, Yard Dog Press, *Continuum Science Fiction* and many others. For more information, and a complete list of William's published works, visit his website at www.williamledbetter.com.

Patrick Thomas is the author of over 75 published short stories and fifteen books including seven in the popular fantasy humor series *Murphy's Lore*. The latest is *Nightcaps*. The others are *Tales From Bulfinche's Pub*, *Fools' Day*, *Through the Drinking Glass*, *Shadow of the Wolf*, *Redemption Road*, and *Bartender of the Gods*.

His stories have sold to various venues including *Sails & Sorcery*, *Until Somebody Loses an Eye*, *Cthulhu Sex*, *Hardboiled Cthulhu*, *Dark Furies*, *Clash of Steel 3: Demon*, *Breach the Hull*,

Bad-Ass Faeries, The 2nd Coming, Unicorn 8, Jigsaw Nation, Crypto-Critters Vol. 1 & 2, The Dead Walk Again, Lai Wai: Tales of the Dreamwalker, Time Capsule and *Warfear*.

Patrick has been an editor for *Fantastic Stories* and *Pirate Writings*, co-edited *Hear Them Roar* and the upcoming *New Blood*. His novellas appear in *Go Not Gently* from Padwolf and *Flesh and Iron* from the Two Backed Books imprint of Raw Dog Screaming. Patrick also writes the syndicated satirical advice column "Dear Cthulhu." Please visit his website at www.patthomas.net.

Jordan Lapp writes computer programs by day and short fiction by night—when he's not running around Gotham in a bat costume. He is most famous for inventing toast, and in 1989, led the first successful expedition to the West Pole.

Jordan writes mostly science fiction, with the occasional foray into fantasy. In 2005, Jordan won the Vancouver Courier Short Fiction contest, and he has recently been picked as a Semi-Finalist in Writers of the Future. Though he has been published in numerous online venues, *Sails & Sorcery* marks his first appearance in a professional anthology.

Gerri Leen lives in Northern Virginia and originally hails from Seattle. She writes in many genres, but her favorites are fantasy or myth-based stories. In addition to the *Sails & Sorcery* anthology, her short stories have appeared in *Fusion Fragment, Mytholog, Shred of Evidence, The First Line*, and three editions of the Star Trek *Strange New Worlds* contest anthology (her story, "The Smell of Dead Roses," won the grand prize in *Strange New Worlds 10*).

Her work has also been accepted by the *Fantastical Visions V* anthology, *Renard's Menagerie, GlassFire*, and *GrendelSong*. She has written a contemporary fantasy novel, which she is currently trying to find a home for, and is working on several other novels. She also writes poetry when the mood hits her, and has one poem published. Her website is at www.gerrileen.com.

T. Borregaard has a Masters of Science in Archaeological Materials (which only sounds interesting), and is listlessly engaged in PhD studies that seem to revolve, in equal measure, around ancient pottery and torturing undergraduates. She is freckled in person, organized by nature, and obsessed with motorcycles, ancient kiln technology, corsets, blue hair, and tea—one of which (or probably all in combination) will eventually be the death of her. Her stories have appeared in *Sword & Sorceress* and various magazines. She's written the obligatory unpublishable fantasy series (there are plans for a rejection-slip database) so is optimistically writing a stand-alone novel instead.

James M. Ward was born, has lived a pleasantly long time, and has been happily married 37 years. He has an unusually charming wife, Janean and three equally charming sons, Breck, James, and Theon. Delightful grandchildren have come into his life: Keely, Miriam, Sophia, Preston, and Teagan. Working here and there, he's managed to write the first science fiction RPG, *Metamorphosis Alpha*, several best selling CCGs including *Spellfire* and *Dragon Ball Z*, and a few novels including *Halcyon Blithe Midshipwizard* and *Halcyon Blithe Dragonfrigate Wizard*.

He likes to fence, the 'sword' type, not the 'put up' type. He spends a great deal of time looking for work. He reads science fiction and fantasy novels and occasionally something else when the cover looks interesting. Recently, he finished designing a board game called *Dragon Lairds* that he is unusually proud of and wants everyone to purchase. If possible, he'd like to end up as the captain of the starship Enterprise, but that job keeps getting taken before he can get his resume in to the home office.

Leslie Brown is a research technician working in the Alzheimer's field. She has previously published stories in *On Spec* and in several anthologies including *Open Space*, *Thou Shalt Not*, and *Loving the Undead*. She is a member of Lyngarde, an Ottawa Writers' Group.

Angeline Hawkes received a B.A. in Composite English Language Arts in 1991 from Texas A&M, Commerce and was recently named 2007 Alumni Ambassador for the Literature Department. She has publication credits dating from 1981. Angeline's collection, *The Commandments*, received a 2006 Bram Stoker Award nomination. Her newest fantasy series is entitled *Tales of the Barbarian Kabar of El Hazzar*. Dead Letter Press published *Blood Coven*, a limited edition novella, co-written with her husband Christopher Fulbright in June 2006. Angeline has seen the publication of her novels, novellas, and fiction in 30+ anthologies, several collections, and short fiction in various publications. She is a member of HWA. Visit her websites at www.angelinehawkes.com and www.fulbrightandhawkes.com.

Robert E. Vardeman is the author of more than fifty fantasy and science fiction novels, as well as numerous westerns under various pen names. Titles include the fantasy *Dark Legacy* and science fiction novel *Ruins of Power*. The reprint of his *Star Frontier* trilogy (from Zumaya Publications) is set for November 2007, followed by the fantasy trilogy *After the Spell Wars* in 2008. Recently, he published another fantasy pirate short story, "The Coins of Darkun," in the anthology *Pirates of the Blue Kingdoms*.

Vardeman is a longtime resident of Albuquerque, New Mexico, graduating from the University of New Mexico with a B.S. in Physics and a M.S. in Materials Engineering. He worked for Sandia National Laboratories in the Solid State Physics Research Department before becoming a full time writer. For more information go to www.cenotaphroad.com.

Renee Stern is a former newspaper reporter turned freelance writer whose articles for trade publications range from building custom furniture to developing agricultural robots. Her short fiction credits include "Oceans of the Mind", "Aeon Speculative Fiction" and "Black Gate". A fan of true accounts of exploration—Lewis and Clark, Thompson, Franklin, Amundsen, and, yes, Shackleton—she is currently at work on a historical fantasy trilogy set in part during the Age of Exploration.

Jeff Houser has been shamelessly raiding and pillaging along the outskirts of Philadelphia for most of his 33 years. As an 11-year veteran of the graphic design industry, Mr. Houser is currently working for a toy design firm in the suburbs of Philadelphia, molding and shaping young minds into his own graven image. He started taking his writing semi-seriously about two and a half years ago, and this story marks his publishing debut—the first in what he hopes to be a long line of published tales of darkness and wonder. Oh, and monkeys. He would like to dedicate this story to his always-encouraging family, his piratical girlfriend, and a certain famous pirate captain who helped inspire this story. . . .

Jeffrey Lyman is a 2004 graduate of the Odyssey Writing School. In 2004, he co-edited the anthology *No Longer Dreams*, and in 2007, he co-edited the anthology *Bad-Ass Faeries*, both with Danielle Ackley-McPhail. He has an epic fantasy story in the upcoming anthology *Blood and Devotion* from Fantasist Enterprises, and a science fiction story in the upcoming anthology *Breach the Hull* from Marietta Press. By day, he is chained to a desk as a mechanical engineer.

Lindsey Duncan is a life-long writer with short fiction and poetry in several speculative fiction publications. She also performs and teaches Celtic harp, and feels that music and language are inextricably linked. She lives in the Cincinnati, Ohio area and is a student at Indiana University, working on a self-designed major focusing on human belief systems. The world of "Currents and Clockwork" is also the setting for one of her novel projects.

Chris Stout holds a Master of Arts in Writing Popular Fiction from Seton Hill University. He also is working to become a Reiki Master. As of the publication of *Sails & Sorcery*, he has attained Reiki II status. Hopefully one or the other of these studies will help him to earn a living and become a better-rounded human being. Feel free to visit him at www.ctstout.com.

Heidi Ruby Miller has always been fascinated by exotic locales and cultural traditions. These dual interests grew into undergraduate degrees in Anthropology, Geography, and Foreign Languages, and later into a Master's from Seton Hill University's Writing Popular Fiction program. It's no surprise that travel writing is her day job, but sometimes the dreamer takes over, and that's when she journeys beyond this world into the speculative. Here or there, it's quite the journey. To see where Heidi's been, visit her at ambasadora.livejournal.com.

Jack Mackenzie's stories have appeared in *Rage Machine Magazine, Raygun Revival* and in the anthologies *The Ghostbreakers, Amazing Heroes* and *Magistria: The Realm of the Sorcerer*. He lives in the wild country of BC's Interior with his wife and two daughters. You can contact him at jackmack676@hotmail.com.

Elaine Cunningham is a New York Times bestselling author of over twenty books and many short stories. A former history and music teacher, she tends toward historical settings and characters who are either musicians or storytellers. She lives five towns north of Newport, Rhode Island, the setting for "Dead Men Tell No Tales." Nearly three centuries have passed since Newport was an important destination for pirates and slave traders, but several of the buildings mentioned in the story still stand. Visitors can still lift a pint in the White Horse Tavern and walk past the Quaker meeting house.

Short stories have fascinated her since first grade, when she came across a collection of funny stories about cats. She is currently editing *Bound is the Bewitching Lilith*, a collection of stories inspired by the Lilith mythology, to be published by Popcorn Press in late 2007. Her next novel will be *Reclamation*, the sixth and final book in the *Forgotten Realms Songs & Swords* series. This will be published by Wizards of the Coast in early March 2008. For more information about her books, please visit her website, www.ElaineCunningham.com.

Danielle Ackley-McPhail has worked both sides of the publishing industry for over a decade. Her works include *Yesterday's Dreams*, its upcoming sequel, *Tomorrow's Memories* (Mundania Press), the anthologies *Bad-Ass Faeries* (Marietta Publishing) and *No Longer Dreams* (Lite Circle Books), both of which she co-edited, and contributions to numerous anthologies and collections, including *Dark Furies* (Die Monster Die! Books) and the upcoming *Breach the Hull*, also from Marietta Publishing. She is a member of the electronic publishing organization EPIC, as well as Broad Universe, a writer's organization focusing on women authors. Keep an eye out; she has four more anthologies coming out over the next year and a half. Danielle lives in New Jersey with husband and fellow writer, Mike McPhail, mother-in-law Teresa, and three extremely spoiled cats. Visit her at www.sidhenadaire.com.

J.M. Martin was born in Lexington, KY, in 1970. He has worked as an illustrator, graphic designer, advertising manager, copy editor, desktop publisher, writer, professional boxing judge, and high school substitute art teacher. He's also had the pleasure of waiting tables, working in a deli, and loading cargo planes during the mid-winter wee morning hours.

J.M. is professionally published in comics, games, and magazines. He was the graphics coordinator for the Detroit-based Caliber Comics and Stabur Press from 1994 to 1998. While there, he wrote 17 issues of the fan-favorite *Legendlore* comic book, a spin-off of the long-running fantasy series, *The Realm*. While at Caliber, J.M. served as the sole graphic designer for the McFarlane Toys Collector's Club. J.M. was also editor-in-chief for the Seattle-based Privateer Press from 2001 to 2004, helping build their *Iron Kingdoms* game environment from the ground up. J.M. conceptualized many of the characters that now comprise Privateer's award-winning *WARMACHINE* tabletop game.

J.M. has lived in Detroit and Cincinnati and now currently resides in Northern Kentucky, where he shares studio space with an obstinate rat terrier and way too many stacks of comped toys and comic books. This is not his first published work of fiction, but it is his best to date (in his own opinion, for whatever that's worth).

Paul S. Kemp lives in southeastern Michigan with his wife, three-year-old twin sons, and their pets. When he is not writing fantasy stories, he slogs away at his day job as a corporate lawyer. This makes him a tool of "The Man", and he yearns for the day when he will be free. He yearns, too, for the day when the world will join hands in peace and, with one uplifting voice, sing the theme song from "Shaft." He is the author of seven novels set in Wizards of Coast's *Forgotten Realms* setting, including the NY Times' bestseller, *Resurrection*. He hopes you enjoy his stories. Paul keeps an online journal at http://paulskemp.livejournal.com, where he posts about writing, life, and politics. Please consider dropping by.

Mark "Cap'n Slappy" Summers" & John "Ol' Chumbucket" Baur say that the afterword they wrote is a fairly accurate representation of how they work and function as a team—although in fairness they take turns being the obtuse one. Despite this, they have managed to create an international holiday—Talk Like a Pirate Day—start a hugely popular web site—www.talklikeapirate.com—have their book, *Pirattitude!*, published by a major publishing company, perform all over the country, be interviewed all around the globe, and have four more book projects in the pipeline. So anything is possible.

W. H. Horner is the Publisher and Editor-in-Chief of Fantasist Enterprises and its comic book and graphic novel imprint, FE Comics. He is currently hard at work editing and art directing *Fantastical Visions IV*, *Blood & Devotion*, and *Veins*, a novel by Lawrence C. Connolly ("We Sail with the Tide"). He is also overseeing work on the comic book titles *Channels*; *The Fracture*, written by Diana Dru Botsford and Chun Lee ("Stillworld: Sailing to Noon"); and *The Karma Game*.

A graduate of Seton Hill University's MA in Writing Popular Fiction program, William is also a student of Tai Chi Quan and Haidong Gumdo, a Korean sword art. You can visit him on the web at www.WHHorner.com, whhorner.livejournal.com, and at www.myspace.com/pantsmagee. Don't ask about that last one, even though it is a funny story.

Coming In 2008

BLOOD &
Devotion

Epic Tales
Of Fantasy

The clash of steel.
The scent of blood.
The heat of fire from heaven.
The cries of the dying and of the dead.

Brave warriors and devotees to the gods follow the paths their faiths have put before them, and when religious fervor meets skill of arms and magic, kings will fall, armies will collide, and men and women will perish for their beliefs.

Edited by W. H. Horner
Illustrated by Nicole Cardiff
$23.00 US / $29.00 Can.
450 Pages (Estimated)
38 Illustrations
Trade Paperback • 6″ x 9″
ISBN 13: 978-0-9713608-8-4
ISBN 10: 0-9713608-8-X

Coming in 2008

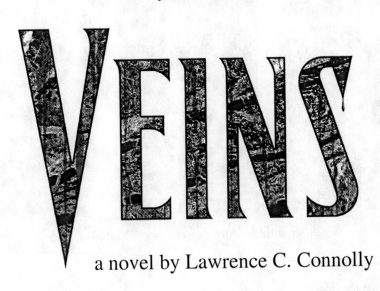

a novel by Lawrence C. Connolly

They are small-time crooks from the wrong side of town. Three men and a woman racing from a botched heist with a briefcase full of cash.

On the run in a restored Mustang, they take a detour down a mountain road that ends at the machine-scarred crater of an abandoned mine. Here they stop—out of gas, out of luck, out of time—determined to keep the briefcase and the hope of making something of their dead-end lives. But they're not the only ones with a plan this night.

Enter *Kwetis*—the Nightflyer—a creature that draws power from the deep veins of unmined coal that still riddle the walls of the valley. Kwetis has planned a heist of his own, and before dawn, the crooks and their pursuers will learn that their arrival at the mine was prophesied long ago . . . and that each of them is a piece of an elaborate plan devised by the spirits of the earth—a scheme to reclaim the land and restore a ghostly mountain once known as the Heart of the World.

Illustrated by Star E. Olson
Trade Paperback • 6″ x 9″
ISBN 13: 978-1-934571-00-2
ISBN 10: 1-934571-00-8

Coming in 2008

the KARMA game

Story by Christe M. Callabro • Pencils by Jason Baroody
Inks by Robert M. Grabe • Colors by Taj

All Lily wants is the man she loves. Of course, being with him would also mean the end of humanity. Then she awakes to the reality that she is, in fact, the goddess Kali. And she's pissed. From the M.O.B. to the Vatican, from lovesick demons to Elvis, the divine must either stand up to her, or stand aside.

the FRACTURE

Story by Diana Dru Botsford and Chun Lee
Pencils and Inks by John R. P. Nyaid • Colors by Axel Medellin

When a disease-ridden alien race fractures Earth's timeline, 5 humans from vastly different times and cultures band together, traveling through history in search of the means to save humanity from extinction.

Channels

Story by A. G. Devitt • Pencils by Brandon Dawley
Inks by Star Olson • Colors by Chrystal Henkaline

Fender, a bargain basement magician, finds himself trapped inside realities based on classic television shows. As if learning how to survive in 80s action-land or 50s sitcoms isn't bad enough, Fender must chase down 36 demons he unwittingly unleashed upon the world. And he must solve the mystery of Tobe, the boy with a television for a head.

www.FEComics.com

Order the Stunning Illustrations of Julie Dillon

The illustrations found in this book are available as 8½" x 11" prints on 80#, white, acid-free cover stock.

Order prints at http://art.fantasistent.com, or use the order form to the right.

Art From Sails & Sorcery

Page # of Illustration	QTY.	PRICE	TOTAL
Cover Art		$20.00	
		$12.00	
		$12.00	
		$12.00	
		$12.00	
		$12.00	
		$12.00	
		$12.00	
		$12.00	
		$12.00	
		$12.00	
		$12.00	
		$12.00	
		$12.00	
		$12.00	

Add $3.00 shipping per print.   Shipping: _____

Please print the following: Total: _____

Name: _____

Address: _____

Address: _____

City: _____ State: _____ Zip: _____

Do Not Send Cash.

Make checks or money orders payable to Fantasist Enterprises at
PO Box 9381, Wilmington, DE 19809, USA

Printed in the United States
91517LV00007B/67-300/A